Sara A. Noë

Phantom's Mask

Chronicles of Avilésor
- War of the Reälms -
Book II

Text Copyright © 2019 by Sara A. Noë
Library of Congress Control Number: 2019913153
All rights reserved.

Printed in the United States of America

First edition, 2020

"You Are My Sunshine" by Jimmie Davis
Copyright © 1940 by Peer International Corporation
Copyright Renewed. Used by Permission.
All Rights Reserved.

Cover font: Black Asylum by Kevin Christopher // KC Fonts
Used by Permission.

Hardcover ISBN 978-1-7325998-5-7
Paperback ISBN 978-1-7325998-6-4
E-book ISBN 978-1-7325998-7-1

Cover design and print layout by Sara A. Noë
E-book layout by Polgarus Studio

PRAISE FOR BOOK I:

— A Fallen Hero —

"*A Fallen Hero* is an explosive beginning to the War of the Realms series."

– LITERARY TITAN
2020 GOLD BOOK AWARD

"Noë's excellent plotting and highly engrossing narrative grab hold of readers' interest from the first page . . . A superb debut!"

– THE PRAIRIES BOOK REVIEW

"Don't be surprised if you say 'one more chapter before bed' and find yourself closing the cover at dawn."

– NAM EDITORIAL

"Noë's tactful narrative and deeply layered plotting offer a unique world that readers can fully immerse themselves in to walk alongside heroes and villains."

– CHRONICLE FOCUS EDITORIAL

"I'm a sucker for found family stories . . . These kids would do anything for each other . . ."

– LAUREN GANTT
TOP 10 FAVORITE BOOKS OF 2019 | *LAUREN'S BOOOKSHELF*

". . . Noë's strongest asset as an author is her ability to make you fall in love with her characters."

– ERIKA DAVIS
BUILDING MY BOOKCASE | *READ TOGETHER PODCAST*

Dedicated to my mom,
who taught me to keep my eyes open . . .

. . . as things aren't always as they seem.

Sara A. Noë

Phantom's Mask

Chronicles of Avilésor
- War of the Realms -
Book II

Voices.

I followed them under an eerie green sky.

The owners of the voices didn't suspect I was tailing them. Ghosts were usually able to sense each other when they came into range, but I was special; I could shut off my power to become undetectable. Although I despised the vulnerability of being powerless, I had to admit it was a useful trick, especially when ghosts were the dominant population. Easier to hide. And when you're the prey, being able to hide is critical.

What a terrifying feeling, being hunted. Even more chilling was the knowledge that safety was an illusion. There was no safe place—not anywhere in this world or the other. I supposed Azar's fugitives fleeing the Ghost Realm must be able to relate to this experience, knowing that ghost hunters would be after them the moment they stepped foot through a Tear. But for me, who'd spent so much of my life as a free human who had never known what it truly meant to be in danger, it was still a relatively new experience.

The three ghosts I was following were dressed in red-trimmed black from their boots to their cloaks, pristine uniforms I'd come to recognize as those of the Shadow Guard. I'd been creeping closer and closer, and now their words were finally in range to hear.

"... decided yet what you'll do with the reward?" a man was asking.

"What reward?" a woman replied. "The captain didn't say anything about a reward."

"Are you kidding? When is the last time Azar put Captain Hassing in charge of a mission instead of Lieutenant Cisco? He jumped chain of command. I'm telling you, whoever brings him an Alpha is sure to get an immediate promotion."

Suddenly conscious of the blatant white Alpha symbol imprinted on the chest of my black shirt, I pulled the edge of my cloak to conceal it, just in case they happened to turn around and spot me.

The hefty guy on the end heaved his shoulders up and down in a shrug. "I don't see what's so valuable about these lab rats. Seems like a lot of fuss over some wretches."

"Hey," the first guy said. "Rule number one: don't question orders. Rule number two: if Azar wants something, you know damn well it's valuable. And rule number three: if there's anything of value to Azar, it's in your best interest to be the one who finds it for him."

I was so engrossed in their conversation that I wasn't careful enough with the placement of my foot, which found an empty can. I cursed to myself and pressed my body into the corner of an alcove, doing my best to blend into the deep shadows.

The Shadow Guards froze. "You hear that?" The woman's voice was hushed.

"Yeah," said the guy on her left. His glowing red eyes scanned the shadows. "But I didn't sense anybody. Did you?"

"No," she replied. The third shook his head.

I held my breath. If I contorted my body any more into the corner, I was convinced I would mold into the space as if I were made of rubber. I could have reawakened my power to become invisible, but I knew I was in their sensing range. The second I let my power flow, the Shadow Guards would know.

I didn't move. There was no electricity here—no streetlights to cast pools of light, no vehicles with headlights. In the dark, I was in Azar's domain.

Finally, the Guards turned away and resumed their patrol. I emptied my lungs in one slow release. *Note to self: avoid being a klutz when you're trying to not get yourself captured.*

The Shadow Guards took a left turn at the next intersection, and I slumped against the brick wall in relief.

A small, furry creature landed on my shoulder from the window above.

Claws pricked my skin through my cloak, and I barely managed to avoid screaming and flinging the black-and-white kitten across the street. I pressed my hand over my racing heart and whispered, "Bloody Scout, Kit, you just scared me half to death."

She flicked her rough tongue across my cheek and nuzzled me, her whiskers tickling my skin, then hopped down and scampered after the Shadow Guards. Instead of turning left in pursuit, she went right. I followed, hesitating at the intersection to look for the Guards. They must have turned another corner, because the road was deserted.

Kit and I both paused and turned our faces skyward when lightning flickered in the green clouds. A low rumble splintered the air in its wake. Kit's ears fell, tail drooping. I walked past her, jolting her attention; she trotted after me. I knelt beneath a broken window, and Kit sat down on her haunches facing me. "All clear?" I whispered.

Her ears swiveled to listen in all directions. She crouched and jumped up onto the windowsill, then leapt into the dim interior and out of sight. That was a good enough answer for me, and I followed her into the building.

The office appeared to be deserted, but the trail of footprints in the dust told me otherwise. I closed my eyes and concentrated on finding my center. To turn my power "off," I had to push the warm spark deep inside myself and seal it away, unfortunately a similar sensation to what the neutralizer did. The difference was that I could reactivate it whenever I wished now that I was free from my shackle.

Once I broke the floodgates, the tingle awakened my blood. I didn't need a mirror to know that when I opened my eyes again, the right one would be glowing blue, the left green. The hot and cold currents of my dual Divinities circulated throughout my core.

Immediately, I shivered. It was a distinct feeling—a cold, sliding sensation along my spine. It happened only when another ghost entered my range.

Or, in this case, when I entered the ranges of five other ghosts.

I strode past the dented filing cabinet, the bare desk, and the chair with a broken wheel. In the doorway, I hesitated.

Shapes were moving in the dark. I could identify the silhouettes of my lab-siblings by the color of their glowing eyes. RC was nearest to me; only one of his violet eyes was aglow. Ash—her smoldering ruby eyes so different from Axel's chilling ones—was kneeling, and I caught the briefest glimpse of light reflected off a cat's eye below her. Two pairs of cobalt eyes observed from the corner. Seeing Finn and Reese alert and sitting up by their own strength was always a relief. One of the twins coughed, the sound echoing in the cavernous room we called Home.

Jay's silver eyes locked onto me. "Cato," he greeted, then paused. "Where's Axel?"

"I thought he was with you."

My spine tingled again, making me shiver.

"Here." A new pair of crimson eyes had appeared out of nowhere.

Jay nodded in acknowledgment of Axel's appearance. "Is everybody ready?" he asked.

I looked at Ash and RC, waiting for them to answer. Yes or no. I'd like to know somebody else's opinion, because I was still hopelessly conflicted about our decision. When they didn't respond, all I could think to blurt was, "Question." Their heads all turned to stare at me in the dark. "Are . . . we sure about this?"

"We already decided," said Jay. "No going back now."

Ash's form reached over her shoulder and pulled a long metal staff from her harness. RC drew his hand out of his pocket, and from the gaping holes in the ceiling, the green glow of the clouds reflected off the metal in his hand. I wasn't ready to summon my weapons quite yet.

The room was suddenly bathed in bright light. I saw, just for an instant, my lab-family. Finn and Reese sitting on a nest of blankets, the backwards hat over Finn's mess of chestnut hair the only way to tell the identical twins apart. Axel leaning against the wall, his clairvoyant eyes peering through locks of his untamed coal-black hair. Kit, still in her fur, sitting next to Ash's boot with her tail curled over her white paws. Ash clutching her staff, a silver band glinting on her upper arm, her ports visible in a line across her forehead. RC's milky blind eye marred by a pink scar, the right sleeve missing from his shirt to expose the gauze winding around his arm. Jay's ashen gray hair swept to one side, the silver whistle around his neck.

I had less than a second to imprint these images.

Then, just as quickly as the light had come, we were lost in darkness again, only silhouettes with glowing eyes in the reverberations of a clap of thunder that made the depths of my bones vibrate.

— Chapter One —

In Thunder's Silence

Lightning illuminated Phantom Heights in a brief washout of white.

Holly Jennings stood in the corner on the terraced stage inside City Hall, her arms folded tightly across her chest. The people around her were phantoms of their former selves. After all of her diligent work to protect them, this was what they had become—homeless refugees battling illness and infection, trapped like rats inside City Hall, surviving on intermittent supply drops from the military and meager yields from raids on the town. The entoplasm dome surrounding the building affected ghosts, not humans, and yet, it felt like a prison, casting its cold green light on the gaunt faces of its skeletal inhabitants.

Holly glared sidelong at the ghost hunter standing by the boarded window. This was all Madison Tarrow's fault. The people hailed her as a leader now; how quickly they'd forgotten that she was the one who had allowed this catastrophe to happen. Madison had let her personal loss lead to more—more families broken, more people kidnapped, more children buried or orphaned. And she'd almost repeated history by negotiating with the Alpha fugitives when they'd abducted her daughter.

Holly shook her head. That was a bad deal, but no one would listen to her. Wesly Cooper had entranced the survivors with wild promises of hiring mercenaries to restore their town and their freedom. He was too cunning for his own good, and his audience had been far too desperate to know any better.

Holly flinched at a sudden *crack* of thunder that set her teeth on edge. Her gaze wandered to the nearest boarded window leaking eerie pale light through the cracks. The entoplasm shield tinted the nighttime clouds green, the low cloud cover broken only by the bright streaks of lightning that turned the sky into a brief puzzle. Was Cato out there shivering like a wretch in this miserable night? Or was he still safely secured underground at the AGC under Agent Kovak's watch?

Pain.

Holly registered it the instant her teeth pulled away too much fingernail, ripping it to the quick. She hadn't even realized what she was doing. Her tongue tasted copper as she ran it along the jagged edge.

"Damn them," Madison seethed, peering through the gaps between boards at the storm. "I told you they'd do this, Wes."

Holly's gaze flicked to the werewolf, who crossed his arms with indignation. "Just because we haven't seen or heard from the Alpha ghosts in a week doesn't mean they backed out of the deal," he defended halfheartedly. Despite the grim circumstances, Holly had to admit that she relished seeing Cooper's usual overconfidence reduced to an almost humble demeanor, at least for the time being.

Madison gestured toward the boarded window. "Nothing has changed! If they're still out there—which I doubt—then they sure as hell aren't doing anything, because there are just as many ghosts, if not *more*, than there were a week ago!"

"The supplies we've been leaving outside the shield are gone every day."

"So?" Madison retorted. "It could be anyone out there stealing our limited supply. My bet is the Alpha ghosts fled into the Ghost Realm the second they had an opening."

Holly bowed her head and watched a red bead swell from the thin line at the edge of her torn fingernail. The Ghost Realm. It was hell for humans. If, against all odds, Cato had managed to escape from the AGC and was now hiding in the Ghost Realm . . . *He'd be fine*, she assured herself despite her churning stomach. The Ghost Realm was where he belonged now. He was probably safer there beyond Agent Kovak's reach, and Holly didn't have to worry anymore. Everything had worked out better than she could have hoped.

And yet, her chest seemed to tighten around her aching heart. Her throat clenched, as if her body was preparing to cry even as she mentally reminded herself that she should be celebrating this victory.

Why doesn't it feel like a victory?

Thunder crashed, and the building trembled in its throes.

Wes, with no rebuttal to Madison's claim, turned his head away. "Maybe I miscalculated," he muttered.

The ghost hunter grumbled, "We could've caught them and claimed the reward from the Agents . . ."

"Don't say that," her daughter said hollowly from her seat on the bottom step. Vivian gripped the paw of her childhood teddy bear and raised her head to glare defiantly at her mom.

Trey was sitting next to her. He shifted and said, "Madison? After touring the lab, I wouldn't wish that fate on my worst enemy."

Madison shook her head and turned away from her apprentice. Everyone in City Hall was solemn as the realization sank in that their mercenaries—their last hope—were long gone.

Holly folded her arms and bowed her head, scoffing at her own low spirits. Perhaps Cooper had managed to stir her hope just a little with his tantalizing speeches. The people of Phantom Heights actually might have had a chance at reclaiming a normal life. Why did it hurt more to have hope revived and then crushed than it did to have no hope at all to begin with?

Outside, the rain pounded, whipped in driving sheets by the ferocious wind. Holly eyed the rattling boards over the windows. A cold foreboding was taking root and spreading throughout her whole body. Was this a natural storm, or the work of a kálos Atmokinetic with the ability to control the weather?

Lightning washed everything in white for a split second in the throes of a deafening thunderclap. City Hall was plunged into blackness—something no one had witnessed in a year and a half. There was a moment of stunned silence. Somebody yelled, "The shield is down!"

Panic.

People started screaming. Somewhere in the darkness, Madison was yelling, begging everyone to calm down. The crowd had been engulfed in hysteria, terrified that ghosts were appearing, unseen, in the blackness. With all the screams, it was impossible to tell if anyone was actually being attacked.

"Shannon!" Holly called, her voice lost in a cacophony of screams. She cupped her hands around her mouth. "Shan! Shannon, where are you?" Bodies jostled her from every direction in the dark. Another flash of lightning gave her less than a second to scan the mayhem for her daughter. "*Shannon!*"

A deafening howl drowned out the screams. Holly yelped and doubled over, clapping her hands over her ears. The howl vibrated her bones, her teeth, the whole building. She squinted when the room was suddenly illuminated in red light.

Madison was standing onstage next to a giant gray wolf, a burning flare held high over her head. "Everybody, calm down! This flare isn't going to last long. I need you all to *stay calm* when the light goes out. All raiders, arm up and form a perimeter. If you see any glowing eyes, shoot. Don't hesitate, and don't ask questions. Pull the trigger."

The townspeople cowered in the center of City Hall as the raiders pushed their way outward. "Excuse me, move, get out of my way, *move*," Holly snarled, unapologetically forcing her way through the throng. The red light was burning away. She had only a few moments, and there were too many faces in the shadows. "Shannon? Shannon, where are you?"

"Mom!"

Holly whirled. She took a breath to call again but hesitated when a hand gripped two of her fingers. Her daughter squeezed between two bodies, emerging from the mass. Holly exhaled in relief and pulled her inward for a tight embrace. "Oh, thank God."

She rested her cheek on top of Shannon's head. Madison was now standing before the barred doors, gripping a two-barreled silver gun. Trey and Wes took up positions in opposite corners. The wolf was growling, hackles raised along his back. The raid team joined the werewolf and the ghost hunters along the perimeter, facing the boarded windows with their backs to the townspeople.

The flare went out.

— Chapter Two —

Perimeter

An angry rumble of thunder rolled over the drone of rain beating the roof.

Distant lightning flickered. Vivian's finger was tight on the trigger.

She squinted in the darkness, barely discerning the outlines of the boards between lightning flashes. She was ready.

But nobody came through the wall.

She glanced sideways at Trey, who was straightening in confusion. He turned to her mom. "I don't understand. Why aren't we being attacked?"

As one, every body rotated. Thousands of expectant stares fixated onto Madison, who pried her stiff finger away from the trigger. "Maybe they're all taking shelter from the storm?" She holstered her gun and strode across the great hall. "I'm going to try to fix the generator while there's still time. Trey, you're in charge of the team. If anything goes wrong, call me."

She wrenched open the door to the basement and disappeared in the pitch black. A flashlight beam appeared, marking her descent. Trey stared at the doorway, looking as though he might throw up with his newfound responsibility to be in charge during a crisis.

Lightning flashed again, followed by a *boom* of thunder that rattled the entire building. A young girl in the crowd started bawling, her cries muffled as her mother pulled her close to comfort her.

The darting beam reappeared up the stairs. Footsteps announced Madison, who halted in the doorway to breathlessly report, "Lightning struck the shield. It repels ectoplasm, not electricity, so some of the conduits on the generator are fried. I don't know if I can fix it."

Vivian leaned back against the wall, her stomach threatening to surrender her dinner of tomato soup and stale crackers. The ectogun in her hand suddenly felt useless against the hundreds of ghosts just outside with nothing to hold them back.

Madison was so flustered that she was talking and thinking aloud at the same time. "It should have hit the rod instead . . . I need . . . parts, tools . . . I can dismantle . . . no, no, that wouldn't fit . . . if I can just find . . ." She vanished down into the basement's depths again.

Wes growled quietly, his ears pricked forward. The raid team stood at the ready, fingers cramping over triggers, bodies tense, senses alert. "Orders?" a woman asked.

Trey didn't answer, as if habitually waiting for his ghost-hunting master to reply instead. Vivian whispered, "Trey?"

"Hold your position," he finally croaked.

Vivian faced the window again. She curled her fingertips between the boards and squinted across town square. From here, she could see the silhouette of the Fruth building across the street, the tallest building in Phantom Heights. The lightning rod on the roof should have attracted the electricity to protect the shield. One stray bolt, and this might be their last night.

Vivian stepped back and exhaled. She checked her ectogun to ensure the safety was off.

Five minutes later, Vivian and most of the raiders had straightened, looking around City Hall with ectoguns loosely gripped in their hands. And when the storm passed and morning's light broke the darkness, they were sitting, weapons lying in their laps or tucked back into their holsters. No one dared to leave or even open the door, but several peered through the cracks between the window boards, and more than one reported seeing ectoplasm bursts and ghosts fighting in the plaza. "Looks like gang clashes," raiders reported.

Wes sustained limbo long enough to announce, "I'm going to find out what's happening."

"You can't leave!" Trey cried.

The wolf, who had started to slink for the doors, paused and metamorphosed again to ask, "Why not?"

Vivian glanced at Trey, who scowled, mouth open, but no answer came when he did a slow sweep of the hall. Vivian followed his gaze and surveyed the crowd. Everyone was calm. There was no reason for Wes to stay here when he could gather information outside. "Well . . ." said Trey, "what if we're attacked?"

"I won't be long," Wes assured, his response almost incoherent in the mess of sharp teeth as he trotted away on four legs. A pair of raiders opened the door for him.

With the werewolf gone, the raid team drew their weapons again.

But the morning passed without incident. Vivian found Trey sitting with his back to the wall. She holstered her weapon, crawled next to him, and sat cross-legged.

"Viv," he said, "why do you think we haven't been attacked yet?"

"Not sure," she answered, feeling strangely calm.

"You think they're waiting for us to lower our guard so they can take us by surprise?"

"I don't know." She leaned back and stared up at the vaulted ceiling high above. "Tell me about the twins," she said, turning to make eye contact with Trey.

"*Now?*"

"Yeah. What were they like?"

He thought for a moment. "Zombies," he finally replied.

"What?"

Trey hesitated. "Well, they watched everything and everyone with these dead blue eyes, but they were . . . I mean, they were kinda creepy because they knew every single thought in your head. On the one hand, I get why Agent Kovak is worried. They're so silent you forget they're there, but I think they observe a lot. Even things never said out loud. I bet they know a lot of secrets he doesn't want leaked to the public. But they didn't say a single word the whole time they were here. I can't see them ever giving up any of Kovak's secrets."

Vivian kept quiet, considering his description. Trey pulled out his Rubik's cube but just held it in his hand, staring at it. "Hey, you solved it!" she exclaimed.

"No. A1 and A2 did. And I still can't figure out how they did it."

Vivian gazed at the solved cube. "The twins solved it? But they're only . . . what, ten?"

Trey narrowed his eyes. "I think they're smarter than they seem on the surface."

"I wish I could have been here. I would've liked to meet the people Jay was willing to sacrifice everything for. He doesn't seem like the type to take unnecessary risks."

Trey was still staring at his cube as if it had hidden answers within and he could find them if he just glared at it long enough. Softly, he said, "It's stupid, you know? Cato bet me twenty bucks I'd never solve this thing. I used to imagine what his face would look like when I showed him this." He shoved it deep in his pocket. "Listen, Viv, I know you brushed off everything that happened for your mom's sake. But please tell me the truth—did they hurt you?"

"No. They didn't. They scared me sometimes, but they never hurt me. Jay is . . . hard to describe. Kovak said he's an aggressive, cold-hearted, calculating killer, but the Jay I met was a thoughtful, patient person who was nervous about even coming near me."

"Well, apparently he's also a liar. And he was going to kill you."

Vivian was silent in response to Trey's cold analysis. "I don't know about that," she said. "What do you think about this deal? Seriously?"

Trey stared down at the prototype gun from the AGC lying in his lap. "Well . . . I keep thinking about . . . about Cato. And what he would do if he were here with us."

Vivian drew her legs up and rested her chin on her knees. "And what do you think he'd do?"

Trey scoffed. "We probably wouldn't be in this mess in the first place. But I think he'd give the Alpha ghosts a chance . . . don't you?"

She shrugged, then tilted her head down so her knee muffled her words. "I miss him."

"Yeah," Trey agreed, the word cracking.

Thump!

Vivian scrambled for her ectogun. The raiders were on their feet, every weapon trained on the doors. *Scritch-scritch-scratch*, then a low whine drawing out into a quiet howl.

"Wes?" called Chase, the raider nearest to the door.

A puppylike *yip* answered.

Chase heaved the bar to the side and hauled the heavy door open. A furry gray head nudged it hard, tossing Chase back. The massive wolf slunk into City Hall, its eyes glowing yellow. In this form, Wes was as big as a draft horse, broad-shouldered with a short dark mane between his shoulder blades.

The ectoguns lowered toward the floor. Wes shook his body, flinging water everywhere and causing a wide radius of disgruntled people to shield their faces with their arms and curse at him. His body shrank, the wet fur yielding to skin, and then the limbo creature was standing on two legs, his tail swishing back and forth to keep his balance on his furry haunches.

"Where's Madison?" he demanded above the grumblings and the questions.

Vivian jogged to the basement door and called down, "Mom! Wes is back!"

Her mom appeared at the bottom of the staircase and trotted up the steps, then halted in the doorway. "What's going on out there?" she asked, wiping her hands on a dirty towel.

Wes shifted, eyes darting, as though he was on an adrenaline high and couldn't keep still. "We've been attacked nonstop since the shield went down."

"What are you talking about? We haven't seen a single ghost."

"It's the Alpha ghosts. They've set up a perimeter around City Hall. They're protecting us."

The gun fell from Vivian's hand and clattered to the floor, the only sound in the wake of silence following Wes's statement. Her mom's eyes were wide as she ogled the boarded windows.

"Maddie, you have to fix that shield *now*. I don't think they can last much longer."

She ran her fingers through her hair. "They actually stayed . . ." she whispered, shaking her head.

Wes strode forward and seized her by the shoulders. She grimaced; Wes still had claws. "Maddie! They must be exhausted! You have to get that shield operational!"

She nodded. "I think I'm close. I just need a few more hours."

Wes released her and turned away. "I'm going out there to help them," he announced, his body shifting again.

Trey stepped forward. "I'm going, too."

"No," said Madison. "No, you have to stay here to guard City Hall in case any ghosts get through their perimeter."

"I can help," he protested.

"You're needed here most."

The wolf loped out the doors again. Trey watched bitterly, folding his arms. "Thank you," said Madison. She laid a gentle hand on his shoulder.

"We should send raiders," he insisted. "The green team can fight while the blue team guards City Hall."

Vivian stood straighter. She and Trey had always accompanied her mom on the green team. Jay needed her help, and she was ready.

Her mom considered the proposal. Police Chief Emerton spoke up: "I don't like that tactical move."

"Why?" Trey challenged before Madison had a chance to.

"Because," he replied patiently, "we employed mercenaries we've never met. We go out and start shooting at ghosts without knowing who's who, and we're likely to shoot our own allies. Fast way to end a deal, don't you think?"

"I agree," said Madison.

Trey clenched his teeth, choosing to stew in angry silence.

Vivian turned away to watch Chase jam the bar back into place over the doors. She understood Trey's frustration. He wanted to be a ghost hunter. He wanted to fight.

And they both knew Cato wouldn't have stood there doing nothing.

— Chapter Three —
Ice

The ghost collapsed with a sickening *thud* into a puddle at my feet.

Raindrops dripped arrhythmically from the lip of my hood, and I tugged at the soaked black cloth covering the lower half of my face. Jay had taken inspiration from my former days as Phantom, and now he, Ash, RC, and I were all hidden behind hoods and masks to conceal our faces and, more importantly, our youth. But I was gasping to force air through the fabric and into my burning lungs, and I yearned to pull the wet cloth away so I could breathe.

My victim stirred, starting to pull himself up again. The trickle of blood from his nose told me he was close to burning out, but he still had a little strength left. I held out my hand, focusing all my concentration on the water he was kneeling in.

I associated my two Divinities with colors. The green power was hot. It was rage and destruction, and when it surfaced, both of my eyes blazed green. The other was cold and blue. This was the one I summoned when I reached for my center, causing my left green eye to change color and match my right blue one.

The puddle solidified; crystalline pillars of ice erupted upward to encase the man's arms and legs. No way he had enough power left in his reserves to become intangible. I let my hand fall.

A sudden chill crept down my spinal cord just before an impact sent me crashing into the wall. *Damn it—too slow.* The ectoplasm bruised my ribs on one side; the wall bruised them on the other. I hit the ground, stunned, and twisted my neck to find my assailant. He was a big man in height and girth, his whole bald head tattooed. I tried to stand, but my muscles didn't want to obey. This battle seemed endless.

I was sleep-deprived and hungry. I'd been drinking from puddles whenever I had a few minutes to catch my breath, and the fatigue was making me slow and clumsy. This was a much bigger arena than what I was used to fighting in. More enemies. More hiding places. Same fight for my life, though.

I pushed myself onto my hands and knees.

Stand up.

My arms trembled. I glared at my reflection in a puddle.

Stand up! I screamed at myself.

The ghost stopped his advance, eyes glowing as electric-blue ectoplasm condensed in his hands. I didn't have the energy reserves left to summon a shield; this was going to hurt.

His smile turned into a grimace, and he went rigid as degraded red ectoplasm suddenly coursed in vicious tendrils along his entire body.

Grade G. The highest form of ectoplasm. Impressive, I thought in a delusional daze, so numbed by exhaustion that I wasn't even afraid of *who* was generating this Grade G ectoplasm, how powerful he or she must be, or how much it was going to hurt if I was the next target.

My attacker shrieked, his body convulsing as the energy ran through it like red lightning shocking his system and snapping across his skin. His screams subsided when he sank to his knees, then onto his side, residual zaps of ectoplasm still crackling across his limp body. A cloaked figure wearing an Alpha uniform was standing behind him.

"Thank you," I croaked.

Axel stepped forward with his fist extended. I seized his forearm and allowed him to effortlessly pull me to my feet. "Just to be clear, I didn't do it for *them*," he said, jerking his head at dark City Hall.

I nodded wearily. Only a few hours ago, I had resented my lab-brother for sitting on a rooftop watching the battle. He still wouldn't fight with us, and even worse, he had the nerve to hang upside down from the gutter and criticize my footwork. Axel could have ended this fight a long time ago. He was the strongest, fastest, most powerful ghost alive, and he was also the most stubborn. I still thought Jay was being a pushover by letting Axel get away with this rebellion, but I could honestly admit, "I'm glad to have you by my side."

An eerie, bone-chilling howl broke above the drone of the rain. I paused, gazing past my lab-brother at the massive animal fleeing from City Hall. The creature loped into town square, glowing yellow eyes fixed on a pair of ghosts fighting with Jay. Wes pounced on his prey. Jay vanished, leaving the two ghosts to the mercy of the wolf's teeth.

A distant squeal of pain—unfortunately an all-too-familiar one I knew belonged to Ash—made me turn. Axel was already gone to assist her. I was on my own again.

I gazed at the white building that housed the human population of Phantom Heights. City Hall had four stone columns supporting its portico, and a domed roof served as the base for its clock tower. My blood-family was inside. I didn't want to think about how I was fighting to protect them right now, because I didn't want to be. They'd disowned me; they didn't deserve my protection.

I shook my head. *I'm not fighting for them*, I reminded myself. I was fighting for Finn and Reese. I was fighting to earn their medicine, and I was fighting to repay the debt we owed for our powers. Not my blood-family.

A figure running toward City Hall jolted my thoughts, and I sprinted in pursuit. The woman must have sensed me; she whirled.

With a battle cry, she swung at me, and in two smooth moves, I'd taken her down. I raised my left fist, sweeping my ice-crusted forearm to the side to deflect her blow away from my head while simultaneously driving my right hand up into her exposed face, smashing the heel of my palm into her nose. The forward and upward thrust of my hand shattered the cartilage and bone with a disturbing *crack*. My opponent screeched and stumbled away from me, her hands flying up to her face to catch the blood.

I shivered, sensing another ghost, and I heard him charging me from behind, his footsteps heavy, his breathing loud and ragged. I knew by listening to his gait that he was much larger than me. I had seconds to react. Intangibility was a useful defense—if I called upon it, he'd pass right through me—but it was costly, not ideal in a long-term fight.

My power reserves were dangerously low as it was.

I crouched lower, preparing myself, listening, and at the last possible moment, I took two steps back, straight into my startled attacker. He'd been committed to grabbing me where I was, and I'd thrown off his timing by moving closer to him. I seized his arm, which was still outstretched to lock around me, and hauled him over my shoulder, using his own momentum to flip him over my crouched body.

The man floundered through the air, then landed with a hollow grunt on his back. The air rushed out of his lungs in a single *whoosh*. I leapt forward and came down on top of him with both feet squarely in his stomach. He tried to gasp, but with nothing left in his lungs to exhale, he just made another strangled grunt. I raised my hand toward the sky, and in the two seconds it took for me to bring it down hard, a ball of ice had formed in my fist, now leaving my fingers and flying the short distance with gravity's acceleration into his face.

I glanced at City Hall for the hundredth time, wishing the Dome would appear so I could rest. *Come on, Madison*, I thought impatiently, as if directing my thoughts at the refuge would goad her into action.

Incoming. Right side.

How I knew that, I couldn't say. Long hours getting the crap beaten out of me in the Arena had tuned my level of awareness. I was used to seeing RC's silver disks zipping through my peripheral and having a split second to react. I clenched my fist and raised my right arm, ducked my head, and turned my shoulder to meet the blow as I reached for my center. A layer of ice hardened into partial armor on my right arm. This minimalistic hardening maintained my power reserves more efficiently than intangibility would have, especially since the latter defense was useless when ectoplasm was involved.

The weapon—it wasn't ectoplasm, but I couldn't catch enough of a glimpse to identify it—struck my forearm. The impact knocked me to the side, but I kept my footing, even used the momentum to spin a full circle and fling a shard of ice back at the source of the attack.

She was quick enough to deflect it, my ice meeting a metal weapon with a *clang* that echoed across the square. But I was faster. I'd already thrown two more deadly shards that whizzed through the air. The first was high, aimed for her head. She deflected. The second was lower, aimed for her rib cage, only half a second behind the first. Not enough time to lower her arm after shielding her face. My aim, guided by my concentration and Divinity, was true, and she went down.

I had no time to celebrate. My feet were yanked off the ground, and I found myself floundering through the air. A cloaked figure with glowing green eyes was pulling me toward him. A Telekinetic, like RC? He veered back with his fist, and I was on course to fly right into the blow. I couldn't stop my trajectory, but I raised my forearms in front of my face and coated them with ice while pulling my knees up and coating my shins as well. His punch, amplified by brass knuckles and my speed through the air, made contact with the ice armor on my arms. My ice cracked, but it protected me.

Then I was flying away from him. I couldn't react fast enough to brace myself when I smashed into a column.

"Bloody Scout," I wheezed. That might have cracked a rib or two.

I was being pulled toward him again. I was pretty sure this wasn't telekinesis. He didn't have RC's finesse to guide me in any particular direction. RC could have flung me from wall to wall and dropped me on the roof like a rag doll; all this guy could do was attract and repel me, as if his body were a magnet and I were made of metal.

I held out my palm and fired ectoplasm to greet my assailant ahead of me. I dropped like a rock and landed hard on the cobblestones half a second before my ectoplasm rebounded and flew over my head. So, my opponent couldn't attract me *and* repel an attack at the same time.

Okay, let's play.

He flung me away again, but this time I was ready. I brought my feet up so the soles of my boots landed on the column. My knees bent to absorb the impact.

He pulled me toward him once more, already veering back for another punch, and at the first shift in direction, I pushed off the column like a rocket. This time, I didn't curl up to take the hit. This time, my ice didn't thicken into a shell to protect me. This time, I waited until a couple of seconds before impact before I reached for my center again, and then I was holding a crude ice spear that would meet his stomach before his brass knuckles could meet my face. I saw the instant realization widen his eyes, but he couldn't reverse his power in time.

My spear passed through his intangible abdomen, my body a second behind. His power broke. I dropped my spear and tumbled across the cobblestones, trying to slow my momentum. I hadn't fully stopped rolling, but I had my bearings, and I threw my arm out, freezing ice needles and sending them flying in his direction as I finally slid to a clumsy stop.

He'd already turned to face me. My ice stopped midair, and then the shards were zipping right back at me. I didn't move; by my will, the ice melted, pelting me as harmless rain. *Damn it. I missed my chance.* Anything I'd throw at him now—ectoplasm or ice—would be repelled. So would I if I tried to charge him.

My focus traveled from his face down to his boots. To his reflection in the puddles. To hardening that water and making it slick and smooth underfoot.

He slipped, arms pinwheeling to keep his balance, but his feet flew out from under him, and he crashed onto his back. I raised my hand, fingers splayed. He jerked with a gasp, staring straight up at the low cloud ceiling. I let my hand fall. I didn't need to check to see if he was dead. I didn't need to see the sharp ice stalagmites that had erupted from beneath him and impaled his body, a growing pool of blood mixed with my melting ice in the rain. He'd given me a good fight, but it was over.

Slowly, I stood. I wiped my nose, surprised to see blood diluted raindrop by raindrop on my fingers. Not good. My power reserves were almost tapped out.

Two more ghosts approached me, their stances indicative of another fight. *Great. Two on one. I'm too tired for this shit.* They halted, seemingly alarmed by something behind me, and then they took off running. Bewildered, I turned.

Shadow Guards were appearing through the Rip.

Okay, I take it back. I prefer the two-on-one odds.

Something hit me so hard and fast I found myself on my back staring up at the clouds in a daze. What struck me? I didn't want to get up again. I wanted to lie there and close my eyes and fall asleep.

But I couldn't. With a groan, I rolled onto my side and pushed myself up. To my surprise and relief, a green spark lit the tip of the clock tower. A single beam shot from the tall spire and fell to the ground like a transparent curtain. I stared at the Dome, and then I chuckled. Next thing I knew, I was laughing hysterically like a lunatic in the downpour. *About time, Madison.*

The Guards had hesitated at the Dome's reappearance, but they were moving into formation. I shivered; Jay was kneeling beside me.

"Close your eyes," he advised.

I obeyed. His hand clutched my shoulder, and I braced myself. A roaring wind filled my ears as immense pressure pushed against me from all directions. When I cracked my eyes open again, I was Home.

Madison emerged from the stairs, wiping perspiration from her brow. "It's working," she announced.

She was answered with a chorus of cheers.

As the ruckus settled, knuckles rapped on the door from the outside. "It's me," came Wes's voice. Trey opened the door, and the werewolf poked his head in. He cleared his throat. Doc handed him a towel to wrap around his waist, and then he slunk inside on dirty bare feet, beaming through the blood spattered on his face. "I *told* you!" he crowed. "Ha! I told you this deal would work!"

Madison sighed, but she couldn't dispute. If Wes hadn't made the deal with the Alpha ghosts, they all would have been in serious trouble when the shield went down. What she dreaded, however, was having to hear Wes boast for weeks on end about it. Even now, he was opening his mouth to continue, but he paused and looked at the whiteboard instead with a hushed, "Oh."

Madison turned.

The marker was levitating from the tray. It wobbled precariously, as if the wielder barely had the strength to raise it. City Hall held its breath as shaky words were written on the board, the handwriting noticeably sloppier.

Exausted need a brake.

Madison nodded. "Yes, of course," she answered faintly. "You deserve it."

The marker fell to the floor with a clatter, the cap spinning separately.

"Thank you!" Madison called, but she was sure the Alpha ghosts were already gone. She wrapped her arms around herself and stared at the floor, still in a state of shock. She had been so sure they'd left Phantom Heights without looking back, and yet here they were, honoring their bargain, risking their own well-being to uphold their word.

"Wes, give me your phone." She held out her hand.

He narrowed his eyes, glaring at her distrustfully. "Why?"

She fixed him with a cold stare until grudgingly, he went to his pile of folded clothes and dug in the pocket of his jeans for his cell phone. Madison dialed the AGC's number and held the phone up to her ear.

"What are you doing?" Wes demanded. "They kept up their end of the deal!"

Madison raised her index finger warningly, signaling him to be quiet. She turned away as a female's voice answered, "You've reached the Agency of Ghost Control. This is a restricted line. If you've dialed by error, please disconnect immediately. Otherwise, state your name and whom you wish your call directed to."

Wes lunged to reclaim the phone, but Madison spun away. "Yes, hi, this is Madison Tarrow, hunter ID 0228. I need to speak with Agent Kovak, please."

"One moment."

Holly's eyebrows lifted in alarm. "You're calling Kovak?"

"Madison!" Wes exclaimed.

"I know what I'm doing," said Madison. "Now *shut it* before I tell him there's a werewolf standing in front of me." Wes took a startled step back as if he'd just been slapped.

Over the earpiece, a man's voice answered. "Kovak speaking."

"Hello!" Madison chimed. Holly frowned and shook her head, but Madison had already realized that her voice was too chipper. She coughed once and said, "This is Madison Tarrow."

"Maddie?" Agent Kovak sounded surprised. She almost corrected the irritating nickname, but she held her tongue as he continued, "This is . . . unexpected."

Trey shook his head pleadingly and mouthed, "You can't do this. It's not fair."

Conscious of every eye still trained on her, Madison replied, "Ah, yes, well . . . first of all, I just wanted to thank you for the weapons you sent us."

"Mm-hmm, always happy to help," Agent Kovak murmured absently. Madison imagined him inspecting his manicured fingernails and fought the urge to roll her eyes.

"Also, we've been keeping an eye out for your missing ghosts, so I'm calling to update you—there's been no sign of them here in Phantom Heights."

The crowd let out a collective sigh of relief, and Wes's hard scowl softened in realization. Holly set her hand over her heart. Madison stood still, listening to silence on the other end of the line.

Finally, Agent Kovak said coldly, "Tarrow, we aren't interested in knowing where our ghosts are *not*. Don't call me unless you've seen them or you have reason to believe they've passed your way."

Although he couldn't see her, Madison nodded. "Yes, sir."

The line went dead. Agent Kovak had surely slammed the phone down, no doubt out of frustration at the pointless interruption and the mocking tone with which Madison had said, "yes, sir."

She shot Wes a smirk as she tossed the phone back. "They kept their end; I thought we should keep ours."

— Chapter Four —
Trial by Stone

The raid team crept slowly, guns drawn, led by the gray wolf slinking through the darkness.

"It's quiet tonight," Madison said, stepping over a window frame. They'd been outside the entoplasm shield for more than ten minutes now without encountering a single ghost.

Trey paused as a shadow flitted a few yards away. He couldn't shake the feeling they were being watched, and the last time he'd disregarded that suspicion, they'd lost Vivian. He wasn't going to make that mistake again. Maybe they hadn't been attacked yet because there was an ambush ahead.

His finger was cramping over the trigger. He almost would have welcomed an opponent just so he'd have an excuse to see how the AGC's modified gun handled. He had yet to fire it, which was beyond strange. He heard light footsteps running quietly through the night, but when he turned, he saw nothing. *Too bad I can't sense ghosts like Cato could*, he thought.

Madison's white-knuckled grip on her gun loosened. "I wonder why we haven't been attacked," she said.

Movement in the shadows drew a gasp from Trey. He tapped her shoulder. When she turned, he pointed at an open door. "I think that's why," he whispered.

Madison stared. When the rest of the raid team followed their glances, they also froze. Lurking in the shadow of a doorway was a cloaked figure with a single glowing blue eye, the other half of his face hidden behind the doorframe. Stitched on the front of his chest, barely visible in the poor light, was part of a white α symbol.

The ghost met their gazes briefly, narrowed his eye, and then he slipped into the shadows.

Trey said, "I think they've been trailing us since we left."

The wolf whimpered and turned in a tight circle, sniffing the air. Madison swallowed. She whirled just as the edge of a cloak vanished around a corner. "They surrounded us," she realized aloud.

"Just like when the shield went down," Chase added.

The raiders murmured among themselves and glanced about nervously. "What do we do?" another asked.

Trey looked to Madison for guidance, as did everyone else.

She considered for a moment, then answered, "Let them fight. We can travel farther and bring back more supplies."

She took off at a brisk jog, and Trey matched her pace. It was a strange feeling, going against all instincts to be cautious, but they had mercenaries at their disposal. Might as well take full advantage.

Trey's gaze wandered up to the shadow that dashed along the rooftop above them, a whisper of footsteps running through the empty building on his right, the edge of a black cloak disappearing around the corner up ahead.

I yanked down the mask and exhaled to calm my pounding heart. I hadn't intended to be seen. I'd been lucky this time; I was the only ghost in the Realms with heterochromia. If the raid team had seen both eyes, they would have identified me immediately, even with the hood and mask hiding my face.

I waited, allowing the humans to put distance between us, and then I refitted the black cloth over the lower half of my face and slinked behind. They'd quickened their pace and abandoned some of their stealth now that they knew we were here.

I gritted my teeth as Ash's screams broke the quiet—another Spasm. The humans faltered. They must think we were torturing someone. That was almost amusing, but just as well because Jay said it was best for them to fear us. He hoped that would inspire them to keep their distance. "Be silent, be quick," he'd instructed. "Nothing more than a passing shadow."

As Ash's cries faded, the raiders continued on. I trailed after them.

The final count was five to two. Axel and I had been outvoted. Axel didn't really care that much; despite the vote, he still refused to aid humankind. To me, the final decision was a devastating blow. I didn't want to be here. These people from my life Before turned on me once, and I had no doubt they'd turn on me again without hesitation, only this time they'd hurt my new family, too. But, like it or not, our services had been employed until the day the humans broke their end of the deal, and until that happened—I knew it was only a matter of time—my personal mission was to protect my lab-family above anyone else, despite our deal.

So, while RC recuperated, we spent several days training at Home. We had to relearn how to use the full extent of our powers, which had been neutralized and filtered for so long. The first few days were long hours of nonstop drills and sparring sessions overseen by Jay. He wanted us to be completely prepared. Once we started fighting, we were sure to make a lot of enemies in a short amount of time. There would be no room for errors.

The plan was to establish a firm hold on one section of the town before gradually widening the radius of our control. We were essentially just another gang claiming territory. But just before we were ready to make our first move, the Dome malfunctioned, forcing us into action to protect our new wards. And now, here we were, our first real "mission" since that impromptu battle.

I quickened my slinking stride into a swift dash through the abandoned buildings alongside the raid team. My long, smooth gait easily overtook them. I paused half a block ahead to crouch below a window, where I set my fingertips on the dusty sill and rose just enough to peer over the edge as the wolf stalked past. His massive paws padded across the asphalt, tail whisking from side to side, nose to the ground, eyes glowing yellow in the night. The swelling moon cast a silver sheen on his gray coat. He still perplexed me to no end.

A few days ago, Jay had asked, "What was your relationship with Wes?"

I'd had to search through my fragmented memories. I didn't remember much about Wesly Cooper. "I think we tolerated each other. He wasn't an enemy, but he wasn't an ally, either."

"Is he trustworthy?"

"My gut says no."

The wolf passed from my vision, and the leader of the raid team sidled into view—Madison Tarrow.

My green Divinity burned hot with hatred while I watched her sweep her gun expertly in front of her body. Her hair was tied back in a ponytail to keep it out of her face. She was slim, similar in stature to Vivian. But much colder. I didn't think she knew how to laugh like Viv, or even smile like her daughter.

"Tell me about Madison," Jay had requested.

I'd emptied my lungs in one heavy sigh. "She's lethal, hates ghosts, and is capable of anything. That's all you really need to know." I had left it at that. A few years ago when I'd been Phantom, she had tried to kill me countless times. I'd been her enemy, but she'd never been mine. That was Before. Now, I considered her one of my greatest adversaries.

Trailing just behind was her apprentice. I cocked my head, studying the teen. We had to be about the same age. He wasn't nearly as deadly as his ghost-hunting master. I could tell just by the way he moved that he wasn't as confident, either. His steps were cautious, and his eyes darted behind a pair of goggles. While Madison was calm and collected, Trey was nervous and jumpy.

It had been sobering to come face-to-face with him for the first time after my escape. In that moment when our eyes locked while I hesitated in the doorway, we'd stood before each other in our true colors—he an armored ghost hunter, I a fugitive hiding in the shadows. How our friendship had devolved over these past few years. I had been beaten down, broken in mind, body, and spirit, over and over, hardened by betrayal and the need to survive. I couldn't help but wonder what happened to Trey after Lastday to turn him into this. I barely even recognized him behind his goggles and patchy beard.

"What about the ghost hunter's apprentice? Is he dangerous?"

"Madison is teaching him everything she knows, so for now at least, we'll have to consider him an enemy too, unless he proves otherwise." I didn't tell Jay that Trey used to be my best friend. My past didn't matter now. The next time I'd face him, we would not be friends. We would be a ghost and a ghost hunter, two people destined to be enemies regardless of who we were in a past life.

I watched the two ghost hunters pass, the rest of the team trooping behind. Interestingly, Vivian wasn't with the group. No doubt Madison had her precious daughter hidden away in City Hall to keep her safe after our kidnapping stunt. It was not only interesting, but also amusing. Madison really did fear us.

I draped my arms on the windowsill and rested my chin on my hands, my gaze following the armed humans making their way down the street. I bet Vivian was bored out of her mind in City Hall. I'd probably never have the chance to speak to her again. Disappointing, but probably for the best. It was too dangerous to get close to her. It was too dangerous for me to get close to anybody from Before.

I shivered. I stood in alarm, skimming the street for the ghost I'd sensed. I turned away from the window to continue trailing the raid team. This mission was particularly difficult; I was surrounded by hostile ghosts while avoiding the hostile humans who were all armed to the teeth with ghost-hunting weapons. Part of our decision to keep our rather conspicuous uniforms was the hope that the raiders would recognize the Alpha symbol on our chests and hold their fire. As Trey just proved a few minutes ago, that turned out to be a wise choice.

None of us would admit aloud that we were secretly attached to these uniforms. They were an important part of us. They were the only taste of freedom we'd had beyond the cage bars and restraints. They preceded pain, yes, but also sweat and exhilaration, unrestricted movement, power—even if only in filtered quantities—and hope to quench the insatiable hunger and thirst as a reward for victory. When I stood in the Arena, I wasn't naked and vulnerable. I had clothes. I had my boots and my metal-studded fingerless gloves. I had my gauntlets to conceal my Marks, and I had my pads, and most importantly, I had my ice. I felt strong. I felt like a warrior instead of a helpless lab rat.

At least, until the match was over and I was stripped to nothing again.

I pushed open a door, emerging into a tight alleyway perpendicular to the raiders. I pressed myself against the wall, turning my head to observe the team pass by. Movement on the other side of the street drew my eye and the attention of the raid team.

Madison pivoted, ready to fire but hesitant, likely doing a double take to ensure she didn't shoot one of us. The figure lurking in the shadows a few feet away was dressed in a green cloak. The ghost's eyes glowed as he raised his hand, but before Madison could pull the trigger, a flash of silver streaked through the night. It passed in front of the ghost, who let out a strangled gasp and clutched his neck as he fell to his knees. Dumbstruck, Madison lowered her weapon, watching the dark blood pour from the slashed throat until the victim collapsed on his side, dead.

The silver object struck the wall and clattered to the ground. Madison approached. She studied it for a moment, then reached out and held it up for the raid team to see. I, of course, recognized it immediately. The raiders stared at it—a metal disk with a hole in the center. But it had changed since the last time the humans saw it when we left one with the twins. Now it had sharp, curved blades that dripped blood.

"It *was* a weapon," Trey whispered.

The blades whisked inward with a metallic *shick*. Madison gasped, releasing the disk. It fell at her feet. The team watched in amazement as the now-bladeless disk rose into the air and then streaked away into the night to return to RC hidden somewhere in the darkness.

A dark shape cut across a patch of stars. My lab-brother had discovered that if he used his telekinesis on an object—his favorites being a trash can lid or a plastic tray from the school cafeteria—he could hover on it and glide through the air like a bizarre surfer. He'd already become quite adept at the art, and he was way too quick for the humans to notice him overhead. He just had to be careful to stay low or hover over rooftops so he didn't fall too far if a Spasm incapacitated him mid-flight.

A woman I didn't know muttered, "They could have killed us at any time."

"They could have," Madison agreed. "But they didn't."

"I don't see why not," someone else muttered. "The only one they needed was Doc. Anybody else was expendable."

Trey swallowed hard and looked at Madison. "Especially you and me. Two less ghost hunters would have been ideal for them."

Well, he isn't wrong.

Madison gazed up at the clear night sky. "I don't understand them. They kidnapped Vivian but didn't harm her. They risked everything to save the weakest in the group, even though the twins took part in helping the Agents experiment on the others. They had ample opportunity to kill us or leave us to die, but they didn't. They had a chance to escape into the Ghost Realm. They didn't take it."

I narrowed my eyes. Nobody had an answer for Madison. Hell, if she'd asked me those questions directly, I wouldn't have had answers, either. The team finally advanced again, walking past the mouth of the alley where I was hidden.

I shivered, sensing another ghost. I turned my head. In the darkness, I could just make out the form of a cat sitting in the middle of the alley. Beyond it in the next street, a cloaked figure was joined by two more, definitely not my lab-family. I walked away from the raid team and cautiously approached the cat.

The fluffy calico didn't move a muscle. It was a silent warning that danger lay ahead. I hesitated, but once I passed the cat, I took off at a sprint after the ghosts. Probably stupid, going after three all by myself when I didn't know what their Divinities were, but I was rested and energetic and eager to test my skills.

They split again so I was chasing a pair, but now I was aware of one running on either side of me, bringing their numbers up to at least four. It was a gang, and they were luring me away from the others.

Again, stupid, but I figured since I knew what they were doing and I was prepared for the ambush, I could handle this myself. I wasn't going to send a distress call for backup unless I ended up in trouble.

Five shadows baited me to a wide street of herringbone pavers on a direct axis with town square's cobblestone plaza. The church steeple loomed at the end of the pedestrian road. The ghosts veered away and vanished inside a building on the left.

I trotted up the stone steps after them. My pace faltered, my attention diverted to the creatures flanking the stairs. I paused in the shadow of a great lion carved out of limestone. I had a childlike urge to appease my wonder by touching the silent guardian.

I stepped up and trailed my palm over the sculpted paw while staring at his partner crouched on the other side. My fingertips fell from the curled tail, and I jogged the last few steps until a pair of doors blocked my path. I filled my lungs with one deep breath before I pushed on one of the double doors. As it swung inward, I automatically lowered into a defensive crouch, my gaze skimming the shadowy room. I took a step and halted to let my eyes adjust.

A musty odor tickled my nose. Tall forms loomed in the dusk. A flash of movement to my left. The gleam of violet eyes before they disappeared.

I exhaled slowly. As my eyesight became accustomed, I realized the strange shapes were wooden cases, the shelves all filled with books. I remembered this place being quiet and peaceful. It was still quiet, but now, hovering over the dark room, which was vast and riddled with many shadows and places to hide, there hung a tension that compressed my lungs. I swallowed, cautiously sneaking forward. The bookshelves rose high on either side, blinding me. My enemies could be anywhere in here.

The door closed slowly behind me. I licked my lips when I reached the end of the aisle and peered out at the shadowy alcoves. I became invisible before I stole through the intersection and into the cover of the next aisle, and then I released the power before I drained my reserves.

My ears strained for the slightest sound to indicate where the other ghosts were, but the building was silent. The only sounds were my own quiet footsteps.

A long *creeeeak* of straining wood preceded a loud crash that paralyzed me for a moment. I turned, staring in horror at the bookcase falling on top of me. I dove to the side as it tipped into the next wooden case, knocking it over, too.

I landed on my stomach with a grunt. The heavy cases came down, and all I could hear were the deafening crashes of cases falling over like dominoes. Books rained down on me, beating, bruising, and burying me. Cases were still falling and smashing into one another as they toppled in procession all around the library.

I didn't move a muscle, even when I heard the last case fall over. Books were still thudding on the floor. I waited until I heard nothing except my own breathing before I coughed in the dust and shifted beneath the heavy blanket of books. The case would have crushed me if the spaces between the aisles had been wider.

I gazed up at the wooden frame a few inches above my head and reached for my center; the books fell through me as I stood up through the solid wood. I stepped on top of the fallen bookcase, but before I'd fully solidified, a powerful force sent me flying. I landed hard on my back with a grunt.

Groaning, I raised myself up on my elbows to gaze at the ghosts on the far side of the room. After pushing over the first bookcase, they'd waited patiently for me to emerge, then shot me with ectoplasm. I gritted my teeth and staggered to my feet as I reached for my center again, my body becoming cold with my blue Divinity. I crossed my arms in front of my chest, then swept them outward.

Molecules of water in the air solidified into ice slivers that flew toward the group of ghosts. Four didn't even flinch—three became intangible, and my projectiles passed harmlessly through them before embedding in the wall. One ghost, to my surprise, stood still with confidence while the ice broke harmlessly against his skin. *An Impenetrable*, I identified. His skin couldn't be pierced, meaning the only way to hurt him would be a concussion strong enough to do internal damage.

The last ghost didn't react fast enough and was caught in the storm of ice needles. My attack was not meant to be fatal—I'd used barely a drop of my power. My intention had been to either hurt my adversaries before moving in or force them to use up their own reserves by becoming intangible. The man stumbled back with a cry of pain.

Pinpricks of blood welled from his skin. One down. One's Divinity identified. That left three unknowns.

They stepped in front of their injured comrade and began their counterattack by firing ectoplasm at me in bursts of brilliant glowing colors.

I fell to one knee and summoned an ectoplasm shield. A disk of glowing green energy materialized in front of me, but my resilience faltered with each blow. Every strike pounded at my shield. I closed my eyes, as if that might somehow help me concentrate on holding the barrier. I was outnumbered four to one; my shield wasn't going to last under this onslaught.

I opened my eyes, timing their throws. The slightest hesitation, that was all I needed to make a move. My shield was about to break any second . . .

"Hold on."

The blasts stopped. Bewildered, I raised my head to stare at the woman who had spoken. Her allies were just as puzzled as I was; they looked at her with equally stunned, stupid expressions.

She smirked and said, "He's a Cryo. I wanna play with him."

There was something strange about her. She bore a mark—a tattoo, I thought—of an odd symbol in the center of her forehead. It reminded me of a four-pointed star with an upside-down arch.

If it was a symbol for something, I couldn't guess what. I wasn't even sure why it drew my attention in the moment. Her violet eyes blazed. She raised her arms, revealing another tattoo on her biceps.

I braced myself. This was the tricky part about dueling opponents with unknown powers. I'd have a few seconds at most to identify her Divinity and devise a counterattack.

The library was still.

I waited.

The crackling of expanding ice popped in the silence as frozen crystals crept up my forearms in preparation. My heart pounded blood in my ears, making me strain all the more to hear the attack that must be coming.

But it didn't. I straightened and looked around. My body felt normal, and nothing unusual was happening around me, so I clambered to my feet and faced the gang. The woman's eyes were still glowing as she exerted power on . . . what? Not knowing was worse than the physical attack I'd prepared for. Her body language gave me absolutely no indication of her Divinity.

I noticed a thin rectangle of light on the floor. It widened, letting more light in. Someone was opening the door. Over the moans of my victim, I heard a new sound, one I struggled to identify. It sounded like . . . like stones grinding together. I didn't sense another ghost, but I did sense *something* behind me.

My eyes burned to swivel in that direction, but I knew better than to turn my back on the gang in front of me. Yet, they'd relaxed. Only the woman was exerting power; the others were waiting to watch the show.

I turned.

A lion crouched in the doorway. *Uh-oh. She's an Elemental, like me. She's a Petrakinetic—she controls stone.*

The limestone creature flicked its tail, its sightless eyes trained on me. I backed away, unsure how to fight this thing. With each step I retreated, it advanced. A man with a matching tattoo on his forehead cupped his hands around his mouth and taunted, "What's a' matter, Cryo?"

I wouldn't give him the satisfaction of breaking my concentration to bother with a retort. The lion, standing at full height, rivaled the size of a werewolf. If I stood next to it, I *might* reach its shoulder. It didn't growl as I imagined a real lion would—it had no vocal cords, after all. It crouched low to the ground in a lifelike move I'd seen Kit execute many times . . . right before she pounced.

And it did. In the split second I had to act, I chose ice over ectoplasm. I called upon the blue power in my center as I turned to the side and made a circular motion in the air with my hand, closing my fingers around the frozen shield on my arm and bracing for impact. The stone cat landed and swiped at me with a massive paw.

The ice shattered. I stumbled back, unsure if my arm was broken or just numbed in tingling pain as sharp as needles.

The spectators whooped and hollered. Flustered by this unpredicted development, I scrambled over the fallen bookcases. The lion bounded after me, its heavy body landing so hard that the massive cases splintered beneath its weight.

How do I fight something that feels no pain and can't be killed?

I made the mistake of chancing a look back and discovered that the beast was a lot closer than I'd thought. And then the answer hit me—break it. *Duh.*

I rolled to the side; the stone beast pounced and landed right where I'd been. I dashed toward one of the support columns erected in the main aisle.

Wha-boom! Wha-boom! Wha-boom!

The ground quaked beneath my feet every time its paws struck the bookcases. The last *thump* was so close that I stumbled.

It was one of those moments when your brain is processing in hyperdrive, like when you stub your toe and have that single moment to think, *Oh shit, this is going to hurt* before the pain signal even registers.

I was falling face-first into a pillar. Warmth swelled in my core, and I instinctively drew upon it, letting it spread. I tucked my limbs inward and passed through the pillar, then rolled across the ground on the other side and twisted so I landed on my hands and knees to watch.

While Elementals could manipulate their element, they couldn't pass on basic powers, which meant the stone couldn't mirror my intangibility stunt. When it leapt, it struck the edge of the pillar. I smirked in satisfaction as the head, front leg, and part of the torso crumbled with a section of the pillar. The statue fell to the ground, lifeless.

"Ha!" I heard, surprised when I realized the triumphant cry had come from my own throat.

The Petrakinetic smiled. "We're not done yet, Cryo."

She wiggled her fingers like a puppet master. At my feet, pieces of stone rolled toward the broken lion. The elation vanished while I watched the rocks merge to re-form the animal. It rose up on all fours once again, most of its body blemished by cracks but still fully functional. It couldn't die, and it couldn't be broken. Even if I pulverized this thing into dust, my opponent could reconstruct it. "You'll have to do better than that!" the Impenetrable called.

I eyed the group, resenting them. This was a game to them. My fingers curled into fists. The Arena fights had been a game. *They*'d placed bets on who would win. I loved fighting; I hated fighting for the entertainment of others.

I didn't mean to trigger the hot green power, but fury had my blood boiling. For some reason, it also cleared my thoughts. The lion wasn't alive, and it didn't think. It couldn't move without the Petrakinetic. I was done playing her game.

My green was doused in blue again. In my hand, I formed a curved piece of ice, and before the stone lion had time to move, I'd veered back and thrown my weapon. It spun through the air, guided by my concentration until it connected with the Petrakinetic's temple. She opened her mouth, but no sound came. She fell to her knees, then to the floor. I turned to the lion again. It stood, unmoving, frozen once more. Whatever life it had possessed was gone.

Invisibility cloaked me, and immediately, the ghosts tensed, eyes shifting, searching for me. They backed away. One threw an orb of ectoplasm where I'd been standing. It exploded against the corner of a fallen bookshelf.

I crept toward them, painfully aware that my power was draining at an alarming rate.

Ice encased my fist. Still invisible, I veered back and swung with all my might as I let go of the basic power hiding me from sight.

The poor guy didn't know what hit him. I punched him so hard in the temple that the ice shattered and he crumpled like a wilted leaf, limp before he'd even hit the floor. The ghost next to him turned toward me, but he was too slow—I'd already driven a shard of ice into his neck. *"Be efficient,"* Jay had advised. *"No time for mercy, and don't expect any in return. We aren't in the Arena anymore. Nobody's going to flip the switch and stop the fight if it takes a bad turn."*

One enemy left.

Or so I thought. With a wild cry, the Petrakinetic I'd mistaken to be unconscious sat up and flung a ball of ectoplasm at me, but I raised a shield just in time to deflect it. I stumbled back. She was powerful; the energy smashed against my shield. A trail of blood streamed down the side of her face, but she was very much alert. She shrieked and lunged at me.

Her fingers grasped my cloak. "Not Guilded?" she snarled, her eyes on my right biceps where the neutralizer used to drain my power. She pulled me closer, spittle landing next to my eye when she continued, "Not good enough for Osias? You're no better than us Fallen."

I jerked free, creating an ice blade in my hand. She lurched toward me again, and as she passed, I spun away and thrust the frozen blade into her side. She gasped in surprise and pain, clutching the icicle protruding from her rib cage and backing away from me.

I brought my right leg up and kicked out. The sole of my boot connected with the side of her knee, and with a screech of pain, she crumpled to the ground, moaning and clutching her leg. Blood was already staining her shirt.

The last ghost, the man with impenetrable skin, gazed at me in terror. He hesitated, glanced down at his accomplices, then pivoted and sprinted through the doorway.

I stood in place for a second, surprised by his cowardice, before I took off after him with long strides. I emerged from the main section of the library just in time to see him disappearing through the wall. I followed, becoming intangible as I leapt through the wall in pursuit.

I appeared in the fresh air just outside the building, and my eyes immediately locked onto the fleeing ghost. I threw a glowing orb of green ectoplasm. To be truthful, I was aiming for his back, but my shot fell short and struck him behind the knee, sending him crashing to the ground.

I dashed at him, and he lunged at me in desperation, deciding to attack me with his hands rather than his powers. That was the biggest mistake he'd made yet.

I vaulted over him, twisting my body in the air to land on my feet behind him. He turned and punched, but I deflected the blow with my ice-coated forearm. Again, he came at me. I ducked, then punched him twice, hard, in the gut. As he lowered his hands away from his head to protect his midriff, I struck him in his unprotected face and throat.

He backed away from my ruthless fists, conjuring an ectoplasm shield out of desperation. I brought my hands up, calling upon the blue power just for a moment to form my familiar icicles, and then I began stabbing at his shield. The ice glanced off the shimmering barrier, but I continued my attack, slowly chipping away at his strength. His passive power meant I could safely assume he was no higher than a Level 2, which also meant his shield wasn't strong. Finally, with one last thrust, I broke through his barrier. He was exposed again.

I drew my fist toward my chest and slashed out with my elbow. My aim was slightly off; I'd meant to hit him in the temple, knocking him out cold immediately. Instead, the hardest point of my body, coated with an even harder layer of ice over the elbow pad, slashed just above his eye, sending him reeling back. Not quite my intention, but the blow I'd delivered was an effective attack. I drew no blood since I couldn't break his skin, but a blow to the head didn't need to be a flesh wound to be effective. He moaned and pressed his palm over the striking point, staggering.

I dropped my icicles and delved into my power supply. This time, I wouldn't miss.

I threw my hands forward at the same time I expelled the power.

Green light separated us, and then he flailed backward and crashed against the brick wall several feet away. His skull made a sickening *crack*ing sound against the bricks.

I lingered, still crouched in my defensive pose, to see if he'd rise again. He didn't.

A breeze stirred, shifting my cloak. Raindrops started to fall from the thin cloud cover. I curled my fingers into fists, summoning the warm power in my core until rays of green light shone through the gaps between my fingers. I tilted my head back and threw underhand with all my strength, then watched the glowing energy shoot high into the air like a pair of green comets and arch down over the buildings.

I shivered. "Tough fight?" a familiar voice inquired. A hooded and masked figure with glowing silver eyes was standing beside me.

I pulled my mask down so it hung around my neck. I shrugged, rather bored by my last opponent's lack of skill.

Jay strode to my barely conscious victim. I blinked, and in the microsecond it took to open my eyes again, Jay and the ghost were gone. With the adrenaline wearing off, the tingling pain was returning to my arm. I made a fist and winced as I slowly uncurled my fingers. Probably not broken. Maybe fractured. *Damn.* Using an ice shield was a miscalculation against a stone opponent. I should have used intangibility instead.

I reached for my center and watched crystalline braces creep along my bare arm. A doctor would no doubt criticize the crude structure, but at least the braces would help stabilize the injury. I was still finishing my creation when Jay reappeared at my side. "He's back in the Ghost Realm."

"Like that'll do a lot of good," I muttered. "It'll never end, Jay."

"Then we won't be out of a job."

I grunted humorlessly, then nodded at the building behind me. "Four more in there." Jay gave me an impressed look that made a bubble of pride swell in my chest. He turned and strode to the library.

I remained where I was, watching the back of his cloak until he disappeared through the doorway. The pride left with Jay, leaving me cold and deflated. I pulled the cloth away from my neck and gazed at it. Dressed in Phantom's mask again, more or less. Phantom was a protector of those who couldn't protect themselves. These humans didn't deserve him.

I turned my back to the library, took a step, and then paused, a colorful object in the doorway of the neighboring building catching my eye. Curiosity bested me, and I wandered closer and knelt to study it.

Blue, bronze, and silver cords were braided together. The band was knotted in the middle, and the ends were frayed, as though it had been tied and then torn against something sharp. I held it in my palm. I'd seen it before. In my mind's eye, I could picture it tied around the wrist of a girl. But I couldn't see the girl's face.

I closed my fingers around the bracelet and tucked it gently into the pouch strapped around my thigh. Why I decided to keep it, I wasn't sure. It might be a key to unlocking memories of Before.

— Chapter Five —
Shields

"I told you to shut up. Open it."

Rewind.

"I told you to shut up. Open it."

Rewind.

"I told you—"

"How many times are you going to listen to that?" Agent Byrn overrode the recording.

Kovak shook his head. "That voice. I don't recognize him. I ran it through our audio database; it doesn't belong to any of our test subjects. So, who the hell found the bug?"

"Wesly Cooper. We already identified the man from the surveillance footage."

"It isn't him." Kovak rewound and played back the recording just a second earlier.

"This is—"

"I told you to shut up. Open it."

Kovak shook his head again. "The voices don't match."

Byrn shrugged. "Don't know what to tell you. Besides, what were you were hoping to overhear in Phantom Heights? It's a ghost town on the brink of collapse. There's nothing there."

Kovak leaned his head back against the chair to stare up at the ceiling tiles. "I don't know. Anything. A lead, maybe."

"If our fugitives are still in this Realm, they'll show up on our radar eventually."

"I suppose you're right." Kovak slumped forward, his head resting in his hand.

He hit *rewind*, then *play* again.
"I told you to shut up. Open it."

Trey sat on the steps to City Hall, glaring at the container a few feet away on the other side of the green barrier. His new gun was lying across his lap. The apprentice blinked a few times to clear the weariness weighing down his eyelids. The steady rain slapped the cobblestones and drummed the roof of City Hall.

Dry under the portico, he rubbed warmth into his arms. The doors opened behind him.

Wes sauntered out and stood at the edge of the first step. "So, how long do you plan to sit out here in the rain?"

"I'm going to catch one."

"What, a cold?"

Trey scowled and gripped his gun with numb fingers. He couldn't kid himself—he was relieved to have the werewolf's company. He didn't *want* to be afraid of the Alpha ghosts. He'd seen where they'd lived at the AGC, how they'd been tortured, how Agent Kovak had starved them and forced them to fight for food and water. Trey had even crawled inside one of their cages. They were victims.

And yet, they were killers, too. Sure, Kovak had molded them into killers if they weren't already before, but tragic pasts didn't put Trey in any less danger trying to cross paths with the fugitives. Maybe he was being reckless setting up this stakeout, but he wanted to meet the creatures that kidnapped Vivian and protected everyone in City Hall when the shield went down.

Wes yawned and stretched his arms high above his head. "Maddie wasn't able to. What makes you think you can?"

"I've got trip wires set up all around." He glanced over his shoulder at the werewolf. "They have to show up sooner or later if they want the—no way!" Trey leapt to his feet, staring at the ground where the container of medicine had been just a moment ago, his traps untouched. "I must have taken my eyes off for two seconds," he said, scanning the plaza for any sign of an Alpha ghost. "Damn it! Did you see anything?"

"No." Wes shook his head. "Very impressive; I have to respect them for that."

Trey bit back another curse—all that time and effort wasted without even a glimpse of Kovak's fugitives. "Respect them? They're killers, you know."

"They're powerful," said Wes with a grin. "And they're working for *us*. I have to say, this is my best work yet."

"You're awful proud of yourself, aren't you?"

"I think I've outdone myself this time. Come on back inside, kid. You'll never catch them."

"Au contraire," Trey said with a smile as he seized a laptop that had been nestled in the shadow of City Hall's stone pillar. "I *did* catch them." Wes leaned down to peer over Trey's shoulder. The screen, which was connected to the security camera over their heads, rewound and played back to show the container sitting in the rain and Trey's back as he sat on the steps. Then Wes appeared, the top of his head just visible in the lower part of the frame.

"Right about here . . ." Trey whispered.

The feed cut out.

His jaw dropped. The static lasted only seconds before visual returned to a very confused Trey and Wes peering into the drizzle. "I don't believe it," Trey whispered, rewinding again. The same occurrence happened right before the Alpha ghost appeared.

"Hmm," Wes murmured in thoughtful appreciation. "They knew you were watching, *and* they knew about the camera."

Trey clenched his jaw and opened another video feed. He'd been so well prepared; he'd activated and hacked the security cameras in front of City Hall, even ventured out to the abandoned shops framing town square and outfitted those deactivated cameras with batteries to make them operational for the first time since the shield had gone up a year and a half ago so he could tap into their feed. But somehow, those, too, were fully functional until the moment before the Alpha ghost made its appearance, and then static.

"I was hacked," Trey concluded in disbelief.

He cracked his knuckles and set to work on the keyboard. "Fine. Two can play at that game."

Now interested, Wes knelt to one knee to watch. "You can hack them back?"

"You familiar with the tale of Hansel and Gretel?"

"Sure."

Trey smirked. "The moment they entered my system, they left breadcrumbs right back to their server." His fingers flew. This wasn't as simple as hacking into the school's network to change the lunch menu from creamed corn to tater tots, which he'd done on more than one occasion. His confidence was still high despite the proof that his adversaries were adept in the art of hacking. But every hacker left an inherent thread behind, and all Trey had to do was follow it back to the source.

His eyes grew wide. "Hell of a firewall," he muttered. "But every wall has a back door for the programmer to access. All I have to do is find it, and then . . . I can . . . ah-ha. Ha! That was easier than I thought it'd be. I . . ."

The words had barely left his mouth when his screen suddenly went black. The small lights on the side winked off. The laptop shut down, as if exhaling its last breath. "What? No! No, no, damn it! Seriously?" Trey tapped at the keys in vain.

"Tough luck," Wes consoled.

Trey hung his head. "Brilliant," he muttered.

He sighed, then nodded in acceptance that he'd been outsmarted. "The programmer built a false door. I got a virus the instant I tried to go through." He wanted to chuck the useless computer into the rain, but restrained himself to shoving it away in angry defeat.

As I rounded the corner, I was greeted by a cold green light.

I hadn't realized how close I was to the Dome until it loomed high above my head. It was eerier in the rain, the pale glow lighting puddles in the cobblestones.

To see the top, I had to tilt my head back and squint through the cool raindrops pattering my skin. I was on the back side where City Hall sat close to the road. Behind me were office buildings, the few intact windows reflecting the brilliant sheen given off by the Dome.

I looked left, then right; First Street was deserted except for abandoned vehicles. Alone in the rain, I crossed the road.

For a long time, I stood before the great Dome, sometimes staring up at the arched edge where the green met gray sky, then leveling my head again to gaze at the swirling patterns on the surface like an image of rolling fog captured in two dimension. It was rather humbling, being so small and meek before something so impressive. The steady rain passed through the Dome to soak City Hall and collect in puddles.

I reached out to touch it. Last time, I'd passed right through and hadn't felt a thing.

This time was different; my fingers met a solid barrier. It was as smooth as polished ice. And yet, just as Ash had described, I could feel the warmth emanating from the surface.

It felt like a Grade A ectoplasm shield. There was that undercurrent of power—that was where the warmth was coming from—and the glowing green coloration, and the gentle swirls on the surface that reacted to the pressure of my fingertips. I glided my hand along the exterior, watching the swirls spin around my fingers.

Humans and animals could pass through it, but ghosts couldn't. My fingers closed around a lengthening icicle I pulled from the air. I raised it to the Dome and pressed the tip against the surface, expecting to meet resistance, but the ice passed right through. I didn't even have to apply pressure.

I took a step back, as if that might put this strange energy into perspective. I raised my hand, palm up, and gathered ectoplasm. Tendrils of green energy converged into an orb hovering over my palm. It was the same color as the Dome. *Exactly* the same.

I shivered, chilled for no apparent reason, and it wasn't because a ghost had wandered into my range. I rotated my wrist, diminishing most of the power until I flicked a tiny shot of ectoplasm at the Dome. When the two energies met, the surface of the Dome reacted, but my ectoplasm was absorbed without a spark or smoke or even a sound, only a disturbance in the swirls.

I leaned against the Dome again with one hand and closed my eyes. I reached for my center. I imagined it was a candle in my heart, and I snuffed it out, the darkness, the emptiness taking the place of the warm tingle in my core that made me feel alive. I fell forward with a jerk, eyes snapping open as I stepped forward to regain my balance. My hand and forearm had passed through the Dome.

I drew my hand back. I couldn't feel the shield anymore, not even the warmth. Whatever this was, it wasn't ectoplasm. I was intrigued by it, even if I didn't know exactly what it was. I relit my Origin, and power rushed through me; by the time my fingers reached the Dome's surface again, it was solid, warm, and smooth.

I wasn't sure what all of this meant. The Dome behaved very much like ectoplasm, even when struck with ectoplasm. But people and objects couldn't pass through a condensed ectoplasmic dome. This unusual energy . . . I couldn't remember ever seeing anything like it.

I looked up. Dusk was deepening as the sun set behind the rain clouds. I turned away, took a few steps, then lengthened my stride into a jog. The Dome dominated the skyline behind me.

When I neared Home, I became invisible, allowing the night to swallow me whole. I glanced around to ensure I hadn't been followed. Time was precious; this basic power drained me quickly. I trotted down the sidewalk, paused beside a broken window, then blew one long, low whistle down the alley.

I waited.

A tabby cat emerged from behind a trash can. It strolled past me, meowed once, and continued on its way. *All clear.*

I leapt through the window, clearing the frame, which had taken some practice to accomplish without being able to see my own body. I landed in a dark office. Still crouched on my hands and feet, I released the power of invisibility before I rose slowly, letting my eyes adjust.

Orange light flickered through the crack of the partially open door. A steady metallic clanging punctuated the echoes of a fight.

I pushed against the door, which opened to a cavernous room with giant, wavering shadows on the walls. A smokeless flame burned bright and true with no kindling on the metal floor in the middle of the warehouse.

I ducked as a metal disk sped toward me and ricocheted off the wall. Ash swung her staff, deflecting another disk. RC was using telekinesis to fling them at her, and as soon as she smacked one away with a *clang*, he sent another from a different direction. Ash was backing up, twirling her staff over her wrist and swinging with quick, controlled strokes.

I watched her for a few moments, admiring the careful precision of each movement. Her eyes glowed in the firelight even with the metal band still encircling her right biceps. At her own request, Finn and Reese had tinkered with the clamp so her neutralizer acted as a filter. Ash was operating on a manageable half of her power reserves to compensate for her lack of total control over her Divinity.

She swept the staff down, smashing the next disk into the ground. RC glanced at me. With barely a shift in his body language, he flicked his hand, and another disk zipped my way. Instinctively, I held my forearm in front of my face so the disk hit the plate of metal in my wrist gauntlet.

And then I was absorbed into the fight. Ash brought her staff down on me as I raised my hands and crossed icicles to catch her weapon in the X I'd made above my head. She spun, and I chased after her amid streaks of silver. She liked to fight close-range; RC liked to fight from a distance. I knew their styles, their moves, as they knew mine.

Ash's exhilaration caused the fire to burn brighter. Our weapons made a rhythm as they collided—Ash's staff and my icicles and RC's metal disks. It was a strange music, and we danced to it as we fought. Whatever this song of ours was, it was three beats to match RC's three disks. His triplet attacks set the tempo, and Ash and I matched it. Everything I did synchronized to the beat—my increasing heartbeat, my steady breathing, my footsteps, the sliding of my soles across the floor, the strike of metal on metal, metal on ice. When we sparred with each other, we were in perfect harmony. Even the flames seemed to dance with our shadows.

I couldn't describe my love for my lab-family with words. In this regard, spoken language failed me to no end. They were the only people in the world I trusted not to hurt me. Axel, if he ever snapped and lost control over his nydæa half, would kill me in a second. Jay, Ash, and RC had never hesitated to beat me to a pulp in the Arena. Finn and Reese used to assist *Them* in painful experiments. Kit was the only one who never did or will hurt me. But that was a different kind of hurt from the one I feared most. They'd never abandon me.

By the time the sparring match was over, all three of us were panting and grinning. There was no winner, no prize, no grudge. We gulped rainwater.

Now that the music of the fight had stopped, I could hear Jay's quiet voice ask, "What's this letter?"

He drew a circle on a newspaper with a blunt pencil. Kit, who was sitting in his lap, cocked her head. "B," she answered.

"And what sound does a B make?"

"Buh."

"Good. What about this one?"

"U."

"And the sound it makes . . . ?"

"Uh."

"Yes, that's right, but U can make two different sounds. What else can it sound like?"

Kit's ears swiveled back in concentration. "Um . . . ooh?"

"Yep. Good." Jay drew a circle around another letter. "How about this one?"

"R." She scrunched her face and growled, "Err . . ."

I smiled. Kit was nestled against Jay, contentedly at ease with his strong, secure arms on either side of her. Meanwhile, Finn and Reese were sitting in the corner. Completely uninterested with the sparring match RC, Ash, and I had just partaken in, they'd partially dismantled ECANI. Finn had a wire between his teeth, held out of the way as he fiddled with the inner workings. Reese was holding ectoplasm in his open palm to shine bright blue light over his blood-brother's workspace.

"What are you doing?" I asked.

They both jumped. Reese glanced up at me, startled out of deep concentration. Finn took the wire from his mouth and twisted it back into place as he replied, "We're attempting to develop a barrier with similar properties to Mrs. Tarrow's."

"You're recreating the Dome?"

Finn turned ECANI over and flicked a tiny switch. Reese extinguished his ectoplasm in his fist and tugged on the special pair of gloves needed to operate the computer. "Not exactly," he said.

"Were you able to examine her generator?"

They shook their heads as a small holographic screen materialized.

"Did Madison explain how it works?"

Again, they shook their heads.

I frowned. "Then how do you plan to recreate it if you don't know how hers works?"

Finn leaned in front of the transparent screen. A scanner analyzed his retina as he answered, "Our own speculations and theories based on the general function of Mrs. Tarrow's shield. Basically, it repels ectoplasm, including the natural source in our bodies." Once Finn's identity was confirmed, the box enlarged to a massive numerical code.

"What good is a barrier like that if Jay, Kit, and I are the only ones able to pass through it?"

Finn didn't answer at first. His eyes were glowing bright, as were Reese's. I knew they heard me, but they were also talking silently to each other, sharing memories and ideas, conferring. Reese's blue eyes were whisking back and forth across the codes. His fingers moved so quickly they were just blurs over a keyboard of numbers.

"All components seem to be in order," Finn murmured as his twin ceased typing.

Reese replied, "Mrs. Tarrow's design appears to be founded on a molecularly altered base of ectoplasmic energy designed to repel anything containing the original source. Her shield is powered by a generator that converts an ectoplasmic by-product from the shield into electricity. It's a positive feedback loop. But it doesn't have to be so complex, and it doesn't require such a large and inefficient generator. We're confident we can create a program in ECANI to simulate the same result."

Reese input a lengthy sequence of code, and the holographic screen shrank into the tiny scanner again. Finn plucked a hair from his own scalp and held it up. A single beam swept over it. They both turned their blue eyes to me. "To answer your question . . ." Reese began.

"Our plan is to enhance Mrs. Tarrow's limited design. ECANI will scan deoxyribonucleic acid and prevent biotic creatures from passing through the shield. Only those with registered DNA will be able to pass through," his brother finished.

"Impressive," I said. Neither twin so much as blinked in acknowledgment of my compliment. They hadn't gone through all this trouble to please anyone.

Reese coughed, but the sound wasn't the painful hacking cough he'd had before his near-death experience. Still, he was flushed, and I knew he didn't feel well despite their interest in ECANI. I inquired, "So, you can make it repel ghosts *and* humans?"

"The concept is basic enough," Finn replied.

Reese continued, "Mrs. Tarrow's shield repels ectoplasm. Ghosts can't pass through it because they have a natural source of ectoplasm in their bodies. To ward off humans, our shield needs to repel anything lacking ectoplasm."

"That wouldn't work," I countered. "You can't make a shield that repels ectoplasm and anything without ectoplasm at the same time."

"Did you know," said Finn, "that cell membranes are formed by a bilayer of phospholipids that have polar heads and nonpolar tails?"

"Uh . . . what?"

Reese explained, "The hydrophilic polar heads align and orient toward water, and the hydrophobic nonpolar fatty acid chains that make up the tails line up in the opposite direction away from water, and the tails of the two layers meet."

"Assuming that the membrane was purely a phospholipid bilayer—which it isn't, by the way—only a small amount of neutral molecules would be able to pass through because the phospholipid layers are both polar and nonpolar."

"See, polar molecules can't pass through the nonpolar part of the barrier, and nonpolar molecules can't pass through the polar part of the barrier."

"Understand?" they finished in unison.

No. Open-mouthed, I gawked at them. For all intents and purposes, the twins might as well have been speaking Latin to me and I would have understood just as much. Either oblivious to my ignorance or choosing to overlook it, Finn excitedly continued, "Our shield is based on the same basic principle. We'll have two layers: one to repel ectoplasm . . ."

"And one to repel anything lacking ectoplasm."

"Polar and nonpolar."

"Our shield is a bilayer."

"Just like only certain proteins can pass through a cell membrane, only people with registered DNA in the system can pass through our shield. The program we're working on will identify the genetic signature as neutral so the person may pass through."

"We've based our model on the processes of the simplest form of life."

The twins stared at me, their cobalt eyes alive with ideas flashing through their synapses faster than lightning. I shook my head. "I don't have a clue what you just said, but I'll assume you know what you're talking about."

Finn smiled faintly as Reese assured, "We do."

I waved my hand through the hologram, my stomach tight. Sometimes, given their ignorance of the simplest things, I forgot just how intelligent Finn and Reese were. Sometimes, I forgot they were being groomed to be the primary architects of the Weapon after the data collection process was over.

It was sobering to see what they could do . . . to imagine what they might have created. "Question. How do you know all that? About the bilayer stuff you just said."

Finn stretched and yawned. "Permeability of cell membranes is basic biology."

"Right," I muttered. "Basic biology. Sure."

I bet I failed biology classes in school.

Reese coughed into his arm, then challenged, "Cato, try to go outside."

I glanced up at the holes in the ceiling, expecting to see a glowing green barrier like the Dome. "But you haven't activated it yet."

They were both staring at me expectantly. I hesitated for a moment, but I was so relieved to see them actually excited about something that I obliged without complaint. Ash, RC, and Jay watched me cross the room, and Kit paused in her reading to look up. I cast one more look back at the twins and reached for a hole in the wall, intending to stick my arm out.

But my hand collided with something solid.

I scowled and set my palm against the surface of something I could not see. I didn't understand—nothing was there. It didn't even feel like Madison's Dome; hers was a transparent barrier of warm energy, but this . . . this was as if the air itself had solidified. My ghost blood was preventing me from passing through.

I closed my eyes and reached for my center, locating the mysterious source of my power and focusing on suppressing it. When I opened my eyes, I knew they were no longer glowing. I extended my hand out once more, but to my surprise, I hit the barrier again. I turned to face the young inventors, letting my warm power refill the emptiness.

Reese motioned for me to return, and as I approached, his blood-brother explained, "Mrs. Tarrow's design is effective for what she intended to accomplish. She used a base of degraded ectoplasm as a support. But for us, an invisible shield is much more practical. We eliminated the ectoplasmic base so the shield is undetectable unless you walk into it."

Finn sneezed hard and remained motionless with his head down for a moment before straightening and wiping his nose with the back of his hand. He sniffed and added, "Our shield isn't constrained to a dome shape, either. It can be, but we can also have ECANI scan the room and create a shield to fill those dimensions. No one with unregistered DNA can enter or leave this room. The shield can't be broken, not even by Axel. The only way to break the shield is to break ECANI."

As I drew near, Finn wordlessly stood, reached up, and plucked one of my hairs from my scalp. I watched in wonder as the black hair was scanned and analyzed by a beam. Reese said, "You're now in the program; you can pass through the shield."

Fascinated, I walked to the hole again and thrust my hand out. If I hadn't just been stopped by the shield minutes earlier, I wouldn't have believed it even existed.

"Not bad, Bot," said Axel.

Kit's ears fell, and she shot Finn and Reese a look of envy that they had managed to earn one of Axel's rare compliments.

I said, "You guys really are amazing. This is . . . fantastic. I mean, Madison must have spent most of her life trying to perfect her Dome, and you've outdone her in a day."

"This is only the first prototype," said Finn, glancing critically over the numbers on the holographic screen. "It's far from perfect. We still have a lot of upgrades to make."

It was perfect to me. I gazed at my lab-family and our ramshackle Home lit by Ash's flame, and a contented peace blanketed me. *Safety*. I had forgotten what that felt like.

— Chapter Six —

Blind Spot

I watched the reincarnation of Phantom Heights.

Over the next several weeks, we fell into an established routine. Ash and I were partnered together for scouting missions, Jay and RC their own team. Kit wandered the town on her own in her fur; she was too young to fight, and Jay didn't want anyone noticing her. Through the network of stray cats throughout the Heights, she gathered useful intel to help us raid hideouts, target places for food and supplies, and avoid Shadow Guard patrol routes. Axel, still firm in his rebellion, roamed without a care or schedule. Finn and Reese spent most of their time sleeping at Home. Jay, RC, Ash, and I took turns throughout the day to check on them. Kit visited them often, and I suspected Axel watched over them more than we realized, but he'd never admit that.

The routine became fairly consistent. We woke before dawn to train in the early morning when it was still cool and dark and quiet outside. Our training varied, sometimes running as fast and far as we could go, other days performing exercises to master our powers. Most often, we sparred with each other. Sometimes we played a game Jay had invented called All-On-One.

At dawn, we split into our groups and spent the day scouting for trouble and foraging for food. The chimes of the clock tower indicated when it was time for one of us to check on the twins. We all returned Home at dusk to share the food we'd collected and store the rest of the nonperishables. After that, we resumed training until late in the night.

We allowed ourselves only a few hours of sleep. The nightmares couldn't haunt us if we didn't spend much time sleeping and if we were exhausted enough that we didn't dream. We'd graduated from lab rats to street rats, and we went hungry sometimes, but we were free. And as we adhered to the deal we struck to save Finn and Reese and RC, I witnessed the dead town resurrect from the rubble.

As our reputation spread, ghosts began to whisper of the powerful new Alpha gang that ruled this human town. Rumors, true or not—and I had the sneaky suspicion that Axel took great joy in feeding and inflating them—deterred ghosts from crossing through the Rip, and the humans became brave enough to venture out of City Hall. For a while, the Dome remained active, but then, several weeks after the last person left the sanctuary, it was shut down.

And thus, the process of rebuilding began. The humans of Phantom Heights trudged on with resilience and courage I'd never witnessed before. As much as I despised every single one of them, I couldn't help but respect them for that. They were survivors.

This town was stranger than any we'd encountered during our travels. For safety reasons, the humans tended to remain clustered downtown and avoid the outskirts. It was as if an invisible circle had been drawn. I could be standing in the middle of a street that had inhabited buildings glowing with lights on one side and desolate, abandoned houses on the other. Entire subdivisions were empty. Now that the Dome was down, electricity had been routed to the center of the town, but not the outskirts where we resided. This suited us just fine. I preferred the dark parts.

Running parallel between Main Street and First was the pedestrian road that connected the church and the courthouse with City Hall's wide plaza in the center of the axis. The ground level was used for shops, cafés, restaurants, boutiques, and the like while apartments occupied the upper floors. These apartments were the first homes filled.

Even though they weren't huddled in City Hall anymore, the humans were keeping close proximity to each other. It wasn't uncommon to see children, parents, grandparents, aunts, uncles, and even friends living in one house. Abandoned buildings were transformed into temporary apartments to replace lost homes.

The result, whether it was intended to be this way or not, was automobiles had become a rare sight. The potholes in the roads were treacherous, and people didn't need cars anymore since almost anyplace they needed to go was now in walking distance. Only occasional police cruisers maneuvered the streets.

In truth, I had only the memories of the various towns we'd passed through when first on the run, but I knew this wasn't the way most cities, if any, in the Human Realm operated. I also noticed that the humans seemed to be taking extra steps to beautify their reborn town. The scorched, half-dead trees lining most of the streets were being nursed back to life. Colorful awnings appeared over the shops. Boarded windows were replaced with clean sheets of glass. Unsightly debris in the streets and alleys was being pushed to the outskirts to further divide the inhabited sections from the forsaken parts. New life had been breathed back into the heart of Phantom Heights and its citizens.

My lab-family and I remained outcasts. This new society did not accept us, and we didn't seek their acceptance.

We dwelled in the shadows of the places humans abandoned. We felt safer roaming the garbage-choked streets, our boots crunching over broken glass, rats scattering in our passing. Humans plowed their garbage into our domain, and we scavenged it for tools and scraps of food.

One afternoon, exactly seven weeks since the Dome malfunctioned, I was standing on a rooftop at the edge of town square watching figures below mill about with their solemn tasks. Volunteers painted over the burn marks on walls, carried lumber, and hammered nails into siding.

Ten on patrol, I noted upon counting a group of policemen in blue uniforms slowly wandering the square in formation.

Jay and RC, each with the ability to travel quickly across town if necessary, usually covered the inner scouting circle while Ash and I patrolled what we called the second circle, which was the residential stretch between downtown and the outskirts that was still under heavy construction as the humans expanded their territory and reclaimed parts of the outskirts.

But when it was Jay's or RC's turn to check on the twins, Ash and I gravitated closer to the Rip as backup. The police had by no means halted passage through the Rip with their patrols. Despite the infrared glasses, invisible ghosts could slip past with the right distraction, and bolder ones wouldn't hesitate to launch a surprise attack the second they stepped foot into the Human Realm. The police were brave, and they were former raiders, but they still weren't ghost hunters, and their equipment was minimal.

I watched the humans far below. The green power was awake in me, and it compressed my lungs with heat. I hated every person down there. The hatred festered inside me like a disease I'd acquired at that place and could never cure. It had only gotten worse these past weeks as I enviously watched human life resume without me. The disgust made me sick, made me hate myself for having so much hate. Such a vicious cycle. As I looked down upon them, I wished I could crush them like the ants they looked like from up here.

Ash was on one knee beside me, her scarlet eyes trained on the blossoming cityscape. "We gave this place a second chance," she said. "Isn't it incredible?"

"They don't deserve it," I snapped.

Ash glanced up at me, her brow furrowing—my blue eye must have turned green to match my left, exposing my hatred. "Maybe," she said. "But I think it's sort of symbolic. We get a second chance, and so do they."

Phantom Heights was Jay's phoenix. From the moment we had glimpsed it from the top of the hill, he'd looked upon the ruins and seen the potential to be reborn from the ashes of destruction.

I didn't.

I wanted to scream my hatred at this place until it was blown into dust and my lungs shattered.

I wanted to eradicate any trace of this town.

Slowly, I exhaled to relieve the pressure before it could explode. I turned my back on town square, sick of looking at the humans below.

We were on the verge of a rooftop garden that was probably beautiful a few years ago, but no electricity meant no irrigation, which had spelled disaster when a past drought smothered the Heights. The once-green leaves were all brown husks now. I scuffed the toe of my boot in the pea gravel and leaned against the arbor overhead. "They should rot in City Hall like we rotted away in our cages. *That* is what they deserve."

Ash still faced the plaza, but she watched me from the corner of her eye. "You've lost your mercy since *They* took you," she noted. "You're more . . . I don't know. Ghostlike, I guess."

"That's a compliment. I don't want anything to do with humankind."

"You can't change your blood."

"No, but I can decide who I want to be. Axel chooses his ghost half over his nydæa half; I choose my ghost half, too."

"How can you choose a half? That would make you incomplete." At my stony silence, Ash rose and held up her hand, palm toward me. "Sorry. Hey. No bars."

I stared at her hand for a moment, feeling my scowl uncrinkle. I straightened from the wooden post. "Right. No bars," I echoed, pressing my open hand against hers.

Ash went stiff and let her hand fall. "I saw a ghost."

I peered down upon town square. The people were still roaming, chatting, laughing. The patrol wasn't engaged in combat. Everything looked normal. "Are you sure?"

No answer. I turned to find that she'd already vanished, and with a quiet curse at her spontaneity, I donned my mask and hood. Through the roof and down four flights of stairs, quick on my feet, barely missing a breath when I reached ground level, I spotted Ash's cloak and took off after her.

We'd watched Phantom Heights enough to know which buildings had been repaired, which were being renovated, and which were still abandoned, and we used that knowledge to choose a route through empty shops flanking town square while using as little intangibility as possible. "Don't take off like that," I chastised as soon as I reached her.

"I thought you were right behind me," she said absently, not even gracing me with a glance. Her gaze was darting through the window, searching for her quarry.

"Where'd it go?"

Crestfallen, she said, "I don't know. I'd hoped we would be able to sense it."

"Are you sure it was a ghost and not a human?"

"It was wearing a black cloak."

No sooner had the words left her mouth than a deep shiver slid up my spinal cord. Ash drew her staff. I conjured icicles in my hands, and we whirled as one to face the cloaked figure standing behind us.

Dressed all in black, a hood over his head, a mask over the lower part of his face, a pair of silver eyes gleaming in the shadows, he didn't move. Jay's gaze flicked between the two of us before he announced, "I found something I think you should see." He then vanished.

Ash and I straightened and exchanged looks, then peered out the window. Jay had teleported to City Hall's portico and was lingering just behind a pillar, waiting for us. I glanced at the patrol on the far side of the square. Now was a good time for us to cross the plaza with a minimal risk of being noticed. I reached for my center and called upon the warmth in my core to envelop me and remove me from sight. Rather than waste even more power with intangibility too, I hopped through the open window frame and sprinted across the plaza. I took the marble steps two at a time and released my power once I was safely behind the pillar and out of general sight.

Ash appeared beside me. Without a word, Jay strode through the wall, and we followed. City Hall swallowed me in darkness before giving way to its vast interior. Garbage and dirty blankets were still strewn on the floor from the humans' departure. A single cloaked figure stood at the far end, his hands clasped behind his back as he stared at a whiteboard.

We felt safe enough to remove the cloths tied around our faces and push back our hoods as we approached him. He didn't look at us. I ascended the terraced steps and studied the list Jay seemed to find so intriguing.

<u>*Project Alpha*</u>

8 escaped

A6 half-breed: Red eyes, fangs, can't speak, growls

A1, A2: Twins, 10 years old, mind-readers, brown hair, blue eyes, obedient

A4 is blind

3 can pass through shield

Jay
Axel
Ash
Seph

Jay said, "Do you find anything strange about this list?"

"What does *Seph* mean?" Ash asked.

Heat burned my face. I turned my head to the side, hoping they wouldn't notice, and I hastened to redirect. "RC isn't completely blind. And they don't know our Divinities?"

"Apparently the only ones they really know anything about are Finn and Reese."

"Well, I don't know," I teased. "I think Axel's description is pretty accurate."

Neither laughed at my joke. Jay said, "After my conversation with Vivian, I think this is the extent of their knowledge about us. You know why, don't you?"

Ash and I exchanged confused looks.

"No," she replied while I shrugged.

Jay turned his head to fix me in his steely gaze. "Because of you."

"Me?" I echoed in surprise. "What makes you think that?"

Jay nodded at the board. "Look at this list." I skimmed it again, still in agreement that it was a bit strange, but not sure why the lack of information involved me personally when there was just as little written about the rest of my lab-family. "Your name isn't up here," Jay said. "If I'm right and this is about you, *They* couldn't give specific details about seven of us and withhold information about one. Too suspicious. I don't think *They* want anyone to know you escaped."

"It's not a secret," I stated dryly. "At the very least, my mother knows I'm here, even if *They* didn't specifically tell her. The moment she learned everyone in Project Alpha escaped, she knew."

"I'm not sure," said Jay, scratching his head. "I'll admit, Cay, this makes me nervous. I don't like stepping into secrets and conspiracies with no idea how deep they go."

I wonder how my disappearance was explained. No way she told the truth. Perhaps she spun a tale about how *They* were trying to rehabilitate me, and I couldn't come home until I was human again. Or maybe she told everyone I didn't want to come back because I was too ashamed, or even invented a story about how I had elected to stay so I could help to build the Weapon and save humankind. Maybe she took periodic trips and pretended she was visiting me.

Whatever lies she told, they worked.

Overwhelmed by an ocean of bitterness, I grumbled, "The only conspiracy is between my mother and *Them*. She won't breathe a word, and she's hoping I stay quiet, too. All she wants is for me to disappear. My escape must have been her worst nightmare." Suddenly feeling weak, I turned my back to the board and leaned against it. "I ruined everything. All the great strides she made in regulating ghost activity in Phantom Heights, and then I blew up in her face. The one mistake that almost cost her career. How could anyone take her seriously after learning a ghost was living in her house right under her nose?" I wrapped my arms around myself.

Jay gently asked, "Is that you talking? Or *Him*?"

I tightened my arms, compressing my rib cage. "I doubt anybody else knows I was sent to Alpha. Just her."

Ash gasped. Startled by her dramatic reaction, Jay and I turned to find her staring out the window. My gaze followed hers to a group of people in black cloaks crossing town square, their destination the Rip.

At first, I failed to see the problem. I knew from their uniforms that they were Shadow Guards, but they seemed to be returning to the Ghost Realm, which meant we didn't have to deal with them.

But on closer scrutiny, I identified the apparent leader—a man with black hair tied back in a short ponytail. He was dragging something on the ground behind him, and when I focused on it, I realized in horror that it was a person. A hood had been secured over his head, and glowing green ectoplasm bound his wrists and arms, a seemingly moot measure since the victim was deadweight as he was dragged across the cobblestones. But through the ectoplasm, I glimpsed a familiar white mark on the chest of the one-sleeved black shirt.

Jay vanished. Ash and I took off at a mad sprint for the doors, concealing our faces with masks and hoods again as we ran. We emerged outside and leapt down the steps of City Hall to analyze the scene.

The patrol was down—dead or immobilized, I couldn't tell—on the ground and unmoving. They'd been brought down without any commotion; it must have been a surprise attack. Any other humans in the area must have fled.

RC was being dragged toward the Rip.

A handful of Shadow Guards were clustered around him and his captor to defend them, but Jay had already lured several away from the group. He was on defense, ducking and sidestepping strange metal rods the Guards were jabbing at him.

"It's Hassing," I said. "He's taking RC to Azar."

With no further hesitation, Ash and I charged forward.

Hassing paused when he saw us coming. "Take them down." His Guards detached to meet us, each brandishing a rod. I'd seen one before when I'd had the displeasure of first meeting the Captain of the Guard, but I still didn't know its function.

Ash pulled her staff over her shoulder, then twirled it in her hand as she ran. She swung at the nearest Shadow Guard, and he raised his rod to meet her staff.

Ash was thrown to the ground in an explosion of red sparks the instant the metal weapons collided.

She lay on her back where she'd fallen, stunned and paralyzed.

I stopped in my tracks. When the next Guard swung his rod at me, I sidestepped out of reach.

He made another wild pass; I leapt back. The rod slashed through the air less than an inch away from my chest. It gave off heat, and I swore I heard a faint sizzle above the *whoosh.* Another Shadow Guard thrust the end of his rod at me, and I spun, seizing his wrist and yanking his extended arm past me and straight into the chest of the first Guard. Electric-like tendrils of violet ectoplasm crackled through the rod and coursed across the man's body. He went stiff and dropped like a stone, mouth open in a silent scream that never escaped.

I had a rough idea about the rod's function now. That was Grade G ectoplasm, no doubt about it. A grade only Ectokinetics and the most powerful Level 5 ghosts were capable of producing. The rod must be a tool to amplify the user's normal ectoplasm into Grade G so it could pack a more powerful punch and down an opponent with a single electrocution.

I made a fist and reached for the blue power in my center. Ice crusted over my hand like a solid glove, jagged shards between my fingers. The second Guard was turning, but he was still off balance. I lunged forward and punched him in the jaw. The mass of ice shattered on contact, his head whipping to the side before the rest of his heavy body twisted to follow the momentum. He crumpled. Blood from his shredded face trickled between his lips and dripped onto the cobblestones. He moaned, the rod resting in his limp hand.

The man who had attacked Ash was coming at me now, and I seized the rod from my victim and used it to deflect my new opponent's strike as I channeled ectoplasm into that hand. My rod hit him in the wrist, effectively batting away his attack while transforming my neutral Grade D ectoplasm into hot tendrils of Grade G. He fell to his knees with a cry but staggered back up.

I crouched to defend myself again. Ash, still dazed, rolled onto her stomach, and she reached out to grab his ankle. Her eyes flared briefly.

Flames erupted, licking at the material of his uniform. She retracted her hand, her work done. The fire could fuel itself now, and it climbed up his leg.

Realizing he was ablaze, the Guard yelled and hopped around, frantically slapping at the flames. I looked past him to see that Hassing was nearly at the Rip now with RC. With a curse, I sprinted after them.

One Shadow Guard remained to guard the captain and his prisoner. She turned to face me, her crimson eyes blazing, but Hassing shouted, "Eldridge, no! Azar wants them alive and intact!"

Whatever Eldridge was about to do to me, she instead chose to charge me head-on with a shock rod in her hand. I swept my arm out in front of my body, creating a transparent round shield of green ectoplasm. She hesitated, but I never broke stride as I slammed my shield into her, knocking her to the side.

Hassing was mine. I screamed his name to make him stop dead in his tracks.

The captain pivoted to face me. The Rip was a few paces away, but he must have realized he wouldn't make it before I hit him from behind. RC was still unconscious, a fistful of his cloak in Hassing's hand.

I sensed rather than heard Eldridge coming at me again from behind and to the left. I turned to dodge the blow.

Something jabbed me between my ribs. I had a single moment to reprimand myself for taking my eyes off Hassing before what felt like scalding electricity coursed through my body. It was a feeling I knew well, but it still took my breath away and made my muscles seize.

The world spun, pain racing through me with an unexpected intensity that left me stunned, a few wild tendrils flickering in a green haze in my peripheral. I was vaguely aware that I was on the ground now, my body throbbing, a low moan escaping from my throat. RC was lying in a heap in front of me.

"When I said Azar wanted to meet you," Hassing said in a low growl, "that wasn't an invitation you could decline."

My eyes rolled so I could find him. I'd expected to see a rod in his hand, but he hadn't used one. Two fingers jammed into my rib cage was all it took to bring me down.

Eldridge hauled me from the ground by the back of my cloak. *She's strong*, I thought sluggishly. Still dazed, I peered up beneath the edge of my hood at Hassing just in time to see glowing red ectoplasm smash into his forehead. The captain staggered backward. Eldridge turned to face the new adversary.

Madison Tarrow was standing at the edge of the square, her ecto-gun level, the barrel aimed right where Hassing had been. She pivoted slightly so the weapon was pointed at my captor. "Drop him."

Eldridge took her word literally and released her hold on my cloak, letting me fall. *Hard*.

I swallowed hot, coppery blood, my chin and tongue throbbing with my heartbeat. *Drop him*, I mimicked irritably to myself.

Eldridge clenched her fists and crouched into a defensive stance, ready to fight Madison, but then she hesitated, glancing past the ghost hunter at the police officers and former raiders converging on the scene. Eldridge was outnumbered. She cast a quick survey of her fallen com-rades, and then she reluctantly raised her arms in surrender.

Madison nodded her head. "I'll let you go. Walk slowly. No sudden movements, or I'll shoot you between your eyes."

A hand seized my ankle and dragged me backward across the cob-blestones before another hand found my throat. "One more move, hu-mans, and I kill the lab rat," Hassing seethed.

My fingers twitched, but I still couldn't control my muscles after that shock of Grade G ectoplasm through my system. With Hassing be-ing an Ectokinetic, it had probably been even more potent than the shock rod.

His grip tightened around my windpipe. "Don't just stand there like you've lost your brain, Eldridge!"

"Open fire!" Madison shouted.

I strained to see the volley of green ectoplasm shots intermingled with a few red ones rain down on Eldridge, who cowered behind an ec-toplasm shield that wouldn't last long under the onslaught.

Hassing grumbled, "Curse King in his godforsaken grave." He let go of me and rose to his feet. When he held out one hand, a smooth, perfect rectangle of shimmering Grade A ectoplasm shielded Eldridge just as her own barrier failed. Hassing's shield was expanding into an impressive wall, and the human-made ectoplasm striking his seemed to be absorbed.

Crack!

The report of a gunshot made me flinch. Hassing fell to his knees with a curse, one hand clasped over his arm, which had probably been the only shot Madison had in that split second before the wall of ectoplasm completely blocked her target. She didn't usually miss a kill shot.

His shield degraded with his concentration. It was bordering on neutral Grade D now, somewhere between a solid and crackling energy, some parts holding firm while others broke apart into tendrils that left holes. A shot of green ectoplasm made it through; Eldridge barely managed to dodge it.

She ran to Hassing and seized his uninjured arm. "We have to go." She hauled him to his feet.

"No." He tried to pull free, but he was unstable. "I did *not* order a retreat."

"I did. We're outnumbered."

"They're only humans! I order you to stand your ground."

"The team is down, and you're hurt." Hassing's shield was failing; more holes were appearing, and shots were finding their way through. He jerked free to wave his hand and flick the incoming ectoplasm away before Eldridge conjured a shield of her own to protect them from the raiders' ectoplasm. Another gunshot *crack* made her squeal in fright even though the bullet missed. She pulled her captain toward the Rip.

"Officer, you will lose your rank for insubordination!"

"I understand. I accept the consequences of my decision."

Madison called, "Hold! Hold your fire!" The *shoom*s and whistling crackles abated. "We'll give you ten seconds to retreat."

Her gun was still aimed level at her target, eyes narrowed, finger curled over the trigger, ready to fire in an instant. Eldridge and Hassing backed away. They were at the fence when Hassing lashed out a whip of ectoplasm that snapped around RC's leg and yanked him toward the Rip.

Move! I have to move!

My body didn't want to obey. With every last ounce of adrenaline-fueled panic and willpower, I managed to flail an arm over RC's torso. My grip strength gone, I clutched at him as best as I could with numb, tingling fingers, but he was slipping out from under me.

My added weight made Hassing falter. The raiders opened fire again, forcing the Shadow Guards to flee back into the Ghost Realm without a prize.

The firing ceased.

My heartbeat throbbed in my ears in the sudden quiet. Madison, gun pointed at the ground now but finger still poised on the trigger, was marching toward us, the armed raiders and officers right behind.

I wanted to run from her, but I was trembling uncontrollably, unable to even push myself up onto my hands and knees. All I could do was hold onto RC's limp body and watch her boots carry her closer and closer, wait for the ghost hunter to descend upon me, to yank back my hood and see my face . . .

A hand latched onto my shoulder, and then the world rushed in on itself in a roar of black wind. Brightly lit town square had vanished. I was lying in a dark building. RC lay beside me, and Ash was sitting up a few feet away. Two pairs of blue eyes gazed at me from the corner.

Madison and the raiders were nowhere to be seen.

I rolled over, but dizziness made my head spin, and I yanked the cloth from my mouth just before I vomited.

"Sorry," Jay said as he removed the hood from RC's head. "I didn't have time to give you much warning."

I moaned and wiped my mouth. I tried to assure him that I was all right, but I was still suffering from vertigo, and I retched again. "You didn't give me *any* warning," I finally choked out.

"Are you two injured?" he asked.

"A bit stunned," Ash admitted while I bobbed my pounding head in agreement. Her voice was muffled behind her mask, which she shakily removed.

RC stirred. "Jay?" he whispered.

"You're okay now."

But RC, dazed and unfocused, sat up. "Lie back down," Jay said.

"My attacker hit me from the right side," RC said. I couldn't tell if he was intentionally ignoring Jay, or if he didn't hear him, or if Jay's command just wasn't processing. "By the time I sensed him, it was too late."

I looked at my lab-brother and the scar that trailed down the side of his face over his blind eye, and then I realized I was staring. I quickly averted my gaze in embarrassment.

"It's not your fault," I said. Since I was on RC's blind side, he had to turn his head so his left eye could find me in his vision.

There was one rule about RC: never ask him about his past. Not only did he throw up figurative defenses, but I was pretty sure he conjured telekinetic energy too, because you could practically feel physical barriers sealing him away. He kept more secrets than whispers from us.

I knew RC had lived in the Ghost Realm with his parents, although I wasn't sure if he had any blood-siblings. I didn't think so, because he'd never mentioned any. His mother died. How, he wouldn't say, but the way his voice caught made me believe that he'd seen her die, and it would forever haunt him.

I couldn't know for sure, but I had a hunch that the reason he ran away from home afterward involved his father. RC never said this directly, but I thought maybe her death put such a strain on their relationship that they fought constantly until RC finally decided to leave. Perhaps each blamed the other for her death; I might never know what exactly it was that drove RC away.

I wasn't sure how long he was on his own before *They* caught him, but it was around that time he became blind in one eye. The details he gave of that experience were the dimmest of all. He was in a fight with a ghost who cut him with a blade. That was all he'd say. When, where, with whom, what provoked the fight, who won . . . I couldn't even begin to guess what had transpired. All I knew was that afterward, RC fled through a Tear, but he was injured and distraught, and *They* caught him after only a few days in the Human Realm. He spent some time in the Quarantine wing of Retention before he joined Finn, Reese, and Jay in Project Alpha.

There was so much more to RC that I'd probably never know. The scar on his eye wasn't the only mutilation on his body. During our captivity, we'd been shirtless and barefoot unless in the Arena. I'd noticed a strange mark on his left forearm—now hidden beneath his sleeve—of two round scars, almost like massive puncture wounds, and whatever did that to him had caused the veins and blood vessels around the scar tissue to turn dark beneath his tan skin.

And there were many more old wounds. His back was a gruesome patchwork of round burn marks and slashes several inches long—he never spoke about those, and I didn't dare ask. I didn't even know if he had those marks before his capture or if *They* had been the ones who scarred him. Jay and the twins would know, but I'd never had an opportunity to ask them in private. Besides, I didn't need to know. The past was behind us, and there was no reason to look back. We all had scars. RC's were just easier to see.

"Not my fault," he echoed in a bitter, dead voice. "What if Jay had been in trouble and needed me?"

I didn't know what to say to comfort him. Jay ordered, "Lie down and rest." He firmly pushed RC back into the nest of blankets. "You too," he added, shooting Ash and me warning looks.

I gave him a crooked smirk and made a show of lowering myself down. I expected sleep to elude me, but on the contrary, the darkness opened beneath me, and I floated into it, gone in a matter of moments.

"My name is Cato," I whispered just before it closed in around me.

— Chapter Seven —

Family

When I woke, dusk was falling.

Ash and RC were dozing, still recovering from the effects of the shock rod. My muscles ached, and I should have been resting as well, but my mind was too active.

Axel was also restless; he was pacing along the far wall, his head down so his sweat-dampened hair hung over his pale face. I suspected he'd be leaving us sometime tonight or tomorrow. Jay was watching out a hole in the wall while Finn and Reese sat together in the corner snacking on crackers. A short distance away, Kit was stooped over a piece of paper. Her tongue poked out the corner of her mouth with intense concentration as she painstakingly traced letters.

I noticed how far away she was sitting from the twins. Even though they were able to read and write, Kit hadn't asked them for help. As affectionate as Kit was, she hardly ever interacted with Finn and Reese, and I found their relationship puzzling. Based on the age divisions, they should have formed a closer bond. Jay, Ash, RC, and I were the oldest, and we were the fighters. By age, Axel was in the middle, the rebel who preferred to be alone most of the time. That left the three youngest with passive Divinities. And yet, the twins didn't pay Kit any attention, and she likewise would go to any of us to snuggle, even half-nydæa Axel who wanted nothing to do with her, but not Finn or Reese.

I watched the three of them. In Kit's defense, Finn and Reese were difficult to connect with. They were distant with everyone and didn't show emotions—if they even had any—not to mention that the twins had done everything *They* had ordered, which included overseeing experiments that caused us pain. Our lab-brothers didn't want to hurt us, but they had, and there was no overlooking that. With all of that in mind, I did understand why Kit hadn't made any efforts to bond with them.

I glanced up in surprise to see the golden-eyed girl standing in front of me holding a sheet of paper. "Hey, Cato, I wrote your name," she said, tugging up one of the indigo arm sleeves that had slipped a little too far down.

"Did you?" I said, pulling her into my lap. "Let's see."

She proudly displayed four crudely drawn letters printed over many faint eraser marks. I smiled. "So close, Kit. But my name isn't spelled with a K."

The Amínyte looked up at me, confusion etched into her brow. "But Cato starts with a *kah* sound, like Kit." She held up her ivory pendant for me to see her engraved name.

"Yes, but there's another letter in the alphabet that sounds just like a K sometimes. Do you remember what it is?"

Kit stared at the paper with intense concentration, her brow furrowed and her lips pressed together. "Um . . ."

"I'll give you a hint. It's the third letter, and it comes after B."

She held up one finger per letter as she recited, "A . . . B . . ." She tilted her head back to look up at me. "Does your name start with a C?" I nodded, and she hopped up, the paper still clenched in her hand.

"I'm gonna try again!" she announced, skipping back to her place by the wall.

I smiled as I watched her kneel and bend over her work, her tongue out again as she pressed the dull graphite tip to the paper. My gaze shifted back to Finn and Reese, and after a minute, I crawled toward their corner and drew my legs in until I was sitting cross-legged in front of them. "Hey," I greeted.

Finn picked at the collar of his gray T-shirt with the faintest hint of an expression that might qualify as disgust on a normal person.

"Dr. Crawford took away our uniforms," he muttered, completely ignoring my salutation.

Reese added under his breath, "Master Kovak will be angry when he sees us wearing these clothes."

They were taking a break from tinkering with ECANI, which was about all they'd been doing these past weeks besides sleeping and eating. By now, they were on their eighteenth version of the shield. Prototype Biodome Model 3.7-5 last I could remember, or were they on 3.8-something now? We'd all started calling their shield Proto for short since we couldn't keep track of the model numbers. To me, it still seemed the same as the first model, but they assured us it was already much more advanced. If it kept us safe and kept them occupied so they weren't bored all day, I wasn't going to contend.

In response to their concerns about the clothing, I replied, "Then it's a good thing *He* isn't going to see you ever again."

Their dead blue eyes found me. They decided not to pursue the argument; we were deadlocked in disagreement. I studied them closely. I'd avoided this conversation for far too long. "Madison was pissed that we took Vivian."

It was a statement, not a question, but they both answered, "Yes."

I stared Reese in the eye and said, "I want you to tell me the truth." My gaze flitted to his blood-brother to meet his eyes. "Did she hurt you?"

They squirmed under my scrutiny. "No," they answered in unison.

"You promise?" I pressed.

They nodded. Finn mumbled, "We were afraid of her."

Reese continued, "But she didn't hurt us."

Finn shivered. "Cato, we're cold." Despite his complaint, his hair was damp with sweat, and the boys were bundled in several layers of blankets.

I checked the medicine supply, muttering, "Okay, hold on," as I unfolded the instructions. I studied the handwriting, then selected two pills. "Here. This should bring down the fevers."

Jay overheard, and he dipped a bowl into our drum of rainwater and handed it to Finn so he could set the pill on his tongue and swallow it down, then pass the water to Reese. Finn mumbled, "Dr. Crawford said we have to go back."

Reese set the bowl down and peered up at Jay. "We don't want to."

Such a simple but powerful request startled me. *Want.* Reese used the word *want*. I'd never heard either twin use that word because it implied desire, which wasn't allowed. They existed to serve without question, not to want. To an Outsider, it might not seem as if they asked for much, but they did.

"You don't have to," Jay replied. He must have picked up on the word choice, too.

Finn muttered, "But she said—"

"I don't care what she said." Though unnerved that Jay was defying an order given by a human, the twins couldn't contain an exhale of relief, although they then looked guilty for it. Jay turned away and started sorting through the various medicines. He uncapped a bottle and poured pink liquid into a spoon.

Finn and Reese eyed it with disgust. Although they didn't complain aloud, Jay noticed their reaction and said, "The instructions say you need it," as he offered the spoon to Finn, who leaned away.

"You just said we don't have to do what the doctor said."

Jay lowered the spoon. "I said you don't have to go back to the doctor. You *do* have to take the medicine she sent."

"But it tastes bad," Finn whined.

"I don't care. We can't lose you again." Jay bowed his head. "I . . . *we* have never been so scared as the moment we thought we were about to lose you forever." He took a deep breath and raised his head enough to glare at the twins through the strands of ashen hair veiling his silver eyes. "Leaving you was the hardest thing we've ever done. Families don't abandon each other. I will *not* lose you again."

Silence resounded in the wake of Jay's speech. Both twins were staring at him with wide eyes, and so was I. Over Jay's shoulder, I saw that RC and Ash had woken and were watching him. Kit had her head turned this way. Even Axel, who had been pacing and mumbling manically to himself, had halted and was frozen in place with his head down, listening.

The conviction with which Jay had proclaimed we were a family, as though the word were sacred, sent a pleasant shiver through me.

Family. Usually when I thought of that word, I associated it with betrayal, but when Jay said it, I thought of loyalty and compassion and protection.

Jay's silver eyes still bored into the twins' startled blue ones. Finn and Reese had experienced even more of Jay's passionate outburst than the rest of us. We heard his words; they heard his deepest thoughts.

Without protest, Finn opened his mouth. Jay flashed his crooked grin and spooned the pink liquid into the boy's mouth. Finn swallowed and grimaced, but didn't make so much as a noise of complaint. No one even moved as Jay tossed the bangs from his eyes and silently poured the medicine into the spoon again, this time for Reese, who also took it without dispute.

As unstable as he was, Axel had a thoughtful frown knitted into his brow. Ash's eyes were closed again, but she was smiling. RC stared vacantly across the room at Kit, who stared back at him and beamed even though he didn't return the smile. The word *family* had a different meaning for each of us.

Jay capped the bottle and stood, his cheeks coloring with embarrassment at our silence and the way we all watched him from the corners of our eyes. He said nothing as he walked to the office at the back of the room. Our stares followed him until he closed the door.

I turned back to the twins. "Family," they murmured in unison, as if testing the word.

"You promise Madison didn't hurt you? I mean it. You're telling me the truth and not just what I want to hear, right?"

"Yes," they said.

Reese tentatively asked, "Cato, could you explain something? Mrs. Tarrow . . ."

"What?" I pried when he didn't finish.

"Well, we know Mrs. Tarrow is a bad person, but . . . she has kind thoughts. Why?"

I pondered for a moment. "What was she thinking about?"

"Her daughter."

Finn said, "She loves Ms. Tarrow."

"Is that normal?"

"For a birth mother to experience such intense emotions about her offspring?"

"Usually," I said. Hurt, I couldn't help but add silently, *But not always.*

"Oh," they said.

I was pretty sure the twins had never met their mother. Prisoners of Gamma were nothing more than livestock bred so the children could be used for experiments. The Project, I'd heard, was divided into two sections. One side of Gamma contained the adults—both men and women undergoing gene manipulation and reproductive experiments. The other side housed the children until they grew up and were inevitably transferred to a different Project or sent back to the other side of Gamma. No direct interaction between the two sections. Finn and Reese had been taken from their mother the moment they'd entered this world.

Hearing Madison worry so much about Vivian must have had the twins wondering what it would be like to have a close relationship with a birth parent.

"Mrs. Tarrow didn't hurt us," Finn repeated quietly.

Reese shifted. "But she did lie to us."

My eyebrows crept a little higher. "Yeah?"

They fidgeted. Reese confessed, "She said Master Kovak told her we were good boys."

"But he would never say that."

"We broke the Rules."

"Master Kovak is going to punish us."

Troubled creases wrinkled their foreheads. Finn was tapping his finger against his knee, and Reese stared at his hands in his lap. I asked, "What's wrong? You can't be *that* upset about Madison lying to you."

Reese blurted, "They wanted us to speak."

"But ghosts should be seen, not heard," Finn recited.

"Humans *wanted* us to break a Rule."

"Why would they do that?"

"Was it a trick?"

I shrugged. "I don't know. You're the Mind-Readers; why are you asking *me* what they were thinking?"

They muttered more to themselves than me, "Is it wrong to break the Rule to obey human orders—"

"—if the order given was to break another Rule?"

They looked at me as if I were supposed to have the answer. I scratched my head, still trying to think of how Jay would respond when Finn said, "It must have been a test."

Reese nodded. "Master Kovak didn't tell these humans the Rules to see if we would still obey them when pressured to break them."

Finn started to gnaw on the jagged nub of his fingernail.

"Stop it." I seized Finn's wrist and pulled it away from his mouth. "You're going to make your finger bleed."

He asked, "Do you think we passed the test?"

"Did we choose the correct Rules to follow?" Reese muttered.

"Maybe we prioritized incorrectly."

"We should have—"

"Enough," I interrupted. Both twins' gazes settled uncertainly on ECANI, as if contemplating using it to surrender to *Him*. "Don't even think about it. That wasn't a test, and you didn't fail."

They acted as though they hadn't heard me. I left to retrieve a book I'd stashed in the corner, then returned to them, purposely standing between them and ECANI. "Here, I almost forgot—I found something for you guys."

They gazed up at me, cobalt eyes aglow. "A book?" they asked in unison, sitting up straighter.

I revealed it from behind my back. "No fair. It was supposed to be a surprise." I set *Introduction to Earth and Environmental Science* down in front of them. "You know how you were asking all those questions about rain and trees? I bet you'll find the answers in here."

Finn had already claimed the book and was skimming his eyes down each page so fast it took him no more than two seconds to flip to the next. Reese closed his eyes. I didn't know for sure, but I suspected he was reading through his blood-brother's eyes, or at least tapping into Finn's mind to glean the content.

I glanced over my shoulder to see if any of my other lab-siblings were within earshot. Axel had resumed pacing. Kit was still printing my name, and Ash was dozing. RC was awake, but he wasn't paying any attention to us. I swallowed and turned back to the twins, trying to find the words to voice the question that burned inside me. "Hey, um, question. I was wondering, while you were in City Hall . . . did, uh . . ."

I couldn't force myself to say it out loud. I cleared my throat. Reese opened his eyes and gazed straight through my tongue-tied silence to hear the question I didn't know how to ask: *Did my mother ask you about me?*

Their inquiry about familial relationships had my thoughts revolving around my blood-family, and that triggered a million unbidden questions only Finn and Reese could hear in the recesses of my mind.

Does she still hate me after all this time? Does my blood-family . . . miss me?

If Finn and Reese had heard a single thought about me in City Hall, even the most fleeting one . . .

Finn didn't pause in his reading, but something close to pity shone through Reese's stare. I braced myself for disappointment and tried to recall what Jay had said about family and the passion with which he'd said it. Gently, Reese told me, "She doesn't know."

My stomach dropped. "What are you talking about?"

"Your mother doesn't know you were admitted to Project Alpha."

I gawked at him for seconds that dragged into eternity. He didn't repeat himself, didn't push me to reply until I was ready. "But . . . how do you know for sure?"

Reese gave me a stoic *did-you-really-just-ask-that* look.

Right, Mind-Readers. I guess that falls into the Stupid Questions category.

"How can she not know?" I pressed my shaking hands together to steady them. "So, what, she just, she signed me away without bothering to ask what was going to happen to me?"

Reese patiently reminded, "We're Mind-Readers. Not Telepaths."

Still reading, Finn added, "We can hear only current thoughts."

"Searching the subconscious for answers is beyond our abilities. All we know for sure is that she is unaware you were assigned to Project Alpha."

"To our knowledge, nobody inside City Hall knew."

I should have been relieved. I could live a new life without worrying that my mother was plotting some quiet way to make me disappear for good this time. But all I felt was emptiness. I clenched my fists on my knees. "I want to know. I mean it—the truth. Did she try to make contact when I was at that place?"

Reese tilted his head at me. "You think Master Kovak might have lied."

"Did he?" I challenged. "Will *you* tell me the truth?"

"We have no knowledge of your blood-family making contact." He reached around my ankle and seized ECANI. "But we can check the logs. There would have been a record."

I shouldn't let my heart run out of control, but I couldn't stop it. This wouldn't prove anything, if there was even a record. This wouldn't change a single thing that happened to me. But I still wanted to know.

Reese pulled on his gloves and activated ECANI, and a grid with names and times scrolled up in front of his face. I squinted at the words, but they were backwards to me, and they were moving too quickly anyway. "There's no record in the primary phone log. But . . ." He swiped his hand, and that hologram disappeared. Another scrolling grid took its place. "Huh." Whatever he saw was surprising enough to break Finn out of his reading trance and make him turn his head to reaffirm.

"What?" I begged.

Brow furrowed, Finn dropped his gaze back to the book. He was almost done with it already. "Your mother called one hundred and forty-three times in the first month of your incarceration."

"What? She talked to *Him* more than a hundred times before she sold me?"

Reese gave me a stern look. "That's not what we said."

"She *called* one hundred and forty-three times," said Finn.

"Master Kovak answered only twice."

"He's the one who initiated contact on the final call, which lasted two minutes and eight seconds."

"After that, there was no correspondence by phone."

"What did they talk about? Were they haggling over money?" I demanded. Reese was studying the phone log. I reached out to seize Finn's book so he'd have to look at me, but he casually held it away without even pausing in his reading as soon as I made my move. "*He* made the last call. *He* must have told her something. Is there any way to know what they said?"

Reese said, "All phone conversations on AGC lines are recorded."

"But . . ." Finn prompted while turning the page.

"*But*," his blood-brother continued, "these calls were all made on Master Kovak's private line. There are no recordings."

"She did sign the visitor's log on one occasion, though," said Finn. He was still reading; I didn't know how he could possibly know that without looking at ECANI.

I couldn't catch my breath. "She was there?"

With a hint of frustration, Reese skimmed through files and muttered, "That's strange. There should be security footage, but there's no other record except a signature on the log. Oh. July eighth." As if that were supposed to be the answer.

He didn't go on. "What happened on that day?"

"We updated ECANI's operating system."

Finn turned the last page, then closed the book. "Surveillance was down for three hours, eighteen minutes, and seven seconds."

"The system went down thirty-three minutes before she signed the visitor's log."

My shoulders slouched. "Awful timing."

Reese closed the holograms and put ECANI back into standby. "Or perfect timing, depending on perspective."

I jerked my head up to glare at him. "You think *He* wanted the cameras off-line when she came?"

"We don't speculate."

"But doesn't it seem like a weird coincidence?"

"Speculation: the forming of a theory or conjecture without evidence."

I rolled my eyes. "Well, we know she didn't come to visit me. She must have been there to see *Him*."

To sign the papers and finalize the deal. I couldn't force myself to say it aloud. I thought of all the times I was in the Arena or other rooms that had one-way glass. Could she have been watching me, and I wasn't even aware she was just a few feet away? I glared first at Reese, then Finn, neither of whom would meet my eyes. "You really didn't know she was there?"

"Cato," said Finn, "we would have told you."

"Even if *He* ordered you to lie?" I fired back.

They hung their heads. Finn mumbled, "Master Kovak didn't command us to lie to you."

"If *He* had," I said slowly, enunciating each word, "would you tell me?"

They squirmed. Reese whispered, "We can't disobey Master."

"What if 'Master' had ordered you to kill any of us?"

Finn stared at the book in his hands. Reese muttered, "We don't concern ourselves with the hypothetical."

"Why?" I challenged. "Because you don't like what your answer will be?"

Finn's knuckles whitened when he gripped the book hard, and Reese raised his unusually bright eyes to glare at me. "Because the hypothetical is irrelevant if it never comes to pass!" Their voices rang in the warehouse, drawing curious looks from our lab-siblings.

Reese twisted the gloves in his hands. Finn scowled at *Introduction to Earth and Environmental Science* and said, "We never met your mother until we came here, to Phantom Heights. She doesn't know you were sent to Project Alpha. That's all we know, Cato."

I stared at him. He still wouldn't look at me. He could be telling the truth, or he could be reciting what *They* had ordered him to say if I ever started asking questions. I liked to pretend *They* were oblivious and too cocky to even consider that *Their* obedient slaves would dare to speak aloud and have full conversations with us. *Ghosts should be seen, not heard* was an ideology Finn and Reese had embraced at an early age. In the presence of their masters, they never spoke unless given a direct order to.

But Jay had convinced them that the Rule applied only if humans were present. I didn't know if *He* had ever figured that out. *He* wasn't stupid. As much as I wanted to believe my lab-brothers—I really, *really* did—I couldn't deny that their loyalty lay first and foremost with their masters, and if *He* told them to lie to me, they would, although they wouldn't see it as a lie. In their twisted logic, a lie was only a lie if they themselves concocted an untruth. If *He* gave them false information to repeat, that was simply "following orders."

"Never mind," I mumbled. "I guess it doesn't matter."

"Cato?" Kit called, holding up her paper. "Did I do it right this time?"

I barely glanced at the paper. "Yes. Good job."

But my mind was far away.

Even after all this time, a tiny part of me had been holding onto the dimmest glimmer of hope that everything was wrong, that my blood-family and the people of Phantom Heights hadn't really abandoned me, that it had all been a lie concocted by *Him*. But it was true. They'd forgotten me. My mother had made sure of that.

— Chapter Eight —
Ice, Water, & Fire

Ash noticed my melancholy mood on our scouting expedition the next day, but she didn't pressure me to talk, and for that, I was grateful.

We were in the park, my favorite place in Phantom Heights. The glassy lake was a mirror of the sky. The water—the founding element and sister to my own—stirred my Divinity and lifted my spirits.

I shot a sly look at Ash from the corner of my eye. "You know, if I remember correctly, there are spooky stories about this lake. Rumor has it there's a monster living in the depths."

She barely humored me with a passing glance, her mood fouling near the water even as mine lightened. "Are you trying to scare me?"

"No. But if you believe the stories, this lake is very deep in the middle, and people swear they've seen a scaly creature surface just for a moment before disappearing again."

Ash scoffed and looked out over the placid water. "I think you were gullible as a child."

And yet, when the shrubs rustled on our left, she jumped and whipped out her staff. Brilliant white flames licked the metal. A telltale shiver tickled my spine, but I chuckled at her as the fearsome beast emerged—a petite woman with a short blue side cloak tastefully clasped at her shoulder to showcase the tattoo on her right biceps. This one was similar to the Petrakinetic's circular tattoo, but instead of straight lines, a curved swath of black formed a symbol reminiscent of a wave cresting over a black circle in the middle.

The stranger stopped dead in her tracks when she saw us, her blue eyes transfixed on the fire in Ash's hands. Immediately, her shocked expression morphed into hatred. "Filthy Pyro scum!"

Ash's response to the immediate hostility was to blink in bewilderment. The ghost raised both arms, and the lake roiled, a wall of water rising high above her. I took a step back in alarm, but Ash just stared up at it, wide-eyed, as the woman dropped her arms and the wave broke over the bank. It knocked Ash off her feet and flowed back into the lake, the undertow dragging my lab-sister with it.

"Cato!" Ash sputtered, clawing at the mud and reaching out to me just before she was pulled under.

Even without the current pulling her down, I knew Ash couldn't swim. On the verge of panic, I splashed into the shallows after her.

The ghost laughed. "What's the matter? Don't like getting your hair wet?" She walked into the lake, hands out, giggling like a madwoman.

Ash was being dragged down to the bottom of the lake; already, she was out of my sight. I held out my hand and called upon my blue Divinity, my eyes trained on the place where she had disappeared. My concentration was on the lake bottom, where I manipulated the water to form a disk of ice. Ice had a lower density than water. After a few tense seconds, my knees weakened with relief when an ice cap broke the surface, a waterlogged figure lying on top. Ash coughed up lake water, shivering. Steam wafted from her wet body.

My hand was still outstretched, and I willed the ice cap to me. It bobbed on the waves like a dinghy as I directed it past me and beached it on the shore. Ash rolled off and landed on her hands and knees, then crawled away, still hacking and gasping.

Now that her life was no longer in immediate danger, I turned to face the ghost who had tried to murder my lab-sister.

The hostility she had demonstrated toward Ash was gone. Her face was blank and confused now as she studied me. "You're a Cryo? What are you doing? We're allies."

"Allies?" I repeated. I knew my memories were fuzzy, but her face didn't trigger even the faintest stirring of familiarity. "Do I know you?"

"Why are you protecting that washed-up trash?"

I was starting to comprehend. My knowledge of the elemental powers was practically nonexistent, but I knew enough to assume that opposite elements would naturally be enemies while similar elements, like water and ice, would be allies. Based on the rules of the Ghost Realm, Ash and I were not supposed to be friends, let alone family. We had just stumbled right into an ancient feud.

I lifted my chin and stated, "Her enemy is my enemy."

The Hydrokinetic gawked at me. She looked at Ash lying in the grass and then back at me. "You'll betray your Guild for that Pyro? Does Osias know about this travesty?"

That was twice now I'd heard the name Osias, and I still had no idea who he or she was. I stepped between Ash and the Hydrokinetic. "If you want to hurt her, you'll have to go through me first."

Her beady eyes narrowed. "Your arm . . . you don't have it. I see— you're neither Guilded nor Fallen. Well, Osias will personally thank me for eliminating a Cryo that defiles his Guild and stands alongside one of Fioren's. You'll bear the mark of the Fallen on your forehead, if I don't kill you first."

I compressed my hands into fists, the water lapping at my calves, the blue power still icy cold in my veins. While Ash had been at a dis-advantage here, I was strongest when surrounded by water.

But so was my opponent. I'd never fought a Hydrokinetic before, and I wasn't sure what to expect. My fight with the last Elemental I'd encountered hadn't exactly been well executed.

I moved my right foot back and bent my knees, prepared for her to make the first strike. The woman moved her arm in a fluid motion, like a deadly dancer. I watched a stream of water rise gracefully into the air, following her hand, but my attention was fixed on the tattoo on her bi-ceps.

Although it was a different symbol than the one imprinted on the Petrakinetic's arm, it was the same diameter in the same spot, and now I wondered if most Elementals had one. The Guilded ones, anyway . . . whatever that meant.

When my opponent snapped her wrist, the water whip shot out, recapturing my focus.

I moved my hand across my body. The stream turned to solid ice and fell with a splash between us. Before the Hydrokinetic could retaliate, I brought my hands up, sending a storm of frozen slivers erupting from the surface of the lake at my target.

With a casual wave of her hand, my ice reverted to water and hovered in the air like rain frozen in time. She redirected the water droplets toward me again. They converged into an orb that engulfed my head. Surprised, I staggered back. My concentration broke, and so did my hold over my Divinity. I held my breath and instinctively reached up, but my hand splashed through the water barrier, which maintained its shape.

Bloody Scout, I'm going to drown!

I stumbled back, desperately trying to shake the water from my head. I became intangible, but the Hydrokinetic was sustaining the water in place. As a final resort, I brought both hands up and called upon my blue power again. I froze the water orb into a sphere of ice, from which I could then become intangible to escape. I inhaled deeply, holding the frozen orb in both hands, then shot it back at the Hydrokinetic, hoping to hit her in the head and either stun or incapacitate her.

Before my ice even reached her, it melted back into water and swirled in the air a few inches in front of her palm. She sighed and let it unwind into a smooth stream, which fell back into the lake without a single drop splashing. "Well. It seems we're too evenly matched."

I was still panting from almost drowning inside the water orb. She was right. We both controlled water in two different forms. This fight was doomed to be a draw. Maybe Ash, who controlled our common weakness, could have tipped the scale, but she was outmatched with only half her power while the Hydrokinetic had access to the entire lake.

I considered my limited options. I was wary of using my second Divinity. Although it would probably guarantee victory, I might very well level all the trees and flood the park. I still had another alternative before resorting to such extreme measures. Engaging our divine powers over a distance had failed. If ice and water couldn't defeat each other, then I'd have to turn this power competition into a close-combat fight.

I conjured a long, lethal icicle in each hand, and before my opponent had time to react, I was sprinting straight at her, a disk of ice hardening the surface of the lake just before each foot came down so I had an even surface to run across. Her eyes widened at my sudden charge—she obviously wasn't trained in hand-to-hand and didn't know how to fight without her element—and after a few vicious slashes, she turned intangible and scrambled away from me, crimson drops diluting in the lake. She squealed in pain and fury as she whirled. A towering wave separated us. Through the wall of water, I watched her run away, her steps sending dainty ripples across the surface until she reached the bank and flailed through the low shrubs.

The wave broke, but I didn't follow. Even when she was out of sight, I could still hear crashing and snapping branches. I tightened my grip on my ice, which shrank in my hands as I reduced my weapons to liquid again. The water slipped through my fingers and back into the lake. I returned to Ash, who had collapsed on the shore with her eyes closed.

I didn't say a word as I lay down on my back beside her and peeled the wet mask away from my face. Her eyes remained shut. I folded my hands behind my head, gazing up at the clouds drifting across the vivid blue canvas high above us while my breathing returned to normal. My mind was still replaying what my opponent had said about the Guilds.

"Hey, Ash," I said quietly, turning my head to face her. "Question. Well, not really, I guess, but I was thinking . . . if the Fire Guild and the Ice Guild are enemies in the Ghost Realm, I guess we would have been enemies if we'd grown up there, huh?"

Ash opened one eye to peer at me. "I hadn't really thought about it."

We lay in silence while she recuperated. I said, "You know, you could have fought back if you had your full power."

Her eyes closed again. "Cato. I have a secret, but I want to make it a whisper. But just with you for now, okay? *They* didn't put this neutralizer on my arm." Her face reddened with shame. "*He* offered it to me on Lastday. And . . . I took it, by my own free will. Nobody forced me."

Horrified, I asked, "But why?"

Her arms circled her midriff. "Because fire burns the people I love."

She turned her head away. I stayed still for a moment, then gently touched her arm. "Not me. You don't have to hold your power back when you're around me. My ice cancels your fire."

"You just don't get it," she muttered.

"I might if you explain it to me."

Silence. I glanced sidelong at the folds of her cloak draped across her back. "Ash . . . you know, back at that place, you were my rock. I want to be the same for you. If you'll let me."

She scoffed. "Oh, please. I'm many things, Cato, but I'm no rock."

"You are to me. You were the first friendly face I saw when I woke up. You were the warm body next to me in that cold metal cage. The sound of your breathing in the dark reminded me that I wasn't all alone. You listened to my stories to try and preserve them when my memories were fading."

"I'm also the one who knocked you out in your first Arena fight."

"Wasn't much of a fight, was it?" I teased.

Ever so slightly, she shook her head. "No. Idiot. You just stood there and let me hit you." She sighed. "You're right; we're both Elementals. But your ice, it's dead in your hands after you've formed it. My fire . . . it's alive. And it's always hungry. And it moves on its own, trying to devour everything and everyone. I'm not strong enough to keep it in check."

"Are you kidding? You're one of the strongest people I know."

She rolled onto her back again, but she still wouldn't look at me. "I don't feel strong."

"You are. You're strong, and kind, and loyal, and pretty, and—"

She sat up so quickly that I hesitated for a few seconds before copying her, though much slower. A troubled scowl had crinkled her face. "What's wrong?"

"Nothing." And yet, she drew her knees to her chest and wrapped her arms around them.

"Did I say something that upset you?"

"No." She rested her chin on her knees and stared moodily at the water for a few minutes, then crawled to the water's edge. I practiced the utmost subtlety as I watched her kneel to gaze at her reflection. She touched her cheek with trembling fingers, then brushed the surface of the lake to smear her reflection with a stroke of ripples. She scowled, plunged her hand into the water, and then chucked the stone she'd snatched, using enough force for it to *plop* far away in the center of the lake.

I approached to sit by her. I had an inkling as to what was troubling Ash, but I didn't know how to broach such a touchy topic, and I didn't know how to comfort her. Ash's nightmares were usually different from mine. I saw *Him* or Dr. Anders, or relived my Lastday. She often saw the night guard who patrolled Project Alpha.

She bared her teeth when she threw the next rock even farther with a quiet, strained grunt, then drove her forearm into the surface again to fetch another. Gently, I said, "Do you remember when I became your lab-brother?" I held up my hand and stared at the worn glove, my dirty, calloused fingers exposed. "You offered your hand to me," I said, turning my palm toward Ash.

She veered back, ready to throw, but then hesitated, her sparkling eyes trained on the water. Smoke was curling up from her cloak. I continued, "You said, 'Welcome to the family.'"

Slowly, she lowered her arm until the stone was cupped in her lap. Her burning gaze found my face. Finally, she raised her other hand and pressed her gloved palm against mine.

I smiled and finished, "No bars now."

"No bars," she echoed in a strained whisper. She sighed and let her hand fall. I kept silent, watching her trace a random pattern across the stone with her thumb. She extended her arm to drop the stone back into the lake, then froze.

A face was staring at us in the water.

"Who disturbed my lake?" the stranger demanded.

Ash and I were both so shocked that we just gaped open-mouthed at the woman rising partway out of the lake. Her ears were pointed, her eyes a dazzling periwinkle and slightly larger than a human's. Her long hair was golden brown and fanned around her shoulders in the water. Below the surface, I saw a spiny protrusion of scales along the outside of each forearm, and although she appeared to be naked, her breasts and lower body were covered in scales. When she twisted, I marveled at the shimmering scales reflecting violet-blue-green in the sunlight. She had two thin, membranous fins at her hips, one long one down the center back of her tail, and two powerful fins at the base of her tail.

"I said, who disturbed my lake?" the stranger repeated.

Ash dropped the stone with a *plunk*. "I'm sorry."

The woman barely glanced at the rock before fixing her glare on Ash. "Not *you*. I'd hardly call a few rocks a disturbance."

"It wasn't us," I said quickly, remembering the giant waves that had disrupted the calm waters.

The woman transferred her cold gaze to me. "*Somebody* did. And you two are the only ones here."

"I'm sorry. There was a Hydrokinetic causing trouble. She's the one who disturbed you." I glanced at Ash. "Anyway, this isn't *your* lake. You have to return to the Ghost Realm."

I received the bitterest of scoffs. "Why should I leave? I was here first."

"This isn't your Realm."

"Yes it is." At our dubious looks, the woman said, "What, you think the Rip was the only Tear here? I've lived in this lake for hundreds of years, before this town was even built. I saw generations be born, grow up, and die, and their children's children's children live their lives. This is *my* lake."

Ash and I exchanged looks. Apparently the lake monster from my childhood was no fable. She just happened to not be a monster at all. Still, our job, as per our deal with the humans, was to send the invaders back to their own Realm. She wasn't a ghost, but she definitely wasn't native to this Realm, and if we broke our deal by letting this creature live in the lake, would the humans punish us?

Under my breath, I asked Ash, "What do you think?"

She shrugged and whispered back, "I don't know. She's not hurting anybody . . ."

I nodded, my resolve hardening. "Right. I say we let her stay."

"Shouldn't we ask Jay?"

"Why? The humans don't even know she's here." Ash didn't agree with me, but she didn't argue, either, so I interpreted her silence to be acceptance.

I turned to the lady in the water and asked, "Are there others here?"

Her stiff expression finally softened. "No. Just me."

Ash asked, "Don't you get lonely?"

"No."

I was trying to identify this creature. I knew her species started with an M, but my mind drew a blank, and I couldn't even guess how many syllables I needed. "Question. Uh, I don't mean to be rude, but . . . what are you?"

"I'm a sirien."

"See-ree-ehn," I echoed slowly, testing the word. Wrong. That wasn't the word I was thinking of. This must be another conflict of ter-minology between the Realms, and just like I still couldn't translate the human word for *nydæa*, the word for *sirien* was also lost to me.

I inquired, "What's your name?"

"Chelvistin. You can call me Chel." The sirien smiled, revealing pointed teeth. "I know who you are." At my frown, her smile widened. "Phantom."

"No," I said quickly.

"Oh yes, you are. There isn't another kálos with eyes like yours. I thought you were dead."

Heat rushed to my cheeks, although why I was embarrassed, I wasn't sure. Flustered, I sputtered, "What? No, um . . . I just . . . I've been away for a while. I don't want anyone to know I'm back. You can't tell."

"Tell who?" said Chel. "Nobody knows about me. *You* can't tell anyone *I'm* here. You keep my secret, I keep yours. Deal?"

"Deal," Ash and I chorused without even hesitating to seek confirmation with the other.

Chelvistin looked directly at Ash and requested, "Your name?"

"Ash."

"Phantom and Ash," the sirien committed to memory with a nod.

"Actually, I don't go by Phantom anymore. You can call me Cato."

She raised one eyebrow and informed me, "I'm still going to call you Phantom."

"Oh . . . kay . . . that's fine, I guess," I mumbled. "As long as you keep it a whisper."

She was confused, so I had to explain to her that a whisper was a secret shared amongst a group of people with the expectation that it wouldn't leave the group. A true secret, by our definition, was something kept to oneself and never shared with another soul. Once Chel understood, she accepted.

Ash still needed time to recover, so we sat in the grass and talked to the sirien until nine rings from the clock tower summoned me.

— Chapter Nine —
All-On-One

Holly paced in her bedroom.

The phone was pressed to her ear, and it was ringing, but she didn't expect him to answer. Not this late. On the last ring, she blew out a pent-up breath, ready to hang up before the voicemail message started.

"Hello?"

Holly froze. His voice was deep and groggy, fresh out of sleep. "Agent Kovak?"

He paused, but when he spoke again, she could hear his smile.

"Holly. It's always such a pleasure to hear your lovely voice. I was getting worried; I'd expected to hear from you before now."

"Where the hell are the supply drops?"

"Ah, that's what I like about you. Always precise and quick to the point. No time wasted on meaningless small talk."

"I mean it, Kovak. Why have you stopped the supplies to Phantom Heights?"

He sniffed and took his sweet time answering. "Isn't there something you were planning to tell me?"

Holly's throat clenched. *He knows?* "What?"

"Maddie's shield is down. It's been down for a few weeks now, correct? I didn't expect a report from Maddie—she's probably still not talking to me, am I right?—but I did expect one from you."

Holly lifted her head. *So, he doesn't know. Not yet.*

"Since when was I required to file reports with you? Yes, the shield is down, but that doesn't mean we have a steady supply in and out of the city limits. You rerouted traffic around Phantom Heights and put up barricades, remember? We still need those supply drops."

"Hmm. My mistake. I'd be happy to reauthorize the drops. One phone call to update me would have prevented this little miscommunication. But you decided the best time to have this discussion was at midnight?"

Holly released a slow breath to settle her racing pulse. "Now that you mention it, there's something else I wanted to talk to you about."

"I hope this means you have good news for me."

She shifted the phone to her other ear. "I don't have any news for you. I want answers, and I want them now. I know when you're hiding something."

"Mmm." He yawned and said, "Remind me never to challenge you to a poker game."

"This isn't a joke. If you don't want to tell Tarrow, fine. But you need to tell me what's really going on in Project Alpha."

He was quiet for a moment. "The less you know, the better. Plausible deniability, right?"

"I've always kept your secrets, haven't I?"

"You have," he acknowledged. "But if my fugitives do show up in Phantom Heights, this could get very messy." Holly stubbornly waited. "You've already guessed, haven't you?"

"I want to hear it from you."

The long pause cranked Holly's nerves tighter and tighter with each heartbeat.

"All right. If you insist, I'll just come out and say it—Cato was in Project Alpha. He's one of the fugitives."

The room spun. She'd been trying so hard to convince herself that her suspicions were wrong. Holly swayed, then plopped down on the edge of the bed.

Kovak continued, "I wasn't entirely honest when I said the Rip was the only reason they might come to Phantom Heights. We thought there was a chance he might come home."

"Oh no," Holly whispered into the phone. She clutched it tighter. "No, you don't understand. Do you realize what will happen if anyone finds out what I did? I . . . it . . . it would be a disaster. I'd lose everything."

"I know."

"Do you?" she shouted, then clapped her hand over her mouth, startled by her outburst. She repeated in a strained whisper, "Do you?"

"That's why we had to limit how much information we gave to Maddie."

"Are you serious? You asked her to hunt them down! What, you didn't think she'd recognize him? You didn't think *anybody* here would recognize him with those eyes of his?"

Kovak took a steadying breath before he explained slowly, as if to a child, "Obviously, I couldn't tell the whole damn town he was one of the fugitives, and I couldn't give a full description of them without revealing him. If he makes a public appearance, there's not much I can do after the fact, but I wasn't going to let the news leak that he escaped before that happened, not while I still have a chance to recover him quietly and keep this catastrophe under wraps."

"I told you before—if you wanted to keep Cato, you had to throw away the key. What part of 'permanent solution' did you not understand?"

"This was an unforeseen event."

"And you didn't think it might be a good idea to give me some forewarning before he showed up here?" Holly ran her trembling fingers through her hair. Her stomach was churning, threatening to upheave her dinner. "Why didn't you tell me you put him in *Alpha*?"

"It wasn't relevant at the time." His tone darkened. "And you never asked, Holly. You didn't want to know, remember?"

She slumped forward. "What am I supposed to do?" she asked, more to herself than Kovak.

"Nothing," he answered regardless. "You keep quiet, keep your ears open, and leave the details to me. Our agreement is still in place, right? You already received your payment."

"I should demand more," she snapped, although they both knew that she wouldn't.

"Be honest. Has there been any sign of them?"

Holly shivered and stared out the dark window. Her worst fear had come to life. Cato was out there somewhere, hiding in the shadows of the night. If Phantom Heights learned how she'd betrayed him . . .

"No," she said. Maybe it was wrong to lie to Agent Kovak. Maybe she should spill everything and beg him to clean up his mess before it blew up in her face. But Cato hadn't revealed himself, and if she let Kovak expose him, the town would never forgive her, especially if losing the Alpha ghosts caused the people of Phantom Heights to seal themselves in City Hall again.

"I'm sorry. I'd tell you if I knew anything."

"And Maddie?"

"What about her?"

"We put her on their trail. Does she know anything?"

"No, not to my knowledge."

"Does she suspect?"

"I don't see why she would."

Kovak was quiet again, and Holly imagined he was nodding at her responses. She swallowed. "What did you tell Cato?"

"What do you mean?"

"I mean . . ." Her voice cracked, forcing her to clear her throat so she could force out, "Does he know?"

"I don't see how that's relevant."

"Answer the question. If Cato comes here, is he going to be looking for aid, or revenge?"

"Honestly, I couldn't tell you. He suffered some memory loss in the lab."

Holly sat up straight. "Memory loss? How much does he remember?"

She could practically hear the shrug over the phone. "Hard to say."

"Don't give me that—"

"Look, the amnesia was a side effect, not an objective. We didn't test his memory to measure the deterioration."

"Does he know the truth? *What did you tell him*?"

The silence on the other end of the line caused her to start gnawing at her fingernail.

"A7 isn't—"

"Don't call him that."

Holly blinked. The words had tumbled out. She wasn't even sure why replacing his name with a number bothered her, but it did. It grated on her conscience for reasons she couldn't quantify. On the other end of the phone, the silence was weighted and mocking.

"Numbers make it easier, Holly. Trust me. A7 isn't stable. In fact, he's very dangerous now, more so than he ever was before."

"What do you mean?"

"People were always so quick to point out that he's half-human, but he's on his way to becoming a very powerful kálos, just like I told you a couple years ago. Did you know that his power level has doubled? He's a Level 4 now. I want you to keep that in mind if you find yourself having doubts. He's more than capable of destroying Phantom Heights. If A7 does come home . . . I don't know what he'll do."

Holly forced herself to pull her hand away from her teeth. "This is all *your* fault," she seethed. "I never should have listened to you."

"What's done is done. Let me handle it. I don't expect you to clean up any messes unless this gets out of hand. You're the only person in Phantom Heights I can trust." Holly bowed her head. He quietly finished, "So . . . this stays between us, right?"

She swallowed hard. What choice did she have? "On one condition." The silence expanded between them. Holly took a slow breath to collect her thoughts. "I knew I didn't mishear when you came to Phantom Heights and said there were *four* primary targets to retrieve. Tell me why you need Cato to build your weapon."

"Because he's special." She could hear the smile in his voice again. "Isn't that reason enough?"

"No. It isn't."

He sighed. "You don't get to twist my arm and make me spill classified information, Holly. It doesn't work like that. You're lucky I respect you and value our professional relationship, so I'll tell you that I need A7 for two reasons. Firstly, he wasn't born with his abilities. I need to understand the physical changes that took place. But second, and most important, I'm interested in his two Divinities. That's a mutation I can't study in any other test subject. Like I said, he's special. He's our best chance at not just surviving, but *winning* this war."

Kovak paused, then added softly, "You know he's safest here, under my supervision. I can keep his unstable powers neutralized to ensure he doesn't hurt himself or anyone else. It's for the best. For him, and for you."

Silence compressed the air. Holly listened to the faint *tick-tick-tick-tick-tick* of her wristwatch. She stood. "Thank you for being honest with me. Good night." She hung up before Kovak had a chance to reply.

"Who was that?"

Holly jumped and spun to face her daughter, who was lingering in the doorway. "How long have you been standing there?" Holly demanded.

Shannon blinked and took half a step back. "I just came upstairs. I'm sorry. I didn't mean to eavesdrop. Is something wrong?"

"No, of course not. Everything's fine. That was Aunt Lorraine."

"Really? You . . . look kind of pale. Is Aunt Lorraine all right?"

"Yes. Sorry. There's no need to worry."

"Do *you* feel okay?"

Holly forced a smile and assured, "I'm just tired, that's all. It's past my bedtime. Past yours too, isn't it?"

Shannon walked forward with her arms outstretched for a hug. "Night, Mom. Love you."

"I love you, too." Usually Holly was the first to let go, but this time she held on a second longer after Shannon released her.

"Mom, are you sure you're okay?"

"Fine. Promise." She smiled and swept a lock of Shannon's hair out of her eyes and behind her ear where it belonged. "Good night."

As soon as Shannon was across the threshold, Holly closed the door, then pivoted and leaned against it. Her back slid down the door until she was sitting with her knees drawn up to her chest. She buried her face in her hands.

It wasn't Cato she saw behind her closed lids. It was A1 and A2 lying on the floor of City Hall, and Doc was pointing out the effects of long-term starvation, and the scars on their wrists, and the holes drilled through their skulls . . . and if Cato had been in the same Project as them . . .

Holly lurched forward. She crawled for a few paces, then staggered to her feet and barely reached the bathroom before she was kneeling by the toilet. She gripped the porcelain and vomited, heaving so hard she thought her stomach might come up, too.

When the bout finally passed, she stayed where she was, her head bowed, tears streaming. "I didn't know," she whispered into the toilet bowl. "I'm so sorry. I swear, I didn't know . . ."

***

The gentlest breeze tossed the leafy boughs around us. I craned my neck to look up at the starry night sky ringed by treetops.

We were standing in a clearing in the park—Kit, Ash, RC, and I positioned in a circle around Jay. Axel leaned against a tree trunk next to Finn and Reese, who were sitting cross-legged on the ground with ECANI. Invisible Proto surrounded the clearing.

I detected movement from my peripheral and looked forward again just as Ash drew her staff. One corner of Jay's mouth turned up. He held out his hand, and moonlight winked on a silver disk. Jay pulled the hood over his head and taunted, "Take it if you can."

And with that, we all rushed at him.

The rules of All-On-One were simple enough. Axel wasn't allowed to participate because he was too fast. RC could use his telekinesis on any object except Jay or the disk. Otherwise, anything was fair game. To win, we had to work together to take the disk from Jay.

Simple, right?

Wrong. We hadn't won a round of All-On-One yet.

Ash swung her staff; Jay ducked it as if she were moving in slow motion. RC jabbed several fast punches; Jay sidestepped and parried every one. Kit was crouched on all fours, her gleaming golden eyes trained on the disk, and she pounced to grab it when Jay leapt away from RC, but he jerked it out of reach just as her fingers closed on where it had been a half-second before.

I went for Jay's feet, hoping to trip him up so another could grab the disk. It wasn't a competition, after all; any one of us could grab the disk, and we'd win as a team.

Just as I was about to hit Jay in the shins, he vanished, and my arms grasped nothing but air when I fell in the grass. I sensed him behind me. I whirled and swung, but he was gone again, appearing a few feet to my left, right in front of Ash. She brought her staff down, her target the hand with the silver disk, but Jay turned his body to the side, and her staff struck the ground.

A rock whizzed toward the cloaked figure, but Jay spun out of its trajectory, his cloak fanning out behind him. I lunged at Jay again. The leader grinned, and I couldn't help but marvel at how effortless it was for him to deflect every one of my blows with his forearms so my metal-studded knuckles glanced harmlessly off his gauntlets. He'd been in the Arena the longest, and the extra time showed. Over his shoulder, I saw Kit crouch and leap; somehow Jay noticed the movement from the corner of his eye, and he ducked so she sailed over his shoulder and landed in a somersault.

Not once had Jay made an offensive move, and yet, we couldn't touch him. I made a desperate leap at Jay from the front at the same moment Ash leapt at him from behind. I was completely focused on the cloaked figure, at the silver eyes that watched me fly through the air at him, at how close I was to finally grabbing him. Just as my arms started to close around his body, he was gone, and I found myself on a crash course with Ash. We were both airborne. It was too late to stop or alter our course. We collided. *Hard*.

I was so stunned that the pain didn't even register when we crumpled together in a heap. And then, it hit me in a cresting wave. With a drawn-out groan, I sat up in a daze. Ash lay still in the grass, moaning softly.

"That's enough," Jay said. He was standing a few yards away from us, barely winded. He had his index finger through the hole in the center of the disk and was causally twirling the weapon around his finger. Ash and I were both still on the ground. RC was doubled over with his hands on his knees. Kit was panting, her ears back and her tongue out. None of us moved.

Jay sighed. "Do you know why you haven't beaten me yet?"

Axel smirked; he knew the answer. So did the twins. But the four of us who actually played the training game exchanged confused looks.

"No," Ash said, finally pulling herself to her knees and rubbing her forehead, which sported a blossoming red mark.

Jay folded his arms. "You won't win until you start working together like a team."

"We do," I argued.

"If that were true," Jay replied, gesturing at Finn and Reese, "this wouldn't have happened."

Life-size holographic images of Jay, Ash, and me appeared in the grass. The twins had been recording us during the match, and now the holograms replayed our final move against Jay. Ash and I both leapt. From this perspective, it seemed there was no way Jay could possibly evade us . . . at least, until he disappeared. The images rewound and played again, slower. I winced; the impact looked even more painful in slow motion. As if reminded, the throbbing in my head intensified.

Jay shook his head. "Cato, you and Ash are partners. I paired you together because your powers are polar opposites and your fighting techniques are similar. You two especially should be working together, and if you had been, you wouldn't have gotten in each other's way. RC, you're my partner. You should be able to read my moves. But not just partners; all of you need to be able to work together as a whole team, and you aren't."

"We're trying," Kit mumbled.

Jay tossed the disk to RC, who held out his hand and let the weapon levitate. To avoid Jay's piercing and disappointed gaze, I watched the holograms until they disappeared. "Not hard enough," the leader reprimanded sternly. "We have to be one cohesive unit. You can try again next time."

He strode away. We watched him go, tired and sore and humiliated once again. Once Jay was out of earshot, Kit's shoulders slumped, and she repeated, "We're *trying*. Why's he so hard on us?"

"Because he cares about us," RC answered, his voice solemn in the otherwise silent night. The Amínyte huffed with indignity. "Kit," he explained patiently, "Jay pushes us so hard because he wants to make sure we're strong. He's afraid of losing us, like he lost his blood-family."

Kit's ears pricked forward. I leaned closer, also curious. I'd heard only bits and pieces of Jay's Before. If Jay had shared his past with any of us, it would have been with RC, who had joined Alpha not long after Jay's own induction.

The Telekinetic gazed at the littlest. "See," he explained, "Jay's mom got sick and died, and when she left him all alone, Jay tried to find his father. He searched all over the Ghost Realm until he wandered through a Tear, but *They* were studying it when he came through."

Kit's eyes widened. "*They* caught him then?"

RC glanced across the clearing and continued quietly, "He literally walked right into *Their* hands." He fixed his eyes—one bright and one dull—on us again, sweeping his gaze over each in turn. "We're the only family he has now, and he's terrified of losing a single one of us. That's why he pushes us so hard. I don't think we'll ever be strong enough to satisfy him."

RC's voice trailed off into silence. Kit's ears were pinned sorrowfully against her head. I stared at the cloaked figure standing on the far side of the clearing, leaning against a tree trunk with his arms folded. His silver eyes glowed in the darkness, watching us. I couldn't guess how old Jay would have been when his mom died, but I imagined him as a child wandering the Ghost Realm alone in search of a family. I didn't know if he'd heard our discussion about him or not—he didn't move or speak.

He turned away from us and strode into the shadows of the night.

— Chapter Ten —
Ghost Hunter's Grave

Men in surgical masks and white lab coats circled a naked teenager on a metal table.

A sheet was draped over the boy's lower half. Scalpels and saws gleamed, so close to his vulnerable flesh. The room, the floor, the walls, the ceiling, everything was white.

Vivian stood in the corner, watching in stupefied horror as the surgeons leaned over the boy, preparing to dissect his still body. She wanted to rush forward, to stop them, but she was frozen, paralyzed, mute.

The boy opened his eyes and turned his head to stare at her—one eye blue, the other green. "Please," he whispered, reaching out to her with his hand outstretched, "help me."

She reached out, but he was suddenly so far away, though not too far for her to hear the sound of saw blades whirring . . .

"No!"

She bolted up with a cry. Where was she? Why was it dark?

She shrieked, shying away from the ghost standing a few feet away. Trembling, Vivian swiped at her tears. "Jay," she whispered upon identifying him.

The ghost narrowed his silver eyes at the sound of her voice. He was garbed in the same uniform he'd been wearing when she had first met him, but there was one alteration—a black cloth concealing his face from the bridge of his nose down. A black cloth that was strikingly similar to the mask of another ghost who used to protect Phantom Heights, a ghost who was standing on a pedestal just a few yards away.

Vivian was surprised to discover that she was in Alvarez Park. She peered over Jay's shoulder at the statue of Phantom. Now she remembered—she'd fallen asleep on the park bench.

"What are you doing here?" she croaked.

"I could ask you the same. It isn't safe for you to be out here alone, especially at night." He cocked his head. "You were screaming."

The way he said that, it sounded as though he had too much experience with people screaming. Vivian buried her face in her hands. "I had a bad dream."

Jay didn't answer, simply stood there, studying her from a safe distance. His silver eyes glowed bright in the dark—*like moons*, she thought. A full moon in each eye, partially eclipsed by a smaller celestial body. She and Jay were equals now, and yet, Vivian still felt like a prisoner under his stern watch. Sheepishly, she asked, "Jay, when you were in the lab, did you ever meet a ghost named Cato? Or Phantom?"

He was silent for a moment, appraising her. "I never met any prisoners outside Project Alpha."

She rubbed one eye with the heel of her palm. "The Agents took him, and . . ." She faltered, unable to continue. "I guess . . . falling asleep by his statue made me dream about him."

Jay turned his head toward the memorial. "So, you commissioned us to take his place," he stated dryly.

Vivian blinked. "No," she whispered, shaking her head. "Of course not. Cato—well, Phantom, I guess—he was a hero. You're just . . . a mercenary. No offense, but . . . it's not the same."

"I see. You . . . miss him?" Jay asked uncertainly.

Vivian swallowed hard. "He . . . I-I, I still think about . . . how I should have . . ." Her voice died.

Jay considered her answer with no insight beyond a thoughtful, "Hmm," as if her gibberish were the most profound piece of philosophy. Finally, he said, "I think you should go home. I'll make sure you get there safely."

Vivian stared at Phantom again, her mind flashing back to the image of Cato lying on the metal table, reaching toward her, calling for help. She sniffed, fresh tears filling her eyes as she nodded and rose.

"Okay. Just . . . give me a few minutes, please."

Jay waited patiently while she approached Phantom's memorial. The statue, she'd always thought, was fierce, but not an accurate representation of Cato. He'd never looked so angry, glaring down his nose at people as if he were above them. Usually he had a smile on his face, never such proud scorn, even behind his mask.

She knelt in front of the memorial, her knees pressing into the soft, cool earth. Some people came to stand before Phantom's statue, meek and admiring, to remember him. Not Vivian, not tonight.

Though she would have liked to be alone, Jay's silent company didn't bother her. She leaned forward and placed a white stone where the grass was torn with rubble. A gravestone used to mark this place. Her brother, deemed a hero for his service, had received the honor of being buried by Phantom's statue.

He used to be alone, but now there were new graves, and Hero's Hollow had become Heroes' Hollow. The grass hadn't had a chance to grow over the upturned soil of the graves on the opposite end of the clearing where the recovered fallen raiders had been laid to rest. Trey would have a place here if he were to have an untimely death. So would her mom, but Vivian didn't want to think about that.

This grave had been the first. Sometimes, Vivian questioned the burial spot. Madison had opposed the decision, but in the end, she'd been too grief-stricken to resist the public outcry. *"He was a hero. He deserves a special resting place,"* people had said. *"He shouldn't be just another gravestone lost in the cemetery."* Some had petitioned to display an urn in the local museum. Madison had insisted upon a burial. Alvarez Park was the compromise.

Jay observed in respectful silence. He didn't ask any questions about her strange actions, and for that, Vivian was grateful.

Someday soon, she vowed, *I'll replace the gravestone and find fresh flowers for you.*

Vivian gazed up at the masked hero standing so confidently above her, keeping watch over her brother's remains. With a sigh, she rose and set her hand on the corner of the pedestal to bid Phantom a silent good night, although she paused when something shifted beneath her hand. She lifted her palm to find a penny sitting on the memorial. She tilted Lincoln's face toward the moonlight, then replaced the offering.

Vivian turned back to Jay, nodding once to indicate she was ready to leave. He was quiet company on the walk home. Through her contemplations, she noticed that he kept a precise distance—close enough to be at her side in a flash, but far enough away that he was out of arm's reach. She tested the theory once, taking a subtle step closer. He was just as subtle about reestablishing the distance. Still, his presence was reassuring, and with him by her side, she wasn't afraid of what monsters might be lurking in the shadows.

Her heart grew heavier in the moment she realized she used to feel this same cloak of perceived safety when she was with Cato. Vivian shivered and wrapped her arms around herself, feeling the raised goose bumps like braille spelling sorrow on her skin. She turned to Jay, but her heart stuttered when she realized he wasn't with her anymore.

"Jay?" she called, turning in a circle, searching the darkness for his silver eyes. She was completely alone in the night.

Vivian backed up a step. The blackness closed in around her like spreading ink. She jumped when something brushed her skin.

Jay was standing behind her, draping a blanket over her shoulders. "Where did you get this?" Vivian whispered, pulling it tighter around her body as Jay stepped away. She squinted at it and rubbed the material between her fingers. "It's . . . mine." She gazed at him. "How?"

Jay didn't answer. He took a step and paused, waiting, and she began walking again as he fell into step beside her. They strolled in silence through the sleeping town.

"I was looking for you tonight," Vivian finally said.

Jay peered at her from the corner of his eye. "And why would the daughter of a ghost hunter be looking for me?"

"Don't label me like that," she snapped. Softer, she said, "I wanted to talk to you."

"About what?"

She couldn't remember. It had been so clear in her head when she'd snuck out, but the nightmare had rattled her thoughts while sleep left her groggy, and now that Jay's bright silver eyes were watching, her mind drew a total blank. What did she want to tell him? Nothing, perhaps. She had nothing specific to say. Simply the desire to meet him under different circumstances, to speak to him as an equal instead of his prisoner, to see if he would become the killer Kovak had described. She still couldn't see it. Jay was too smart, too calculating to be the ruthless man she'd been told he really was. And yet, he and his small band of fugitives had made Phantom Heights safer than it had been when Phantom himself was here.

Vivian couldn't understand him, and it was hard to think with the stern statue and the white stone on her mind. Her dream was still too fresh. Agent Kovak, the man who took Cato away, the person who condemned Phantom Heights to die a slow, cruel death, the last face her brother probably saw before his vision went dark forever . . . The very thought made her sick. She wished it had been her face, or their mom's. Not Kovak's. Why did it have to be *him*, his face still sharp while everything else turned to black, his emotionless gaze the final image to blur away?

She and Jay were connected. Did he realize it? Did he comprehend that the man hunting him was the same man Vivian could never forgive, that they shared a bond forged in hatred of a common enemy?

Of course not. Why would the powerful leader of the Alpha ghosts care even for a second about the dead ghost-hunting protégé he never met? Jay would deem her a fool for so wholeheartedly embracing such a connection. He was a lab rat; she was the daughter of a ghost hunter. The only connection was his scheme to kidnap her.

"Here." He halted.

Vivian stopped short. "Huh?"

The Alpha leader nodded forward. Vivian finally took stock of her surroundings and realized they were on her street. The sight of her familiar house was both a comfort and a wound; she was glad to be safe at home, but depressed by the thought of two empty beds upstairs instead of just hers.

She wiped the corner of the blanket across a stray tear as she slowly trudged up the porch steps. She turned around to say, "Thank y—"

But Jay was nowhere to be seen.

Vivian stood at the top of the steps for a few minutes, gazing up and down the dark street, but there was no sign of the Alpha ghost.

***

"It's not like you to fail me, Hassing. I can't find the words to express my disappointment."

The captain fell to his knees, staring at the floor. Never before had he been forced to kneel before the Warden in such shame. "I know, sir. You have my humblest apologies. Our targets have proven to be skilled and formidable. And . . . something strange is happening in Cröendor."

Azar folded his arms. "You're going to try my patience with excuses for your incompetence?"

"No, sir. Actually, I think my problems are related to Rayven's."

The Warden glanced at the bird perched on the back of his chair. Rayven tilted his head at Hassing, who asked, "Have you shared your theory?"

The slave blinked but otherwise remained immobile.

Azar said, "Well? You have something to report, Rayven?"

The bird glided from its perch in eddies of smoke, then landed as a man on his knees in front of Azar, head bowed, long black hair brushing his toes, scars gleaming across his bare back. "Master, I prefer not to report until I've verified the facts."

Hassing glared at him. *Damn pest, making me look like a fool.*

Azar smirked and said, "While I appreciate your thoroughness, I'd like to hear this theory of yours."

Rayven raised his head. "I believe there may be another Amínyte in Phantom Heights."

"Oh? And what gives you reason to think that?"

"The corvids have reported unusual organization among the feline population. I command the skies, Master, but I believe another Amínyte has created a spy array on the ground. If this Amínyte is a member of

Project Alpha, that could explain how they have eluded the Shadow Guard. Our targets may have many eyes watching—more eyes than I have, and I have fewer every day as my spies fall. But I haven't found the Amínyte yet, Master. I haven't been able to prove my theory."

Before Azar could respond, Hassing blurted, "Whoever is killing Rayven's crows has also taken out my best trackers just as they start to close in. Guards have reported blacking out in Cröendor and waking up in Avilésor. *Level 4* officers, caught completely unaware, eclipsed without even realizing they were under attack. We're talking about someone with an immense amount of power and stealth. Must be Level 5."

Azar snapped, "You should take a lesson from Rayven. His hypothesis is grounded."

Hassing's cheeks flamed. "Yes, sir. I just . . . It's as if there is a shadow guarding these fugitives."

"*I* am master of the shadows," Azar seethed.

Hassing inclined his head in acknowledgment. "All of my intel indicated that the subjects in Project Alpha were specifically chosen for the program due to unique Divinities or high power levels."

Azar rubbed his chin. "And yet, Lieutenant Cisco wasn't able to sense any power at all, basic or divine. When he finishes his current mission, I might send him back to Cröendor to see if the circumstances have changed. In the meantime, you need to restrategize."

"I'm doing the best I can, but morale is low, and many good Shadow Guards have been injured."

Azar turned away and opened a desk drawer. "Then I suppose you need more."

Hassing's head jerked up. "R-really? You'll give me more troops?"

"No," Azar snapped. "You've exhausted more than enough of the Shadow Guard."

"Then . . . I don't understand, sir."

Azar disregarded him and gazed down at a checkered board on his desk. Black pieces were aligned on one side, white on the other.

"Hassing, do you know what this is?"

"It looks like it came from Cröendor."

"That it did." Picking up the tallest black piece topped with a cross, Azar explained, "It's a game of strategy, although I don't know the rules. A scarback from Cröendor told me this piece is the king, and it's the most important." He set it down, then indicated a carved horse figure. "You, of course, are at my side." He gestured to the other unique black pieces. "Veto, Inalli, Cisco, the Guard, they also serve me. Then there are the pawns beneath us."

Azar turned the board so the white pieces were nearest to him. Whereas the black pieces had been organized so the king was in the middle protected by a ring of higher pieces behind an arc of pawns, the white pieces had been arranged differently. The white king was surrounded by a circle of pawns. Azar picked it up. "The AGC is the most important opponent in this war. They hide behind the human citizens. But it seems there are some new pieces in our little game." Azar set the other seven white pieces in the middle of the board. He studied them intently, then pushed them toward the white side.

Hassing watched in silence, too afraid to interrupt.

"Ironic, isn't it, Hassing, that people fear the darkness because they can't see the monsters that lurk in it. People always choose the light with the misconception that it will illuminate the danger. Instead, they allow themselves to be blinded. But soon enough, they'll see it's in the darkness where their salvation lies."

Azar picked up the white queen and held it in his palm. "I want the leader of the Alphas," he said, his voice hard again. He set the queen down and moved the black horse to the center of the board beside the white queen, then shifted all of the black pawns toward the horse.

Hassing glared at the board. "I don't understand. Why move your lowest pieces there? You should be using your more powerful ones."

Azar chuckled. "That's why you don't know how to win this game. And that's precisely what it is—a game. Strategy, Hassing. I control all the pieces, and soon enough, they'll fall into place. But you see these white ones here?" He pointed to the cluster of figures separated from the king and pawns. "They're on the wrong side of the board. Do you understand?"

"Yes, sir." Hassing reached over and seized one of the black pawns. "But if you expect me to succeed, give me more powerful pieces to use."

He blinked in surprise when the Warden handed him a single sheet of paper. Hassing frowned as he skimmed the writing, then peered up at Azar.

"I suggest you start spreading the word. This is a generous offer. Let the pawns do their work."

Hassing nodded, clutching the paper as he set the pawn down. "Yes, sir."

Azar crossed his arms. "My patience has reached its limit. I don't want to demote you over this." He unfolded his arms, set one finger on top of the black horse, and tipped it onto its side.

Hassing bowed as he backed away. "Yes, sir, I understand, sir," he mumbled. Azar scowled after him until he retreated from the office and closed the door.

Azar sighed and rubbed his temples. "Rayven, I'm sending you back to Cröendor for reconnaissance. See if you can confirm the presence of another Amínyte there . . . as well as Hassing's mysterious Level 5 'shadow-kálos.' But be careful. I don't want you to end up dead on the ground with a broken neck, too."

"Understood, Master," said Rayven in the instant before he transformed in black smoke and flapped through the open window, leaving Azar in solitude to gaze lustfully at the white queen and the six white pieces near it on the board. He slowly slid one white pawn to join the cluster. An Amínyte in Project Alpha. What an interesting potential development. Amínytes were not all that powerful, but, as Rayven had proven time and again over the decades, they were immeasurably useful as slaves.

The seven white pieces had become eight.

Seven to bring the Seventh, but Eight are the key. They will decide what the fate of the Realms shall be.

Seers were known to be arcane, and many kálos had met a foolish end by misinterpreting a prophecy. Despite the empty words about sons without wings and whatnot, Azar had no doubt the Eight referred to the Alphas. But this Seven had him absolutely perplexed. Perhaps seven worthy and powerful foes were destined to make history with a lowly slave serving them, making eight in total?

Frustrated, he rested his cheek against his hand and nudged the black king with his fingernail. He had to be careful; prophecies were not always meant to be taken literally. If Eight were the key, he'd focus on them and perhaps find the Seven along the way. Whatever the Seven and the Eight had to do with this war, the rest of the prophecy was clear—the Sixth Dynasty was about to come to a close.

— Chapter Eleven —

The Teacher

Mayor Correll's voice, amplified through the microphone, reverberated off the buildings to echo around the crowd gathered in town square.

The mayor was talking about a new proposal city council was considering that, once passed, would ensure a safer Phantom Heights. He was being irritatingly vague on the details, instead choosing to emphasize the importance of preparing for the future so when the town's mercenaries inevitably failed or turned against them, the town would have a plan of protection in place.

City council's plan was drastic, and it would be sure to trigger heated debates, but for now, Correll was simply making efforts to prepare the citizens so it wouldn't be such a shock once it passed. And it was likely to pass. Holly Jennings had persuaded most of the council to back the proposal.

Madison took a sip of warm tap water from a plastic bottle, thoroughly bored standing at the mayor's side beneath the portico of City Hall. *This is degrading.* When the town was under siege, she'd been the leader at the forefront of the raid team. Now, although she did still have valued input on any ghost-related activities, she was more of a trophy Correll liked to show off, an image rather than a leader. He needed her support, not her expertise. Because "the people trust her," he said. The usual political bullshit she typically tried to avoid.

Trey was almost dozing on his feet beside her. She subtly jabbed him with her elbow, causing his head to jerk up. She was still readjusting to seeing him with a clean-shaven face. The absence of his scruffy beard had returned some of his youthfulness, as if time had been rewound just a little and he had another shot at enjoying his teenage years. His gray eyes were unobstructed now, his goggles traded in for contacts.

Madison let her gaze wander, trying not to look as distant as she felt. Many in the crowd shared her lack of enthusiasm and were busy whispering their own more exciting conversations. The mayor really wasn't telling them anything. Madison suspected most were here hoping for news of the mysterious Alpha ghosts, since the local news channel and newspapers were forbidden to report anything even hinting about the Agents' fugitives in case Kovak caught wind of the story.

Wesly Cooper was in the front row. He seemed to be the only person listening to Correll, and his furrowed brow indicated he wasn't liking what he was hearing. Madison's gaze skipped over him and continued to wander across the restless crowd until a man standing three rows back ensnared her attention.

The stranger was the only one besides Wes who was actually listening. Now that she'd seen him, she could focus on no one else. The closer she looked, the more out of place he seemed. His clothing was unusual; he wore a light-colored tunic with leather wrist gauntlets tied on his forearms. His light brown hair was pulled back into a short ponytail, his beard trimmed close. Clasped around his neck was what a kálos would call a two-fold-style hooded full-length cloak. The base hung near his ankles, with a second piece of fabric—sort of a half-cloak— sewn on the top half, giving the midnight-blue garment two layers.

When he raised his vibrant blue eyes to look at her, they glinted in the sunlight.

Madison drew her weapon and aimed at the man's chest. Trey, startled to attention, mirrored her movement, immediately picking out the odd wardrobe from the crowd. The stranger didn't so much as bat an eye at the two ghost hunters who now had him in their crosshairs.

The anxious crowd fell silent—the town meeting had just become much more interesting. Police officers rested their hands on their holstered ectoguns, awaiting Madison's orders.

Correll trailed off. He spotted the intruder, blanched, and took a quick hop-step to hide behind Madison.

"Wait, *wait*!" Wes cried, breaking away from the crowd with his hands up. "Don't shoot!" He turned his back to Madison to face the intruder. "What are you doing here?"

"You know him?" Madison asked, lowering her gun.

"Don't put that down," Correll whimpered over her shoulder. She paid the coward no heed.

The ghost smiled and strode toward Wes, extending his hand as humans rippled away from him in fear. "My apologies. I did not mean to interrupt," he said as they clasped forearms.

"No, no!" said Wes with a genuine laugh. "Eh-lai! It's great to see you! I take it this means you received my message?"

"I did. Shall we speak in private?"

"Not so fast," Madison intervened. "Wes, you know how I feel about you bringing your contacts here. Keep your underhanded business in the Ghost Realm."

The stranger glanced at her sidelong, his eyes crinkling as if he was amused by her. "A contact? Is that all I am, Wes?"

"Of course not. Maddie," said Wes, facing the ghost hunter, "Ero is a close friend. I asked him to visit. I'm sorry; I guess I should have let you know he might come."

"You think? You're lucky I didn't shoot him where he stood."

Ero was grinning in a way that made her feel as though she were a child threatening him with a toy gun, and Wes's smirk had the air of a taunt, too. Neither was taking her seriously. *What the hell is this ghost's Divinity?*

Wes shrugged. "My bad. Honestly, I didn't think you'd come. Last I heard, you were still training in Nagem."

"On the contrary, I have been without a student for several years now. I found your letter intriguing. I am eager to meet the prospects."

Wes nodded. "Maddie, Ero is here to . . . uh . . . well, I'm hoping to help us reconnect with the twins. He's a teacher who instructs young Mind-Readers and Telepaths in controlling their Divinities, so I thought he might like to meet A1 and A2—if the Alpha ghosts are permitting. If they aren't . . . well, being a Telepath, he can be very persuasive. My hope is that Ero will be able to reestablish communication with them."

Ero advanced up the stairs and extended his hand. "You must be the infamous Madison Tarrow. A pleasure."

Mayor Correll shied away, but the ghost hunter seized his hand and shook, reluctantly holstering her weapon. She had a natural distaste for Wes's shady acquaintances, but Ero seemed polite enough. His readiness to shake her hand—which was a human, not a kálos gesture—impressed her. Still, he was a ghost, and ghosts were not to be trusted, especially one who was an associate of the werewolf. "A Telepath, huh? Okay, what am I thinking?"

Ero, perfectly at ease and quite merry despite the hostile reception, laughed at the challenge. "That you do not trust me. But then again, it does not take a Telepath to know that. It is written all over your face."

Madison scowled at him, though that didn't make his smile waver. "You want to teach the twins?" she asked, surprised and suspicious. As time had passed and there had been no sign of the boys, she had tried to find an Alpha ghost to inquire about the twins and request that they bring A1 and A2 to Doc for a checkup as originally instructed. But she had quickly discovered that the Alpha ghosts were harder to catch than minnows. By the time she glimpsed one, the fugitive's cloak was already vanishing around a corner. This was Wes's solution? Bring in a Telepath from the Ghost Realm to get close to them?

Ero shrugged. "We shall see. As I understand from Wes's letter, these potential new pupils have ten years, and I rarely take on a new student beyond seven years of age. Since they have missed the window of opportunity when their Divinities might have evolved, they are most certainly not Telepaths. I would like to meet them, though, to assess how well they can control their abilities. If they do not need my assistance, I have no reason to stay here."

"I didn't know mind-reading evolved into telepathy," said Madison.

"Telepathy is an advancement of mind-reading, but only a minuscule percentage of Mind-Readers ever evolve. I travel across Avilésor in search of children who need help learning to master such a strong Divinity."

"Hah, good luck getting near the twins," said Trey. "I don't think Wes told you what you were getting yourself into."

"I am well aware of the risks. Rumors about your fugitives have spread throughout Avilésor. I truly do apologize for interrupting your meeting, though. My intention was to speak with Wes afterward. Unfortunately, my curiosity got the better of me."

Madison asked, "How long have you been here?"

"Approximately ten passings," he said, his sapphire eyes flashing as he read Madison's mind.

"Ten minutes," Wes translated.

Madison felt her cheeks burn. *Ten minutes?* She must not have been paying much attention at all if a kálos had been standing right in front of her for so long not even trying to blend in. She glared at the Telepath, furious that he'd sensed her own self-criticism. "Would you like to speak to the Alpha ghosts now?" she asked.

"Right now? Well, yes, I would be grateful if you could put me in touch with them."

The crowd, realizing their mysterious mercenaries were about to be involved, stirred with excitement. Wes faced her and muttered, "How do you plan to do that?"

Madison ignored him and turned to the whiteboard that had been brought outside just in case the Alpha ghosts decided to initiate communication. "Let's see if this works again," she muttered, then raised her voice to call, "Hey! Are you listening? Did you know there's been a kálos here for ten whole minutes, and you haven't done a thing about it? I thought we had a deal! You're slacking, Jay!"

She held her breath, waiting . . .

Ero cocked his head in interest as the marker rose from the tray.

Our job is to protect humans from hostile ghosts, not peaceful ones.

Madison could feel herself blushing again. They knew Ero was here? Perhaps Agent Kovak was right . . . Maybe she *was* getting soft.

She jumped when Trey muttered, "Somebody's been studying."

"Huh?"

He nodded at the board. "Same handwriting, but now the spelling is correct."

Ero was also studying the board. "That is an interesting trick," he said, a sly smile denting his cheeks.

"Can you tell where they are?" Wes asked.

"That is what is so interesting. I am unable to hear their thoughts, which means they are not nearby. However . . . I may be able to . . ."

Ero trailed off, his eyes glowing bright, his face drawn in concentration. "Ah-ha," he murmured just as the cord from the microphone wrapped around his foot and hoisted him upside down. He dangled for a moment, comically shocked, his arms hanging limply toward the ground with his cloak. He chuckled.

Madison was aiming her ectogun, searching in vain for a target.

"Nothing to shoot," Ero said good-naturedly. "They are not here. Excuse me?" he called louder. "Would you please let me down?"

Ero continued to sway back and forth. Then, the cord went slack. He hit the ground with an "Oomph!" and rose to his feet again. Casually brushing himself off, he said, "Thank you. Now, unless I am mistaken, I believe that must have been the work of a Telekinetic, am I correct?"

Wes moaned and slapped his palm to his forehead. "Duh! I'm an idiot. That's how they make the marker move without actually being here. Back when we were in City Hall and the shield was up . . . that's how they did it, Maddie—"

"*Madison*," she corrected.

"—they weren't inside the shield at all!"

Ero's attention was on the board. He had his hand over his mouth, his index finger tapping his lips in thought. "Only one sentence, and I have already learned much about them."

Everyone's interest was directed to the printed words Ero seemed to find so informative. "Maybe you'd like to share, then," Madison suggested after a stiff pause.

"Certainly. They are resourceful. They have made contact without revealing their presence while staying outside your range as well as mine. They knew I was here. They have been watching me, and yet they did not confront me because I have not given them due cause. But this . . ." He tapped his finger against the word *ghosts*. "This is a human word for us. No one in Avilésor would use it to describe our race. I would guess your friends have been in captivity for some time if they are using your terms instead of ours."

He withdrew his hand as the marker moved across the board by its own accord.

What do you want?

Ero smiled graciously. "Perhaps we could speak in private."

No

The Telepath blinked in surprise. "You would rather speak here with such a large audience?"

Yes

Wes frowned. "Odd."

"Not particularly," Ero replied.

"No? They don't trust humans. Why would they want a public conversation?"

"I presume they trust me even less. This method of communication is safer for them because my telepathy is not a factor." Ero shrugged and asked, "Would you mind if I took more of your time?"

When the cowering mayor didn't make a peep, Madison took it upon herself to reply, "Not at all, Ero. I'm interested to see how this pans out."

Ero nodded. "Very well, then." He turned to face the whiteboard. "You will have to forgive me, but I must admit I do not know much about you. With whom am I speaking?"

All of us

"I see. I usually have the luxury of meeting potential students and their families in person."

No doubt it's easier to convince people to let you into their lives when you can control their minds.

"Well now, with all due respect, we do not know each other. It is hardly fair to make assumptions like that."

Telepath, Level 4. Middle-aged, probably about 300 years old, 5'9" 178 pounds. You walk a lot. Your boots are worn on the soles. Your heart rate is 57 beats per minute faster than normal. Your most recent meal was a snack of nuts. Before that, you ate salted pork with greens, and for breakfast you had toasted bread with jam and fruit. Your blood sugar is slightly elevated, and there's been an increase in cortisol since you passed through the Rip. Your eyes haven't completely adjusted to the sunlight, have they? Your pupils are con-stricted, and you blink three times as often as you should. You're a significant threat, but only if we enter your range. The easiest way to kill you

Not a single person dared to interrupt while the marker hovered. Rather pallid, Ero stared at it, waiting for the end of the sentence. A flash of silver—all he had time to do was flinch as something sharp and fast zipped by a hair's breadth from his neck. A disk ringed with wick-ed razor blades had embedded in the side of City Hall, still quivering from the impact.

a quick slice through the trachea.

The bulge in Ero's throat jumped. He couldn't react beyond gazing at the weapon that had just barely missed him.

"Damn," Trey whispered weakly.

"Ero," Wes croaked, "you don't have to do this."

The Telepath's voice was impressively strong when he replied, "Do not patronize me, Wes." He took a long breath and then lifted his chin. "The rumors do not do you justice. I am most certainly at your mercy right now."

The marker didn't move, but the silver disk dislodged itself. It orbited Ero twice before the curved blades disappeared inside the shell with a *chink* and the shining weapon rocketed off. Though visibly unnerved, Ero cleared his throat and said, "It is my understanding that you have two Mind-Readers in your group."

There was a pause while the eraser swept away every word except one:

Yes

"I see. And they have ten years, correct?"

A line was drawn under the word.

"Although you seem to know quite a bit about me, I would like the opportunity to introduce myself. My name is Ero, and I am a teacher. If you would allow it, I would like to meet the Mind-Readers."

No

"May I ask why?"

They don't need a teacher.

"I respect your opinion, but—"

The twins are not Telepaths. They don't need your teachings.

"Perhaps if I could meet them, I could judge for myself if—"

NO OUTSIDERS

Ero released his breath through his teeth, eyes dancing as he deliberated his next method of persuasion. "Tell me, when they call upon their Divinities, are they able to determine whose mind they hear, or do they read the minds of everyone within range because they have no control?"

When he received no answer, he nodded. "As I assumed, they have had no instruction. If their telepathic powers have not emerged by now, then I am certain they are, as you said, Mind-Readers, not Telepaths. But I can still teach them."

The marker continued to hover in place as the Alpha ghosts considered Ero's offer. The Telepath waited, then added, "For now, all I wish to do is meet them for a completely painless and noninvasive evaluation of their abilities."

We don't trust you.

"I understand. If it would make you more comfortable, perhaps we could talk inside City Hall. You can monitor the conversation from your current position without fear of me interfering with your thoughts and decisions."

They know information you have no right knowing.

"I will hear only what they consciously think during our conversation. You have my word that I will not dive any deeper into their minds than the surface. After we are done, you may take—I apologize, but may I ask their names? I do not feel comfortable referring to them as 'the twins' all the time."

"They don't have names," Madison answered before the marker could write a response. "The Agents called them A1 and A2."

Ero shook his head. "Surely you do not call them that, do you?"

Finn and Reese

Madison mouthed the names in bewilderment. Why had the boys insisted their names were A1 and A2 when Doc had asked them?

"Good names," Ero acknowledged. "Did you name them?"

A second line was drawn under:

Yes

"I see. As I was saying, once our meeting is finished, I will report my analysis to you, and we can determine how best to proceed. Are you satisfied with that proposal?"

If you harm them, we will kill you where you stand.

Ero raised his eyebrows in amusement. "I guarantee their safety. As I said, I am a teacher; I care for the well-being of my students."

They aren't your students yet.

There was another pause before the marker added beneath that sentence:

We agree to meet you in City Hall.

Ero hesitated. "I understand your desire to be present. However, when first meeting students, I prefer to speak with them alone. It is best for me to evaluate their abilities if I have their full attention and they are not distracted by the thoughts of an observer."

The marker lingered in hesitation.

Alone?

"Yes," said the Telepath with abundant patience. The marker spun slowly in the air as one might twirl a pencil when contemplating. The eraser swept the board clean before the marker printed:

You haven't lied. That's the only reason we're agreeing to this meeting. If you touch Finn or Reese, you will die. If you infiltrate their minds, you die. If you harm them in any way, you die. The second they tense up or act scared, you're done. It's in your best interest to make sure they stay calm and comfortable . . . without telepathic interference. We'll know if you're manipulating them.

Ero nodded. "I understand and accept all of your conditions."

Sudden movement in Madison's peripheral made her head turn. "Do you?" challenged a male's voice. Her hand landed on the ectogun holstered at her hip, but by the time she'd turned enough for a full view of the intruder, he was gone. His appearance had been so quick she'd barely glimpsed the afterimage of a cloaked figure standing a few feet away from Ero, there and gone in a second. *Damn, he's fast!* Her heart was flying. She hadn't even had a chance to draw her weapon. If his intention had been to strike her down . . . she would have been completely defenseless. She'd never felt so unprepared before.

People in the crowd were whispering in awe and fear. Although Ero hadn't turned his head, his eyes had shifted to stare at where the Alpha ghost had briefly appeared. He remained composed but solemn. "I do," he answered. "And I am fully aware of the consequences for violating any of your conditions."

Finn and Reese are waiting for you inside.

Ero forced an uneasy smile. "Thank you," he said, turning on his heel.

"Hold on! I'm coming with you," called Doc, detaching from the crowd and trotting up the marble steps. Ero held out his arm to stop her.

"I am afraid I cannot allow that. Not only did I give my word that I would come alone, but your presence would also interfere with my diagnosis."

"But I need to see my patients. I have my own diagnosis to make." She pushed past him and marched toward the doors.

Ero remained where he was, watching. He heaved a sigh but made no move to stop her. To everyone's surprise, the doctor halted of her own accord.

Ero strolled past her, his blue eyes glowing bright. Her vacant eyes were also glowing blue. The Telepath paused to glance at the woman seemingly frozen in time. "I apologize, but this is a delicate matter."

Doc took two steps back and stood obediently in place.

Madison drew an ectogun and took aim at Ero's back, her finger curled over the trigger. "You're controlling her mind," she accused.

"Yes," Ero said, turning his head to glance over his shoulder. His sapphire irises flared again, and Madison's anger cooled instantly. Her thoughts slowed to a crawl. "Put the gun away," he ordered gently, his voice echoing as if from the far end of a long tunnel. "There is no need for violence. I came here with peaceful intentions."

In a daze, Madison holstered her weapon.

"Thank you," Ero murmured. He opened the door to City Hall and stepped inside, then closed the door behind him.

Madison blinked, completely befuddled. "What just happened?" She stared at Doc, who looked equally confused.

Wes chuckled. "You picked a fight you couldn't win."

Madison ground her teeth. "Ero turned us into human puppets."

She drew her ectogun again and marched for the doors, but Wes intercepted her. He seized the wrist of the hand that held the gun and begged, "Don't. Ero isn't an enemy; I promise. Please, Maddie, he may be our only chance to make contact with the twins again."

"I've got half a mind to shoot *you* for bringing him here," Madison snapped, jerking her hand away. "We have enough ghost problems without you inviting more to Phantom Heights."

"Trust me. Ero is a good man. His entire life has been spent mentoring children who need his help."

"Then why on earth would he befriend the likes of *you*?"

Wes let out a halfhearted chuckle. "You know, I'm still trying to figure that out myself, actually."

Madison shook her head, glaring at the doors, but she shoved the weapon back into her holster. "Fine."

— Chapter Twelve —

Diagnosis

Ero was right—we were high above town square, too far for him to telepathically locate us without intense concentration and a great expenditure of power, too far downwind for Wes's sharp nose if he changed into his wolf form, too far for Madison or her apprentice to get a clear shot with their guns.

We were on a rooftop high above the proceedings. Jay paced along the edge, constantly shooting anxious looks at City Hall and the crowd of humans below us. My gaze followed his hypnotic path. "I didn't think it would take this long," I said.

"Ero seems interested in 'em," Axel replied with a careless shrug. "I don't know why. Bot ain't even answering his questions."

Ero was powerful; Axel could sense it, and Ero had demonstrated it himself with the stunt he'd pulled on Madison and the doctor. If we ventured too close to him, the Telepath could eclipse us, or alter our memories, or who knew what else. We'd have no way of differentiating reality from whatever Ero wanted us to believe. While I hated leaving Finn and Reese alone with him, at least from this distance, Axel could monitor them without Ero's telepathy playing tricks. Madison and the doctor had both exhibited physical reactions when he took control. Axel was confident he would know immediately if Ero tried to invade the twins' minds.

Jay continued, "Right, but this is part of Wes's scheme, and Ero's an Outsider. Plus he has a dangerous Divinity."

"Everything he promised was the truth," Axel said, dangling his feet over the edge. I'd been keeping a good distance from the verge of the roof, and seeing Axel halfway over it dropped an extra pit of worry into my stomach, but he was perfectly at ease. "I don't like him either, but he didn't lie to us."

Ash met my gaze and shook her head, troubled. "I'm not sure about this," she said. "What if Azar sent Ero? How do we know Ero isn't digging around in their minds and gathering information?"

I shared her concern, but Axel didn't seem worried. "Finn and Reese aren't stressed," he replied casually. "I mean, they're nervous, sure, but they're calmer now than when Jay left them. Heart rates are normal, breathing's normal—everything's normal. And I don't care how powerful Ero thinks he is; if he so much as twitches a finger to hurt them, I'd hit him so hard and fast he wouldn't even know I was coming until it was too late."

The black-and-white kitten leapt into Jay's arms and began purring as he absently stroked her back. "What have they been talking about then?" he asked.

"Nothing special. Ero hasn't said a single word about their Divinities. He's talking about Outside, how blue the sky is . . . pointless crap." Axel paused, tilting his head. "But Bot's dozing off."

"This is too much stress for them. I knew it would be."

Axel cocked his head the other way. "Ero's getting up."

Jay stopped his restless pacing, and Kit jumped onto the rooftop again. He vanished. Kit rubbed her head against my leg and started winding her small, furry body between my feet.

Jay reappeared with an exhausted twin clutching each arm. They blinked wearily at us in the sunlight, tired but unharmed. "You're okay?" Jay asked. Finn yawned while Reese nodded. "Sit down and rest. You can go to sleep if you want." Jay turned to Axel. "What's happening down there?"

Axel narrowed his eyes, his attention on the minuscule people down below.

* * *

Correll had been fumbling through the rest of his speech even though nobody was paying any attention to him as he stumbled over empty words while blotting his large, shiny forehead with a handkerchief. The moment the cloaked Telepath stepped out of City Hall, Madison interrupted, "Ero! What happened?"

The town collectively seemed to hold its breath, eager to hear the Telepath's diagnosis. Doc stepped forward. "First, how did they seem? Coherent? Any sign of injuries? Symptoms of illness?"

Ero seemed to be lost in his thoughts. He was walking slowly away from the doors, scratching notes into a small, leather-bound journal. He glanced at Doc for a brief moment, then continued writing as he said, "A bit flushed. No visible injuries that I could see. Exhausted. I would have loved to chat some more, but unfortunately, they were starting to fall asleep." He closed the notebook and smiled. "Fascinating kids. Absolutely fascinating."

"*Really*?" Wes said dubiously.

"They actually talked to you?" Madison asked, unscrewing the lid of her water bottle.

"No, not aloud. But since I could read their minds, speaking aloud is rather irrelevant."

"But they aren't mute? They *can* talk?" Madison inquired just before she lifted the bottle to her lips and took a drink.

"Oh yes, absolutely . . . in eighteen different languages." Madison gasped and choked, spraying water as she doubled over, coughing.

"Really," Wes said again, this time in appreciation.

Ero chuckled. "They are exceptionally bright. When I asked why they refused to speak, their answer was because ghosts should be seen, not heard." He fixed the ghost hunter with a stern look of silent blame.

"But they didn't seem that intelligent when they were with us," Madison sputtered. She wiped the back of her sleeve across her mouth.

"Finn and Reese woke up in an unfamiliar place, surrounded by hundreds of strangers. They did not understand what was wrong with their bodies or where the rest of their lab-family was. That, and they have had no instruction with their powers, so whenever they activated their Divinities, they were listening to every single thought of every single person. Can you imagine all that chatter? It must have been a disorienting and frightening experience for untrained Mind-Readers who, until that point, had never been in the presence of more than a handful of people at a time."

Madison argued, "But we asked their names. They insisted their names were A1 and A2."

Pity briefly contorted the Telepath's face. "The others in Project Alpha are the only ones who have ever addressed them as Finn and Reese. You are human, so when you requested their names, they responded with the names humans have always called them by."

"What about their powers?" Wes asked.

"Ah, yes, their powers. Most interesting," Ero murmured, his eyes glazing as he drifted into his thoughts again.

The Alpha ghosts rejoined the conversation when the marker cap tapped on the board to draw everyone's attention, and then the marker scrawled:

Wat dus that meen?

Madison stared at the words. Why were they spelled wrong now?

Ero rubbed his beard. "I am not entirely sure. I have never encountered anything like it before."

Wes scowled at the vague answer. "You've taught every Telepath and almost every Mind-Reader in Avilésor. What do you mean you've 'never encountered anything like it before'?"

"Well . . . yes, but none of my other pupils were raised under the conditions Finn and Reese were. I believe they are, in fact, Telepaths, but . . . something seems to have gone wrong."

Rong?

Ero nodded slowly and flipped through his notes, buying time to put words to his thoughts. "If a child's mind-reading Divinity is going to advance into true telepathy, those specialized abilities typically manifest between the ages of four and seven as their comprehension skills develop. But the twins were raised in an environment where they were continually punished for any minor mistake. This is nothing more than a working theory, but I believe as their telepathic powers began to expand, they suppressed them for fear of being punished. Rather than allow their Divinities to take them into the minds of the humans they served, Finn and Reese focused all their power on each other, and as a consequence, their telepathic powers sort of . . . backfired."

"What do you mean *backfired*?" said Wes. "That doesn't make any sense. They're either Telepaths or they aren't."

"Correct, that is how it should be. But as we were communicating, I noticed that Finn and Reese actually 'talk' to each other, so to speak, through a mental connection that flows in both directions. At first, I assumed that was because they are twins and they share Divinities, but *sending* thoughts is a telepathic trait. It appears that their telepathic powers partially developed, in a sense—I am not quite sure how to describe this—linking them. Finn and Reese literally share minds."

"Share . . . minds," Madison repeated, frowning. "Is that possible?"

"Well, no. Perhaps I explained that incorrectly. What I mean is . . ." Ero seized the levitating marker and drew two circles on the whiteboard. "Say these represent their minds."

He drew a line connecting the circles to each other. "Their Divinities tethered their minds, so let us say one learns a new language. The other twin can actually tap into his brother's memory through this connection as if it were his own memory. Now, twin brothers or not, their condition should not have happened naturally. To put it simply, Finn and Reese started their lives as individuals and now are essentially two halves of one consciousness sharing thoughts and memories. It is intriguing."

He uncurled his fingers to let the marker rise again. Next to the Telepath's drawing, the floating marker wrote:

Can it be undun?

"I do not believe so," Ero answered. "What absolutely amazes me is that Finn and Reese seem to have a nearly infinite amount of memory. The brain really is a remarkable thing. Look at what *one* is capable of processing and remembering. Theoretically, the twins' capacity has been doubled."

So thay ar or ar not Telepaths?

"I wish I could provide a more satisfying answer. I believe the connection occurred around the age of five when their Divinities began maturing. If I am correct in my estimation, the twins have essentially had their telepathic powers for five years, although they have been primarily dormant. I fear that despite the state of semi-dormancy, their Divinities still continued to grow, and it is only a matter of time before they manifest. When that happens, the twins will likely experience the full-fledged telepathic powers that have been building for all those years."

Wen?

"Impossible to say, unfortunately. Extreme emotions or stress could potentially trigger them. I am astonished that the shock of coming Outside for the first time did not initiate their powers. The real problem is that as their minds are linked, I am afraid their Divinities may be as well. That will make it all the more difficult for them to control their abilities when and if they manifest."

How powerful wil thay be?

"For their age group, they will be unparalleled. Not to boast, but I am presently the most powerful Telepath in Avilésor. As adults, their powers will likely exceed mine. But I can still help them." He turned to glance at the werewolf standing nearby. A slow smile spread across the Telepath's face. "Wes, my friend, you may very well have stumbled across two potential Level 5's. I have never had the pleasure of teaching one. I myself am only Level 4."

Wes's eyes widened. "Level 5?" he repeated. "No, Ero, they're only Level 2."

"Right now, yes, you are correct. But if their Divinities grow the way I predict . . ." Ero trailed off in thought.

Wat do we need to do?

Ero gazed down at his closed notebook. "They need proper training. Of that, there is no doubt. If I can work with them now while their powers are still dormant, hopefully the damage that will inevitably occur when their Divinities fully awaken will be minimized. Of course, you are their guardians, so the decision is completely up to you. Will you allow me to take them on as my students?"

"Hell no," said Axel.

My gaze traveled from him to Jay, whose brows were furrowed in deep deliberation. "Not so hasty," he murmured.

"We can't let an Outsider in," Axel insisted. "Especially not someone so dangerous."

"You told me Ero never lied about his intentions. Finn and Reese need a teacher before their powers grow out of control."

"*If* they grow out of control," Axel snapped.

Jay rubbed the back of his neck. He looked down at the boys snoring at his feet. "I'm worried about them."

"That's bullshit—"

"Axel."

"—you weren't worried about them until Ero started putting ideas in your head. They're fine. Look at them; there's nothing wrong with them."

Jay remained silent. I shot a look at Ash, who shrugged at me, and then I glanced over at RC, but my lab-brother's attention was still down below on the marker hovering in the air, his lips pressed tight in extra concentration since Finn and Reese weren't spelling the words out for him. Ash pointed out, "Ero could be an ally."

Axel folded his arms and grumbled, "We don't need an ally. We're doing just fine on our own. What happened to 'no Outsiders'?"

Jay said, "Let's give him a chance." Axel opened his mouth, but before he could argue, Jay added, "But we aren't going to take our eyes off him for even a second."

I studied the sleeping twins. *Two halves of one whole*, Ero had said. Maybe Axel wasn't so far off when he nicknamed them Bot. Finn and Reese had always had identical personalities since the day I met them. Without Finn's hat, I couldn't even tell the two apart unless I checked their Marks.

So . . . their minds were telepathically linked. I knew something was odd about them, but I never would have guessed that anomaly. They must have been so frightened. Five years old—were they in Alpha yet, I wondered?—locked in cages. I could only imagine the moment of panic when their newborn telepathic powers started to expand and they accidentally slipped into *Their* dark minds, so they directed the power at each other instead. And now . . .

I watched them for a few more seconds before shifting my gaze to follow Axel's. I squinted down at the Telepath far below. Vivian had been the first Outsider we'd had prolonged contact with. But Ero . . . I didn't like the thought of letting him into the fold. It wasn't him, per se, so much as I cringed at the idea of any Outsider getting too close— close enough to hurt us. And this particular Outsider had a Divinity that could destroy us without any forewarning or opportunity to defend our- selves.

I knew how to fight a physical battle, but one in my mind against an unbeatable opponent? That, I'd have no way to prepare for. I'd have to trust Jay's judgment.

I crouched at the edge of the rooftop. *All right, Ero. You've got one chance. Let's see what you do with it.*

***

Madison held her breath in wait as Kovak's fugitives deliberated. If they agreed, Wes's friend would have direct access to the Alpha ghosts. Even better, he was a Telepath, so he could compile information from their minds—powers, vulnerabilities . . . the possibilities were endless. Ammunition for her to take them down when this shaky deal collapsed.

The edge of a cloak brushed her shoulder, and a voice whispered in her ear, "I will not spy on them for you. I am a teacher, Madison, and I refuse to betray the trust of my students."

She clenched her fists, angry that the Telepath had read her mind like a diary. "There are five others besides your possible students," she hissed back, but Ero shook his head.

"If you want information about them, you will have to obtain it from another source."

He pulled away as the marker wrote:

How offen will thes lesons hapin?

"I would prefer to have them daily."

We can not pay you mony.

"I ask for shelter and a minimum of two meals a day, a fee Wes has graciously absorbed. However, I do require some form of sacrifice from the family of my students. Those who can afford to pay me a monetary fee do so. Those who cannot find an alternative payment. I am open to trades and will accept anything of value that you have to give."

We'll moniter the ferst lesson and then decide if you can trane Finn and Reese

Ero nodded. "That is a fair answer. When and where shall the first meeting be?"

He waited patiently, staring at the board, but the marker continued to hover. After a few minutes, people began to stir impatiently.

"Hello?" Ero called.

We wil find you wen its time

The marker clattered into the tray. Ero was silent, his posture straight and his cloak fluttering in the gentle breeze. Madison watched him, aware of just how out of place he looked. He turned away, his hands clasped around the notebook behind his back. "I do apologize for interrupting your meeting. I shall leave you to continue now."

"Ero," Madison called. He paused. "We've had a lot of problems with kálos in Phantom Heights. Tread lightly; you don't want to cross me."

The Telepath smiled, amused by her threat. "I would not dream of it. But I will keep your warning in mind," he said, striding down the steps. The crowd parted to let him pass.

Madison folded her arms. As soon as Ero was out of earshot, Wes chuckled. "Maddie, you don't stand a chance against a Telepath. Not that Ero will cause any problems, mind you, but he already proved that you aren't a threat to him."

The thought of a ghost with that much power roaming Phantom Heights left her unnerved, but if Ero turned out to be a problem, dealing with him would be the Alpha ghosts' responsibility.

Unless he turns them against me.

Madison sighed and faced the crowd. Councilwoman Jennings, visibly livid at the way Madison had handled the situation, had her locked in a deadly stare, and yet, the only thoughts reeling through Madison's mind were of the two kids she'd helped nurse back to health from the verge of death. According to Ero, they were intelligent beyond belief, destined to grow into two of the most powerful kálos in history. Yet they'd seemed so hollow and innocent. Had Kovak realized what an asset he'd had at his disposal?

An apparition in the back of her memory dredged Agent Kovak's voice from his last visit: *"I've become very attached to those kids, Maddie. I'd do just about anything to get A1 and A2 back. Even if it costs me all the other Alpha ghosts, I want those two."*

A deep chill in her bones made her shiver. He knew, all right. He may not be aware they were actually Telepaths, but he most certainly knew they were special. His mysterious visit was starting to make a little more sense.

Madison rubbed the goose bumps on her arms and looked away from Holly's death glare. What exactly had Phantom Heights gotten itself into by sealing the deal with Kovak's fugitives?

— Chapter Thirteen —

Payment

The next afternoon, I was standing in a secluded area of the park.

The sunlit lake hidden behind a thicket of shrubs cast an occasional sparkle through the leaves. A light breeze tickled my skin and stirred my cloak, bringing flickering memories of summer vacations and picnics, gone as soon as they came.

Finn and Reese sat cross-legged in the dappled shade. "Nervous?" I asked. They hesitated, then nodded. "You'll be fine. Jay, Axel, and I will be here the whole time. RC is close, too."

Reese anxiously plucked blades of grass while his twin turned a stone over in his hand. "We're defective," said Finn.

Axel, who was pacing nearby, said gruffly, "You'll be fine, Bot. All Telepaths need training."

The twins were silent, but I could tell by the faint furrows in their brows that they were dissatisfied with his answer. I soothed, "You're not defective. You're just different, that's all." At their insistent downtrodden expressions, I cast a glance over my shoulder. "Look at Ax and me. We're different. That doesn't mean anything's wrong with us."

All I earned for my efforts were blank stares from Finn and Reese and a withering look from Axel. "We're unique," I finished.

Axel stopped pacing to roll his eyes and snort. "Oh yeah, we're unique. We're so goddamn *unique* that only this band of outcasts nobody wants will take us. Welcome to the freak club."

"Axel!"

Reese twisted his fingers through his hair as if the end of the world were upon us. "If *They* find out . . ." he whispered. Finn turned a shade paler.

"The hell are you talking about?" Axel demanded.

"*They*'ll test on us again."

"*They*'ll know. *They* always know."

Finn gasped. "What if *They* send us to the Arena?"

"Hey," I interceded. Two pairs of frightened blue eyes found me. "Relax, okay? *They*'ll never know."

In eerie unison, they whispered, "*They*'ll find us . . ."

Over my shoulder, Axel muttered, "Oh, nice job, you got them all worked up."

I bit back a colorful retort Jay would have scolded me for. Instead of taking the bait, I said, "Question. Are you positive Ero wasn't making all that up? I mean, if he is an enemy, this could all be a ruse."

"He didn't lie."

"But maybe—"

"What part of 'he didn't lie' aren't you getting?" Axel snapped. "Unless you're saying I screwed up?"

"Don't twist my words. I just want to be sure, that's all."

Axel bristled, ready for a fight. Instead, he froze. "They're coming."

I let the argument go and promised, "It'll be all right," as I seized the lowest branch above Reese, ignoring Axel's farewell gesture of a middle finger. I vaulted up, climbing higher and higher. Far above the ground, I crouched down to wait and survey the twins sitting below me. Axel still paced with restlessness. He didn't even bother to pull the hood down over his eyes; no use trying to hide his identity from a Telepath.

I leveled my head and scanned the trees across the clearing. Somewhere beyond my sight, RC was well concealed, no doubt with a silver disk in his hand at the ready. I should be high enough to be out of Ero's range, but if I wasn't, RC definitely was. Jay and Axel were the primary defense, I was the secondary, and RC was our final line. Ash, in my opinion, would have been a better candidate to take my place considering the importance of keeping my identity hidden, but with her power partially neutralized, her fighting style required close-combat conditions—not ideal for fighting a Telepath. Distance was better so Ero would have to focus harder to extend his power, giving us a better chance of escape or resistance.

I drew in a shaky breath. Telepathy wasn't a power I was overly familiar with, nor was it one I was keen on facing. Ero's abilities terrified me. My own physical powers would be useless if he already had his hooks in my mind. In a single second, he could wipe my mind clean, or replace my life with false memories, or eclipse me without even touching me, just like he'd done with Madison and the doctor.

Breathe. Relax. Chances are he won't even know I'm here. I'm just an observer.

I watched Axel pace down below. Jay's strategy was risky. Axel was our best distance observer, able to see and hear all the way across town. He could sense if we were being manipulated by telepathy. But Ero had already demonstrated a taste of his great power at City Hall, and Jay wanted to show off our own trump card as a warning not to trifle with us. Axel was more than twice as powerful as Ero.

The problem was, if Ero revealed himself as an enemy and telepathically eclipsed Axel, it would be game over. Our own lab-brother would hunt us down in a matter of seconds. Despite Axel's confidence that he was strong enough to resist Ero, I wasn't convinced.

Movement on the ground caught my eye, and yet, my body didn't shiver. Jay and Ero had appeared from thin air, but they were out of my sensing range, and I theirs. Ero swayed as if drunk. He leaned against the trunk of the very tree I was perched in. Faintly, his voice carried up to me: "I have never Blinked before. A little warning would have been appreciated."

Jay muttered a brief apology. Axel halted and stood still and stiff, eyeing the Telepath with contempt radiating from his body so strongly I could feel it way up here. Ero found the twins sitting in the grass and greeted, "Hello again, Finn, Reese," making a point to address them individually. "Wonderful to see you again." They gazed up at their new teacher, but they didn't speak a word in return. I was saddened by the immediate difference in their personalities. The moment Ero had arrived, they'd transformed into shadows of my lab-brothers. I knew I wouldn't hear their voices again until he was gone.

The Telepath turned back to Jay and Axel. "And it is an honor to meet you," he said, extending his hand. "Finn and Reese certainly hold you high in their respects." Jay hesitantly reached out to shake his hand, a human custom we'd witnessed countless times, but Ero seized Jay's forearm instead of his hand. Jay froze, surprised, and Ero studied him with equal surprise before releasing him. "You obey a human custom," he noted.

Jay retracted his arm. "I, uh, I didn't know," he mumbled, cradling his hand to his chest.

Ero nodded slowly. "You have not been to Avilésor in quite a while, have you?" The Telepath sized up our leader, then turned to the red-eyed teen brooding at Jay's side.

My stomach clenched. I couldn't analyze Ero's reaction from way up here, but he didn't give Axel the wide berth most people subconsciously did. In fact, he almost seemed relaxed. "And you must be Axel. How interesting. I had heard the formidable A6 was a beast, yet your thoughts are quite clear."

"My name's *not* A6, asshole."

Jay bowed his head, likely accompanied by a sigh, but Ero held up his hands. "My sincerest apologies. I will not make the mistake of calling you that again." He offered his hand, but Axel just glared at it.

Ero's hand fell to his side. "Impossible. You . . . are a nydæa."

Axel must have been wondering if Ero knew, and his worries betrayed him. He clenched his hands into fists at his sides. "I'm a kálos."

Ero observed my lab-brother's defensive reaction and inclined his head. "I see."

"I don't like you."

"Perhaps I can change your opinion."

"I doubt it."

Ero hadn't even glanced up at me. My sigh of relief was cut short when Ero called, "Are you going to come down so we may be properly introduced, Cato?"

My fingers tightened around the branch. Ero still hadn't looked up. If he hadn't called me by name, I wouldn't have been sure he was talking to me. I hesitated, but then decided that staying in my perch was pointless since my location had been revealed.

I swung down and alighted from branch to branch until I dropped to the grass and straightened. Only then did Ero turn to me. He extended his hand. "So, the Demikan. A pleasure. I must confess, there was a time when I did not believe you existed."

There had been multiple instances when I knew a ghost word I was unable to translate to human terminology and vice-versa. *Demikan* was not one I'd ever stumbled across, and I wasn't sure if I should be honored or insulted that Ero had addressed me as such. I gawked at him before I had the sense to ask, "What did you call me?"

"The Demikan," he repeated, visibly surprised by my confusion. "Demi—half—kálos and human."

Is that what ghosts call me? The title lit a thrilling flutter in my chest. I'd never known what I was. Not human, not ghost. Something in between. Mutt, half-breed, those terms were accurate but demeaning. *Demikan* . . . I was the Demikan. There was a name for me, even if I'd always be alone in the category.

Reality punctured my selfish elation. I scowled at Ero, frustrated that he not only caught me, but also identified me. "This stays between us."

He nonchalantly let his arm fall. "I beg your pardon?"

Jay warned, "If you want to train the twins, you'll keep Cato's name and Axel's number a secret."

Although he was visibly puzzled by Jay's adamancy, Ero inclined his head. He skimmed his perceptive gaze over the three of us, analyzing our motley group. Jay and I had our masks and hoods covering our heads as usual, but I still felt completely exposed. Ero could see who we really were. "I have heard a great many rumors about you, and to be honest, you are not at all what I was expecting. All of you seem to be very young."

Jay's voice was hard: "Your students are Finn and Reese. They're the only ones you need to be concerned with."

"And if you hurt them or any of our family, I'll kill you," Axel added.

Ero cocked his head at Axel, and to my surprise, he smiled. "A bold threat," he acknowledged. "Very convincing. But the truth is, your greatest fear is that someday you *will* kill someone."

Axel took a startled step back as if Ero had just slapped him across the face. The Telepath noticed our silent alarm and hastened to add, "Please, let me be clear. My intent is to teach Finn and Reese to master their Divinities. What they do with those powers once I have taught them all that I can is up to them. Your support is necessary for me to be successful, so I hope to establish a trusting relationship with all of you. Do you have any questions for me?"

I said, "I thought Wes was your friend."

It wasn't a question, but Ero answered, "He is. But my purpose is to teach, and Wes will not interfere with that. He will complain profusely, I am certain, but I give you my word."

"How long do you think it'll take to train them?" Jay asked, looking down at Finn and Reese. The twins gazed back at him for a moment before staring up at their new teacher.

Ero regarded them thoughtfully. "I honestly cannot answer that. Every student learns at a different pace. Some can be taught in a few months. Others need a few years. As I said, I have never encountered anyone like Finn and Reese. In their case, it is impossible to predict exactly when or if their telepathic powers will manifest. It could be any day, or it could be a few years from now, or it could never happen. I have no definite answer. Please be patient and give me some time with them. I may be able to provide you with a better answer once I understand more about their Divinities."

The twins exchanged looks of barely contained horror. Ero watched them, intrigued. "Absolutely fascinating," he murmured. He raised an eyebrow as he listened to their silent conversation. "I can assure you that coming into your telepathic powers will not hurt at all. It will be a confusing time, and you will certainly be frustrated, but you do not have to handle it alone. With the right instruction, you have absolutely nothing to fear. I am here to help you."

They didn't look particularly reassured. "What's the first step?" Jay asked.

"We get to know each other," Ero replied. "I will observe them, talk to them, learn how their minds and their powers currently work, and then we will start some simple exercises to help them master mind-reading. For now, my focus is on developing the powers they have rather than the powers that have yet to awaken. But first, what do you have to offer as payment?"

Jay met Ero's expectant gaze. We had nothing to our names—no money, no possessions. We'd thought long and hard last night about what to give Ero. Jay nodded at Finn, who stood and solemnly extended his fist. The Telepath held out his hand.

Finn gingerly placed a smooth, round stone on Ero's palm.

Ero studied it. We all held our breath, waiting. That stone had come a long way. It had been plucked from a creek in the woods, and Finn had asked me if it was alive. It had been an alien artifact then, a mystifying new discovery before he started to understand this Outside world, and he'd held onto it all this time as a reminder of the wonder and mystery of that very first day of freedom.

The Telepath stroked it with his thumb. "I asked you to give me something valuable." He curled his fingers over it, and I was certain he was going to throw it into the trees. "Too often is sentimental value underestimated." To our surprise and relief, he pocketed the creek stone. "I accept your payment. Now, you are more than welcome to stay, as I know you do not trust me alone with your brothers, but I will ask that you remain quiet and give us a little space so we may concentrate."

Jay and I exchanged glances, and we wordlessly strode to the other side of the small clearing and seated ourselves in the grass. Axel glared at Ero for another moment to accentuate his earlier threat before he reluctantly joined us and stood as still as a statue with his arms folded across his chest, glaring at the three beneath the tree. Ero pulled out a small leather notebook and pen, and he spoke to Finn and Reese in a hushed voice. Although they never answered, Ero sometimes smiled or nodded as he jotted notes.

I muttered, "I'd hoped that since Ero isn't human, they'd be willing to talk to him, but apparently not."

"They'll come around," said Axel. "Look at how tense they are. When they relax around him, I'm sure they'll start talking."

"So, what do you think so far, Jay? Did we make a good choice?"

"Too soon to tell. I'm worried that Ero knows about you."

My gaze was drawn to Jay's chest where the silver whistle should have been hanging. Without it, he seemed incomplete. Wherever RC was, it was around his neck, just in case Ero eclipsed Axel. I muttered, "At least he doesn't know about RC."

"Oh, he knows," Axel said.

"He didn't say anything," I said in surprise.

"He can't sense RC, but he can hear our thoughts. He knows RC is watching from somewhere safe. He just doesn't know where."

Jay heaved a sigh and muttered, "Well, at least one of our defenses worked." He shot me a glare from the corner of his gleaming silver eye, as if it were my fault Ero had found me in the canopy.

"Shh," Axel hissed loudly. Ero, Finn, Reese, Jay, and I stared at him. He lowered his voice and said, "Humans are coming."

No one moved, each of us straining to listen. Not until several minutes after his announcement did I hear the faint footsteps on a nearby path and low voices as a couple strolled through the park. We were hidden from view in the thicket, and they passed by without even realizing we were there. Once they were gone, Ero heaved a sigh of disapproval and closed his notebook. "Interrupting our lesson every time someone passes does not create a conducive learning environment. Why not have the lessons in the privacy of your home?"

"Because we aren't stupid," Jay snapped. "We aren't going to show you where we live."

Ero looked rather amused by that statement. "I do not underestimate your intelligence, Jay. Why do you feel so threatened by me? I am here to help you."

"We'll see about that."

"If you do not trust me, so be it. Where would you be most comfortable meeting?"

Jay hesitated, considering. "We'll find new places for you to have your lessons, and then I'll come to retrieve you, just like before."

"That seems like a major inconvenience on your part."

"That's the way it's going to be."

Ero glanced at the twins, noticed they were already rubbing their eyes with fatigue, and pocketed his notebook as he rose. "My students are tired, so we will continue this whenever you are ready. I assume you will call on me when Finn and Reese are more attentive and you have found a new place?"

"Yes," said Jay.

Ero made a point to engage eye contact with the leader. "I have no problem allowing you to Blink me, Jay, but there is no need to sneak up from behind and grab me unawares. Next time, please approach me, and I will come willingly."

Jay broke his gaze, embarrassed. "Sure."

Ero's attention fell onto his students again. "Although our lesson was brief, I have enjoyed spending time with you. Until our next meeting." He turned away, but over his shoulder, he acknowledged, "Jay. Axel." In a secretive tone, he added, ". . . Cato." And with that, he strode down the path, leaving us alone beneath the tree.

None of us said a word until we were sure the Telepath was out of hearing range.

Axel scoffed. "*Lesson*. Like he actually taught them something."

"So," I said. Finn and Reese turned to me. "What do you think of Ero?" They pondered the question longer than I'd expected, prompting me to add, "Don't you like him?"

Finn mumbled, "He's nice."

"Patient," Reese added.

"A good teacher."

"But we can't hear his thoughts."

"His mind is shielded."

"We don't know what he wants."

Their fragmented speech was a sure sign they were exhausted. They still hadn't returned to full strength after their near-death experience, and I was beginning to wonder if they ever would.

Jay and I each scooped a twin into our arms. I was holding Reese, who closed his eyes, exhaled, and snuggled into a comfortable position against my chest. Jay told Finn, "Maybe it's good that you can't hear what Ero wants from you. It's time you started doing what *you* want, not what everybody else wants. So, do you want to see Ero again and let him teach you?"

Too tired to answer aloud, Finn and Reese nodded. Jay glanced at me and said, "That's good enough for me."

Axel shook his head. "Well, I don't like him. You do realize that Ero could literally turn us into mindless zombie puppets and make us do whatever he wants?"

I countered, "But if what he said about Finn and Reese is true, they could do the same to us when their telepathic powers mature."

"*If* they mature."

The twins were already snoring softly. Jay gazed down at Finn, considering both arguments. Quietly so as not to wake the boys, he murmured, "I'm reluctant to let an Outsider in, but . . . he seems genuinely interested in helping them. Yes, he could potentially harm us all, but just because he has the power to do so doesn't mean he will. You should be able to relate to that, Axel."

The half-breed stiffened, his lips curling back over his short, deceivingly harmless-looking fangs as if he were about to snarl, but instead, he turned away, scowling resentfully. "I ain't letting Ero out of my sight."

"Good," Jay replied.

I shifted Reese in my arms until he was nestled in one and I was able to set my other hand on Jay's shoulder. The world rushed in, and the sunlit park was replaced with the dark walls of Home.

Wes opened the door and stepped aside so Ero could enter. "You are certain this is no trouble?" the Telepath inquired, trailing his hand down the carved bedpost.

"Not at all," Wes assured. Ero wandered to the window to admire the gorgeous vista of Alvarez Park across the lawn. "I'd be insulted if you stayed anywhere else while you're in Phantom Heights. Welcome to Saros Manor. Just, uh, stay on the ground floor. The upper levels are mostly used for storage."

"I appreciate the hospitality. This is a beautiful home."

Wes leaned against the doorframe and ran a critical eye over the guest bedroom. It was smaller than his master suite, although not by much, and the southwest view toward the woods of the park was certainly enviable. He had no doubt that Ero would enjoy the pleasantries Saros Manor had to offer—the sunroom overlooking the bluestone patio with a fire pit; the library; the great room, complete with an open bar, a large fireplace, and an impressive forty-foot vaulted ceiling. And yet, the manor was in desperate need of maintenance. The house had, understandably, become a coveted prize in a turf war between gangs during Wes's absence, and the ongoing battles for ownership had left the mansion in complete disarray by the time Wes had been able to reclaim his home. "You should have seen this place in its former glory."

"Have you always lived here?" Ero asked as he opened the closet door.

"No, actually, I used to live in Colorado. I realize that means nothing to you; it's about four hundred leagues due west from here. My old home was in a hot spot; Tears would come and go every day, and then they stopped forming, so I moved here to be by the Rip. This manor was owned by the Fruth family. They were very wealthy—came from old money—and they were responsible for a lot of the development in the early days of Phantom Heights. Anyway, this house wasn't even for sale, but I made the owner an offer he couldn't refuse, and here I am."

A wan smile dented Wes's cheeks. "Quite a change of scenery. I'll admit, I miss the mountains. Of course, the Rockies aren't half as impressive as the Razorbacks. No mountain range in this Realm can compare. I . . . uh . . ." Wes suddenly went pale when Ero, who hardly had anything at all to hang in the closet, reached up and pulled down a wooden chest that had caught his eye from the top shelf.

"Wait—" Wes protested, but too late; Ero had already opened it.

Wes bowed his head. "I forgot I had that in there."

Ero scowled at the contents before he pinched a corked vial and lifted it. "Well," he said distastefully. "I am guessing these are illegal."

Wes snatched the chest and the vial, which he gingerly replaced inside the box before shutting the lid and backing away. "In Avilésor. Not here."

Ero gave a little grunt. "And if humans knew what those were, I am sure they would be quick to ban them here as well. Have you used Witch's brew on humans?"

"Not recently," Wes mumbled. "And most of these are harmless, anyway."

Ero shook his head and shut the closet door. Wes set the chest on the dresser and casually stretched his arm out to rest his palm on the doorframe. "So, tell me . . . what are the Alphas like?"

Ero rolled his eyes. "I knew you would broach the subject eventually, but I am surprised by how little time you wasted."

"They know what this mysterious weapon is in the AGC. They *know* things, Ero—things the Agents are keeping secret. Heck, *they're* one big secret the Agents are trying to cover up."

"I am not going to betray their trust."

"I'm your friend. You can trust me."

"But they do not. You may as well just drop the subject, because I will say nothing more on the matter."

Wes growled softly in frustration. "The point of you coming here was so you could get close to them for me."

Ero's eyes flashed dangerously. "Wes, I am not a pawn in one of your schemes, and I am saddened that you see me as such."

Shame warmed Wes's cheeks. He hung his head and mumbled, "I don't see you as a pawn."

"A tool, then. A means to obtain what you want." Wes said nothing, and Ero glared out the window at the spacious backyard overlooking Alvarez Park.

Wes said, "I'm sorry. You aren't just one of my contacts, Ero. You're a friend." He paused before he added, "But . . . you don't have to betray their trust. You can just dig around in their minds a bit, and they wouldn't even know."

"I am disappointed in you. I will not use my Divinity so negligently on the very people whose trust I am trying to earn."

"You'd use your telepathy on Madison and Doc, but not them?"

Ero fixed him with a cold look. "Fine," Wes relented, "although I thought that since we were friends and I'm the one who contacted you about new students, you'd be on my side."

"I am on the side my students need me to be on. I hope that will not strain our friendship."

Wes was silent for a moment, considering Ero's position. "I understand," he grudgingly replied. "I just hope *you* understand that as docile as the twins are, the others are merciless, and by trying to earn their trust, you might just end up dead."

"That is an interesting observation, considering I know for a fact that you have not met the others."

"I know enough about them," Wes grumbled, rubbing his head at the painful memory of his first encounter. "Just . . . be cautious." He reached into his pocket and withdrew a coin, which he offered to Ero. "Here."

Ero stepped forward to hold out his hand, palm up. Wes dropped a penny dark with patina into Ero's grasp. "Your first payment."

One of Ero's eyebrows crept up. "What is that expression you are so fond of using? Déjà vu?"

"Not this time," said Wes with a smile, remembering his first encounter with Ero in Avilésor when he'd tried to pay the Telepath with human currency out of ignorance. "Guess the grade."

Ero's other eyebrow shot up in surprise and awe.

"Ninety-five," Wes said smugly. "When is the last time someone paid you with an ąez?"

Ero lifted the penny close to his face to examine it. Wes, pleased by Ero's reaction, went on, "And would you believe that little penny is the lowest valued coin here? Next to worthless in the human market."

Ero gave Wes a sidelong look. "Hmm. No wonder you have accumulated wealth, if you can so easily obtain copper at such a high grade here."

Wes sifted through the contents of his pocket for more coins. "Actually, they're not as common anymore." He held up a shiny new penny that gleamed in the light. "Only the old ones are worth anything. Humans stopped using copper decades ago and started making pennies out of zinc with a thin copper coating instead. But anyway, that's just a first payment for you. There's more to come."

"You are too generous."

"It's nothing," said Wes with a careless shrug. "Really. I'll let you get settled in now. Dinner's at six."

He seized his wooden chest and sauntered into the hallway.

Ero watched him leave. He waited until he was sure Wes was out of earshot before he said softly, "Were my answers satisfactory, Axel?"

With a whisper of a breeze, the half-breed appeared in the corner, his arms folded. "How did you know I was listening? I was too far away for you to read my mind."

"A fortunate guess. I assumed you would have me under surveillance, and I imagine the hearing range of a nydæa is on par with that of a Clairaudient." He grinned. "You did not disappoint."

Axel was silent for a moment then said, "I'll still be watching you."

"Understood," Ero said lightly.

Axel growled at Ero's careless tone; he clearly wasn't used to having his threats taken so casually. "Watch your back, Ero," he warned as he turned away, and then he was gone.

Ero smiled faintly.

"I most certainly will," he said to the empty room.

— Chapter Fourteen —

Ghost, Hunter

The ceiling fan whirred—a quiet, soothing sound in the dark room.

At least, it used to be soothing. Now all Trey could hear was the whine of drills spinning above a metal table he saw every time he closed his eyes.

He sighed and rolled his head to look at the red numbers smoldering in the darkness. 12:31. Again, he couldn't sleep. It wasn't just his mind that was restless, either; his muscles were twitchy, and lying still made him want to scream.

"Weren't you his sidekick?" drifted Agent Kovak's voice.

Trey threw off the covers. He knew every squeaky floorboard to avoid and was able to navigate his room in the dark well enough to find the trunk at the end of his bed and grab the clothes that weren't exactly clean but weren't dirty enough to go in the hamper yet. Minutes later, he was easing the front door shut and trotting down the porch steps as he cinched his heavy weapon belt around his waist.

He tried not to dwell on the knowledge that this was the first night he'd ever snuck out without Cato. Two and a half years ago, he would have been on his way to meet Cato in the schoolyard, and then they'd roam the town together looking for trouble. Trey hadn't done much of the fighting then—that he'd left to Phantom—but Kovak was wrong. He wasn't a sidekick. Trey liked to think that if Cato had been with him tonight, things would have been different. Trey had trained hard since the last time he saw his friend.

He tilted his head back to look up at the cold stars. He was on his own tonight.

He stopped in the middle of an intersection and shivered, unsure which way to go. He halfway considered tossing pebbles at Vivian's window until she woke. But he wasn't in the mood to talk, and besides, he didn't want to reveal his vulnerability to her.

Trey yawned as he strolled down the deserted street. What a team they'd made when they had been separated from the other raiders. Too bad Viv had no interest in becoming a ghost hunter. They'd really been in sync that night, although she had been too upset over losing her bracelet to notice.

Trey stopped. Vivian's bracelet. If he could find it . . . He felt a goofy grin split his face as he imagined her reaction when he presented it to her. She'd squeal and throw her arms around him, thank him over and over again, maybe . . . maybe even kiss him. Okay, that was a long shot, but not beyond the realm of possibility.

He changed direction and jogged toward downtown. They'd been by the library—he was fairly sure he recalled noticing the stone lions nearby. Trey drew a small flashlight from his belt. He remembered kicking in a door and was confident he'd recognize that door once he saw it; the problem was finding it. He spent almost half an hour sweeping the light back and forth from door to door until his heart started beating faster. This place was familiar. He was close.

He rounded a corner, and here should be—he aimed the circle of light on the wood—yes, the clear imprint of a boot in the center of the door. The hinges had been repaired after he broke them with a strong kick, but the door hadn't been repainted yet. Heart flying, Trey pressed against the shop window and shined his flashlight over every inch of the bare floor and into every corner. Vivian's bracelet was gone.

His spirits fell. He shouldn't have been surprised after all this time, but he'd let his hopes climb too high. He pocketed the flashlight and shoved his hands deep in his pockets, still not ready to return home and lie in bed staring at the clock, which he knew would read 1 a.m. because the bell tower of City Hall sent one clear ring over the sleeping town.

He adjusted his belt, itching for a training session. Madison kept canceling on him lately. But why did he need to wait for her? Phantom never had any formal training. Cato's "training" had been real experience looking for ghosts to fight.

Trey jogged down the street, eyes and ears strained for the slightest hint of trouble.

By the time City Hall's bell tower tolled twice, his determined jog had slowed to an aimless walk. Either the Alpha ghosts were really good at their job, or traffic through the Rip had just about stopped, because Trey hadn't encountered a single ghost to fight. He wasn't even listening for one anymore, just mindlessly roaming. His feet had carried him into Alvarez Park.

He scratched his cheek, startled yet again when his fingers touched skin instead of hair. He hadn't liked his embarrassingly patchy blond beard that had sprouted during the survival days in City Hall, but he somehow felt more vulnerable without it, as if an extra protective layer had been stripped away and his naked skin was more susceptible now. His clean-shaven face felt like a mask, as if he was pretending everything could go back to normal when he knew that was impossible.

Trey stopped short when he found himself face-to-face with Phantom. He blinked, startled out of his wandering thoughts. "Hi, Cato," he whispered sadly.

The trees ringing Heroes' Hollow rustled in the summer breeze. His hand magnetically rose and draped over his friend's boot. The cold of the metal startled him; for some reason he'd expected it to feel warm and real. His head drooped as his eyelids closed. The last image he had of Cato was one he wished he could forget. The moment before the doors closed, his friend trying to rise with his hands bound, a panic-stricken look passing over his face as though somehow he'd *known*—he'd known that would be the last time he'd see Phantom Heights.

That had been the image Trey's tormented mind always replayed. Now, he actually wished that were the one he'd see again, because new images conceived in the darkest folds of his imagination had taken its place—Cato, naked and muzzled, pounding on the one-way glass and begging for help just before he collapsed; Cato, hoisted up and restrained against the wall, his body covered in wires, screaming as he was electrocuted; Cato, strapped down to the metal table, staring up at the bright fluorescent lights and the metallic instruments and the whirring drill . . .

Agent Kovak never even said Cato had been on that table. Maybe he hadn't. But Trey's imagination had already conjured the scene, and it would never be erased. Damn Kovak! Just thinking about what that man had done to Cato made Trey sick.

"I took Phantom out of the spotlight. It's all yours now when you're ready to step up and take it. Your turn to be the hero. You're welcome."

Trey fell to his knees with a quiet cry of anguish. "This wasn't how it was supposed to happen." He folded his arms on top of the pedestal and buried his face in them.

"You and me, Cay. One day the two of us are going to run this town."

A branch snapped. Trey stood and whirled, his face on fire, beyond furious that someone dared to intrude. A figure cloaked in white was moving between the trees. Trey cast a look up at Phantom, narrowed his eyes, and drew an ectogun. He took off in pursuit.

The night was quiet. I couldn't sleep. The alley was littered with pieces of construction debris, and I kicked a chunk of wood out of my way as my fingers twisted the broken bracelet.

My thoughts revolved around Ero. He'd been in Phantom Heights for five days now. Five lessons. And I still couldn't figure out his true motive. Was he really as selfless as he seemed on the surface? Or was it all an act to worm his way in? Maybe Azar had—

A sudden crash nearby sent my heart into my throat. I'd been keeping to the tight alleys for the sake of avoiding unwanted company, but a telltale shiver indicated at least one ghost was involved, and I supposed it was my job to deal with the disruption.

I pocketed the bracelet and donned my mask and hood as I approached the sounds of the scuffle, rather annoyed to have my thoughtful stroll interrupted. As I drew near the intersection of perpendicular alleys, I glimpsed a figure in a white cloak darting past, followed by red ectoplasm orbs fired half a second too late each time. I'd expected to find two ghosts fighting, but as I emerged into view, I found to my surprise that one of the fighters was human.

Trey had one eye squeezed shut, the other trained on his opponent. He needed both hands to keep his gun steady, but even as I watched and gauged the fight, I noticed that the ghost was circling back toward him. Much closer, and that gun wasn't going to be very effective.

The man in white ducked another shot and stooped to snatch a piece of rebar from the alley floor before charging.

Trey must have realized his gun was about to be useless because he backed up a step. A sickening sound of metal on bone resounded when the rebar struck his skull. He went down, hard. The ghost loomed over him and raised the bar again.

"Hey!" I yelled, pitching an ice ball at his head.

He staggered on impact and whirled, finding me immediately. A slow grin appeared as he lowered the rebar. "Ah. A much more suitable challenge." And with no other introduction, he sprinted headlong at me.

His direct approach took me by surprise; his Divinity must be passive or better suited to close combat rather than ranged attacks. He veered back and then swung with all his strength as he drew near. The rebar was coming down on my head, but I'd already formed an icicle to counter it. Ice and metal collided with a dull *clang*.

He was too strong for me to stop the blow, but I was able to redirect it away from my body. The rebar was knocked out of his hand.

I planted my feet, poised to deliver a strike to his exposed throat.

He was fast—faster than I'd anticipated—and rather than dodge or deflect, he seized my fist in one hand and gripped my bare arm with the other.

As soon as his skin made contact with mine, I felt a prickling tingle and, to my horror, a current of energy flowing from my core, through my arm, and into his hand. My brain performed a split-second calculation—Siphon or Elicitor. The latter could steal an opponent's Divinity from either an attack or direct contact. A Siphon could steal raw, undeveloped power from my Origin, raising his overall level while depleting mine. Since he hadn't baited me into using my Divinity, I'd bet this guy must be a Siphon. And he was draining my power.

Rather than struggle, I took a deep breath and reached for my center, then pushed it away once I found it—deeper, deeper inside of me until it was extinguished.

The Siphon ogled me. "What in King's cursed name? You just had the reserves of a Level 4. There's no way I already—"

I narrowed my human eyes at him and veered back with my free left hand to deliver the solid punch to his trachea I'd originally planned. He let go of me and fell to his knees in a fit of violent coughing. A kick to the head sent him sprawling, and as he rolled over onto his back to stare up at me, I glared down at him and seethed, "I'm done letting people make me feel powerless."

To accentuate my point, I raised my knee and stomped my heel on his face. The cartilage gave way beneath my boot. Seeing the blood stain his pristine white cloak filled me with a strange sense of satisfaction.

He tried to take my power away. Memories of being powerless—numb—empty—were still raw. I shuddered, fury surfacing in a green storm that boiled in my core. *That bastard.*

As if his spirit were still awake and attacking, I'd swear I could feel his hand still clasped over my biceps, or was that the neutralizer my skin hadn't forgotten? *No. Not powerless, not again.* Not from a lowlife bastard like *this*!

I kicked him as hard as I could, and it felt good. "You . . ." I whispered, sick to my stomach at the thought of what he'd almost done to me. Ice crystallized across my hands despite the green heat burning in my chest like a supernova.

And then I was on top of him, slamming my fists down again and again on his stupid face, again and again until my hands were red and his face wasn't a face anymore, and again, and again, over and over and over and over.

Finally, panting through gritted teeth, I stilled. My surroundings slowly seeped back into recognition. The man beneath me was so mutilated I couldn't even distinguish his features anymore. I gazed at the bloody mess, then lifted my hands to stare at my stained fingers, crimson streaming in rivulets and dripping onto the faceless man below. How long had I been hitting him?

I leaned forward and pressed two fingertips under his jaw to feel for a pulse. Finding nothing, I stood. I felt no remorse. He'd tried to steal my power and kill Trey. He deserved to die.

There was a time when I would have been repulsed by taking a life in such a brutal manner. That time had long passed. Survival had a way of hardening one's capacity for empathy.

I seized the hood of his cloak and dragged the body down the alley. I was a little light-headed after being partially drained by the Siphon, but at least I was still standing, which was more than I could say for Trey.

I discarded the body in the street and returned to Trey's still body. He was out cold. I couldn't leave him here defenseless like this, but I couldn't take him Home, and I didn't remember where he lived. I supposed I could take him to the Tarrow house . . . or not. No, if Madison spotted me setting her unconscious apprentice at her doorstep . . . well, I could only imagine how that scenario would unfold.

I sighed and glared at my new ward lying face-down on the filthy alley floor. After an uncomfortable hesitation, I knelt beside him.

I reached out, my fingers pausing a few inches from his shoulder, and then I poked him and yanked my hand back, tense, ready for him to react. He didn't move. I exhaled, then gently rolled him onto his back, watching his face to see if his eyes would flutter. They didn't. He looked peaceful on his back now, except for the raw lump on the side of his head.

I leaned back on my heels, my gaze traveling from his face to the ectogun lying near his limp fingers. I stared at it, then picked it up and turned it in my hands, inspecting the weapon. I knew Madison had invented it, and although I couldn't have cared less Before, now I wondered how she'd managed to imitate a ghost's natural-born power in this human-made weapon without replicating the Origin.

I leveled the gun and aimed down the alley, closing one eye as I set my finger on the trigger and pretended that I had the barrel pointed at an invisible enemy. I held the position for a moment, then opened my eye and let my arm fall. On a whim, I pointed the gun at the night sky and squeezed. The trigger was locked.

I studied the gun, turned it over. There was a safety switch. I flipped it into the off position, aimed at the sky again, and pulled the trigger. The weapon made a high-pitched whine as it charged, then a *whoosh*ing sound when it recoiled. I watched an orb of red ectoplasm shoot upward in an arc over the buildings.

My gaze flitted back down to the ectogun in my hand. I didn't like wielding it. It was a cold, hard piece of machinery. I was disconnected from it. My own power was so warm and exhilarating, and it was a part of me. Humans might be able to recreate ectoplasm, but they couldn't experience the rush of true power.

A quick glance at the unconscious teenager nearby reassured me that he hadn't roused yet. I started to set the weapon down when I froze. Imprinted on the butt of the gun was a symbol I recognized: ζ.

Why did my old friend have a gun from Project Zeta?

I traced the symbol with my finger. After a moment's hesitation, I made sure the safety was in place and then holstered the weapon in the waistband of my pants, tucked away so it was hidden behind my cloak. I glanced at Trey's closed eyes, and when he still didn't move, I felt brave enough to reach for his belt and rifle through everything he had in his possession. Most of the armaments were the same as what Vivian had carried in her weapon belt. I handled various guns, canisters I'd guess contained noxious smoke, and a Taser. I discovered a set of keys and a wallet in his pocket, and a weird colored cube. I reached inside a pouch on his hip.

The pain struck without warning.

It wasn't a Spasm—this was different. It was hot, like a thousand scalding needles embedding in my whole body while my hand caught fire. On some level, I registered hitting the ground, but I couldn't see in the green haze. Ectoplasm. I was being electrocuted by high-grade ectoplasm. *My* ectoplasm.

The longest fifteen seconds dragged by, and then, just as suddenly as the ectoplasm manifested, it was gone. I was sprawled on my back beside Trey, drawing ragged breaths into my lungs and staring up at the twinkling starscape.

I lay still for several long minutes to catch my breath before daring to stir. Something was resting in my hand. I sat up and inspected it. The little gadget that had been in Trey's pouch was scorched now, faint tendrils of smoke reaching for the night sky. It was small and resembled a microchip, but it had knocked me right off my feet and completely incapacitated me before shorting out, and even then, I needed a few extra minutes of recovery time. This was another one of Madison's inventions, no doubt.

Bloody Scout, where does she come up with this sadistic stuff?

I returned the keys, wallet, and cube, and replaced the weapons in their respective compartments before I stood. Trey didn't stir.

My muscles were still tingling and throbbing from the unpleasant encounter with the zapper. I wandered toward the building and leapt to seize the lowest rung on the ladder of a fire escape, then pulled myself up and sat down on the first landing, one knee drawn to my chest and the opposite foot dangling over the edge. Bored, I glanced up and down the alley, but it was deserted. I was alone with the apprentice.

I sighed and tilted my head back to face the stars, then down at the alley floor to stare at the teenager below. He was a ghost hunter, and yet, I didn't hate Trey the way I hated Madison, despite his apprenticeship. We'd been friends once.

Now look at us. Me, a half-breed fugitive, and him, on his way to becoming just as lethal a ghost hunter as his master. He was training to hunt creatures like me. The betrayal was an ache. I shouldn't be so insulted—after all, even though I was technically part kálos, Phantom had been a ghost hunter too, and I supposed I still was now that I'd been employed as a mercenary—but I dreaded the day I'd be staring into the barrel of Trey's gun instead of Madison's. The question was, would he pull the trigger?

What made his betrayal so complete was the knowledge that he was one of the few in my inner circle during my days as Phantom. Why would my best friend, knowing his ghost-hunting master had the power to negotiate my rescue but wouldn't, continue to study under her?

Shadows of half-erased memories wafted just out of my reach, and the harder I tried to grasp them, the farther they drifted. I sat for at least an hour more, pondering our past relationship and our future as I absently turned the Zeta ectogun over and over in my hands. The early morning hours were starting to roll in when he finally stirred.

My heart raced. I'd had all this time I could have used to plan what I would do and say, and I hadn't even considered my course of action for when Trey awakened. I was never planning ahead as I should be— as Jay did.

I stashed the ectogun in my waistband, closed my hand into a fist, and summoned an orb of ice. I kept part of my attention focused on manipulating the orb, on causing it to grow and shrink and morph in my hand so I was constantly drawing on the power to sustain my blue eyes. I adjusted the cloth over my nose just as the apprentice opened his eyes.

I remained motionless, my fingers working the ice behind my back while I watched my old friend from my perch. He focused on the buildings high above him, blinked a few times, then gasped and seized an ectogun from his belt as he sat straight up. He clutched the weapon in both hands, pointing it wildly in every direction.

Finally, he spotted me sitting on the fire escape, and he took aim. Our past friendship held no bearing. He didn't see *me*; he saw a dangerous, blue-eyed fugitive staring at him in the dark. I wouldn't even blame him for a single panicked twitch of the finger.

I didn't move. Madison would have shot me. Trey was not as ruthless, and I wasn't afraid of him. Not yet, anyway. Whether it was a residual feeling of trust or my perception of his body language, I was confident he wouldn't shoot.

My fingers continued to play with the cold orb in my hand. I found the action calming, enabling me to meet his gaze. He kept the gun leveled at my chest. He was waiting for me to attack him, and when I didn't, he hesitated, as I'd expected. The Trey I thought I once knew would not fire on an opponent who hadn't given him due cause.

He frowned. "You . . . y-you saved me?"

I said nothing, and for some reason, my silence and immobility satisfied his question. He slowly lowered the ectogun.

Trey and I stared at each other in silence. He shook his head with a curiously slow, jerky motion, as if trying to jolt his fuzzy mind into focus. "You . . . wow, you're actually one of the Alpha ghosts. In the flesh."

Fresh confusion found a place in his expression when he frowned and touched his head, then winced upon discovering the tender lump. "Where are we?"

I hesitated with my answer. Would he be able to recognize my voice after all this time? I swung my other leg over and slid from my perch, then landed on the ground in a crouch. Trey started and tightened his grip on his gun, but he didn't aim it at me as I straightened. He couldn't see any distinguishing features that might give me away, but just in case, I decided not to respond.

Trey didn't seem particularly surprised by my silence. He groaned and shoved the ectogun into his holster. "It's morning? How long have I been here?"

I cleared my throat and kept my voice low when I replied, "A few hours."

He closed his eyes and tilted his head back with an exasperated sigh. "Shit. Mom and Dad are gonna ground me."

Ground him? As in what, bury him in the ground? At least with the mask muffling my words and the probable concussion clouding his perception, he hadn't noticed that my voice was even remotely familiar. He was too preoccupied patting his empty holster. "Oh no, my ectogun. It's gone."

"It's right there," I said, conscious of the weapon pressing against my lower back.

"Not that one. I had another one."

I looked away from him and pretended to survey the alley. "You probably lost it in the fight. We could retrace your steps."

That made him falter. He blinked a few times and admitted, "I . . . I don't remember which way I came."

I relaxed a little and transferred my ice orb to my other hand while I tilted my head to study his reaction. "Question. What were you doing by yourself in the outskirts in the middle of the night?"

Trey stared at me long and hard, and I tensed again, wondering if I was out of line for questioning him. I wasn't entirely sure what the boundaries were between a ghost and human in the Outside world. Was the human race really as high above ghosts as *They* would like me to believe?

He shook his head and mumbled, "I was looking for a ghost—erm, I mean, a kálos—to fight."

I leaned back against the wall and folded my arms, surprisingly relaxed in the presence of a ghost hunter. "You probably would have been killed if I hadn't found you." I didn't mean to include such a biting edge in my tone, but it escaped nonetheless.

He nodded, either choosing to brush it off or completely oblivious to it. "I know. It was stupid. But, um, what happened to the ghost?"

"He's dead."

"Oh." Trey stared down at his hands. "Do you know what his Divinity was?"

"He was a Siphon."

"A Siphon?" Trey repeated, jerking his head up. "Are you sure?"

"Yeah."

"A Siphon. Damn it." He slammed his fist down on the asphalt. "They're usually only Level 2. And that Divinity is useless on humans. I should've been able to take him by myself." His whole body slumped in defeat.

I let him wallow for a minute before I said, "Get up. I'll take you home."

He heaved a great sigh and stood, but he wobbled and took a few steps like a toddler learning how to balance on two legs before he was able to stabilize. I watched him, rather enthralled. This was like kidnapping Vivian all over again, but different—my first direct communication with another human of Before. When he leaned against the wall, I requested, "Let me look at you."

He gave me a certifiably weird look. "What?"

"Your eyes," I justified. "To see if you have a concussion." Without any further explanation, I circled in front of him and halted. He held still while I gazed at him. He wasn't in my photograph, and because of that, his face was always blurry in my memories, his essence there but not the details. I absorbed his features: his pronounced cheekbones, the slight cleft in his wide chin, his gray eyes, his tousled blond hair. This version of Trey was closer to how I thought he'd looked Before—no beard, no goggles. I recommitted him to memory so now, even if he was a little out of time, I could put a clear face to my memories.

"So?" he inquired, startling me.

I shrugged and muttered, "I don't know," still taking in his face and the expressions he made.

"What do you mean you don't know?"

"Do I look like a doctor?" I walked away, pleased that even though I wasn't looking at him, I could still conjure a clear mental image. He followed, and I had to adjust my stride to make sure he was in my peripheral at all times so I'd have forewarning if he made a sudden move. I didn't think he'd attack me, but I didn't know where his loyalties lay, and I knew better than to turn my back on a human, especially a ghost hunter in training.

"I've been to Project Alpha," he announced.

I glowered at him from the corner of my eye but said nothing. He swallowed hard in the silence and continued, "I saw where you lived. I sat in one of your cages, and I ate your food. I stood in the Arena. I . . . was in the same restraints you were in. The ones on the wall."

"I'm not sure what you think you're proving."

He shook his head and gazed up at the night sky beginning to lighten with a dusting of dawn's violet. "I know. That's all. I know more than any human in Phantom Heights what hell you came from. That doesn't excuse what you did, though. I just want to say, if you ever mess with Vivian again, I'll come after you, and I won't hold back. Fair warning."

The hostile undercurrent beneath his sharp tone was hard to miss. I glanced at him sidelong, an explosion of contradicting responses sparking. Anger—*who does he think he is to threaten me?* Pleasure—*I'm glad Vivian has someone to look out for her.* Jealousy—*she doesn't belong to him.*

I stared straight ahead and coldly replied, "Back off."

His face wrinkled into a scowl. He took a step closer. It was an aggressive move, one that automatically stiffened my body in defense. "I mean it, you touch her again and I'll—"

His hand was coming toward me. I didn't think; I just reacted. I whirled, seized his wrist, twisted his arm behind his back, and pulled it upward until he cried with pain. My foot was already hooked around his ankle. In one move, he was lying on his stomach with his wrist pinned between his shoulder blades, my knee in the center of his back, and his face smashed between my palm and the pavement.

A flash of a memory, painfully clear, pulled me away.

The sun was shining. I was in the grass on my back. Someone was on top of me, pinning me down, hands tight on my wrists, and yet, I wasn't scared. I was staring up into Trey's flushed face, and we were both laughing. "You know," he said, "if you're going to be a hero, you'd better get stronger."

His soft groan brought me back. Horrified, I released him. I hadn't meant to hurt him. I'd zoned out, acting on my fighting instincts. He was slow in hauling his body up onto his hands and knees, but when he raised his head, he was grinning. "Can you teach me how to do that?"

I gaped at him. At first I thought he must be teasing me, but his eyes were shining with eagerness to learn. "No."

"Why?" he demanded, seemingly forgetting our previous conflict as he scrambled up.

"I shouldn't have done that to you when you probably have a concussion."

I started walking. He followed, then advanced so he was a step ahead of me to lead the way. "Or you're afraid of me. It wouldn't be in your best interest to make a ghost hunter more lethal."

A soft snort escaped under my breath. "You think you're lethal? You're *barely* a ghost hunter."

Again, I'd baited him, and yet, he simply shrugged in acknowledgment that he *was* only an apprentice. There was something I liked about him—the cockiness that was still reined in by humility. Even though he'd lost his fight and almost died, he still wanted to learn. I admired his confidence. He would have made a much better hero than I did. He wouldn't have been left in that place; somebody would have come for *him*.

I shivered and halted. Trey kept going for another few paces before he realized I wasn't with him. He paused and turned back to face me, but I wasn't looking at him. "Something wrong?" he asked.

I turned in a slow circle, ears strained. "I thought I sensed a ghost."

He didn't question me, didn't ask if I was sure—which I wasn't. His ectogun was already out. He closed the gap between us, his back to mine, and we completed the rotation. Weird, how easily we synced to one another, as if on a deeper level than either of us was aware, our friendship remained undamaged. I trusted him to have my back, just like I thought he subconsciously trusted me.

"I don't see anything," Trey whispered. "You?"

"No." I straightened out of my defensive stance.

Though I detected nothing, my skin still crawled. I felt as though I was in someone's crosshairs. "Stay alert, though."

Trey nodded and holstered his gun. I stared at the array of weapons around his waist, even when he retracted his hand and resumed walking. "Ghost hunting," I said. "That's an intense career choice. Can I ask what made you decide to do it?"

I didn't think it was a stimulating inquiry, and yet, Trey scowled at his feet and shoved his hands deep into his pockets. "Personal reasons," was all he'd tell me. That, of all the things I'd said to him tonight, put him in a silent, bitter mood. I had the impression there was a lot more behind those two words than he was willing to share with a stranger.

We walked for two whole blocks in silence before I said, "So . . . Madison Tarrow. Why do you still train with her?" It was harder than I'd thought, keeping the desperation from seeping out.

He pondered his answer before he finally replied, "She's the only ghost hunter in the area to teach me, plus she's one of the best. And, you know, I get to see Vivian a lot, too."

"What does she have to do with anything?"

Trey, caught in the heat of a flush, floundered, "Oh, uh, n-nothing, never mind." He puffed out his chest and proclaimed, "Someday, I'm going to take Madison's place as the lead ghost hunter in Phantom Heights. I really hope we're still allies when that happens."

I couldn't tell if he was being sincere or if there was a veiled threat buried in that last sentiment, but our walk wasn't going to last much longer, and I was running out of time to question him. "What about Phantom?"

Trey's carefree demeanor vanished. "What *about* Phantom?"

There was no mistaking the hostility as cold as the ice in my hand. Problem was, I couldn't ask him questions about a person I was never supposed to have met. All I could safely say was, "I suppose he's my predecessor, isn't he?"

"Yeah, well, if you think you replaced him, you're wrong. Phantom was a hero."

"Being a hero isn't in my job description," I retorted. While Trey stewed, I took a deep breath to calm down. I couldn't let my anger surface and turn my eyes green. I tilted my head back to look up at the cold stars. "Did you ever visit him?"

"Yeah, right. You know Agent Kovak; you really think he let me drop in for a visit?"

"Did you try?" I pressed, unable to completely bury the hurt and hope in the question.

Trey, thankfully, didn't notice. He was too wrapped up in his own thoughts. "No."

I couldn't help it; I had to ask, "Why?"

This answer took a long time—too long, each second dragged out, our time together ticking away, until finally, he said, "I guess . . . I don't know, I waited because . . . I guess I thought he'd come back, you know?"

"Yeah." The word cracked in my throat. I did know. I used to think I'd come back too, though under drastically different circumstances.

Trey said nothing more for our walk, which was fine by me. My head was reeling. Madison was a clear enemy. Trey . . . I couldn't decide. My best friend who never tried to make contact with me and was still training under the ghost hunter who had tried so hard to destroy me on multiple occasions. *How could he betray me like that?*

It was a question I could never ask him.

I couldn't read him, couldn't determine if he was loyal to her or just using her as a resource to become a ghost hunter, and my time was up. He was walking up the steps of his porch, and I had so many more questions I wished I could ask him.

Trey had always been ambitious. His life dream was to be a ghost hunter, and if being associated with me hindered that chance, well . . . his unfaithfulness hurt, but it wasn't a mystery.

I leaned against a light pole and watched him unlock the front door to his house. My fingers were busy working the hard but malleable ice ball in my hand as he stepped inside, paused, turned to look back at me once more, then closed the door.

The moment the door latched shut, I melted the ice into water and allowed it to trickle between my fingers. I hung my head and expelled the air from my lungs. What a long night.

I turned away from the Selmans' house. Each day, Trey trained under the supervision of his ghost-hunting master, and I trained with my lab-family. Each day, we both grew stronger, and I had to face the horrifying reality that one day, I might have to stand before my friend as an enemy.

I was aware of a sudden clamminess to my skin, a pit in my stomach, and I realized I was afraid. Not of Trey, but of our seemingly inevitable fate. The ghost facing the ghost hunter.

I shivered in the chilly air and wrapped my arms around my midriff. I traveled a few more steps before my sluggish brain fixated on a realization that made me halt again.

I was a Cryokinetic.

An early morning breeze wouldn't make me shiver.

I whirled in alarm, gaze darting suspiciously up and down the deserted street. "Axel?" I retreated a step. Did I feel the familiar charge in the air, or was I imagining it? "Ax, this isn't funny!"

"Nobody's laughing." A woman's voice answered me.

I spun to find a figure standing beneath a streetlight. The stranger didn't move. Her cloak shifted in a slight breeze, her red eyes glowing. I assumed a fighting stance, ready for the assault, but she remained still.

Something was wrong. Suddenly, terribly wrong. My blood felt as if it were thickening, turning to cement. My balance failed, causing the world to tilt. I swayed, dizzy, ears ringing with a high-pitched whine growing louder and louder above my deafening heartbeat. *Blink.* I tried to force the world back into focus. *Blink again.* I was only making it tilt more. *Blink.*

I'm falling.

"Trey," I whispered. A call for help—one he couldn't hear.

The cloaked figure walked toward me, blurry, then clear for an instant, darkness encroaching on the edges of my vision, ground plane tipping further and further. Everything was spinning. I had a moment of wild panic, and then a wave of blackness slammed into me before I even hit the ground.

— Chapter Fifteen —
Project Zeta

Footsteps.

Sure, even footsteps.

A breeze.

Someone was carrying me.

Waking felt like trying to pull my body out of mud sucking me down, filling my nose and mouth and clogging my veins so I couldn't move. My senses returned at a crawling speed, but even when I had limited awareness, I was still too disoriented to make sense of anything beyond the state of my own body. I became aware that my right arm was dangling at my side, my left draped over my abdomen. My cheek was pressed against someone's chest. Whoever was carrying me had me lying limp in his or her arms like a rag doll.

I should have been in the throes of panic. I was too weak to move, completely helpless, and probably in the Ghost Realm far away from my lab-siblings. But the fear switch in my brain hadn't clicked on yet. I was too drowsy to be afraid.

The only thought meandering through my sluggish mind right now was that I was being carried. Someone had taken the time and effort to actually lift me up and hold me, not drag me across the ground. I couldn't remember the last time an Outsider showed me that kindness. For all I knew, it could be Azar or a Shadow Guard or bounty hunter holding me, and yet, I kept my eyes shut for a moment longer so I could pretend I was a child again and my mother was carrying me to bed. I could almost hear her singing that song—the one about gray skies.

I tried to swallow the acrid taste in my mouth.

"Ah, good to see you returning to the world of the conscious."

A man's voice? Hadn't I been confronted by a woman, or did I remember that incorrectly?

My head throbbed like it always did after a Spasm, and I labored to force my heavy eyelids open. Ero smiled down at me.

Ero. Damn it, of all people, it had to be him, the person able to read my mind. He was probably silently mocking me, thinking I was an idiot for enjoying that tiny fantasy of my old life. I needed a long moment to focus on his face before I tried to ask, "Where am I?" Instead, it came out as, "Weh-mm-ah?" I shifted in his arms with a quiet moan.

"Easy, now," he soothed. "I am taking you to Saros Manor."

Saros Manor? That's . . . that's Wes's place. "No." I squirmed again, but my limbs felt as if they'd been turned to stone. "Wha-ditcha-dooda-me?"

"Me? Absolutely nothing. You, my young friend, made the unfortunate mistake of crossing paths with a Hemokinetic."

"A whuh?"

"One who controls blood. She stopped the circulation to your brain so you would lose consciousness. But, luckily for you, I enjoy walking early in the morning so I can watch the sunrise. I sent her back through the Rip."

I turned my head away from Ero's chest to find that he was now carrying me up the front steps of the porch stretching across the front of Wes's mansion. I'd seen Saros Manor from a distance but never ventured this close. "Am I gonna be okay?"

My speech was more coherent; that must be a good sign. Ero became intangible, passing his power on to me, and we phased through the closed door. Once we'd solidified, he answered, "You just need to rest. I would have taken you to your lab-family if I knew where you were living."

I struggled and insisted, "I can walk."

Ero tightened his grip to maintain his hold. "I would not recommend it just yet."

My strength and my wits were returning, but Ero was still able to overpower me with minimal effort. We were in a foyer that had probably been grand at one point in time but showed signs of abandonment—cracks and ectoplasm burns on the walls, missing rods from the balustrade leading upstairs, sheets covering chairs and sofas in the parlor to our right, cobwebs veiling a crystal chandelier dangling on a long chain from an impossibly high ceiling that renewed my dizziness in a swooping wave.

I inhaled the distinct smell of fresh paint. Somewhere off to the left came the quiet sound of a door closing. *Wes!*

"Ero, please, Wes can't see me," I whispered, my resistance growing stronger.

A figure emerged from an arched doorway leading into what appeared to be a library. I caught my breath and froze. The werewolf, his pajamas covered by a silk robe and his hair still disheveled from sleep, sauntered into the foyer with a steaming mug in his hands. He stopped in his tracks.

"Good morning," Ero greeted cheerily, as though there were absolutely nothing out of the ordinary about carrying a masked, semiconscious fugitive through the foyer at dawn.

Wes's eyebrows slowly rose. "Um . . . morning," he repeated.

Ero carried me away and called over his shoulder, "Perhaps you could bring a glass of water for our guest?"

Completely befuddled, Wes just stood there. "Uh . . . yeah. Sure."

"Ero," I protested, "please. I can walk Home now."

"Oh, really?" He paused, dropped the arm that was behind my knees, and swung me down. Unfortunately, my numb legs had forgotten how to work. As soon as my weight settled, they betrayed me and buckled. Ero hoisted me back into his arms. "Just as I thought."

I didn't even try to squirm free now; I leaned my head back and let him carry me. We were heading toward a wall made mostly of glass, although upon closer inspection, I identified three sets of French doors spaced between windows to frame a panoramic view of a patio ringed by a stone seating wall before a backdrop of trees in the distance.

At first, I thought Ero was taking me to the patio, but as we neared the doors, he turned toward a hallway with a normal-height ceiling that made me feel much less small. He carried me through the door on the right.

This room was mercifully dark compared to the open foyer and great room. I noticed a pool table on the far end, a massive flatscreen TV that was so thin it was almost flush with the wall, a leather sofa, a fireplace connecting to the great room on the other side, and several recliners.

I bartered, "If you take me outside, I can contact Jay, and he can Blink me."

"Blinking is very disorienting, and that is something you do not need right now. Humor me and rest for ten passings before you try to move around."

"Ten . . . what?"

"Ah. I believe the word I was looking for was *minutes*. My mistake."

He bent over and gently laid me down on the sofa. As much as I didn't want to be here, I couldn't deny that lying down felt so blissful when my weight settled into the cushions, although something hard pressing into my spine caused me to wince in discomfort. I reached under my back and withdrew the Zeta gun I'd taken from Trey.

Ero eyed it curiously as I clutched it to my chest, but he said nothing. He reached for my face. I shrank away, but his fingers seized my mask and pulled it down so I could breathe better.

"Ero, I can't focus my power. Wes will see my eyes and—"

"Yes, he will. But he will not recognize you."

"How can you know that?"

"The problem is not his eyes, but rather his mind making the connection to past memories. Trust me. He will not recognize you." We turned at movement in the doorway. Ero winked and said, "Watch." His sapphire eyes were bright with power.

More alert and definitely curious, Wes approached with a glass in his hand, his glowing blue eyes fixated on me. "So, who do we have here?" Wes asked.

"Cato," Ero said matter-of-factly.

My jaw dropped. How could he? Just like that, he'd ruined every-thing. And he didn't stop there.

"You know Cato, right, Wes? The Demikan. He used to be Phan-tom."

I gaped at the werewolf, too horror-stricken to even deny Ero's pro-clamation. I waited for recognition, maybe even alarm. And yet, Wes didn't bat an eye. He set the glass of water on a table near the armrest of the sofa and said, "Cato. No, doesn't ring a bell."

"Huh?" The syllable slipped out of my mouth.

Ero pleasantly informed his friend, "Poor Cato had a run-in with a Hemokinetic a little while ago, and I thought he should rest before re-turning home."

"Sure, no problem. They can be tough to deal with, especially when they sneak up on you, eh, Cato?"

"Um . . . yeah. I guess so."

Wes yawned. "Well, I should get dressed. Let me know if you need anything. Oh, there's a fresh pot of coffee in the kitchen if you want some."

"Ah, wonderful," Ero called in his wake as the werewolf strolled back into the hall. He peered down at me. "I have become quite fond of that drink."

I lay completely still, too scared to move. If Ero had intended to impress me with that display of power, he'd failed miserably because I was petrified.

His voice casual, he said, "See? Wes saw you and knew your name but was not able to connect that information with his memories to re-cognize you. I did not need to control him or erase any memories. I simply blocked the pathways needed to access memories or form new ones. He will not remember this encounter."

"Yeah? And how do I know any of this is real?"

"If not for me, you would no doubt be in Avilésor right now, prob-ably in Azar's Prison."

I grumbled, "Thank you."

"Please," he said with a wave of his hand. "I do not ask for gratitude. What would Finn and Reese do without their lab-brother?"

"I feel better." I tried to sit up, only to find my body sluggish and heavy with unusual resistance. Though I cringed at his touch, I allowed Ero to slide his arm behind my back and assist me. The gun fell into my lap.

"Here," he said, pressing the glass of water into my hands. I eyed it suspiciously. I didn't trust food or drink given to me by an Outsider; I'd been drugged too many times. "I promise it is clean," he assured upon hearing my worries. "No drugs, no poison." His sapphire eyes glowed brighter, and I believed him.

Still, I insisted, "I'm not thirsty."

"That may be so, but you are an Elemental within the Water Pinnacle. Dehydration is particularly detrimental to you. Drink up. I promise it will help." He further coaxed me by setting one finger against the bottom of the glass and tipping it to my lips. I obliged. I felt quite calm in his presence, regardless of his handling. I was aware that his telepathy probably played a significant role in that, but whatever power he was pushing into my mind was minimal and meant only to soothe me . . . I hoped.

Although I really wasn't thirsty, once I started drinking, I couldn't stop. Was it Ero's doing, or was he right about my Divinity being so closely related to the element of water? I lowered the empty glass and let out a deep sigh as I leaned my head back against the cushion. Ero took the glass from me and set it on the table. "Better?"

"Yes." I felt a touch of heat in my cheeks. I rather liked having someone take care of me, and for some reason, that felt like a weakness.

"Cato." I heard it in his voice; he'd been listening to my thoughts. His tone was saturated with tenderness. "There is no shame in relying on others."

"I know."

"I am not certain how old you are, but I know you have not yet reached your second coming of age. Possibly not even your first."

"I don't know what that means."

Patient with my ignorance, he explained, "You are not considered an adult until your second coming of age when you reach a hundred years. You have been on your own, hunted to the brink of exhaustion while protecting your lab-family and standing against both humans and kálos without a single ally in the midst of a gathering war . . . Surely you must be tired of being strong for so long."

He was right. As though his very words weighed me down with the realization, my body had never felt so leaden. What was the harm in letting Ero adopt a fatherly role, just for a little bit while I rested? I felt so much older than I really was—the training, the fighting, the scouting, the scarce meals, the stress, the nightmares, the Spasms, the hatred, the fear, the sorrow, it had all taken a devastating physical, mental, and emotional toll on me.

But rather than admit this aloud, I rubbed my temples and moaned. "Bloody Scout, I feel like that Hemokinetic pounded the inside of my skull with a mallet."

"Her power is no longer affecting you. It just takes a little time for your body to return to equilibrium. You are lucky her intention was to incapacitate and not kill. Otherwise, she might have induced a stroke or heart attack, or bled you dry."

I stared down at the gun in my lap, still trying to remember what happened last night. My memories were in choppy vignettes with too many blank periods in between. The Siphon cloaked in white, Trey, the woman standing under the streetlight, blackness, Ero carrying me . . .

He might have rescued me, but the sense of security under his watch was starting to waver as I considered the night's events. "So . . . you just happened to be walking past?"

"You do not believe me?"

I fixed him with a glare, silently conveying the depth of my distrust. He smiled warmly. "I enjoy walking through the town early in the morning while all is quiet. I was on my way to the lake. Chelvistin and I have made a habit of watching the sunrise together. Unfortunately, I will have to miss this one, but hopefully she will not mind."

"Chelvistin? You . . . know about Chelvistin?"

"I do."

"And she actually entrusted you with her whisper?"

"I have given her no reason not to . . . just as I have given you no reason not to trust me, either." He sat down beside me on the sofa. Instantly, a bubble of panic expanded in my chest. He was too close; I wasn't in a good position to defend myself. And then, just as quickly as it had come, the fear subsided, and I relaxed into the cushions.

He studied me closely. A little too closely, actually; I started to feel uncomfortable. "Cato, may I ask you a personal question?"

I tensed. *Even if I say no, he can pull the answer out of my mind anyway.*

"I guess so."

The Telepath pondered his inquiry for a moment before posing it: "Is it true that you have two Divinities?"

I was so startled by such a simple question that I blinked in surprise. "Yeah."

"Cryokinesis and sonokinesis, correct?"

I nodded. "Why do you want to know?"

"It is an unheard-of phenomenon, and I was curious if the rumors were actually true. Is that why your eyes are two different colors?"

His inquiry jolted me. "My eyes? What do you know about that?"

Ero observed me with keen interest. "You do not know?" I shook my head, awaiting his explanation. "I do not have a definitive answer."

"I'd like to know your opinion, though," I pressed, trying to mask the eagerness in my voice. I didn't know what had happened to me when the Flash changed my body. Nobody had explained it to me because nobody else knew either, not even *Them.* I wanted an answer, even if the most Ero could give me was a hypothesis.

He stared me straight in one eye, then shifted his gaze slightly to my other one. "Do your eyes ever change?"

"When I use my cryokinesis they're both blue, sonokinesis green."

"Could you demonstrate?"

I held up my right hand and curled my fingers into a fist as I sought the cold Divinity in my core. It ran through my body, turning my blood cold, and I channeled it to my closed hand. When I unfolded my fingers, a delicate ice crystal was sitting in my palm. I didn't need a mirror to know what Ero was seeing—when the crystal was forming, both of my eyes glowed blue. As the power receded, my blue left eye faded back to its natural green color.

Ero took the crystal from me and studied it. "Interesting. I have met two Cryokinetics in my lifetime, and they both had blue eyes. If I am not mistaken, green is the most common eye color for Sonics."

He peered at me over the ice crystal, appraising me. "A kálos is meant to have only one Divinity or none at all. But you have two very different divine powers competing inside you, and I believe that is the reason your eyes are two different colors. When in a neutral state, both powers are in a state of equilibrium. But when you pull one Divinity to the surface, your recessive eye changes color to match the dominant power."

I nodded slowly, considering his theory.

Ero continued, "No other kálos can boast of having two Divinities. You were a legend in Avilésor, you know. Phantom, the Demikan, protector of humankind."

I frowned at the ceiling. "That was a long time ago. I'm not Phantom anymore."

"Not so long ago," he reminded me.

"Well, it feels like a lifetime. Do I live up to your expectations?"

"No." Surprised, I turned my head. "You exceed them. You are more powerful now than you ever were as Phantom. More formidable, I should say. Granted, I did not know you back then, but if the rumors are true, then you have grown a lot since that time in your life. I doubt you knew how to fight and kill so efficiently back then."

"No," I whispered. "I learned that in the Arena." I used my thumbnail to scrape the dried blood flaking off my knuckles. Uncomfortable with his inquiries about Phantom, I changed the subject.

"Ero? Um, I have a question for you."

"Certainly."

"What do you gain by training Finn and Reese?"

"What do I *gain*?" he repeated in surprise. "My friend, has your captivity caused you to forget the personal satisfaction of helping others?" Instead of answering my question, he asked one of his own: "Why did you become Phantom?"

I shook my head, trying to remember.

"Hmm." Ero tilted his head slightly, studying me. "Great power can be used to harm or control those weaker than you, or to protect those who cannot protect themselves. You chose to help people, as did I. My gain is the fulfillment of watching my students mature and find confidence in themselves."

I stared at the gun in my lap, pondering his answer. Rather than look him in the eye, I tilted the weapon until I could see his bright blue eyes reflected in the barrel. "Are you a father?" My gaze flicked up to witness an expression of great sadness carve sorrow lines into his forehead.

"No, I am not. My job requires much traveling—not very conducive to settling down and raising a family, I am afraid. I have temporarily become a part of many families over the centuries, and I like to think of all my students as my children."

"Is it hard to move on when their training is done?"

"Yes, it is. But in moving on, I always find a new child in need of my help."

I nodded slowly. Again, I experienced the rare pleasure of pretending, just for a moment, that Ero could play the role of a father. I didn't know what happened to mine, anyway. He wasn't in my photograph, but why? Had he died? Walked out on the family? If he was somewhere out there . . . I wondered if he would accept me even though my mother couldn't.

I subtly observed the Telepath from the corner of my eye. Despite these alluring thoughts likely woven with telepathy to influence my opinion, he was not my father; he was an Outsider. The calm, safe feeling passed when I remembered that technically I was his captive.

I stared him down and asked, "Will you let me go now?"

"I will, but on one condition. I want to watch you walk across the room and back."

I wriggled my toes to make sure they were operational before planting my feet on the ground. I scooted closer to the edge of the cushion, letting my legs take on a little weight at a time until I was ready to stand. I was still weak, and my knees wobbled, but I could hold my own weight.

I shoved the gun back into my waistband and stood in one place for a few more seconds to ensure I had my balance under control. Ero leaned against the armrest and observed me as I took one unsure step, then another, and by the fifth, I was moving normally again, if a little slower than usual. I shuffled across the carpet, touched the pool table, and then returned to stand before the Telepath.

I brought my hands to my neck and covered the lower half of my face with the mask. "Thank you," I told him again, this time sincerely.

He nodded. "Will I see you later today for a lesson?"

I hesitated before answering, "Probably not. Axel, um . . . he's . . . sick."

I was afraid to look Ero in the eye, not that it mattered because I couldn't hide my thoughts from him. Sure enough, when I did summon the courage to face him, he was watching me with deep thoughtfulness clouding his blue eyes. "Is he, now?" he murmured knowingly.

Uncomfortable, I rubbed my right arm and assured, "As soon as Axel's well again, we'll come for a lesson. Maybe tomorrow."

He was still watching me, his eyes drilling into my soul to see the truth. "Very well. At your earliest convenience. I do not like skipping days."

"I know," I said apologetically, but what could we do? Jay wanted Axel present to supervise, and the hybrid was too unstable right now. Ero understood this. He might not like it, but he understood.

Lowering his voice theatrically, he confided, "You know, if you ever need help, please do not be afraid to ask."

"I'll keep that in mind," I said as I turned away and left him sitting on the sofa.

Wes was nowhere to be seen as I wandered into the hallway. This time, I could appreciate my surroundings, and I took my time in leaving.

Across the hall, a door led into a sunroom practically glowing with light streaming in through the windows and glass roof. Unfortunately, the plants inside hadn't survived the town's downfall; they were brown and crispy.

I turned back toward the great room. The French doors lined my right side, and perhaps I would have been wiser to leave through the back and circle around outside the manor to ensure I didn't cross paths again with the werewolf, but my curiosity bested me. I could see the trees of Alvarez Park across the lawn, giving me my bearings; that direction must be south. A railed walkway connecting the east and west wings of the second floor jutted above the French doors, and ahead of me, another door opened onto a covered porch.

I rounded the corner and was gazing down the central axis of the manor again. The fireplace I'd seen in the other room connected to this open space through the wall. Next to it, before the flared staircase, there was an open bar with stools, although the shelves behind the bar were mostly bare. I imagined Wes throwing grand parties here a few years ago, those shelves gleaming with top-shelf booze and sparkling glasses.

My footsteps, quiet as they were, seemed to echo in this place. I wandered past the bar, tilting my head to peer through the first of a pair of arched doorways on the right wall. As I'd guessed earlier, it opened into a library. Bookshelves lined the walls around a table and chairs, and a metal staircase twirled up in a tight spiral in the corner. I noticed a door on the far wall, and since Wes had come through here with fresh coffee, I presumed that door must lead to the kitchen.

I passed the library and continued toward the front doors. Through the next archway on the right, I found an elegant dining room table beneath a smaller chandelier. Large windows lined the north wall, oil paintings of peaceful landscapes the south wall. A display of fine china gleamed in a glass cabinet. To my left, across from the dining room, was the front parlor I'd noticed when Ero had carried me in, the dusty chandelier in the center a perfect match to its dining room twin.

I opened one of the double front doors and trudged onto the porch, then closed the door and leaned against it. I'd wondered how Wes was able to finance the reconstruction of Phantom Heights. After seeing his "house," I was well convinced that his wealth was limitless. I wanted to close my eyes and fall asleep right there, upright, slumped against the door, but I leaned forward and forced my feet to start walking.

The trek Home was a sleepy fog of exhausted confusion while I tried to sort my scrambled and fuzzy thoughts. Whenever I was around Ero, I felt my guard dropping under his kind voice and warm smile, and only in retrospect could I look back and question the encounter. I hadn't noticed a hole needing to be replaced by a parental figure before, but Ero . . . he was practically a stranger, and yet, he treated me like a son. And I liked it. Not a lab rat, not a killer, not a fugitive. A son. Something my own mother wouldn't grant me.

And yet, I wondered . . . were my thoughts my own? Or was Ero planting these ideas in my mind? I didn't even know if I'd really been as out of it as he made me believe, or if he was sedating me with his power. What if I hadn't met a Hemokinetic at all? What if Ero had tricked me with illusions so he could have the opportunity to "save" me and win my trust?

I was too tired to sneak through town, let alone torture my mind with these musings. Phantom Heights was beginning to stir, which forced me to tap into my reserves to turn my green eye blue. I played with a malleable ice orb in each hand.

As I passed, humans gasped, pointed, and backed away from me in wonder and fear. No one dared to follow. They just stared, except for one little girl who beamed at me and stepped off the curb, only to find her mother's hand wrap around her wrist and yank her back. "Stay away from him; he's dangerous," the woman scolded, shooting me a glare. Her daughter batted her dark eyelashes at me and secretly waved.

I did have the sense to check my surroundings once I reached the outskirts to make sure I didn't have any unwanted shadows tailing me, but all was quiet, and after one long whistle, a black cat strolled across the alley without pause. All clear.

Finn and Reese were the only ones Home. Finn passed along the message: "Jay said you're exempt from training."

I let out a groan of relief and collapsed in the nest of blankets. Moments later, the blackness pulled me under.

When I opened my eyes, beams of sunlight were filtering through the holes in the roof and walls. "Hello, Cato," welcomed a pair of identical voices.

Cato. My name is Cato. I'd forgotten to say that before I fell asleep.

Finn and Reese were sitting nearby, watching me. Usually they were still sound asleep when we woke before dawn to train, so a greeting from the twins upon awakening was an unusual but pleasant surprise.

"Morning," I said groggily. I rubbed the sleep from my eyes, frowning. *Bloody Scout, I feel like I slept on a rock.*

My eyes flew open. I reached under the cloak and discovered the hard contours of an ectogun, which I drew and set between us. "Hey, question. What do you know about this?"

For a moment, they just stared at it. Finn leaned forward and picked up the weapon. "This is a prototype ectogun from Project Zeta. Where did you get it?"

"Doesn't matter. What do you know about Zeta?"

Finn handed the gun to his blood-brother, who took and inspected it. Reese answered, "Our research was constrained to Alpha."

"Don't give me that excuse. You knew everything that went on in that place. Zeta isn't even classified, is it?"

"No, it isn't," Reese confirmed.

Finn explained, "Project Zeta is focused on ectoplasm technology. Zeta produces cutting-edge ectoguns and other ghost-hunting equipment. The most recent project underway is sustainably converting ectoplasm into an energy source that can be a substitution for nonrenewable fuels."

I nodded slowly in thought. Ectoplasm technology. An image of the transparent green Dome surrounding City Hall surfaced in my mind.

"Madison Tarrow," I stated, then waited a moment to gauge their reactions. They seemed uncomfortable but unsurprised by the name.

I leaned forward. "Before you met me and learned about Phantom Heights, did the name Madison Tarrow mean anything to you?"

"Yes," they answered simultaneously.

Reese bowed his head while his twin traced the tattoo on his left arm with one finger. *2296*, Finn's read. Beneath that number was the Greek letter γ. He wasn't a numbered Gamma; only the permanent residents used for breeding were numbered. The children born in that place were branded with the symbol to indicate they had originated from Gamma, but they weren't identified as a resident of the Project unless they were circulated back into the breeding program.

Finn moistened his lips with the tip of his tongue, knowing that I was waiting. "Madison Ann Tarrow, hunter ID 0228, registered as an independent researcher since before we were born."

Reese held up the gun. "This was her design. The basic form, at least. This version has been modified from the prototype of the first ectogun she patented."

I frowned and reclaimed the weapon. "So, she works for *Them*," I deduced dryly.

"She did," Reese corrected. "Not anymore."

I stared at the gun in my hand. "What was Madison working on when she quit?"

"We don't know," Finn said with a little shrug. "Like we said, she was an independent researcher."

Reese explained, "She wasn't required to file regular reports since she wasn't an employee. There's no way of knowing what she was in the process of studying when she ceased disseminating her research."

I rubbed my temples. A headache was starting, although that wasn't surprising after the night I'd had.

"Is it possible Madison was also searching for the Origin?"

Finn and Reese looked at each other, eyes glowing as they shared an unspoken communication. I waited patiently for them to voice their thoughts.

"Maybe," Reese admitted.

Finn added, "We hadn't considered the possibility, but . . . it's plausible."

I felt sick. What if she was searching for the key needed to create the Weapon? If she found it, that would result in one of two scenarios—either she'd sell *Them* everything *They* needed to build It, or there would be a race to see who could patent It first.

"Cato," Reese said uneasily in response to my dark thoughts, "we don't know for sure if Mrs. Tarrow is involved with the Origin."

"But we don't know for sure that she isn't," I retorted. I held up her apprentice's ectogun. "How recent is this model?"

Finn swallowed. "Master Byrn was negotiating with investors from South Korea about the cost of developing a working prototype."

"So, Madison got this after we were gone," I summarized coldly.

I glowered at my distorted reflection in the sleek silver gun, then slammed the weapon on the ground in anger. I felt so stupid for letting myself and my lab-family be exploited by humankind. Again. The fall of Phantom Heights had cut off a valuable independent researcher from *Them*. We'd liberated the town and freed the ghost hunter to aid our enemies.

— Chapter Sixteen —

Gravestone

On Monday morning, Shannon Jennings took a deep breath and decided that LeahRae Harris High School smelled exactly the same as it had before.

Students milled about all around her, chatting and getting reacquainted with old friends, and yet, she felt completely isolated in the current of moving bodies.

It was too surreal to be real. Her shoulders felt too light without the weight of a backpack. Her hands felt empty without a pile of books. And her heart felt just as empty as she stared down the hall. It used to be so packed it was nearly unnavigable. Now, with only a fraction of its students left, LeahRae Harris High felt sick and weak, as if the flow of students had been the school's lifeblood and now it was in its death throes even as Phantom Heights took new breaths.

The warning bell rang, jarring her attention. Five minutes until the first class in over two years.

"Good morning, Ms. Jennings," came a pleasant voice.

Shannon forced a smile. "Morning, Principal Solwitz."

The woman inclined her head and continued her rounds, her high heels clacking with confidence and authority. Shannon had always been on good terms with the principal, especially during the last semester of school when she'd been involved with the student council.

She leaned her temple against the cool edge of her locker. It hadn't changed since the last time she'd opened it, and she found that rather depressing because she *had*. When her life had been normal, she'd covered the interior of her locker door with photographs of her family, her friends, and her cat, Jezebel, who had run away just a few weeks before the entoplasm shield enclosed City Hall.

Shannon scowled and slammed her locker shut. She spun away, only to collide with Trey, who caught her by the wrists as she stumbled backward and muttered an embarrassed apology.

"Don't worry about it," he assured with a crooked grin. "I wasn't watching where I was going."

Shannon scrutinized him. "Yikes. Rough night?"

"What?" he asked innocently, letting go and taking a step back.

"*What*? You look awful. And is that *makeup* on your forehead?"

"What? N-no."

"Uh-huh." Shannon's gaze fell to the ectoguns holstered at his waist. "I thought only teachers were authorized to carry weapons."

"I'm the apprentice to a ghost hunter," he said, a pointlessly stated well-known fact that somehow doubled as an explanation.

The pair glanced up at the ceiling when the second bell rang. Trey rubbed the back of his neck. "What's your first class?"

"English. You?"

"Algebra."

Shannon nodded, eyes downcast. "Don't wanna be late," she said, although she didn't move.

"Yep." Trey sighed. "See you around."

She strode toward the classroom at the end of the hall without a look back.

Trey procrastinated for a few extra seconds to watch her leave, and then he turned away. He didn't have the energy to lift his feet completely off the floor as he shuffled down the hallway. This was hell. He felt as if the school were full of ghosts—real ghosts—*moorlins*—including Cato's spirit.

A shoulder knocked into him and nearly sent him sprawling, but as Trey opened his mouth to apologize, a mocking voice snapped, "Watch it, loser."

Chase sneered at him as he passed. Anger boiled in Trey's chest. He clenched his fists and took a breath, but his mind drew a blank for a clever retort, and instead, he hung his head with a long sigh. Two years fighting side-by-side on the raid team, surviving together, past rivalries seemingly forgotten, and somehow, old habits were settling right back into place.

Trey glared at Chase's receding back. *Don't let him get to you*, he reminded himself. *He's just mad that I outranked him as a raider and I'm allowed to be armed at school while he isn't.*

He let out a long, steadying breath and continued his walk. *I bet he wouldn't mess with me if Cato were here.*

Actually, he might. Cato certainly hadn't been spared the myriad of bruises in the past, although circumstances might have been different now that everyone knew he and Phantom were one and the same. Trey couldn't count how many times Chase had pushed the two of them against walls, lockers, tables, chairs, whatever was in range when he passed, always a hard shove followed by, "Watch it, losers."

A few times, Cato had been enraged enough for his eyes to glow green, forcing Trey to intervene and pull his friend away before his secret was revealed.

That felt like a lifetime ago.

"Good morning, Mr. Selman," his teacher greeted warmly the moment he stepped through the doorway.

Trey managed to force a smile. "Morning, Ms. Tighe," he replied, painfully conscious that not only had he never walked in alone before, but he'd also never received that greeting from Ms. Tighe, either. In a past life, she would have said, "Good morning, you two," and he and Cato would have synchronized the answer he'd just given by himself. Coming from his mouth alone, the familiar greeting felt all wrong.

The feeling of solitariness was further accentuated when he sat down at his old desk and noticed the empty one beside him. Cato's seat wasn't the only vacant one; at least half were unoccupied. The final bell rang, and two stragglers dashed in, proclaiming breathlessly, "We're not late!" as the final note echoed in the hall.

Ms. Tighe shook her head and glanced at her attendance sheet.

"Alyssa and Nicole, I see you're starting the first day off with the same bad habits. I'll give you some leeway today, but please don't make me hand out detention slips already." The girls nodded but snickered as they took their seats.

Ms. Tighe shut the door, then turned and smiled at her class. "Glad to be back?"

She was answered with a chorus of groans. "I know," she sympathized. "I'll try to make the review sessions as quick and painless as possible. But we lost two years; we have a lot to cover in order to get you prepared. Unfortunately, we no longer have a complete set of classroom books, and I don't expect you to have school supplies, so most of the lessons will be oral and group participation. As long as you pay attention, we'll get through this together, all right? Let's do roll call, and then we'll get started. Bartow?"

No answer.

"Brayden?"

Empty desk.

Erika Davis was the first student to answer the roll call.

Trey set his cheek in his hand and stared out the window. The few agonizing seconds of silence in the wake of another missing student's name were unbearable. Devereaux—gone. Ehresman—gone. Fuller—gone. Gantt—"Here!"

Grayam, Gruenbacher, Idella, Kolbri—gone.

Kuhns—here. Ortega—here. Reed—gone. Rodriguez—gone.

So many names without answers. Names of victims who had died or fled, or gone missing, likely enslaved in the Ghost Realm. A body blocked Trey's view of the old maple tree, and he peered up into Ms. Tighe's thin face. "I guess I'm going to have to mark Trey Selman absent," she said.

"I didn't hear you call my name. Sorry."

She made a check on her paper and strolled down the aisle.

"Thomas?"

No answer.

"Todd?"

"Here."

"Wheeler?"

The dead silence in the wake of the final unanswered roll call was suffocating. Ms. Tighe set the clipboard down on her desk and perched on the corner. "Now that we have that out of the way, let's start with some review exercises to get your brains back into school mode."

Despite the teacher's call for attentiveness, Trey couldn't focus. His eyes constantly zeroed in on the clock as he counted the hours, minutes, seconds until the bell would ring. He traced random patterns on the desktop with his fingertip, only half listening to the lecture. More than once, his peripheral tricked him into believing Cato was there, but every time he turned his head, the ghost of his friend was gone.

Second-period US history with Mrs. Dermody, third-period English with Mr. Hartwick. When the bell finally freed him for lunch, he rushed to the cafeteria and scoped the crowd for Vivian. He lingered behind her for a few seconds to smooth his unruly blond locks before saying, "Hey."

"Hey," she echoed with a glance over her shoulder. They meandered to the line. "How was class?"

Trey shrugged. "You know," was his vague answer. "You?"

He seized a tray and scooped mac-n-cheese as the line advanced.

Vivian followed, but she'd brought her own lunch from home in a paper bag. "I can't focus," she admitted.

Right, he wasn't the only one seeing ghosts—moorlins, to be more precise—in the school. He shoved his hand into his empty pocket, then frantically patted his jeans. "Crap. I thought I had a five in my pocket."

"Here," Vivian offered, handing him a bill. "I got you today."

"Thanks. I owe you."

They strode through the cafeteria to the open doors on the other side. Although the cafeteria was full of tables and chairs, most students preferred to eat outside when the weather was nice. Trey and Vivian walked through the doors to be greeted by the shouts of a group of boys playing football on the open lawn beyond the big maple that shaded the tables. A mass of students was gathered nearby.

"What's going on?" Vivian asked.

Trey shrugged and answered, "Dunno." The two ventured closer. A memorial had been erected for all the students who had lost their lives or gone missing over the past two years. Flowers and candles and toys were arranged in the grass in front of the wall where photographs had been posted on a large bulletin board. The center of the display read, in great, looping letters:

Gone But Not Forgotten

A girl from Vivian's class touched her arm and said, "You should put a picture of your brother up there."

Vivian stared at all the faces, all the lives stolen. "He died before the invasion," she said in a numb monotone. "He was already honored. This is for the people who didn't have that chance." She touched her naked wrist.

Trey turned away, his cheeks warming with embarrassment that he had witnessed her brief spasm of pain. If only he'd been able to find her bracelet that night. Hopefully the surprise he'd planned for her after school would be a fitting consolation.

He politely yielded a step when a girl came forward and, silent tears cutting trails down her cheeks, pinned a photograph of her boyfriend among the others. She blew a kiss and backed away.

Trey caught a glimpse of Shannon standing in the crowd. As soon as their eyes met, she turned and walked away.

"Phantom wouldn't have let this happen," Trey mumbled.

"Phantom is gone," said Vivian, turning away.

"Gone but not forgotten," Trey said, following. Vivian said nothing as she selected a table and sat down. They ate their meals in silence.

Trey stole secret glances at her, wishing he had the Divinity of mind-reading. Her eyes had a glazed, vacant stare. She was lost in her thoughts, her thumb unconsciously stroking the blue vein on the soft, pale skin inside her wrist. Just as well; Trey didn't know what to talk about anyway.

He let his own attention wander across the yard, rather amazed that the same old cliques had reconvened. One lunch table was occupied by six skinny boys and one mousy girl crowded together around a single schoolbook in a desperate attempt to cram material before the first review exam. The football players wrestling in the grass had drawn in a group of girls who liked to giggle every time one of the boys glanced in their direction, resulting in more eyes watching the girls than the ball. A handful of teenagers dressed all in black were playing a card game in the shade of the maple. Trey snickered in amusement as he watched a couple of boys crawling on their hands and knees in the grass, searching for a lost wallet.

Slowly, the smirk faded. The normalcy of the scene was surreal . . . and all wrong. *I should be a senior now*, Trey found himself thinking. A lot of the kids eating lunch weren't really kids anymore. *Two years gone, and here we are as if nothing ever changed.*

"Aw, look! There's a kitten!"

Vivian's voice made him jolt. "Hmm?" Trey glanced at her, then followed her gaze to the black-and-white ball of fur near the dumpster. "Oh yeah, that's Casper."

"Casper?"

"Yeah, he's been hanging around here since school opened this morning, so he's been deemed our honorary mascot."

"But he's wearing a collar," Vivian observed. "He belongs to someone."

Trey shrugged. "Some guys tried to catch him, but he's too fast. If you wanna give it a shot, go for it. I wouldn't say no to some entertainment while I'm eating."

"Very funny. But seriously, somebody's probably missing him."

A group of girls walked their trays back to the cafeteria, tossing scraps on the ground near the dumpster as they strode past. Casper hesitated, staring intently at the food, then dashed forward and swallowed the morsels before retreating to the safety of the dumpster.

Vivian scowled in disapproval. "He'll never go home if people keep feeding him."

"So?"

"We should try to find his owner."

"Tons of animals were abandoned," Trey reasoned. "You can't return every stray."

"I know."

Trey bit into his burger. Mouth full, he said, "If you want to go on a quest to find Casper's owner, be my guest. But you'll never catch him. He's scared of people, and after the trauma of being chased by half the basketball team, he's not going to let you come near him." He tore some of the meat off the side and set it on his tray.

Vivian frowned. "What's wrong with that piece?"

"Nothing. It's for Casper."

"Trey!"

"What?"

"You're impossible."

He answered with another shrug. Vivian leaned forward, seized Trey's scraps in her fingers, and marched over to Casper, who was crouching beneath the dumpster. Trey swallowed and set his lunch down, then wiped his hands on his jeans as he stood and followed.

"Hey, Casper," Vivian was cooing when he approached. The kitten peered at her from the shadows, tail twitching. "Hi, kitty-kitty. Come here. I have some yummy food for you."

"Hypocrite," Trey joked, making her jump. "I told you he wouldn't come to you."

She scowled at him. "I'm trying to see the tag on his collar." She turned to the kitten again. "Come on, kitty-kitty. Come here. I won't hurt you." Casper pinned his ears and crawled backward, farther away from Vivian's reach. She sighed and leaned back on her heels.

A piece of paper caught Trey's eye when she shifted. Rather, it wasn't the paper itself so much as the black symbol printed on it.

"Hey," said Trey, pointing over her shoulder. "What's that?"

Her gaze followed his finger and settled on a crumpled piece of paper lying by the corner of the dumpster. A sane person would have been disgusted by the thought of touching garbage by the school dumpster, but the faded word *Alpha* must have evoked Vivian's curiosity too; she reached out and unfolded the wad. "Whoa," she whispered.

Trey knelt down beside her to read. "Wow," he echoed. "Should we show this to your mom?"

A girl's voice from behind said, "Hey."

Startled, Vivian and Trey both turned in sync. Vivian stood quickly and brushed off her jeans with one hand while shoving the flyer into her back pocket. Trey remained crouched on the balls of his feet for a few extra seconds. He took his time setting his hands on his knees and rising with a casual grin to ward off the impression of embarrassment.

Shannon and her best friend Amber were gazing at them with well-masked criticism. Amber held a clipboard in one hand, her nose wrinkled just enough to betray her repulsion.

Shannon was much better about concealing hers. "Cute cat, huh?" she said. "Reminds me of Jezebel."

"Yeah," said Vivian. Trey continued to battle Amber's blatant disgust with a careless smirk. She huffed through her nose but didn't say a word. If the girls were going to pretend they hadn't just caught Vivian and Trey crouching together by the school dumpster picking up trash, he wasn't going to contend.

Shannon tucked her hair behind her ear. "So listen, I'm organizing a group of volunteers to clean up Phantom's statue." Amber offered the clipboard.

"There are a lot of names," Vivian commented as she accepted the clipboard and scrawled her own.

"I know! We'll have his memorial cleaned up in no time," Shannon said, smiling as she reclaimed the clipboard. "What about you, Trey?"

His body immediately turned cold and clammy, his chest tightening as his stomach dropped. He reached up and scratched the back of his head. "Oh, um, I . . . I can't."

"Why?"

He scuffed his toe on the asphalt. "I can't . . . um . . . I can't look at Phantom." *Not in a crowd*, he thought silently. If he was going to visit the memorial, he wanted solitude.

Vivian looked just as puzzled by his reaction as Shannon. Amber said, "I don't understand what the issue is."

"Me either," Shannon agreed.

Trey's fingers twitched, ready to touch the weapons in his belt for security, but instead, he shoved his hands under his armpits. He barely recognized his own meek voice when he explained, "Agent Kovak told me . . . some of the things he did to Cato. I really do want to help, but I just . . . I just can't."

Vivian stared across the schoolyard, as if she'd completely tuned out the conversation, but Shannon's gaze bored into Trey while Amber shifted uncomfortably beside her. "What happened to Cato?" Shannon asked.

"Don't ask."

"I want to know."

"No, you don't."

"You can tell me, Trey. It's okay."

He backed away. "I'm sorry. I'm not ready to talk about it, and trust me, you're way better off not knowing." He turned his back and walked away. Vivian jogged after him, leaving the two girls behind.

The breeze changed direction, wafting the nauseatingly sweet and acrid scent of rotting garbage baking in the hot metal dumpster into Shannon's nostrils. Although Amber shifted, Shannon's feet remained planted.

"Hey." Amber touched her arm. "You okay?"

Shannon's gaze was fixed on Trey's back as he strode away from the clusters of students toward the grassy knoll behind the maple with Vivian tailing. She whispered, "Yeah."

"You sure?"

Shannon nodded. "Yeah. He's probably right; I'm better off not knowing."

"Forget about Trey. We've already got a long list."

Shannon didn't answer. The breeze swept a few loose hairs over her eyes, but she didn't tame them. "Hey. I have . . . sort of a profound question for you."

Amber clutched the clipboard to her chest and said, "Okay . . ."

"Have you ever wondered if the last words you ever told a person were meaningful?"

Shannon raised her head to meet Amber's puzzled stare.

"Where is this coming from all of a sudden?"

"I don't know. It's just . . . you know, thinking about all the people we've lost these past few years. I can't remember the last words I said to my little brother. He was here and then gone, and I don't think my last words were very important. I should have said something memorable."

Amber was silent. She stared at the clipboard, solemn, then lifted one hand and said absently, "Oh. My ring. Did I forget to put it on after I showered? Shoot, I hope I didn't lose it."

Shannon glanced at her, annoyed. Amber hadn't lost anyone. She couldn't understand. Vivian would, but Shannon wasn't going to confide in her. She did wonder, though, if Vivian had made her last words count. If she knew them by heart. Was it a mark of carelessness, to not remember the final sentiment uttered in one moment that seemed just as inconsequential as the next? How could anyone know a moment would be the last until it had already passed?

"C'mon, Shan. This garbage stinks. Let's go talk somewhere else."

Shannon watched Casper's tiny white paws bat playfully at a poor beetle trying to skitter past the dumpster. "Okay," she said with a sigh.

Amber fell into step beside her, fiddling uncomfortably with the clipboard. "You know, Shan . . . just because you don't remember your last words doesn't mean he didn't."

When the last bell rang, Vivian was the first student through the classroom door. She made her way straight to Trey's locker to find him donning a jacket.

He slammed the door shut and greeted, "Hey," as he turned. The two strode through the dispersing crowd of students.

As soon as they stepped outside, Trey grabbed her wrist and pulled her in a different direction.

"Our houses are that way," Vivian protested.

"I know," he replied, grinning broadly. "I want to show you something."

"What?" she asked, perking up a little as she followed Trey through the schoolyard. Casper was perched on top of the dumpster, staring at them, his tail twitching. Vivian glanced at him, considering another attempt to see his collar, but Trey was adamant about their detour.

"Where are we going?" she asked. They were heading for a section of town that was under construction.

"It's a surprise."

She rolled her eyes but allowed him to lead her forward. They journeyed several blocks away from the school and were passing behind Joe's Bar & Grill when she jerked her hand out of his grip.

Trey stopped short and turned around. "Viv, what's—"

"Shh," she whispered, cautiously taking a few steps in the direction from which they'd just come. Trey tiptoed after her, brow furrowing.

The two peered around the corner of the building. A figure cloaked in black was rifling through the contents of a large dumpster. A violet eye glinted in the shadow, but what caught Vivian's attention was the white symbol on the front of the shirt—α. Before Trey had a chance to stop her, Vivian walked boldly out of their hiding place and said, "Hi."

Immediately, the ghost straightened in surprise. Only his left eye was glowing, as if to counterbalance the missing sleeve that had been torn away from his right side. Vivian opened her mouth to speak, but the Alpha ghost took a nervous step back and then fled into the wall.

"No, wait!" she called in disappointment. "I just wanted to . . . never mind," she finished in a whisper. She walked to where the ghost had been standing and set her hand on the edge of the dumpster, then frowned and knelt down.

She turned toward Trey, holding up a backpack partially filled with an assortment of discarded food. "I don't believe it. They're eating garbage."

Trey exhaled and gently pulled the pack from Vivian's hand. He set it down at their feet and said patiently, "Viv, I sympathize with them. I really do. It sucks. But could you please forget about school and a stray cat and the Alpha ghosts for just a few minutes? What I have to show you is really important."

She met his eyes and saw the fiery excitement of whatever his surprise was. Vivian glanced down at the backpack and realized she couldn't do much to help if the Alpha ghosts didn't want any help in the first place. On a whim, she dug into her own backpack and pulled out a crumpled brown paper bag—the leftover half of her sandwich from lunch. She shoved the present into the backpack and leaned it against the dumpster. Trey steered her forward again.

They were on the edge of the outskirts now. Vivian gazed around with interest. The street they turned onto was still littered with broken glass and debris. Teams of volunteers were busy sweeping off the pavement and carrying paint cans and lumber into the buildings that were being repaired.

Trey pulled her into an empty alley and stopped, looking at her expectantly, his face cracking under the grin that he couldn't contain any longer.

Confused, Vivian stared between the buildings. Trey's "surprise" was nothing more than a tight alleyway strewn with piles of garbage. She looked at him and found him watching her, waiting for her to share in his thrill. She opened her mouth, shaking her head wordlessly.

"They found it yesterday during cleanup," Trey explained, nodding at an object lying at their feet.

Vivian gazed down. Her eyes grew wide. She knelt to one knee, gently pulling away a piece of tarp. "It's . . . the gravestone," she whispered.

"Well, what's left of it," Trey corrected, appropriately solemn now.

True enough, a large chunk was missing from the top left corner, and the bottom half had broken away. A long diagonal crack split the remaining piece, which was scratched, scuffed, and chipped. Vivian reached out and traced her fingers along the etched words:

JAXON TARROW

She softly read aloud, "A beloved friend, son . . ."

Her throat clenched. She skimmed the debris for the bottom pieces, but they were absent.

". . . brother, and hero. He will never be forgotten," she finished from memory. "Did anyone find the missing pieces?"

"Not yet."

Vivian latched her fingers along the jagged edge and hauled the stone from the debris. She wrapped her arms around it and strained, heaving it up as she staggered to her feet. "Whoa, careful, Viv! That's really heavy."

"I know," she said through gritted teeth. Her arms were already trembling under the weight, but she was determined to carry it home. The challenge and pain actually made her feel better; it allowed her to redirect her grief into something productive.

Trey fell into step beside her, ready to reach out and help if needed. Vivian said between pants, "He deserves . . . a gravestone that's . . . intact . . . and . . . I'll get him . . . a new one . . . but . . . I want to . . . keep . . . this one."

"Okay, but you could leave it here and come back with a wheelbarrow or something. You don't have to carry it all the way home. Jeez, you're going to throw your back out."

Sweat was trickling down Vivian's face, and they were only just now emerging from the mouth of the alley. It was going to be a long trek home. She stubbornly locked her jaw and continued forward. Trey, realizing that she couldn't be swayed and she needed to concentrate on placing one foot in front of the other, fell silent. The gravestone had been mutilated already; she wasn't going to leave it lying in that alley like a piece of garbage. He stayed by her side, but she would still bear the burden alone.

She always bore her burdens alone.

— Chapter Seventeen —

S - O - S

There was something I liked about the church.

It was big but empty, quiet and calm, the soft light filtered through colored windows and a sense of peace slowly unwinding the tension in my muscles the longer I lingered in its illusion of safety.

Finn and Reese were sitting at the altar. I'd been having a staring contest with the bronze sculpture of a man mounted on a cross above them for several minutes. Time seemed to slow down in this place.

My lab-brothers looked up the instant Ero, Jay, and Axel appeared out of thin air in the main aisle. I broke my gaze, forfeiting the stare-down.

Axel was accustomed to Blinking with Jay, and he was unfazed as he strode toward me and leapt onto the back of the wooden pew, where he perched on all fours. He pushed his hood back and shook his ink-black hair out of his eyes.

Ero, on the other hand, swayed and seized the back of the nearest pew for support. "That will still take some getting used to," he murmured, but he managed to flash me a weak smile.

"At least you didn't puke," Axel muttered with a sidelong glance at Ero.

The drawn look on the Telepath's face made me wonder if vomiting wasn't outside the realm of possibility quite yet. "Good to see you again, Cato."

I inclined my head in silent acknowledgment as Ero turned to his students. "And the two of you, of course. I heard you are feeling well this morning."

They nodded. "Excellent," their teacher said as he straightened, his gaze lingering on the beautiful stained-glass windows and the light casting rainbow patterns on the floor.

Ero took a few unsteady steps and plopped down on the lowest tier of the altar. Although his voice was soft, every word carried clearly across the vast church. "Ah, how beautiful. We do not build such magnificent structures in Avilésor anymore. If anything like this ever existed, it has fallen into ruin. This seems like a wonderful place for meditation and solitude."

Jay strode down the aisle without a word. Axel and I exchanged looks, then followed the leader to the last row where we sat down in the pew to give the teacher and his students some privacy. Ero's low voice was still audible, but I couldn't decipher the words now.

Axel was watching Ero with narrowed eyes. I glanced at him and noticed the telltale way the corners of his mouth turned down. "What's up?" I muttered under my breath.

"That's eight lessons he's had with Finn and Reese now."

"So?" I whispered, careful not to speak loudly enough for the Telepath to hear me across the vast room. *Like it even matters. He's probably reading our minds.*

"*So,*" Axel said, "he said he came here to teach them, but his 'lessons' haven't taught them a damn thing. All he does is talk to them. And not even about their powers. He's still talking about this stupid church. What does that have to do with training them to master mind-reading? Makes you wonder what his real agenda is if he isn't teaching them anything useful."

I nodded slowly. During the last lesson, Ero had brought a thick science textbook that was so advanced I didn't even know what it was about because I couldn't understand the title. He'd handed it to Finn and said, "I would like to time how long it takes you to read this entire book." Just under five minutes later, they'd finished, and Ero had taken the book away and asked, "Can you tell me the content of chapter nineteen?"

Whatever he saw in their minds must have impressed him, and his questions became more and more specific. "Can you tell me the third sentence of the fifth paragraph on page 449? What was the 151st word on page 83?"

After a few more technical questions to verify that they had indeed memorized the entire textbook and could recite it verbatim if requested, Ero had ended the lesson. Although I didn't know the content of the book, I knew it had nothing to do with mind-reading or telepathy. Axel was right; Ero didn't seem to be teaching the twins anything about their Divinity.

"I know," Jay said. "But Finn and Reese seem to enjoy the lessons. I've never seen them connect with any Outsider like this before."

"Yeah, that's what worries me. Ero's getting too close to them."

Jay rubbed his chin. "You think he's working for Azar?"

"I don't know," Axel admitted.

"What does your gut tell you?"

Axel considered for a long moment. "No, I don't think he is, and I haven't caught him reporting to Wes, either. But something doesn't add up."

I asked, "What do you think we should do, Jay? Confront Ero?"

"It's a delicate situation, considering Ero's Divinity."

Axel growled quietly. I demanded, "So what, then? We let Ero do whatever he wants because he's more powerful than us?"

"Not me," Axel said before Jay could respond. "Ero might be able to read my mind and know what I'm going to do, but he isn't fast enough to stop me. I can take him."

"Just wait," Jay said sternly. "Nobody's 'taking' anybody. Not yet, anyway." He watched the Telepath gesture to the stained-glass windows, our lab-brothers staring at him intently. "Let's talk to Finn and Reese first."

"Fine," Axel grumbled.

Hiding secret intentions from Mind-Readers and Telepaths was no easy task. When the lesson ended, I did my best to blank my mind as Ero bid us farewell, but as soon as we approached our lab-brothers, they frowned and asked, "What's wrong?"

Jay quickly shushed them, glancing back at the sound of the great doors closing. He whispered, "Can Ero still hear our thoughts?"

"We don't know," Reese said.

Finn added, "We can't read his mind."

Axel exhaled through his nose and gave Jay his *I-told-you-so* look, which the leader disregarded by shifting so his back was to Axel and he was directly facing the twins. He said, "I need you to answer this truthfully, okay? It's very important. Has Ero asked you any questions about that place?"

Their frowns deepened in puzzlement at the question, and they shook their heads. Axel scoffed. "That doesn't mean anything; he could be digging around in their heads, and they don't even know it."

"He hasn't," Reese insisted.

"You just admitted he won't let you into his mind. Maybe you already told him everything, and then he wiped your memory."

Finn countered, "But you've been watching every lesson."

"He could have wiped my memory clean, too."

I muttered, "Okay, my head is going to start hurting if we think like that."

Jay said, "Agreed. And if Ero were fishing for information and already took everything he wanted to know by force, there'd be no reason for him to stay and continue the ruse. For now, we'll give him the benefit of the doubt. But he still has questions to answer."

The twins' eyes glowed as they glanced at Jay, Axel, and me in turn.

"Jay," said Reese, "we like Ero. Please don't harm him."

We stared at them in surprise. "You *like* Ero?" I repeated.

They nodded enthusiastically. "Yes," Finn said. "He's intelligent."

"And kind," Reese added.

"And we can have conversations without breaking the Rules."

Jay asked, "But he's never let you into his mind? Not once?"

They hesitated. Reese said, "He always keeps his thoughts shielded from us."

Jay nodded slowly. Finn asked, "You really think Ero is violating our minds and stealing classified information?"

"Yes," said Axel.

"*No*," Jay disputed, shooting a quick glare at the half-breed. "We don't know for sure. But it's a possibility we have to consider."

Finn and Reese always knew what a person was thinking. Deceiving them was usually impossible, so the idea that Ero might be manipulating them and gently harvesting one secret at a time had them anxiously biting their fingernails.

That night at Home when we voiced these concerns to the rest of the family, RC didn't say a word, but his brow knit in concern while Ash quietly admitted that our fears were very real possibilities, although she also pointed out that we had no proof. If Ero wasn't actually training Finn and Reese, then what did he want from them? One way or another, we needed to find out. We couldn't let this potential risk to our family go ignored.

Just before sunrise, Jay, RC, Axel, Ash, and I gathered in the street in front of Wes's mansion. "Okay," Jay muttered, his focus trained on the house, "we have to be fast if we want to catch Ero off guard. After we Blink, you'll have to get your bearings immediately."

We nodded. All there was to do now was wait. Jay and RC rubbed their gloved hands together in the chilly dawn. I squatted low, eyes trained on Saros Manor on the other side of the wrought-iron fence and manicured lawn. My breath escaped in clouds, and after a while, I turned my gaze downward to my wrist gauntlets, where I absentmindedly froze the abundant moisture in the air into tiny jewels of ice. The frozen drops spread in a crystalline lattice, reinforcing my battle armor.

Axel announced, "Ero's up."

I rose with a glance upward at the lightening sky. He was up, no doubt, to see the sunrise with Chelvistin, which we'd anticipated. Ash drew her staff. We waited a few more minutes for the Telepath to dress. Axel whispered, "Now."

I seized Ash's wrist, already reaching for my center. She and RC grabbed Jay, and then there was wind and darkness and a crushing pressure. We were standing in a hallway. I had seconds to take in my surroundings and focus on the man with glowing blue eyes in front of me. Ero, as if expecting us, seemed completely unfazed that Ash, Jay, RC, Axel, and I had him surrounded.

He glanced at the three silver disks with blades whirring near his neck and casually requested, "I would be grateful if you would please move those away. They are a bit too close for comfort."

We tensed, expecting him to use his telepathy on us, but nothing happened. The lethal blades hovered in place, testing our opponent. Ero's vivid blue eyes studied each of us in turn until RC, by his own free will, finally directed his disks away from Ero, although they still hovered nearby. "Thank you," the Telepath said as he flashed a warm smile. "May I say, good morning to you all."

Axel stepped forward and seized the front of Ero's cloak in his fists, then pulled him down to eye level, their faces mere inches apart. "I don't know what you're doing, but I don't like it."

"There is no need for the violence," Ero said, impressively calm considering he was staring into the red eyes of the strongest, fastest, most powerful, and possibly most short-tempered ghost in the Realms. "You already have my undivided attention."

Axel reluctantly released Ero, but he was still growling under his breath. I tightened my grip on my ice daggers but remained stationary, watching Jay for our next move.

The leader glared at Ero. "You told us you came here to instruct Finn and Reese. But you haven't. You haven't done a single thing to teach them how to control their powers."

Ero smoothened his cloak, which had been wrinkled in Axel's grasp. "I see. Ambushing me was unnecessary if that was all that was on your mind."

"We don't trust you," Axel snarled.

Ero frowned but nodded. "How unfortunate. May I ask what I have done to cause you to lose faith in me?"

"We need to talk," Jay said coldly.

"As I said, I am listening."

Jay held up a silver band. "Prove it. Will you talk to us with your powers neutralized so you can't interfere with telepathy?"

Ero eyed the neutralizer in Jay's palm with wary distaste. He sighed and answered, "If that is what it will take for you to trust me, then yes." Jay seized Ero's wrist, slipped the neutralizer over his fingers, and yanked it up Ero's arm to his biceps. He grasped it in both hands and twisted in opposite directions, then released and took a step back.

Ero's vivid blue eyes dimmed until he looked like a human dressed in outlandish clothes. The Telepath craned his neck to study the metal band. He touched it and murmured, "This is an unpleasant sensation. I have never felt so empty before."

I demanded, "If you aren't teaching the twins, then are you here to spy on us? Who are you reporting to?"

"Not a soul," Ero assured me, still completely calm. "You have my word."

I pressed, "Not Azar?"

Ero chuckled, as if I'd told an amusing joke. "No."

Jay's eyes narrowed. "Then explain yourself."

Ero eyed the lethal disks still hovering near RC's head, the icicles clenched in my hands, and the metal staff in Ash's grip before he answered, "I am here to instruct Finn and Reese. The problem, as I have mentioned before, is that their particular case is an isolated and unprecedented incident, and I cannot proceed in my usual fashion. We have not begun their actual training because it is important for me to understand how their minds and their Divinities work before I begin. My instruction must be tailored to the student, as every student learns differently. The real training can be . . . intimate. We will be working within each other's minds. Needless to say, I have to establish a strong sense of trust before attempting that, and I do not believe your lab-brothers are ready for that step yet. Please be patient and give me time; Finn and Reese are in good hands, and I *will* teach them. But I am afraid of rushing into their training without fully understanding how their Divinities evolved first."

"Then why keep your mind sealed so Finn and Reese can't hear your thoughts?" Jay demanded.

Ero blinked in surprise. "Do I?" He laughed. "My apologies. Force of habit; I do not even realize that I have my barriers raised."

We all looked to Axel, whose expression didn't change as he continued to glower at Ero. Only when Jay cleared his throat did the half-breed grudgingly admit, "He told us the truth."

Jay said nothing. He gave us no signal, cue, or command. His only movement was the relaxation of his stiff posture, and immediately, we all let the tension drain from our bodies. RC pocketed his weapons, Ash sheathed hers across her back, and I melted mine.

Ero rubbed his chin, his attention on RC and Ash. "Not the best circumstances to meet," he acknowledged, but he held out his hand nonetheless. "You are the Telekinetic, I presume?"

"I am," my lab-brother replied, cautiously grabbing Ero's forearm in a traditional Ghost Realm greeting I was unaccustomed to.

Ash stepped forward and introduced herself next. Ero clasped her forearm too, although I knew Ash had never honored that custom in her life.

"A beautiful name," Ero praised. "Fitting of your Divinity."

"Thanks," she mumbled, looking away with a rather bitter expression.

I reached into my pouch and removed the clamp, then passed it to Jay, who stepped forward to fit it over the neutralizer on Ero's arm. Jay flipped the latch, triggering the red light, and then he slid the latch downward. "Sorry about that," he said as Ero's eyes rekindled to their glowing sapphire splendor. "I hope you understand why we had to take the precaution."

"I do. And I hope this will strengthen our relationship." He smiled at us, but it was forced, as if his skin had suddenly become stiff and he could stretch it only so far. I was suddenly attuned to how drawn he was, how stress lines were carving a map of worry on his features.

When the smile broke, he looked even wearier, especially when he leaned against the doorframe. "I must say, in light of the current circumstances, I did not expect you to turn your aggressions on me. In fact, I had hoped you would see me as an ally."

I wasn't sure what to make of his comment. Everybody—Jay, RC, Ash, even Axel—looked just as confused as I felt. Jay asked, "Why?"

Ero studied us for several long seconds. "Ah. So, you do not know."

A feeling of foreboding was slithering inside me and condensing into a pit in my stomach. Axel demanded, "Know what?"

Ero paused, deliberating his words, and I wished he wouldn't. If something was wrong, I wanted him to just come out and say it without wasting time being delicate.

"You are aware the humans have held several town meetings lately? And city council has been convening regularly?"

"So?" Axel said. "What of it?"

"The topic of their discussion is a new law concerning kálos. They are calling it the Shoot-On-Sight doctrine, or S-O-S. If this law passes, the patrol in town square will be replaced with a firing squad that has rifles and ectoguns trained on the Rip at all times. Should anyone or anything enter this Realm, these officers will open fire at the first sign of movement. No dialogue. No negotiations."

"S-O-S," I whispered, horrified at the thought of the bloody massacres about to be committed in town square.

"The hell?" Axel exclaimed. "They can't do that!"

"Hmm," was Ero's solemn response. Ghosts had no rights in this Realm, as if anyone had to tell Axel that.

Jay was quiet when he said, "What about you? What if you took a trip into the Ghost Realm and then came back?"

"No exceptions. The few seconds wasted to identify a traveler would be an opportunity for an enemy to attack. The squad would open fire without hesitation."

"But what about Wes?"

"No exceptions," Ero said again, his voice heavy. "I know you do not trust me, but we find ourselves in a similar dilemma. I fear this anti-kálos campaign is just beginning, and it will raise tensions in Avilésor, too. No doubt Azar would view this as an act of war and use the aggression to rally people to his cause. A full invasion would likely not be far behind."

I shook my head, so flushed with anger at humankind that the hot green power awakened and rose to the surface. At times like this, I didn't want to associate myself with them at all. Ero continued quietly, "It is interesting, in a way. The two races focus so closely on the differences between each other that they overlook some striking similarities. War is in our nature, as it is in theirs. I do not mean to pry, but I did wonder . . . if war breaks out, have you considered your course of action?"

That was a good question. I hadn't, but Jay always planned ahead for everything. I turned to him, curious to hear his answer. Yet to my surprise, he admitted, "I haven't given it much thought."

Ero nodded. "Understandable that you do not wish to ponder such dark contemplations. But you do realize that sooner or later, you will have to make a decision."

"What will *you* do, Ero?"

"My decision will be tied to yours if I am to continue working with Finn and Reese."

Jay nodded, but the motion was jerky. He looked rather ill.

"Ero," I said, my voice strained, "when will S-O-S be passed?"

He scratched his neck. "The doctrine was officially announced last night. Wes was quite worked up about it. This afternoon, there will be a public debate to gauge the community's support, and if enough people approve S-O-S, it will be passed almost immediately. You should know that Wes is fighting it, though."

Good for Wes. I'd never thought very highly of the werewolf, but at least he was trying to stop this.

Jay asked, "Are you taking any action?"

"Me? No. No, as much as I have to say on the matter, it is not my place, and I fear the human community would be affronted if I were to speak against their laws."

"I don't get you, Ero," said Axel. "You're a Telepath. You could walk into City Hall and change the council's minds."

"I caution you, my friend," the teacher warned sternly. "That mind-set is the root cause for the friction between humans and kálos."

"So," Jay said, "there's nothing we can do, then? Just sit here and wait for humans to pass S-O-S into law and start slaughtering?" The leader's unusually melancholy voice reeked of defeat.

All Ero had to say was, "I suppose we shall see what happens to-day."

Jay took a step back. "We've bothered Ero too long."

Ero forced another smile. "You are never a bother, I assure you. Please feel free to stop by any time. But knock first, and I will gladly invite you in. No need to break down my door."

I felt the color rise in my cheeks as I backed away, flushed in the heat of humiliation. I succumbed to Jay's darkness, the compression, the wind, and then we were Home again. The sun was rising; it was too late in the day now to train.

But when Ash and I were running through the morning dew on patrol, my stomach was still sick, and it wasn't a residual aftereffect from Blinking across town. Shoot-On-Sight. Humankind was making an offensive move, and there was a good chance it would spark the war.

And we might be caught in the crossfire.

— Chapter Eighteen —
Silent Vote

Vivian was running late.

She was trying to tie her shoe, dig the keys out of her purse, close the front door, and not drop the sandwich clenched between her teeth. Of all those tasks, the only one she managed to accomplish was closing the door before someone bore down on her. "Tarrow!"

Vivian jumped with a stifled yelp, tripped on her shoelace, dropped her purse as she fell, and landed hard enough on her butt to open her mouth with a quiet cry, losing her sandwich to the front porch. Bewildered, she looked up to see Shannon Jennings standing in front of her, legs braced apart, hands on her hips, forehead etched into a deep scowl.

"What the hell, Shannon?" Vivian snapped as she snatched her purse and continued to rifle through it for her house keys. "Were you just waiting to jump me, or what?"

"Not *you*. Your mom. Where is she?"

"Downtown, I guess. I don't know. Why?"

"Damn it."

"What do you want with my mom?" Vivian asked, finally digging her keys free and locking the front door. She turned back around to find Shannon holding a stack of papers.

"This is a petition against S-O-S. I already have four hundred signatures."

"Four hundred? How did you get so many already?"

"There are a lot of people against this."

"So am I," retorted Vivian, defensive about the insinuating tone.

"Prove it."

"Fine. I'll sign your petition." She snatched the papers. "But it's not going to change anything."

"It's better than doing nothing." As soon as Vivian finished looping the W, Shannon reclaimed the stack. "This'll open city council's eyes," she stated. "Maybe enough to outvote my mom."

The whole town had congregated in front of City Hall for the debate. There was a buzz in the air somewhat akin to the energy Axel expelled, except this was caused by hundreds of excited, jittery bodies all talking at once. S-O-S had stirred Phantom Heights like a hornet's nest.

I sprinted across the asphalt, keeping to the alleyways to avoid groups of latecomers making their way to town square. The debate had already started. Speakers had been set up all around the square, and now Madison's voice boomed, "Good afternoon, everyone."

Her voice spurred extra energy in me, making me run faster. Her words echoed around me from all sides: "Today, we're here to discuss city council's Shoot-On-Sight proposal. I don't have to emphasize how important this debate is for the future of Phantom Heights. We're going to keep this civilized. Police officers will escort anyone causing a disturbance off the premises. Here's how it's going to work—I am here to argue in favor of the new doctrine that will give our officers the authority to use immediate lethal force against ghosts who enter our Realm through the Rip. Speaking against S-O-S is Wesly Cooper."

I rounded the corner and shivered as I paused in the middle of the street. "Where?" I called.

"Here," came Axel's cool reply.

I found him half a block ahead, standing with his arms folded while he leaned against the exterior wall of an office building. A black-and-white kitten was sitting on the doorstep.

This was the Fruth building. M.G. Fruth had been some important benefactor back when Phantom Heights was at the peak of development, and he was responsible for more than half of the office buildings downtown, including this one. Why I knew that, I couldn't say, and I was frankly annoyed that of all the priceless memories I had forgotten, somehow this trivial piece of knowledge had stuck with me.

"As I said," Madison's voice thundered, "this exchange will remain civil. City council wants to gauge the community's support. So, if you don't agree with S-O-S, stand on the west side of the plaza before Mr. Cooper. If you believe in this defense plan, stand on the east side before me. You are welcome to switch sides at any time if we address an issue that changes your mind. When this debate is over, hopefully we'll have a clear indication of where the community stands."

I trotted over to them. "Top floor," Axel said.

Kit, tail erect in perfect poise, trotted inside the building to lead the way. I strode past Axel, who stood like a sentry and didn't move. Even in the dark entryway, with the walls muffling Madison's amplified voice, I could hear the ghost hunter's words: "We survived together. We will continue to survive together, and that means we must make decisions together. This demonstration is to show you that city council is listening, and your opinions influence the direction our town takes."

Kit led me to a stairwell and scampered up. I sighed and tipped my head back. The Fruth building, with five flights of stairs to climb, was one of the tallest buildings in Phantom Heights.

Above me, Kit poked her head through the rails. Her long black hair fell down over her shoulder. "What're you waiting for, Cato? Let's go!"

"Yeah, I'm coming."

Kit pinned her ears with a devilish smile. "I'll race you."

"A race, huh?" I took my time walking up the first few steps, trailing my hand along the railing. "I don't know . . ." With a grin, I took off. Kit squealed in delight and pulled her head back through the rails as she turned to smoke and resumed her fur. The black-and-white kitten streaked up the stairs.

I chuckled and slowed my pace. Kit was way too fast for me to even hope of winning. I lost sight of her almost immediately and was left to jog up at my own speed.

At the top, she was waiting for me in her skin. "I win!" she sang as I walked to her. I shivered, sensing my lab-family nearby.

"I never had a chance." I patted her on the top of the head as I entered the room. Finn and Reese were sitting in front of the window with ECANI while Ash, RC, and Jay lingered nearby. Kit skipped in after me.

I walked to the window and peered out. The office overlooked town square directly below us. Something big hit the glass with the softness of a feather, blocking my view. I yelped and stumbled back. RC cursed under his breath, and Ash set her hand over her heart. I fixed Axel with a resentful glare as he became intangible and then leapt through the window and landed soundlessly on his feet.

"Did you jump from the ground?" I asked, stepping forward again to peer down at the cobblestones five stories below.

"Focus," snapped Jay. "What happens down there will affect us." He set both hands flat against the windowsill and gazed down at town square. "This is a tipping point. If it tips the wrong way, we're looking at war."

He was right. Until now, I thought *They* were the ones inflaming the conflict while the humans of Phantom Heights were victims caught in the middle. But if S-O-S passed, the aggression would invoke retaliation. Tensions were going to explode if this debate went the wrong way, although Ash raised a good point: "The war will happen eventually, whether this passes or not."

Jay muttered, "Later is better than sooner."

I stood beside him and peered down on the minuscule figures in town square. Wes was already arguing, "This new doctrine assumes that every single creature coming into this Realm is our enemy, and that isn't true. Some come here in peace seeking asylum from the violence in their Realm. How can we even be considering S-O-S when we have a small kálos community living here in Phantom Heights?"

Madison's scoff crackled in the speakers. "I'd hardly call Ero and the Alpha ghosts an entire community."

"S-O-S is an overreaction."

Madison paused to sip at a water bottle before replying, "The ghost community still sees us as cowards hiding inside City Hall. They think we're weak. We have to prove that we're strong enough to hold them back ourselves without the assistance of ghosts. We have to prove that we *humans* can stand our ground on our own."

"But you're proposing a firing squad! We should *regulate* passage through the Rip, not blindly open fire. Ghosts aren't the only creatures in that Realm. Are you going to gun down a human slave trying to escape? And besides, if we have trigger-happy cops shooting at glowing eyes, there's going to be an accident when one of the Alpha ghosts gets caught in the middle."

"The *Alpha ghosts*"—she spat out the words as if they had a bad taste—"are luring us into a false sense of security. What happens when this deal fails? We have no plan of protection in place. We need to be able to defend ourselves without them."

"Come on, Maddie. You know S-O-S is good only for small numbers of ghosts caught unaware. What you are proposing is an offensive strike. You know what that warrants? A military response from the Ghost Realm, which is exactly what Agent Kovak is afraid of. What are you planning to do when an army comes through the Rip? We're signing our death warrants."

I felt one eyebrow rise. *We? He's using the plural loosely; I bet Wes will be long gone the second Azar's troops storm in.*

Despite the initial call for civility, a group of people in the crowd started making a ruckus. Fed by the noise, Wes raised his voice above it and called, "The Ghost Realm won't see this as an act of defense! They will interpret it as a call for war!"

Wes was a strong orator. Now he just had to convince enough humans to believe him. Couldn't they see the consequences of initiating a lethal assault against ghostkind? But my fear was much more personal. What would happen when we defeated an opponent and Jay Blinked the ghost to the Rip to be returned to its home Realm? If they appeared out of thin air, Jay would be greeted by a barrage of bullets. Shot on sight, no exceptions.

I turned my head to look at him. He hadn't moved since the debate began. Even now when he spoke, only his lips moved: "I can't stand here and let humans dictate our lives like they always do."

"It's more serious than that, Jay," I said. "They're trying to phase us out."

"I don't think—"

"Cato's right," Axel interrupted.

Stunned by his proclamation, we all gawked at him. He actually agreed with me for once? Axel glowered at each of us in turn and said, "What? He's right. They hired us when they had nothing to lose. Now, they think they don't need us anymore, and they'll sell us out to the highest bidder."

Jay needed only a brief moment to consider. "Let's do something about it."

"Like what?" I snapped. "Even Ero's keeping out of this. Besides, it's not like we can change anything."

"That's the problem," Jay said, his silver eyes flaring. "I'm sick of being helpless at the mercy of humankind. I want to vote, whether it makes a difference or not, but if we want to be heard, we can't make a sound. Got it?"

No. Too ashamed to admit that I had no idea what he was talking about, I glanced at my other lab-siblings to see if I was the only one. Apparently not; they all looked completely lost. Axel grumbled, "What the hell kind of dumbass riddle is that?"

Jay held up one finger and said, "Language," then a second finger. "And it's not a riddle. There are rules set in place. Madison and Wes are the only ones allowed to speak. We have to follow those rules, which means the debate must be done by Wes. All we can do is vote. But at least that's something. Are you with me?"

Ash, RC, and I exchanged uneasy looks, but our lack of refusal must have equated to *yes* in Jay's eyes because he nodded and held out his hand. "Kit, Finn, Reese, stay here inside Proto. Anybody else who wants to vote, come with me."

RC gripped Jay's cloak. Axel shrugged and stepped forward, wordlessly granting Jay permission to set his hand on Axel's shoulder. Ash seized RC's arm and extended her other hand out to me. "Cato?" she asked.

I stared at her open, waiting hand. The idea was both thrilling and terrifying. Voting . . . would we even be taken seriously? We were ghosts. In this world, that didn't amount to much. But standing before all of Phantom Heights . . . that was a terror ripped right out of my nightmares. Lastday all over again.

But this time, I wouldn't be alone. Axel, Jay, RC, Ash, they'd all be right there beside me. Against my better judgment, I drew a breath and took Ash's hand.

Jay warned, "No matter what happens, you'll have to keep a constant flow of power so your eyes are both blue. Can you do that?"

I nodded. Jay's silver eyes flared bright, and a surge of panic made me balk. I tried to let go of Ash, but it was too late; I was falling in darkness, collapsing under the pressure, and then my feet were on the ground.

I couldn't sense humans, and yet I felt the presence of a crowd—or at least, my mind was convinced that I did. Already forgetting Jay's advice about my eyes, I opened one, then, surprised, I opened the other. We weren't in town square. We were inside City Hall.

Jay stood before us, grim and determined. He fixed the mask over his face and waited for us to do the same. "If we're in danger, grab me, and I'll Blink us away." We nodded. Ash was looking a bit off-color now; I wasn't the only one second guessing this ploy.

Jay faced the window. "Eyes, Cato," he reminded me. I reached inside for my center and let the cold fill me. Inside my fist, ice solidified. Jay didn't look back, but he glimpsed my reflection in the window and nodded in satisfaction. "You too, Ax. Don't let anyone see that your eyes are red."

"Don't worry," Axel said, which didn't actually appease my concern in the slightest.

Jay was gone.

I rushed to the window. He had appeared in the center of the portico behind Wes and Madison.

Wes, completely oblivious, continued his rant: "We don't protect the borders of our country with a line of soldiers and machine guns mowing down refugees indiscriminately. We have customs. We allow people to enter with passports. What we need . . .''

He trailed off at the crowd's stirring. People whispered in puzzled surprise, stunned, excited, bewildered, and fearful at the sight of our leader's debut appearance. That, and I was sure they could sense Axel's aura nearby—that curious pulse of energy that created natural tension in the air. The uniformed police officers drew their guns, all aimed at Jay, and I caught my breath, afraid they were going to enforce S-O-S already. He may be fast, but I didn't think he was fast enough to race bullets.

Jay stood perfectly still. If he was alarmed by the weapons trained on him, he didn't show it. The debaters, after observing the peculiar behavior of the crowd, finally turned. Madison gasped—I could actually hear the intake of her breath through the glass and over the murmurs of the crowd—and rested her hand on a gun holstered at her waist. But she didn't draw it. Wes just gawked open-mouthed at Jay.

The initial noise from the crowd died. They must have thought Jay was going to make a speech. He surveyed them coolly, only his bright silver eyes visible through the gap between the mask and hood. Without a word, he took a step toward Wes. The guns followed him, along with hundreds of eyes. My lab-brother solemnly walked behind Wes, past him a short distance to make his position clear, then halted. He put his hands behind his back and stood militantly.

Axel—I hadn't even noticed him leave us—appeared next to him, head down, hood so low over his head that only his chin was visible. RC stepped through the wall to join them.

I couldn't swallow, couldn't breathe. *There are so many people out there.*

Ash took my hand. I was thinking too fast, moving in slow motion; I let her pull me after her. We became intangible. I closed my eyes as the wall swallowed us in darkness.

Light fell on my face. I tightened my grip on her hand and clenched my other tighter around the ice, which I focused on morphing. Only then did I open my blue eyes.

Wes was closest to us, but he hadn't moved. He'd found the sense to close his mouth, and now his lips were pressed together into a confident smirk. Behind him, the crowd stirred again. Whispers made the air hiss. One man gave us the most disdainful look and took a few steps toward the east side of the plaza—toward Madison's side. A few more followed.

Maybe we had made a mistake. Maybe the people of Phantom Heights truly despised us, and by rejecting S-O-S, we were encouraging them to vote in favor of the proposal.

Then, a miracle happened—a massive wave of movement shifted most of the east crowd to the west. Madison turned to watch in dismay as her followers changed sides.

Our appearance lasted a minute at most, and Jay had already Blinked us back to the office in the Fruth building. We were all fighting grins. For the first time ever, humans had listened to our opinions.

And we hadn't said a word.

— Chapter Nineteen —

Speak

Finn and Reese had a lesson.

I'd expected their teacher to hold an understandable grudge, and yet he was as merry as ever, not a single mention of our confrontation. With Wes out of the mansion, we had come to Saros Manor for the lesson.

Axel sulked out in the hallway; Jay and I stood guard by the door. Finn and Reese were sitting cross-legged on the floor of Ero's bedroom while their teacher sat perched on the edge of his bed, waving his hands through the air as he told a story, the twins' spellbound blue eyes following the movements as if hypnotized. Reese tried to stifle a cough to avoid interrupting.

I left to find the kitchen and fetch water for them, and when I returned with three empty glasses stacked in one hand, I was surprised to discover Jay in the hallway lingering by the half-open door. "Hey," I greeted, but he hurriedly shushed me.

Confused, I leaned closer to hear him whisper, "They're talking."

My eyes widened in disbelief. I peered around the doorframe to discover the impossible—Finn and Reese speaking in low voices with Ero. And not only were they talking aloud, but they were in the middle of an animated discussion. They seemed perfectly at ease, as if Ero were an old friend. I pulled my head back to look at Jay. "When?" I whispered.

"Just a few minutes ago. Ero's been great with them."

I glanced at Axel, who was leaning against the wall with his arms crossed over his chest and the hood thrown low over his head. "So," I said quietly, "Ero's earned their trust." Axel raised his head enough to peer at me from the shadow of his hood, but he didn't speak.

"Looks that way." Jay peeked through the doorway again to watch.

"Ax?" I asked, seeking his opinion.

He grunted and muttered, "Ero will always be an Outsider."

"Yes," Jay whispered without turning around. "But he's proven himself to be an ally."

Axel's response was a soft growl as he dipped his head so his gleaming crimson eyes were hidden beneath the hood again. He wasn't happy, but because he didn't argue, I took his silence to be reluctant agreement. I scratched my head, craning my neck to watch Ero laugh at something Reese said. Even if I didn't trust Ero, I should trust Finn and Reese. Being privileged enough to hear their voices was a rare honor, a gift they didn't share with just anyone. "Okay," I concurred.

An hour passed, then two, and still never a lull in the conversation. I'd never seen the twins so talkative. I lingered in the doorway with Jay, listening to a story Ero was telling that had our lab-brothers entranced. Curious, I stepped forward and said, "What are you talking about?"

Ero paused, smiled, and beckoned me closer. I separated the glasses I had brought from the kitchen and summoned my Divinity, freezing water from the air and melting it into the containers. Finn and Reese both seized a glass and drank deeply.

Ero took a polite sip and explained to me, "The Senses. Five of them, to be exact, and they are one of the oldest legends in Avilésor. Olf, Opti, Audi, Tacti, and Gusta. What they are exactly, no one knows. Not kálos, not human. Perhaps fay, or at least partially. Supposedly, these creatures live deep in the Razorback Mountains. They are identical sisters, and if the fable is true, they have been around for thousands of years. But here is what makes them interesting—each sister has use of only one sense. All are blind except Opti. All are deaf except Audi. Olf can smell; Gusta can taste; Tacti can feel. All can perceive pain, hunger, exhaustion, et cetera. Now, what I find fascinating is that the sisters have some sort of telepathic connection. The other four can see what Opti sees, hear what Audi hears, et cetera. They perceive their environment through the senses of their sisters."

"Are they Telepaths?"

Finn and Reese glared at me for interrupting, although Ero didn't seem to mind. "Unlikely. There is never any mention of mind-reading in the stories. But my fascination is that this tale, whether it is true or not, describes a condition similar to what your lab-brothers have. Finn and Reese share thoughts, dreams, opinions, memories, and knowledge, and the women in this fable share senses."

Jay had wandered closer to listen while Axel remained stubbornly posted outside in the hall. I pondered Ero's tale for a moment, then asked, "Are the Five Senses real?"

"Ah, nobody knows. Perhaps, perhaps not. If they do exist, they do not wish to be found. But does that mean they are not real?" Ero took another sip of water before continuing, "People tell stories of the sisters roaming Avilésor in search of naughty children from whom the Five will steal a sense. That part of their story is undoubtedly a fable. I am simply intrigued by the connection between the sisters. I will admit, I always doubted such a link, but after meeting Finn and Reese . . . well, now I wonder if the Senses do exist after all."

Ero consulted his pocket watch before he closed his notebook and rose. "I have enjoyed this lesson very much, but we have talked the afternoon away. Jay, I have dinner plans with Wes tonight but otherwise am free at any time if you should need to call on me. Tomorrow is a clear schedule, so I will be ready at your convenience."

"Right." Normally Jay would say a quick goodbye and Blink the twins Home, but he hesitated. "Ero, uh . . . I'm not sure we ever properly thanked you for sacrificing so much to train Finn and Reese."

Ero paused, noticing the deviation from routine. "I assure you, the pleasure is mine. I would hardly consider this a sacrifice; it is my life's work."

"Right," Jay said again. He shifted his weight, still postponing our departure.

Ero inquired, "Is something wrong?"

Jay looked up at the ceiling and shook his head. We'd never extended our trust beyond the lab-family before. "You mentioned dinner plans later. Are you busy . . . now?"

Axel was braced in the doorway, and his unblinking red eyes hadn't left Ero for a second. He didn't say a word, just glared menacingly at him, silently warning him that he still wasn't one of us. Ero paid no heed to the hybrid's hostile looks. He smiled kindly at Jay and said, "Did you have something in mind?"

"You know damn well we got something in mind," Axel grumbled.

Jay didn't even correct his language this time. He took a deep breath and blurted, "Ero, we'd like to show you our Home."

That was all he said. He didn't mention that the twins' decision to speak had granted access into our inner circle or that Ero had finally, officially earned our trust. He didn't have to. The gesture of taking Ero to Home said all that and more.

Ero must have realized the significance of the invitation. His features softened, his eyes bright with excitement but his voice humble as he said, "I would be most honored."

Jay nodded, looking rather relieved. Finn and Reese clasped hands; Reese seized mine while Finn grabbed Jay's. Ero smiled and fitted his hand into Jay's other. The world collapsed to black wind, and then we were Home, this time with our first Outsider since Vivian.

Ero turned a slow circle, observing the garbage pushed into the corners, the industrial drums of rainwater situated beneath the holes in the ceiling, the dirty, wadded-up nest of blankets where we slept, the holes in the wall that RC had crudely patched with boards and nails. I studied him as he studied our home, noticing how the corners of his mouth turned down in disapproval. "This is where you live?"

"Yes," Jay answered.

Ero shook his head in pity. "I am not surprised Finn and Reese became so ill."

Axel growled and muttered, "Not everyone is privileged enough to live in a mansion."

"But you were not planning on living here during the winter, were you?"

Jay ignored the question and asked, "Would you like to meet Kit?"

Realizing the faith we were placing in him, Ero smiled cordially. "I would love to."

Axel warned, "If you betray this trust, I will hunt you down no matter what Realm you're in."

The Telepath assured, "There is no danger of that, and I would not dream of testing your threat, Axel. I know when I am outmatched."

Ero's gaze shifted to the black-and-white kitten sitting in the doorway. Kit changed to smoke and stood up in her skin as a little girl with long black hair, golden eyes, and silky cat ears that flitted back and forth nervously.

We watched Ero warily, ready to step between him and Kit.

He smiled and knelt down to Kit's level. "Hello there," he said warmly, extending his hand. "It is a pleasure to meet you."

Kit's ears swiveled forward, and she shyly approached and placed her small hand in Ero's large one, ears falling again as they shook hands. I relaxed. Ero was a teacher; he knew how to speak to kids and make them comfortable in his presence. His eyes were glowing again, and I knew he was reading Kit's mind as well as all of ours, adjusting his recourse appropriately to ensure everyone remained at ease.

Kit retracted her hand. The Telepath said, "My, you are adorable. Will you tell me your name?"

He knew her name, of course, but he wanted to give her the chance to introduce herself. To my surprise, timid little Kit did answer, her voice soft as silk. "What a pretty name," Ero said in approval.

Kit grinned and gazed down at her dirty bare feet in embarrassment. She asked, "Are you going to teach Finn and Reese how to be Telepaths?"

"I am."

She looked up again and tilted her head to the side, scrutinizing Ero. "How old are you?"

"Three hundred and twelve years."

"That's really old."

He chuckled. "To someone with your years, I suppose it must seem so. But I still feel quite young."

My lab-sister giggled back and announced, "You're nice. I like you."

"I am very glad," Ero said with a smile.

Kit beamed at him, then skipped over to Jay and leapt into his arms. "Is Ero gonna live with us?"

"No," Jay answered, sweeping a loose strand of hair out of her eyes. "He'll just visit sometimes to teach Finn and Reese." At the mention of the twins, I glanced at them to see that they were studying their teacher with their heads tilted down so they could avert their eyes if Ero caught them watching.

I suggested, "Hey, why don't you guys show Ero ECANI?"

Immediately, they jerked their heads up. "Really?" Reese said.

"We can?" Finn asked. They looked to Jay for permission.

Jay replied, "It's your invention. You can show it to whoever you want."

The boys turned as one and asked Ero in unison, "Would you like to see it?"

"Absolutely."

Jittery with excitement, Finn rushed to ECANI while Reese reached for Ero. He hesitated, then did the unimaginable; he seized the edge of Ero's cloak and peered up eagerly at his teacher. The Telepath allowed his student to lead him over to Finn, who was already tugging on the gloves.

I crossed my arms and leaned against the wall, watching Finn and Reese explain their incredible computer to Ero while flipping through holograms. Although Ero continued to nod, I had a feeling he was completely lost while they went on about the various codes and sequences that formed the core of the ECANI's Matrix and the complex design of Proto, which was now on model thirteen-dash-something.

Ero humored them and occasionally asked a thoughtful follow-up question, which they gleefully answered. I couldn't help but smile.

— Chapter Twenty —
Defining Humanity

Vivian traced the jagged edge of the gravestone with the tips of her fingers.

She silently vowed that she wouldn't stop searching until she had every piece back. The mutilation made her sick, as if her brother himself had been attacked instead of just the stone marking where his remains were laid to rest. At least this piece was safe with her now.

Vivian's world had fallen apart years ago. Now, it seemed as if the rest of the world was collapsing, too. Ghosts in cages, ghosts dead in the streets, riddled with bullets from a firing squad . . .

It all sickened her. What did humanity even mean anymore? To have pure human blood flowing through one's veins? Didn't it used to mean something more than that?

Vivian pulled her hand back and cradled it over her heart. Phantom had been living proof that humanity didn't have to be based on blood type or birth race. She'd always thought his mixed blood could have been the Realms' salvation. If only he'd had time to grow up to be the hero he was meant to be, he could have been the guardian of the Rip, a link to bridge the races. The Alpha ghosts were doing a good job, but a hero couldn't be replaced by mercenaries.

A quiet knock made her jump. Trey was leaning against her doorframe. "Hey."

"Hey yourself."

An awkward silence expanded the void between them. "So," Trey finally said. "S-O-S failed."

"You weren't in favor of it, were you?"

He scratched his head. "No, but I haven't told your mom. I guess it doesn't matter now."

Vivian's forehead wrinkled. She turned back to the gravestone. "I wonder what the outcome would have been if the Alpha ghosts hadn't shown up."

"The Alpha ghosts." Trey's serious tone pulled her attention back to him. "That's actually the reason I wanted to talk to you. I, uh, I've been doing a lot of thinking lately and . . . I haven't told anyone this, okay?"

"Okay," she echoed uncertainly.

Trey's eyes rolled up toward the ceiling so he wouldn't have to meet hers. "I've been having trouble sleeping. I saw some things at the AGC that really bothered me." Trey's next words were strained. "Agent Kovak told me some of the things he did to . . . him—to Cato. Kovak was trying to test me. Viv, he . . ."

She felt the blood drain from her face. How vividly she still remembered the day the Agents had taken Cato away. The clouds moving in from the west, the way the Agents had shoved and yanked Cato around as if he were a criminal, the mass confusion written on every person's face in town square, the cold horror that had frozen Vivian's feet to the cobblestones as she locked eyes with Cato's concussed blank stare, the look of terror on his face when he was thrown unceremoniously into the back of the truck . . .

"Cato's gone," Trey said.

Those words, even if they were true, stabbed Vivian hard enough to make her physically wince. She could hear the sound of that truck door closing with fatal finality again.

He continued, "We have to start looking ahead, not back. S-O-S was supposed to ensure we aren't completely defenseless again if the Alpha ghosts stop doing their job. Since it didn't pass, that leaves one more option I can see."

Vivian scowled at Trey. "Why are you telling *me* this instead of my mom?"

He held up a piece of folded paper. "This was in the hall just outside your door. It must have fallen out of your pocket."

Her frown deepening, Vivian stood, marched over, and snatched the paper. Upon unfolding it, she discovered the wanted flyer they'd found under the dumpster. Trey lowered his voice in excitement. "We don't need S-O-S as long as they're here, and the best way to make sure they stay is to form a real alliance with them. When the Agents took Cato, I—I felt so helpless, you know? I felt like I was just a kid, and this was an adult problem, and there was nothing I could do. In some ways, I still feel like that. But we're not as helpless anymore, Viv. We couldn't help Cato then, but we can help the Alpha ghosts now, and maybe that's a start. They were tortured, and they lived in these tiny cages where there wasn't even enough room to lie down or change positions. I can't blame them for hating humans after what happened to them. But after all that, they gave us our lives back. We wouldn't be here without them."

Vivian was speechless. She needed a few moments to gather her thoughts before she could say, "I had no idea you felt that way." She folded the paper and slipped it back into her pocket. "Everyone is afraid of them. Don't get me wrong, Trey—I want to help them, too. It's just that . . . well, I don't want to cause any more tension between me and Mom."

"But Viv, don't you realize how important this is? I know we'll probably make Madison mad at first, but eventually she'll understand."

Although Vivian nodded, her stomach twisted with dread. "I need some time to think."

His face fell. "I thought you'd be with me."

Vivian directed her vacant stare toward the gravestone on the floor. "I'm not against you. I agree with everything you've said. But . . ."

Trey turned away. "I shouldn't have said anything. Forget it."

"No, wait!" He paused. "I haven't been sleeping so well, either. It's only fair that I tell you what's been going through my mind ever since they kidnapped me."

She turned away and wandered back into her room. Trey followed, silent and slow in her wake, letting her collect her thoughts. "I feel . . ." She trailed off, overcome by the heat of a blush. Vivian reached for a framed photograph sitting on her dresser. "It's stupid, probably. But I feel like I'm connected to them now. I can't explain it, but I feel like it's no accident I was taken."

"It wasn't an accident," Trey calmly reminded her. "They took you to target your mom."

"But I think our paths crossed for a reason," she insisted. "I know this might sound far-fetched, and maybe it is, but think about it. Does it seem like an accident that the same people chasing these ghosts are the ones responsible for my brother's death, and of all the towns for the Alpha ghosts to come to, they came here to Phantom Heights, and of all the people to kidnap, they chose *me*? When they kidnapped me, they made me a part of something. I feel like we're connected now in a way they don't even know." When she caught Trey scratching his head dubiously, she challenged, "You think I'm a lunatic."

"No," he said quickly. "It's just . . . I don't know, Viv. I think it's a coincidence, and you're drawing a personal connection that isn't really there. The Alpha ghosts have nothing to do with anything that happened before when—"

Before he could finish and crush the tether her wild desperation had cast to the fugitives, Vivian shoved the frame into his gut, evoking a grunt. Trey claimed it and held it up, his expression softening. The little boy in the photograph had his thumb stuck in his mouth and gazed out of the frame with wide eyes, and the girl, her hair braided with a pink ribbon, clutched a teddy bear, her eyes squeezed shut as she bared her teeth—the front two missing—at the camera.

"Kovak killed him," Vivian stated. Her voice was a cold knife.

Trey stared at the young faces behind the glass. He shook his head and set the frame back down on the dresser. "He didn't *kill* him."

"He didn't save him, so he might as well have," she shot back without missing a beat. She seized the framed photograph again and gazed at it. "I refuse to accept the garbage that Kovak forced down everyone's throats. It's complete bullshit. *That*—" Vivian jabbed her finger at the broken gravestone in the corner "—didn't have to happen."

Trey wandered forward until he was kneeling in front of the stone.

"So . . . what, you think helping the Alpha ghosts will avenge his death?"

Vivian blinked. "I don't know about *avenge*. But the enemy of my enemy must be my friend, right?" She cradled the frame to her breast. "Okay."

He twisted around to look at her. "Okay what?"

Resolved, she bobbed her head in a slow nod. "I want to help you."

— Chapter Twenty-One —
Slave's Confession

The reverberations of a bell tolled through Phantom Heights.

I turned to look at the spire of City Hall's clock tower above the trees of the park. "Three chimes," Ash counted.

"I'll wait for you by the lake," I promised.

Ash nodded and sheathed her staff before she took off at a steady run toward Home. I watched her billowing cloak and dark-red hair until she disappeared behind a cluster of tree trunks, and then I strolled along the shore before discovering a mulched path that meandered into the woods. The canopy cast dappled shadows shifting on the ground. Birds twittered, and a gentle summer breeze stirred the leaves. I wondered if I'd come here Before as often as I did now. Had I realized how beautiful Nature was back then, or had I failed to learn that lesson until I was locked in a cage for so long?

My gaze followed a cardinal flitting from branch to branch, its vibrant ruby feathers a stunning contrast to the dark foliage. Below the tulip tree where it was perched, two women were sitting together on a park bench.

I froze for an instant, panicked, before whirling and pressing my back to the nearest tree where I dug my fingernails into the bark, working a piece free and letting it fall before fretfully prying off another. What were my mother and blood-sister doing here, *now* of all times?

I closed my eyes and strained to hear them. Just barely, I could discern the faint sounds of their voices, but no clear words. I squeezed my eyes tighter and pretended that they didn't hate me, that we still loved each other, that I was still part of their family. Their soft voices were familiar echoes of childhood, sounds that evoked comfort and longing and sadness and fear and anger and betrayal all at once.

I considered the consequences of using my power to become invisible and move closer, but the thought of approaching them terrified me. Instead, I craned my neck to peer around the thick trunk while keeping my back pressed against the rough bark. They were too far away for me to gather the minuscule details, but from this distance, they looked just as they did in my photograph, if maybe a little older and a little wearier.

My blood-sister leaned forward to embrace our mother, who held her close in a genuine, protective hug. She still had love for her human child. I had to turn away. I closed my eyes again, but that image was imprinted on the backs of my eyelids, burned there forever, and I couldn't escape. I was empty, cold, so cold that frost was crystallizing on the bark behind me. I shuddered and exhaled a frosty cloud, trying to compose myself.

I needed no further proof that they'd moved on with their lives. I'd been forgotten.

This realization caused a pain in my heart deeper than any syringe or scalpel had ever penetrated. *That* pain eventually went away. This pain would never be soothed. It drilled deeper and deeper the longer I stayed here in my hometown, and yet, something bound me here.

I couldn't leave; I loathed staying. I was like a moorlin trapped in limbo, unable to move on, unable to let go, living an existence of eternal pain.

All thoughts of drawing nearer to them were banished. I had nothing left to do but run away.

I was always running away.

I turned invisible and took off. This was not a controlled, long-distance pace; this was a mad sprint, a desperate attempt to escape from the pain. Perhaps if I pushed myself hard enough, I could outrun it. Perhaps the burn in my muscles would overpower the ache in my chest.

The green power was awake and clawing at my lungs. I raced faster, determined to keep sprinting at full speed until I had no breath left to scream.

Every time I closed my eyes, even in the fraction of a second it took to blink, I saw them embracing, holding on as if each was a life-line to the other, because that was what family was supposed to be.

***

Vivian kicked at the dead leaves as she walked along the mulch path that wound through the woods. Every time she closed her eyes, she saw the broken gravestone, a persistent afterimage that wouldn't fade. Madison still didn't know she had it in her room. Vivian couldn't convince her mom to step foot in Heroes' Hollow; no way Madison would be able to handle seeing the actual gravestone.

Vivian stopped at the edge of the clearing. Her grip on the bouquet of wildflowers tightened until she felt stems break. A woman and a girl were standing by Phantom's statue.

The woman turned at the sound of Vivian's footsteps halting in the leaves. She left her daughter's side to approach and extend her hand. "Hello, Vivian," she greeted.

Still startled by the surprise company when she had anticipated solitude, Vivian wordlessly shook the woman's hand. Holly Jennings had a tight grip; tight enough to hurt. "I've been seeing your mother a lot lately. You're doing well, I hope?"

Vivian nodded. She subtly clenched and unclenched her fingers behind her back to regain feeling.

Shannon turned away from Phantom. "Hi," she greeted solemnly. Her eyes found the flowers in Vivian's hand. "Oh." She respectfully looked down at the white stone nestled in the grass. "I'm sorry about the grave." Shannon patted her pockets, then withdrew a small object. "Here." She set it on her thumb and flicked it up at Vivian, who caught it one-handed. When Vivian uncurled her fingers, a penny gleamed in her palm.

Shannon shrugged with an apologetic smile. "I, uh, I never seem to have a flower on hand."

Vivian inclined her head. "Thanks."

Holly kept her gaze averted; she wouldn't look either of them in the eye. Her blouse was perfect, her skirt pressed without a wrinkle, her eyes pinched and her lips small, as if her face was used to being scrunched into a scowl, or just cinched from her hair being twisted into a tight bun all day.

Shannon faced Phantom again. "Just came by to see what needs to be done. We have a lot of work to do, huh?"

"Yeah," Vivian agreed without much emotion. She made a point to look Holly in the eye when she inquired, "Will you be participating in the volunteer effort too, Mrs. Jennings?"

Holly didn't answer at first, waiting a few seconds to maintain a measured but civilized stare-down. "No, unfortunately not," she said, voice level. "I have a previous engagement I can't reschedule."

Vivian's gaze dropped under Holly's unwavering cold stare. She and Trey had talked for more than an hour, and she had adamantly disagreed when he wanted to involve a third person with his plan.

"Shannon can help us," he'd insisted.

"We don't need her."

"C'mon, Viv, what's with you two? Why do you hate her so much?"

"I don't *hate* her."

"Look, even if we can convince your mom, that's not enough. We need city council's backing, and Shannon can make that happen. If we get Mrs. Jennings on our side, we've practically got the whole council."

"That's never going to happen."

"We have to try," Trey had stated passionately. "I think Shannon will help us."

Vivian sighed. Trey was convinced that Shannon would be sympathetic to the Alpha ghosts. Problem was, even if Shannon got involved, Vivian couldn't see any possible way to sway Councilwoman Jennings.

Vivian took a deep breath, seized Shannon's wrist, and marched forward, cheerily announcing, "Let's take a closer look."

Shannon instinctively yanked her hand free. Mrs. Jennings was watching. Vivian forced a smile and gave Shannon a meaningful look, reaching slower for her hand one more time.

Picking up on the message, Shannon let Vivian tow her toward the statue, but she eyed her guide skeptically. "Okay, what's gotten into you?" she muttered as soon as they were out of her mom's earshot.

They stopped in front of Phantom. Vivian tilted her head and pretended to study the graffiti. "Trey wants to help the Alpha ghosts," she said, barely moving her lips.

"What's that got to do with me?"

Vivian's jaw clenched with irritation, and she had to unlock it before she could whisper back, "I just want to know your position. Where do you stand when it comes to them?"

Shannon had to think for a moment. She kept up the act by pointing at a dent in Phantom's arm. "Not sure," she admitted. "They're no replacement, but . . . I don't know. We wouldn't be here without them."

"We need them," Vivian stated, watching Shannon's reaction.

Shannon took a few moments before she reluctantly said, "Yes."

"Does your mom agree?"

Shannon shot Vivian a frigid look from the corner of her eye, bearing a rather frightening resemblance to her mother in that instant. "Does *yours*?"

Vivian gestured toward Phantom as if indicating an area that needed extra work. "The Alpha ghosts are living in the ruins and surviving off garbage. It isn't right. Trey and I are going to try and convince Mom and Wes to make a real alliance with them. Any chance you can do the same with your mom?"

Shannon wandered forward, careful to step over the white stone, and touched the plaque on the base of the statue. *Phantom: A Fallen Hero.* "Cato had human blood in him," she said, as if Vivian weren't aware of that fact. "And see what happened? How am I supposed to convince Mom to endorse pureblood ghosts?"

"You're smart," Vivian answered. Even she could hear the haughtiness in her own voice. "I'm sure you can think of something."

Without turning around to look at her, Shannon replied, "And what makes you think *I* want to endorse them?"

"Cato."

Shannon bowed her head. She wasn't the only one capable of manipulating people; Vivian knew how to utilize words to strike a blow too, although she loathed drawing that connection between herself and Shannon Jennings.

Shannon glanced over her shoulder at Vivian, then farther back to her mom, who was waiting at a well-established distance from the statue. "Are you ready yet?" Holly called impatiently.

"I'll see what I can do," Shannon whispered as she passed Vivian.

"Thank you."

"I'm not doing it for you. I'm doing it for Cato. I don't want to see history repeat itself."

Vivian turned in time to see Shannon smile broadly at her mom and announce, "I'm starving, Mom. Let's go. See you around, Vivian."

Holly seized a picnic basket lying near the threshold of another path leading into the woods. "Tell Madison I said hi," she said. Vivian remained frozen in place, watching their backs recede. Shannon didn't even look over her shoulder.

Vivian waited until the trees hid them from view and she was alone in the clearing with Phantom, who made her feel as if she wasn't really alone after all.

She sighed and turned to face him again. Her footsteps were quiet in the grass as she approached him with the bouquet in both hands. She stopped just in front of the statue and knelt in the soft earth, bowing her head as she set the harvested wildflowers next to the white stone.

"Hey," she whispered. "I haven't been to see you in a while. I'm sorry. I miss you so much, you know. Mom does, too. I almost got her to come with me this time, but she couldn't do it. Someday, I promise she'll come to visit."

Vivian stared at her hands cupped in her lap. "You know, I think about this a lot, and I know Mom does too . . . why didn't you come back as a ghost? A real ghost, I mean—a moorlin. Just for a few seconds. Just for one last goodbye. I guess I don't really know how it all works. Maybe you couldn't. Maybe you did, and we just couldn't hear you, and if that's the case, I'm sorry."

No answer, of course. The trees rustled around her, and the breeze felt cooler here in the shade. Vivian sighed and hung her head. Voices from memories rushed back to her like waves that crested and fell, washing cold, empty pain into the void and then retreating, dousing her with bits of memories seeping in one at a time.

"How could you let this happen?" her mom cried.

Kovak's sympathetic voice: "Maddie, I understand how upset you must be. Believe me, this was a terrible accident . . . I tried to save him . . . I'm truly very sorry for your loss . . ."

A brief image, a snapshot of a memory too painful to replay in its entirety. *Madison leaning over a white sheet that had been pulled back just enough to reveal the dark hair and deathly pale face of a teenager. Agent Kovak standing nearby, watching with his emotionless eyes as the grief-stricken mother sobbed. Her hand beneath the boy's head, her fingers entwined in his hair, her forehead pressed against his . . . her tears falling on his cold skin . . .*

Vivian swallowed and leaned back on her heels. "I want you to know that I've decided I'm going to help the fugitives of the man who let you die. I don't know if it will bring you any peace, but I think it'll bring some to me."

Run. Faster, farther, run.

I wanted to sprint as far away from my blood-family as possible, but I was at the edge of the park when I remembered that Ash was expecting me to be there waiting for her.

I slid to a stop, only my chest moving as my lungs heaved. *I have to stay,* I realized in horror. Even though my blood-family was in the park.

Pain. It struck as suddenly as lightning on a clear day. I gasped and fell to my knees, twisting my fingers in my hair as I pressed the heels of my palms to my temples before I collapsed the rest of the way into the grass. I tried to silence the screams by clenching my teeth together, but I couldn't stop the muffled groans from rising into wails. I was vaguely aware that I was on my side now, my knees drawn up as my muscles automatically tensed in response to the agony. I screamed, wishing it would stop. Who was there to beg? God? Would He make it end? I had prayed to Him in the beginning, but my prayers had long since run dry, so I suffered alone.

Why did it always hit me so quickly but take forever to recede?

The pain transformed from unbearable agony, to a sharp stabbing that pulsed with my racing heartbeat, to a deep, dull pounding that lessened with each throb until it was a tolerable headache. I shuddered, my skin clammy after the episode. Still gasping, I rolled onto my back and dragged my fingertips down my face. I lay still for a few minutes to watch the clouds drift above me and let the final remnants of the Spasm dissipate before I sat up.

My headache was faint but still present. I inhaled and then exhaled deeply, rubbing the round ports across my forehead.

Remembering that my mother and blood-sister were still somewhere in the vicinity, I scrambled to my feet and looked around. I must have run far enough away for my screams to go unnoticed by my blood-family, because I was alone.

I spun in a circle to gain my bearings. Ash was supposed to rendezvous with me at the lake. As I returned to the water, I was alert to my surroundings with a superior hyper-sense bordering on an anxiety attack. A squirrel scampering in the leaves sent my heart into my throat. I tried to stand still, but I was too restless, and I took to pacing along the water's edge, my eyes darting with paranoia. What if my blood-family came this way? I wasn't able to sense them like I could ghosts. My ears strained for the sound of their voices or footsteps.

Finally, I couldn't take it anymore. I climbed a tree with natural agility until I was high enough to feel safe. I leaned against the tree trunk and stared moodily across the lake, trying to tame my runaway heart and steady my breathing. My mind replayed that image of my mother and blood-sister embracing each other. Over and over and over again. Eyes open or eyes closed, I saw them.

I exhaled and leaned my head against the bark to gaze up at the canopy overhead. A shiver racked my body as a sudden chill slid along my spine. I peered down below. A girl walking on the path paused and looked around as if she'd sensed me, too. Relieved for welcome company, I climbed down to the lowest branch and leapt to the ground. Ash didn't flinch when I landed nearby.

"Any trouble?" she asked.

Trouble? I swallowed and cleared my throat. "Um . . . n-not really, no. I didn't come across any ghosts. How are Finn and Reese?"

"Fine. They were asleep when I first got there, and I was going to leave, but they woke up and were hungry, so I stayed with them while they ate."

I nodded, still distracted as we started walking around the perimeter of the lake. Ash casually stretched her arms above her head. "So, where should we head now? Park seems pretty quiet, so maybe we should go back into town. What do you think—outskirts, or second circle?" she asked.

"Yeah, sure."

"That's not an answer." Ash frowned. "You okay?"

"Fine."

She narrowed her eyes suspiciously. "Are you sure there wasn't any trouble while I was gone?"

I didn't respond at first. But her anticipatory gaze was starting to make me squirm, so I admitted, "My blood-family was in the park."

Ash digested the news with a stoic expression. "Did they see you?"

"Of course not," I snapped. I hung my head. "And I wish I hadn't seen them."

"Maybe they were going to visit your statue. Maybe they miss you."

Although she'd tried to placate me, her suggestion only made me hot with anger potent enough to awaken the green power again. "If they missed me, then they would have come to visit *me* instead of a stupid metal replica. All that time at that place, and not one visit. Ever."

Ash gazed out across the water and stopped in her tracks. I paused and glanced back to find her squinting at the opposite shore. "Hey, Cato . . . is that . . . ?"

She trailed off.

I followed her gaze, and my heart stuttered out of rhythm.

Two women were sitting on a blanket with a basket between them. They were too far away for me to identify them with absolute certainty, and I hadn't been paying any attention to what they were wearing, but both women were slender with dark hair. I had no doubt who they were.

"Let's go," I whispered urgently, afraid my voice might carry all the way across the water if I spoke at a normal volume.

Ash didn't move; she seemed to be fascinated by the pair on the other side of the lake. "Ash, come on." I seized her wrist and gently but firmly pulled her with me.

There was a lake between us. I didn't know why I was so frightened, but I was jittery now, on the brink of a panic attack. Ash was with me. I had to protect her and the rest of my lab-family from my blood-family.

No matter what, I couldn't let my two families cross.

The rough blanket made Shannon's bare legs itch.

She shifted, watching her mom arrange paper plates, napkins, cups, a pitcher of iced tea, a carton of strawberries, and bagged sandwiches. Holly was particular in her methods, and Shannon knew it was best to sit still and let her mom organize the picnic before they could both relax and enjoy it.

But Shannon's mind was spinning after the encounter with Vivian. What a jolt, standing in front of Phantom and realizing that his legacy had been passed on to a group of mercenaries who had escaped from the same place that consumed Cato. She didn't want to believe he'd been replaced. What had ultimately made Shannon agree with Vivian was a combination of suspicion and curiosity. Her mom had been acting strangely ever since Agent Kovak came to Phantom Heights seeking help, and Shannon wholeheartedly believed that Finn and Reese might be the only people who could pick apart the lies and expose the truth.

Shannon kept her head down while she watched her mom open the plastic carton of strawberries. It was in a daughter's nature to want to trust her mom and believe every word she said.

But Shannon wasn't naïve. She'd grown up surrounded by political masks, and she had learned to don them herself and see through others'. Her mom was hiding something, and Agent Kovak, as skilled as he was in the art of manipulation, hadn't been able to hide the fear in his eyes. If Shannon wanted to uncover the truth, the Alpha ghosts were her best bet, and the best way to ensure an opportunity with them was to make sure they had an incentive to stay here, at least for a little longer.

Her mom, finally satisfied with the layout of the picnic, seized the pitcher and poured iced tea into red plastic cups. "It's been a long time since we did this, huh?" she said merrily.

Shannon closed her eyes in a pained grimace. The last time they'd had a picnic, three places had been set. "Yeah. I suppose we have the Alpha ghosts to thank for making this possible again."

Her mom went stiff. Maybe Shannon shouldn't have broached the topic so early, but her mind was on one track now. She casually accepted the iced tea from her mom's frozen hand and took half a sandwich. Holly blinked to regain her composure and selected a strawberry. "Oh, I don't know. I think Tarrow and her apprentice get some of the credit, too. Not to mention the efforts of the police and the volunteer raid team. And, I suppose, Mr. Cooper."

Shannon sipped at her iced tea. Her mom didn't want to give ghosts credit. She barely wanted to credit a werewolf. "You know we'd still be in City Hall if it weren't for the Alpha ghosts."

Holly bit into the strawberry and sucked out the juices before they could dribble down her chin. "Perhaps. Who's to say what might have been?"

Shannon inhaled the smell of peanut butter just before she took a delicate bite, still watching her mom. She liked to think of these discussions as chess matches. Her mom always used to dominate any civilized disagreement when Shannon was younger, but over time, Shannon had learned to hold her own, and now their matches were more even. "Hiring them to be mercenaries was a smart play. I think we made the right choice to trust them."

Check.

Holly snorted delicately. "There's no trust involved with this deal. It's just business."

Check.

"Sure, I guess. But business requires investment, right?"

Feigning ignorance, her mom inquired, "What do you mean?"

"You're a member of city council. You represent the interests of the people, and the people seem to be better off with the Alpha ghosts. Shouldn't you try to communicate with the Alpha ghosts? Find out what they want, if they're happy, how we can better coexist?"

Check.

"Coexist? What makes you think we're better off coexisting with *ghosts*?"

"Well, to start, we're sitting under a tree in Alvarez Park having a picnic instead of rationing scraps in City Hall."

"Yes, and we wouldn't have been trapped in City Hall if not for ghosts, or did you forget that already?"

Check.

"Of course I haven't forgotten. But these ghosts are different. I know you see them as mercenaries now, but they could be more than that if we invest in them."

Check.

Her mom stared at her long and hard, still as a statue. Shannon defiantly stared back, but after a full ten seconds of the standoff, her confidence wavered under her mom's unbreakable gaze, and Shannon conceded. Finally, mercifully, her mom broke the silence with the quiet words, "You think they're a replacement for Phantom."

"Not a *replacement*," Shannon quickly refuted. She blinked a few times to clear the excess moisture in her eyes; she would not cry in front of her mom.

Holly closed her eyes in either feigned or genuine pain—Shannon couldn't tell which. "Honey . . . pretending these fugitives might bear even the slightest resemblance to him . . . You're being irrational."

A single tear escaped. Shannon swiped at it and turned her head away, furious at herself for losing control. To her embarrassment, her voice was husky when she growled, "Cato has nothing to do with this."

Holly released a long sigh. "I'm going to tell you something I've never told you before."

Shannon raised her head. She couldn't move. She had heard her mom's voice adopt many different tones over the years, but this was something different. It was cold, hard, like a knife about to cut out a heart. "Okay," she said weakly.

"This stays between us. Understand?"

"Yes."

Holly nodded. "I was twenty-three. A few months after graduating college, I had just put down a security deposit on my first apartment in Virginia. I was an intern at the mayor's office. I had my whole life planned, and everything was all lined up for a promising future. And then, in the middle of the night, I was attacked by a ghost."

Shannon's brow furrowed, her narrowed eyes scanning her mom's face for the truth. As usual, she was staring at a perfect politician's mask. "But . . . ?" She couldn't even put words to her question.

Holly inclined her head, unsurprised by her speechlessness. "What I remember about my assailant is that he smelled like clay and his eyes glowed red in the dark. He beat me, raped me, beat me some more—the sick animal—tied my hands, and dragged me into the Ghost Realm. In retrospect, I'm sure the intent was to sell me as a slave. At the time, I was sure my life was over."

"Wait, he . . . he raped you? Then, am I . . . ?"

"Half-ghost?" Holly barked out a bitter laugh. "No, of course not. You, my dear, are a pureblood human. Take one look at your daddy's picture, and there's no doubt."

"You don't keep any around," Shannon muttered. Her mom's lips pressed together in instant disapproval, and Shannon quickly redirected, "So, how did you escape?"

"I kept my head down, pretended to be submissive. The Ghost Realm took my breath away. Honestly, it was beautiful, but it was a fool's paradise, nothing more than a pretty illusion so you forget you're in the outermost circle of hell. The sky was yellow with green clouds, and we were in a village with cobblestone roads and unicorn-drawn carriages. Humans are nothing there, just things to be used—labor, sex, target practice, a punching bag—whatever the need may be. The moment my captor's attention shifted, I tripped him, kicked him where a man hurts most, and ran as fast as I could. Of course, nobody believed me when I claimed a demon with glowing red eyes dragged me through a mirage to a fantasy world with a yellow-and-green sky. Your loving grandparents sent me away for psychiatric treatment."

Holly's lips pulled apart in a forced smile, as if to escape a bad taste on her teeth. "The doctors had almost convinced me that I'd hallucinated the whole ordeal—they said the mind has strange ways of coping with trauma after being assaulted, and I'm sure they were convinced drugs had been involved. Then, I met Agent Kovak. He wasn't the head of the AGC yet, but he was quickly working his way through the ranks, and he had ears in many places; whenever he heard rumors about ghosts, he investigated. He interrogated me, then pulled some strings to get me out of the facility. It was a blessing, it really was, to meet someone who didn't think I was crazy."

Shannon wished her mom would look away. Most people would have been avoiding eye contact while telling this story—picking at the frayed ends of the blanket, staring up at the shifting leaves, watching the clouds drift by on their journey. Holly's piercing eyes were fixed on Shannon. She hardly blinked. Even when Shannon let her gaze fall to the ants roaming across the blanket, she could still feel that penetrating stare.

"I almost became an Agent myself. But I've never had any interest in ghost hunting. I wanted to educate the public and warn people, but Kovak advised against it. Occurrences with the Ghost Realm were isolated instances, pretty rare still at the time. Instead, he encouraged me to pursue my political path and directed me to Phantom Heights. The Rip didn't exist yet, but this place has experienced more Tears than anywhere else in the country, so people here knew exactly what kinds of monsters exist on the other side of a mirage. I could make a difference and start reforming laws, which will be desperately needed throughout the country when ghosts begin invading in greater numbers."

Holly leaned forward, drawing Shannon's gaze up once more to meet her mom's intense emerald stare. "I was a *slave*, Shannon. Madison Tarrow is not a ghost hunter; she's actually a demon hunter, and those monsters come straight from hell. Don't ask me to put my faith in demons to protect us. That is *my* job, and Madison's, and Trey's."

Shannon clenched her fists and bowed her head. "I'm sorry."

Holly leaned back, selected a fat strawberry, and bit into the fruit. "You didn't know, and that was my fault. Maybe you would have understood more a couple of years ago."

Shannon jerked her head up. "How do you know for sure that I'm not half-ghost?"

"You aren't."

"How do you *know*?" Shannon shot back. "How can you—"

"Shannon." Holly's voice dropped to a lethally cold monotonous tone. Her dead eyes stared straight through her daughter. "If there had been any question of your blood, I wouldn't have carried you to term."

Shannon couldn't breathe. Holly used her thumb to wipe away a trickle of red juice creeping down her chin. "You're pure of blood. I know. Your DNA was tested by Madison herself before you even left my womb."

"Does Dad know?" Shannon croaked out.

"Know what? That there was a brief moment when I wasn't sure if the fetus I was carrying might be part demon? No. I never told him."

The rush of relief made Shannon feel suddenly light-headed.

As if her mom could read her mind, Holly continued, "That isn't why he left. He just didn't understand how important my work was. I think he believed having a family would distract me from my career. When he finally realized that I wouldn't settle down and be a good little housewife, he decided this wasn't the life he wanted. You can blame me if you want."

"I don't. Whatever his reasons were, he walked out on us, and that's inexcusable. I blame him, not you."

Holly set the decapitated green top down on the lid. "You know, it's a beautiful day, and this wonderful picnic is being ruined with all this unpleasant talk. Let's eat, shall we?"

She reached for another strawberry.

Shannon stared at the half-eaten sandwich in her hand, her appetite gone.

Checkmate.

— Chapter Twenty-Two —
Gameplay

Gathering the key players together wasn't hard.

Vivian simply asked her mom if she could set three extra plates at the dinner table for the Selman family. Then she rode her bike to Saros Manor and announced, "My mom would like you and Ero to join us for dinner tonight."

Wes stared dubiously at her in the doorway. "*Madison* . . . wants Ero and me . . . to join her for dinner," he repeated suspiciously. "All right, what does she want?"

"Nothing. It's just a friendly gesture."

"Right. Madison making a friendly gesture with no ulterior motive." Vivian folded her arms, and Wes sighed. "You look just like your mother when you do that.

"Come on, please? She wants to make sure there aren't any hard feelings about S-O-S."

Five minutes before dinnertime, Trey walked through the back door and was perplexed when Madison asked when his parents were coming. Then the doorbell rang, and Madison opened the front door to find Wes and Ero on her front porch. She scowled and snapped, "What are you doing here?"

Wes stammered, "Ah . . . you invited us for . . . dinner?" Ero's blue eyes were glowing as he glanced between Wes, Madison, and, over the ghost hunter's shoulder, Vivian. An amused smile pulled up the corners of his mouth as he understood.

Madison glared at Vivian, who chuckled nervously and muttered, "You said we could have guests."

At her mom's silent wrath, she quietly implored, "Come on, Mom.

They're here, and you cooked plenty of food and set extra places at the table."

"Vivian Madison Tarrow, you lied to me."

"Can we talk about this later? We have guests."

Madison's lips pressed into a tight line. Flushed, she marched into the kitchen, snapping over her shoulder, "Well, you're here now, so you might as well sit down."

While the others migrated after her, Ero remained stationary on the porch. "It was not our intention to intrude on your dinner uninvited," he said.

"Come in and sit," the ghost hunter commanded. "I prepared too much food for just the two of us, anyway."

Ero inclined his head and closed the front door. "We brought hash browns for dessert," he said, holding up a covered dish.

"Uh, brownies," Wes corrected, poking his head out of the kitchen. "Those are brownies. Hash browns are what we had for breakfast."

Ero flashed a good-natured smile. "Forgive me; I am still learning your cuisine. What a charming abode you have," he said as he followed Madison through the living room.

"It's no Saros Manor, I'm sure," Madison muttered.

"True," he agreed, "but I appreciate the homey charm."

Trey leaned closer to Vivian and whispered, "You didn't tell her they were coming?"

"I thought it would work better this way."

He was quiet for a moment, then said, "I didn't know Madison was your middle name."

"Lame family tradition," Vivian grumbled.

"I don't think it's lame," he said quickly. "Coulda been worse. It could have been your first name instead, and you might have been named Madison the Second, or Madison Junior, and we would have called you Jr. for short."

Vivian grinned despite herself. "You're such a dork."

"Maybe. But this dork got you to smile." Her grin broadened, and he looked away, the tips of his ears blazing vermillion.

"So, okay, if you have a daughter someday, her middle name would be Vivian?"

"If I continue the tradition."

"What if you have a second daughter?"

Vivian rolled her eyes. "Why are you so fascinated by this?"

"I don't know," he replied with a shrug. "I think it's a neat tradition."

"Well, it's reserved for firstborns. I could give my second daughter whatever middle name I wanted."

So, if you had a son . . . ?"

She let her annoyance escape in the form of a long sigh. "*If* I would decide to continue the tradition, my firstborn son's middle name would be his father's first name. Can we drop this, please?"

"Sorry." His ears were still burning red.

The guests took their seats around the dining room table, which was rarely used except on special occasions. Vivian's hands were shaking. *Maybe this was a miscalculation.* Her ghost-hunter mom, who had been advocating the Shoot-On-Sight solution to regulate activity through the Rip, was sitting across the table from a ghost and a werewolf who probably took great offense to the violent proposal.

The only sounds punctuating the miserable silence were the clock ticking on the wall and the clinking of silverware on plates. The roasted chicken, mushrooms, and potatoes filled Vivian's mouth with savory undertones below delightful pops of zesty seasonings, but she was having difficulty forcing the food down her dry throat.

She kept stealing glances at Trey, trying to read him. His attention remained painstakingly focused on his plate and no one else at the table. If he wouldn't start the conversation, she'd have to.

"S-O-S," she blurted. The silence was so stifling she felt as if she were underwater. "We're all thinking it," she added quietly.

Madison shot her a poisonous glare. Wes tapped his fork against his plate and kept his eyes down. Ero, on the other hand, set his elbow on the table and rested his cheek against his fist in amusement. "Another Mind-Reader in Phantom Heights?" he said lightly.

Madison set her fork on the table. The action wasn't forceful, but it spoke loudly enough to command everyone's attention. "You know it was nothing personal, right?"

Wes slammed his fork down. "Shoot on sight? What if S-O-S was in place when Ero came? What if I were returning from a trip into the Ghost Realm?"

"I already made my point at the debate. I failed Phantom Heights once. I have to make sure it doesn't happen again."

"There's a better way to do that, Mom." Vivian tilted her chin down and gave her a serious look. "Trey and I think the Alpha ghosts are the best bet for Phantom Heights." Madison rolled her eyes, but before she could speak, Vivian demanded, "Why not? People believed in Phantom."

"It's not the same, Viv."

Wes sipped at his water and added, "Phantom had a vested interest in protecting this place. Kovak's lab rats don't. Without our deal, they wouldn't even be here still."

"Then let's give them a reason to care about Phantom Heights," Vivian replied. She cleared her throat and finally asked the question on her mind: "What would happen if Azar finds them?"

Wes stared at her. "Azar?" Madison repeated. "Who's that?"

Ero grimly passed his gaze over each person, ending on his friend to speak. "The tyrant of the Ghost Realm," Wes replied bitterly. "He's the self-appointed lawmaker, police chief, judge, jury, prosecutor, and warden."

Ero added, "How do you often phrase it, Wes? Azar rules Avilésor with a steel gauntlet."

"Iron fist, but close enough," Wes muttered in mild amusement. "Anyway, what would possess you to ask about Azar?"

Vivian pulled the wanted flyer from her pocket and held it out to Wes, who accepted it and skimmed its contents. "Huh. Azar is offering complete immunity from all crimes, as well as a hundred copper pieces per head for the live capture of each Alpha. Were you aware of this?" he asked, sliding the paper across the table to Ero.

The Telepath glanced down at it. "I had heard rumors that Azar was growing impatient," he admitted. "But I had no idea he had taken it to this level."

Vivian asked, "Ero, do you think the Alpha ghosts would join forces with Azar? I mean, they wouldn't . . . right?"

He shrugged. "Hard to say. They are not the most predictable."

"Oh, come on," said Wes. "You know them better than any of us do."

Ero took a delicate bite as he considered his reply. "It all depends, I suppose."

"On what?" Madison politely pressed.

"On what is in the best interest of the group." He took a drink of water before explaining, "Jay is a compassionate but sensible leader who considers the opinions of the others and draws the conclusion he believes will benefit the group. From what I have seen, they typically trust his final judgment. When facing tough decisions, they vote. So, to answer your question—if breaking your deal to join Azar would be best for the group—then yes. They likely would."

Vivian and Trey exchanged worried looks. Madison had a thoughtful, uneasy scowl knitting her brow. Wes reclaimed the flyer and read over it again. "This seems a bit extreme for a first meeting. Did Azar already contact them?"

"Not to my knowledge," said Ero, his eyebrows lifting at the question. "They have not mentioned encountering Azar. But then again, I did not ask."

Madison jabbed her fork in the direction of the flyer in Wes's hand. "Azar is paying bounty hunters. Obviously he's an enemy, not an ally. They won't join him."

"Are you sure?" Trey challenged softly. "What if this Azar ghost—um, kálos, I mean—offers them a better deal?"

She paused in consideration. Vivian immediately seized the opportunity. "Mom, we took Phantom for granted and didn't realize it until he was gone. Now we're starting to take the Alpha ghosts for granted, too." She paused to fix her mom with a fierce gaze. "Cato defended our town, and we created a statue to remember what he did. The Alpha ghosts are protecting us too, but they're living off the streets and eating from our garbage. It's not right."

She'd expected some guilt at her proclamation, but instead, Madison scowled. "They can take care of themselves. In fact, that's what they want. They don't want anything to do with us. It's best to just leave them alone."

"But they're heroes. They shouldn't be living like rats on the streets."

"They're not *heroes*, Vivian. They're mercenaries, and that's a big difference you need to recognize."

"May I say something?" Trey asked. "We understand the difference. And we also understand that a mercenary's allegiance depends on who offers the best compensation. Our deal was strong when we first made it, but now it's pretty weak. We've given the Alpha ghosts their powers—okay, that leverage was good for one play, and we've already used it. Medicine, which they can find other places besides here. And protection from the Agents—any gh-kálos can offer that. What if Azar or someone else makes them a better offer?"

Madison was frowning as she listened. Trey continued, "We've always known they aren't our allies. There is absolutely nothing stopping them from turning on us if a better deal comes along. They've proven themselves to be efficient and deadly, and honestly, I don't even want to think about having to potentially face them as enemies."

Madison glowered at her daughter and apprentice. "Impressive speeches." Vivian blushed and stared down at her plate as her mom directed her cold gaze to Wes. "Did you have anything to do with this?"

"No." He threw his hands up in surrender. "Honest, Maddie."

Madison sighed. "I'll be the first to admit we didn't plan very far ahead when we originally made our deal. But the problem, like I said, is that they don't seem to want anything to do with us. I'm afraid if we interfere too much, that alone will drive them away. This is . . . a touchy situation."

"We haven't even met them face-to-face," Wes added. "Well, I correct myself—Vivian and Ero have."

Trey scowled and stabbed a potato but kept quiet.

"But my point is," Wes continued, "they haven't established contact with any human in this town. I'm inclined to agree with Maddie; I think they want to be left alone."

"Wes," Vivian said coyly, "you have a lot of influence in the Ghost Realm even though you're a weir. And that's because you surround yourself with important people. Well . . . the Alpha ghosts are supposed to be very powerful."

Wes pressed his fist against his lips. "Establishing a relationship with them *would* be beneficial," he agreed. "But that would mean siding against Azar, and that's a nasty business altogether. I've been very careful to avoid the Warden."

"But if you had to choose a side, which would you pick?"

"I'd rather stay neutral."

Vivian scoffed in disgust. "Right. You'd stay neutral until you knew who was winning, and then you'd pick your side."

"That's how you survive," he retorted with a careless shrug. "Avilésor, as Ero can attest, is an unforgiving place. Let's consider the odds. Azar has an army. Our mercenaries from Alpha are a group of five warriors and two ten-year-olds, plus a vicious monster probably far away slaughtering people."

"Five warriors who cleared out hundreds of hostile ghosts by themselves," Vivian reminded.

That gave Wes reason to pause. "Yes, that is impressive. Very impressive."

Madison interrupted, "I think before we make any decisions, we should arrange a meeting with them and actually *talk* to them. And I don't mean talking to a whiteboard, either. If we meet, it has to be in person this time."

"Are you going to get a permission slip from Jennings and Correll before arranging this little conference?"

Madison kept her gaze trained on her plate when she answered, "I don't need to. Holly has given me free rein to deal with the fugitives as

I see fit."

Wes gawked at her for a full five seconds before he said, "Seriously? Control-Freak Jennings? Are you sure we're talking about the same woman?"

"That's . . . weird," said Trey. He gave his ghost-hunting master a questioning look. "Isn't it?"

Madison admitted, "I did find it a bit strange—"

"Especially given her track record," Wes muttered under his breath.

"—but Holly trusts my judgment," Madison finished, glaring at him for interrupting.

"Since when?" he interrupted again.

Madison continued as if he hadn't spoken: "I'm expected to keep her updated on any developments, but as for actually corresponding with the Alpha ghosts, she doesn't want to be involved. For reasons she didn't divulge, she prefers to keep her distance."

Wes said, "Think she's got an ulterior motive?"

"Like what?"

"I don't know. What if she's setting you up? So if Kovak makes a move, her hands are clean."

"I doubt that."

"Why?" he challenged. "Everybody knows Kovak paid the bill for her last campaign to get her in office. She has history with him."

"So did I. Things changed."

Wes shrugged. "Whatever. Holly's going to stay out of the way? No complaints here. But if we're actually going to go through with this, we need to remember that Kovak's fugitives are dangerous. If we meet them face-to-face, I think we should send seven armed raiders to meet the seven of them."

Trey reminded, "The twins aren't a threat."

"Then we pick a team of five," Wes revised.

"Wait a minute," Vivian said. "Jay's the leader. I think instead of sending five people, we should send one to meet Jay."

Madison asked, "Who?"

"Ero, obviously," said Wes. "He already has a good rapport with them."

The Telepath shook his head. "I will not risk their trust by engaging in your politics."

"Then Madison," said Trey. "The leader of the Alpha ghosts should negotiate with the ghost hunter of Phantom Heights."

Vivian negated, "Jay would never agree to meet a ghost hunter. And I think he's afraid Mom has it out for him after he kidnapped me."

"I do," Madison muttered. "What about Trey?" she suggested, eyeing her apprentice. He sat up straighter.

"No ghost hunters," Vivian repeated.

Wes offered, "Vivian, then? They trust her more than they do the rest of us."

Although Trey nodded in approval, Madison tensed. "Absolutely not."

"But Mom—"

"This is not open for discussion. You aren't going."

Wes grumbled, "No offense, Maddie, but you've been overprotective with your daughter ever since you lost your son."

Vivian gasped. Trey quickly bent over his plate and shoveled potatoes into his mouth. Madison froze, staring at Wes with wide eyes. "Don't you dare judge my choices."

"She's an adult."

"I'm still her mother! I still have to protect her!"

"You can't protect her from everything."

"Stop!" Vivian pleaded.

Her cry rang in the air above the awkward pending silence until Trey swallowed his mouthful and broke it by suggesting, "What about Wes?"

Vivian and Madison turned to stare at him. Wes raised an eyebrow. Trey explained, "He came up with the terms of the original deal. Plus, Wes isn't human. They might be more comfortable around him."

Madison turned to the werewolf. "What do you say?"

He shrugged. "Like I told you before, I have a talent for making offers that can't be refused. Ero? Can you convince Jay to meet with me?"

"Convince him, no," the Telepath said, setting his fork down on his empty plate and then dabbing a napkin to the corners of his mouth. "But I can pass along the message that you wish to meet with him."

254

— Chapter Twenty-Three —

New Deal

Wes paced slowly, glancing at his watch. 8:09.

Ero had asked Jay to be there at 8:00. Wes lowered his arm with a slow, impatient exhale. "I'll give it five more minutes," he muttered aloud to the empty room as he turned on his heel to pace in the other direction.

Vivian's suggestion that he establish a relationship with the fugitives had been eating at his thoughts ever since she'd implanted the idea in his head. Wes was, after all, only a weir, which didn't account for much in the kálos society of Avilésor. He'd made his fortune and his reputation by striking deals and forging alliances with both the powerful and influential leaders as well as the lowest criminals in the Black Market. It was in his best interest to seek the company of those who could benefit him. And the thought of having a connection to the infamous Alpha gang left him itching to bargain with the leader. Even if Jay couldn't prove to be a worthy ally, he was still valuable with a high price on his head. Who would pay more for him? Azar or Kovak?

Wes's last journey into Avilésor had unearthed absolutely no new information about the fugitives. The trip had been a complete waste of time; not a single one of his contacts knew a legitimate detail except that the fugitives from Project Alpha were at the top of Azar's bounty list. There were rumors about their great powers and fighting skills, but no one could identify them, which puzzled Wes because they hadn't been lab rats forever. With the exception of Finn and Reese, they must have lived outside the AGC before the Agents captured them. So why didn't anyone know who these kálos were?

The only validated information Wes had to work with were the facts the Agents had provided, but he was well aware those details had been skewed. Vivian had told him everything she could about Jay—how he kept his distance; how he was quiet and analytical; how he took great care in choosing his words before speaking; how although he didn't look intimidating, he was physically very strong and had forcefully moved her aside once with hardly any effort.

Then there was what Jay's actions said about him—how he kept his team in line; how successful they were under his direction; how he'd managed to outsmart the Agents and the entire armed raid team without his powers; how he protected the twins, who were without a doubt the weakest and most vulnerable of the group. Wes was feeling confident. After all, he'd already solidified one deal with the fugitive. Jay was smart, cautious, and calculating . . . but so was Wes. The werewolf was eager to match his wits against the Alpha leader.

Except that chance didn't seem to be tonight.

Wes growled softly and looked at his watch again—8:13. Jay wasn't going to show.

Just as Wes turned to leave, the lights began to flicker. He paused, eyes narrowed, glancing up as the light bulbs on the other half of the room exploded in procession with small *pop*s, plunging that half into shadow. A cloaked figure was standing in the dark corner as far away from Wes as he could possibly be. On the chest of his black jumpsuit was the white symbol α.

Wes smiled warmly and extended his hand. "Hello," he greeted. "You must be Jay."

The stranger remained frozen, his silver eyes trained warily on Wes's open hand. His face was completely hidden, the top half covered by the hood of the cloak, the bottom half by a black cloth. He made no indication of even considering stepping forward to return the handshake.

Wes dropped his hand. He had to fight the urge to wrinkle his sensitive nose at the smell. Kálos didn't suffer from the body odor humans did, but he could still smell the sweat and blood and filth trapped in the man's clothes. He wanted to take in the finer details, but Jay was intentionally cloaked in shadow. All Wes could make out was the black cloak, the irises glowing silver, the white Alpha symbol, and a whistle around his neck. A whistle that had a twin Wes had seen before.

Jay, likewise, was studying Wes. The werewolf suddenly experienced the sinking feeling of dread; despite everything he knew about Jay, he didn't have the slightest clue what the fugitive's Divinity was. It must be incredible for him to be able to subdue the other Alpha ghosts and assert his dominance as leader. Surely Jay must be a Level 4.

When it became apparent that Jay had no intention of initiating the conversation, Wes moistened his lips and said, "It's a pleasure to finally meet you. Please, have a seat." He gestured at the chair across the table, but Jay simply glanced at it, then back at Wes. His silver eyes couldn't keep still, as if Jay were expecting an ambush. Vivian was right—despite the fact that he was powerful, strong, and dangerous, he was skittish. Hopefully Wes could manipulate that in his favor.

In an attempt to put his visitor at ease, he sat down and folded his hands on the table. "I hope you don't mind, but the door is locked so no humans interrupt our meeting."

Now that Wes was seated in a non-threatening manner and Jay had the advantage of already being on his feet, the Alpha leader relaxed a little. The shift in his body language was subtle, but still he didn't speak, leaving Wes to continue, "I suppose some introductions are in order. My name is Wes, though I'm sure you already knew that. I'm a lunos."

His voice trailed to silence. Jay made no response, not even a single nod to indicate acknowledgment. Wes remembered Ero's comment about how the test subjects had been in captivity for so long that they'd adopted human terms, and he wondered if Jay had understood. He cleared his throat and added, "Erm, a werewolf, that is." Still nothing. "So, ah, perhaps you could tell me a little about yourself?"

"Not much to tell." Jay's voice was quiet, muffled behind his mask to confound Wes's ability to estimate his age.

"Sure there is. Let's be fair, I don't know much about you. I've shared my abilities . . . what are yours? What's your Divinity?"

If Wes didn't know any better, he'd have thought the cloaked figure was a statue. Jay didn't move and didn't answer.

Time for the first offensive move in this game. Wes reached beneath the table and pulled out a covered dish, then set it on the wood and opened the lid. Steam billowed out, followed immediately by a mouthwatering sweet and zesty aroma of meat, cheese, and Italian spices.

The Alpha leader stared at the dish. "It's homemade lasagna," Wes said, studying his adversary's reaction. "I thought you might enjoy a fresh, hot meal for a change. You're welcome to eat while we talk."

Jay tried to remain impassive, but Wes noticed how he swallowed, his eyes drawn hungrily to the food. Offer a starving person a good meal, and the negotiation would most certainly follow smoothly in Wes's favor. The werewolf replaced the lid, set a fork on top, and slid the dish across the table.

He watched, waiting for the leader to give in to hunger, to lose his self-control, remove his mask, and scarf down the meal. But to his surprise and disappointment, Jay stepped forward, moved the sealed dish to the corner of the table, and returned his attention to Wes. He'd resisted the temptation. "Thank you," he said.

Wes narrowed his eyes. He had to admire the enormous amount of willpower Jay had just demonstrated. "It's the least I can do. In fact, I should be thanking *you*." Wes brought out two wine glasses and a bottle of cabernet. He filled both glasses halfway and passed one down.

Jay studied his glass but didn't drink.

"It's not poisoned. I promise," said Wes, swirling the liquid in his glass and breathing in the subtle profiles of cherry and black currant above the dry, spiced undertones before he took a delicate sip. "We're drinking from the same bottle."

Still, Jay didn't touch the wine. "It looks like blood," he noted uneasily.

Wes chuckled, although it sounded forced even to him. "It's wine. Top shelf, I might add." Annoyed by Jay's insistent hesitation, he added, "You know, it's rude to refuse an offering from your host."

Jay sighed and picked up the glass. He dipped his head so the hood shadowed more of his face when he tugged his mask down around his neck to expose his mouth. Wes watched in satisfaction as Jay brought the glass to his lips, sniffing cautiously before taking a tentative sip. He set the wine back on the table and replaced his mask immediately.

The pleasantries dispatched, Wes began, "Let's get down to business. It's been a crazy past few days, huh? That whole S-O-S catastrophe . . . what a mess. I'm not sure I would have pulled that victory off without your help." At Jay's stony silence, Wes took another sip. "May I ask you something? Why did you keep up your end of the deal?"

Jay blinked at the question—Wes had caught him off guard. He averted his gaze as he considered his answer. Finally, he said, "We gave you our word."

"Sure, but we didn't expect you to keep it."

"We don't have anything else to give. If our word means nothing, then what do we have?"

"Hmm, so you have a set of values, then. That's interesting. Please," he encouraged, "have a drink, Jay. This was an expensive bottle."

The change in Jay's body language was subtle but noticeable. His muscles tensed in dissatisfaction, and when he shifted his mask down to take another sip, it was with great reluctance. He managed only one forced swallow before replacing the glass on the table.

"Well," Wes murmured in interest as he leaned back in his chair. He'd gotten a glimpse of Jay's bare chin just before the Alpha leader replaced the black cloth to cover his face once more. "You're younger than I expected. Have you even reached your second coming of age?"

Jay maintained his persistent silence.

"The problem," said Wes, leaning forward again and pressing his fingertips together, "is that when we constructed this deal of ours, it covered a short-term dilemma. At the time, we were both desperate for a quick fix, am I right? We have some issues to address. Vivian Tarrow claims she saw you taking food out of a dumpster."

"We weren't stealing it. Nobody wanted it."

Stunned by Jay's defense, Wes said quickly, "No, of course not. I wasn't insinuating that you were stealing. But while our lives have resumed a sense of normalcy, you're eating garbage, you haven't had a break, you're wearing the same filthy clothes from the accident—how many months ago was that now?—and you're living off the streets. That doesn't seem fair, does it?"

Jay looked down at his clothes as if surprised by how ragged they were. Wes interlocked his fingers, completely in negotiating mode now. "Here's my proposition: we alter our deal so it's more of a long-term arrangement."

"Alter it," Jay repeated. He pinched the stem of the wineglass between his thumb and forefinger and turned it. "We're not interested in renegotiating our terms."

"Perhaps I misspoke," Wes said, then drained his own glass and poured more wine for himself. "I don't mean we change what's already in place. We'll continue to do what we've been doing—we'll give you medication for the twins and keep the Agents' attention directed away from Phantom Heights. But we'll add some incentives. To start, would you be open to adjusting the supplies for Finn and Reese? At this point in our arrangement, it seems rather senseless to give you daily rations. What if you collected once a week instead?"

Jay thought briefly about the amendment, then nodded. "Okay."

"Good. Now, accommodations. I . . ."

Wes paused, a sudden thought illuminating a new opportunity, and then he smiled. "You know, the third floor of Saros Manor is an old ballroom. I don't use that space, so it's been sitting empty for several years. With a little construction, I could turn it into a home for you."

Jay stared at Wes for a moment as if unsure he'd heard correctly. "You . . . want us to live in Saros Manor with you?" he summarized uncertainly.

Wes's initial goal had been to forge a stronger alliance with Jay, but why couldn't he benefit as well? Despite the fact that he'd financed downtown's reconstruction almost single-handedly out of the goodness of his heart, his requests for construction crews to Saros Manor had been denied. *Low priority* was Councilwoman Jennings's favorite pair of words. But opening his home to the Alpha ghosts would not only put them in his debt, it would also force Holly's hand so Wes could have access to the resources she kept denying him.

Wes said, "Sure, why not? It's certainly big enough. The entire third story would be yours to do with as you please. You'll have access to all the amenities in the house, food in the kitchen, my spacious backyard overlooking the biggest natural park in Phantom Heights . . . I even have a small gym you can use to exercise. Ero is living on the first floor, so it'll be more convenient for the twins' lessons. Saros Manor can be your home. That's better than making you deal with the hassle of an apartment, a lease, all that nonsense, right?"

Jay's eyes were narrowed suspiciously. "Nothing is ever free. There's always a catch."

Wes unlocked his fingers and laid his hands flat on the table. "You're a smart man, Jay, and I respect that. I'm extending this generous offer to you because you've done more than your fair share, and we need to compensate for that. But you're right—there is a small catch. You can collect your medical rations from Dr. Crawford only after she has examined the twins."

"No."

"Then no deal, I guess."

"Fine," said Jay, turning away.

"Whoa, wait!" cried Wes, rising halfway out of his chair. The cloaked figure paused in the shadows. Wes growled in frustration; he hadn't expected Jay to break off the deal so easily without even attempting to negotiate the terms. The werewolf closed his eyes and exhaled, trying to regain control of the conciliation. "You drive a hard bargain, you know that?"

Jay turned his head to gaze at the werewolf with one silver eye. "Finn and Reese are not up for negotiation."

"What value can those kids possibly have to you?"

"What do you care?"

Wes slowly lowered himself back into the chair. "You'd rather let them live on the streets than receive the care of a doctor to keep them healthy?"

"To be stabbed with needles, injected with drugs, poked, prodded, and scanned all over again? That's right."

Wes held up his hands. "Okay. I can't even begin to understand your relationship with them, but for now we'll forget about the doctor, all right? Let's just focus on giving them a better home. Good food; clean water; a warm, dry place to sleep—that seems like a good start, wouldn't you say?"

Jay, still tense with suspicion, turned to face Wes again. "We'll all be able to live in the same room?" he asked.

"If that's what you want, sure. I can turn the upper story into a suite for you." He winked and said, "But no wild parties unless I'm invited."

Jay didn't laugh at the joke.

Wes unfolded a piece of paper from his pocket. He held up the flyer and asked, "Did you know you were wanted by Azar?"

"Yes."

"Do you realize what a powerful, influential man he is?"

"Yes," Jay replied again, folding his arms. "We encountered Hassing before we ever made the deal with you."

Wes gaped at him in awe. "You confronted Azar's second-in-command without your powers?"

"Yes."

Wes teased, "Is that the only word you know now?" Jay just stared at him. "Well, apparently your sense of humor is nonexistent," Wes muttered under his breath.

"Maybe it's your comedic skills," Jay offered.

"My point is, you need a safe place to live. Give me a week to prepare your suite. Any special requests?"

Jay thought for a moment, then said, "We like to see the stars."

"Uh . . . hmm. Okay, I guess I can make that work. However, considering my generosity, there is one small favor I feel I have to ask of you. In fact, I'm making it a condition of our arrangement. If you want to live in Saros Manor, you have to present yourself before the town.

All seven of you have to be there. No more games in the shadows, Jay. It's time to stand in the spotlight."

The werewolf smirked as Jay clenched his fists, trying to find a way around the stipulation. Wes rose to his feet before Jay could have time to think of a counterargument. "Sunday afternoon, then. You give us the opportunity to thank you for your service, and my home is yours. If that's all, I guess I'll see you in a week," he said with a smile. "It was a pleasure to finally meet you."

Jay glared at him, but sensing that the meeting was over and he couldn't talk his way out of Wes's demand, he touched the covered dish and disappeared with it. Wes blinked, surprised by Jay's quick departure. Had he turned invisible, or had he left?

Wes hesitated for a few moments, then decided that he was alone. Jay had left his full glass of wine sitting on the table, barely touched. Wes's plan to get him to loosen up by way of alcohol had certainly backfired. He shook his head in dissatisfaction and drained the rest of his glass.

— Chapter Twenty-Four —

Seph

What had started as a simple announcement that the town's mercenaries would be making a public appearance had somehow swelled into a full-blown festival in town square by the time Sunday arrived.

Madison stood in the middle of the crowd with a bottle of root beer in her hand. All around her, people were enjoying themselves. Children played tag, giggling and dashing between the legs of the adults. A local band played upbeat jazz. Christmas lights had been strung around the light posts and cast into the street trees. Smoke was in the air, and it carried the tantalizing wafts of burgers, hot dogs, tacos, shish kabobs, and grilled vegetables. Kids licked ice cream dripping down cones. Adults clanked beer bottles after toasts to the future.

The people needed an outlet, a celebration, a time to relax. Yes, the festival was in honor of the Alpha ghosts, but it was also in honor of freedom for Phantom Heights.

Madison alone seemed restless. She couldn't stop her gaze from roving in search of the mercenaries who were supposed to make their grand appearance tonight. Thus far, they were nowhere to be seen.

Evening was starting to fall, and the festival had been going strong for several hours, leading Madison to believe they weren't planning to show. She couldn't picture them with this lively crowd, anyway. The anticipated entry point for the guests of honor was, of course, City Hall's portico, the grand architectural stage overlooking the plaza. A banner reading *THANK YOU* had been strung up between the columns.

Lingering near the steps was a group of people Madison had been keeping an unwavering eye on. City council, with Mayor Correll, Police Chief Emerton, and a small guard of uniformed officers, had maintained their position since before the festival officially started.

Although most of them chattered and laughed with drinks in hand, Madison eyed them with distrust, especially Councilwoman Jennings, whose cold eyes continually scanned the crowd every few minutes.

Madison sipped at her pop, glaring at the group. Whatever game they were playing, she didn't like it. Any interaction with the Alpha ghosts was supposed to be her responsibility, not theirs.

A hand on her shoulder made her start as a sweet voice chimed in her ear, "Hey, Mom!" Vivian, who had towed Trey behind her, grinned and looked around. "Isn't this great?"

Madison nodded. She straightened when she found Ero talking to Wes, the werewolf laughing heartily and brandishing a half-eaten corn dog in one hand while holding a beer in the other. Madison had almost forgotten the full moon was in two days; Wes looked more feral than usual, his normally brown eyes glinting with yellow flecks, every tooth sharpened to a point, his hair looking rather unkempt and bedraggled. People were giving them both a generous berth, suspiciously eyeing Ero's odd clothing and Wes's early signs of transformation, but Ero seemed unconcerned with the distrustful glares he was receiving, and Wes simply ignored them. Madison licked her lips and approached, motioning for Trey and Vivian to follow.

Wes was still laughing when they drew near. "Maddie!" he cried, raising his corn dog in greeting.

"Madison," she corrected coldly. "How much have you had to drink?"

"I'm fine."

"You're tipsy at best, if not drunk already. Damn it, Wes, I needed you to have a clear head tonight, not just for this meeting, but also to make sure you keep your inner animal under control."

"Such a buzzkill," he muttered. He took a swig from his bottle.

Ero was much more polite as he inclined his head in acknowledgment and said, "Hello, Madison, Vivian, Trey. What a festive gathering."

"Yes," Madison agreed, glancing around. "But the point of it was to thank our guests of honor. Where are they?"

Vivian added, "Yeah, they're coming, right?"

Wes sobered up and looked at his friend. Ero shrugged and said, "The last time we spoke, they had every intention of making an appearance."

"When?" the ghost hunter demanded. "After everyone goes home?"

Ero smiled. "Time does not seem to be a concept they fully appreciate, but their word is their honor, so if they said they will come, I have faith they will."

Madison habitually touched the holster of an ectogun sheathed at her hip. Wes scowled at the array of weapons in the belt. "Maddie—"

"*Madison.*"

"—whatever you do, don't turn this into a fight. We don't know what most of their Divinities are."

"All the more reason to be prepared for anything."

"But one could be a Necromancer and kill you with a single touch. Or . . . or an Apportator who could teleport you into the middle of the Ghost Realm with a snap of the fingers. Or an Inflictor. Those are the worst, Maddie. They stimulate every nerve in your body to feel intense pain."

Ero chuckled and teased, "You are letting your imagination get the best of you."

Madison folded her arms. "Wes, what is your point?"

"My point is, I highly recommend you don't draw any of those guns," he snapped. "Kovak *handpicked* them for a classified Project, remember? Who knows what they're capable of? I have a feeling an ectogun isn't going to be much of a deterrent if they want to kill you. Am I right, Ero?"

He evaded, "This can be a peaceful meeting if all parties remain calm."

An icy voice said, "Well then, let's make sure that happens."

Wes went as stiff as a board. His head swiveled to locate the person standing just behind him. "Councilwoman," he said, performing a surprisingly graceful hop-pivot to face her while simultaneously putting distance between them.

She forced a smile, her dark red lipstick contrasting her perfect teeth. "My, you aren't looking so well. Haven't been breaking any laws lately, have you, Cooper?"

"No, ma'am," he replied, shaking his head.

Bristling, Madison said sharply, "What are you playing at, Holly? You and the other council members planning to jump the Alpha ghosts as soon as they arrive?"

Holly turned to her, feigning polite surprise. "Of course not," she said innocently. "We're just here to observe. The people have chosen the Alpha ghosts over our proposed Shoot-On-Sight doctrine to protect Phantom Heights, so we intend to evaluate these 'protectors.' The floor will be all yours, of course."

Madison glowered at the councilwoman, not even bothering to hide her disdain and suspicion about Holly's ulterior motives. "Right," she muttered.

Holly inspected her fingernails and asked without looking up, "I trust our guests will be making their appearance soon?"

"We're assuming," said Madison, barely curbing the irritation in her voice.

Holly glanced up, but her gaze went straight to Ero. "And Jay is aware of how important this is?"

"He is," Ero said, inclining his head. "We discussed it."

"Discussed what?" Madison blurted.

Holly, Wes, and Ero stared at the ghost hunter as if they were all in on a secret she wasn't supposed to know. She glowered at each one in turn, ending on Holly, who smiled faintly and tilted her head ever so slightly. "I'm sorry, Madison. No one informed you?"

"I'm afraid I must have missed the memo."

Through the last bite of corn dog, Wes said, "All the Alpha ghosts will be here."

"Oh, really?" Madison snapped. "And here I thought this festival was just for fun."

Holly rolled her eyes. Wes swallowed and lowered his voice. "Nobody's going to miss a chance to see them. I guarantee every single person in Phantom Heights is here right now."

"And?"

"*And* Ero's going to scan the crowd so we can pick out any potential traitors thinking about contacting the AGC for the reward."

Madison's gaze snapped to meet Holly's green eyes. "You approved this?"

"It was my idea, actually."

"Since when do you care about protecting them? And what happened to 'my mind is my own and nobody has a right to invade my privacy'? I thought you were completely against mind-reading and telepathy."

Ero cleared his throat. "Madison, I think you misunderstand the intentions here. I will not be manipulating anyone. Once the focus is turned onto Jay and the others, I will simply skim the vibe of the crowd and zero in on the negative reactions. My role here is only to identify potential threats."

"And then what? You'll reprogram the perpetrators on behalf of city council?"

Holly said, "Oh, for God's sake, Madison. Are you actually accusing me of taking away people's free will? *Really?*"

Ero's expression hardened immediately. "I would do no such thing even if it were asked of me."

"I'll be handling the potential traitors once they're identified," said Holly.

Madison glared at her. "Why was I left in the dark about this covert operation?"

Wes used the stick to pick out his sharp teeth. "Sorry."

Holly smirked and monotonously added, "I apologize for not going through the appropriate channels."

Madison jabbed her finger at her and seethed, "You crossed into my jurisdiction. Don't pull strings behind my back. I'm in charge when it comes to dealing with the Alpha ghosts. With *any* ghosts, including Ero." The Telepath's eyebrows shot up in amusement. Madison finished, "We already agreed on this. You made it clear you want nothing to do with them. I don't appreciate you circumventing me."

Holly's grin never wavered. "Of course. I apologize. I thought Cooper was going to fill you in." The werewolf jerked his head up with a scowl, but Holly continued, "As I said, the show will be all yours. You handle the ghosts. I'll be handling the humans. Business as usual."

Madison clenched her fists, trying to quiet the furious tremors that made her want to scream in frustration. She glared past Holly, her gaze landing on City Hall overlooking town square, the wide stone steps spanning the front of the white building. The portico formed the perfect stage. All that was missing were the Alpha ghosts.

***

Inside City Hall, I leaned against the wall, my gaze following Jay as he paced back and forth, back and forth. His anxiety was contagious.

"We don't have to do this, you know," I told him.

The kitten perched on the windowsill beside me flicked her ears back at the sound of my voice.

"Yes, we do," Jay said sullenly. "Wes practically ordered it."

Axel barked out a humorless laugh. "Oh yeah? Well, Wes can take his orders and shove them right up his furry—"

"Don't you dare finish that sentence," Jay warned.

I swallowed, my stomach performing nauseating acrobatics. "We can't go. Come on, Jay, you want to give up all our secrets just like that? What about Axel? And Kit? And . . . me?"

"Do you trust me?"

I crossed my arms. "That's irrelevant."

"It's not. Do you trust me?"

I let out a pent-up breath, which Jay interpreted as *yes*. He had that look that always came over his face whenever he was scheming. "Wes specifically said all seven of us have to be present."

"Seven?" I said, glancing at my seven lab-siblings, eight counting me.

"Seven," Jay repeated with assertion. "If you exclude A6."

Axel stiffened. "If you're going, I'm going."

"I planned on that," Jay said. "Kit isn't going."

"I'm confused," RC muttered.

Ash agreed, "Me too. I thought you just said Axel isn't going."

"No," Jay said patiently, "I said A6 wasn't going." He tossed a scrap of black cloth to Axel, who held it in his hands with a blank look.

Jay pointed at the whiteboard mounted on the far side of the room. "They think one of us is blind. We're going to hide your red eyes so they won't know you're A6."

Axel pinched the cloth between his thumb and forefinger and raised it in disgust. "Forget it."

"It has to be this way, Ax. What do you think is going to happen if the humans see your red eyes and your fangs and figure out who you are?"

"Who cares?"

"They'll break the deal and send us back," Jay snapped. "Besides, do you *want* them to look at you like a monster? Because that's how they'll see you if they know your number."

Axel scowled and turned away. Jay rubbed the ports embedded in his temples. "It's for the best we keep you hidden, Ax. You and Cato both. You understand, right?"

I nodded; I didn't want to be recognized, anyway. To the people of Phantom Heights, I'd much rather be seen as an escaped fugitive than as myself. It was best if Axel and I stayed off the radar.

I closed my eyes. "I think I'm going to be sick."

Behind me, just on the other side of the wall, the citizens of Phantom Heights laughed and talked and feasted. I could feel the vibrations of the music and hear the white noise of voices broken by laughter. They were celebrating their own freedom, but we all knew the real reason they were here was to see us—the infamous fugitives who had started as enemies but evolved into their protectors.

I didn't want to face them. I squeezed my eyelids tighter, remembering the final day of Before when they had all watched me with distrust. My classmates, neighbors, teachers, best friend, mom, blood-sister—everyone I cared about—all present. And every one of them stood in that very same plaza and watched *Them* take me away. Now I was going to have to stand in front of them again.

"This isn't like Lastday," Ash soothed. "You aren't alone, Cato. We're all here with you."

I took a deep breath and exhaled slowly. "I can't do this."

"Hey." I opened my eyes to find Ash standing beside me with her right hand up, palm facing me. "No bars," she said.

I forced my lips to twitch into a feeble smile. "No bars," I repeated weakly, pressing my palm against hers. She curled her warm fingers between my clammy ones.

Axel tied the cloth over his eyes, blindfolding himself. He jerked his hood over his head. Jay leaned back to study the cloaked creature. "Can you navigate?"

Axel didn't need his eyes to give Jay *the look.*

I wasn't confident this would work. Even with his clairvoyant red eyes concealed, he still possessed that feral aura around him, and he was too cocky and sure of himself. Would they buy that he was blind?

Jay redirected his critical gaze to me. "You'll have to keep your eyes blue for longer this time."

I considered what he was asking of me. Maintaining enough focus to sustain a steady flow of power wouldn't be an easy task, not to men-tion it would also be physically taxing in addition to the already high level of stress. "Jay, I can't do this. You guys go. I'll stay here."

Axel snapped, "All you have to do is stand there and keep your mouth shut and your eyes blue."

I didn't have the heart to engage in an argument right now. Jay crossed his arms and informed me, "You're coming. Either hold your ice Divinity so both eyes are blue, or suppress your power so your eyes don't glow at all."

I weighed my options—deplete my power by using it continuously, or make myself human?

Ash whispered, "Ready?"

If I opened my mouth, I might throw up, so I answered her with a weak nod. Jay swallowed hard, glancing out the window. "I'll go first. The rest of you hang back until I'm sure it's safe. And Cato . . . we'll get through this." He gave Kit a nervous pat on the head as he pulled his mask up.

And then he was gone.

Ash, RC, and I concealed ourselves with our hoods and masks and peered out the window. Jay was standing in the shadow of City Hall's pillar, surveying the festival. At first, no one noticed him. Then, a few people spotted him, gasped, and fell silent, and the effect of his presence was immediate.

Like a ripple, silence washed over the crowd, which turned to face him as the music came to an abrupt stop mid-song. The police at the front of the crowd rested their hands on the holsters of their guns but didn't draw. A few people clapped. The pathetic smattering of applause quickly died as the crowd observed Jay with a sense of wonder.

His attention was immediately trained on the three people walking up the steps to meet him—Madison, her apprentice, and the werewolf. At the bottom of the stairs, Ero offered a reserved smile and nodded in encouragement.

"Hullo, Jay!" Wes greeted enthusiastically.

"Yes," said Madison, forcing a frigid smile as she reached the top. "We've been looking forward to meeting you. No need to be shy. Why don't you come into the light where we can see you?"

My lab-brother hesitated. Finally, slowly, he eased his way around the pillar and stood in full view, clenching his fists and surveying the humans before him.

Madison's gaze traveled up and down his figure, absorbing the cloak, worn thin, tattered, and torn; the long-sleeve uniform soiled with dried mud and blood; the hood covering the top half of Jay's face; the black cloth tied over his nose and mouth to conceal the rest of his face, leaving only his gleaming silver eyes visible; the whistle dangling around his neck on a cord.

"Jay," Wes said, his originally jubilant attitude eclipsed by a stern expression, "you seem to be six short. I thought I made the conditions clear."

"They're coming."

Madison folded her arms. "Now that's a familiar look. Take off that mask so we can see your face."

"I respectfully decline, Mrs. Tarrow."

I smirked as her eyes widened and her nostrils flared. "Oh, you *respectfully* decline? Too bad that wasn't a request. This town was almost destroyed once before because of masks and secrets."

Her answer was silent disobedience. She glowered at Jay, clearly ready to start a debate, but then she changed her mind and instead pursed her lips, searching for words. "You're not very . . . I mean . . . well, I don't know what I was expecting."

"Sorry to disappoint."

I tried to see Jay from the humans' perspective. He really wasn't all that menacing outside the shadows we liked to hide in. His stance wasn't assertive. He was taller than Madison, but only by a few inches. His build was impossible to tell beneath the tattered cloak, so it was hard to gauge his muscle mass. I knew firsthand from Jay's strikes that he was strong, but it was a lean, clean-cut strength, not a bulky form that immediately intimidated in a standoff.

"You think you're Phantom?" Madison demanded.

"No."

"*No*," she repeated, almost mocking. "But you think you're clever for that blackmail stunt you pulled a while back, don't you?"

Jay considered for a moment, then rolled his shoulders and said, "I think *you* think I'm clever."

I didn't know how he did it, how his challenge was so bold and yet artfully subtle. He earned himself one of Madison Tarrow's famous withering looks, something I'd thought she kept reserved for Phantom, although by Jay's attire, maybe she saw him as a suitable surrogate.

Her voice sharp as a blade, she seethed, "You want to know what I think of you? I think you're a villain who's having some fun dressing in the hero's cape for a little while. But I think you're going to get bored.

You're going to screw up, and by the time I'm done with you, you'll be begging me to send you back to Kovak."

If Jay was afraid of her intimidation tactics, he did a remarkable job of hiding it. "That isn't going to happen." Softer, he added, "I'd beg you for death before I'd beg for that."

A broad man at the base of the steps cleared his throat with a deep cough to break the tension. The ghost hunter broke her gaze away from Jay to give the man a measured glare. He was carefully positioned behind two officers, but he was shorter than they were, and he looked rather ridiculous standing on his tiptoes and stretching his neck to smile nervously over his guards' shoulders. "Ah-hem, uh, Jay, I'm Mayor Correll. Sorry about that little unpleasantness there. On behalf of Phantom Heights, I'd like to thank you for all you've done."

The mayor didn't approach Jay. He wasn't going to get any closer to my lab-brother than he had to.

Jay inclined his head and replied politely, "Yes, sir."

Correll chuckled nervously. "Yes, *sir*," he repeated, smiling at the ghost hunter while blotting his damp forehead with a handkerchief. "I like him."

Despite the mayor's claim, he couldn't back away fast enough to melt into the safety of the uniformed officers. Madison took a brazen step toward Jay. He took a step back. She paused, watching him curiously. She held out her hand, but Jay simply stared at it. "What's the matter?" she taunted. "Are you afraid of a handshake?"

He narrowed his eyes. Yes, he was. Human hands always brought pain. *Always.* Sometimes humans made their intentions clear; they were rough as they pulled us out of our cages, gripped us with iron fingers, dragged us across the floor, strapped us down, hurt us with sharp instruments. Sometimes humans were deceitful; they spoke gently and approached slowly, but then when we let our guard down, they made their move to harm us. Our fear of the human touch had been instilled by a long history of abuse. I'd rather face a Scout in the Arena with clear intentions of killing me than try to guess the motive of a ghost hunter offering her hand.

I didn't expect Jay to shake Madison's hand, but he seemed to be considering. His gaze kept shifting between the weapon belt around her waist, her spiteful face, and her waiting hand. He leaned forward.

But his brief surge of courage died, and he quailed away from Madison, taking another step back farther out of her range.

Madison didn't seem as surprised by his reaction as she was smug. She said, "Let's be clear: I don't trust you. I think it's safe to assume the feeling is mutual."

Jay folded his arms, listening in silence.

"But whether we like it or not, we do need each other, and it's been brought to my attention that your living conditions are inadequate. I've discussed your predicament with city council, and we've decided to collect a portion of our taxes on your behalf. You'll receive payments so you don't have to survive on garbage anymore."

Jay stood a little straighter. "You're paying us? Like a real job?"

"No, not *like* a real job. This *is* your job, and you have to earn your paycheck. You—uh, eh-erm . . . you, you've been doing good work so far." She paused, then snapped, "But if you *ever* touch my daughter again, so help me, I will personally send you back to the AGC."

Despite her final threat, Jay remained impassive. His gaze danced over the deathly silent crowd again. "You're going beyond the original terms of our deal. On behalf of my lab-family, I thank you for your extra hospitality."

Madison's jaw dropped. Jay's open gratitude must have caught her off guard; she'd no doubt expected him to be crude, not so mild-mannered. I could practically see the silent argument churning through her head as she had to remind herself how much she hated Jay for traumatizing her daughter. "Yes, well," she said, flustered, ". . . you deserve it."

The crowd erupted into applause. Jay leapt back, startled by the sudden noise.

"No, no, it's okay," Madison soothed. The gentleness in her voice surprised me; she seemed to have surprised herself. But despite her reassurance, Jay was still uneasy. The applause had spooked him, and now he was edgier than before, the silver irises beneath the lip of his hood darting.

"No one here is going to harm you," Madison assured, stepping toward him again.

She halted. Jay wasn't alone anymore.

The atmosphere changed the moment Axel came into sight. The humans had gazed upon Jay with wonder, but they eyed Axel with unease. He did have that effect on people. They must feel that otherworldly charge pulsing in the air. On a primal level they'd never experienced before and couldn't truly understand, they sensed the danger about him, the predator dormant within.

The contradiction between Axel and Jay was undeniable. The leader was cautious, wary, his eyes dancing, his body tense. Axel, on the other hand, was perfectly relaxed. Although Jay had half a foot of height on Axel, the half-breed reeked of confidence, his head turned toward the ghost hunter. The roles between lab-brothers almost seemed as though they should have been reversed.

Madison studied Axel, sizing him up. Something besides his aura was off. It was the blindfold, I was sure, that perplexed her.

Wes snickered. "I think you missed the memo. The mask goes over your face, not your eyes."

"Wes!" Madison scolded quietly. Through clenched teeth, she said, "Show some respect. He's blind." Wes immediately sobered into bashful silence.

I exhaled in relief. Axel's nostrils flared as he inhaled, analyzing the scents of his environment. If I didn't know myself that he was A6, I never would have connected the snarling, crouching beast of legend to the blindfolded ghost standing cool and calm beside Jay. As long as he didn't do anything stupid, we might actually pull this off.

The crowd stirred with renewed excitement kindled by Axel's attendance. Madison asked, "What's your name?"

My lab-brother took his time in answering, waiting until Madison was growing restless with impatience and about to repeat her question before replying, "Axel."

She adjusted the belt holstering her weapons. "Allow me to formally introduce myself. I'm—"

"Yeah, Madison, I know."

Jay swiftly elbowed our lab-brother in the gut. Axel didn't flinch, but the gesture was clear, and the half-breed did pause to turn his head. "Show some respect. It's Mrs. Tarrow."

Axel sneered. "She's lucky I didn't call her Bitch instead."

Beside me, Ash gasped. I closed my eyes and sighed. "Oh no."

The kitten transformed in black smoke, and then a soft voice whispered, "Is Axel allowed to call her—?"

"No," RC cut in quickly.

On the other side of the window, Jay exclaimed, "Axel! Bloody Scout, how many times have I told you to watch your mouth?" His hand disappeared beneath his hood as he rested his forehead against his palm and let his breath out in a frustrated sigh. "I'm so sorry, Mrs. Tarrow." He glowered at the hybrid and muttered, "Axel doesn't know when to keep his mouth shut," then turned and shot a meaningful look at the window where the rest of us were watching. His message was clear: time to make our appearance. *Now.*

I swallowed. My body went cold, although whether it was from terror or my ice Divinity awakening in response to my distress, I couldn't tell. RC tied an extra piece of fabric at a diagonal across his face to hide his scar and milky eye.

Ash gripped my hand. "Ready?"

I balked, pulling away from her. "I can't. I can't do it. I can't stand in front of all those humans and pretend I'm equal to them."

"You aren't equal," Reese said.

Finn added, "Humans are superior."

Ash shushed the twins while RC, his blind side to me, stared out the window and said quietly, "Cato, you don't have to prove yourself to anybody."

Ash took my hand again. "And we'll be right beside you."

I was so numb I couldn't feel her reassuring squeeze. "Good luck," Kit whispered just before changing in a swirl of smoke and leaping up to reclaim her place on the windowsill. I closed my eyes. Ash was moving forward, pulling me with her, and together, we stepped into the wall, leaving our sanctuary and emerging in front of the crowd.

I bowed my head and squeezed my eyes shut to hide from the reality in front of me just a little longer. This was different from casting our vote at the S-O-S debate. This time, I had no other purpose than standing before these traitors so they could gawk at me, analyze me, and judge me. Again.

I noticed the sound first—the whispering like wind rustling leaves.

Voices.

I couldn't breathe.

White waves of white noise.

I curled the fingers of my free hand into a fist, searching inward for the cold power I harbored deep in my core.

Rushing whispers made the air hiss like wind tearing through wild grasses.

Ice formed in my hand. I worked it with my fingers, frowning, focusing on the solid object. Even if I had no control over anything else, I had control of my power.

I opened my blue eyes and glared down at my feet. I didn't need to raise my head to know the humans were staring right at me.

Eyes bored through me . . .

I exhaled. *Don't look at them. Look at my lab-family. They're the only ones who matter.*

Ash let go of my hand, and without her anchoring me, I felt as if I were falling. My heart stalled. I wanted to reach out and grab her again for reassurance, but I had to put on a brave front, so I focused on the ice. I moved my fingers, morphing the shape of the solid orb.

I finally found the courage to focus on the three biggest threats— Madison, with her cold and calculating green eyes so similar to and yet so different from Vivian's; Wes, who looked as if he might turn full wolf any second; and Trey, my former best friend, ready to do his ghost-hunting master's bidding. I looked over his shoulder at the uniformed policemen at the base of the steps separating the crowd from us.

They hadn't drawn weapons yet, but their hands were on the holsters of their guns.

When I had stood here on Lastday, I'd been searching for familiar faces in the crowd. I didn't want to do that this time. I didn't want to look at any of them. I had the irrational fear that if I made eye contact with anyone, I'd be recognized. That was probably paranoia. But, if Finn and Reese were wrong, there was one person in Phantom Heights who knew I was here. This was the closest we'd been to each other since Lastday. Even with my blue eyes, she must know.

My mother.

My chest hurt, as if my heart pumped ice instead of blood now. I could feel her gaze drilling into me. I was so much stronger now than the last time we'd faced each other, and yet, I was petrified of her. If we made eye contact, her hatred was going to pierce my soul, possibly even destroy me. I looked at Axel instead and wished I could borrow some of his confidence.

Madison's voice jolted me: "Phantom Heights, I present to you—the Alpha ghosts."

A wave of sound slammed into me. People were clapping their hands as they'd done before with Jay. Then, I'd been separated by a wall. Now, the unfiltered noise was deafening. Slowly, I lifted my head, tightening my fist around the ball of ice, staring vacantly at the crowd as they cheered and yelled and screamed and whistled like wild animals. Their hypocrisy made my stomach turn. These were the same faces as Lastday, but this was a different crowd.

I didn't search for my blood-sister. The people were just a faceless mass of movement and noise. From the corner of my eye, I noticed that my mother had her arms folded and refused to clap. I was a Cryokinetic, and yet I couldn't rival her coldness, which seemed to affect me and only me, a coldness so deep beyond my own abilities that it felt alien and lethal, even as I clenched ice in my hand.

The applause reverberated in my bones, echoing in the cavern of my emptiness. I tried to separate myself from my mother, to be aware of her entity but keep my concentration on my lab-siblings instead.

The noise continued for several long minutes, unbroken with no sign of stopping. Madison raised one hand, and the people quieted, although they still shifted with restlessness. They weren't sure what to make of us, and we them.

A thin, dark-skinned woman detached from the crowd and advanced up the steps, her gaze fixed on the twins.

Axel crouched low with a vicious snarl. Ash whipped the staff out of her harness and twirled it expertly in her right hand before trapping it in her other fist, the weapon snapping into position as a diagonal warning in front of her. RC seized the three silver disks from his pouch.

I tensed, taking a step back. I couldn't form a visible weapon because I didn't want anyone to connect me to Phantom, who was known for his ice ability, so instead, I expanded my orb into a thin layer of frost, just enough to keep my eyes blue as I moved behind Finn and Reese and clasped my hands on their shoulders.

My fingers must have been cold, but the twins didn't flinch. They leaned into me, as if secretly soothed by my touch. Their small, frail, warm bodies pressed against mine. I could feel them breathe, even feel their hearts beat. Just like the night of our escape, I experienced the overwhelming desire to protect them. I'd made that promise once, and I'd failed. This time, I was able to fight, and if I had to, I would stand between them and the hundreds of humans in town square, even my blood-family. Finn and Reese, upon hearing my thoughts, peered up at me.

And just like that, the ruckus was gone. Only a steady growl remained above the petrified silence. The woman had halted at the top of the stairs.

Between snarls, Axel warned, "One more step, and you're dead."

Madison drew an ectogun. The police officers at the front of the crowd took aim at us, waiting for the ghost hunter's order. I tightened my grip on Finn and Reese. Axel sank even lower onto all fours. The blades slid out of RC's disks.

Instead of steeled anger when Madison spoke, her voice wavered with uncertainty. "Why are you so protective of the kids who helped torture you?"

Jay retorted, "I'm not obligated to explain it to you."

I was torn between the two threats. In front of me, there was the ghost hunter with a weapon drawn and ready to fire, and on my right, there was the doctor with her sights on my lab-brothers. Despite the fact that Madison had a gun and I knew she also had a steady shot, it was the older, unarmed woman who charged every cell in my body with fear.

In physicality, she bore no resemblance to Dr. Anders—gender, skin color, height, build, voice, demeanor. But her eyes knew how to find the right veins for her practiced hands to insert needles, and her knowledge of the body's balance between life and death and all its inner workings was a dangerous parallel to the cruel man who had left the scar on my chest and the ports embedded in my skull.

Irrational as it might be, I feared her more than I feared the ghost hunter. Madison, I could fight. I knew how to fight. It was second nature now, a trust of my body, my power, my instincts, my ingenuity.

Doctors were more underhanded. They liked to cheat with drugs, to attack only once you'd been incapacitated, restrained, and stripped of your power. They attacked when you were helpless. And all they had to do was get close enough to stab you with a needle, and then you were at their mercy.

The woman held up her hands, as though that would somehow indicate she was harmless and we should trust her. I narrowed my eyes. I knew that trick.

"I mean no harm. I cared for Finn and Reese when they were sick. You were supposed to bring them back to me so I could evaluate their health, remember? I'd just like to give them quick checkups, that's all."

Her voice sounded sweet and docile. She crept forward, slower this time. Although Ash was armed and the human approaching her had no weapons, she retreated a step, as did RC. I stiffened, the cold power flaring in my core and causing an accidental layer of frost to crystallize on the twins' shirts.

To my surprise, a transparent red barrier shimmered in the air, cutting between the doctor and us. Relief weakened my knees, and I exhaled. *Thank you, Ax.*

The woman paused again. Madison was less threatened now, almost intrigued by our reactions. "You're afraid of Doc," she realized, sheathing her ectogun. The police, though reluctant, followed her lead, dissipating a trace of the tension.

"I can understand that," said Trey.

"What do you mean?"

The apprentice was still watching us, although I avoided my former friend's gaze and continued to survey Doc for any sudden movement.

Trey said, "There are a lot of similarities between doctors and the Agents."

"Such as?" Doc inquired. I despised the way she continued to study Finn and Reese.

"The laboratory has a weird sterilized smell. The Agents wear lab coats and latex gloves. And they use a lot of medical equipment." He explained to us, "I've been to the AGC. I've seen where you lived."

Axel straightened and snapped, "So what, Selman? You think you know everything about us because you've been in that place?"

Trey raised his eyebrows, clearly taken aback that Axel knew his last name. He shook his head. "No. I don't pretend to know very much about you at all."

There was energy in the air; it suffocated me. I didn't know if it was coming from Axel or if it was just the adrenaline in my own blood making me dizzy. Jay's gaze flicked meaningfully to Wes. "I don't remember agreeing to an examination."

The werewolf glanced at Madison and Doc, then shrugged. "He's right." Doc opened her mouth to protest, but Wes added, "Back off for now, okay?"

She sighed but stayed in place, then put on her warm smile again and called sweetly, "Hello, Finn, Reese. I like those names much more than A1 and A2. You remember me, right?"

I squeezed their shoulders to give them silent reassurance. They had to face these humans alone last time. I wanted them to know they wouldn't have to do that ever again.

"I've been very worried about you." Doc held out her hand. "Will you please come here?"

Even though it was posed as a question, the intent behind it was clear. The twins stiffened beneath my grip. They couldn't disobey a direct command from a human, no matter how polite. They both took a reluctant step forward.

I tightened my hold on their T-shirts and pulled them back. "No," I said in a low voice, then cleared my throat. *I will use ectoplasm if you try to pull any stunts with intangibility. Stay by me.*

Undeterred, Doc sat down on the step and continued cheerily, "That's okay. Maybe next time. I'm so glad to see you alive and well. How are you feeling now? Better?" They hesitated, then nodded. She asked them many questions, such as, "Are you congested? Have you been taking all the vitamins I sent? Do you drink water every day? You look tired—have you been sleeping a lot?" When Finn coughed, she added, "Does it hurt when you cough?"

The twins were starting to shiver. At first, I thought terror must be making them shudder, but then I noticed how ice was creeping down their backs, hardening their shirts and raising goose bumps on their bare skin. I forced my frozen fingers to open with a crackling chorus of thin ice breaking at the knuckles.

Sorry, I thought, in case they were still listening.

I made the mistake of looking at the crowd. I froze when I found all those eyes trained here, on the stage, on us, on me, watching . . .

I gasped, reliving Lastday. I took a step back into Ash and flinched, not realizing how close she'd been. Her warm hand shot out and seized my wrist.

"We're with you, Cay," she whispered.

I nodded, concentrating on steadying my breathing to calm myself. I was afraid, and that made me angry at myself. I was supposed to be strong for my lab-family.

Ash's finger tapped my wrist, and I realized in surprise that I'd formed an icicle in my moment of panic and was now clenching the long shard of ice at my side. I channeled my power back to my hand so I could re-form the icicle back into an orb to keep my hand and my mind busy.

Ero strode up the steps, his midnight-blue cloak trailing over his shoulders with sophisticated grandeur. Axel dissipated his shield so the teacher could approach. Ero said, "Finn, Reese, I think you should thank the nice doctor for taking such good care of you when you were ill."

The twins blinked, glanced at Doc, then at Ero, and then questioningly at Jay. They hung their heads. Ero knelt down to one knee. "It is not forbidden for kálos to speak in the presence of humans. I have not been reprimanded or disciplined. Neither has Jay."

"That's right," Doc added, following Ero's lead. "We would very much like to have a conversation with you."

Finn and Reese looked at each other. Finn faced the doctor, opened his mouth, and took a breath, but then hesitated. He seemed to deflate as his courage failed him. He clamped his mouth shut again.

"So," Madison interrupted icily, "will we be graced with your names, or do we have to call the rest of you by your numbers?"

We shifted uneasily and looked at Jay. The leader nodded once, and only then did the figure next to him with one glowing violet eye answer, "RC."

The ghost hunter nodded and looked at the next in line. My lab-sister said shyly, "Ash." She shifted, clutching her staff closer. Sunlight glinted off the neutralizer on her right arm.

Madison noticed. "That band . . . did the device we stole for you not work?"

Ash stiffened. "It . . . it did."

"Then why are you still wearing a neutralizer?"

"I-I . . ." Ash looked around, desperate to find a suitable distraction so she wouldn't have to answer. "Um, I . . . I mean, my Divinity is . . . I can't really . . ."

"It doesn't matter," Jay intervened. "She's able to do her job without her full power."

Before Madison could ask any more questions, RC clutched his head and collapsed, a strangled scream clawing its way out of his throat. "What's happening?" Madison demanded. "What's wrong with him?"

Doc stood to approach, but Axel's shield reappeared to block her passage once more. RC writhed on the ground, trapped in the throes of a Spasm. The townspeople stared, confused and horror-stricken. Some backed away, as if they were afraid he'd been possessed by a demon. Finally, he lay still, panting.

"Most unpleasant," Ero said, rubbing his own temples. I wordlessly offered my hand to my fallen lab-brother. He clasped it and allowed me to pull him to his feet.

"The side effect," Trey murmured. I glanced at him, then averted my eyes. He added, "Agent Kovak told us you suffer from a side effect caused by one of the experiments."

A side effect? That's what He *calls it?*

Axel's shield dissipated again. "I'm fine," RC mumbled, embarrassed. "Happens all the time."

"All the time . . ." Madison whispered in a horrified echo.

Finn yawned, and Reese was swaying on his feet. Jay put a tender hand on Finn's shoulder and said gently, "You can sit down if you need to." They plopped down cross-legged at our feet. Ero lowered himself the rest of the way to the ground beside them.

I was ready to leave. The last time I'd been here . . .

"Don't you ever forget."

"I'll come get you, Cato! Be strong. I'll get this mess straightened out."

Despair brought with it a surge of my ice power, making me cold inside and out. I tried to tune it out, but I heard *His* voice: *"See, she was too ashamed of you . . ." I was crammed in a small cage, staring in horror through the bars at the paper* He *was holding, the neat signature on the bottom line. ". . . a half-breed that shouldn't even exist."*

"And don't think we've forgotten about *you*," came a cutting voice.

I jolted to face Madison, who was staring straight at me. My mouth was suddenly cotton dry. In retrospect, I was an idiot for not anticipating this question. She wanted to know my name. I opened my mouth. What was I supposed to tell her? I had four names, and none could be used. *Cato. Phantom. 5292. A7.*

No, wait. I do have another name. "Seph," I answered on a whim, glancing away from Madison just in case she could read my lie. *Five now.*

Axel blatantly snickered. My face was on fire. Madison didn't seem to notice as she nodded at each of us, reciting, "Jay, Finn, Reese, Axel, RC, Ash, and Seph. Good start. Now, your Divinities?"

Jay gave her a stern look. "That's a very personal question."

"Yeah," Axel chimed in. "C'mon, Tarrow. We barely know each other. Gotta be friends before we start sharing weaknesses with one another, right?" He expelled the most theatrical yawn and suddenly proclaimed, "*Bloody* Scout. This is so boring. Are we done yet?"

Jay glanced briefly at him, then over his shoulder at Finn and Reese. I followed his gaze to find that the twins had already dozed off. They were still so weak from being sick that when their bodies needed to rest, they just couldn't keep their eyes open any longer. Jay finally betrayed his wavering patience with the public spectacle when he announced, "If you're satisfied, we'll be going."

"Already?" Madison asked. "But this festival is in your honor."

"We should go." He bent down and scooped Finn into his arms. The boy stirred, and his eyes fluttered open. He looked at Jay through half-open lids before closing his eyes and leaning his head against his lab-brother's chest, a contented sigh escaping from his parted lips. I lifted Reese.

"Wait," said Wes. "I, uh, I hope this is the start of a stronger alliance, Jay. You're part of this town now."

Jay scoffed. "We may fight on your behalf, but that doesn't make us part of the town."

Madison's hard expression indicated that she agreed with Jay's stance. Wes argued, "But you live here now, and that does." While Jay contemplated, Wes continued, "All I'm saying is we have to start communicating with you. I know we don't trust one another, and that needs to change."

Jay gazed down at Finn sleeping in his arms. "The deal was structured so we wouldn't have to rely on trust."

"When we first made it, yes, but we have a mutual codependence now." Wes held out his arms to the spectators. "This entire celebration was our way of officially welcoming you. You're just as big a part of Phantom Heights now as Phantom himself was."

I closed my eyes in a grimace. It was official, then. Phantom had been replaced. *I* had been replaced. It was ironic, really, that one of Phantom's substitutes was actually the former Phantom himself, but of course the humans didn't know that. Did it matter, anyway? Would their knowing change anything? Wes spoke of Phantom—of me—like a dim memory of a past most people didn't want to remember.

Jay's response was silence. We left on the heels of another roar of applause.

Humans wanted heroes to celebrate. But I knew trusting any of them would end in disaster because heroes were built up so they could fall, either as villains or martyrs. But they did fall. It was inevitable.

We weren't heroes, though. We were mercenaries.

Question was, would that spare us the fate of a hero?

— Chapter Twenty-Five —

Remember

Finn gasped in my ear as his arms tightened around my neck.

We were standing in a bright, open room. The southern side was more glass than wall; large windows and a set of French doors lined a railed balcony that faced Alvarez Park. Plush sofas, armchairs, and a low table had been tastefully arranged to break up the openness of the huge room. Behind me to the left, an arched doorway similar to the swooping architecture of the library and dining room on the ground floor opened into the sleeping quarters, where three wide bunk beds and a regular bed lined the far wall. To my right was a door I assumed led into the bathroom. And the best part—cut into the ceiling were skylights so we could still look at the stars.

"This is really ours?" Ash asked in wonder, turning a slow circle. I knelt into the plush carpet so Finn could clamber off my back, his twin climbing down from RC's.

Kit skipped to the sleeping quarters, and we trailed after her, watching her scamper up to one of the top bunks and giggle as she bounced on the mattress. "We sleep on these?" she asked. At Jay's nod, she beamed. "I never ever *ever* had a real bed before," she proclaimed joyously, falling back onto the mattress. I couldn't help but smile as she snatched the soft pillow and cuddled with it.

I wandered back into the sitting area, my fingers trailing along the arm of a sofa. Finn and Reese were mesmerized by the balcony. They tentatively opened one of the French doors and crept outside with slow, cautious steps, as if afraid the floor might collapse under their feet. They gripped the railing and stared at the clear blue sky, their gazes following the path of a hawk gliding over the trees of the park.

Jay set a backpack down on the floor. "Before we settle in, would you set up Proto, just to be safe?"

The twins took a few more seconds to appreciate the stunning view from the third story, then obediently returned to Jay and knelt by the backpack. Finn pulled out the gloves while Reese removed the sophisticated computer, set it down, and flipped the switch on the side.

Finn donned his gloves and leaned toward the tiny holograph that appeared in the air. ECANI beeped upon identifying his retina, and then the small square expanded to a large screen and a keyboard flickered into existence. Finn's fingers flew silently over the transparent keys. He brought up the program of their newest Proto model, and after a moment, the screens vanished again as ECANI entered standby mode.

Finn leaned back and reported, "Proto is active."

ECANI made a strange set of beeping sounds as though speaking in a mechanized language I couldn't understand. "Low power," Reese translated, glancing at Axel.

Without a word, Axel strolled over to ECANI and held his open hand right above the machine without actually touching it. Red ectoplasm crackled around his glove and was drawn into the small black box, absorbed immediately. Any of us could power ECANI if we had to—Finn and Reese had been responsible for feeding it at that place— but with Axel's unlimited power supply, the depletion from him would be like taking a glass of water from the ocean.

"Hey, Cato," Axel said, a mischievous grin making a foreboding appearance. "I was wondering . . . wherever did you come up with the name *Seph*? It's so creative."

I shot him a look of daggers, which he returned with a fanged smile. "It's short for 'seven,'" I mumbled.

"You think of that all by yourself?"

I turned away and announced, "I want to clean up." Axel chuckled at my back, but I walked into the bathroom and shut the door.

I shouldn't let him get under my skin.

I spent a few minutes admiring our clean new home—white cabinets, tiled floor, marble countertops, a stained-glass window of warm colors in a symmetrical design—but it was too pristine. I was dirty and unworthy to be in this perfect place.

A dormer jutted out from the middle of the room, and situated in front of the window, nestled comfortably in the three-sided nook, was a massive bathtub. I peered out the window, pleasantly surprised to find that directly below was a fenced-in garden. It looked rather weedy and neglected, but blooming flowers displayed pops of red, yellow, white, pink, and purple.

In the back corner of the bathroom, a frosted glass encasement caught my attention. I tentatively walked past the tub and opened the door to see what was inside.

I froze. A chilling memory of Detox floated to the surface—a shower with manacles dangling from the ceiling and high-powered hoses rank with the odors of chemicals. I quickly shut the glass door.

The toilet, on the other hand, I found to be nothing short of a miracle. I hadn't been allowed to use one at that place, just a bucket once a day. I didn't need to use it now, but I flushed it and watched the water swirl in a whirlpool. Once the bowl was refilled, I flushed it again, just because I could.

I approached the sink next. I flipped the faucet on, off, on again. I left the water running while I unfastened my cloak and dropped it to the floor, then untied the wrist gauntlets. I removed my gloves. The dark marks tattooed on my bare forearms snared my attention. Slowly, I lifted my hands. My heartbeat pounded in my ears above the running water.

I couldn't remember looking at this tender skin with faint blue veins when it was Pure. I felt as though I'd been Marked forever. I closed my fingers, forming my hands into fists.

I'm not A7-5292. My name is Cato.

"Cato," Jay had said a long time ago. The first time my name had ever passed his lips. *"Listen to me carefully, Cato. You have to remember that name. It's very important. They'll try to take it away from you. They'll try to unname you and make you believe that you are A7, not Cato. Don't let* Them. *You have to remember who you are."*

I peeled off layers of clothing until I was naked in the middle of the bathroom. When I looked in the mirror above the sink, a stranger stared back.

I approached the reflective glass, watching the young man copy my movements. I set my hands on either side of the sink and gazed into the unfamiliar face.

My blue-and-green eyes glinted beneath the overhead light. I stared at them for several long minutes, then hung my head and exhaled. I searched for the power source inside of me, and I felt it pulsing subtle warmth in my core with every heartbeat. It was a part of me, a part of who I was. Usually when I sought it, I then called upon it and let the warmth rush through me. This time, I forced it away, deep down out of reach. When I raised my head and opened my eyes, they were no longer glowing.

I covered my blue eye with my palm. I used to look like this once. Had I grown up human, perhaps this face wouldn't be that of a stranger, but one I saw every day in the mirror.

I broke the dam and let the warmth fill me again as I lowered my hand, my eyes flickering to life again in the mirror. I tilted my head, then knelt down to extract my photograph from the pile of clothing on the floor. I held it up in front of me so I could compare this testament of the past to the person in the mirror.

The boy in the photograph was smiling. He was well-loved and healthy with short, glossy black hair. I, on the other hand, stared at the mirror with eyes that were tired and haunted, shadowed by dark circles accentuating a gaunt face. My dull hair was longer, unkempt. A long scar trailed down the center of my chest. I was still emaciated from long-term starvation, but physically in such great shape that the lean muscles made me appear less sickly. I had been re-formed and hardened into something not human anymore. I was nothing like the boy in the photograph.

With a sigh, I set my treasure on the counter and glared at my reflection. My fingers drifted up and caressed one of the small, round metal ports in my forehead. I could still hear the high-pitched whine of the drills and the *chink* of sliding metal every time the NMS was threaded through the holes in my skull to analyze my brain while I fought in the Arena. Both sounds set my teeth on edge and sent an unpleasant tingle through every nerve in my body.

Light-headed and nauseated, I turned away. Maybe not having mirrors in that place had been a blessing. Seeing myself made me remember not only how much my life had changed, but also how much I had changed. I didn't even want to look at myself.

I explored the cabinets until I found a washcloth, and then I rinsed it under the stream of icy water.

I scrubbed away not weeks' but months' worth of dirt and blood and filth. I was rough on my skin, determined to cleanse myself of the foulness caked on my body so I could be worthy of this spotless abode. Eventually maybe I'd be brave enough to examine the tub and figure out how it worked, but this was a start.

I worked the matted knots out of my hair, shuddering when I heard the drills again. The overhead light seemed to flare brighter. Whirring drill bits and cold metal and painful white lights and I didn't want to think about this but I couldn't stop; all I heard were drills, and then . . .

Quiet. It was a noisy quiet, the kind where many voices fade into a wordless drone in the background—a white-noise kind of quiet. I was sitting inside the cafeteria at school. Lazy, fat snowflakes fell softly outside the frosted windows. Trey was across from me, but I'd turned to face Vivian, who was perched on the edge of her seat next to me.

She smiled and tucked her hair behind one ear, revealing a bracelet made of blue, bronze, and silver cords tied around her wrist.

The realization slammed into me so hard it actually took my breath away. I stood stone still as the stream of water continued to swirl down the sink. "It's Vivian's bracelet," I whispered over the sound of falling water, as if saying the words aloud would confirm my statement.

My mind was blank as I used the washcloth to finish scraping the grime off my body, and then I dunked my head in the sink to let the water wash away the rest of the matted filth I'd loosened in my hair.

Every time I closed my eyes now, I saw Vivian and that bracelet tied around her wrist. How could I forget?

I knelt beside my pile of clothes, shoved my fingers into the pouch, and retrieved the bracelet, then settled my weight on my knees and stared at it for a few long, heart-pounding minutes. I knew I should return it, and theoretically, doing so would be simple. I'd just have to find a way to get Vivian alone, and then I could give her the bracelet and . . . and what? How would I explain how I knew it was hers without revealing my true identity?

I gazed at the woven cords in my hand. I couldn't deliver it personally to Vivian, but perhaps I could put it someplace where she was sure to find it. I shoved it back into the safety of my pouch. For now, I'd keep it. After all, how badly could she miss a broken bracelet?

My clothes were still soiled, but since I had nothing else to wear, I donned them again. The boots were worn. The pants were dirty. The fabric of my shirt was stiff and crusty, and the smell wasn't exactly favorable. I didn't mind, though. I still felt safest in my Arena uniform. And despite the dirty clothes and my newfound dilemma, I felt refreshed.

I opened the door and stood on the threshold to admire our new Home. Finn and Reese were sitting with their backs to me, alone. I took a breath to ask where the others were, but the words evaporated on my tongue.

Hovering in front of Finn and Reese were thousands of holograms, most of them arranged in columns of tiny little squares off to the side. The twins were facing two big screens. One showed Jay, RC, and Ash walking down a side street. The other, at first glance, showed a deserted alleyway, until I spotted a black-and-white kitten snoozing on a warm dumpster lid. Even as I watched, my three lab-siblings walked out of sight of the camera's view, and that screen rapidly shrank and joined the column of squares as a tiny screen near the bottom expanded and shifted to take the other's place as the dominant main screen. The new image still showed Jay and RC and Ash, but from a different angle.

"What is all this?" I asked.

They turned. "This," said Finn with an unusual gleam in his eye, "is the visual execution of the program we designed to prevent us from being digitally tracked."

Reese added, "It's usually running in the background. But sometimes we like to watch."

Finn gestured to the columns of little squares and explained, "This is every open-source camera in Phantom Heights."

Reese pointed to the large screens and said, "This footage is being deleted from the sources in real time. With its precise facial recognition, ECANI locks onto your image and automatically switches cameras depending on which direction you're heading and which cameras are in range. Most of these images are coming from security cameras."

Sure enough, when our lab-siblings walked out of sight again, that screen was minimized and replaced with two more big screens, one from a street corner and the other apparently from the inside of a store window.

"Where's Axel?"

Finn replied, "Axel has an impressive talent for avoiding the cameras. It's extremely rare for him to ever show up on the screen, and if he does, it's only for a moment."

"Do you always watch us when we're on patrol?" I asked.

They quickly turned back to the screens to avoid looking at me. Finn admitted, "Well, we can't go on patrol with you . . ."

"So, we like to know where you are and what you're doing," Reese finished.

I was touched by this unintentional show of compassion, but also a little unnerved. I stared at the thousands of tiny screens to the side, rather solemn as I realized just how much effort it took for ECANI to keep us off camera. I'd had no idea there were so many opportunities for humans to record us. The program Finn and Reese had created included all open-source devices, from cell phones to satellites and everything in between. All this time, I thought I'd been sneaking around unnoticed in the shadows when in reality, Finn and Reese had been cloaking me from technology's invisible eyes.

The sobering notion struck me how much we had to rely on the twins without even realizing it. One flip of the switch, and ECANI would cease protecting us from *Their* network.

I bowed my head, watching the backs of my lab-brothers' heads from the corner of my eye. It wouldn't take much to make that program turn off. One command from a human. One moment of second-guessing the decision to defy their masters. One accident.

"Did Jay leave a message for me?"

"No," they answered in unison.

"Okay. Are you going to be all right here if I leave?"

Finn glanced at me over his shoulder, and Reese asked, "Why wouldn't we be?"

I shrugged. "I don't know. It's just a new place—a big adjustment. I want to make sure you're comfortable."

"We're fine," Finn dismissed.

Despite the assurance, I shifted. "You promise you'll stay inside Proto?"

"Yes," said Reese.

"And you won't let anybody in? Even if it's Ero?"

"Yes," said Finn.

"Do you need anything from the kitchen before I go?"

"Cato," they said in reserved exasperation. "We're fine."

I nodded. Ash, Jay, and RC were being recorded a few blocks from the school, so I tied my mask in place, threw the hood over my head, and departed to find them.

As Wes had promised, the entire third floor had been reconfigured to suit our needs, so there was no hallway; the door opened onto a short landing at the top of the staircase. I trailed my hand down the balustrade, the smooth oak sliding beneath my fingerless glove as I descended to the next floor. I shouldn't dally at the risk of being unable to find my lab-siblings by the time I made it to their last location, but I lingered at the foot of the stairs on the second floor, my curiosity begging me to explore.

Like the ground-level staircase, this one had an elegant flair at the base, opening with a flourish onto the second story. I opened the door at the end of the hall and found Wes's study, although it didn't seem to be in current use. Next to the staircase was another door that opened into a closet filled with boxes, many of which were labeled with holidays.

Past the stairs, I had the option of going straight or right. I chose right. The hall took me deeper into the west wing, intersecting with another hallway. I opened doors and discovered unused bedrooms filled with furniture beneath cobwebs and dusty white sheets.

Upon returning to the stairs, I ventured down the unexplored hallway, which ended at a massive window where it connected with the railed walkway I'd seen from down below. I knew from my first visit to Saros Manor that the walkway spanned the three sets of French doors leading out to the backyard patio. Tall windows lined the walkway all the way to the east wing.

As much as I was tempted to explore the east side of the second story, I'd lingered too long already. I returned to the staircase again, although I couldn't resist the urge to open the door right beside the stairs going down. Locked.

No doubt it was locked for a reason, and I shouldn't be snooping around Wes's home, but I couldn't help myself. I reached for my center and summoned intangibility, then leaned into the door.

I couldn't phase through.

I frowned and stepped back, then lifted my hand to stare at my glove. My body had a slight transparency to it; I was definitely intangible. With the exception of the Dome, I'd never been unable to phase through a solid object.

I cut the flow of power before it drained too much from my reserves. Interesting. A locked door that ghosts couldn't phase through. Now I *really* wanted to know what was inside.

Realizing I'd wasted way too much time and at this rate Jay, RC, and Ash weren't going to be anywhere near where I'd last seen them, I hurried down the last staircase with recklessness I soon cursed myself for, because lurking in the foyer was a giant wolf.

I froze.

So did Wes.

The longest second passed before I snapped to my senses and dipped my chin while reaching up to seize my hood. I pulled it down low over my left eye, hoping Wes hadn't had enough time to see my unfortunately unique eyes.

This was the closest I'd been to the creature since returning to Phantom Heights. He was colossal. One swipe of his paw could easily send me flying across the great room. His gray fur was thick and coarse, raised up in a dark mane between his broad shoulders and partially down his back. The wolf bared his teeth at me.

I took a step back in alarm, and yet his body language didn't match the hostility of showing his teeth. He was growling, but I didn't think he was growling at me. He almost seemed to be grimacing.

His muscles taut, he sank to the floor, snarling and whining, eyes closed in strain. Slowly, amid the painful pop and grind of bones, the wolf's body shifted. I waited a full minute, watching, transfixed and horrified by the pain he seemed to be experiencing and unsure if this was an intentional transformation or if something was wrong with him.

Finally, he'd changed enough that he was sort of in limbo, still more wolf than man, but capable of speech. He lay on the floor and opened his yellow eyes to look at me, and through elongated teeth set in a partial muzzle, he croaked, "I . . . apologize for . . . startling you. It's . . . almost full moon . . . and . . . I can't . . . change. Sorry."

I stared at him. He whimpered in agony, struggling to maintain the partial limbo he'd managed to achieve.

"Sorry?" I felt myself grinning kindly at him behind my mask, sympathy connecting us in a way he didn't even know. "You don't have to apologize for what you are."

He blinked his yellow eyes at me, visibly stunned even in his distorted form. He said nothing more; his body had changed beyond the point of words, and he was a wolf again. He rose, still comically surprised, ears forward, tail moving just a little from side to side.

I couldn't linger, not with his superior olfactory senses drawing in my scent with each passing moment, so I left him in the grandiose foyer and departed to find my lab-siblings.

— Chapter Twenty-Six —

The Letter

Holly locked the door to her office before she ran her hands down her face with a frustrated sigh.

So, Cato was going to play this game as Seph. Fine. It gave her more time to figure out how to handle the situation. His performance had been convincing; not even Madison had recognized him. If Holly hadn't been specifically looking for him, she wouldn't have known his true identity, either.

But he couldn't live under this alias forever. Phantom's mask had been ripped away, and eventually Seph's would be too, especially now that Cooper was involved. "Damn it," Holly muttered under her breath. She stormed over to the window and yanked down the blinds so nobody might happen to look up and see her pacing in distress.

When she'd met with him to discuss Ero analyzing the crowd when the Alpha ghosts made their appearance, Dog-Breath had conveniently forgotten to mention that part of his negotiation with Jay involved sharing Saros Manor with the fugitives. Why did Cooper have to get in the middle of this mess? Never mind—that was a stupid question. He'd seen an opportunity to leverage resources and manpower to fix his mansion, and he'd taken it.

But of all the places for Cato to go, why there? He was smarter than that. A mask over his face might fool everyone else, but even if Ero knew—how could he not?—and was maintaining the secret, Cato couldn't conceal his scent from a werewolf with an impeccable sense of smell. He had chosen the riskiest place in Phantom Heights to live.

"What were you thinking?" Holly muttered. She plopped down in her chair.

Everything on her desk was in perfect order, except the corner of one sheet of paper in an otherwise neat stack. She adjusted it to its proper alignment, then leaned back to weigh her options. Wesly Cooper was a problem, but one she knew how to deal with. His loyalty could be bought. Was it better to forewarn him about his "guest" and buy his silence?

But that would be such a mess, and then that entitled jackass would likely blackmail her. No, Holly didn't want to deal with that, not while she was preparing for the biggest campaign of her life. Mayor Correll had no idea she was planning to end his reign. She was confident she could beat him in an election. The only obstacle potentially standing in her way was Cato. Her past mistake might cost her everything.

She stared at the list of twenty-three names on her desk. "No one expressed the clear intention to contact the AGC," Ero had told Wes, who had relayed the message to her since Holly was still doing her utmost to stay out of the Telepath's range whenever possible. "This list consists of the least accepting members of the community who reject the idea of hiring kálos for protection."

Twenty-three. Such a conservative number; she'd expected more. But nonetheless, it was a good statistic to keep in mind.

No wonder S-O-S had failed so miserably.

Holly's next step was to schedule an individual meeting with each person on her list, but her mind was elsewhere right now. She shifted the list to reveal the unfinished letter beneath it. Thus far, she'd written only one word:

Cato,

There was so much she wanted to say, but the words eluded her except for two: *I'm sorry*. Two words that wouldn't count as an explanation, wouldn't stand as a threat, wouldn't negotiate a deal.

Two useless words blocking any other sentences from appearing in ink, and she couldn't bring herself to give those two words life because then the guilt would be real, and she'd be staring right at it.

Holly crumpled the paper into a ball and threw it across the room. The wad bounced off the rim of her trash can and rolled across the floor.

It was still too early in the game for her to reveal her hand. She wasn't even sure how much Cato knew. Kovak could have told him the truth, or he could have spoon-fed him lies, and Holly wasn't sure which was worse. Cato might be a bomb counting down to detonation. And this bomb, if Agent Kovak was right, was now powerful enough to obliterate Phantom Heights.

A knock on the door made her jump. "What?" she snapped, hand pressed against her chest to keep her heart from bursting out of her rib cage.

A muffled voice shyly answered, "It's me. Nikki."

"I said no interruptions."

"Oh. Yes. I'm sorry. I . . . I have the transcripts you requested from the last meeting."

Holly closed her eyes, took a deep breath, and rose. She tugged at the bottom of her blouse to pull out any wrinkles and calmly smoothed her skirt with her palm as she drifted across her office. She turned the lock and opened the door to find the secretary offering a folder. "Thank you," Holly said, a little too sweetly.

She started to close the door, but Nikki said, "Did you get a copy of *The Herald* today?"

"No. I haven't had time." *Go away*, Holly wanted to snarl while she maintained her toothy smile. She pushed the door a few inches more.

"Caslynn Swan wrote an article about the Alpha ghosts."

"*What?*" Holly yanked the door open again and snatched the newspaper out of Nikki's hand. She skimmed the headlines for the word *Alpha*.

"Page three," Nikki said meekly. "At the bottom."

Holly opened the paper and located a narrow article titled **Code Word: Rogue**. She skimmed the first few sentences and then lifted her head in angry confusion. "What the hell is this?"

"Oh, she wrote in code," explained Nikki, needlessly pointing at the newspaper in Holly's hand. "I, um, well, I think it's clever. Everyone in Phantom Heights will know who she's really talking about."

Holly scowled and read: *For more than two years, there has been a hero vacancy in Phantom Heights. That post has now been filled. The PH Herald is investigating leads in regards to a mysterious new team of heroes. Believed to be former members of Madison Tarrow's raid team gone rogue, these ghost hunters have taken Phantom's persona to heart. Heroes? Perhaps. We have little information on this new organization we call Rogue, but there have been sightings of Rogue raiders wearing masks similar to Phantom's iconic look. The recent festival revealed an overwhelming approval rating for the ragtag team of new heroes. Time will tell if they are here to stay and if they can fill the shoes of their predecessor.*

Nikki was watching Holly, looking for approval. Holly folded the paper. "I specifically told Caslynn she was not allowed to report on the Alpha ghosts. Apparently Ms. Swan doesn't seem to be concerned that the Agents aren't complete idiots capable of figuring out that *Rogue* is code for *Alpha* and this tale she spun about former raiders is a farce."

"W-well . . ." Nikki rubbed her arm and stared at her feet. "*The PH Herald* isn't publishing online. Only in print. Nobody outside Phantom Heights will even see these articles unless they come here and pick up a real newspaper."

"I think I'm going to have to have a talk with Ms. Swan." Holly tucked the paper into the folder and clutched it loosely to her breast. "Thank you, Nikki."

The secretary blinked at her like a doe before she realized she'd just been dismissed. "Oh. Yeah. You're welcome." She smiled uneasily and took a step back, but then stood there smiling even while Holly slowly closed the door.

Holly waited one, two, three seconds until she heard Nikki's footsteps recede, and then she let her shoulders slouch. She wandered to her desk and set the folder down.

Great, as if Wesly Cooper weren't bad enough. Caslynn will have a field day if she discovers who's under Seph's mask.

Holly rubbed her temples. All this worrying was giving her a splitting headache. She took a deep, cleansing breath and pivoted. Head held high, she marched to the wad of paper next to the trash can, picked it up and flattened it, then inserted it into her shredder to ensure the evidence disappeared. She had to make sure nobody tied her to Seph. The longer Cato remained a moorlin in the shadows, the better. Eventually she would have to deal with him.

But she needed more time to set up her pieces before the inevitable endgame.

Vivian Tarrow pocketed her key as the front door swung open. She closed it with her foot while absently flipping through the mail. Bill, bill, another bill, a letter from her cousin Terra, and . . .

She slowed to a stop in the middle of the living room. Madison was coming down the stairs. "Anything for me?"

"Bills," Vivian said distractedly. She held up a manila envelope with the AGC's insignia in the top left corner and Madison's name in the middle. "And this."

Her mom quickened her pace and jumped the last two steps to rush at Vivian and swipe the envelope away before Vivian could inspect it.

"Mom, what is that?"

"It doesn't concern you." She marched into the kitchen, her destination the closed door that led to her lab in the basement.

Vivian followed. "But it's from Agent Kovak." When her mom ignored her, she raised her voice and accused, "I thought you didn't work for him anymore."

Her mom froze with her hand on the doorknob. "I never worked *for* him. This is just . . . something he owed me. I called him a few days ago and asked him to send it."

"And what is *it* exactly?"

"Test results, I think."

"On what?" Silence. "*On what?*" Vivian repeated louder.

"Not what. Whom."

Vivian felt as though she'd just been punched in the gut. Before she could speak, her mom said, "Don't tell anybody I have this—do you understand? I'll be in my lab, so don't disturb me. You can heat up leftovers for dinner."

"Wait a minute," Vivian protested, but her mom had already slammed the door shut behind her, leaving Vivian alone in the kitchen. She stood in absolute bewilderment before she sank into the nearest chair. The thought of heating up last night's lasagna turned her stomach.

Not what.

Whom.

— Chapter Twenty-Seven —

Bonds

"There is a cave high up in a mountain so tall that the top is never seen from below the clouds. Freezing rain falls in sheets, and thunder booms so loudly it causes rock slides. In the cave is a dragon named Asiana."

Ero's deep voice was mesmerizing, even from my place in the doorway. Finn and Reese were sitting cross-legged on the floor gazing up at him, enthralled by his story.

"There is a trespasser in Asiana's cave this night. Thirteen-year-old Osidius is lost in the storm when he stumbles upon the dragon's treasure. He describes it as a 'glittering mountain within the earthen mountain.' Gold and silver coins, jewels, swords, goblets, crowns, anything that twinkles, all gathered in one pile and guarded by the great dragon herself. Steam erupts from Asiana's nostrils. She accuses, *Thief!*"

"Does she eat him?" the twins chorused.

Ero laughed. "Now, now, how can you expect me to finish the story if you keep interrupting?"

They mumbled, "Sorry," to which Ero gently scolded, "Never apologize for an inquisitive mind. Now, where was I? Ah, Osidius. He is a Mind-Reader. He tells the dragon, 'Thief? Perhaps to a soul who first gazes upon this great treasure, the temptation would prevail, but not I. You see, O Great One, I have now seen the guardian of the treasure. I cannot understand why you collect such dull trinkets when all these jewels pale in comparison to the beauty of your scales. Never before have I seen such magnificence.'

"Dragons know a great many tongues and speak by means of projection, intrigued by riddles but easily distracted by flattery. Cunning Osidius gauges the effectiveness of his words and then says, 'Mighty

"

Dragon, if I may so humbly ask a favor of you, I would like to see your scales in the light.'

"Asiana replies, *Your words are sweet poison. To see my magnificence in the light, you say, Little One? But the weather is foul, and there is no light but that of the lightning, which is too brief and bright to truly admire my colors.*

"'Ah,' says Osidius, 'but there is heat in your heart that can blossom to the gentlest and warmest of lights. Will you not grace me with your splendor?'

"Pleased by the Mind-Reader's praise, Asiana gladly lights a fire to show off her lovely blue scales. Osidius admires and compliments her, all the while edging nearer to the glowing embers to fend off the chill and dry his clothes. As the night waxes, the dragon and boy become friends, talking of more important things than scales and jewels. They speak of their travels and toils, of how Osidius never knew his parents and Asiana's mate was slaughtered by another dragon.

"When the weather clears, he stays with Asiana. He learns to hunt in the mountains, and scale the rocky cliffs, and craft his own fire by striking the mineral rocks in the caves. He is even allowed to sit between Asiana's dorsal spikes and fly with her high above Avilésor. He is one of a sparse few to ever fly above the clouds and see the sun, the moon, and the stars. As the decades pass, then the centuries, he learns the art of projection until he speaks like a dragon with his mind instead of his mouth.

"Eventually, Asiana becomes ill with a sickness that kills her fire. She dies, leaving Osidius alone again. He takes but one treasure from her mountain—a single sapphire scale from her breast. He roams the land and spends much time meditating, focusing his mind until he can do more than simply project his thoughts. He can summon memories from below the surface of the consciousness and twist them or erase them, although this he does only to the unsavory characters he meets on his travels, the wickedest souls who cause others pain. He never lives in one place for more than a few nights, so determined is he to see every place he and Asiana flew over. Then one day, he meets an Empath whose eyes are the same color as Asiana's scale, and he marries her. She bears him three children. Two carry his Divinity of mind-reading, and to them, he passes on the wisdom of the dragon and the art of telepathy.

"So you see," Ero finished, "if the legend is true, we can trace our Divinity's origin back to the dragons. All Telepaths are descendants of Osidius's bloodline. You and I are, though probably very distantly, related."

The teacher paused, noticing me lingering in the doorway. "Hello, Cato." I didn't reply to his greeting, but he continued, "Perhaps you would be willing to help us? We need someone for the twins to practice on."

"No."

Ero tilted his head. "You do not trust them?"

"I trust Finn and Reese; it's you I don't want inside my head. Why don't you ask Axel to volunteer?" I asked, glaring at my lab-brother standing at the window with his back to us and his arms folded. Axel hadn't moved during the entire training session, and he didn't bother to answer or even grace us with a glance. I didn't need to be a Mind-Reader like Ero and the twins to know his silent answer was *Fuck off.*

"Fair enough," Ero said casually. "I understand. It is one thing to open your home to me, but another matter entirely to open your mind." He turned back toward the twins but studied me from the corner of his eye. "Too bad, though. I bet your friend Trey would have volunteered."

I did my best not to react to his bait. "Former friend," I corrected.

"Hmm. What about Vivian?"

I couldn't help it; I automatically stiffened. I knew he said that on purpose, testing me, monitoring my reaction to coax conscious thoughts so he didn't have to dig. That was the one aspect I hated most about Ero—I couldn't hide anything from him. The twins too, of course, but they were my lab-brothers. I had nothing to hide from them.

Although Ero swore he never used his powers irresponsibly, a small part of me still wondered if he actually did, then reprogrammed us to believe nothing had happened. It was a confusing and frightening notion, making it hard to let me give the Telepath the trust he should have already earned.

Ero smiled at my thoughts. "I am not altering your mind, Cato. I do find it curious, though, that of all people on the raid team you could have kidnapped, you chose perhaps the most carefully guarded and difficult target. That is something that has puzzled me."

"It's not that puzzling. We did it to keep Madison in check. Simple as that."

Ero cocked an eyebrow. "Is it?"

I ground my teeth in frustration because he was right, although I'd never admitted it aloud. I did have an ulterior motive for selecting that human from all the others.

"So I also wanted to see her again. Who cares?"

Ero was studying me so intently that I began to fidget. "Is that all?"

I turned away, embarrassed that he was aware of the satisfaction I had in knowing that I'd successfully caused Madison to squirm.

He said, "I have noticed that you harbor an unusually strong abhorrence for Madison."

"Oh, please," I snapped. "Every ghost that's ever passed through Phantom Heights hates Madison. Go ahead; I challenge you to find even *one* that came through the Rip and doesn't hate her."

Ero set his elbow on the chair arm and leaned his cheek against his fist. "Yes, but your disdain seems much more . . . *personal*. May I ask what—?"

"No, you may not. Our history is none of your business."

He paused long enough to make me regret being so rude with my interruption before he said, "I see. Then let me ask you this: why are you still hiding behind a mask? Is it out of fear, or is it something else?"

"Why do you care?"

"I simply wonder what caused you to sever your ties with humankind. Your friends, your loved ones—they do not know you are here. Why? Why are you still in hiding, Cato? Why have you not returned to your blood-family?"

I should have been angry that he insisted on prying into my personal life. But the anger that had been boiling inside me just a few moments before had cooled, drowned in a deadly cold pain that opened inside me like an abyss. I squeezed my eyes shut and hung my head.

Agent Kovak leaned over my cage. "It would be so much easier for you if you stopped fighting me." I glared up at him through the bars. "They aren't coming for you."

"Yes, they are."

"No, they aren't. We legally own you now."

"You're lying," I whispered, conscious of the other Alpha subjects watching silently.

Kovak pulled a piece of paper from his lab-coat pocket and unfolded it, then held it down so I could read the print. Mom's fluid signature was scrawled neatly at the bottom of an agreement that transferred custody of me for the sum of ten thousand dollars.

"She signed this yesterday."

The cold despair of abandonment knocked the wind out of me. "No."

"Oh, yes," he replied with a cruel smile. "You belong to us now. See, she was too ashamed of you—a half-breed that shouldn't even exist. She doesn't want you."

I shook my head. "No," I whispered weakly. She had promised. She promised . . .

My voice grew stronger. "I don't believe you. She said she'd come get me."

"She was distressed." Kovak sighed, shaking his head as if I were an ignorant child that failed to understand a simple concept. "Now that she's had time to settle down and think, she decided she couldn't keep you. After all, you're a high-risk, dangerous kálos with unstable powers. She knew she wouldn't be able to handle you. You're safer here, where I can make sure you don't hurt yourself or anyone else. We've been working out the arrangement for a few days now, and we finally agreed on the terms yesterday."

He was holding the signed document in his hand, and yet I con-

tinued to shake my head in denial. He chuckled and said, "You can't really be that surprised, can you? Your mommy is a highly regarded authority figure, and then you came along and made her look like an incompetent fool. Didn't you wonder why you've been here for three weeks and she hasn't visited? Hasn't called? Hasn't even sent a letter? Tell me, why do you think that is?"

I swallowed, reeling to think of excuses while I stared at her signature. "She . . . uh . . . she's probably just been . . ."

"What, busy?" Agent Kovak taunted. He folded the paper and tucked it out of sight in his pocket again. "The truth is, she hasn't contacted you because she needed time to think this through logically without you biasing her decision. I already transferred the money. The deal is done."

"I want to hear it from her," I insisted, as if hearing these words from Mom's mouth instead of his would convince me this was really happening.

"Well, unfortunately she won't see you," Agent Kovak replied coldly. "It's easier for her to move on with her life if she doesn't look back. I recommend the same for you. Like it or not, this is what your mother wanted. She donated you to science. I don't intend to waste her gift."

I swallowed. The lump in my throat was a painful ache. "I don't have any loved ones here anymore. My blood-family doesn't want to see me . . . and I don't want to see them."

Ero frowned at my memory. "Let me see if I understand this correctly: your mother sold you to the Agents?"

I didn't answer. I liked to delude myself with words like *abandoned* and *disowned* because they didn't seem quite as harsh as the truth. *He* hadn't whisked me away and hidden me in a secret place where I couldn't be found. There was no miscommunication, no misunderstanding. I hadn't just been cut out of the family; I'd been sold. It was a clear legal transaction. *He* had paid my mother and promised to make me disappear so she could salvage her life and carry on with nothing more than an embarrassing memory of me.

Axel turned his head ever so slightly, one narrow red eye watching me. My throat was cinched almost shut; the words actually hurt when I forced out, "She would take me back only if He could 'cure' me. But I can never be human again, so that means . . ."

I trailed off, but the thought unreeled for Ero to hear in the wake of a sigh: *I can never go back.*

Finn and Reese both had their eyes averted. They already knew all this, and my pain was making them uncomfortable. Axel turned to the window again. Ero's silence was solemn and respectful. "So," he murmured, "when she found out your transformation was permanent, she sold you."

I shrugged as if I didn't care, but really I was trying to slough off the weight dragging me down. "*He* didn't even try. *He* just told her no, and that was it. She signed the paperwork, took the money, and forgot I ever existed. Easiest solution." An image rose from the murk of my mind—a moment frozen forever of two women sitting in the park holding onto each other. "My fam—my *blood*-family—moved on. They don't want me in their lives anymore, so I should honor their wish."

"But—"

"They *disowned* me, Ero. If they want to move on with their lives, why should I hold them back? I have a new family. I don't need them."

Ero raised his hands in surrender. "I see. But are you trying to convince me . . . or yourself?"

I scowled, opened my mouth, then closed it and stormed away. I wasn't angry at Ero so much as I was angry that his words struck true. I marched through our sleeping quarters and phased through the window to emerge onto the gently sloping roof on the north side of Saros Manor.

The sun was shining, though a gentle breeze kept the heat at bay. I wanted to scream at the world until there was nothing left, but I couldn't, so as always, I locked it away inside myself. It had been a long time since I'd let the green power out. I was starting to wonder if smothering all this rage and frustration was slowly killing me. I sat down on the rough, warm shingles and buried my face in my hands.

Why did everything have to be so complicated?

A few long minutes passed before I drew my knees to my chest and stared at the buildings of Phantom Heights. Of all the towns for us to take refuge in, it had to be this one. It had to be mine.

I drew the worn photograph from my pocket and held it in my hand as the breeze ruffled my hair. We all looked so happy, so carefree. They had moved on . . . Why couldn't I?

I let go. The photograph fell at my feet, fluttering gently in the breeze. I didn't need any more reminders of what I'd lost. With a deep sigh, I rose.

Pain exploded in my head without warning and slammed me back down on the roof. I wilted in on myself with hoarse shrieks that faded away as the Spasm split my head apart and displaced my senses.

Couldn't hear my own screams. Couldn't feel the rough shingles beneath me. Couldn't see in the blackness consuming me behind eyelids squeezed tight. *Roof . . . edge . . . fall . . .*

On a primal level, abstract and disjointed without the cohesion of language to form a true sentence, I remembered that I was on a rooftop and I was in danger of falling, and I shouldn't thrash, but this pain was something wild, something that made me buck and writhe beyond conscious control. I wouldn't even register falling off the roof in this state.

I pressed my palms against the ports in my skull, gripping my hair in my fingers, pulling, focusing on the sharp bursts of pain from my hair follicles to ground myself into this world and slow my freefall into the consuming abyss. Seconds felt like hours. It wouldn't stop . . . It wouldn't leave me in peace . . . It just wouldn't *stop*!

Finally, as if it were a living creature, the pain slowly retracted its claws from my skull. I opened my eyes. Gray-and-black peppered tiles were arranged in neat rows. *Not tiles. Shingles. Not grass. That's good.* I stroked the edge of a shingle with one finger, feeling the coarse surface against the ridges of my skin. My eyelashes were heavy with tears, which itched when the breeze swept over me. The sun was hot on my back.

I moaned, pushing myself onto my hands and knees. My throat

hurt, and my voice would be hoarse for a few hours, no doubt. I froze, my gaze settling on the creased photograph in front of me. The breeze, which felt colder than it had before the Spasm, caught the paper.

My heart skipped a beat. I scrambled up. Just as my photograph floated over the verge of the rooftop, I snatched it back and held it in my trembling hand. I couldn't let it go. It didn't matter that I hurt every time I looked at it, or that it was an immortalized lie, or that it teased me with a life I could never reclaim. I couldn't let it go.

Exhaling in defeat, I tucked it back safely inside the pouch strapped to my right thigh, then wrapped my arms around my body. This pain was different but just as devastating as the Spasms. Loneliness. Why was I lonely? Like I'd told Ero, I had a family. Finn, Reese, Jay, RC, Ash, Axel, Kit. I didn't need anybody else.

I reached for my power to become as empty as I felt. I let the roof swallow me whole, cutting off the sunlight in darkness, and then I landed in the second-story hallway, knees bent to absorb the impact. I stabilized my balance with my fingertips and stayed crouched on all fours for a minute to let my eyes adjust from the bright sunlight to the dim interior of Saros Manor, and then I bowed my head, sighed, and rose. My body felt heavy, old, weary.

I lingered in the hall, halfway considering going into one of the furniture rooms and peeling the plastic off a bed or couch so I could sleep alone in the dark without company. But with a deep sigh, I trudged down the hall, turned left to reach the staircase, and slowly ascended up to the third floor.

I opened the door at the top of the stairs. The twins, worn out from the lesson, had wandered to the sofa by the window and were dozing. Axel and Ero, thankfully, were gone.

I quietly closed the door and retreated to our sleeping quarters. Despite feeling drained and sore from the Spasm, I didn't want to sleep on a bed. It wasn't familiar yet. I still clutched that lingering sense of loneliness, and sleeping by myself on the mattress would leave me feeling exposed and vulnerable. Instead, I crawled under the bed and curled into a tight ball.

The darkness and tightness of the space reminded me of my cage. That wasn't exactly a soothing realization, but my cage had been a safe place where *They* didn't hurt me. Outside the cage—that was where the pain came. I felt secure under the bed where the world was nice and small and not nearly as confusing. *I'm inside Proto*, I reminded myself. *I'm safe.*

I closed my eyes. For a while, the image of my mother and blood-sister embracing on a park bench illustrated the backs of my eyelids until eventually the darkness pulled me down, deep down, made my body even heavier, calmed my anxious mind, allowed me to escape . . .

"Cato," Jay begged, "please, you have to eat."

I gazed at the cup of paste sitting beside me in the cage. My stomach hurt; it was an endless, aching pain of emptiness, as if it were a black hole causing me to cave in on myself. I hadn't eaten in days.

I closed my eyes, too tired to shift my cramped body from the position I'd been lying in for so long. My joints and muscles ached in protest. "This isn't going to solve anything," Jay continued quietly in an attempt to persuade me. "They aren't going to let you kill yourself; you're way too valuable. Having Them nurse you back to health will just cause you unnecessary suffering."

I ignored him, retreating into a restless doze to temporarily escape from the pain.

"Cato—" he pleaded again, but he fell silent at the warning sound of A6's growls. The doors slid open. Two sets of footsteps strode purposefully toward my cage.

I opened my eyes as the cage door was yanked open. A hand reached inside and snatched the untouched cup of paste that was supposed to be considered food.

"Still not hungry?" a cold voice taunted.

The handler touched a key card to a sensor on my cage. My muscles automatically went stiff as a low electric current paralyzed me so the man could seize my ankle and drag me out. He needn't have bothered—paralyzed or not, I had no energy, no will to resist. There was nothing to fight for anymore.

I lay motionless on the tiles, staring up at the painfully bright fluorescent lights. Each man grabbed one of my arms and dragged me across the floor, past the row of cages where the other prisoners of Project Alpha watched. Ash curled her fingers around the cage bars; Jay and RC watched with grim frowns and tight lips; A6 paced back and forth in his electricity-charged cage, snarling in discontentment.

The doors slid shut behind us. I watched the lights pass above me in procession as I was lugged to wherever my captors were taking me. I didn't care. They could do whatever they wanted with me. It didn't matter anymore.

We entered a chamber with six doors, each leading to an isolated room. The handlers hauled me through one of these doors and lifted me up onto a padded table. Without the strength to hold my own body up, I had to be supported to remain upright.

I swept my half-closed eyes around the space, which resembled a hospital room with its tubes and wires and machines. Quarantine.

Two more men were already in the room, and I recognized them immediately—Agent Kovak and Dr. Anders. Misery always befell me when those two were together

They didn't look happy. The doctor grumbled, "Is there a particular reason you brought one of the Alpha subjects for an unscheduled trip into Quarantine without my clearance?"

Equally pissed, Kovak added, "And interrupt me in the middle of a meeting with the Board of Directors?"

Their voices rang with an eerie echo. We were in the same room, and yet they sounded so far away.

The handler on my left cleared his throat and explained, "We wouldn't waste your time or break protocol if it weren't of the utmost importance. A7 hasn't touched his food or water from last night, sir. Agent Enzo had yesterday's feeding shift, and he reported that A7 didn't eat or drink then, either."

The other sheepishly added, "The test subject is lethargic and unresponsive. We decided it was necessary to invoke emergency Quarantine removal."

A vein throbbed in Kovak's forehead, but his fury had shifted from his subordinates to me. The handlers held me firm while Dr. Anders pressed the edge of a cup to my lips. "Drink," he commanded, breathing the sickeningly strong scent of peppermint in my face. The instinct to survive made my dry throat want so desperately to swallow, to taste the good water, but . . . no. I couldn't. If I gave in, my heart would never stop beating. I just wanted to die.

I clenched my teeth, rolled my lips together, and closed my eyes, silently refusing.

Dr. Anders let out his breath through his nose, his teeth working at the wad of gum. He gripped my chin so tightly it hurt as he forced me to look at a tube and a catheter. "Your choice. Either you start eating and drinking, or this needle is going into your vein and this tube is going down your throat. You remember the last time that happened, don't you? It wasn't fun. You want to do it again?"

The only sound in the room was the rattle of a pill being shaken out of a plastic bottle and into Agent Kovak's waiting palm. He popped the pill into his mouth and swallowed, watching me, waiting. I didn't respond. "The hard way it is, then," he muttered.

"Fine," said Dr. Anders. "Strap him down."

The handlers pulled me back onto the table and fixed restraints around my wrists and ankles. I didn't struggle, simply watched with disinterest as Dr. Anders slid the needle into a vein in the back of my hand. He loomed over me, tube in hand as he gripped my jaw again. This time he squeezed, forcing it open, and the tube traveled down my throat.

Instinctively, I thrashed weakly against the restraints. I needed to cough the foreign object up to free my airway. My eyes burned, but I was too dehydrated to produce any tears. I couldn't even cough with the tube in my throat.

Dr. Anders let go and stared down at me through the clear lenses of his wire-rimmed glasses, not a trace of sympathy in his brown eyes. "Did you think we'd let you go so easily?" He shook his head. "You don't get to decide when you die. We do. When we're done with you,

you'll go to Project Omega, and I'm going to dissect you slowly and carefully . . . but you won't be dead yet. See, your Origin dies when your heart stops beating, so we need to observe how everything inside a ghost works while it's still alive—"

"Cato, wake up . . ."

"—we'll keep you alive for as long as we can while we cut you open, but you won't last too long—"

"Can you hear me?"

"—then, and only then, we let you die."

"Cato!"

I jerked awake with a cry and instinctively kicked out at the face hovering beside me. I was in a cramped space, but I wasn't restrained, and my strength was back; I could hurt *Them* now. I could fight back.

But the face was gone, and my boot slashed through air. I rolled out from under my dark sleeping place and leapt to my feet, crouched in a defensive position.

"Cato, you're in Phantom Heights, remember?"

I whirled to find Jay standing in the corner well out of reach.

Slowly, I became aware of my surroundings—the bunk beds, the skylights, the plush carpet, the tan walls. This wasn't Quarantine.

The light had changed. Several hours must have passed. I swallowed and ran my trembling fingers through my hair. "Bad dream?" Jay asked.

"Bad memory," I corrected.

I could still hear *His* voice echo, *"I told you I'd break you."*

Jay nodded in sympathy—no questions, no prying. A surge of gratitude coursed through me; Jay always pushed us to our limits during training but never about tough memories or troubled pasts. "Sorry I didn't make it back in time for the twins' lesson. RC and I ran into some trouble in the second circle. Everything went okay?"

"Yeah, it was fine," I said, although I was struggling to recall the exact details from before the vivid nightmare. "Ero was telling stories. Something about dragons and the origin of telepathy." The adrenaline was seeping out of me fast, and I felt my shoulders sag. "Hey, Jay . . .

question. Have you ever thought about looking for your father again?"

Jay raised his eyebrows at my unexpected inquiry. Although I'd caught him off guard, his voice was level with certainty when he answered, "No."

"Why?"

My lab-brother rubbed his forehead, his fingers circling one of the ports, as if it might help him remember while he pondered his answer. "I can't remember his name. I don't think I ever met him. If he's alive, he either didn't want anything to do with me or has no idea I even exist. The only reason I tried to find him was because I was alone. But I'm not anymore."

I nodded, but Jay frowned. "What's really on your mind?"

"Ero mentioned that maybe . . . I should seek out my blood-family."

"Do you want to?"

He was supposed to say what a terrible idea that was, that Ero must be crazy for suggesting it and I must be crazy for considering it. Not "do you want to?"

Such a simple question, and yet I couldn't decide on an answer. I wanted to say yes, but then I was immediately guilty for even thinking such a thought, and the old hatred rekindled when I forced myself to remember what they'd done to me.

"I don't know." I raised my head. "They abandoned me, Jay. I can't forgive them." I pressed my shaking hands together to steady them.

"Nobody said you had to forgive them. That wasn't what I asked. Do you want to see them?"

I stared out the window at the sky warming with color. "I don't know," I said again.

"Then what *do* you want?"

"I want . . . I don't know. I want . . ."

The muddled snags of thought suddenly aligned into a single desire that stunned me in its simplicity. "I want my mother to acknowledge me." This wasn't a declaration so much as a realization.

What I really wanted above all else was the courage to stand before my mother and look her in the eye so she would finally have to face me. She had tried very hard to make me disappear; I wanted to be brave enough to take off my mask and confront her. I wanted her to *see* me, to be subjected to *my* judgment, to explain to me *why*. Even if I'd been disowned, I was still her flesh and blood, and I wanted to make her acknowledge that.

My knees felt weak. I backed up and plopped down on the bottom bunk. Head down, I withdrew my photograph again and held it in my lap so I could stare into her flat green eyes, loathing and missing her at the same time. Jay watched me for a moment, then asked, "May I see it?"

I handed it over. My lab-brother studied it as if it were an ancient and priceless artifact. "They have your eyes. Or at least, one of them." I didn't respond to that observation. I was still simmering and didn't want to let him deter my hatred. Jay returned the photo and sat down beside me. "Do you remember when you joined our family?"

"Vaguely," I said, frowning as I sought the exact moment it became official.

"It wasn't an easy decision. We weren't sure we could trust a half-human. But you know, it was hard watching you give up. I think part of you died after *He* showed you the custody transfer."

I stared straight ahead, saying nothing, letting his voice revive distant memories.

"We talked while you were recuperating in Quarantine. By then, you'd been there long enough for us to realize that you would be a permanent resident of Project Alpha, and like the rest of us, you had no blood-family anymore. So, it wasn't unanimous, but we agreed to make you a part of our family . . ."

I closed my eyes. I did remember.

I hadn't spoken aloud in so long I wasn't even sure my voice still worked. My pain was beyond words. I stared vacantly through the bars of my cage, unable to sleep, nothing to do to pass the time. My world was a fog now. Nothing I did mattered anymore. Nothing that happened to me mattered, either. Lately I'd been considering asking Kovak to send me to Project Omega. He could dissect me and find the Origin he was searching for, and I could finally die. We'd both get what we wanted.

A voice echoed through the fog. I blinked, focusing on the voice. "Cato . . ."

Cato? Right, that was my name. I'd almost forgotten . . . For a moment, I was convinced I'd always been A7. But no, I used to be Cato.

The voice called me a second time. "Cato . . ."

I raised my head. My gaze wandered to the gray-haired ghost three cages down. "What?" I croaked. Apparently my voice did still work.

He smiled, visibly relieved to see me finally responding, but then he became serious again in an instant. "Cato, I know you're upset about your family leaving you. I'm sorry; we're all sorry." He paused to see if I'd speak, and when I didn't, he continued, "You know, none of us have real families. Unfortunately, it seems to be a condition of Project Alpha that nobody Outside wants you. So, we've sort of made our own family. We've been talking, and, uh . . . w-well . . ." He took a deep breath. "We'd like you to be a part of our family."

Jay fell silent. All the Alpha ghosts were watching me, even A6. It took a few painfully long seconds for his words to make sense, and when they did, I didn't know what to say besides, "What?"

RC said, "We want you to be our lab-brother."

I swallowed hard, the fog partially lifting. I'd thought I was alone, abandoned, unwanted. But someone did want me. I had a chance to be a part of a family again.

I nodded and whispered, "Okay," but my voice was so hoarse I had to repeat myself to be heard. Jay nodded in approval.

Ash set her open hand against the bars between us. I hesitated, then pressed my hand against hers. "Welcome to the family," she said.

I opened my eyes. "You gave me something to live for again. But it wasn't unanimous, huh? Let me guess—Axel."

Jay shrugged. "He came around eventually."

Despite my melancholy mood, I felt my lips twitch with a weak grin. "The only good part about being sent to that place was that I met all of you."

Jay rose. "I know how difficult it is for you to be back here. The humans from your past may have moved on with their lives, but I want you to remember that you weren't born into this family. We chose you. No matter what happens, we'll never leave you behind."

He removed the gauntlet from his right arm and held up his fist so I could see A3 clearly tattooed in dark ink on his pale skin. "We may not share blood, but we do share this."

I nodded again. Jay was right—the bond of blood was nothing compared to the bond we'd forged in that place. That bond could never be broken.

— Chapter Twenty-Eight —

By Lab, by Blood

A crow flew over Wes's head.

The werewolf cast an uneasy glance up, his gaze following the bird's path until the building hid it from view. "One for sorrow," Wes muttered. It was a bad omen. He faced forward again, but stopped short. A man was standing in his path.

The man himself was unfamiliar—black hair tied back into a short ponytail, a closely trimmed beard, and gleaming green eyes set in a stern face—but the uniform Wes recognized immediately.

The kálos held up his hand. "Eh-lai," he greeted.

Wes backed away. "I'm just—"

"It's rude not to acknowledge a greeting. I know what you are, lunos. And I think you know who I am."

Wes sensed movement from behind and swiveled his eyes just in time to see three more Shadow Guards emerge from the walls to pen him in while he faced the leader. Despite the trap, Wes's shoulders relaxed as he let his feigned confusion fall away. When a large raven with a white-tipped wing landed on the man's shoulder, talons clutching an ivory pendant, his suspicion was confirmed.

"Only by reputation, Captain. Eh-lai."

Hassing critically eyed the narrow street. "No pack?"

The raven tilted its head at Wes, who cleared his throat and answered, "I've had better fortune on my own."

The Amínyte ruffled its feathers, as if mocking him. Wes returned its beady glare. Captain Hassing said, "Rumor has it you made a deal with the Alpha fugitives."

"Well. You can't believe every rumor you hear."

"Azar has a bounty on them. Harboring fugitives is against Law, regardless of which Realm you're in." The Shadow Guards crept closer. Wes swallowed. Hassing continued, "I hope you don't misunderstand my intentions. I don't plan to arrest you tonight."

"No?" Wes murmured, his gaze darting over his soon-to-be assailants. A transformation would be quick and easy with the full moon only a few days ago. But there was no telling what the Shadow Guards' Divinities might be.

Hassing said, "You strike me as a smart man who likes making deals."

Wes nodded. "You want the Alpha fugitives." Rayven squawked, making Wes jump. Hassing didn't even flinch. "I, uh . . . I don't have the connection with them you seem to think I do."

"Maybe not yet," Hassing replied. "But you're in contact with them. I think you can get closer, maybe earn their trust. What do you say, Wes? Azar would pay you handsomely for information about them. Imagine what he'd offer if you actually delivered them to him."

Wes forced his shaking fingers to adjust the cuff on his sleeve, feigning disinterest. "I'm a businessman," he began. "I like to weigh the opportunity costs of any arrangement before I commit. That's not to say I have any loyalty to the fugitives. I wouldn't lose a second of sleep if I were to turn them over to you." He took a moment to think through the implications. "If I were to gain their trust and guide them into a position for your Shadow Guards to make a move . . ."

"Azar would reward you lavishly," Hassing finished with a smile that disappeared in an instant. "But if you were to deceive us . . . I'd imagine Veto would come pay you a special visit."

Wes blanched at the mere mention of Azar's torture master. He nodded that he understood. Captain Hassing stepped forward and extended his arm. "Do we have a deal?"

Rayven leered at Wes, his sharp beak close enough to peck, but the bird kept still when Wes and Hassing gripped forearms. "I'll see what I can do."

Hassing nodded as he stepped back.

"Just remember, wherever there are shadows, Azar has eyes."

"A sentiment I have never forgotten," acknowledged the werewolf.

The Shadow Guards wordlessly marched past Wes and fell into place beside their captain.

"I do hope we'll be in touch soon," said Hassing as he turned away.

Dr. Anders loomed over me with a syringe in hand. "I'm going to take you to the brink of death, my friend. But not to worry . . . I promise I'll bring you back . . ."

I breathed in peppermint as I went under, deep into the blackness, deeper than I'd ever gone before, beyond the black and into green light where a woman's voice called, "Cato? Cato! Can you hear me?"

"Shouldn't we take him to the hospital?"

"He's coming to."

Another flash of green. All I could see was green. Green light all around me, in me, until I ceased to be a physical entity. I was light.

"Don't forget."

"I'll come get you, Cato! Be strong. I'll get this mess straightened out."

I jerked awake.

Her voice echoed in my head. I stared up at the skylights, willing myself to go back to sleep. The cold moisture soaking my eyelashes made my eyes heavy. I closed them.

"I'll come get you, Cato!"

Her voice continued to repeat itself over and over and over in my mind, torturing me. I sat up.

The twins were snoring softly. Kit was curled in a little ball of fur on top of Jay's chest, and he was comfortably tangled with Ash and RC. Axel was nowhere to be seen.

We'd rearranged our sleeping quarters because we had all been miserable the first night. My bed had been too big, too empty, even with my lab-siblings in the same room. I'd barely slept, and even when I was finally able to doze, every moment my eyes were shut had been plagued with nightmares. The others had fared no better.

We were used to sleeping together in the corner at our old Home. Even at that place in my cage, I'd always fallen asleep touching Ash and Kit through the bars. So, we had pulled three of the mattresses off the beds, pushed them together in the middle of the room, and slept on the floor instead.

In my tossing, I'd rolled away from the group. Perhaps it was missing their touch that had woken me in the echoes of a broken promise. I rose in the darkness and gazed down at my lab-family. I had to do something, hit something, go somewhere, anything to drown out the voice in my head.

As quietly as possible, I tugged my boots on and donned the black cloak. I took an extra moment to bury my face in the fabric of the cloak and inhale. Ero had talked us into letting him wash our uniforms, and although my clothes were still torn and threadbare, they now had a clean, fresh smell I found rather comforting. The cloak felt softer than it had before.

I knew all of my lab-siblings were light sleepers, and although I was careful not to make much noise, Kit stirred in her sleep, and her movement made Jay groan softly. Ash let out a strained whimper, likely trapped in a nightmare as well. "Please," she whispered. "Please stop. You're hurting me. Please . . ."

I knelt beside her and gripped her shoulder. "Ash." Startled by how hot her skin was, I yanked my hand back.

Her unfocused glowing eyes snapped open and stared straight through me. She shied away. "Don't touch me."

"It's okay, Ash. It's me. Cato. I'm not going to hurt you."

"Where's my staff?" she demanded, as if she hadn't heard me.

I leaned over and seized it in my fist, then pressed it into her hands. "Right here."

She gripped it tight, her eyelids falling over the smoldering embers of her irises. "I'm in control," she murmured, resting the metal staff against her forehead. The weapon glowed faintly as she channeled heat into it. "Come what may." Her words blended together as she drifted back into slumber.

Come what may, her haunting voice echoed, the glow fading from the staff. A rather eerie phrase she sometimes used to ground herself. In context, it translated to, "I'm not helpless now. I have my power, and I have my weapon. Any pain that befalls me from here is my own fault."

She'd often said it right before we began an Arena match. That was the only place we'd had any semblance of control. If I was injured in the Arena, it was because I had miscalculated or my reaction time had been too slow, and those direct cause-and-effect repercussions were something I'd come to treasure. It was my pain. I could learn from it. I could avoid it, if I were strong enough and fast enough. I didn't have that dominion over pain when I was stripped of my power and bound in restraints, at the unforgiving mercy of *Them*.

I remained on my knees, staring at the still forms of my lab-family for a moment more. Then, I became intangible and slipped through the floorboards.

The night was clear. A breathtaking tapestry of stars unfurled high above me as the swollen moon lit my way.

My footsteps were light in the dewy grass. I focused on the rhythm of my body—the steady fall of my feet, the increase in my heart rate, the expansion and contraction of my lungs, the sound of my breath cutting through my teeth. I sprinted as fast as my body's limit would allow, leaving Saros Manor and the memories behind me.

My mother's voice was drowned out by my gasps, my heartbeat, my footsteps, my cloak flapping behind me. My muscles began to burn with exertion, but it was a welcomed ache, and I preferred the physical strain to the emotional. I pushed myself harder. I felt fierce, elated, ready to challenge anybody who crossed my path. I'd welcome a good fight right now while I was on an adrenaline high.

The town was quiet. I ran everywhere and nowhere, choosing no specific direction and just letting my feet take me away. Eventually the burn in my muscles spread, becoming more intense until I could run no more. I slowed to a walk, panting for breath.

Trees surrounded me. There were no streetlights here, and I realized I was in the park south of Saros Manor. I emerged in a clearing, and standing in front of me, arms folded, a sculpted scowl looking down on me, loomed the statue of Phantom.

I approached the figure. For a while, I remained as still as the statue, the rise and fall of my lungs evening out. Phantom glared at me with lifeless eyes. He was so stern and intimidating that I had a hard time believing he was actually me. Maybe he looked so severe because the mask hid most of his face. I tied my own mask over my nose and mouth, and then I pushed my shoulders back to stand up straighter. If someone saw me, what would they think? Was I more formidable than my past self? Or did that statue cast me in a shadow I could never overcome?

I stepped over a white stone in the grass to touch my hand to the plaque. "A fallen hero," I muttered.

What inspired me to do this, I couldn't say, but I climbed up onto the base so I could look Phantom in the eye. He was much more intimidating from below when he was looking down from his pedestal. Apparently he'd been crafted to be life-size, and apparently I had grown since it was made, because now I was a good two inches taller. But even with my height advantage, I still felt insignificant before Phantom.

I glared at him, the symbol of my past life standing there with that defiant look on his face, taunting me with memories that had faded so much I hardly remembered being him.

My fist connected with his masked face.

I would have smashed my hand if not for the padding beneath the metal studs in the knuckles of my gloves. I shivered, sensing a ghost nearby, and turned away from Phantom, crouching down defensively on top of the pedestal. I swept my gaze around the empty clearing.

"Show yourself!"

"Someone's jumpy tonight."

I straightened. I knew that voice. "Are you spying on me, Axel?" I continued to scan the dark landscape for my lab-brother.

Finally, I spotted a pair of red eyes and the silhouette of a dark figure crouched in a tree. I hopped off Phantom's pedestal and started to walk toward him, but Axel warned, "I'm not feeling so good. Don't get too close."

I felt it now—the charged air humming, not pulsing. Jay had been trying to make Axel eat in the hopes that his body would adapt to human food, but it wasn't working. Axel's sense of taste was just as advanced as the rest of his senses, and yet he claimed food didn't taste good or bad—it just *was*. His teeth weren't designed to chew, and lately he'd been swallowing food whole; a few nights ago, I'd watched him open his mouth wide, too wide—his jaw dislocated—to shove a whole meal down his throat like some bizarre snake-man.

There had been no improvement. Axel was not designed to be an omnivore. I wasn't even sure *carnivore* was the right word. He'd probably leave us tomorrow, maybe even tonight. Where he went and what he did, I hadn't asked. I didn't think I wanted to know. What concerned me was that Axel seemed to be getting worse. When he returned from his trip each week, he looked as though he was already halfway through his cycle.

I took several steps back. Axel exhaled and asked, "What's on your mind?"

"Nothing," I lied, tucking my head down and away to avoid his clairvoyant red eyes.

"Oh please, Cato, I'm insulted."

I clenched my teeth, frustrated that Axel could see through me so easily. "She promised," I whispered, unable to hide the hurt in my voice. "I can't help but wonder what I did wrong . . . you know, what changed her mind."

Axel knew, somehow, exactly who and what I was talking about. He stayed completely still on his perch. "You want me to kill her for you?"

"Yes."

He provided an empty smirk at my answer but said nothing. He hadn't intended his question to be taken seriously, and I knew that, although I wasn't sure if my answer had been truthful or sarcastic.

Finally, he said, "Is punching that statue making you feel better?"

I felt the color rise in my cheeks, and I glanced at Phantom, embarrassed. "I just needed to hit something."

"I don't think that hunk of metal is a worthy opponent." He leapt down and straightened, red eyes staring at me in the darkness. My lab-brother placed one hand behind his back and held the other out, palm facing me.

"I thought you didn't feel well."

"If this is too much, we'll stop."

Still, I hesitated. "You really expect me to come at you after what you did to the leader of the Talon Gang? No thanks. I'd rather not have every bone in my hand shattered."

Amused, he assured, "I meant to hurt him. I won't grab you. Hit me as hard as you can."

I did need to vent, and Axel really was the best person to help me do that. I approached him and halted in front of the half-breed, then bent my knees into a fighting stance and leveled a strong punch at his hand. When my metal-studded knuckles smashed into his palm, he didn't even flinch, although now that I was closer, I could see that his mouth was drawn into a tight line and the part of his face that was visible beneath the hood was paler than usual in the moonlight. His eyes also didn't seem as bright because his pupils were dilated.

I threw my other fist at Axel; his open palm absorbed my blow. Channeling my frustration into a powerful, physical attack was exactly what I needed. My next punch was aimed at his chest, but Axel casually moved his hand to adjust.

He and I moved together, I using my entire body to throw hard strikes, he moving his hand to block me as effortlessly as if I were moving in slow motion and barely even tapping him. Axel could feel pain, I knew, but not by the hands of a weak mortal like myself hitting him, even with the metal in my gloves. He was as impervious to my attacks as Phantom, who watched our one-sided bout from his pedestal. I spoke through clenched teeth, punctuating my words with each strike: "I *hate* her, Ax, *but . . . she . . . why?* I don't under-*stand* why she a-*ban*-doned me after she *prom*-ised . . ."

"Money," he answered, completely calm, his breathing normal even as I was becoming more and more winded. I stepped back and leveled a solid kick at his waiting palm. "And humiliation." I spun and kicked again; he blocked me with his forearm. "I mean, as far as we know, you and me are the only half-breeds. If my parents were still alive, I bet they wouldn't want me, either."

I let loose a series of fast punches. "Okay, but you're half-nydæa. I'm just . . ."

In the wake of my pause, he finished, "Half-ghost?"

My knuckles landed in his palm one last time. I froze in my stance, panting, staring down at the dewy grass. "Yeah." Usually I thought of myself as half-human, as if I'd been a ghost my entire life. I was silent for a moment before pulling away. "Part of me wants to confront her. The other part never wants to see her again." My throat cinched, trapping the lump so I couldn't swallow. I looked away from Axel and stared into the trees.

His chuckle was dark, cold, and unforgiving. "Aw, Cato misses his human family." Though I didn't answer, my jaw locked at his mocking tone. He giggled again, half-crazed. "Cato J—"

"*Don't* say it," I snarled, whirling on him before he could finish the next syllable.

"What?" he asked innocently, his sharp white teeth cutting a devilish smile in the darkness. "Your *name*?"

"That's not my name anymore, and you know it." I'd surrendered my full human name and didn't want to hear the words put together ever again. I was just Cato now. I wouldn't claim the same name as my blood-family.

We stared each other down. I stood firm before the hybrid, refusing to blink and break contact from his dark, dilated eyes. I didn't know how long we faced off, but Axel was the one to break his gaze. I couldn't tell if he gave up because he was late in his cycle and feeling ill, or because he knew he'd crossed a line and this was his way of apologizing. Either way, I won, and I would hold onto that victory because I'd probably never have another one.

He muttered, "I guess being half-nydæa to kálos parents would be as bad as being half-kálos to human parents."

That was the closest to an apology I'd get. "Your parents never saw you like this. They died loving you." I heaved a deep sigh. "They never had the chance to betray you."

Cross again in an instant, he snapped, "What do you want me to say? I'm sorry I can't completely relate to you because *They* murdered my parents in front of me when I was still a pureblood? You want sympathy? I don't got any for humans. They're all worthless pieces of garbage who will turn on you the second it benefits them, and like it or not, that includes your blood-family."

I bowed my head, not in the mood to argue with Axel anymore tonight. "Question. Finn and Reese said my mother signed the visitor's log. She did come."

What I could see of Axel's expression was difficult to read. "That ain't a question."

"I'm getting to it. Do you remember her coming? You wouldn't have known who she was at the time, but maybe you heard her talking to *Them* about me."

"Nope."

He didn't even pause to think back. "Are you sure?"

"Look, if I ever heard *Them* say 'Alpha' or any of our numbers, I always listened. I woulda noticed *her*. You sure Bot ain't messing with you?"

"I don't think they'd make something like that up."

"Then isn't there proof? Like camera footage?"

"ECANI was off-line."

"Huh. That's convenient. When was ECANI ever turned off?"

"Well . . . I don't know. Are you saying Finn and Reese are lying?"

"I'm saying that I trust them only because I can read them. But they could tell *you* just about anything, and you'd swallow their story like a bad pill because you're too trusting. You know they'll recite whatever

He programmed into them if you ask the right trigger question."

I gripped my arms and stared into the dark. "So, you don't think she really came."

"I didn't say that. I'm just saying I don't remember it, and isn't it a little suspicious that ECANI happened to be down so there's no record except a signature that may or may not be real? And besides, does it matter? Even if your mommy did come, she didn't come to see *you*. She signed the visitor's log and then went to *His* office to sign the paperwork and collect her money."

My head bowed. Axel's voice softened, and he added, "Hey, if you really want my advice, I say forget about your blood-family."

"Forget?" I repeated, rubbing my throbbing hand. "I've been trying to hold onto what few memories I have left."

Axel stepped away from me. "You're driving yourself insane trying to figure out what you did wrong when *they* are the ones who couldn't accept you. They forgot about you, so you should forget about them. Move on."

"Easier said than done."

Axel shrugged. "I never said it'd be easy. I know you miss them, but don't forget that you have another family that cares about you."

I raised my eyebrows. "That's the most sentimental thing I've ever heard you say."

"Wow," Axel fired back. "I just might throw up."

I chuckled; I couldn't really see him in the dark with the hood thrown over his face, but I imagined he was scowling. I started to turn away. "Thanks, Ax."

I received no answer. When I glanced over my shoulder, my lab-brother was gone. With his passing, the air, which had been flexing with energy, relaxed, as if the whole world had been holding its breath and was now exhaling. Alone again, I faced the judgment of Phantom's soulless eyes.

My fingers found the knot at the back of my neck and loosened it until I was able to pull the mask away. I stood before Phantom, the black cloth hanging limp in my open hand. I studied the creases made by the knot, the frayed corners, the way it shifted in the night breeze.

This isn't what I want.

The realization reverberated through my being, startlingly strong in the wake of all the uncertainty. What I wanted was a fresh start with my lab-family. At all costs, I wanted to shield them from the mistakes of my past. And yet, here we were, following in my own footsteps. Hiding behind Phantom's mask, protecting humankind, shrouding ourselves in secrecy . . . every mistake I had made Before was being repeated. I feared that if we continued down the path I'd already tread, the one that led me to my own demise, we were going to end up with the same catastrophic results. And I didn't know how to stop history from repeating itself.

I crushed the mask in my fist and walked away from Phantom. *Forget*, Axel had told me. *Move on.* He was right, of course. And yet . . . I felt as if doing so would erase the rest of my memories, the final pieces of my life Before that I'd been desperately clinging to.

And that terrified me.

I wandered through the park, calmer now, but not ready to return to the manor quite yet. The cool night air was refreshing.

Crickets hummed a shrill song, distant and soothing above the leaves rustling in the light breeze. I meandered along the edge of the still pond, admiring the gleam of the moon on the surface and wondering if Chelvistin was asleep in the dark, cold depths. The lack of ripples disturbing the moon's reflection led me to believe she probably was.

Axel's words gnawed at my thoughts. I knew Finn and Reese would betray me for *Him*, but they had seemed genuine when I'd asked them about my mother. And yet, Axel didn't remember her coming, and he could hear everything in that place, even *His* private phone calls in *His* office on the top floor. Unless . . . Axel was the one who was lying. Maybe that *wasn't* the end of it. Maybe my mother had said something Axel didn't want me to know. He'd made it clear that he didn't like my blood-family. Maybe he was afraid that if he told me the truth, I might choose them over my lab-family.

That was ridiculous, of course, but maybe . . .

She still signed the papers. She still sold me. That, I knew, was not a lie, because I'd seen her signature with my own eyes. One hundred and forty-three phone calls in the first month, then nothing after the paperwork was done. She'd probably been haggling with *Him* over how much I was actually worth. And Axel was my lab-brother; I shouldn't doubt him.

My wandering was aimless. Along the winding paths through the trees, past the townhouses at the outskirts of the park . . . Eventually I found myself walking down a familiar street. As soon as I realized where I was, I halted.

I was standing beneath a streetlight staring at the gray house with the white door.

They were sleeping inside. Through that door and up the stairs.

I wondered if they ever dreamed about me. I was the ghost, but they would haunt me for the rest of my life.

Swallowing hard, I crept toward the door. This was insane. It was a bad idea. I was going to regret it. But, as if I were in a trance, my feet continued forward. I ascended the porch steps, eyes fixed on the white door. I was becoming light-headed, and after a moment, I realized I was holding my breath. I swallowed again and inhaled deeply, then reached for my center and became intangible. I stepped through the locked door and emerged into the living room.

What am I doing here?

The house was dark. Warm ectoplasm gathered in my hand to shed dim green light on my surroundings. The room was much more like I remembered from my scattered memories. In a different time, I could have been in my pajamas tiptoeing down the staircase for a midnight snack.

I extinguished the light and allowed the house to be washed in a cloak of darkness again, concealing me—its unwelcome visitor.

I stole up the stairs, careful to avoid the creaking fourth step. In the hallway, I froze, staring into the darkness.

I held my breath, ears strained for the slightest sound. All was quiet except for my loud heartbeat. I crept toward my blood-sister's room.

Her door wasn't closed all the way. I pushed; it swung open on quiet hinges, and I slipped into her room with the stealth of a shadow. My gaze immediately fell on the figure lying on the bed.

Moonlight streamed in through the window, highlighting her features. I slunk farther into the room and hesitated at her bedside. Her dark hair spilled over the white pillow. I tilted my head, studying her. Somehow, her expression was so peaceful in slumber. Did she always sleep like that? Was I so accustomed to seeing Ash and Kit grimacing through nightmares that this normalcy struck me as an anomaly?

I knelt, and there I remained for a long time, simply watching this stranger sleep. Time became a ravenous thing I was suddenly conscious of—how long I'd been in this forbidden house, how quickly the night was slipping away, how much time had actually passed while I was locked up in that timeless place. I should have been here, growing up with her. What would she think of me if she woke and saw me? Would she even recognize my face? Or would she see nothing but my eyes glowing in the dark and take me for a monster, screaming and fleeing from me?

I rose and backed slowly away. My heartstrings ripped a little more with every step. I'd known this would be a bad idea.

I lingered in the doorway to watch her for a few more minutes, imprinting the sight of her sleeping in the moonlight into my unreliable memory. Finally, I turned away.

I stepped into the hall and paused, glancing at the room at the end of the hall. This was another bad idea, I knew, and I might very well do something that I'd most certainly regret later, but I eased my way toward the door and entered the dark room.

My mother was sprawled on top of her blankets, her limbs splayed across the bed. Waves of hatred and betrayal ricocheted through every cell in my body as I watched her from the doorway.

I remembered. I was much smaller, still human, tears sliding down my face, and even then, she was sleeping alone.

"Mommy," I whimpered.

She stirred at the sound of my voice and sat up. "Wuz-a-matter?"

she asked groggily

Thunder shook the house, and I yelped and ran to her, then leapt onto the bed and into her safe arms. "Okay," she whispered, stroking my hair. "It's okay. You're safe. I'm here." A melody softened by the soothing lilt of her voice played through my mind.

"You make me happy, when skies are gray," she sang. I buried my face against her, trusting her to protect me.

The memory faded, leaving me a little emptier. I cautiously left my place in the doorway and tiptoed forward, my heart pounding so hard it hurt my ribs, my brain screaming that she'd send me back to that place if she awakened and caught me.

I'm a mistake. She's ashamed of me. She will lock me away forever so she can pretend I no longer exist.

I loomed over the woman who had raised me, who had held me when I was afraid of a storm, who had hummed lullabies to me, who had promised to rescue me when *They* took me away, who had abandoned me. I used to wonder if she ever cried for me.

I'd told Jay I wanted to confront her so she would have to acknowledge me. I couldn't ask for a better opportunity than now. We were alone. We'd both been putting on fronts in public, but now was our chance to face each other as we really were—a fugitive and a traitor.

And yet, the thought of waking her was terrifying enough to turn my blood to ice. I couldn't make myself move. Why did I fear her? She was sleeping. She was an unarmed human, and I had my full power. I was stronger. I could kill her now, if I wanted. Maybe I should. Then she couldn't betray me again, and I wouldn't have to live in fear that she was waiting for the right opportunity to send me back to that place.

My fingers closed around a long icicle. *This wouldn't be revenge*, I told myself. *She's a threat to my new family. If she hurts them, I'll never be able to forgive myself. I have to protect them from her. I have to . . .*

My grip tightened. My vision blurred. I closed my eyes, forcing the tears out. They trickled slowly down my cheeks and fell from my chin.

One landed on her hand. I stared at it glistening on her skin. "Mom," I whispered wretchedly.

She frowned and stirred, and in a panic, I leapt back and crouched to the floor, allowing my warm power to render me invisible. I held the icicle out like a blade to defend myself. She inhaled sharply, then exhaled and rolled over onto her side, facing away from me.

I straightened and cut the flow of power. She wasn't Mom anymore. Every time I saw her, I wanted to drive a dagger of ice through her black heart so I could hurt her like she'd hurt me. But now, as I looked at her sleeping so vulnerably, all I felt was emptiness. I melted my weapon.

I backed away from her still form and retreated down the stairs with my head down. Lurking beneath the hatred and the sadness was the guilty desire to love them again. But *He* was right—my mother was afraid of me. Maybe if I were a Level 1—if my ability were passive, like communicating with animals or self-healing—then maybe things would be different. But I was one of the dangerous ones. I could destroy a whole city by myself in a matter of minutes. She was afraid of the power harbored inside me, and *He*'d paid good money to salvage her status and hide me away forever.

Hadn't she ever considered that I was afraid of that power, too? That I needed her to help me understand, to learn how to control it . . . to not become a monster.

— Chapter Twenty-Nine —

A Thief's Business

The next night, I sprinted through the darkness in silence, nothing more than a phantom of a shadow passing beneath the streetlights.

This was becoming a bad habit, I knew, but now it was an obsession. I couldn't help myself. Their voices had woken me again. I had to see them.

I dashed down the familiar street. My gaze darted beneath the hood, searching for prying eyes, ensuring that no humans saw me—a cloaked, hooded creature with glowing eyes—phasing through the white door of the gray house. I emerged and stood in the living room for a moment, inhaling deeply. The smell of the house was soothing, a reminder of my childhood.

Stooped in a low crouch, I stole up the stairs. I didn't even need to consciously think about skipping the creaking fourth step; it was a habit from Before. When I reached the top, I turned down the hallway. The darkness was my cover, my solitude. I pushed open the door.

My breath caught in my lungs when my gaze fell on the sleeping form of my blood-sister again. Time itself stood still; it was just her and me now. This was the only way I could see her without giving her the chance to hurt me or my lab-family.

I slowly approached, pushing the hood back. She was sound asleep, so I didn't have to worry about concealing my face and my eyes. She breathed so deeply, so peacefully, and I wondered what she was dreaming about. I wished I had the twins' Divinity.

The sheets had been thrown back around her waist. She was cradled on her side, arms curled inward like a wilting flower.

Afraid that she must be cold, I reached out to gently pull the blankets over her shoulders, but she stirred unexpectedly. I took a startled step back. The floorboard creaked under my weight, and with a gasp, she sat straight up.

I didn't have time to become invisible. Her eyes locked onto me.

I was frozen in disbelief and panic. Several long moments passed before I finally had the sense to call upon my power and vanish, but the damage was done. It was too late. She'd seen me standing there with my hood back, my green-and-blue eyes glowing in the dark.

Invisible, I watched her, waiting for her reaction. She was still staring at me even though I'd passed from her sight, but she seemed disoriented and confused. "Cato?" she whispered blearily, her gaze sweeping the room. I held my breath, knowing that I should retreat before I burned out. But I couldn't unlock a single muscle. *She said my name.* I shivered with guilty pleasure and wished she would say it again.

She frowned, still searching. Her eyes were unfocused, and I slowly realized that she wasn't fully awake. She was in a hypnopompic state, stuck in that strange limbo between dreamland and awareness. I slowly released the air trapped in my lungs. Clearly befuddled, she lowered herself back down, then sighed and closed her eyes.

Despite the acute realization that my power was leaking from me at an alarming rate, I remained completely still until her breathing evened out again and I was sure she was asleep. Something wet dripped from my nose, and a dark spot appeared on the wooden floor. Dizzy, I resumed visibility and wiped the drop of blood away with my glove, then swiped the back of my arm across my nose. Close call. All I could hope for now was that if she remembered the encounter by morning, she'd pass it off as no more than a half-forgotten dream.

I lowered myself into a crouch so I was balanced on the balls of my feet and my fingertips as I watched her sleep. I knew I needed to leave now before she woke again, but I was afraid that moving might disrupt her light sleep. Only now did I realize I was trembling.

A particularly violent shiver racked my body. I tensed; a ghost was near. *Here?* I whirled, rising partway out of my crouch to defend my blood-sister from the cloaked creature lurking in the doorway.

Smoldering eyes stared back at me. I straightened.

Ash.

I swallowed with guilt. Her gaze flickered from me to the still form of my sleeping blood-sister, then back to me. With a sigh, I crossed the room. Ash backed out of the doorway to let me pass. We stood in the hallway, staring at each other in the dark, saying nothing. Finally, I choked out in a whisper, "What are you doing here?"

"I wondered where you went every night."

I averted my eyes. "I didn't think it was too much to ask to have a little time alone."

Ash glanced into the dark room again. "I didn't realize how much you missed her."

I scowled and started down the stairs, Ash trailing behind. Tonight had been too close. I couldn't come back here anymore. I couldn't risk losing everything again just to sustain my selfish and pathetic desire to be with my blood-family, even if the only way that was possible was when they slept. Ash's presence in this house made me remember that I had a whole new life separate from this old one, a new family to think about, and any consequences from my unnecessary risks would harm them.

Becoming intangible to walk through the front door was more difficult than it should have been—a clear sign I'd used too much power. The cool night air helped to clear my head.

"Cato," Ash said as she appeared behind me, "I'm sorry. I didn't mean—"

"No, it's okay. I won't be coming back here. Tonight was my last night."

"Because of me?"

I shook my head. "No. I was almost seen. I won't risk it anymore. Do, um . . . do the others know where I've been going?"

"I don't think so."

"Don't tell them. Please?"

Ash looked down at her feet as we walked away from the gray house. "Okay."

I could see it in her glistening eyes—she was wondering if she wasn't a good enough sister, if I wanted my first one back instead. My heart was being torn in two, ripped apart by my lab-family and my blood-family. It shouldn't even be a choice. One disowned me; the other welcomed me with open arms. Why did I have to keep looking back and wishing for more?

The bell signaling the beginning of class wouldn't ring for at least ten more minutes. Trey folded his arms and leaned back against the chain-link fence. "Your mom keeps canceling my training lessons." He glanced sideways at Vivian, who wouldn't look at him.

"Oh," she said softly.

"Did I do something to make her mad?"

She shrugged. "I don't think so."

"You're about as talkative as Madison's been lately."

"I'm sorry. It's just . . ." She glanced around and lowered her voice. "Mom got a file from Agent Kovak in the mail, and it's . . . test results."

Her voice cracked on the last two words, and Trey's eyes widened in understanding. "Whoa, seriously? She has Cato's file from the AGC? What's she doing with it?"

Vivian shrugged again. "Don't tell her I told you, okay?"

"Sure." Trey dug his Rubik's cube out of a pouch on his weapon belt.

Vivian watched him twist a few rotations. "That glove you're wearing on your left hand," she finally said. "Did my mom give it to you?"

Trey paused. He gripped the cube in his bare right hand and held up his gloved left. "Yeah." He gave her a sly look from the corner of his eye. "Know what it does?"

"Uh, yeah. It short-circuits. Did she not tell you that?"

"What?" Trey splayed his fingers and stared at the metal nodes embedded within a mesh of thin wire filaments. "No. Are you sure?"

"Yeah. That glove is supposed to dissipate ectoplasm, right? Except it sort of short-circuits when it comes into contact."

Trey curled and straightened his fingers. "I think she fixed it."

"Are you sure?"

"Ah . . . n-not entirely, no. She wanted me to test this prototype." Vivian raised an eyebrow, and Trey quickly added, "Don't look at me like that. She's wearing one, too. We're both testing the updated version." He slumped against the fence and cradled the cube in both hands with his head bowed. "I'm not her guinea pig."

Vivian was quiet for a minute before she said, "I'm worried about you."

"Why? I'm fine." He turned the rows back into place. Ever since the twins had solved the Rubik's cube, he'd been careful to remember each rotation he made and put the colored squares back into their proper order after only a few turns to ensure he didn't forget.

"Are you? You haven't been acting like yourself ever since Mom sent you to the AGC. Would talking help?"

Trey turned the top row. "No."

"You can't keep it bottled up inside. It's going to destroy you."

"Jeez, Viv, I said I don't want to talk, okay? Telling you how Kovak tortured my best friend isn't going to give me any closure." He glanced at her pale face, then snapped, "Don't give me that look. What did you think happened to Cato in the AGC?" Trey threw the cube onto the ground and turned away, curling his fingers around the links of the fence as he glared across the street.

In his peripheral, he noticed Vivian staring at the Rubik's cube in the grass. "I thought you went to Project Alpha."

"I did. Kovak said all new subjects are taken to Alpha first for some preliminary tests before they go to their own Project. And that bastard put me in the restraints . . . the same damn restraints Cato was in when he was electrocuted."

"What?" Vivian whispered.

Damn it. Trey slammed his open palm against the interlaced links of metal, angry at himself for saying that, angry at Vivian for drawing it out of him, angry at Kovak for doing it, angry at Cato for letting it happen, angry at everybody. He squeezed his eyes shut and leaned his forehead against the fence. "I shouldn't have told you that."

Vivian bent down to pick up the cube. She stared at it for a moment, then offered it back to Trey. "That isn't all you know, is it?"

He turned his head just enough to look at her from the corner of one eye. "No." He reclaimed his Rubik's cube. Vivian walked to the fence and stood beside him, her back to the schoolyard. Across the street, the kids of Heavilon Elementary were laughing and cavorting on the playground. Trey watched them in envy. It must be so blissful to be so carefree.

"Cato was electrocuted," Vivian whispered.

Trey shook his head. "I didn't even know until afterward, when . . . oh my god."

"What?"

He stared across the schoolyard without seeing. "Oh my god."

"Trey, I'm going to need a little more context than that."

He turned to stare at her. "Shannon was right."

Vivian folded her arms. "Right about what?"

"Oh my *god* . . ."

"Trey!"

He jolted. "Finn and Reese. Project Alpha. Cato."

"Okay, better. But now try speaking in complete sentences."

Trey took a deep breath. "Finn and Reese were present for the experiments. I knew that, but I was so focused on stealing that device to rescue you that I didn't put two and two together. It didn't even occur to me . . . Finn and Reese had to have met Cato, at the very least for that one test in Project Alpha."

Vivian sagged against the fence. "Not just met him, either," she said. "They're Mind-Readers. They got inside Cato's head. They'd be able to disprove Kovak's claim that Cato had a mental breakdown."

"Or confirm it," Trey sullenly countered.

"So now you believe Kovak?"

He shrugged one shoulder. "It just doesn't seem as far-fetched now. I know I would've gone insane in there." He kept his head down when he mumbled, "Viv? You, uh . . . you don't think I'm just a sidekick, do you?"

"What?"

"Well . . . I mean . . . I was just thinking . . . What the hell?" he muttered, watching a flickering golden light arch over LeahRae Harris High. It dissipated above the roof. "Viv, did you see—?"

"Hey," she interrupted, tugging his sleeve to get his attention. "Hey, look."

He turned to spot a cloaked figure strolling down the sidewalk. The white letter α was clearly emblazoned on the front of his long-sleeve black shirt, and his eyes were hidden behind a blindfold under the hood.

"It's Axel," Trey identified in surprise, welcoming the distraction. He jumped on the opportunity to change the subject. "What's he doing walking around by himself? Do you think he's lost?"

"Let's go talk to him."

"Are you crazy?" He seized her shoulder. "I don't know why, but I'll be honest, Viv, he scares the hell out of me."

"He's blind. He's probably scared because he was separated from the other Alpha ghosts. We should help him." Still, Trey hesitated.

Vivian gasped. "Oh no," she whispered. Trey's attention returned to Axel. A ghost twice his size had appeared behind him. Trey reached for his holstered weapon, but he already knew he'd be too late. The ghost was reaching for its blind victim.

Vivian clutched the chain-link fence. "Axel, *look out!*"

Axel never broke stride.

Raw power crackled around him like red lightning erupting from his pores. It jumped from his body and onto his assailant, who shrieked and reeled back, falling to the ground and thrashing in agony as the degraded ectoplasm swarmed around him.

Vivian and Trey stood in dumbfounded shock as Axel strode away from his victim without so much as a glance over his shoulder. Students, drawn by the commotion, crowded to the fence for a better view. "Whoa. Did you see that?" Vivian asked above the excited murmurs.

Trey nodded as the energy finally dissipated around its victim. The ghost was either unconscious or dead on the sidewalk. Trey said, "For someone who's blind, Axel can sure handle himself. Do you think that was Grade G ectoplasm? Hey, Viv, wait!"

She'd already rounded the end post and taken off at a brisk jog for the retreating Alpha ghost. He rolled his head back to send an exasperated sigh at the sky, then trotted after her. A girl with long black hair tailed him.

The air was dense and charged in Axel's wake, almost pulsing with residual energy from the massive amount of ectoplasm he'd just unleashed. "Hey, Axel," Vivian greeted when she finally caught up.

He continued walking as if he hadn't heard her. Trey slowed, giving Axel a wider berth than Vivian did. Shannon started to walk past him; Trey shot his hand out to catch her wrist. "You should stay back," he advised.

"I'm not afraid," Shannon asserted.

"Hey."

She jerked her wrist out of his grip.

He grabbed her arm. "*Hey.*"

She froze. He could see it in her eyes—she was thinking of the day she'd snuck out with the raid team and hadn't been able to pull the trigger when they fell under attack.

"Shannon. You don't have to prove you're brave."

She stared him down for a few seconds. Then her shoulders sagged.

He let go, and they both watched Vivian boldly reach out to tap the Alpha ghost on the shoulder. Trey's hand found the holster of an ectogun. Her fingers were inches away when Axel said, "Touch me, and you'll end up like him."

Vivian yanked her hand back. "I thought you were blind."

"Humans rely on their eyes too much."

She jogged to walk abreast with him. Trey drew his ectogun halfway from its holster. He so desperately wanted to call her back to him, away from the danger. He flipped the safety off. Just in case. *Shit, what am I doing? I can't shoot one of the Alpha ghosts. That would violate our contract.*

But what if Axel hurt Viv?

He wouldn't.

Trey swallowed.

He might.

Trey tailed the pair at a safe distance, Shannon half a step behind.

Vivian asked, "So . . . how are you?"

"Fuck off, Tarrow."

"What's got you in such a foul mood?"

"You."

"*Me?*" she repeated. "What did I do?"

Axel growled deep in his throat like Wes did when he was irritated. *He's in a bad mood,* Trey realized in a panic. *Get away from him!*

But Viv, in her openhearted kindness, said, "Listen, Axel, if you're lost and you can't find the other Alpha ghosts, I can help you. I can lead you back to Wes's house."

Axel snorted, his nose wrinkled in a sneer. "I know exactly where I am and where the others are. If you're done insulting me, go away."

"You know, if it weren't for Trey and me, you'd still be living on the streets and eating garbage. You could try to show a little gratitude."

How Axel, blindfolded and hooded with half his face covered, managed to execute such a contemptuous look, Trey couldn't fathom. Red ectoplasm flickered dangerously across the knuckles of his fists. The air seemed to flex, and such a ferocious snarl issued from the Alpha ghost that Trey feared Vivian's life was in jeopardy. His grip tightened on the ectogun. Before he could raise it to defend her, Axel was right in her face. "Don't think for one second I have to tolerate you just because your name is Tarrow."

Axel vanished. Trey waited, knowing that maintaining invisibility was incredibly taxing for a kálos and Axel should reappear at any moment, but he never did. Vivian was a statue, as if she were afraid to reach out in case her hand might find his solid body still in front of her.

Ectogun drawn but pointed at the ground, Trey approached to stand beside her. "Viv," he said weakly, "please do me a favor and don't piss him off. You saw what he did to that ghost."

"I was trying to help."

Shannon, who was preoccupied inspecting her cell phone, joined them from behind. "Okay, Axel is definitely my least favorite Alpha ghost," she said.

Trey glanced at her. "It's weird, you know? I would've thought the blind one of the group would be the least intimidating. But Axel . . . I'll take Jay over him any day." He shuddered. "You know, that makes me wonder what Jay's Divinity is. He must be crazy powerful if he's able to keep someone like Axel in line."

"Hey, Trey, you're good with tech, right?" Shannon interrupted.

"I know a few tricks. Why?"

"I took a picture of Axel, but I'm getting this error message that says the data is corrupt and the image can't be displayed."

"Weird. Let me take a look." He holstered the ectogun and accepted the phone. As his fingertips slid across the screen, he muttered, "I've been reading Madison's book about creatures in the Ghost Realm. I wonder if Axel has a Divinity that compensates for his eyes, like one of the clair powers."

Vivian said, "You mean like clairaudience? Super-hearing?"

"Maybe. All six types have fangs, although it looks like Axel has two sets, which is kind of weird. Clairs also have pointed ears, but I can't tell if Axel does since I've never seen him without his hood on. My guess—clairaudience or clairsentience. It wouldn't surprise me if he has super-touch and can feel things like air currents moving around objects to gain a sense of space."

Vivian nodded enthusiastically. "Makes sense. Axel carried me on his back once. I swear, Trey, we were jumping on rooftops. How else could a blind person navigate like that?"

Trey considered, but he wasn't convinced. "Thing is, though, the clair powers are passive, and Wes told me passive Divinities are rarely higher than Level 2. I can't imagine a Level 2 being able to produce the kind of ectoplasm he just did. Actually . . . I've never seen ectoplasm like that. Maybe he's an Ectokinetic."

"You know a lot about ghosts, right?" said Shannon. Trey glanced up from the phone with a proud smile. "I have a hypothetical question for you."

"Okay, shoot."

"Can a ghost and a human have a baby together?"

The trio paused by the fence post marking the schoolyard. Trey and Vivian both stared at Shannon, who met their gazes and added, "Hypothetically."

A warm breeze stirred their hair, turning Trey's collar up. Vivian blurted, "Why?"

Shannon gave a little shrug. "Just curious. The thought popped into my head, and I wondered what the outcome would be."

"Yeah, ghosts and humans can procreate," Trey said, turning his attention back to the error message on the screen. "I think."

"And, uh, what would the baby be like?"

"I'd have to do a little research to be sure, but I'm almost positive the offspring wouldn't have any powers, and its eyes wouldn't glow. Even with mixed blood, it'd be considered human as far as ghosts are concerned."

"But would there be any way to tell that it's a hybrid?"

"Not really. I mean, the eyes *might* give it away if they were a weird color like violet or red or gold, but the kid could have blue or green eyes, too. I think it's pretty rare for ghosts and humans to, uh, you know. Make a baby." Flummoxed, Trey finally admitted defeat and returned Shannon's phone. "Sorry, I don't think the image can be recovered."

Shannon reclaimed it with a glum, "Oh. Thanks anyway." She clutched her phone and looked Vivian in the eye. "I couldn't convince my mom."

"I'm not surprised," said Vivian with a frigid edge.

"Viv," Trey reprimanded lightly.

Shannon lifted her chin. "Don't count me out yet."

Vivian scoffed. "If you couldn't get through to her, nobody can."

"I just need more time. I have another idea." She dug into her pocket and withdrew a long ribbon, black on one side and shiny silver on the other. She handed it to Vivian, then pulled out another and gave it to Trey. "Trust me," she said before she strode away.

Trey stared at the ribbon draped across his palm, then watched Shannon's long ponytail sway over her back as she picked her way between the tables near the school where students were waiting for the bell to ring. Vivian was also watching her.

No, Trey realized. *Not Shannon.* Vivian's gaze had been drawn beyond Shannon to the black-and-white kitten sunning itself on top of the dumpster.

"Casper's asleep," she whispered, as if speaking at a normal volume would awaken the kitten from across the schoolyard.

"So?" Trey said, but she had already shoved her ribbon into her pocket and was stalking past the tables toward the dumpster, her eyes trained unblinkingly on her dozing quarry. Trey sighed and followed.

Casper's collar tag was lying under his chin, hidden from view. Vivian licked her lips and reached out, her hovering hand prepared to flash down on the unsuspecting ball of fur. She reminded Trey of a patient heron waiting to snatch a fish. The kitten's ear flicked in her direction.

Casper's golden eyes opened. Upon realizing how close Vivian was, he leapt from the dumpster and dashed beneath it to safety.

She cursed softly and fell to her hands and knees, peering at the kitten cowering well out of arm's reach. "Here, kitty," she coaxed, patting her lap. "Come here. I won't hurt you."

Casper hissed at her and hunkered low to the ground.

"Why do you care so much about that cat?" Trey inquired from behind.

Vivian leaned back on her heels. "He has a collar. He must belong to someone who misses him."

"I haven't seen any posters for a lost cat."

They both glanced up at the sound of the bell ringing. Trey offered his hand and helped Vivian to her feet, and the two joined the throng meandering into the school, leaving a pair of golden eyes watching from beneath the dumpster.

— Chapter Thirty —

Project Safe Haven

Madison couldn't breathe.

Her legs felt as if they had turned to rubber. She could face a kálos without breaking a sweat, but standing in front of Councilwoman Jennings's desk, waiting in the suffocating silence, had her knees shaking. Late-afternoon sunlight streamed in at a slant through the window.

Holly set the folder down on her desk. "City council will not approve this."

The ghost hunter bristled. "City council won't? Don't you mean *you* won't?"

"Isn't that what I said?" Holly asked with a smile.

"Why not? All the paperwork is in order."

Holly raised one eyebrow. "It is," she agreed. "But this exception is going to undermine the ordinance we've already set in place barring civilians from driving vehicles in the city limits."

"No, it won't. We're not talking about regular citizens. These are raiders. I'm trying to set up patrols and emergency crews to assist the police."

"Your raid teams were a hodgepodge of volunteers, including high schoolers. The current wording of this exception would let unlicensed teenagers get behind the wheel and potentially clog the streets for police cruisers and paramedics. Besides that, your raid teams were in constant fluctuation. Who qualifies as a raider, and how is it determined? Anyone you deem fit should be allowed to drive on the roads? I don't think so."

Holly leaned back in her chair. "I'll make an exception for *you*. And," she added as an afterthought, "your apprentice . . . once Mr. Selman has passed a driving test and secured a valid license. I can have your permit tomorrow."

Madison clenched her fists. She detested politics; she'd rather be allowed to focus on her research and hunting, but that required funding, which required catering to the politicians. And, like it or not, Holly Jennings was the one most likely to fulfill Madison's requests. They were a reluctant team working toward the same goal, albeit usually with opposing strategies. Correll might hold the title of mayor, but Madison knew Holly commanded the respect of city council.

"Is there anything I can do to make you reconsider?"

"No. But I'm glad you dropped by for a visit. I've been meaning to speak with you." Holly opened a drawer and unceremoniously dropped the folder into it. "Are you as concerned about Cooper's involvement with the Alpha ghosts as I am?"

"Wes didn't act on his own. I was part of the decision to make contact with the Alpha ghosts."

Holly's lips flattened into a thin, displeased line. "You decided it was best to have them live in Saros Manor?"

"Well . . ." Madison shifted before admitting, "Wes went off script on that part."

"Do you condone his actions?"

Madison opened her mouth, waved her hand in an attempt to draw the words out, then sighed and rubbed her neck. "I'll admit I don't like it. But he's not breaking the law."

"Not in this instance, no. But although the law has yet to catch up with him, Wesly Cooper is a criminal. It was irresponsible on your part to let him put a claim on the Alpha ghosts like that."

"He hasn't *claimed* anything or anyone. I'm not happy about it either, but . . . I don't understand why you're upset."

"He's sure to be a negative influence. Don't be surprised when they start taking liberties with our laws just like he does."

Madison's temper was starting to flare at the insinuation of incompetence. "I can assure you, I've been watching Wes. I have him on a leash."

"Then tighten it," Holly ordered without missing a beat. "And while you're at it, get some collars on the Alpha ghosts, too."

"With all due respect, I'm a ghost hunter, not a babysitter. I—"

"I prefer *liaison*, but you will be whatever this town needs you to be. And what we need is to make sure our good little mercenaries are under control. Jay has to be held accountable for his team."

Madison lowered her gaze, but nodded. "I understand."

"Good." Holly leaned forward again and folded her hands on the tabletop. "You aren't on the Agents' payroll anymore. You work for the city of Phantom Heights, and we need you to take charge. Got it?"

Again, Madison nodded. Holly stood, the chair legs scraping across the floor to make Madison cringe, although Madison was convinced that wasn't an accident. "I'll see you out."

Holly strode for the door. Madison followed, her boots quiet beneath the *clack* of the councilwoman's high heels. Neither spoke a word as they walked down the hall and descended the staircase. When Holly stopped before the back doors of City Hall, the ones that led to First Street instead of the plaza, Madison also halted.

But when Holly reached out and snatched one of the ghost hunter's ectoguns from her belt, Madison's reflexes were too sluggish for her to react. She simply gawked at the councilwoman.

Holly held up the weapon. "You must really hate them," she murmured.

"Actually, no. I find them intriguing."

"Interesting. Wasn't it a ghost that killed Jaxon?" Madison caught her breath but didn't dare speak while Holly studied the ectogun. "If I could, I'd seal the Realms forever." Holly leveled the weapon and closed one eye. "Tell me, Madison. If you don't hate them, why hunt them?"

Madison reached her hand across the span until it hovered over the ectogun. She pressed down. Holly submitted to the weight, letting the ghost hunter push the muzzle toward the floor. She relinquished the weapon to its rightful owner.

Madison held it in both hands, perplexed by the councilwoman's simple question that had no simple answer. "The things they can do," she started, hoping her purpose would illuminate itself as the words unfolded. "They're just . . . fascinating. My job brings me as close to their level as a human can get. I like standing my ground against them. It makes me feel . . ."

"Empowered?"

Madison nodded. She holstered the gun. Holly's gaze was still on the weapon, a hint of obsessive madness in her eyes. "I know how you feel. I have a proposition for you."

"What?"

"We both know Correll is nothing more than a figurehead. His term ended, and he's overdue to step down. Now that things are settling . . ." Holly glanced to either side as if searching for eavesdroppers before lowering her voice. "I want to run for mayor."

Madison didn't react. Somehow, the announcement didn't surprise her. "Let me guess—this campaign will be on Kovak's dime again?"

"Not this time."

Madison folded her arms. "Well, now it all makes sense."

"What?" Holly asked, frowning in what appeared to be genuine puzzlement.

"Shoot-On-Sight. I'd wondered what sort of insanity got into your head to push that doctrine through. So, that was a political ploy. You're setting up the pieces for your election, and you used me. That whole 'debate' you staged was just a show."

"On the contrary, I never start anything I don't have the intention of seeing through to the end. I rushed S-O-S a little too soon, that's all. It did get people riled up though, didn't it?" Holly smiled. "I've always vowed to protect Phantom Heights. S-O-S was proof that I'm willing and ready to take aggressive action. Correll is not. When it's time to vote, the people want a proactive candidate. Your support would help me win."

At Madison's hesitation, Holly added, "We'd be a great team. I'd make you an official consultant and put you in charge of designing weapons and training police officers to use them. The city would fund your research and anything you needed—equipment, assistants, maybe even a new lab. Between the two of us, we could stop traffic through the Rip."

Madison touched the holster of an ectogun. "It sounds great, but . . . well, I'm just not sure it's a good idea to stir people up over an election. What they need right now is a familiar face in charge."

Holly snorted delicately. "Correll proved to be incompetent in a crisis. People don't need a familiar face; they need a leader. I'm sure they would vote for you in a heartbeat, but you don't have time for an office job, and I know how much you dislike politics. So, let me handle it. With you backing me, there's no way I'll lose. You'll come out on top, too."

"That's, um . . . that's a generous offer."

Holly was too sharp to miss the hesitation. "Think about it."

Madison nodded a little too vehemently. She slipped her hand inside her bag and drew out a folder. "I, uh, I received this from Kovak a few days ago. I thought you should know I've been in touch with him recently."

Holly, upon reading the words in the top corner and deducing what its contents contained, shifted her foot back half a step. "I'm not sure what you think you'll accomplish with that."

"I want to know, that's all." Madison thumbed through the papers in the folder. "The file's obviously been censored. I was thinking about making a trip to the AGC so—"

"I strongly advise against that."

"Why?"

Holly adjusted the hem of her skirt. "You don't want to do anything that might make Kovak turn his attention back to Phantom Heights, do you? We wouldn't want him learning about our little secret here."

Madison stared at the folder. Holly glanced around again for eavesdroppers, then pointed at the file. "That's what you were promised, and that's what you got. Leave it at that."

The ghost hunter reluctantly replaced the folder in her messenger bag. "Have you been in contact with Kovak lately?"

Her answer was a harsh scoff.

They both jumped when one of the doors slammed open. A young woman strode into City Hall and stopped short when she sighted Holly and Madison, who stared back at her. She was slim, her short bleach-blonde hair tipped with red and styled up and forward. She wore skinny jeans tucked into black boots, and beneath the edge of her black leather jacket were the holsters of a weapon belt.

"Madison Tarrow?" she asked. Her husky voice carried the smell of stale smoke.

"Yes," said Madison uncertainly. The stranger came forward to shake Madison's hand.

"Huh. You're older than I thought you'd be." Madison had to force her smile to stay in place as she slipped her hand free. "Name's Jules."

Her gaze fell on Holly, who offered her hand and introduced herself: "Holly Jennings, city councilwoman."

Jules shook Holly's hand with a grunt of acknowledgment and turned her attention back to Madison, who shifted her bag behind her back and politely inquired, "What brings a fellow ghost hunter to Phantom Heights?"

Jules rolled her shoulders. "This used to be the place to go for a score, but it looks like you cashed out all the bounties, eh Tarrow? What's your secret?"

"Secret?" Madison and Holly shared brief glances. Madison stammered, "Ah . . . no secret, really, I guess. I, um, well . . ."

Holly cut in, "Madison organized systematic strikes to combat the little infestation we had. As you can see, we've had a lot of success under her leadership."

Jules folded her arms. Her gaze had flickered to Holly when the councilwoman spoke, but it settled right back onto Madison, who could only smile and nod. "Uh-huh," said Jules. "So, any sign of those escaped Alpha lab rats? Still got a big bounty on their heads, and I haven't heard any updates on them lately."

Madison gave a little shrug. "If you want my opinion, they're probably in the Ghost Realm by now." She hesitated. "I'm not in network.

Just out of curiosity . . . what is Kovak offering?"

"Hundred k apiece. Double for A1, A2, and A6."

Holly let out a low whistle. "That much, huh?" Madison croaked.

"Well, they have to be alive, of course, which makes it a little trickier." Jules shrugged her shoulder to indicate the rifle strapped across her back. "Nothing a little tranq can't handle, though. Just put 'em to sleep, nice and easy, and it's a hell of a payday, eh Tarrow?"

"Sure is," Madison mumbled.

Jules studied Madison closely, her eyes narrowing as she drummed her fingers against her arm. "Rip's still active, right?" Madison nodded. "I'd like to check it out. If you don't mind."

Again, Madison's and Holly's eyes found each other in a shared look of alarm. Madison grudgingly replied, "That's fine."

Holly cleared her throat with a quiet "Ah-hem," then said sweetly, "I don't mean to be rude, Jules, but I'm sure you'll understand that this town has a deep loyalty to Madison, and people won't take kindly to another ghost hunter being here."

Jules appraised the councilwoman with a faint smirk. "No worries, just passing through." She turned back to the door. "I'd love to bag-and-tag a ghost, but if there aren't any around, well, no need to waste my time. I don't want to cause any trouble." She was already pulling out a pack of cigarettes and a lighter as she kicked the door open.

Holly waited until the door closed behind Jules before she whispered, "Should we warn the Alpha ghosts, do you think?"

"Yeah. Just to be safe." Madison stared at the door as if waiting to see if it would open again. "I bet she'll be gone in a few hours as long as she doesn't find anything." She paused, then frowned at Holly. "So, what inspired the sudden change of heart?"

"I beg your pardon?"

"You were so outspoken against our deal with the Alpha ghosts in the beginning, but I've noticed you've been rather protective about them lately. Why?"

"Nothing personal," Holly said as she inspected her fingers and picked at a chipped nail. "As Cooper would say, I'm just safeguarding an investment. Speaking of Cooper, you can be the one to call him. I'm not in the mood to deal with him right now."

"Fine. He can warn Ero, too."

"Hmm?"

Madison raised one eyebrow. "*Ero*, who would also be in danger with a ghost hunter in town. Or does he not have enough short-term value to warrant protection?"

"I was more concerned about the ones who don't have the ability to control minds and erase memories. I think Ero can handle himself. Anyway, I meant what I said earlier. Your job is to defend this town, and if you need Cooper and the Alpha ghosts to help you accomplish that, fine. But get your guard dog on a tighter leash and make sure those lab rats are kept accountable. Jay and Cooper report to you, and you report to me. Got it?"

Madison rubbed her arm. "I understand."

Holly turned her back with these parting words: "Good. Your paycheck might come from the city of Phantom Heights, but really, you work for me." She strode down the hallway, her heels clacking on the marble.

Madison watched her until she rounded the corner. She hung her head in submission, her mind on the ghost hunter outside who was free to do whatever she wanted and answered to no one but herself.

Madison couldn't help but feel a tinge of envy.

***

That evening, Holly didn't take her usual route home.

She stood on the marble steps of City Hall, watching the fenced-off Rip until the streetlights came to life.

Holly rubbed the back of her neck. All this stress was tying her muscles in knots. She needed a hot bath and a deep tissue massage. Jules, as far as Holly knew, was gone, but still, today had been a close call.

"Damn it, Cato," she muttered under her breath. There was only so much she could do to protect him while distancing herself as much as possible. He had no idea how much he was shredding her nerves. Holly was exhausted.

Even bending over to pick up the briefcase made her muscles complain. Rather than start the fifteen-minute walk home, she descended the steps and crossed the cobblestone plaza to stand before the Rip. In the fading light, the disturbance inside the barbed-wire fence was nearly impossible to see, but it was there.

Holly's grip on the handle tightened. An adrenaline rush accompanied the thrill of terror that chilled her blood. Sometimes, her nightmares sucked her back into the Ghost Realm, reminded her how it felt to wear rags and chains and answer to a sharp whistle like a dog. A year, a lifetime, it was all the same. It was hell. Nobody but Agent Kovak fully comprehended what she'd been through, and that wasn't about to change anytime soon. Perhaps she shouldn't have revealed so much to Shannon, but even that was only a ripple on the surface of what had really happened. It was a secret she intended to take to the grave.

Inside her jacket pocket, her thumb stroked a small, square gadget. She never walked home without an e-zap in her hand. It gave her a small sense of security—at the very least, a fighting chance if she was attacked. It may have been Madison Tarrow's invention, but Holly had funded the development of the tiny weapon with her own savings, so she felt as though in part, it was hers, too.

She backed away, too afraid to turn her back on the sinister Rip in case a ghost might reach out behind her and drag her inside. Her gaze skimmed town square. It was strangely empty . . . where was the patrol?

A pair of shadows behind the fence made her freeze. She waited, petrified in place on the cobblestones, but the figures didn't cross through the Rip. Holly squinted at them. They weren't in the Ghost Realm, she finally deduced. They were behind the Rip, which had distorted the figures, but they were definitely humans, and they were huddled just inside the alleyway conversing in hushed, suspicious tones.

Holly, pretending she hadn't noticed them, casually made her way toward the shops edging town square. As soon as she was out of the men's sight, she quickened her step.

She reached the sidewalk and turned, then hurried down the street to circle back to the opposite end of the alley. She peered around the corner just in time to see a long-haired man dressed in shabby clothes hand something to a businessman in a suit, then skulk away toward the Rip.

Holly squared her shoulders and marched toward the man in the suit still standing at the mouth of the alley watching his accomplice leave. By the time Wesly Cooper turned and realized he wasn't alone, Holly was already halfway down the alley, and he had no chance to make an inconspicuous getaway. "Councilwoman," he greeted nervously, taking a step back and subtly hiding his fist against his spine. "What a pleasant surprise. Didn't expect to meet you here."

Holly reached him and halted, her free hand drifting up to settle on her hip. "All right, Cooper. I'm going to pretend I didn't just witness what was probably an illegal transaction with someone who looks like a scarback from the Ghost Realm. I'm also not going to ask you what's behind your back."

Wesly forced what he probably hoped was a nonchalant grin, but Holly noticed how it wavered. He was nervous, and that solidified her suspicions. "I appreciate your discretion."

"My discretion comes at a price."

"Naturally," he muttered, shoulders sagging.

Holly slipped a folded piece of paper out of her pocket and handed her list to him. She'd been intending to meet with him anyway; this was just too perfect an opportunity to pass up. Blackmail was a much better price than whatever he would have demanded in exchange for these items.

He skimmed the cursive, his brow furrowing. "Charms are illegal without papers."

"I can't imagine that would be an issue on the Black Market."

He lifted his eyes to stare at her. "A Charm to sense kálos would have to be a special request. These Witch's brews shouldn't be hard to get. What do you want this stuff for, anyway? I thought you hated everything about the Ghost Realm."

"Although it's really none of your business, I want those items for self-defense. And you're in the perfect position to get them for me."

Cooper folded the paper, now looking Holly up and down in appraisal. "How would someone like you know about Charms and the Black Market of Avilésor? Actually . . . come to think of it, how would you know the term 'scarback'?"

Holly's heartbeat pounded in her ears. "As difficult as this might be for you to process, I know quite a bit about the Ghost Realm."

He leaned closer, eyes narrowing. "I bet even Maddie doesn't know about these types of Charms and brews. I've always wondered what caused you to hate kálos so much. You wouldn't happen to be a scarback yourself, would you?"

Holly's breath caught in her chest. Her ears rang. And yet, she maintained her perfectly composed politician's mask despite the sudden itch on the layers of scar tissue on her back. He was leaning too close, eyes dancing, as if he was considering reaching under her blouse.

"If you touch me, I'll mace you."

He took a step back, but his perfect white teeth gleamed in the frame of an eerie smile. "I almost missed your little slip-up. It's hard using the right terminology for the Realm, isn't it?"

"I have no idea what you're talking about."

"Fine. Keep your secrets for now, Councilwoman. As far as payment goes—"

"Your payment is me keeping quiet about whatever you're still hiding behind your back. Besides, this is the least you can do. You and Tarrow circumvented my authority when you organized a meeting with the Alpha ghosts and didn't consult me."

"What? No. We—"

"Here's the deal, Cooper. If there are any developments concerning them, you come to me first before you breathe a word to Madison. Got it?"

He tilted his head a little. "What sort of developments?"

"Any. Are we clear?"

"So . . . you want to know if one of them is allergic to peanuts?"

Holly waited a few seconds to make sure her irritation was evident before she asked, "How far do you think sarcasm is going to get you in life?"

"Well, it hasn't steered me wrong yet," he replied with an arrogant smirk.

"Let me put it to you this way: I don't like you. You're a thief and a liar and a—"

"Weir?"

Holly glared at him. She despised being interrupted, and he knew that. "Yes. You skirt on the edge of trouble without actually incriminating yourself, and someday your luck is going to run out, and you'll bring all that trouble here where innocent people will get hurt. I didn't know what you were before, and since this town was laid to siege, you've been answering to Tarrow. But guess what, Cooper? The old rules are back in play. *My* rules."

Undaunted by her threat, Wesly shifted his weight and tucked her unusual grocery list into his pocket. "I see," he said quietly. "You want me to go behind Maddie's back."

"I want to know that your loyalty lies with me."

He rolled his shoulders in a slight shrug. "It's hard to pledge loyalty to you when there's a ghost hunter threatening to report me to the AGC."

Holly's lips flattened into a tight, thin smile. "You're afraid of Agent Kovak?" She leaned closer. "I'd do more than just make a quiet phone call to the AGC. Your face would be all over every news network. There would be no safe place in this country for you, nowhere to hide in the developed world. Everybody would know exactly what you are."

Wesly held her steady gaze for several long heartbeats. Softly, he finally said, "And people wonder why Cato hid behind a mask."

Holly caught her breath. *Does he already know?* She scrutinized his features in the dark. No, she didn't think so. He didn't have that arrogant smirk he always wore when he knew a secret he shouldn't. "You would have been better off if you'd never revealed yourself."

"And you'd probably be dead by now."

Her coy smile returned. "And yet, here we are."

He nodded. "Here we are."

A murder of cawing crows flew high above them. Holly glanced up at the dark bodies flapping above. "How much did you bribe the patrolmen?"

"What?"

She leveled her glare at him. "Don't make me repeat myself."

"*Bribe* is such a negative word. They worked so hard today . . . I generously bought pizza for them and offered to guard the Rip until the next shift comes in ten minutes. Out of the goodness of my heart," he added with a smile.

"And naturally you were going to honor your word and stay here until the next shift. Right?"

"Naturally," he said, his smile unwavering.

Holly turned away from him. "You better sit and stay like a good dog. I'd like those items delivered as soon as possible. Try to be discreet, would you?"

She strode away without waiting for an answer.

Holly let a shaky breath hiss through her teeth once she was out of earshot. Why was she trembling?

She glanced around to guarantee no one was watching when she ducked into the alcove of a recessed doorway and sniffed, thumbing away a rogue tear without smudging her makeup. Damn it, why was she crying? Wesly Cooper was the only person in Phantom Heights who had the ability to rattle her.

Holly tilted her head back and slumped against the bricks. She blinked rapidly to clear the excess moisture from her eyes. No one could see her shed a tear, especially not Shannon. She had to be perfectly composed by the time she walked through the front door.

She closed her eyes, gripped her briefcase tight, and stepped out from the shadows.

Holly maintained a brisk pace on her walk home. One thing she'd learned from her experience as a slave was to not *look* vulnerable. Hold your head up. Be aware of your surroundings. Pay attention. Pay *visible* attention; let people see your eyes so they know you're looking.

The prime targets were people who radiated submissiveness. Assertive slaves were undesirable in the Ghost Realm. That, or they were broken before final sale. Either way, the result almost always ended in scars.

The e-zap was comfortable in her hand. Just a little insurance. She would feel even safer if Cooper could get his hands on a Charm that would allow her to sense a ghost's presence. Then she wouldn't have to be constantly glancing over her shoulder in fear, even though she detested the idea of having any similarities to the demons or even touching one of their cursed relics. But until human technology was sophisticated enough to compete with kálos Charms, she would have to compromise.

Holly paused on the sidewalk in front of C-Sully's Café. Someone had tied a ribbon around the door handle.

The breeze caught the ribbon's edge, its black face fluttering to reveal a shining silver back. Holly pursed her lips and rubbed at the building ache between her temples. She shook her head and walked on.

All down the street, black-and-silver ribbons on doorknobs waved in the breeze.

When she opened the front door of home, an enticing aroma greeted her. The living room was dark, but the kitchen was glowing with warm, welcoming light. Shannon smiled when Holly paused in the doorway. "You're late. I made spaghetti and meatballs. Yours is probably cold by now, but I can heat it up for you."

Holly didn't say a word. She set her briefcase down on the table.

Shannon pushed the buttons on the microwave and turned away with a flourish. "What would you like to drink? Water?" She hesitated. "Looks like you had a rough day. A glass of wine instead?"

Holly popped the clasp on her briefcase, pulled out a folded newspaper, and tossed it on the table. "Tell me what this is."

Shannon's smile fell. She leaned forward to study the print, and then her grin returned. "Cool. Ms. Swan didn't tell me it would make the front page."

Holly jammed her finger down on the headline that read **Rogue: Project Safe Haven** and seethed, "I specifically told you to stay far away from the Alpha ghosts."

The microwave beeped. Shannon opened the door and removed the bowl, filling the kitchen with the aroma of Italian herbs, marinara, and meatballs. "I haven't had any contact with them," she said, setting the bowl down in front of Holly. "I had an interview with Ms. Swan, and I talked to just about every store owner in Phantom Heights, and I met with a lot of students and teachers at school. But I didn't break my promise. All I did was hand out ribbons. Would you like water or wine with your dinner?"

Slowly, Holly lowered herself into her chair. "Pinot noir. The bottle on the top left."

Her gaze followed her daughter's graceful path to the wine rack above the sink. "I noticed there's no ribbon on our front door."

Shannon froze, her fingers around the smooth neck of the wine bottle. Quietly, she said, "The ribbons are to show the Alpha ghosts where they can go for food, shelter, or care if they're in trouble. Safe havens. And you're right; I didn't tie a ribbon on our door."

Holly twirled the pasta around the tines of the fork. The only sound was the *pop* of a cork followed by the smooth pour of the wine. Holly chewed, swallowed, closed her eyes. The headache was back.

"I put his room back the way he left it."

Holly kept her eyes closed for another few seconds. She didn't want to look at her daughter right now. Her voice was husky when she said, "I don't know why you wasted your time." She finally opened her eyes just long enough to see the glass of wine. She gripped the dainty neck and lifted the rim to her lips.

Shannon sat at the table and answered, "No reason other than it was therapeutic for me."

Holly set the glass down and let a long sigh escape. *Why?* Why did Shannon have to test her, today of all days? "I wish you hadn't done that. I told you I was planning to turn it into a guest room."

"In your spare time?" Shannon muttered under her breath.

Holly ground her teeth. *Now how am I going to be able to open that door upstairs?*

She cut a meatball with her fork and twirled the proper meat-to-pasta ratio on the tines. Shannon was silent, her eyes gliding back and forth as she read the article.

Holly finished the last bite and set the fork in the empty bowl. "I don't suppose you have any more of those ribbons left."

Shannon peered up at her without lifting her head. "I do. Why?"

Holly downed the last swig of wine and stared into the empty glass. "I wouldn't want to be the only house on Spitler Avenue without one. A poor example to the rest of the neighborhood, don't you think?"

Shannon didn't answer, although the tiniest smirk dented her cheek.

Her gaze fell back to the paper as she reached into her pocket and slipped out a black-and-silver ribbon that shone under the kitchen light. She draped it across the table.

— Chapter Thirty-One —

Fallen

By midweek, a series of storms had drenched Phantom Heights in an unseasonably cold rain.

Trey's numb hands were shoved deep in his pockets, his shoulders slumped against the chill. The rain struck the umbrella with a steady *tap-tah-tap-tap*. He glanced sidelong at the girl holding it. Their walk might have been romantic had they not both been frozen to the bone while Vivian's vacant gaze wandered, her mind far from him.

"Lovely weather, isn't it?" he said sarcastically, then cringed.

Lovely weather? That was the best he could come up with?

Although she didn't break her distant stare, she replied, "Are you sure you want to train in this nasty weather?"

"Your mom's been busy. I gotta take any time she'll give me. Besides, we'll be dry. She's going to teach me how her entoplasm generator works while she does a maintenance check on it."

"Hmm, sounds like fun," muttered Vivian less than enthusiastically. The pedestrian road connecting the church to City Hall opened into the cobblestone plaza where colorful umbrellas dotted town square above hunched patrons shuffling in the damp drizzle.

"Hey, Viv," said Trey as they turned to stroll under the covered walkway in front of the shops edging the plaza. The low roof silenced the sharp taps on the fabric above their heads, washing the world in pleasant white noise. "Have you ever thought about an apprenticeship? I mean, don't you want to follow in your family's footsteps?"

"I'm not a ghost hunter. I respect what you and my mom do, but it's not for me." She lowered her voice. "Have you been thinking about your theory?"

"Yeah."

"And?"

"And I still haven't figured out how I can get Finn and Reese to talk to me."

They walked a few strides in silence. "Me either."

He shook his head in frustration, his eyes rolling up to watch water droplets trickle across the teal fabric of the umbrella. "We tried, in City Hall. A lot of people tried. The twins wouldn't even say 'ah' for Doc. I wonder if they have a trigger word, you know? Some kind of secret command. The Agents wouldn't have wasted time teaching Finn and Reese eighteen different languages if the twins never spoke."

"Hmm. Maybe Ero can find the truth for us."

"I guess it's worth a shot."

The drizzle was lightening. Vivian nodded at a pair of figures standing on City Hall's portico. "Is Wes part of this training session?"

"He's not supposed to be."

The werewolf spotted them approaching, and with one last word to Madison, he nodded to her in farewell and trotted lightly down the steps. Madison raised her hand in greeting. Trey waved back with a grin, and Vivian lifted the umbrella in acknowledgment.

Trey's smile vanished. A dark, amorphous figure had appeared behind Madison. There wasn't time to cry a warning before the cloaked man raised his hand and struck her down with a heavy object. Trey's ghost-hunting master crumpled like a rag doll, her grunt lost in the rain.

Vivian shrieked. She threw the umbrella to the ground and dashed toward her mom, Trey on her heels, one hand already gripping the holster of his ectogun. The ghost descended halfway down the steps and shouted to all of town square, "I challenge the Alpha rats to a duel!"

Wes snarled on the bottom step, his brown eyes flickering yellow, but the enemy leveled his fist at Wes, displaying his weapon—a loaded crossbow attached to his forearm. He must be a Fusion, one with the Divinity to fuse anything to his own body and make it a functional component. The sharp *twang* of a bowstring resounded through town square. Before Wes had the chance to transform, the bolt pierced his thigh. He fell to the ground, clutching the shaft protruding from his leg.

Trey's ears strained for gunshots to break the droning downpour. None. Why? Where was the patrol? Why weren't raiders here to guard the Rip?

Vivian launched herself up the stairs and fell to her knees over her mom. All around Trey, people were scattering in blind terror. He alone stood still among the chaos.

The ghost laughed as he reloaded. "Come on, Alpha scum! Come out and face me! Humans are going to die until you do!" His crossbow arm drifted in front of his body, taking leisurely aim at various moving targets.

The taunts sounded distant beneath the pounding of blood in Trey's ears. This would be only the second battle he'd ever fought alone . . . and the first hadn't ended well.

Okay, be smart about this. Think tactical. I can do this. His body looks lumpy under the cloak. That makes sense . . . he wouldn't have challenged the Alpha ghosts with only a crossbow. What do I know about Fusions? Damn it, I'm blanking. Level 2. It costs power to fuse new objects but also to utilize them after they've been fused to his body. Every time he fires that crossbow, he uses his Divinity, but probably only a tiny amount of power. Whatever big weapons he has hidden under his cloak, I bet he's saving for a fight against the Alpha ghosts. He won't want to waste his main weapons and power reserves on a human like me. That gives me an advantage.

Trey drew his ectogun and aimed at the quiver of bolts dangling at the Fusion's hip. *I really hope I'm right.* A charging whine preceded green ectoplasm erupting from the barrel. His shot knocked the ammo loose, causing the ghost to flinch and accidentally fire. The bolt harmlessly glanced off the cobblestones. The quiver hit one of the columns and rolled down the stairs.

Trey was already running. The ghost was slow to react, and before he could snatch the quiver, Trey kicked it away. Bolts skittered across the ground.

The Fusion's hands glowed red with his eyes.

Trey realized the danger but couldn't react fast enough; the ectoplasm sent him sprawling in a flash of red. He landed hard on the steps near where Wes was groaning in pain. Trey gripped the cold, slick marble step. His eyes weren't focusing quite right, and his head pounded. He must have knocked his skull in the fall. The ectogun . . . it was gone. He'd lost his grip on it when he landed. Where was it?

Trey blinked, hard, trying to refocus his vision. The falling rain, the reflections in the puddles gathered between cobblestones, the water rolling down the smooth marble treads . . . it all blurred together and made him nauseous. *Gun. Get up. Find the gun.*

There! It was lying by the pillar. He lurched forward and scrambled clumsily up the stairs on all fours, seized the weapon with a trembling hand, and rose to meet his opponent.

But the Fusion was standing with a bolt loaded in the crossbow, his fist aimed at Trey, the point leveled at Trey's heart.

Trey met the eyes of his soon-to-be executioner. His gun was at his side, pointed at the ground. No time to raise it.

Odd, how clearheaded he suddenly was. How the patter of the rain rose in a crescendo in his ears, as if it were about to wash him away through the curtain separating the Realms. He wasn't afraid. He exhaled and relaxed, accepting the inevitability coming to fruition.

Two nearly simultaneous sounds above the rain.

Click-twang.

An impact hit Trey hard and fast. He was falling. Had it been a clean shot through the heart? He'd felt no pain. But he wasn't falling into darkness or light . . . He was just falling.

He smacked the marble, and the air rushed out of his lungs. *That hurt.* That shouldn't have hurt, not if he was dead. His right shoulder throbbed with pain that alternated between sharp with his heartbeat and dull in the pause between.

I landed on my side. I should have landed on my back.

Trey's hand drifted up to his chest. *I'm . . . not hit*, he slowly comprehended. He coughed and rolled onto his hands and knees to find the cloaked savior who had shoved him out of the way just in time. The white Alpha symbol filled his vision, light glinting off a metal whistle.

Jay groaned and jerked his hand up to clutch the bolt embedded in his upper arm, raising his head to glare defiantly at the Fusion with bright silver eyes beneath the lip of his hood.

The shooter was just as surprised as Trey as he stared at his victim pinned to the wall of City Hall. He lowered his crossbow arm, a dry chuckle rasping in his throat. "Ha! Ha-ha! Would ya look at that? Ha-ha-haaaaa!" He pointed at Jay. "I *got* ya, rat! And ya know what? Given how hard it is to catch any of you slippery vermin, I think I'll demand triple the payment from Azar."

Trey slowly reached for his ectogun, which had fallen a few feet away when Jay pushed him. "I don't think so," growled the Fusion, reloading and taking aim once again. Trey froze.

In his peripheral, he saw Vivian slip a gun from her mom's belt, but before she could raise it, the Fusion swung the crossbow to face her instead.

She swallowed hard. Trey was reaching for his weapon again, but he already knew he'd be too late. Jay, still pinned to the wall, could only watch helplessly.

A streak of silver zipped in front of the Fusion. He stood still for a few heart-pounding seconds, eyes wide, and then his hands rose to his throat. His last breath came out in a gurgle—teeth red, fingers red. He crumpled, dead before he hit the marble. The crossbow bolt rolled down the steps and came to a stop in a shallow puddle on the cobblestones.

Trey seized his ectogun and took aim at the body, his hands trembling uncontrollably. His finger wouldn't even bend over the trigger. He didn't need the weapon anymore; the assailant was dead. The rain was washing his blood in a waterfall down the stairs.

Madison was just starting to groan softly as she came to.

But another, agonized moan commanded attention.

"Oh, Jay," Vivian whispered, gazing at the Alpha ghost in sorrow. She cried, "Somebody find Doc!"

Jay closed his eyes. Vivian rose and stepped hesitantly toward him.

The silver irises reappeared. A translucent barrier sprang up around him, blocking Vivian's passage.

Trey cautioned, "Careful, Viv." He didn't think Jay would hurt her, but the Alpha ghost was like a cornered, wounded animal right now, and anything was possible.

She reached out and set her open hands on the shield of ectoplasm. It looked like a solid, low grade from Trey's vantage—a defensive, not offensive concentration. Her face didn't wrinkle with pain. Jay's barrier seemed to weaken, flickering at times like a candle about to die at the end of its wick. Vivian said, "Jay, I want to help you."

His fingers were still wrapped around the bloody shaft. He swallowed, but the shield remained.

"I promise I'm not going to hurt you."

"No," he whispered, voice hoarse.

"Please," Vivian beseeched.

"No." He tried to straighten and pull himself away from the wall, but he was securely pinned. He tugged at the shaft, then cried out. His shield flickered again. Maintaining a high or low grade required ample power and concentration; the pain must be inhibiting Jay's ability to focus on the shield, even if he had enough power reserves.

Trey shook his head with a scowl. What was he doing? Now wasn't the time to be analytical. He couldn't help himself; it was one thing to read about ghosts in Madison's books, and quite another to study them firsthand and up close.

Vivian asked, "Can't you phase through it to free yourself?"

She spoke to him softly, as if he were an old friend, and for some reason it evoked an uncomfortable twang of jealousy that made Trey's brow twitch.

"I tried." Jay's head bowed. "I can't."

"What do you mean you can't?"

"I don't know what it's made of. Intangibility didn't work."

Trey holstered his ectogun. He turned, skimming town square in the hopes of spotting Doc in the crowd, but he was met only with curious onlookers beneath a rainbow of umbrellas.

"Please lower your shield," Vivian continued to beg. "Let me help you."

Jay didn't answer this time. His barrier remained intact.

"Trey?" Vivian called, immediately returning his attention to her. "I don't think his shield is very strong. Can you bring it down?"

He hesitated. He took a few slow steps toward the wounded Alpha leader pinned to the wall. "Jay? I'm so sorry. I was too slow. You saved me, and now you're hurt, and it's my fault."

Jay didn't answer. Trey lifted his left hand and stared at the nodes on the glove. "Sorry, Jay. I know it doesn't seem like it, but we just want to help you."

He turned his palm toward Jay but hesitated again, remembering Vivian's warning about the short-circuiting malfunction in the proto-type.

I'm sure Madison fixed it, he told himself. *She wouldn't have given it to me otherwise.*

He took a deep breath and set his open hand against Jay's shield, immediately cringing and turning his head away with his eyes squeezed shut.

Bright light flashed when the ectoplasm met the nodes on his fingers, and with a faint crackle like the final sparks of a distant firework fading into the night sky, the silvery shield dissipated.

The ghost and apprentice met each other's gaze. Jay's eyes were dim in the shadow of his hood. He didn't try to summon another shield. Defiant, he lifted his chin . . . and vanished.

Jay, arrow and all, had disappeared, leaving a bloody smear on the wall in the wake of rolling thunder as another chilling downpour moved in again.

Ash and I lingered under an overhang. "I hate the rain," she muttered ruefully.

I shrugged. "I like it."

"Of course you do," she said under her breath.

A jagged cut of white light forked through the clouds, followed by a deep rumble that vibrated in my bones. I didn't particularly like the light and sound, just the drone of rain and the tap of water on my skin and the smell in the air. Ash may have claimed to hate the rain, but I'd noticed the way she stiffened with exhilarated pleasure every time the sky was split by a streak of light. The electricity in the air appealed to her. Lightning and water, opposite elements clashing in one beautiful storm.

A point of light illuminated the underbelly of the clouds in blue. It arched up from the ground, resisting gravity above the rooftops for just a few moments before it was pulled back down, and, in defiance, it flickered and went out before the ground could claim it.

"A distress call?" Ash identified.

My heart lodged in my throat. A single ectoplasm orb shot into the sky—yes, that was our distress call. Finn and Reese were the only ones with blue ectoplasm.

Ash and I faced each other in shared terror, reading our concurring reactions. We sprang into the storm, splashing through puddles, squinting through the rain that blurred colors into a gray-washed landscape. Ash didn't even complain about the water causing her skin to steam.

My head spun as my imagination concocted horrible scenarios. What could have possibly gone wrong for the twins to call for help? Weren't they safe inside Proto? Maybe they were sick. Or someone was hurt. I didn't know how they could have seriously injured themselves in the room, unless maybe one had a Spasm and hit his head when he fell or, or . . . I didn't know.

As we drew near enough to see Saros Manor looming through the mist at the top of the hill, Ash pointed and said, "Up there."

I squinted at a figure standing on the roof. "Check the room," I told her.

She nodded and veered toward the front door as I slid to a clumsy stop in the wet grass, head tilting up as I squinted into the rain.

I couldn't see the person on the rooftop from this vantage. I found my center, and my divine power flowed through me as I rotated my wrists. With this steady rain at my disposal, my power barely diminished when the water in the grass froze and converged beneath my feet into a disk.

I'd seen RC perform this move many times; I raised my arms, and the ice beneath me levitated. It wobbled precariously despite my jaw-clenched concentration, so I turned my gaze up to the eaves and stopped trying to think so hard, focusing more on where I wanted to go rather than how I was going to get there. I leapt onto the shingles of the porch as soon as I was within reach, cutting the power and letting my makeshift elevator fall to the glistening lawn below. Sky-surfing might be a suitable mode of transportation for RC, but I preferred to keep my feet on solid ground.

I peered up into the rain. Saros Manor had two balconies, but they both faced south toward the park, and I was on the north side.

I scrambled up the roof, forming handholds out of ice on the steeper slopes. Someone was standing on the second-story rooftop with his back to me.

"Reese?" I called.

He turned at the sound of my voice, shivering violently, raindrops dripping from his hair and running nose. He pressed his sopping T-shirt to his chest as he tried to rub warmth into his bare arms. "Y-you saw," he stammered.

"What are you doing up here?" I demanded.

"C-Cat-o, J-Jay's h-hur-t."

"Okay," I soothed, holding out my hand. "Everything's going to be all right. Ash and I are here. Let's get you back inside and dried off, okay?"

He stepped toward me, slipping on the wet shingles, and I grabbed his thin arm before he fell. I called upon my basic power and let it warm me with energy I passed on to him as I pulled him toward the window. We phased through the glass and landed in front of the closet by our sleeping quarters. Reese had to trot to keep up with my long strides.

In the middle of the sitting room, Jay was kneeling with his fists on his knees, head bowed, eyes squeezed shut. The bolt of a crossbow protruded just below his shoulder. Kit was sitting beside him, her ears pinned and her brows drawn together in worry. Finn was near Ash, who was pacing with short, frantic movements. "He's hurt," she said. "Oh, bloody Scout, he's really hurt."

"Okay, calm down," I said in a stupor.

Yet my feet remained planted, my eyes fixated on our fallen lab-brother. Although I hadn't succumbed to panic, I didn't know what to do. Ash spun away and marched into the bathroom, then returned with several towels. She tossed half to me and knelt next to Jay, but then paused, unsure how to treat him with the bolt still lodged through his arm.

Movement at the window stole my attention from Jay; I turned just in time to see RC land on the balcony. He phased through the French doors, leaving the plastic tray he'd stolen from the school outside.

Jay ripped the cloth away from his face and begged, "Get it out."

RC hesitated.

Teeth gritted, Jay whispered, "Just make it fast. *Please.*"

I had the sense to give one of my towels to Reese before I crouched down to my knees. His face hard, RC solemnly held out his hand. He closed his eyes in a grimace and turned his head away before he gave his hand a quick flick. The bolt ripped through Jay's flesh and into the far wall, where it quivered in place.

Jay screamed. Ash and I leaned forward, pressing our towels to the wound. Jay's entire body was rigid, his face pasty white and his jaw clenched so hard that a vein in his temple throbbed. Kit reached out and set her small hand on top of his glove, but he didn't react to her touch.

Desperate to look away from Jay's suffering, I watched RC cross the room, seize the crossbow bolt, and jerk it out of the wall. He held it in his hand, scowling.

"Where's Axel?" I asked. "He needs to know what happened."

RC shot me a severe look. "I'm sure he knows. Jay and I were patrolling the second circle when Axel told us there was an attack in town square. You know Jay, he was there in an instant. By the time I caught up . . ." He shook his head.

Jay was trembling so hard his teeth chattered. The towels were already red.

"What do we do?" Ash asked helplessly. "Cato? What should we do?"

"Me? I don't know."

"Ero," said Reese.

"He can help us," Finn agreed, bobbing his head.

When Ash and RC offered no alternatives, I swallowed my pride and misgivings about Outsiders and headed to the first floor to knock on Ero's door, hoping the Telepath was in his room.

"Just a moment," he called from the other side. I shifted from foot to foot with impatience. The bed frame creaked, and the muted sound of a hardback book closing preceded casual footsteps before the knob turned and the door slowly swung open.

"Cato," Ero greeted. He frowned. "What is the matter?"

What's the matter? He should know! He could read my mind!

But he hadn't. He had respected my privacy. Maybe later I'd feel grateful.

I wanted to babble the whole story to him, but all I could force out was, "We need your help."

He offered me a kind smile. "All you ever have to do is ask."

Finn had already disabled Proto when we returned so Ero could enter. The teacher immediately surveyed our situation and ordered, "Get Jay out of those wet clothes. We need to warm him up. Ash, keep applying pressure on the wound." He hesitated, then admitted, "I am not a Healer. I would feel better if we took him to Dr. Crawford."

I firmly shook my head. "Whatever you do will be good enough."

Ero sighed at my stubbornness, but relented. "I will see if Wes has supplies."

Relieved to have an adult giving us directions so we weren't fumbling around in confusion, we obeyed without question.

While Ash stripped Jay of his soaking uniform and RC prepared a bed with all the blankets, I warned Jay he'd be very cold for a moment but then dry. I didn't think he'd processed that yet when I froze the water on his skin and whisked all the ice into my hand. I could dry him, but I couldn't warm him; as Ero cleaned and dressed the wound, Ash took her cloak off and pressed her hot body against Jay's to share her heat. By the time we put him to bed and covered him with blankets, his shivers had subsided.

I tended to an equally cold Reese by removing the water from his skin. Naked, he curled his chilled body into a tight ball in Ash's lap with her arms around him. I covered them with a blanket; her natural body heat would be trapped quickly, and Reese should warm up in no time. Still, the cough already taking root deep in his chest concerned me.

Ero left only after we promised to fetch him if Jay's condition worsened, and I suspected he agreed only because Wes kept pounding on the door and disturbing Jay. Once Ero was gone, Wes didn't knock anymore.

That night, Jay barely slept, and neither did we. The usual quiet of the big house was punctuated by his haunting moans. Dawn was pushing away the darkness when he finally lapsed into an uneasy and restless doze. Exhausted with worry, I abandoned any further attempts at rest and wandered to the balcony for some solitude.

The rain was moving on, and I could see the first signs of a pale sunrise beneath the receding storm clouds. I sensed that I wasn't alone. I glanced up to find Axel sitting on the edge of the roof, facing east with his knees drawn to his chest. He didn't look at me, but I knew he knew I was there, so without an invitation, I leapt onto balcony railing and hauled myself up onto the roof to join him.

We watched the sunrise in silence for a few minutes until I cleared my throat and reported, "Jay's sleeping."

"I know."

I licked my lips, unsure how to start. I considered easing into the conversation until I could work up the courage to speak what was on my mind, but I decided that doing so was a waste of time, and Axel would call me out anyway. I said, "You knew about the attack." It was both a statement and an accusation.

I kept my head straight but swiveled my eyes to watch him from the side, waiting for a reaction. I'd expected his infamous short temper to lash out in defense, but instead he remained stationary, not even blinking at my hostility. "Yes."

"Why didn't you do something?"

"What was I supposed to do?"

He was too calm, too emotionless. "Jay wouldn't have been hurt if you'd dealt with it yourself."

Finally, a sigh of guilt. "I thought he could handle it."

I glowered at him. "Are you willing to let one of us get hurt or die just because you refuse to help humans?" Axel said nothing, but he hung his head. I was on a roll now. "When are you going to start caring about this family? Honestly, sometimes I wonder why you even bothered to find us after we escaped."

That finally evoked a reaction. Axel glared at me sidelong and retorted, "If it weren't for me, *They* would have caught you before the first sunset."

"And what have you done to contribute to this family since?" I challenged.

Axel's frown softened. He hesitated, then averted his eyes. I stood and snapped, "You call yourself a brother. Do you even know what that means?" Determined to get the last word, I left him sitting alone on the rooftop.

— Chapter Thirty-Two —

Promise

Jay was restless and feverish.

Ash brought food from the kitchen, but he wouldn't eat, and he drank only a few sips of water.

We all jumped at the sound of knuckles rapping softly on the door. Nobody moved; even Jay stilled and held his breath.

"May I please enter?" came Ero's voice from the other side.

We breathed a collective sigh of relief and opened the door. The twins' teacher was holding a basket with a sling, rolls of gauze, antiseptic, a corked vial containing greenish sludge, and a bottle of medication with handwritten instructions. "I consulted Dr. Crawford," Ero explained.

The last thing I wanted to do was drug my lab-brother, but one look at Jay's pale, drawn face, and I was already reaching for the pill bottle. Ero held it away from me. "Not so hasty."

"He's in a lot of pain," I said.

Ero nodded sadly. "I am not surprised. It is common for Traders to dip blades and arrows into various toxins to further incapacitate prey." He pushed the basket into my hands and removed the pill bottle and vial. "This is from the doctor," he explained, holding up the plastic bottle. I'd already surmised that much, but I kept quiet to let him finish. "I do not know how effective human drugs are, but these should alleviate some of his discomfort once they have had time to absorb in his system." He held up the glass vial. "This is Witch's brew. The effects will be more immediate. You may choose which one to give Jay, but I do not recommend giving him both at the same time."

I hesitated. "Witch's brew? Where did you get that?"

"From Wes." Ero dropped his voice and added, "Many are illegal. I do not know where this one originated from."

Despite the warning, I was eyeing the vial instead of the pill bottle. "Will it heal him?"

"No. Healing brews are incredibly complex to make and require rare and contraband ingredients. All this one will do is stabilize his condition, eliminate his pain, and put him to sleep so he may recover."

That was all I needed to hear; I snatched the vial from Ero. He didn't follow me into the room, simply said to my back, "Please do not hesitate to call for me if you need anything. I will be downstairs."

I knelt beside Jay. Ash propped his head up while I uncorked the vial. "Drink up, Jay," I murmured, lifting it to his lips.

He took a sip of the green sludge, gagged, and coughed. "Tastes even worse than it looks," he croaked.

"It'll help," I promised. He managed to down the rest of the brew. The effects were instantaneous; his muscles relaxed, and his eyes clouded with drowsiness before Ash had even finished lowering him back down on the pillow. She gave me a concerned look. "He'll be okay," I reassured weakly. She stroked Jay's damp hair off his forehead without a word.

Although we didn't want to leave him, our job didn't stop just because someone was hurt. RC, Ash, and I would have to be a team of three for now. Finn and Reese were asleep, but Kit promised to send a distress call if Jay awakened and needed us. We were about to leave when a weak voice called, "Cato."

I was already at the door, but I paused and turned to find a pair of dopey gray eyes on me. I told the others, "I'll meet you at the church," then returned to our fallen lab-brother.

I knelt beside Jay and asked, "Are you still in pain? Do you need these pills from Doc to go to sleep?"

"No," he whispered. "I can . . . barely keep my eyes open."

"Then rest."

His eyelids closed again, then fluttered open before he could succumb. "Cato . . . 'm trusting you to lead the team."

I stared at him for a moment until the meaning of his words sank in. "Me?" I squeaked. I cleared my throat to unearth my normal voice, accidentally causing Finn and Reese to stir. "No, I can't. Why me? Why can't RC do it? He's your scouting partner."

Jay's eyes were dull, and yet when he fixed them on me, I could still see the spark of dedication. "RC's a skilled fighter with a strong Divinity," he acknowledged.

I knew he was going to say more, but I cut him off by encouraging, "Right. The two of you have been training in the Arena the longest. He's a better candidate."

"Mm-hmm, true. We've been fighting longer. But RC was a mess when he arrived. His eye, his blood-family, his home . . . so . . . I took care of him." His brow furrowed from a different kind of pain the brew couldn't alleviate. "Tried my best in that place, anyway. He's strong. But not a leader."

"Then Ash—"

"Lacks self-confidence and direction. You know that."

"Jay, I—"

"Stop. Unless you'd rather I gave Axel the responsibiziny . . . re-responsibility, that leaves you."

I let out the breath I'd been holding for my argument. "I'm not sure I can do it, Jay. I'm not you."

He stared at me for a moment. "I'm not asking you t' be." He shifted to bring his hand out from under the blankets, and even with the influence of the Witch's brew, the movement made him wince. He held out his fist, and his fingers opened to reveal a gleam of silver in his palm.

I stared at the whistle but didn't take it. I couldn't. Where Jay had summoned this confidence from, I couldn't even guess, because I had none whatsoever. He must not be thinking straight with whatever drugs were in his system. I bowed my head and glanced up at him. "Jay—"

His eyes were closed. My words died in a breath of disappointment. "Never mind." I rose and turned toward the door.

"Cato."

I peered over my shoulder at my lab-brother, who was watching me again. "Do you know why I . . . why I paired you with Ash?"

I did, actually. "Because we're both Elementals, we have similar fighting styles, and our Divinities are exact opposites, so we cancel each other out."

Jay's eyelids fell as he gave a weak nod. "But that's not the only reason."

My throat clenched. "Is it because . . . because Ash was the one who was next to me at that place? Because she helped me . . . adjust?" I sniffed and wiped the back of my arm across my nose. Bloody Scout, why was I getting emotional?

"Hmm. I like your track of thought. Train, I mean. But there's another reason."

Jay didn't continue. His chest rose and fell with deep, even breaths. This time, I was sure he was asleep. I shook my head at his delirious and puzzling conversation but had barely turned away when I heard, "She's like RC." His voice was so weak, I halfway wondered if he was talking in his sleep. When I returned to kneel by him, his eyes didn't open. Had he actually said something, or had I imagined that?

He took a breath and whispered, "RC follows my lead." His eyes fluttered open for a moment before they slid shut again. "Ash follows yours."

Me? A leader? No, I'd always relied on Jay. Sometimes I hated myself for being so dependent on him, but the point was that I was a follower, too.

But then I thought about my days on patrol with Ash. She always asked me where we should scout; she never made the decision on her own. And now that Jay had drawn attention to her passive nature, I realized he was right. Ash was always caught in the heat of the moment. When it came to actually making a strategic decision, that was all me. She was too spontaneous, since her element in and of itself was wild and untamable, and perhaps it was the structured nature of my own element that gave me the cool-headedness for guidance.

"You had to be paired with one of them," Jay whispered. "Ash made the most sense."

"But Jay, I—"

"Cato. Do . . . you trust me?"

"Yeah."

He whispered, "Well, all right then," as if that response were the solution to everything.

The floorboards creaked when I leaned back on my heels. "You asleep now?"

I received a weak grunt as an answer.

My responding nod, even if he couldn't see it, was slow and thoughtful. "I'll do my best," I promised, leaning forward and gingerly plucking the whistle from his limp hand. "But hurry up and get better."

He didn't respond this time, although I noticed—or at least, I thought I noticed—the tiniest twitch at the corner of his lips. I rose, surprised by the difficulty I had in staggering to my feet. As if a yoke had been placed on my shoulders, a great weight held me down. Already, I was feeling the burden of responsibility. Leadership was not something I pretended I was qualified for. It was one thing to risk my own life, but knowing that every decision I'd make from here would risk the lives of my lab-siblings caused my stomach to flip.

Then there was Axel—I had no idea how I was going to keep him in line—and supervising the twins' lessons with Ero, and keeping tabs on Kit while she wandered around on her own, all the while rotating the teams so no one had to scout alone. And Madison . . .

Bloody Scout, I hoped Jay could resume command before a confrontation with the ghost hunter inevitably erupted. I cupped the whistle in my hand. It was so small and light. I couldn't help but wonder when I'd ever done anything to make Jay see the potential for leadership in me. I'd always lingered safely in his shadow.

I filled my lungs with a deep breath as I set the cord over my head, the whistle dangling over my heart.

Before I closed the door, I cast a look back at Jay, who was sleeping soundly with Kit curled up in a little ball of fluff on his stomach and the twins snoring softly beside him.

The Witch's brew had left Jay's face clear of pain and his breathing deep, even, and calm.

When I reached the church, I found Ash and RC loitering in the shadows. We greeted each other with melancholy silence. They didn't ask what Jay said to me, but I knew they saw his whistle around my neck.

Though I never would have noticed this before, now I observed how they both waited for me to choose a direction, and then they followed half a step behind. Could I really lead them? It was only a few days, after all, and they seemed to have subconsciously consented to my guidance.

I broke the silence: "Okay, so . . . I, uh, I was thinking . . . the best way to do this while Jay's out of commission is to rotate the teams."

I monitored their responses. Ash had her head tilted slightly, and RC eyed me with wariness. He asked, "What do you mean?"

I cleared my throat and explained, "Well, somebody checks on the twins every hour anyway. So, I was thinking, one person could stay at Home for the whole hour in case Jay needs anything. The other two will scout the town as a pair, and we'll just . . . you know, rotate every hour."

My words hung in the air. I held my breath in the silence. If Jay had come up with this idea, no one would have questioned it. But I wasn't the established leader, and they needed time to consider my reasoning. It'd be a little weird switching the partners Jay had originally paired, but I also thought it would be a good exercise. It might even prepare us to beat him when he became well enough to play All-On-One again. Still, I could read the doubt in their eyes. They trusted me as their lab-brother, not their leader. I couldn't blame them; I'd done nothing to prove to them that I was capable of leading the family.

But my idea seemed to be a success. RC volunteered to take the first shift on the hour, leaving Ash and me to scout as if everything were normal, even if it wasn't.

There was a strange, invisible force between us that kept us quieter than usual. Our attempts to scout downtown were thwarted by the constant presence of humans. I didn't remember them being so bold around us before we'd made our guest appearance at City Hall.

One shop owner, a hefty, bearded man in a stained white apron, was even brash enough to block our path and tell us, "You're always welcome in my store. Anything you want, you name it. No charge. It's yours. And please, don't worry about sneaking through the back. Use the front door."

Ash clutched her staff and took a step back. "Thanks," I muttered, reaching back to grip her wrist and turn away. Under my breath, I muttered, "Sure, the front door. So we can promote his business."

Ash said, "I think I liked it better when they were afraid of us."

"We just need to have Axel with us. I guarantee people will give us a wider berth."

"He still hasn't come back," she noted in concern. "Where is he?"

I couldn't meet her worried gaze. I hadn't seen Axel since I had confronted him on the rooftop and accused him of being a selfish lab-brother. I'd asked why he'd even bothered finding us after escape. What if he'd decided that I was right, and he'd run away to be on his own without saying goodbye? The others would never forgive me for driving him away, especially Kit.

"I don't know," I told her. It was the truth, but it tasted like a lie. If I'd already driven away a lab-brother, maybe I should give the whistle to RC now before I screwed anything else up.

A group of kids was playing a game in an empty lot, but when they spotted us, they scattered like a flock of startled birds, calling for their parents. Ash and I stopped short when a lone boy darted in front of us and braced himself. He was wearing a bandana tied over his nose and mouth, much like the black cloth I was wearing. Fists clenched at his sides, he proclaimed, "Stop right there, ghosts! I'm Phantom, and if you don't do what I say, I'll freeze you where you stand."

An amused smile broke behind my mask. "You're Phantom, huh?"

He held out his hands, palms out to me, expression serious. Feeling playful, I went stiff and called upon my blue Divinity. A frozen crust crept across my uniform, freezing me in place.

The self-proclaimed Phantom gasped and stumbled back, gawking at me, then at his hands as if horrified by a newfound power. I wondered if I'd looked like that after the Flash when I had first realized what I could do.

I chuckled and melted the ice. For the first time in the presence of a human, I let the blue power recede completely so my eyes could revert to their normal state. "Hey," I said, "you're very brave. But your mom and dad need you to stay by them to make sure they're safe. Leave the ghost fighting to us, okay?"

Wide-eyed, mouth open, he nodded slowly. "This is our little secret." I winked at him and retreated with Ash, my eyes already glowing blue again thanks to the frozen orb I was manipulating in one hand.

"Was that smart? Letting him see your eyes?"

"It was just for a second, and he's a little kid. Even if he tells, who's going to believe him?"

She glanced over her shoulder, and I followed her gaze. The kid was a statue standing right where we'd left him.

I didn't admit this to her, but as we scouted Phantom Heights, I was really searching for Axel. When she took the next shift to check on Jay, I asked RC to do an aerial sweep of the town and casually mentioned that he should keep an eye out for our lab-brother. Upon his return, he reported no sign of Axel.

RC was quiet company on patrol, which suited me just fine while I mulled over worrisome thoughts. He'd never been much of a conversationalist since I'd met him, although I had wondered if he and Jay talked much when they scouted together. Either I wasn't a suitable replacement for his partner, or he still wasn't keen on conversation and preferred to keep mostly to himself, just as he'd done when we were locked up in that place.

I respected RC, but I had to admit I still didn't know much about him, and so far, we weren't exactly bonding as a scouting pair.

The clock tower signaled that it was time to switch shifts. I waited until Ash had rejoined us, and just before parting from my lab-siblings, I asked, trying valiantly to keep the desperation out of my voice, if Axel was at Saros Manor.

"No," she said. "Do you think he's okay?"

"Sure," I dismissed, hoping I portrayed more confidence than I felt. "Come on, it's Ax. I'm sure he's fine." I couldn't catch my breath.

What have I done?

I left them, and though I should have been hurrying back to care for Jay and Reese, who had developed a low-grade fever, I took a detour to search in secret for Axel. No sign of him. Near the mansion, I called his name. He didn't come.

I trudged to the front door, on the verge of panic. I hoped the twins were both asleep so they wouldn't hear my thoughts and learn that I'd already broken the family Jay worked so hard to keep together.

I shivered as I opened the door, so demoralized that I almost collided with the person standing in the foyer. A pair of red eyes glared at me, and a familiar voice growled, "What do you want?"

Apparently my few heartbeats of stupefied silence was enough to annoy him, because he added, "You called me, so what?"

I blinked. "You came back," I whispered, so weak with relief that my knees trembled and I almost knelt before him.

Axel shot me a queer look. "What the hell are you talking about? I never left."

Too embarrassed to admit that I was afraid I'd driven him away, I replied, "Well, nobody's seen you."

He shrugged. "I've been around."

"With Jay?"

"No."

I stared at him, the guilt retreating. *So, it isn't me he's been avoiding.* I took a step to pass, but he blocked me with one sinewy arm. "I know he gave it to you."

My hand crept up to grasp the whistle around my neck. When I'd accepted it, I had thought of it as a symbol of leadership. I hadn't imagined using it, nor had I considered the impact it would have on Axel.

He trusted Jay to carry it. I had no right to wear it without his blessing.

Heat flushed my cheeks. "I—"

"Jay made a promise. If you plan on wearing that, you gotta make the same promise."

I stared at him in horror. I didn't like to think of Axel as a deadly monster, which was stupid because the chances were high that someday he'd snap and we'd have to deal with him. *By any means necessary.* Having Axel in such close proximity to such a large number of humans was a recipe for catastrophe. Still, I preferred to pretend nothing would go wrong, even if it was a fool's dream.

"I can't kill you, Ax. Even if you . . . aren't yourself."

He locked his intense red eyes onto mine, trapping me in his hypnotic stare. "Even knowing I'd rather die by your hand than live with the knowledge that I'd killed one of you?"

"Don't talk like that," I said in a panic.

The intensity in his eyes seemed to fade, his expression sagging into something wretched and unbefitting of him.

"Promise, Cato. If you're going to keep that whistle, you have to do two things. One, you can't use it unless absolutely necessary. And two, you have to be prepared to use it if it comes to that."

"Ax—"

"And *if it comes to that*, I need to know that you can keep your promise and protect the rest of the family from me. That might mean you have to kill me."

I stared at the whistle in my palm. I was afraid of making such a drastic commitment. Kill my lab-brother?

"I promise I won't misuse it."

"And?" he pressed.

"And . . . I'll use it only to stop you if you lose control." *Stop you. Not kill you. Not if I can help it.* If I were smart, I wouldn't ask this, but I blurted, "I need to know something. If Jay hadn't been there, would you have saved Trey?"

Axel stared at me, his blood-red eyes as hard as his features. He turned and strode away.

— Chapter Thirty-Three —

Sacrifice

I was returning to switch places with RC when two figures approaching ahead of me on the sidewalk made me freeze in my tracks.

Despite the distance and their heads down in deep conversation, I recognized them, and my head buzzed with panic. I ducked around the corner of the building and pressed my back against the wall. I felt light-headed, breathing hard but getting no oxygen, and I cursed my pounding heart for inhibiting my ability to listen for the quiet footsteps.

I turned my head but kept myself flattened in the shadows of the building, watching. I could hear their voices, which stirred echoes of memories, and my runaway heart suddenly seemed to go silent.

"No, actually, I'm meeting her in the square. We're having dinner at C-Sully's."

"Ah, so you're the reason she canceled on me this time."

"Sorry."

"No worries. You both need some time to unwind; I get it."

I swallowed hard as the pair walked into sight, then paused just in front of me. If either turned, they'd see me watching. My old friend Trey, and beside him, Vivian.

"I'll see you tomorrow," she said as he turned away.

"See ya," he called, stepping into the street to cross.

Vivian watched him walk away. Slowly, she turned her head, frowning. I plastered myself to the wall and reached for my center, vanishing just as her gaze settled on me.

She stared straight through me for a moment, then sighed and continued her journey down the sidewalk.

I became visible again, but I didn't move. She had been so close, I could still smell the floral scent of her shampoo.

I peered around the corner to watch her. If I approached her as Seph, would she be happy to see me? There was no way to know; my feet were frozen in place. A coward, I turned away. I hung my head, staring at my feet as I walked.

Caws captured my attention, and I turned my gaze skyward to count ten crows flying above the alley. A shrill scream cleaved the air, echoing through the spaces between the buildings, sending a shiver up my spine.

I couldn't breathe. I'd heard that scream before . . . in a dark building across from the shimmering Dome around City Hall . . . Madison standing on the marble steps . . . Jay asked Vivian to scream so her mom would cooperate . . .

Vivian.

I pivoted and sprinted back to the street corner. *Damn it, where is she?* I summoned my blue power as I pounded down the sidewalk in the direction she'd been heading. My gaze darted beneath the lip of my hood, searching. A violent shiver racked my body. When I reached town square, I halted.

A crowd of humans had gathered in the plaza—whether unfortunate victims of circumstance caught in the wrong place at the wrong time or hostages rounded up like cattle, I couldn't say. I crept forward, slowly now, in a daze, taking in the scene with wide eyes.

Axel was already here. In the center of the crowd loomed a tall ghost with red eyes glinting in the sunlight. Something was strange about him. Although the sun was shining brightly, the light didn't seem to touch him. His skin was so dark it was almost black, as if he were cloaked in shadows. The man towered over every single person around him; he had to be at least seven feet tall. A black cloak cascaded over his shoulders, so long that the excess material spilled across the cobblestones, the edge tattered, yet tastefully and purposely so.

His presence in and of itself stole my breath. Somehow, without any introduction, I knew who he was. It was one thing to defy the Warden when we were separated between Realms; it was quite another to meet his chilling red eyes in person as he stared me down.

Captain Hassing was standing next to him holding a glowing green whip of ectoplasm like a leash. I followed it to find Vivian ensnared in its bonds, a burly Shadow Guard standing behind her with a dagger to her throat. Surrounding them were a dozen Shadow Guards. Madison stood before Vivian's captor, her fists clenched, her jaw locked, and her weapon belt lying at her feet.

But the ghost of the shadows wasn't focused on Madison or his captive; his red eyes were trained on Axel and me. "Well, if it isn't the infamous fugitives from Project Alpha," he said. "I'd hoped you might honor us with your presence."

I shoved my fist behind my back under my cloak and clenched an icicle. I made brief eye contact with Vivian, who stared at me pleadingly, her wide eyes brimming with tears. A sudden movement on my right made me flinch, but I wasn't under attack. Trey must have heard Vivian scream too and come running. He was panting, ectogun in hand, gaze darting over the scene.

Azar smiled at him. "Ah, I was expecting you as well." He held out his hand. "The apprentice should be up front with his master, agreed? No sudden movements, though. I think your master would be very disappointed in you if you made a poor decision that resulted in her daughter's death." Azar's extended hand gestured Trey closer. "Come on, don't be shy."

I stared at Trey. Even if I wanted to help, I couldn't move.

Trey swallowed hard and took a timid step forward. His shaking hand clenched the weapon with a white-knuckled death grip. Azar maintained his perfect, unwavering white smile as people parted to let Trey approach. "Very good. Come along. Nobody has to get hurt."

Trey crept toward Azar, every muscle stiff and ready to flee or fight. He stopped abreast with Madison. Azar gestured him even closer. Trey hesitated, then took a few small steps forward again. Azar loomed above him, dark and menacing, and poor Trey looked like a little kid holding a toy gun and quailing before a shadowy demon. Azar held out his hand. "Give me your weapon."

Trey clenched it tighter.

Azar stared him down. He had a naturally soft and slow speech; he was clearly used to his orders being obeyed immediately without the need to raise his voice. "Give me . . . your weapon," he repeated, the words rolling even slower, more sinister now with a hint of fraying patience.

Trey glanced at Vivian. Then, after another moment's hesitation, he raised his shaking hand and set the ectogun in Azar's waiting palm.

"Good. Now, disarm."

Trey's fingers fumbled with the clasp on his weapon belt. When it finally came free, he held it out, but Azar didn't take it. "Step back. I'm not interested in you."

Trey dropped his belt on top of the pile on the ground. At first, I was puzzled why there were so many weapons collected—no way Madison carried that many on her at one time—but then I realized the patrol must have been forced to disarm as well. Trey shuffled back until he was a few steps behind his ghost-hunting master.

Azar turned his attention to Madison and shot her a taunting smile. "Such a well-trained apprentice," he commended.

Madison's whole body was trembling, but unlike Trey, who was quaking in terror, she was quivering with barely tethered rage.

A shiver slithered down my spine. Ash and RC must have sensed the intruders—there were so many, how could they not?—and the pair appeared across the street, surveyed the crowd, and then skirted the mass to join Axel and me.

"Welcome," Azar said, his burning red gaze following their movement. "So glad you could join us. Allow me to introduce myself—my name is Azar, Warden of the Prison and Lawmaker of Avilésor. I'm sure you remember Captain Hassing, my second-in-command."

Axel growled. His taut body instinctively crouched lower in preparation to attack. He was finally facing the person he held responsible for chasing his parents to their deaths and driving him into the hands of *Them*. Azar was the catalyst to the end of Axel's life Before. I understood my lab-brother's fury, but he might compromise this already risky situation.

I touched Jay's whistle. *Can I use it on him?* I'd accepted it as a symbol of leadership while telling myself it was just for show. Now that the responsibility of keeping A6 from being unleashed was a very real possibility, I wasn't sure I could hurt Axel, despite my promise to him.

But he wasn't my concern. Vivian was a hostage. She was sickly pale, her lips tight, her eyes swimming with tears. The blade caught the sunlight, gleaming against her exposed neck.

I was the leader now. This was my impasse to defuse. And yet, I just stood there, numbed by the odds and too overwhelmed to even process what was happening, let alone have the sense to start thinking ahead and planning. I dimly registered a silver flash in RC's hand. Ash drew her weapon but held it loosely. We couldn't act while that dagger was at Vivian's throat.

They were waiting for me to decide what to do.

I flinched when Azar said, "I don't usually make public appearances, but I was so gravely disappointed when you refused my invitation. I hope I now have your attention. You should be honored that I came all this way just for you. I rarely make exceptions like this, but I've been so impatient to meet you."

Axel's deep growl was a borderline snarl. The Warden glanced at him and then passed him over as he skimmed our group. "Which of you is the leader?"

None of us moved. I felt my lab-siblings' gazes dart to me and then back to Azar, but my tongue was thick in my cotton mouth. I stared into the blazing red eyes, too petrified to answer. The Shadow Ghost glowered at us in silence for a few more seconds. "I don't like repeating myself. Which one of you is the leader?"

"I am." The words croaked weakly from my throat as a voice in the back of my mind called me an imposter. I didn't feel like a leader, and with every eye piercing me, I wanted to melt.

As if my less-than-authoritative tone didn't betray me enough, Madison blurted, "What?"

"I'm the leader," I said stronger.

"No. I am," came a familiar but unexpected voice. I turned, stupefied to find the real leader standing at my side. Jay was in full uniform, and he'd foolishly abandoned his sling for the appearance of normalcy, as if he weren't hurt at all. But he was. His eyes weren't as bright as they should have been.

What are you doing?" I demanded.

"Trust me," he said. In his absence, I'd been more than ready to pass the responsibility to anyone else. Now that he was here, a surge of protectiveness crested in me. I took a breath to tell him to back down, but he'd already stepped forward, and Azar's red eyes were fixated on him. "I'm the leader."

Of that, there was no question. He held the confidence I clearly lacked. There was no point in disputing; everyone could see which of the two of us commanded respect. I would stand by my lab-brother's side, but it was his show now, and stirring in the shadow of my relief was resentment that he'd given me leadership but didn't believe in me.

Madison snapped, "Jay, don't do anything stupid."

"Now, now," Azar interceded. "It's not polite to interrupt." He muttered something that sounded like "*heathen*" under his breath.

One of his Guards held out a hand and directed her violet gaze at the ghost hunter. Madison staggered, gasped, and was forced to the ground with a quiet cry of resistance. I mentally listed the Divinities that could have caused that—telekinesis, gyrokinesis, biokinesis—as if it mattered. Azar had fifteen Shadow Guards with him, no doubt with Divinities across the spectrum.

He didn't even glance at the ghost hunter pressed on her face at his feet. Our leader had his undivided attention. "Jay, is it?" he greeted with an uncomfortably wide smile. "So nice to finally have a formal introduction."

"What do you want?" Jay coldly asked.

Azar's smile never faded, his white teeth such a sharp contrast to his ebony skin. "There's no reason for us to be enemies, although it's hard to extend an offer of friendship when you continually refuse my gracious requests to meet. We could have introduced ourselves under much more pleasant circumstances than these. I must confess, you've been causing me quite a bit of trouble. I don't understand why you're wasting your talents on these humans."

"We made a deal," Jay murmured. He tugged at his mask as if he were having trouble breathing through it. Jay's eyes were shifting, taking stock of the enemies, noting potential human casualties in the modest crowd standing captive, cataloging escape routes. Hopefully that meant he was also plotting out a strategy.

"A deal!" Azar laughed. "All you've done is trade one form of enslavement for another. I can give you true freedom. But it's a one-time offer on the table."

Axel snarled under his breath. "I'm not listening to this shit." He strode toward the Warden with long, confident steps, as if daring someone to try and attack him. The Shadow Guards stiffened but held formation, their eyes glowing bright.

"Wait!" Jay seized Axel's cloak with his right hand, keeping his left arm stiff, but the half-breed didn't falter. He kept walking, dragging Jay along behind. The leader was forced to let go and skirt around Axel to press his palm against our lab-brother's chest and beg, "Axel, don't!"

He finally halted. I clutched the whistle around my neck. Jay should have taken it from me. What should I do? Should I use it? No, I had to give Jay a chance to talk Axel down. But what if he couldn't? *Bloody Scout, what was I thinking? I should have given him the whistle back!*

Axel folded his arms and pushed past Jay. "Do you know who I am?"

"Forgive me for not being able to recognize you with a hood hiding your face," Azar said coldly. I immediately noticed the change in his voice. No doubt he was frantically combing through memories to remember which of his unfortunate victims was now branded with the Mark of Project Alpha.

"You wouldn't remember me. I was a little kid when you persecuted my parents."

"I think you mean prosecuted," Azar corrected.

Axel growled, wild ectoplasm flickering around his fists. "No, I don't. It's *your* fault. I'ma kill you," he seethed, taking a menacing step forward. Two Shadow Guards stepped in front of Azar. Jay seized Axel's arm and hissed something into his ear. Axel froze, then reluctantly straightened, but he was still growling softly.

Azar studied Axel with a calculating look that eerily reminded me of Jay when he was thinking. The Warden was powerful; he had many people under his command, and yet he didn't seem quite sure how to proceed with us now. Apparently he hadn't anticipated a past incident tainting his reputation and withering his shallow attempt at friendship.

Cheek still pressed to the cobblestones, Madison flicked her gaze between Jay and Azar. Vivian was staring at Jay, silently pleading for help. He nodded at her and negotiated, "She isn't a part of this. Let her go."

Azar waved his Guards aside. "Hmm. See, I can't do that, because as soon as I do, I lose my leverage."

"What makes you think she's leverage in the first place? Why would we care if the daughter of a ghost hunter dies?"

I caught my breath. Madison begged, "No, please!"

Jay was playing a dangerous game against a skilled player, and Vivian's life was the stake. He was taking this way further than I'd been prepared to. Was he being reckless on painkillers, or did he really have a plan?

Azar narrowed his eyes. "I think you're bluffing." He shrugged and turned to the Shadow Guard holding Vivian. "All right. Kill her."

She gasped, eyes widening as the ghost tightened his grip on the handle.

I watched, transfixed in dread, unable to look away even though I had no desire to see the crimson blood pour from her neck.

"Wait!" Jay cried.

The Guard paused, awaiting an order. Azar chuckled. "That's what I thought."

Jay shook his head, jaw clenched in frustration. "Oh, Jay." Azar sighed like a disapproving father. "Your selfishness is so disappointing." At our leader's angry silence, Azar continued, "I had such high expectations of you when Hassing delivered the report of your escape. And yet, here you are, standing as a traitor against your own proud race, protecting the monsters who tortured you instead of trying to liberate your fellow prisoners. Do you care that kálos are still suffering in that laboratory? Have you even considered saving them?"

The guilt made my stomach turn. I was ashamed to admit that after all this time Outside, I hadn't given a passing thought to anyone else locked away in that miserable place. Maybe my impartiality was because I'd never met any prisoners outside Project Alpha, with the exception of the animals we'd fought and killed from Theta.

I knew other prisoners existed. I knew there were children in Project Gamma. I knew medical experiments were being conducted on the victims in Project Lambda. I knew people were being dissected alive in Project Omega.

But had I once thought about trying to rescue them? No. Was that wrong of me? Was it wrong that while we'd been enjoying our freedom Outside, other prisoners were still dying and wishing for death in their cages, and we never even discussed the possibility of liberating them?

Now, for the first time, my mind wandered willingly back to that place. I wondered if the other prisoners knew about our escape. Did they fantasize about us returning to set them free?

My innards squirmed. *They probably don't even know*, I rationalized. *They* wouldn't want prisoners to think escape was possible. *He* was probably pretending that Project Alpha was continuing according to schedule.

Jay bowed his head. A single, bitter chuckle jerked his body. "Save them? You think we can save them?" He raised his head to glare at Azar. "We wouldn't make it through the doors. My family is the only thing I care about. We won't take that risk."

"But I will," said Azar. "I can destroy your enemies for you."

Jay snapped, "Nobody saved *us*."

"But you have that chance now. Instead of protecting humans, you can liberate your brethren."

Jay was quiet again. Azar waited, but when it became clear Jay wasn't going to respond, his expression hardened. "Perhaps we can revisit this conversation later. Here's how it's going to work," he said, pacing slowly in front of Vivian. She swallowed, sending a trickle of blood inching down her neck. Axel was growling, crouched on all fours now; Ash gripped her weapon tightly in both hands; RC's three silver disks spun near his head. Ice was creeping over the edges of my wrist gauntlets and up my bare arms. The Shadow Guards tensed, anticipating a fight.

Azar's red eyes were glowing as more shadows gathered around him and spread over the crowd, dimming the town.

"I gave you a fair chance. Now, I know for a fact that the Agents are developing a weapon in Project Alpha, and they plan to use it to exterminate us. I'm going to destroy them and their weapon before that happens. So, if you won't cooperate, which is truly a grave disappointment, we'll trade. I want the slaves. You give me the twins, and this human gets to live."

Time seemed to screech to a halt. Azar's proposition resounded through my thoughts until the meaning finally seeped in.

Finn and Reese for Vivian.

Axel's growls increased in intensity. He was a coiled spring, ready to rip apart the enemies. But even with his strength and speed and ferocity at my side, his presence didn't ease the hopelessness that had settled in with the impossible ultimatum we'd just been given.

I turned to Jay, never so desperate for his guidance before. The tension in his body didn't bode well, and his eyes danced as he considered the options. RC leaned forward and whispered, "I think I can get the dagger."

Jay shook his head. "No, it's too risky. One slip, and she's dead. And there would likely be a lot more casualties than just Vivian." His shoulders slumped, his silver eyes disappearing behind his lids. Was he giving up? He couldn't give up! RC's plan was better than condemning Vivian to death or giving up Finn and Reese.

Jay took a reluctant step forward. "What about me instead?"

"Jay, no. What are you doing?" I demanded. He held up his hand, signaling me to shut up.

Azar blinked, surprised by the counteroffer. "You? No, I want the slaves."

Jay swallowed. "You want to know about the Weapon, right? I can tell you what you need to know. Isn't the leader worth more?"

The rest of us watched in horror, wanting to intervene but trusting that somehow Jay must know what he was doing. Finally, Azar nodded, smirking at the thought of having Jay in custody. "I accept your surrender."

"Jay," I pleaded, "don't do this. I'll go inst—"

"No."

I lowered my voice. "But I know as much about the Weapon as you do, and Vivian—"

"I said no."

The drugs must have rattled his judgment. I couldn't let him do this. I stepped in front of him, looked him in the eye, and held up the whistle. "You put me in charge."

"Temporarily. I'm here now."

He tried to step around me, but I blocked his path. "And if I challenge you for the title of leader?"

Rarely had I been able to best Jay, and even when I'd managed to pull off a miraculous victory in the Arena, I was pretty sure he had let me win. But he was weak now. I could beat him if I had to. He'd been avoiding my gaze, but now his silver eyes locked onto mine with such ferocity I actually believed I heard them click into place. I'd surprised him. Hell, I'd surprised myself.

But under his stern glare, I faltered again. My leadership was constrained to Jay's absence, and he was here now, so I was expected to back down. By challenging him, I'd overstepped my boundary. Even if we fought for the title, Jay might actually be able to defeat me one-handed, which would be a humiliating loss. What would I have done if he'd yielded to me, anyway? My only plan would be to sacrifice myself.

Prison . . . I couldn't handle a cage again. I wasn't able to ask Jay if he had something else planned, but surely he must.

He promised, "I'll be okay," and I believed him. I let my pent-up breath escape through my teeth in defeat and stepped aside, trusting that he knew what he was doing, that he wouldn't abandon us, that he'd somehow save everybody and return to us safely. Axel snarled as though about to attack, but Jay shook his head. "Don't follow," he commanded, stepping toward Azar.

"Jay," Ash whispered miserably.

"Don't," he repeated over his shoulder.

We watched our lab-brother approach Azar, whose smile returned. Jay had to stop short when a small body darted forward and planted itself between him and the Warden. For one heart-stopping moment, I thought it was Kit. But no—it was a boy with a bandana tied over the lower half of his face. He squared off against Azar, who could probably squish him under his boot, and proclaimed, "Phantom won't let you hurt anybody. Right?" he asked, turning to look at me.

Shit. Every pair of eyes followed the kid's expectant gaze, surveying the group of us with curiosity. At least my eyes were still blue— *wait, they are still blue, aren't they?* I dove deeper into my cold Divinity, just in case. The kid was watching me, waiting. I barely shook my head.

His brow creased, and he took a step toward me. "Tell them, Phantom. Make them leave." I was frozen in a stupefied trance. Even Azar was looking at me, and Hassing. What now? This kid had just revealed my identity. I was waiting for the shouts of recognition and the wave of movement, but everyone else seemed just as stunned as I was.

Jay knelt and set his hand on the kid's shoulder. He spoke softly, his words too quiet for anyone but the boy to hear. Whatever he said, the kid didn't like it. He backed up, jerking free, and he faced me again with fists clenched. "You can't give up! Phantom never gives up! I thought you were a hero! You're not the real Phantom!"

His words hurt, but he was right. I wasn't the real Phantom. Not anymore.

A woman I assumed must be the kid's mother took a few uneasy steps from the edge of the crowd, but she stopped. She was deathly pale and trembling like a leaf, too scared to claim her son and carry him to safety. RC acted instead. He extended his hands, and the boy was yanked through the air. He cried out and flailed, and when he landed in RC's arms, he continued to struggle, but my lab-brother gripped him tightly with one arm and muffled the protests by pressing his palm over the bandana.

Jay hung his head and heaved a deep sigh. He was slow in rising to his feet again. Head down, he shuffled forward once more with the resolve of a man on death row taking his last walk. All eyes left me to follow Jay.

He came to a stop in front of Azar, his gaze flitting briefly to Vivian. She shook her head ever so slightly, risking a deeper cut.

"I have your word?" Jay asked.

"She'll go free," Azar promised.

"And my lab-family."

Azar hesitated, glaring at the rest of us. "For the time being," he reluctantly agreed. "That's the best I can promise."

Jay's head dropped in submission, although he was trembling in anticipation of the rough hands about to grab him.

A Shadow Guard stepped forward and lifted her hand, eyes glowing. Jay's arms, as if he'd suddenly become a marionette, contorted behind his back. He bit back a cry of pain. Captain Hassing, still maintaining the whip that bound Vivian, snapped his other wrist, sending a second stream of green ectoplasm out to encircle Jay's torso like a python that squeezed him tight.

Azar smirked. "How disappointing. The mighty Alpha leader is willing to sacrifice himself for a lowly human. I'm curious—what value could this girl possibly have to you?"

Jay glanced at Vivian and then away. "None," he whispered.

"Hmm. I'm not sure I believe that." He lunged forward and threw his fist into Jay's stomach. My lab-brother grunted, doubling up and falling to his knees. Axel snarled again, furious that he was unable to act. The kid in RC's arms squirmed as if he was ready to charge Azar and beat him with his small fists.

Tears streamed down Vivian's face. I understood Madison's helplessness. I wanted to scream in frustration. The hot power awakened, overtaking the cold one I'd been sustaining to keep my eyes blue. I was sure my irises were green now, but I was too worked up to change them back. No one was looking at me, anyway.

The Warden knelt down and reached for Jay's head. My lab-brother instinctively shied away from his hand. Azar mused, "Let's see what the mysterious leader looks like under there," as he pulled the mask down and threw back the hood of the cloak.

His eyes widened, and those at the front of the crowd gasped. "You're a child!" Azar exclaimed.

Jay raised his head to meet Azar's gaze, his expression defiant. Azar's red eyes flashed. "You tried to fool me. Kill her. Then him."

"No!" Jay cried. "Check my arm. I'm A3-3616!"

Azar studied him dubiously for a moment, then dug his heel into the center of Jay's back and pressed his captive's body to the ground. My lab-brother groaned through bared teeth. Azar nodded at Hassing, who allowed the ectoplasm bonds to part just enough for Azar to remove Jay's gauntlet and inspect the tattoo beneath. He touched Jay's skin to ascertain the ink was genuine.

Slowly, he stood. "So, this really is A3. How many years do you have?" Jay ground his teeth and remained silent, scowling. Azar moved his foot to Jay's shoulder and pressed down. My lab-brother cried out. "How many years do you have?" Azar repeated coldly.

"I don't know."

"You don't? Then you better think hard." He shifted his foot to Jay's upper arm, right where the wound was fresh, and twisted his heel. Jay yelped.

I grimaced at the sound of my lab-brother's pain. I'd become well accustomed to each of my lab-siblings' cries at that place, and I'd hoped I would never have to listen to one of them make a sound like that again. Azar was demanding an answer Jay honestly didn't have.

Please, Jay, I silently begged, *make something up so he'll stop hurting you.*

"Hey!" shouted Axel. Azar and Jay both turned their heads to look at him. "His file says he's nineteen."

"Is he really?" I whispered, barely moving my lips.

Axel nodded. Just as quietly, he replied, "According to Finn." It took a moment for me to process that, and once I did, I was surprised enough to glance at him sidelong. He was so fast I hadn't realized he'd left us and returned with the answer.

"Nineteen," Azar echoed, turning his attention back to his victim and relieving some of the pressure. "So, you haven't even come of age yet. But it doesn't make sense you would choose a child to lead you. Unless . . ." Azar's eyes widened as he realized the obvious answer. "You're the eldest, aren't you?" He threw his head back and laughed. "All this time . . . You're children! I don't believe it!"

Madison stared at us, mouth open, brow furrowed as she grasped the unbelievable truth. The Warden's laughter died just as quickly as it had come. He glared down at her and accused, "You exploit kálos children for human gain."

"No!" she insisted.

"Even by your standards, he's a child."

"I-I didn't know!"

Jay blurted, "No, it was my fault, I—"

"Shut up." Azar pressed down again, transforming any more of Jay's words into a long groan. "Does that hurt?" He peered at Jay beneath his boot. "Because that's nothing compared to what Veto will do to you if you're less than cooperative during our little chat when we get back to Szion. Understand?"

"Yes," Jay whimpered. He exhaled in relief when Azar removed his boot.

"Interesting," Azar murmured, stepping back and seizing a fistful of Jay's gray hair so he could haul our lab-brother onto his knees. He squeezed Jay's biceps and then prodded his abdomen, causing his prisoner to grunt at the sharp jabs. "So young, and yet you've managed to elude my best Guards. You've even bested Captain Hassing and Lieutenant Cisco." The captain glowered at Jay, contemptuous in contrast to Azar's admiration.

Jay tried to twist his head away, but Azar seized his face and brushed his hair back to look at his ears. I'd never noticed this because Jay's hair was always covering them, but the tips of his ears were pointed, elf-like. They were strange to me, but probably not all that uncommon in the Ghost Realm. Azar then forced Jay's mouth open to inspect him like a slave before purchase. His actions were odd to me until I realized he was checking Jay for physical traits that might reveal his Divinity, or at least rule out others. "Are you pure of blood?"

Jay wrenched his head free and turned away, glowering at the cobblestones. Azar's eyes flashed. His hand darted out, and he grabbed our leader's face again and forced his head around. "Look at me when I'm talking to you! Are you pure of blood?"

"Yes," Jay growled, his voice muffled in Azar's grip.

"And your Divinity?"

This time, it was me Jay's eyes found for a fraction of a moment so brief it almost didn't happen. "Sonokinesis," he whispered. The first lie I'd ever heard him tell.

"*Really.*" Azar leaned closer so his face was near Jay's. "Most Sonics have green eyes."

Jay met his skeptical gaze and said, "Guess I'm unique. Do you need a demonstration?" He made a big show of filling his lungs with a giant breath.

Azar clapped his palm over Jay's mouth. "No."

I understood my lab-brother's genius. I'd wondered why of all the Divinities he could have claimed, he'd chosen mine instead of his own. It was one of the few that no one, not even Azar, would demand proof of.

The Warden released Jay and stepped back. "Well. You're intriguing, but to be honest, I'm disappointed. I had hoped we would be equals. But you . . ." He trailed off. As if I'd suddenly become a Mind-

Reader, I could imagine how his thought ended: *you aren't the power-ful allies I was hoping you would be.* Maybe *ally* wasn't even the right word. *Adult.* Azar wanted powerful adults, not a rejected gang of kids.

"Let Vivian go." The voice was so small and meek I barely recognized it as Madison's. She squirmed feebly, still plastered to the cobblestones by an unseen force.

Azar sneered and said, "You're tempting me to forgive Officer Maven if the blade slips."

It was me, not Madison, who cried, "*Don't!*"

The power behind my voice was dangerous. I managed to keep it in check, although if I had been any more careless, glass would have cracked under the pressure of that single word. The ghost hunter's eyes swiveled to find me. Azar turned. My lips quivered, and any more pleas shriveled in my lungs.

Jay, calm when I was panicking, said monotonously, "Humans lie. Apparently your word is as meaningless as theirs."

The Warden glared down at him. "My word is good," he promised, his crimson eyes finding Madison once more. "And I give you my word that I will destroy humankind before I allow you to continue hunting us like animals and torturing our children." He studied Jay again. "Usually I don't accept ignorance of Law as an excuse for breaking it, but contrary to popular belief, I'm not a heartless man. I think you'll find I can be very reasonable. I'd wager a guess that most of your short life must have been spent in this Realm, so I suppose I really can't blame you for your insolence."

Jay refused to meet his gaze. Azar finally looked away from Jay to face the rest of us. "That being said, there are six more of you I could interrogate. I need only one, which means as valuable as he is, he's also expendable. If you follow, he will be executed. Do you understand?"

None of us answered. "And *you*," Azar seethed, reaching down. He seized Jay's shirt in both fists and hoisted my lab-brother off the ground. "Are you going to behave on our trip back?"

"I already surrendered to you, didn't I?" said Jay.

"That you did." He shoved Jay at two of his Guards, who caught him and held him up. "Now, let's make sure you don't pull any tricks." Azar drew his fist back and punched Jay squarely in the face.

I winced at the sound of knuckles cracking the cartilage in Jay's nose. Axel snarled, then vanished in a blur, gone. Ash's hand flew to her mouth as Jay reeled back and went limp in the arms of his captors. RC remained frozen.

If Jay really were a Sonic, a broken nose was good incentive to not scream shock waves. That lie came back to hurt him.

Our lab-brother labored to raise his head. His eyes were unfocused, and yet somehow, they found us. Through a river of blood streaming from his nose, one corner of his mouth twitched up in the slightest grin. He nodded once.

This was what he wanted.

The Guards hauled their prisoner toward the Rip. Captain Hassing let Vivian's bindings dissipate so he could follow and keep Jay restrained. The chain-link fence had been warped, as if someone had melted it, and I stood helplessly as Jay was dragged through the Rip. Vivian's captor threw her to the ground and followed.

Azar was the last to leave. He paused before the distortion in the air. "I'll be back for the rest of you after Jay and I have a little time to bond one-on-one. You have my word," he promised, stepping through the Rip and into the Ghost Realm.

— Chapter Thirty-Four —
Miscalculation

Eerie silence suffocated the crowd.

There were too many people gathered for it to be this quiet.

I was still waiting. I thought Jay had a plan. I thought he'd find a way to send Azar and the Shadow Guards back into the Ghost Realm, save Vivian, and walk back to us, weary but satisfied, and say, "See? Told you it'd all work out."

So I waited, staring at the Rip, expecting to see Jay walk back out. Each second wound my chest tighter and tighter around my heart.

He isn't coming.

I pushed away the voice at the back of my mind. Jay would come.

He isn't coming.

No. No, no, it wasn't supposed to happen like this.

I was ashamed to acknowledge this, but a tiny part of me, so small I was able to pretend it didn't even exist, had hoped Azar could help us. I'd thought if everything fell apart, if humankind had us cornered and we were driven from this Realm, Azar might offer sanctuary.

But he'd hurt Jay. He'd taken our lab-brother from us, eradicating that sliver of hope. My courage snapped. I actually felt it, like breaking a stick, and now it was a thousand shards of shrapnel lodged in my chest. Never aloud, but I'd admit it—I wanted to break down in tears. I wanted to let the despair drag me all the way to my knees while I begged for my mommy to come fix everything and make it all right again like she used to, as if I were a child and the world were still that simple.

How stupid to wish for her help, to even grace her with a passing thought. I was . . . lost. I was lost right now. How could I lead when I was lost? How could Jay ask that of me? It wasn't fair. It wasn't fair for him to make me leader; it wasn't fair for him to leave us.

I looked to Ash and RC, and they looked back at me. None of us knew what to do. Jay had specifically told us not to follow, and without Axel, we'd never be able to reach Jay before they killed him. I hadn't realized just how much we relied on them. Our efficient team had been crippled in a matter of seconds, and I resented Axel for ditching us in our time of need.

Ash and RC were waiting for me to come up with a plan, but the harder I tried, the more I began to panic when I failed. Every second wasted took Jay farther away. Why had he told me he'd be okay? He wasn't okay. He wasn't coming back like he was supposed to.

The young Phantom finally ducked low to escape RC's hold. He marched straight to me, his hands balled into white-knuckled fists. "You didn't *do* anything!" he screamed, beating my abdomen. And I let him, because he was right. I'd frozen when I needed to act, and now Jay was gone. "Why? Why didn't you save him? You didn't even try!"

Now that Azar was gone, the boy's mother was brave enough to cross the span and seize his wrist, then jerk him away from me. She didn't say a word, didn't scold him, didn't apologize, just pulled him back to the solemn wall of humans.

Vivian stormed over to us. "Whatever the plan is, I'm in," she said fiercely.

I blinked in surprise. Her voice broke the spell over me. This was really happening. Jay wasn't walking back through the Rip, and I had to do something. Something braver than breaking down.

None of us answered. Vivian hesitated, rather puzzled by our lack of response. "You do have a plan, right?"

Jay's last order had been to stay put. What should I do? Obey his final wish? Ignore it and go after him, even without Axel? Damn it, I wished Finn and Reese had been here, or Ero. I needed to know what Jay was thinking.

Ero! Maybe Ero can help us. If he can eclipse the Shadow Guards to keep them from executing Jay . . .

Vivian shook her head in disbelief. "What is *wrong* with you? Jay needs you!"

I stared blankly at her. She'd interrupted my sluggish train of thought, and I needed a few extra moments to process what she'd said. When she still received no answer from us, she turned away with a huff and marched to the pile of discarded weapons. "Fine. I'll save him without your help." She seized a belt and cinched it around her hips. "Mom? Trey? Come on, let's get the raid team." She tossed belts to them both. "Wes? Are you with me?"

Wes hung his head. Trey glanced uncertainly between Vivian and Madison. "You heard Azar, Viv," he muttered. "If anyone follows, he'll kill Jay."

"And if nobody rescues Jay, he'll be tortured." Tears were still sparkling in her emerald eyes. "It's my fault he's in this mess. I'm not abandoning him."

Ash leaned toward me and whispered, "Should we stop her?"

Yes or no? Why was every decision so difficult? At least this was one I didn't have to worry about; Madison seized her daughter's arm just as Vivian was about to reach the mangled fence surrounding the Rip. "You are *not* going into the Ghost Realm," Madison snarled, her relief masked by the sharp order. She jerked Vivian back so hard the girl stumbled.

I was between them. It happened so fast, I didn't even know how I got there. Jay had sacrificed himself for Vivian, and all I could think of was protecting her. Somehow, I was gripping Vivian's arm, and Madison was in front of me.

She stared at me, stunned that I'd ripped her daughter out of her hand. Fury hardened her expression into a scowl. She reached for her belt.

Defensive, I pulled Vivian farther away, harder than I intended, causing her to cry out. There was wind in my ears, or blood, I didn't know, and I was staring into the barrel of an ectogun trained between my eyes, but I wouldn't let go.

Madison snarled, "You've got two seconds before I blow your face off."

"Mom, don't," Vivian ordered, calm under duress. "*Don't*. Can't you see they're upset? Drawing guns is just going to make it worse. Let me handle it."

She twisted in my grip to push the gun away and stare me straight in the eye. "Seph. You're hurting me." I blinked, focusing on her green eyes. "Let go. It's okay, Seph. I'm okay, but you're hurting me."

I croaked, "I don't want to hurt you."

"I know. You can let go now." Puzzled, she said, "I thought you had blue eyes."

I didn't even need to consciously activate the cold power; the shock of her statement immediately chilled my blood so when my fingers unclenched, ice was already crusting on my fingerless gloves. "What?"

She stared at me hard, head tilted slightly to one side, as if she was trying to decide if it had been a trick of the light. "We have to rescue Jay now. Do you understand?" I did, but I couldn't think straight. Her hand reached for my heart, and she lifted the silver whistle. "You're the leader now. That's what this means, right?"

I dazedly reached up and took the whistle back, held it, numb. I was the leader. I didn't want to be.

"We can't go," said RC. Vivian and I both turned to stare at him. "Jay's final order was to stay."

"What if it was the wrong order?" I asked weakly.

RC shook his head. "I trust Jay. I won't disobey him."

First Axel, now RC . . . My team had officially crumbled. Even if I could convince Ash to follow me against Jay's wishes, the two of us didn't stand a chance if we crossed through the Rip in pursuit, even with the raid team.

Vivian stepped back. "I'm going after him," she said. How did she inject that assertiveness in her voice? She made a better leader than I did. "Seph, I want you to come with me."

"You are not," Madison seethed. She lunged for her daughter again, and I instinctively reached out to intercept, but Vivian was faster than us both, and she spun away with natural grace.

She wheeled to face the ghost hunter. "Mom, I—"

She trailed off, staring over Madison's shoulder. I caught my breath. Every insignificant face around me seemed to fade away as I stared at the boy with gray hair who had appeared out of nowhere.

All around us, the air came alive with whispers. Madison paused, gazing at Vivian in confusion, and then she turned just as Jay collapsed hard onto his knees, cradling one arm to his chest. His eyes were closed. Blood poured from his nose and dripped off his chin.

I should have gone to him. But I didn't, because I stared at this stranger and wanted to be relieved, and yet, I didn't recognize him. Jay was our fearless leader, the voice of reason in panic, the one with a plan. He was the only one unstoppable Axel would listen to.

But this boy was weak. He was hurt. He wasn't the leader I knew.

Vivian tentatively called, "Jay?"

He tipped forward and vomited blood all over the cobblestones.

Finally, my feet carried me forward. Vivian was approaching Jay, but I forced myself between them and gently but firmly pushed her away as Ash slid onto her kneepads beside him. She caught him as he collapsed onto his side with an agonizing moan.

"Miscalculated," Jay slurred. "D-distance." Shivering violently, he coughed up more blood and spat it onto the cobblestones.

"Please don't talk," said Ash, cradling his head in her lap. "You need to rest."

"Cursed be King, Jay," Wes broke in. "Are you . . . ? I don't believe it. Are you a Blinker?"

Jay's empty gaze wandered until settling vacantly on the werewolf in a way that made me wonder if his ears were working but his vision wasn't quite right. "Between the Realms . . . so . . . *cold*," he whispered. He was bleeding from his right eye and left ear in addition to the stream still flowing from his broken nose.

Ash took his hand in both of hers. "Shh, Jay. Please."

Vivian was still staring at Jay as if she didn't recognize him, either. "I owe you my life. Trey and I both do now. But . . . is it true? That you're the oldest?"

She received no answer, but she didn't need one.

RC turned away from Jay and faced the shops edging town square. He extended his hands and rotated his wrists. Humans flinched and retreated from him, afraid for no reason other than he had the potential, even if no motive, to harm them.

At first, nothing seemed to be happening. I followed RC's intense gaze and finally noticed the screws of a door's hinges were turning and growing until they hovered free for a moment and then fell with a faint *clink*. RC rolled his arms with movements as fluid and elegant as a dancer or a martial artist. The door came free and levitated parallel to the ground. When he drew his hands back to his body, the door followed.

Humans parted to let it pass. They stared at it, understanding how this bizarre occurrence was happening but still awestruck by the oddity of a door levitating past their noses.

RC telekinetically set the door beside Jay, then gently lifted Jay's body while Ash and I guided our fallen lab-brother onto his transport. Jay's eyes were squeezed shut in pain, his red teeth bared, but fatigue melted the tension out of his body the instant we laid him down.

The door rose, and RC started to take him away. "Wait," Madison called.

RC paused, and Jay's bloodshot eyes fluttered open when she called his name. He coughed, spraying her face with a red mist, but she didn't even wipe the blood away. "Vivian means the world to me. But to you . . . she's just a human, the daughter of a ghost hunter. Why would you risk your own life to save her?"

He whispered, "Because I promised." He managed a half-smile, half-grimace before his eyelids slid shut again, setting free a single blood tear that cut a crimson trail down his cheek.

Madison extended her hand. "Let me help you."

I snarled, "You've done enough," as I grabbed her wrist and twisted.

Her whole arm rolled with the motion in an attempt to relieve the pressure, and, off balance, she fell to her knees with a quiet utterance of

"Damn it." She rose, but I was between her and Jay. She had no right to touch him.

RC was making his way through the crowd. Most humans backed away, and those who didn't, he pushed away with telekinesis. The door floated behind him, carrying its passenger.

Voice low, I accused, "It's your fault this happened."

"*My* fault?" she said in disbelief. "If anything, it's *your* fault!"

"We almost lost Jay!"

"I almost lost my daughter! Azar wouldn't have come here if it weren't for you!"

I stepped dangerously close to the ghost hunter. "Azar held Vivian hostage because of you. Every time she's put in danger, it's because of *you*! Did you think we were the only ones smart enough to figure out the quickest way to disarm you is to take the daughter you love so much? You put Vivian *and* Jay in danger this time! Maybe if you were capable of protecting your family—"

"*Don't*," she seethed, drawing an ectogun.

Ice crusted my gloves and gauntlets. "Shoot me. I dare you."

"Stop!" two feminine voices rang in sync. Vivian grabbed Madison's shoulder, and Ash fit her warm hand into my cold one, melting my ice.

"Please, Mom," Vivian implored. She set her hand on the gun.

"Let's go," Ash said. "Let's go see Jay." She took a step back, pulling my arm with her, but my feet remained planted, and despite Vivian's pressure, Madison kept the gun trained on me. We glared each other down. In my rage, my eyes should have been green, but the ice creeping up past my elbows was enough to keep the blue power active. Steam wafted where Ash's hand met mine.

Madison snapped, "I don't know how old you are, but apparently you never learned respect."

Ash's grip was tightening, but I continued to resist her pull. I retorted, "My age is irrelevant; I respect those who show respect to me. But you never will, because you're never going to accept us. It wouldn't matter if we were ninety-nine percent human; that wouldn't be good enough. You look at our glowing eyes, and you hate us. That's never going to change."

Finally, I succumbed to Ash's steady pressure and turned away from the ghost hunter, halfway expecting a shot in the back.

It never came.

— Chapter Thirty-Five —
Long Walk Home

Jay should have been sleeping, but he was sitting on one of the beds, propped against the wall and holding a towel to his face.

His swollen nose had transformed to a grotesque purple tinged with yellow. I couldn't fathom how he was still clutching at consciousness by sheer willpower. His eyes were completely dull as if he were wearing a neutralizer, and he kept wiping away blood gathering in the corners of his mouth. His eye had stopped bleeding at least, and the red line from his ear was crusted now.

Finn and Reese were sound asleep. They were oblivious to what lengths Jay had gone to in order to protect them. Axel still hadn't returned. The others were guarding the Rip in case Azar was pissed enough to launch a full-scale invasion after Jay's stunt.

I gazed down upon him. "You didn't do that for Vivian."

"No," he agreed in a hoarse voice that sounded centuries older.

I stared at the bloody towels lying next to him. He'd done it for me. "Why?"

Jay sighed and made eye contact, trapping me in his gaze. "Because you still love her, whether or not you'll admit it."

"You should have let me go instead."

"It had to be me. I'm the only one who can Blink between the Realms."

His argument was logical, and yet I was still riddled with guilt. "Isn't it hard for you to Blink between the Realms at *full* strength?" He broke his gaze to stare at the floor while subtly wiping his mouth again. Even sitting down, he was unsteady and had to keep righting himself to stop from falling over. He'd come dangerously close to a complete burnout. Actually, I was certain that stunt almost killed him.

"Never tried before today," he admitted.

"It still should have been me. You could have Blinked into Prison and rescued me."

Without looking at me, he replied, "I barely made it alone. There's no way I could have Blinked between Realms with a passenger."

"Bloody Scout, Jay, you can't . . . you can't *do* this anymore."

"What?" he asked innocently.

"*Don't*. Do you think this family could survive without you?"

"What were my other options? Let Trey take a bolt to the heart and Vivian a knife to the throat?"

"You're going to end up killing yourself to protect the people who betrayed me. How did you even know?"

"Axel."

One word, and it was all I needed. Axel knew I couldn't do it. Why was I so surprised? Of course he knew. One look at me in town square, and he knew I was caving under the pressure.

Still, even if that was true, he had no faith in me, and the betrayal stung. I turned away from Jay, who beseeched, "Please don't be like that, Cay."

I held up the whistle and demanded, "Why did you make me leader if you didn't believe I could do it?"

"I do believe in you. But I didn't expect you to confront Azar by yourself."

"You didn't give me the chance to succeed or fail on my own." That wasn't fair, and I knew it. Vivian could have died through my indecision, and then I'd be blaming him for not intervening.

"I'm sorry." Jay closed his eyes and leaned his head back, his whole body sagging with fatigue. "I'm not going to be able to help you for a while now."

The silence was so thick I imagined I could freeze it if I wanted. "Jay? Question. Do, uh . . . do you think Azar is right? Should we have gone back and tried to save the other prisoners?"

Jay opened his eyes. Despite his weariness, his voice was sharp when he snapped, "Do you think any of them would have returned for *us*?"

"But we could. Really, if you think about it. Finn and Reese already hacked the Grid once. They could shut down the whole security system, open all the automatic doors, control the elevator, and—"

"Cato."

He was staring at the sleeping forms of the twins. All he said was my name, and yet, it was as if he'd just spelled out exactly why my proposal was impossible, and I saw. I, too, watched Finn and Reese sleep, and I understood. My faith was ill-placed. They wouldn't betray their masters. They'd betray *us*.

I still didn't know what Jay had whispered to Reese the day he convinced the twins to disable all communications in the area and lock the Grid, but he'd somehow convinced them to hide from their masters.

Or so I thought. Watching their chests rise and fall with steady, shallow breaths, I wondered now if they hadn't been hiding, but rather waiting. I'd like to believe they'd helped us because they had a change of heart, but now I saw that they'd just bought us a little extra time Outside because that was what Jay asked for, and all along they'd been waiting to return to their masters' sides. They weren't fighting us, not trying to escape. Just waiting to be found.

Even though they'd broken the Rules once, they would never initiate a direct strike with the intent to harm their masters. If we tried to storm that place, Finn and Reese would immediately yield to *Them* and probably lock our cages themselves if it would increase the chance of *Him* forgiving them. And yet, even knowing they would betray us, Jay loved them. And so did I.

"Doesn't it bother you?" I asked.

Jay's lips twitched before he answered, "Knowing they'd betray us isn't what bothers me. It's thinking about what *They* did to Finn and Reese to warp their loyalty."

"Look, I don't want to say it . . . and you probably don't want to hear it, but Azar has the ability to take down our enemies. He offered us an alternative deal. We could—"

"No."

"How long are we going to keep hiding, Jay? How long are we going to stay here in Phantom Heights pretending to be heroes when we're really just waiting for the people we protect to turn against us? *Again*, Jay. It's not a matter of if; it's a matter of when. They've already done it to me once."

"Cato," he said, the calmness in his voice juxtaposing with my frustration, "what do you think Azar will do to Finn and Reese when they refuse to betray their masters?"

I fell silent. Jay did too, letting my own imagination answer his question. If Azar couldn't convince our lab-brothers to give up *Their* secrets, he'd likely try to torture the information out of them. And if that didn't work—which was a strong possibility, considering how much torture Finn and Reese had already survived—I feared he'd find a way to attack their minds somehow and extract what he needed, regardless of whether the twins survived intact.

"Besides," said Jay, closing his eyes again, "I'm pretty sure I just blew any chance of an alliance today. I don't think Azar is going to forgive my insolence a second time."

The soft rap of knuckles against the door made us both jump. "Hello?" a girl's voice called. I set my hand over my throbbing heart. "Um, it's Vivian Tarrow. Is anybody in there?"

Jay and I stared at each other. He managed to lift one corner of his mouth in a rather pathetic, exhausted, crooked grin. "Well?"

The day's events smashed into me harder than one of Axel's punches. "She came to see you. You're the one who saved her, not me." Even though I knew why it had to be him, I still resented him when the words left my mouth.

"Open the door."

"I can't."

"Cato—"

"No."

"Cato—"

"Jay, I *can't*. What if she—?"

"Seph."

The use of my false name caught me off guard. He looked me in the eye and said, "You have the chance to start over."

I swallowed, turning as she knocked again, a little firmer this time.

I hesitantly walked toward the door and rounded the corner, then paused and glanced at Jay again. He encouraged me with a nod. I took a deep breath, exhaled, pulled the hood over my head, fixed the mask over my face, and reached for the bolt.

"There's a noticeable difference between Cato and Seph," Jay reminded me.

My eyes widened. I closed my left hand into a fist and searched for my center, letting the cold creep from my heart to my hand until it materialized. My clumsy fingers fumbled with the lock. That was stupid. I'd almost let Vivian Tarrow of all people see my bicolor eyes.

Stupid mistake. Stupid, stupid, stupid.

I pulled the bolt back, then cracked the door open to find a pair of green eyes gazing back at me. "Hi, Seph," she greeted, looking rather surprised that someone had answered. "Um, is Jay here?"

"Yeah," I croaked. I cleared my throat and said, "Yeah," stronger this time, swinging the door wider and glancing around the corner into our sleeping quarters. "He's . . ." I paused, finding to my surprise that Jay was on his side, eyes closed, chest rising and falling with deep, even breaths. "Um . . . asleep, I guess," I finished, silently cursing him for leaving me alone with Vivian. Under normal circumstances, I'd call him out for faking, but he might very well have finally passed out.

"Oh." She scuffed the toe of her sneaker on the doorframe. "Um, well . . . I just wanted to thank him for saving me."

I hung my head and muttered, "I can give him the message."

We lingered in awkward silence. My nervous fingers fiddled with the ice in my hand. Vivian tucked her hair behind her ear.

"Well, I guess I'll just go." She turned away.

"Uh, wait!" She glanced back at me, frowning. "Maybe . . . um, maybe I should walk you home? T-to make sure you make it safely this time."

Vivian considered my offer. "Sure, I guess."

My heart stopped. Was I relieved or horrified that she accepted?

I closed the door and followed her down the great staircase. My heart had started again, and it was running wild. My lungs, on the other hand, had forgotten how to work. My guard was still up; I hadn't forgotten Vivian's ghost-hunting background. If she made a sudden move, I had to be ready to react.

"This is some house," she said, her head rolling as she took in the majesty of Saros Manor on our way down. I nodded. I didn't think she saw me, but she didn't seem to have expected an answer anyway.

We crossed the grand foyer—I staying at least an arm's length away—and stepped outside. Wes's front lawn sloped down to the wrought-iron fence edging the sidewalk below. Vivian had her head tipped back now, watching the clouds drift high above on lazy atmospheric currents without the slightest inkling that this wasn't the first time we'd walked together like this. Though a different route, we'd done this a thousand times with heavy backpacks slung over our shoulders.

The bracelet in the pouch strapped to my right thigh felt like lead weighing me down. Now was probably the most opportune time I'd ever have to give it to her. But how to broach the topic? I was drawing a blank.

Her voice interrupted my thoughts: "So . . . is Jay okay? He didn't look so good in town square."

"Jay? Yeah, he'll be fine. He burned out; he just needs to rest for a while."

"That's good. I was worried about him."

I rubbed my right biceps and muttered, "Yeah, Jay can be a real idiot when he decides to play hero."

Vivian dropped her chin and smiled shyly, sweeping her dark hair behind her ear again. "Well, I owe that 'idiot' my life. If there's anything I can do for him, or the rest of you, just let me know. I mean it, anything at all."

"Sure."

She kicked a stone down the sidewalk. The awkward silence thickened the air between us until she broke it again: "Beautiful day, isn't it?"

I nodded.

"So, Jay's nineteen. And you're even younger, right? How old are you?"

"I don't know."

"Why not?"

"I just don't, okay?"

"Oh. I'm sorry."

Heat burned my cheeks, and I mumbled, "It's fine."

She was quiet for another block, and this time when I snuck another glance, I realized she was also stealing glances at me.

"You know, Seph, there's something really familiar about you. You remind me of . . . someone I used to know."

I tensed, wondering if I'd pushed my luck. Was it my voice that was familiar? The way I talked? Should I leave now, before Vivian realized who was really walking beside her?

She stopped again. I hesitated, my unease engorging rapidly as she tilted her head and scrunched her eyes, studying me. I looked away; I couldn't meet her gaze, and I was terrified of making eye contact with her. She said, "Your eyes are so bright. Brighter than any of the other Alpha ghosts'."

Had she already guessed that I was drawing upon my Divinity? My grip tightened on the ice.

"I know you're younger than me. Why do you still cover your face up?"

I was trying to find my faltering voice, but I was afraid I'd swallowed it. I was grateful my body didn't sweat anymore; otherwise I'd no doubt be a pathetic puddle on the sidewalk by now.

"Personal reasons," I finally choked out.

"I'd like to see your face." She reached for my hood.

It wasn't a sneak attack. She moved slowly, deliberately, giving me time to grant permission by holding still or deny her by retreating. Her hand drew nearer, but I didn't move. She didn't scare me as much as other humans. But that didn't mean I was going to stand there and let her touch me; her fingers were inches from my hood when I seized her wrist.

She didn't resist. We stood there like that for a long minute, her wrist in my right hand, ice in my left. She was staring at me with alarming intensity, trying to discern features visible in the shadow of the hood above my mask. "I know not all kálos look human. Whatever you think you need to hide, I won't judge. I promise."

I almost laughed in relief. Was that what she thought? That I kept my face hidden because I had some kind of deformity, like horns or scales? I shook my head and opened my fingers, letting her hand fall back to her side. Vivian deflated with disappointment, but she accepted my silent refusal and said nothing more on the matter.

As we drew nearer to the Tarrow house, my stress skyrocketed. I enjoyed being with Vivian. Madison was an entirely different matter, especially since she might still take me up on my dare to shoot me. I hesitated on the bottom step.

Vivian was on the porch when she realized I was no longer following. She turned, and her head tilted as she sized me up again. "Are you sure we've never met?"

I shrugged. "Sorry."

"Please, Seph. All I want is the truth. Have we met before?"

She said that as if it were the simplest request in the world. I stared into her eyes, spellbound by the wounded note in her voice. I knew how it felt, to beg for the truth.

She was waiting for my answer. I opened my mouth to do exactly as she asked me not to and lie. No, we never met.

"Yes."

Wrong word. *What am I doing?* Panic laced my chest tight, but then cautious hopefulness bubbled within, straining against the cords until I might burst. I held my breath. Her eyes widened a little, but the rest of her reaction was contained, as if she already knew.

"You were in Phantom Heights before you were taken to the AGC.

You came to this Realm through the Rip." It wasn't a question, and I didn't answer. She rubbed her wrist. "And my mom? That's why you don't like her, isn't it? I bet she tried to send you back to the Ghost Realm, didn't she?"

Something like that. It was too late to go back now. I may have just ruined everything by pulling on this forbidden thread.

But Vivian seemed so . . . innocent. Like a marionette bobbing helplessly at the end of a string, I nodded.

She was commendably calm with this information. My heartbeat hurt. It kicked my sternum so hard I imagined tiny fractures cracking as it tried to break free. "How long ago?"

"I don't know," I croaked. "It was a long time." *At least, it feels like a long time.*

"I understand now. That's how you knew so much about me, and my mom, and this town. I should have realized the only way you could have known was if you'd been here to—"

"Vivian," I interrupted. "You can't tell anyone. I didn't leave this place on good terms. I—" *Want to tell you, but* . . . "uh . . . look, I—" *Am the leader now.* "I—" *Can't.*

I sighed. "I'm trusting you."

Unbridled hope tingled in my chest. If Vivian passed this test—maybe, just maybe, if she proved herself trustworthy—I could take off the mask, throw back the hood, allow my eyes to revert back to normal, and face her judgment. Maybe . . .

That was dangerous thinking, especially with my lab-family relying on me to lead them right now. Vivian's gaze fell to her feet. "I get it. It's hard enough convincing people in Phantom Heights to trust you. You need a clean slate, and you won't get that if people know you orig-inally came here as an enemy. Okay," she said, nodding. "I won't tell Mom. And . . . thank you. For walking me home."

My voice was gone again; all I could do was nod back. I reached into my pouch one more time, catching my breath as my fingertips brushed the bracelet inside. It was time to return it.

Vivian turned away before I could. Her voice wafted back: "See you around, okay, Seph?"

She shut the door, leaving me standing on the porch step alone, filled with exhilaration and hope and regret. I couldn't take back what I'd said. I sighed and held the bracelet in my hand. *So close.*

I wrapped my fingers around the broken cords. Who was I kidding? This would never work. The idea had been tantalizing in theory when Jay said it, but now I knew that I was wasting my time. Seph could never have the same life as Cato.

I lifted my head to stare at the closed door. A black-and-silver ribbon tied around the handle hung limp and lifeless. A safe haven? Here? Really?

My fingers tightened, and the ice exploded.

— Chapter Thirty-Six —

Origins

"Ero!" said Wes upon discovering his friend in the kitchen making a sandwich.

The Telepath glanced up inquisitively.

"Did you know Jay is only nineteen?"

"Is he?" Ero asked in genuine surprise. He held up a yellow bottle. "What is this?"

"Mustard."

"What does it taste like?" he asked, popping the lid and sniffing.

"Like . . . I don't know, tangy, and . . . I don't know. It's good for sandwiches. You'll probably like it. Would you focus, please? Jay is *nineteen.*"

Ero took his time squirting mustard onto a slice of bread, and then he replaced the bottle in the refrigerator. "I knew he was young, but I never did ask his true age."

"*Really.*"

"Really," Ero insisted as he sat down at the small table by the bay window. "Only nineteen, you say? Hmm, I thought he had at least a half century. He certainly acts mature for his years."

"He hasn't even reached his *first* coming of age. Why didn't you tell me?"

Ero took a bite and chewed slowly, watching Wes. He swallowed and said, "Oh. I like this. What did you call the yellow sauce? Mustard?"

"Ero!"

"Wes, I already made it clear that I would not divulge personal information about them."

"This seems a little important, don't you think?"

"If it was so important, perhaps you should have inquired about his age before making a deal with him. Are you upset because Jay outsmarted you and now you know he is just a child?"

Wes tensed. "Jay has never outsmarted me." Ero smiled and took another bite. "Stop changing the subject."

"I think you are overreacting. So, they are young. Do you doubt their capabilities now that you know?"

"Well . . . yes."

"I see. Then perhaps that is why they chose to keep their ages a secret?"

Wes was silent for several long moments, considering. He finally asked, "Do you think it's wrong for us to hold them to the deal?"

"Not at all," Ero answered. "If they have chosen to honor this bargain, why are *you* so uncertain now?"

"Some people are uncomfortable with hiring kids as mercenaries."

"Some people? Not you?"

"I haven't decided yet if the gain is worth the consequence," Wes admitted.

"But consider this—these kids were exploited, tortured, and caged like animals. When they came here, you gave them responsibility. They have a purpose now, and they would see the loss of such responsibility as a punishment."

"Well . . . I suppose if this is really what they want . . ."

"Please, join me for lunch."

Wes obliged, quickly crafting a ham, cheese, and pickle sandwich and pulling a beer from the fridge before joining the Telepath in the breakfast nook. "So, he's really a Blinker?"

"Ah, so you know!" Ero cried in delight.

"Yeah," Wes said, too thoughtful to share in Ero's enthusiasm. "I guess the Triad of extinct Divinities isn't the Triad anymore."

"True, but then again, we knew the day would come. Extinct Divinities are never truly extinct, just dormant in recessive genes. But how thrilling, to witness the rebirth of one."

"Yeah," Wes said again. "By King's grace, how did Agent Kovak stumble upon the first Blinker of this Dynasty? And why does he need a bunch of kids to make this weapon in Project Alpha?" Ero chewed in silence, his gaze falling to the tabletop. "You know," Wes realized.

"I suspect," corrected his friend. "They have told me nothing about Project Alpha, and I have not pried. As curious as I am, it is not my business."

Wes used his tongue to loosen a piece of ham caught between his teeth. "Agent Kovak said he handpicked these kálos for Project Alpha," he muttered, more to himself than to Ero. "Finn and Reese are special. So is A6. So is Jay." His gaze flicked up to meet Ero's. "Are they all so unique?"

Ero finished chewing before he replied, "Some more so than others, based on your definition of 'special.' They are not all one-of-a-kind. You already know RC is a Telekinetic, and he is just that—a Telekinetic. Powerful, but not 'special,' as you would put it."

Wes took a swig of beer, his thoughts still spinning. "But Kovak didn't seem nearly as interested in retrieving Jay. He said the high-value targets were the twins and A6. I bet he doesn't realize just how rare Jay is."

"That is certainly plausible."

Wes coveted deeper answers he already knew Ero wouldn't surrender, so he redirected, "Speaking of the twins, how are your lessons going? Or are you not allowed to tell me that?" He took a generous bite.

Ero pondered for a moment before answering. "To be honest, I am struggling to connect with my students."

"Really?" Wes said through his mouthful. "But you love kids. And kids love you."

"Yes. With minimal effort, I have always been able to establish a relationship with even the most rambunctious student. Yet Finn and Reese are not like anyone I have ever encountered."

"They're beyond your skills?"

"I did not say that. I am enjoying the challenge they have presented me. May I show you something?" he asked, pulling a piece of paper from his pocket. He unfolded it and set it on the table.

Wes glanced at it. "Sudoku," he said, wiping the corner of his mouth with a napkin. "I never had the patience to find the appeal."

"Nor I," Ero agreed. "However, Finn and Reese enjoy puzzles, and I discovered a book of sudoku in your library. Do you know how quickly they solved this once I read them the rules?" Wes shrugged. "Thirteen ticks."

The werewolf's eyes grew wide. He dropped his sandwich, snatched the paper, and stared closer at it. "Not possible."

"I timed them myself. Their minds automatically find patterns and missing numbers. I could write out a list of numbers from one to a million, and they could take one look at it and tell me which number was missing."

"These can't be the same kids I met in City Hall. Honestly, Ero, I was convinced they suffered from mental retardation."

"I do not think you comprehend just how deep their subservient fear of humankind runs. And as brilliant as they are, they are also astonishingly ignorant in the most basic subjects." Ero reclaimed the sudoku puzzle. "I have found that I cannot seem to challenge Finn and Reese. They absorb knowledge like sponges, and their stamina is incredible. You know, most Mind-Readers and Telepaths activate their Divinity only when they wish to delve into a specific mind. Every time I have been with Finn and Reese, they have constantly been using their abilities, likely because at the AGC they had to be listening for silent orders at all times or risk a punishment. Now, if I could coax their true telepathic powers awake, their potential would be . . ."

He shook his head, as if unable to grasp the right words needed to finish his train of thought. "I have taught many students, each with his or her own unique personality and learning style."

Ero paused, then grinned. "But I must say that in spite of my difficulty connecting with them, Finn and Reese are among my favorites. I have had only glimpses into their amazing minds, and I know I am barely scratching the surface of what they are capable of. Thank you for contacting me to instruct them."

Wes took a deep drink to wash down his sandwich. He set the bottle back down on the tabletop with a heavy *clunk* and belched quietly behind closed lips. "I knew ten was outside your age range, but they clearly hadn't had any instruction, so I figured it couldn't hurt for you to meet them. I just didn't plan on you befriending all of them and keeping me in the dark."

"Are you still upset about that?"

"Yes." Wes was brooding, but he dropped the subject. "Any signs of their telepathic powers starting to manifest yet?"

"No," lamented Ero. "I have been encouraging them to speak with me telepathically, but thus far they can project thoughts only to each other."

"Maybe they aren't really Telepaths."

"That is possible. As I said, this is an unprecedented case. I could very well be wrong about them. Perhaps their telepathic powers have evolved as far as they ever will. Time will tell, I suppose."

The werewolf shoved the rest of his sandwich into his mouth. "Wes," Ero said hesitantly, "this is a bit off subject, but I have a question for you."

"Shoot," Wes replied, his voice muffled.

"Well . . . I was wondering if you could tell me about Phantom."

The werewolf froze, mouth still full. He shifted the mushed food against his cheek. "Phantom?" he repeated in surprise. He swallowed. "What makes you ask about him?"

"Curiosity. This is the Demikan's home, but I must confess that I really do not know much about him."

Ero waited, his gaze unwavering and unblinking. Wes wouldn't look at him. "It's a sensitive topic. You shouldn't ask people about him."

"I am not asking people; I am asking my friend. Why does no one want to discuss Phantom? I was under the impression he was a hero." Ero cocked his head. "Interesting. Are you having trouble collecting your thoughts, Wes?"

The werewolf nodded. "It's complicated, but if you want to know about him, I don't see why you shouldn't. His human name was Cato."

Ero set his chin in his hand and leaned forward. "I am aware of Phantom's human background. Tell me, what was your relationship with him?"

"With Phantom or Cato?"

"Were they not the same person?"

Wes considered for a moment, disregarding Ero's last question to answer, "We coexisted, I guess. Phantom and I weren't exactly enemies, but he certainly wasn't my ally."

"So, you were not close."

Wes chuckled at a memory. "I didn't make a good first impression on him. When the Tears near my home in Colorado sealed, I purchased Saros Manor so I could be near the Rip. I knew there was a ghost hunter here, and I was prepared to deal with her, but I hadn't heard of Phantom. Imagine my surprise when we crossed paths one night. He wasn't very powerful or confident or even coordinated—must have recently become a half-breed. Our duel caught Maddie's attention."

Enthralled by the story, Ero watched his friend with an unwavering gaze. Wes nudged his half-drunk beer across the tabletop. "While Phantom and Maddie were focused on each other, I turned back into my human form. You should have seen the look on Phantom's face when he saw me lying naked on the ground. I don't think he'd ever encountered a weir before. I, uh . . . well, I lied. I told Maddie that he'd robbed me and beaten me, and they turned against each other. Phantom escaped, and I let Maddie help me back to my house while she apologized for not getting there soon enough to stop him from harming me. That's how I met both Madison Tarrow and Phantom."

"That does not sound like you had a mutual relationship."

"No, our first encounter wasn't a good one. He tracked me down later. I'm ashamed to admit it, but he caught me off guard and eclipsed me so we could have a more formal introduction. I explained to him that I just wanted access to the Rip, and he agreed not to expose me as long as I didn't cause trouble. After that, we had minimal contact. I was introduced to Cato on another occasion."

Wes snorted. "It just occurred to me that I thought I was meeting him for the first time, but he already would have known who and what I was."

"What I find interesting is that you refer to Cato and Phantom as two separate people."

"For all intents and purposes, they *were* two separate people. Cato was a typical teenager. He went to school, spent time with his friends, laughed a lot, liked to have a good time. Phantom was much darker, much more serious, and he didn't speak much at all. One was human, one was kálos. Honestly, Ero, if I hadn't been there the day Phantom's identity was exposed, I never would have guessed he was Cato."

"I am curious to know the Demikan's history."

"I don't know the specifics. Like I said, Phantom was already here when I came to the Heights."

"Surely you know his story, though. You know how a pureblood human became the only half-blood in history to possess kálos abilities."

Wes drummed his fingers against the tabletop. "Maddie has a lab in the basement of her house, right below the kitchen. Ectoplasm fascinates her; that's primarily what she studies. Every modern-day ectogun on the market is based on her original design. If I'm not mistaken, the day of the accident, she was attempting to destabilize a sample of ectoplasm and reform it into the first working prototype of her entoplasm shield. There was an explosion, and . . . well, Cato happened to be in the wrong place at the wrong time. He and Maddie were the only two in the immediate radius of the explosion."

Ero frowned. "If she was exposed to the same explosion as Cato, why is she still human?"

"Maddie knew she was experimenting with volatile samples, so she was wearing protective gear. Cato wasn't supposed to be down there."

Ero's eyes widened. "Madison created Phantom."

"Maddie didn't *know* she created Phantom," Wes clarified. "Nobody knew. Cato recovered from the accident seemingly unharmed. Phantom made his first appearance a few weeks later, and everyone assumed he'd come through the Rip."

He paused to take a drink. Ero waited patiently until Wes set the bottle down on the tabletop with a heavy sigh. "I don't know much about the accident. I know Vivian had been tutoring Cato after school, but at the time of the accident, she was supposedly on the second floor, and Cato and Maddie were in the basement. I don't think Trey was present. Why Cato wandered down there in the first place, I have no idea. All I do know, if the rumors are correct, is that he was very sick for about a day, and then he was fine. There was no reason to suspect anything was wrong."

"No one noticed his glowing eyes?" Ero asked dubiously. "Or that they were different colors?"

"Cato could suppress his powers and make his eyes stop glowing, and I found out later that Trey provided him with colored contacts. As long as Cato's eyes weren't glowing, the contact made his blue eye look green. Who would have made the connection? And when Cato wasn't dressed as Phantom, he looked like a normal human teenager. He could even walk through the first prototype of Maddie's entoplasm shield."

"How did the Agents catch him?"

Wes stared at his beer. "They had been in town collecting data on the Rip, so Cato and I were both trying to keep low profiles. But there was an attack in town square. One Agent and three civilians died, and more would have if Phantom hadn't stepped in. I watched him take a blast of ectoplasm head-on. It stunned him long enough for his attacker to expose his identity, and then the Agents took him away. Just like that. It happened so fast, you know? One minute he was there, and the next . . ." Wes shook his head. "I still can't believe I met Phantom and Cato on separate occasions and never put the pieces together."

"Did you try to liberate him?"

Wes tensed. "*Me*? What was I supposed to do? I wasn't going to get in the middle of that mess and expose myself."

"I see. Then what did Cato's family do?" asked Ero as he leaned closer.

Wes bowed his head. The cell phone started to vibrate in his pocket. Wes took his time in removing the phone, and then he stared at the screen as the device continued to buzz in his hand. "What was there to do?" He rose with a sigh. "I have to take this. If you really want to know more about Phantom, the person to ask is Trey Selman."

Ero watched his friend stride out the swinging door that led into the dining room. He knew Phantom's origins now, although he hadn't had the chance to probe Wes as much as he wanted.

"Well, Cato," Ero murmured thoughtfully to the empty room. "No wonder you have issues with Madison."

Chapter Thirty-Seven

Weakness

Madison Tarrow sat slumped in the armchair in her living room, knees drawn to her chest, hands locked around her ankles, eyes staring at nothing.

The shades were drawn over the windows. Only the *tick* of the clock on the wall broke the silence.

She narrowed her eyes at the sound of something swishing through the air and a great weight causing a floorboard to creak. "You know," she said coldly, "in this Realm, proper etiquette is to knock on the door and wait to be let in."

A massive gray paw stepped forward, and Wes came into view, his tail swishing. He was in limbo form, eyes glowing yellow in the shadows. He didn't answer.

Madison closed her eyes and leaned her head back against the chair. "I don't know what to do with these ghosts from Project Alpha." She chuckled once. "I feel ridiculous. Did you know I was actually afraid they were going to take over Phantom Heights? Stupid, right? They're just a bunch of kids."

Wes quietly noted, "You made the same mistake with Phantom."

Her voice was hoarse when she whispered, "I know." She drew her hands into her lap and used her thumb to stroke the metal nodes embedded in the glove covering her left hand. "What do you think we should do?"

He shrugged. The movement was stiff; his body wanted to settle into one form or the other, and the shoulder blade grated against the shifting joints. "Ero thinks we should let them fight."

"And what do you say?"

"It's not the fighting I'm worried about," he admitted. "Here's the thing, Maddie—kids do have comparably weaker powers than adults, but in a way, they can be more dangerous because their powers are maturing, so they tend to have less control over their Divinities. And if the Alpha ghosts are exceptionally powerful for their age group . . ."

"Then their powers are likely unstable," Madison concluded.

Wes bobbed his distorted head. "You see the problem. Ash already admitted she can't control hers. Although . . ."

"What?"

The werewolf pressed his furry hands together. "I can't for the life of me figure out the connection between them. Project Alpha has me absolutely baffled. Eight test subjects, right? Their powers aren't even remotely close. You've got low-level powers like Blinking and mind-reading, and then high-powered ones like telekinesis, and then there's A6, whose power was supposedly off the charts. Passive, active, all over the spectrum. The only real connection between them is their youth. But why does Kovak need kids to build his weapon?"

"Does Ero know?"

"If he does, he won't say."

Madison shook her head. "How do you think we should handle the situation now?"

"I don't know. You're the parent, not me."

She scoffed. "They're living in *your* house."

Wes flicked his yellow gaze up at the ceiling. "I never had any interest in fatherhood. Besides, they seem self-sufficient. I don't think they need a guardian."

"All kids do," Madison replied heavily.

Wes gave another stiff shrug. "I never asked for that job."

"Well, you got it, whether you like it or not."

Wes was silent for a moment. He scratched at his floppy ear and said, "I have some news I think you'll be interested in hearing. Jay is a Blinker. I know his weakness."

Surprised, Madison straightened. "You do? What is it?"

Wes shook his head, staring thoughtfully at the ceiling again. "His eyes are silver. I knew that had to mean something. Granted, silver eyes aren't completely unheard of in the Ghost Realm, but until today, Blinking was considered to be an extinct Divinity. Anyway, his weakness is light. And I don't mean regular sunlight; I mean a bright flash, or better yet, a series of bright flashes, like a strobe light. It disorients a Blinker, which, if you're lucky, will give you just enough time to incapacitate him before he can teleport away."

Madison's mouth turned up in a faint smile as she traced a random pattern on the armrest with one finger. "Good," she muttered. "Any leverage I can use is good. What about the others?"

"What about them?"

"Their weaknesses. Do you know what they are?"

"Planning to build your arsenal for war against them?" Madison gave him a steely glare, effectively wiping the grin off his face. He cleared his throat and shifted. "I haven't identified all of their Divinities. RC is obviously the Telekinetic. You could inhibit him by binding his hands, which you can think of as training wheels for his power. Young Telekinetics utilize their hands to guide the objects they're moving. If you want to completely eliminate his telekinesis, you'll need to blind him. He can't move what he can't see. Well . . . to an extent. He could still send out waves of telekinetic energy to defend himself, but he wouldn't be able to target specific objects."

Madison nodded, adding the mental note. Wes went on, "Seph slipped up and lost control of his Divinity when you two last faced off. He's a Cryokinetic."

"Really?" Madison sat up straight.

Wes smirked. "Ironic, isn't it, that Phantom's replacement has one of his Divinities."

Madison stared past Wes. "Fate has a twisted sense of humor."

"Anyway, that one's a no-brainer. Seph's weakness is heat. That, or you could cut off his supply of water, but that's no easy task considering he can draw it out of the air and his own body. Ash I haven't figured out yet, and Axel . . . he's something else. I haven't got a clue."

"What about Ero?" Wes gave her a funny look. "What? Every kálos has a weakness, even a Telepath. Right?"

"Sure," Wes reluctantly acknowledged. "A Telepath can't use his power if he can't focus. Same with Mind-Readers. But a master like Ero has spent centuries teaching himself how to tune out distractions. You really don't stand a chance against him."

"And what's your weakness, Wes?"

He smiled uneasily. "Oh, come on, Maddie. It's suicide to give up your weakness to your enemy."

"You consider me an enemy?"

"Depends on the day."

She didn't push him for an answer because she already had a magazine of pure silver bullets in her weapon belt, as well as a knife with a silver blade. A regular bullet could get the job done too, but pure silver was toxic to weir, so the special bullets were extra insurance in case she missed the kill shot.

She didn't turn around when Wes stepped back. "I'll be going," he said as he crouched down to all fours. His voice was growing huskier as fur rippled across his naked torso. His hands expanded into massive paws, and then the great wolf was crouching in the gloom. It blinked once at Madison and turned away, then padded into the kitchen and through the open back door.

The ghost hunter wrapped her arms around her legs again and sank deeper into the cushion. The silence was loud in the wake of Wes's departure. She reviewed the list of weaknesses he'd provided, mentally planning out scenarios she might have to respond to when dealing with the Alpha ghosts. She'd need to equip her cache with a flash bomb in case she ever had to incapacitate Jay. Blind RC, overheat Seph . . . probably easier said than done.

Her stomach flopped. Cryokinesis. Ironic indeed. She hadn't noticed Seph use his ice power during their last confrontation, but he must have at some point for Wes to be able to identify it.

Madison hadn't known Phantom was a Cryo in the beginning of their feud. Perhaps he hadn't mastered the ability, or maybe he simply wasn't keen on using it. She ran her hands through her hair. Her past confrontations with Phantom should have prepared her to handle Seph's power, but that wasn't the case. In all their skirmishes, not once had Cato ever used that Divinity offensively against her, and as she envisioned how a battle with Seph might unfold, she felt as ill-prepared as ever.

Cryokinesis was bad news against a human adversary. Kálos could phase through ice, but Madison would be helpless if Seph froze her solid. If he had decent control over his Divinity, he could form weapons in an instant, anything from a sword or spear to a shield, or worse—a barrage of projectiles Madison wouldn't be able to avoid. An all-out fight against Seph could turn lethal in an instant. He definitely wouldn't hold back like Cato had.

Although her conscious thoughts were on the Alpha ghosts, her mind kept hearing Kovak ask her if Phantom made her hesitate before pulling the trigger now. "Would you like to oversee the procedure on him?" he'd asked her two years ago.

His voice had been mocking, his smile a taunt. He thought she was weak. Madison had turned away from his scorn and answered in a razor-sharp voice she barely even recognized as her own, "No. Do whatever you need to, but I don't want to see it. Just the results. My only interest is the file when you're done."

Her gaze found the folder sitting on the small table next to the chair. She reached out to touch the corner. Yes. She did hesitate now, every single time she had to pull the trigger.

That boy today, Nikki Kaminski's son—Madison couldn't remember his name—had been so sure one of the Alpha ghosts was Cato. The kid was, after all, Phantom's biggest fan. It was almost sad to see how he'd so vehemently embraced the delusion that his hero had returned in an Alpha uniform.

She stroked the edge of Cato's file. In some ways, Madison felt she was a half-breed, too. Half-mother, half-ghost hunter. She'd never confronted kálos children before, so her ghost-hunting half had always been unrestricted, allowed to act independently and as ruthlessly as necessary. It was armor to protect the vulnerability of a mother inside.

But these Alpha ghosts were different. Part of her acknowledged their deadly supernatural power, their ferocity, the danger they presented. Part of her wanted to cook them a hot meal and tell them they didn't have to be afraid anymore. Kovak, he'd let her real son die, her own flesh and blood, and then he'd unknowingly given her seven children of kálos blood—enemy blood—to care for. She was so confused.

A vibration shattered the silence. Madison jumped. She turned her head to stare at the cell phone trembling on the table. The name on the screen made her tighten her arms around her body, as if she could bar the rest of the world from interrupting just by shielding herself with her own arms.

She sighed and snatched the phone. "Councilwoman," she greeted.

"Hello, Madison."

On the other end of the line, Holly Jennings was standing at her office window.

The people in the square below her milled about, not nearly as cautious as she felt they should be so close to the dangerous Rip. A couple of raiders were repairing the fence while a dozen others armed to the teeth were stationed with rifles trained on the Rip, almost exactly as Holly had envisioned for the Shoot-On-Sight doctrine. "What an eventful day."

"What do you want?"

Holly wrinkled her nose and plucked lint off the shoulder of her blouse. The ghost hunter had a tendency to be a bit curt sometimes, but Holly kept her voice pleasant. "Correll wants to know where you are. City council has been in a meeting for three hours straight concerning the little, ah, *development* this afternoon. You're supposed to be in charge of the Alpha ghosts, remember?"

"I haven't forgotten. I've been caring for Vivian."

"Right," Holly quickly sympathized. "How is she?"

"Resting. But let's keep this restricted to business."

"Fine. We have a little problem, don't you agree?"

Quietly, Madison asked, "What do you think we should do?"

Holly didn't answer immediately. As much as she abhorred relinquishing power, this was a delicate situation she didn't want to be held accountable for. "You're the ghost expert. In the end, it's your decision." The last word caught in her throat. That had been harder to force out than she'd expected. *The more distance, the better*, she reminded herself.

A pause, then Madison's breath crackled the speaker. "They're just kids. I mean, they're all still T.H.A. for God's sake."

"You'll have to forgive me, Madison; I'm not up to date with all the latest ghost-hunting terminology."

"True to human age. They're so young that they're still aging at the same rate as human kids."

"Oh, Madison." Holly sighed. She watched a little boy down below run across the square to his mom, and for a moment, her heartstrings twanged until she steeled herself again. "Mothers do have a soft spot for children, don't we? But ghost kids aren't as innocent as they seem. They grow up to be monsters. There's nothing you can do to change that."

"Finn and Reese?" Madison challenged. "Do they seem like monsters to you?"

"Ah yes, innocent little Finn and Reese, who will likely one day have the power to control people's minds and obliterate a lifetime of memories."

"There's a chance we can instill a sense of humanity in them. Children can learn."

"A snake will still grow up to be a snake, regardless of how you raise it. It's best to crush the egg before the beast hatches and grows big enough to bite you and kill you."

Silence on the other end. Holly cleared her throat and added, "I won't tell you what to do, but if you decide to try your little experiment and invest in these kids, you need to be prepared for the day you have to stand against them. Can you do that, Madison? Can you care for them with the knowledge that they'll grow up to be dangerous enemies and you'll probably have to destroy what you've nurtured?"

"I don't know," Madison admitted.

That was a weak answer, but at least she was honest, even if it wasn't the reply Holly wanted to hear. "Then I suggest you think long and hard before you decide what to do. Now, back to business. I'm sure it's no surprise that we've been discussing the Shoot-On-Sight doctrine again."

"S-O-S failed," said Madison, a hint of startled panic in her tone.

Holly gazed at raiders in the square and almost smiled. "It did. But we think that in light of today, we'll be able to regain community support. I predict our current arrangement with the Alpha ghosts isn't going to last much longer. But here's the thing—people just don't have much faith in the government. They need somebody more relatable . . . somebody who took control and led them in their darkest hour."

She was answered with silence. Holly picked at peeling flecks of paint on the windowsill, watching a blonde head bob across town square away from City Hall, a notebook clenched in the figure's hand.

Caslynn Swan was furious. She had come to City Hall looking for Nikki, but once Holly had learned about the story she was chasing, she'd sent the reporter away.

"Come on, the biggest story in Phantom Heights just unfolded between Jay and Azar, and I'm not allowed to report a single word about it," Caslynn had complained. "All I have for a consolation story is a child imagining that one of the Alpha ghosts is actually Phantom. That I can work with. I'll be careful."

"Andy has an overactive imagination," Holly had dismissed. "And I do hope Nikki disciplines him for behaving so recklessly in the middle of a crisis. He put himself in danger, not to mention the hostage."

Caslynn had insisted, "It's an innocent story. The kid believes his hero has returned, and he claims Phantom even has a girlfriend. I truly think I can soften up some of the hostile opinions of the Alpha ghosts if people are able to make a connection between them and Phantom."

"You can't report that," Holly had said, perhaps a little too quickly. Caslynn had folded her arms, suddenly alert to the councilwoman's distress. Holly had to clear her throat before continuing more calmly, "Nothing about the Alpha ghosts is allowed in the local news. For their own protection."

"I know that," Caslynn had replied with a casual wave of her hand. "I'll write in the Rogue Code."

"No." Holly had remained firm. Sure, on the surface the story was innocent enough, but what if it made people start to wonder if maybe there was some truth to it? If Seph came under close scrutiny, someone was bound to discover his true identity. "It's too risky. I forbid it."

"*Forbid* it? You were never in favor of this deal with the Alpha ghosts. Why are you suddenly so concerned about their safety?"

"If you run this story, there will be legal action taken against you. Am I clear?"

Holly had sent the fuming reporter away. She'd never seen Caslynn so angry before, her hands shaking, face flushed, as if she wanted nothing more than to wring Holly's neck. Her frustration was understandable. Nothing made a good reporter more furious than censorship. And yet, Caslynn's final venomous glares were not what had imprinted in Holly's mind. She couldn't care less if she'd made another enemy.

He claims Phantom even has a girlfriend . . .

Could that be true? Holly, still waiting for Madison's reply, leaned her shoulder against the window frame. A girlfriend. Ash, that was the Alpha girl's name, wasn't it? Cato and Ash. Holly allowed a small smile to appear for a moment before she composed herself. Maybe all her guilt was superfluous. Cato's life at the AGC couldn't have been too miserable if he'd managed to fall in love.

She was aware that the phone had been silent for a long time. "Madison? Are you still there?"

"I am," the ghost hunter said weakly. "I'm just . . . I need some time to think."

Holly frowned. "What is there to think about? Don't tell me you're losing your nerve."

"I'm not. I will do my job without hesitation. But I have to ask you, Holly . . . does S-O-S have anything to do with what happened to your son? Are you trying to make a point?"

Holly stiffened immediately. "I should ask you the same question."

"This anti-kálos campaign isn't going to change what happened . . . to either of them."

Holly's focus shifted ever so slightly from the humans in town square to her own reflection watching from the glass. She looked pale in her white blouse, transparent. Ghostly. "Enough," she snarled into the phone. "My head is clear. Yours needs to be, too."

The line went dead.

— Chapter Thirty-Eight —

Shades of Gray

Jay hadn't roused since passing out.

I had to refrain myself from constantly checking to make sure he was still breathing. *A burnout, that's all*, I kept telling myself. *He just needs to sleep it off, and he'll be fine.* But he needed to hurry, because I could already feel any perception of control I might have had slipping through my fingers.

I held my palm up, idly channeling my power to form a delicate ice crystal, its irregular facets catching the sunlight streaming through the windows and casting tiny rainbows on the walls. After the catastrophe with Azar, I'd decided we should regroup and strategize, although really I just wanted everybody safe inside Proto for a while so I could worry a bit less. Surely Madison and her team were capable of handling their town for a few hours.

I didn't know why I was trying so hard not to look as terrified as I felt. Axel sensed it, the twins could read my mind, Kit was too perceptive for her own good, and no doubt Ash and RC had noticed how I'd been fidgeting with Vivian's bracelet before tucking it away in favor of distracting myself with ice. They didn't comprehend the gravity of our dilemma. Our only value to the humans was as their mercenaries. If they'd lost faith we were capable of doing that job . . .

I poured more power into the ice crystal suspended over my palm and watched it swell.

Axel folded his arms and grumbled, "Why the hell is everybody moping like it's the end of the world?" When he failed to stir up responses from us, he continued, "So what if everyone knows we're young? We'll just have to remind them why they feared us in the first place."

"*We*?" RC asked.

Axel paused. "I still ain't fighting for humans. But I'd *really* love to get my hands on Azar."

Without taking my eyes off the ice crystal in my hand, I warned, "Just cool it. It's one thing to fight him if he comes here again, but you shouldn't go out looking for trouble. We have enough problems as it is."

I summoned ectoplasm to the same hand that was holding the crystal and let the light shine through so speckles of green danced on the walls in place of rainbows. I had to keep it together a little longer. Just until Jay was well enough to take control again. I glanced over at him to make sure his chest was still rising and falling. The ice exploded with a tiny *pop!* when I accidentally released too much ectoplasm.

"You okay?" Ash asked.

I hung my head, setting my hands on my knees and curling my fingers into tight fists. "No," I whispered. "It's over."

"It isn't—"

"Yes, it is. I know when Jay wakes up he's going to deny this, but the truth is we've taken Phantom's place." I peered up to find Ash shaking her head in rebuttal, but before she could speak, I said, "We fight ghosts to protect humans. My life Before ended the moment my mask was pulled off. And our masks were just yanked away today. You know what comes next?"

Ash's wide eyes smoldered like embers as she stared at me. Finn and Reese remained stone-faced and impassive while Kit crawled under RC's arm and snuggled against him. Axel wore an odd expression of bitterness and worry, denial slowly being cracked by reason. I stared out the window at the beautiful park. I understood their attachment to Phantom Heights; I really did. But clutching at fantasies wasn't worth being sent back to that place.

Ash quietly asked, "But what does that mean for us? Our backup plan was to escape into the Ghost Realm. That's not really an option anymore . . . is it?"

"I don't know," I admitted.

"We got company," Axel announced.

Despite the early warning, I started at a knock on the door. Sure enough, the werewolf's voice on the other side called, "Hello? Anybody home?"

We exchanged looks, but no one answered. Wes heaved a sigh on the other side. "Will somebody please talk to me?" After another pause, he said, "Ah-hem, uh, I was hoping you would grace me with your presence at dinner tonight. What do you say? Not to brag, but I'm an exceptional cook."

I wasn't sure if that statement was supposed to entice us into joining him for dinner or if he was indeed bragging, but my skepticism didn't waver. Ash leaned forward and whispered, "He's never invited us to dinner before. Why now?" I shrugged.

"Come on," Wes pleaded through the door. "One dinner with Ero and me? I'm your host, and you're my guests, and we haven't really acted our parts, have we?"

"Think there's a catch?" RC muttered.

"With Wes?" I whispered darkly. "There's always a catch."

His calloused hand scraped down the wood. "Well, if you'll join me, I would be honored. Dinner will be served at six o'clock. I really do hope to see you there."

In one unanimous motion, everyone turned to me. The weight Jay had placed on my shoulders doubled, crushing me. Did he always feel this way when we turned to him, waiting for his decision, relying on his judgment?

I had to think about my answer, and despite the impatience of my lab-siblings, I wouldn't be rushed. I had to consider Wes's motives. What would Jay do? Part of me wanted to wake him and ask for guidance; the other part didn't want my lab-siblings to see me fail to make a simple decision by myself.

By the sixth chime of the grandfather clock, the six of us were standing in the grand dining room. The long table was set with glistening silverware and clear glasses beneath the crystal chandelier. Though

I wouldn't admit it, part of what had swayed my decision was the mouthwatering aroma of cooking meat. I had promised Kit that I'd sneak her some since she couldn't join us.

Ero and Wes were already seated. Wes had anticipated our attendance; every place at the table was set, every plate heaped with steaming food. Our host beamed and stood, extending his arms in exuberant welcome. "Friends, I'm so glad you decided to join us."

"I ain't your friend," Axel grumbled. He clearly didn't care whether or not Wes saw his face now that our youth had been exposed; he plopped down in a chair as far from Wes as possible and threw back his hood. Strands of his coal-black hair hung over the blindfold still masking part of his face. Ash, RC, and I kept our hoods on as we chose our seats. Finn and Reese sat next to their teacher.

We'd learned after years of cruelty at that place to not hesitate with food or it would be taken away. As soon as we sat, we were using our fingers to shovel food into our mouths. Wes watched us, surprised, then shrugged and set down his fork and supplemented it with his fingers. Ero smiled politely but continued to use his silverware.

I wasn't sure what I was devouring, but Wes's self-proclaimed title of "exceptional cook" was valid from my perspective. I'd initially been disappointed to see rice on the plate, as that was often an Arena prize that was only a slight improvement over our usual meals. But Wes had done something to this rice—it was brown, not white, and seasoned in some kind of sauce with sautéed vegetables. I couldn't identify the meat on my plate, but it was tender and juicy on the inside and crusted with breadcrumbs and spices on the outside. Fresh green beans were piled beside a fluffy white tomato wrapped in brown skin—wait, no, *potato*—that was glistening with butter, herbs, a dollop of creamy white sauce, and bits of something salty and crunchy. A golden-brown roll was perched on the edge of my plate, and I discovered that I could mop up the sauces to pack even more flavor into the soft bread. This was ecstasy. This was the first true, home-cooked meal we'd had Outside, not counting the cold but tasty lasagna Jay had brought Home after his first meeting with Wes.

As I scarfed down my meal, I gripped the edge of my chair with my left hand and let the cold power flow, sending tendrils of ice creeping down the legs. I was going to have to be extremely careful not to lose focus and let my left eye turn green. As if this weren't doomed to be challenging enough.

Axel, Finn, and Reese hadn't touched their food yet. The twins kept stealing desperate, starving glances at Wes. "You can eat," I told them through my mouthful. They looked at me, then back to our host, still waiting. I swallowed and said, "Wes, tell them it's okay."

"Yeah," he said in puzzlement. "Dig in." Only then did the twins oblige. I watched Wes as I chewed. He hadn't said anything beyond the vapid welcome, and I wondered if, despite having the meal prepared for us, maybe he hadn't really expected us to join him for dinner. He awkwardly cleared his throat, inadvertently causing Finn and Reese to sit straight up as if they'd been electrocuted, eyes glowing, awaiting a silent order. "Hi. Hello. Um . . . thank you for coming."

We gazed silently at him, adding to his discomfort. Axel bowed his head and snickered. His open mockery made Wes even more flustered, although I suspected that had been his intention.

The werewolf drummed his fingers on the tabletop. "Listen, I . . . I just want to say that I'm not . . . well, to be honest, I'm not really sure what to do now. I mean, don't get me wrong, you've been great houseguests so far. Low maintenance, no trouble . . . In fact, I've barely even seen any of you since you moved in. But Maddie seems to expect me to . . . Look, I'm not a father."

We stared at him. Axel tipped his chair back on two legs and burst into wild laughter. "Are you sure, Wes? I really wanted to start calling you Daddy."

Above Axel's chortles, I said, "Nothing has to change. We don't need you to take care of us."

Wes exhaled, visibly relieved. "Okay, good. Good, we're, uh, we're on the same page then." He nodded as if reaffirming, and then he sneered, as if he'd suddenly remembered a joke. He glanced at each of us in turn. "So . . . the deadly Alpha gang sits before me. You really caught everyone off guard. Aren't you a little young to be playing superhero?"

A few moments of silence passed before I remembered Jay wasn't here to rebut. "*You* employed us," I said.

"I employed who I thought were powerful warriors," Wes retorted.

"You did," I said with a wan smile.

Wes leaned back in his chair, looking much more at ease now that he'd identified me as the surrogate leader. "You know Tarrow is having a fit about all of you now, right?"

Axel said airily, "Yeah, we know she's a bitch."

There was a moment of silence I habitually expected Jay to fill with a warning, but when his scolding didn't come, the words fell meekly from my own tongue: "Watch it."

I'd never corrected Axel like that before. Heat flushed my cheeks when he snapped back, "She is. And don't pretend to be Jay."

Although Wes didn't verbally concur, he made a face and shrugged in silent agreement. "Here's the thing—Maddie can wave her gun around all she wants, but this is really *my* town. I paid to rebuild it. Phantom Heights exists because of me."

I gaped at him. Was he really so naïve he thought humankind wouldn't turn on him because he'd paid to build their homes?

Axel mumbled, "Big talk for a dog."

"I am *not* a dog, and I suggest you show me a little more respect considering I gave *you* a home, too."

I cringed and braced for the explosion. Just in case, I touched the whistle.

Axel snarled. Tendrils of ectoplasm flickered around his forearms just for a moment before dissipating, but I could still detect the venom in his voice when he seethed, "I don't need *anything* from a mongrel like you. And if I were at the bottom of the power ladder—or lower, since you're pretty much human in that form—I'd think twice before talking down to someone who's a hell of a lot stronger than you."

Wes snarled back, "And if I were a kid like you, I'd show some respect to your superiors."

My fingers tightened around the whistle. "Stop," I intervened before Axel could retort. "Please." Though I lacked the authority Jay somehow mustered when requesting anything of the half-breed, Axel did give me the courtesy of pausing.

He bowed his head and grumbled, "Moron ain't worth my time anyways."

Ash leaned forward and shyly asked, "Mr. Cooper?"

"Please don't call me that. Wes is fine."

"Sorry. Wes. Does Mrs. Tarrow expect us to replace Phantom?"

Whether or not it had been her goal, her quiet voice effectively shattered the tension between the werewolf and half-nydæa. Though I deliberately kept my head stationary, my eyes swiveled to find Wes. I gripped the chair tighter, my food temporarily forgotten.

Surprised by the question, he repeated, "*Replace* Phantom? Of course not. Nobody expects you to replace Phantom."

I knew Jay would disapprove, but after briefly weighing the consequences, I said in a low voice, "If you ask me, we've not only replaced Phantom, we've surpassed him."

The werewolf's gaze bored into me. "You'd better not let anyone hear you talk like that."

I really wanted to press the issue, but I'd aggravated it enough already, so I bit my tongue and silently stewed while I nibbled at my food. A sharp elbow jab into my rib cage made me glance at RC, who frowned and pointed to his eye. I understood and redirected my focus onto my melting ice to change my green eyes back to blue.

Oblivious, Wes went on, "You know, Phantom ended up at the same place you escaped from."

"Is that so?" I kept my eyes down and voice neutral as I popped a green bean into my mouth.

"Yeah. And get this, I heard Maddie received Phantom's file from the AGC a few days ago."

I gasped. Unfortunately, I hadn't had time to swallow or even chew the bean, which flew to the back of my throat. Everybody stared at me while I choked and seized my glass, but I ended up spraying half of the water back up in the fit. Eyes watering, I rasped, "Why . . . the hell . . . does Madison . . . have m—Phantom's records?"

"To study them, I presume," said Wes said. He was watching me, baffled by my overreaction. "Phantom has always been a mystery, and Maddie's been wanting to get her hands on those documents for some time." I was still trying to contain my coughs. Ash graciously handed me her water. "Why do you care that she has Phantom's records?"

"I don't."

Bloody Scout, even swallowing hurt. Wes folded his arms, scrutinizing me with alarming intensity. "I bet you came into this Realm through the Rip, didn't you, Seph? Did you meet Phantom?"

"No."

Had I said that too quickly? Probably, because he was eyeing me doubtfully. I glanced across the table and thought, *Ero, if you can hear my thoughts, give me a sign.*

The Telepath and everyone else was watching me. I waited for a small nod of the head, or a wink, or any indication that he'd heard me, but he didn't move.

I can hear you.

I jumped in surprise. Ero's voice chuckled in my head. *Do not be alarmed. Just think what you want to say.*

This is really weird. Too late, I realized Ero heard that. I quickly channeled my thoughts into the inquiry, *Does Wes know?*

He is fishing. He has not connected you to Phantom . . . yet. I will caution you to be careful with your answers, though.

Ash cleared her throat, jerking me from the silent conversation taking place in my mind. She was fiddling with her napkin and kept her eyes downcast when she said, "Wes, um, I have a question. A-bout Phantom." She took a deep breath after the stutter before looking the werewolf in the eye. "Are the humans planning to send us away like they did to him?"

"Whoa, now wait just a minute," Wes answered loudly, his face reddening as if Ash had offended him personally. She shrank deeper into her chair. "I think you have a gross misunderstanding of what actually happened."

I bristled. Ero, knowing I wanted to challenge that statement, held up his hand to warn me not to speak. He said, "Perhaps for their benefit, you could explain what happened."

Wes shrugged. "Bad circumstances. Phantom happened to be in the wrong place at the wrong time."

"It was more than that," I seethed, slamming my palms on the table and making everyone jump. The hot power resurfaced for a moment, long enough that my blue eyes probably flickered green. *Damn it, if I don't keep my power in check, this is going to turn into a disaster.*

Wes stared me down and challenged, "For someone who claims not to have met Phantom, you seem to think you know an awful lot about him. I happened to have met him, so between the two of us, I think my account is a little more credible, don't you?"

I glowered at him. It was all I could do to keep the cold blue power above the hot green one.

Quieter, Wes said, "I was there the day the Agents took Phantom away. I promise you, every single person standing in town square was in shock. No one wanted that to happen. He was their hero. This entire town fell apart after we lost him; I doubt anyone is willing to gamble that the same outcome won't happen again if the Agents take you away, too." He scratched his neck. "You know, there are so many other things we could talk about. This wasn't meant to be a business meeting, but while you're all here, I do have some business to discuss."

I might have challenged his not-so-subtle change in topic had I not realized what a dangerous slope we were sliding on, so I let it go. He set an envelope on the table. "I have your first payment from the city. Now, I can give you the check and let you deal with the hassle of creating a bank account and buying what you need, or you can let me handle your finances. I'd be more than happy to use your money to buy clothes and whatever else you need and invest the rest into a savings account for you. I'd . . . take out a small fee for my services, of course, and I do have to buy food and basic household—"

"Fine," I dismissed without much thought.

Wes acted surprised that I'd agreed so quickly, but we really didn't comprehend the value of human money. I could identify it, sure, but it was just paper and metal; I doubted I'd appreciate its proper worth. We had little need of currency as long as Wes provided everything we needed. My only fear was developing too deep of a dependence on the unreliable werewolf, but I didn't think Jay would object to my decision.

My mind was still buzzing with Wes's news of Madison having my file. I felt violated, knowing that she was reviewing every invasive test Dr. Anders had conducted on me. Why? Did Madison view me as a science experiment, or was she trying to find the Origin, too? Either way, the ghost hunter with her hands on my test results from that place was nothing but bad news. I bet I could steal them from her. How hard could it be?

I shouldn't have, but I'd tuned out the ongoing conversation. What jarred me from my contemplations was Wes finishing a sentence with, ". . . A6?"

Immediately, the atmosphere flexed to the point of suffocation, though the werewolf's eyes were shining with gold flecks in his eagerness. A dark chuckle broke the quiet, directing my attention to Axel, who was sneering. "A6," he murmured, leaning forward. "You're stupider than I took you for."

"Curious," Wes corrected. "You've seen the beast, right?"

Axel leaned back, amused. Although none of us answered, Wes rambled, "Is it really the most powerful being in the Realms? Level 9? What does it look like? What kind of hybrid is it?"

Axel clasped his hands behind his head. "If you're a smart dog, you won't mess with A6."

Wes fought a smile. "I just . . . can't imagine that much strength and power in one individual. I wish I could see A6."

"Is that a death wish?"

I reached for my glass and took a drink. The cold water soothed my irritated throat. Wes leaned back, lost in his disturbing thoughts of monsters. "Well," Ero said, drawing out the word as he spread butter on a roll, "I know everyone is a bit tense about Azar's appearance today, but there is some good news about him knowing of your youth. You do have a limited degree of protection now."

I peered at the Telepath over the glass, then slowly lowered it back onto the table. "What do you mean?"

"Oh, yeah," Wes cut in. "The age decree."

Ero replaced the butter knife on the table and inclined his head. "Correct." To the rest of us, he explained, "In Avilésor, murder is not taboo like it is here. There are many blood feuds between families, and oftentimes battles end in a fight to the death. However, regardless of the circumstances, it is illegal to kill a child who has not yet reached the first coming of age."

His announcement should have eased me, but all I could say was, "So . . . when Azar threatened to execute Jay if we followed . . . he was bluffing?"

Ero, who had raised the roll to his mouth and already parted his lips for the first bite, paused. He set the bread back on his plate and sent me a compassionate expression across the table as he sensed my guilt. "Most likely, yes."

I closed my eyes briefly. I'd made a mistake, then. The team had been mine to lead, and I'd just stood there like a brainless idiot when Jay was dragged away. The real leader would have called Azar's bluff. My miscalculation could have cost me a lab-brother.

Ero soothed, "But may I remind you that even though it is against Law, Azar bends and breaks the rules to his liking, and no one can stop him. That, and there is more to Azar's strength than just his Divinity and sway over Law. Let us not forget those who serve him."

"Hassing," I said immediately.

"Yes, but there are others. Captain Hassing is second-in-command, the one who reports directly to Azar. He and Titon have a formidable reputation."

Ash asked, "Who's Titon?"

Wes and Ero both looked at her. The werewolf replied, "Hassing's mount—a black valdenar."

Her face still blank, Ash stammered, "I . . . I'm sorry, I don't . . ."

Ero patiently explained, "A cross between a unicorn and a zephr."

"Hassing rides a winged unicorn?" Axel snickered. "Wow, that sounds intimidating."

"Don't think so lightly of a valdenar," Wes warned. "Despite the lack of respect humans in this Realm have for unicorns, I can assure you there's absolutely nothing whimsical about them. They're big, dangerous animals. One kick can break your skull, and their horns are sharper than any sword. Valdenars are worth a small fortune on the Black Market. In fact, I heard Titon was a colt being sold on the Market when Azar led one of his raids. Titon was confiscated merchandise, a gift from Azar himself to Hassing."

Ero finished, "With Titon, Hassing can easily outrun you on the ground or swoop down on top of you from above. Then there are two lieutenants beneath the captain."

"Cisco and Inalli," Wes recited.

"Correct. One to command the Shadow Guard, the other to rule the Prison Guard."

"And don't forget Veto."

"Ah, yes." A shadow seemed to pass over Ero's face. "Veto. He is the torture master—an Inflictor. His power is pain. He can ignite every nerve in your body in the most intense agony you have ever experienced."

Wes added, "You know why they call him Veto, right?" We all stared at him in silence, even Ero. Wes lowered his voice theatrically. "Because nobody, not even his own parents, wanted him. I heard he was the only kid ever rejected from the Youth Training Program. There's something wrong with him, mentally, you know? Azar hired him as a mercenary because he wasn't fit to be a real Shadow Guard."

Ero sternly said, "Do you have any basis for that tale, or are you simply spreading rumors?"

"You know it has to be true," Wes retorted.

"Regardless, with Hassing, Cisco, Inalli, and Veto carrying out his orders, plus his Amínyte slave turning any corvid into a spy, Azar has absolute control over Avilésor."

"Avilésor," Axel repeated, brash in his overconfidence. "Not this Realm."

"No," Ero agreed. But he added ominously, "Not yet."

Wes said, "Azar's gotta be fuming after losing Jay. And if he doesn't already know *you* are here, he's going to be even more pissed when he finds out."

Ero coolly replied, "I do not view Azar as my enemy."

"He sure sees you as one."

"Why?" I asked.

Wes took a drink before answering, "Telepathy is an incredible Divinity. Obviously, Azar would love to recruit as many Telepaths as he can, but thanks to Ero, his ranks are practically nonexistent."

Ero gave us a reassuring smile. "Not intentionally. The time I spend with my students so early in their development forms a close bond. Although I do not forcibly impose my own morals onto my students, I suppose I leave an impression on them by the end of their training. Shall we say, most are not keen on volunteering to join the Shadow Guard."

Wes muttered under his breath, "Something Azar's never forgiven you for."

I hadn't seen Axel take a single bite, and yet his plate was somehow half-empty, only the vegetables and rice left. I was alarmed and yet unsurprised to see a white-tipped tail under his chair. Damn them, why hadn't they forewarned me? I didn't know how good Wes's sense of smell was in his human form. If Kit was discovered . . .

I subtly watched the werewolf for any signs of suspicion, but he obliviously speared several green beans onto the tines of his fork, seeming not to notice the extra dinner guest. He continued, "Anyway, my bet is Azar will make the first move to hit the Agents before they're prepared. I think all that's holding him back is his reluctance to rush in without enough intel first, though he'll definitely retaliate if S-O-S rears its ugly head again."

"S-O-S?" I said, partly out of curiosity, partly out of dread, and partly to keep the conversation moving so Wes didn't happen to notice an Amínyte under the table. "I thought that was over."

Wes shoved the beans into his mouth and, between chews, he answered, "People are having doubts now that they know you aren't as old or powerful as they thought."

"Madison?"

Wes swallowed. "It's not that black and white. Maddie may be the face of S-O-S, but the masterminds behind the doctrine are the politicians. Idiots. There's a good reason the Agents are investing all their time and resources into a different kind of weapon. They could have sent the military in a long time ago, but they know better. Bullets might do some initial damage when kálos are caught unaware, but when they actually fight back . . . well, you know. Unless the bullets are made from vidon, they'll do no good against someone who's intangible. From what I've heard, it's Councilwoman Jennings who's really pushing S-O-S, although that's no surprise. She has a reputation for trying to pass tough anti-kálos ordinances. Let's just say she's out for kálos blood, which she expects Tarrow to deliver."

So. There was more to this than what was apparent on the surface. I was surprised by the relief I felt in knowing the exact nature of my mother's involvement, as if I'd been trying so hard to see the big picture that I had been forcing the wrong pieces into the puzzle, and Wes had just placed a few of the right ones in my hand. While the puzzle was still incomplete, I was closer to seeing the whole. It was much bigger than I'd thought, and though I might not understand how the maze of politics worked, I saw now that there were unseen forces to contend with.

"Question. How did you do it?" I asked quietly. Perhaps this wasn't the one I should be asking, but it was the only one that mattered all of a sudden. "How did you survive when Phantom couldn't?"

Wes had somehow traversed through the web of invisible lies and agendas in the game of politics when I'd been ensnared. Was there a secret? Was there a safe path to tread that could prevent my lab-family from getting tangled the same way I had?

"Hmm," the werewolf mused. It wasn't a question he'd expected, but it was definitely one he was intrigued by. "It's all about understanding and playing the system. Phantom's mistake was jumping into the hero role and asking for nothing in return. I waited until humankind was truly desperate before I revealed my hand. That's the key, right there. You have to make people *need* you. Actually, no, that's not entirely accurate. You have to make people *realize* they need you. At the end of the day, it's just a business deal. I could help you, if you'd like. I can help you make the right connections in both Realms."

The offer was enticing; it really was. Wes had an entire network to manipulate. But he was a cutthroat. He maintained connections only as long as they benefitted him. In fact, I was sure he'd be one of the first to betray us to *Them* or Azar in exchange for his own freedom.

Even without acceptance of his offer, he was already babbling: "First piece of advice—keep your heads down and just do your job. Don't try to get involved with the political side of this. They might appear to be allies, but there's a lot of friction between Maddie and Holly. And while we're on that topic, you should avoid Councilwoman Jennings altogether. There is no human in Phantom Heights with a stronger hatred of kálos. You'd have a better chance of forming an alliance with Maddie, who made a career out of hunting your kind professionally."

Irritated that my mother was still a part of this discussion, I snapped, "We aren't interested in an alliance with either of them."

No way Wes missed the acidity in my statement. It was enough to shock him into brief silence. My mind was spinning with so much information that I was having a hard time keeping my eyes blue. This room seemed smaller than it had when we'd first arrived. I was startled to realize I was standing. "Thank you for dinner."

My lab-family rose in immediate response, except Axel, who leaned his chair back on two legs without a care. Kit was gone; she must have snuck away unnoticed.

Wes stood. "Don't you want dessert?" I wasn't sure what he meant, but I shook my head. "Did . . . I say something wrong?"

"No," I said. "Good night."

— Chapter Thirty-Nine —
DNA

Shannon took a deep breath. She lifted her fist, exhaled, rapped her knuckles against the door, and then waited.

She swallowed hard, glancing left down the deserted road, then right. The streetlights were just now sputtering to life in the deep violet dusk. She shifted her weight, watching the black-and-silver ribbon tied around the doorknob flutter faintly in the evening's breeze sweetly fragranced by honeysuckle blooming in a neighbor's garden.

She jumped when the knob turned and the door opened. "Yes?"

Shannon swallowed again. "Hi, Mrs. Tarrow. I'm, uh, I'm sorry to bother you. I didn't interrupt your dinner, did I?"

"No. Is something wrong?"

"No," she said quickly. "Not wrong, I just . . . I-I wanted to ask a favor."

Madison looked her up and down, then glanced over Shannon's shoulder to see if she had company. "Would you like to come in?"

No. This is a bad idea.

"Yes. Thank you."

Madison opened the front door wider and stepped aside. Shannon followed, her throat tightening when she stepped over the threshold.

"Were you looking for Vivian? She's up in her room."

"No, Mrs. Tarrow. Actually, I came to see you. I . . . well, my mom doesn't know I'm here. Please don't tell her."

Madison closed the door. "Are you in trouble?"

"No. Like I said, I have a favor to ask. I understand . . . when my mom was pregnant with me . . . you did a DNA test."

Madison's eyebrows shot up. "Yes. I did."

"Would you do another one? Just to be sure?"

Madison was gazing intensely at Shannon. "Is there a particular reason you want the test done?"

Shannon clenched her jaw. All this stress made her want to break down in tears. "I know," she forced out. "Mom told me what happened to her. I just want to be sure."

Madison rubbed her chin, still nodding in silent deliberation. "Okay. I can do the test. If you want a quick yes or no, I can tell you in about five minutes. If you want me to completely analyze your genome, that'll take considerably longer, but I can—"

"A yes or no is all I need. What do you need from me? Blood?"

"Saliva will work just fine for the basic test," said Madison. "Why don't you come into the kitchen? I need to grab a swab from my lab."

"Okay." Shannon eyed the staircase, praying Vivian wouldn't come downstairs. She tucked her chin down and followed Madison through the living room, the carpet absorbing their footsteps until they reached the tiled floor. She lingered near the table by the window while Madison opened the basement door and descended the stairs, closing the door behind.

Shannon wiped her moist palms on the back pockets of her jeans, blinking back unbidden tears. Maybe the test would come back the same as it had before her birth. Or maybe it had been incorrect the first time. Older, less reliable technology. Or . . . maybe Madison had suspected that Shannon's life would have been terminated if she gave the wrong answer, so she gave the only one that would save the fetus, regardless of the true test results.

Footsteps on the stairs. Shannon swiped her thumb under each eye, careful to wipe away the evidence of tears without smearing her eyeliner. Madison opened the door and quickly shut it behind herself, as if there were something secret downstairs in the lab that she didn't want to escape.

"Okay," Madison said, standing in front of Shannon. "Open wide, please."

Shannon started to tremble. "Mrs. Tarrow . . . if the test results are

. . . not what they should be . . . do you promise you won't tell my mom? Or report it to the AGC?"

Madison lowered the swab, appraising Shannon, who could feel hot tears returning to make her vision swim. One overflowed and rolled down her cheek. "You have my word," Madison said gently.

Maybe she was too trusting, but Shannon believed her. She closed her eyes and opened her mouth. The swab made a quick, painless pass across the inside of her cheek.

"You can sit down and make yourself comfortable. We'll have the results in a few minutes."

"Thank you," Shannon whispered, probably too quietly for Madison to hear. The door closed behind the ghost hunter again, and Shannon was left alone in the kitchen with white cabinets, the faintest scents of lavender and vanilla from Madison's shampoo lingering in the air.

Shannon wandered to the table and pulled out a chair, then situated herself before allowing her shaking knees to give out. She clasped her hands together to keep them still.

Her thoughts had been tumultuous ever since the picnic. Spearheading the Safe Haven project had been a welcome distraction to lessen the constant worries gnawing on her mind, but lately the anxiety had been building and building until she couldn't catch her breath.

She'd spent hours with her nose less than an inch away from the surface of the bathroom mirror, staring at her reflected irises, wishing she had brown, gray, or hazel eyes, because then she'd know for sure she was human. But no, they were vibrant and green. Her mom's green eyes should have eased her worries; Shannon had the right genes for them. But ghosts had colorful eyes too—red, gold, violet, blue, *green*. Was she staring at human eyes in the mirror? Or ghost eyes that didn't glow because powers couldn't be passed to humans?

Except for Cato.

She thumbed away another pair of tears trying to journey toward her chin, her gaze locked on the basement door. What if Madison was calling her mom? Or the AGC? Maybe this was a mistake. Maybe Agent Kovak was already on his way to come throw Shannon into the back of the same transport truck that had carried Cato away.

Footsteps.

Shannon stood quickly when the door opened. Madison was examining a piece of paper on a clipboard. "Well?" Shannon blurted.

The ghost hunter used her foot to close the door. She peered up at Shannon and smiled warmly. "One hundred percent human."

The relief made Shannon so weak she was afraid she might melt onto the floor. "Are . . . are you sure?"

"Well, technically 99.99 percent human, but that's perfectly normal. A lot of us have a diluted drop of Avilésian blood in us thanks to our ancestors interacting with creatures and spirits from the Ghost Realm when Tears were more frequent. Here, take a look." She offered the clipboard. Feet planted at the risk of falling over if she tried to move, Shannon craned her neck to see. The dots on the paper might as well have been an alien language, and Madison's voice sounded far away at the end of a long tunnel as she pointed to various patterns and explained how the configuration would have been different if kálos DNA so close on the family tree had been present.

Shannon nodded, numb. "Thank you," she whispered.

"No trouble at all. I'm sorry your mom ever put the idea in your head. Crossing bloodlines between humans and ghosts is possible but extremely difficult. The DNA doesn't blend well, so the chances of you having mixed blood were astronomically slim. I didn't have any doubts about my findings the first time I tested your DNA, but I figured running the test again would ease your mind."

Shannon continued to nod. Why were the tears still coming? She sniffed, and then she couldn't contain the overwhelming relief anymore, and she threw her arms around Madison, sobbing.

Madison stood frozen for a second, startled by the outburst, and then she set the clipboard on the table and put her arms around Shannon. "I'm sorry," Shannon blubbered into Madison's shoulder. Sorry for letting these raw emotions out—sorry for going behind her mom's back—sorry for Cato, whose test results hadn't been so lucky. The tears wouldn't stop. She sniffed to keep her nose from running, breathing in the sweet scents of lavender and vanilla and finding them inexplicably soothing.

Madison rubbed her back with a mother's soft touch. Shannon hic-cupped her sobs under control and pulled away, swiping her fist across her eyes without concern for the eyeliner no doubt smeared across her face now. "Thank you. I'm sorry I bothered you. I should go."

"Do you want to take the test results with you?"

"No. I don't want Mom to know what I did. Please destroy them." Shannon backed away. "Thank you, Mrs. Tarrow."

Azar ran his finger down the list of printed names. The ancient book on his desk was massive, but it was only the last page that had his attention. As his black fingernail passed over the final name, he leaned back in his chair. "No Jay," he said quietly. "Tell me, Rayven, isn't it Law for all newborns to be reported in the Census?"

His voice was calm. Too calm in the wake of the storm his fury had unleashed when his prisoner had disappeared. Rayven had huddled in a corner while Azar screamed and cursed, threw objects across the room, slammed doors, and broke windows. The poor captain had to endure a long rant about how Cisco would have been a more valuable asset on the mission. Azar had turned a deaf ear when Hassing reminded him that the lieutenant's sensing Divinity had been ineffective on the Alpha fugitives during his last mission in Cröendor, and when Hassing tried to explain that Cisco was unavailable because he was leading a raid on the Black Market, Azar had bellowed, "Then you should have led the raid, and I should have taken Cisco with me instead!"

Even after the anger had cooled, after Azar had dismissed Hassing and requested Rayven to fetch the Census, after Rayven had retrieved the heavy book and staggered down the long hallways to deliver it to his master before cowering in the corner again, the Amínyte was still braced for residual rage to cause him pain. Trembling, he stuttered, "Y-yes, sir. It is Law."

"I see," Azar murmured, still horrifyingly composed. "Then answer this: for what reason would a child's name not be listed?"

Rayven wrung his hands together. "Ah, w-well, children born of slaves in the Black Market would not be reported. Kálos children born in Cröendor aren't written in that book either, nor are those whose parents violated Law and live in hiding."

Azar rubbed his chin. "All plausible explanations," he acknowledged. Rayven shuddered and sank lower to the floor as the tension in his muscles melted with relief. The Warden leaned over the book again, this time skimming for a different name. "So . . . let us see if there is an Axel . . . ah." A smile parted his lips as his finger stopped. "Well, well. Our young friend Axel has fourteen years now, born of a Remote named Vera and a Xenogloss named Simial."

Azar's features suddenly twisted into a violent scowl that caused Rayven to cringe deeper into the darkening shadows. *Remote-viewing, the ability to gather information by meditating, and xenoglossy, the ability to temporarily know any language instantly after hearing or reading only a few words*, Azar mentally reviewed. *Both low-level Divinities, passive and altogether unthreatening.*

"Insolent pest," he seethed, "challenging me like that. Based on his bloodlines, he must have a weak passive power, no higher than a Level 2 at best. Who does he think he is to threaten *me*?"

Azar shook his head, jaw set, and after a few breaths to calm himself, he turned his attention back to the Census. "Vera and Simial," Azar said. "Why are those names familiar?"

"I don't know, sir," said Rayven.

Azar glared at the Census. In the last nineteen years, only fifty-three children had been recorded. As Rayven had pointed out, there were probably a dozen or so unlisted. Rayven himself was not in the Census; he'd been born in an illegal Amínyte breeding facility tied to the Black Market. Azar had only two Alpha names to search, but the others must be in here.

He closed the book with slow, thoughtful deliberateness. So, Project Alpha required children. But why? Children were weak with undeveloped Divinities. If the Agents wanted to build a weapon, what contribution could such young kálos possibly make? The real power lay in the elders, not the young. And yet, this could play to Azar's advantage. Humans torturing innocent kálos children . . . that could be the spark of anger he needed to unite a revolution; all he had to do was fan the flame.

Azar leaned back in his chair. "Do you want to know something strange, Rayven? When I looked into Jay's eyes, I saw fear. But I also saw defiance. Do you know how long it's been since someone looked at me like that? It was . . . almost exhilarating." His gaze flicked over to his slave still cowering silently in the corner. "Isn't that curious?"

Rayven didn't answer, but Azar hadn't expected him to. The Warden glanced at the game board on the desk, the only object in the room that hadn't been thrown or smashed. Partly to Rayven, partly aloud to himself, he said softly, "I think it's time to change the game."

The park was quiet.

Wonderfully, mercifully quiet in the middle of the night, just the lull of shallow waves on the lake gently slapping the pilings below. I sat on the pier, alone, the serenity lost in the hurricane of disturbing thoughts ripping me apart. Did Jay ever have to do this? To leave the family and be alone to try and make sense of it all?

Still numb, I replayed a conversation I'd had with Axel after dinner. "You ain't gonna like what I have to say," he'd warned.

I should have listened, but like an idiot, I'd challenged, "Just say it."

Axel had fidgeted, uncharacteristically uncomfortable. When he finally spoke, his voice was subdued. "It wasn't easy to make me like this, you know. Genetics, physiology, decades of research. Every single detail was recorded in my file."

Annoyed, I had snapped, "What does this have to do with me? The Flash wasn't documented, so *They* couldn't put any details like that in my file."

"I'm not talking about that file."

"I . . . I don't understand what you're . . ."

"You know exactly what I'm saying. You and me, we're both mistakes, but it takes a lot of effort to defy nature. Can you look me in the eye and tell me, without any doubt, that you're *sure* you were an accident?"

His words fell with an odd ring, like a hammer striking a metallic note in my ears. What he was implying was . . . crazy. All I could stutter was, "I . . . you . . . th-that's insane. *You're* insane. The Flash was an accident."

"Well," he'd said softly, "there's only one person who knows for sure. And that person now has your file from *Them*. You don't think that's a little suspicious?"

I yanked off my boots, removed my socks, and then rolled up my pant legs before dangling my feet off the edge of the pier and into the water. The Flash had been an accident. Madison hadn't known I was there . . . had she?

I summoned my blue power and lifted my hand. A pearl of ice rose from the surface, rotating slowly, then faster, spinning, growing, engorged by delicate frozen crystals rising from the lake like snow falling in reverse. I refused to believe Axel's theory. Accepting such madness would mean the ghost hunter had experimented on me against my will.

My hand fell, and the ice plopped into the lake. I extended my Divinity to push it down, down, deeper into the depths. What if the accident had been staged? What if Madison was in her lab right now with two files? What if she was comparing her notes about my transformation to *Their* findings?

A face was staring at me from the water. I jolted, startled when Chelvistin rose from the surface. The sirien held up her hand, her webbed fingers clutching a solid orb. "Ice floats," she told me, followed by a knowing smile. "It takes a Cryokinetic to make this sink to the bottom. I thought I'd find you here, Phantom."

"I told you, my name isn't Phantom anymore."

Chel just blinked her large eyes at me.

We both froze at an eerie cry in the night that sent a shiver rippling across my skin. I looked up just in time to see grotesque, winged creatures pass over the moon. Demons, I would have called them, but Chel said, "Gargoyles."

"You mean the stone sculptures on buildings?"

"No, I mean the ones from Avilésor. Nasty little beasts. If you see a gargoyle on a building in Avilésor, it's no sculpture. It can sit completely still for days without moving, waiting to swoop on prey."

I chewed the inside of my cheek in deliberation. I should probably track down and kill those monsters before they swarmed a human, but I didn't move. Obsessed with my current train of thought, I said, "Question. How do you find an answer when you can't ask the only witness?"

Chel pondered my riddle. "Hmm . . . I'd consult a Seer."

She didn't even question the peculiarity of my inquiry. But, disappointed with her solution, I grumbled, "The answer I need is in the past, not the future."

"A Seer's Divinity isn't limited to precognition; they use retrocognition, too. If a past event had enough of an impact to affect your Future, they'll know. But their services aren't cheap."

My head was swimming. A Seer. How would I even find one?

Chel set her arms on the pier and rested her chin on them. I stared at the scaly crest along the outside of each forearm. She asked, "Why do you need a Seer?"

I glared out at the dark water. "No reason."

"Come on, Phantom. You can tell me."

My head drooped, and I glanced away at the rustle of a bird in the tree off to my right to avoid Chel's unblinking gaze. "There's nothing to tell."

"You're not a very good liar." She raised her tail, moonlit jeweled droplets rolling down her scales and falling into the black water in a symphony of ripples. "Heard your leader got hurt. Does that mean you're in charge now?"

"Yes." I slowly kicked my feet, watching the water curl with the motion and spawn tiny whirlpools away from my ankles. "I don't suppose you've heard any rumors about what Azar is up to?"

Chel lowered her tail so it floated on the surface. "Other than he's been recruiting more Shadow Guards, no."

"S-O-S . . . what do you think about that?"

"I think the humans are losing their minds, that's what I think. Let me tell you something: the reason Azar hasn't really fought back yet is because he's waiting. He doesn't just want to the send the Shadow Guard through the Rip; he could've done that ages ago. He wants the support of every kálos in Avilésor backing his military strength. That

Realm has been in discord for a long time. Azar needs to unite the people to his cause. He's counting on the Agents' secret weapon to accomplish that, but if humankind does something stupid like S-O-S first, well, that's just the sort of push Azar is waiting for. Doesn't really matter to me one way or another. I'll still have my lake, regardless of who has dominion over the land."

My feet stilled. I stared at the moon's reflection on the tranquil water, troubled by her words. "I wish I could live here with you and not have to deal with any of this."

"You'd drown," she said bluntly.

I shot her a look from the corner of my eye; I hadn't intended my statement to be taken literally. I rubbed the ports in my forehead.

Chelvistin, bored with my insistent lack of conversation, bid me good night. I thought I answered. She dipped below the glassy surface, leaving me alone in the silence to think my disturbing thoughts. Axel had said something else to me after dinner, something that still echoed: "We're in the one place Outside that has the answers about what happened to you. And you haven't even tried to find them."

I stared at the final ripple of Chelvistin's departure. He was right. Rather than confront my past, I'd shied away from it. And yet, on the eve of war, questioning the past seemed like a waste of time.

Madison had barely slept in her bed since that mysterious envelope arrived from the AGC. She stayed locked in her lab, alone, poring over the file, looking for . . . Vivian didn't know what.

Wrapped in a soft robe, Vivian stood in the dark kitchen. It was after midnight; surely her mom must be asleep by now. Every move Vivian made was slow and deliberate—turning the knob, easing open the door, tiptoeing on bare feet down the basement steps. She gingerly opened the second door at the bottom of the stairs. A desk light was on in the lab to guide her way. The machines along the wall were silent, no lights or humming to indicate they were running. Disassembled parts from a dozen ectoguns were scattered across the table.

Her mom, as Vivian had predicted, was sitting on a stool at her worktable, her arms cradling her head, chest rising and falling with deep, even breaths.

"It wouldn't matter if we were ninety-nine percent human; that wouldn't be good enough. You look at our glowing eyes, and you hate us," Seph had said. Madison had brushed his words away without a second thought, but Vivian had been mulling over his word choice. Ninety-nine percent human . . . was Seph referring to mixed blood?

Phantom . . . that raised a whole new mess of questions she had no answers to. As she lingered in the doorway, her mind started to wander, and she didn't stop it.

Cato, fourteen then, sat at the kitchen table next to her in the afternoon light. He groaned and slumped forward, sprawling over the books, papers, calculator, and pencils scattered on the tabletop.

"It doesn't make any sense, Viv," he said, his voice muffled behind his arm.

She'd been a patient tutor, but even she could feel the weariness and frustration weighing her down. It was an effort to not show it; anything less than a positive and encouraging attitude would no doubt shut Cato down. He was dangerously close to quitting as it was. "Don't you give up on me," she ordered, her voice gentle. "You know this." Cato didn't raise his head, and she teased, "Are you trying a new method? Absorbing algebra through your skin?"

Disgruntled, he shifted enough to shove the book away so he could set his cheek on the cool wood, his eyes still covered in the crook of his arm. "Math isn't supposed to have letters in it."

Vivian pushed her chair back and stood. The sound of the legs sliding on the tiled floor made Cato turn his head to peer curiously over his arm at her with one green eye. She grinned at him and said, "I think I still have my notes from that class up in my room. They might help, since yours suck. No offense." That coaxed a weak smile out of him.

When she'd turned her back on him draped over the kitchen table, she'd had no idea that would be the last time she would see him as a human. To this day, she wondered what it was that had driven Cato to his fate. After she'd left, had green light spilled from the edges of the basement door and beckoned him? Was that what had caused him to rise and open the door, to wander down the stairs, so focused on the light that he hadn't paid attention to the note taped to the door at the bottom of the steps warning to stay out?

And then the explosion, the blast so violent it had knocked Vivian off her feet on the second story. She'd been standing here—right *here* in this exact spot at the foot of the basement steps—when she found her mom kneeling over Cato's body. Vivian had been certain he was dying. His body was racked by intense shivers, his skin clammy and pale, his breaths shallow, his eyes wild and unseeing. But still green. How could she have possibly known then? How could anyone have guessed the changes occurring in his body even as he lay there trembling?

It could have happened to me.

Such a thought had never taken anchor, but now that the hook was in her mind, it was so startlingly clear she could think of nothing else. What if she hadn't left him alone? What if she'd gone downstairs to ask when dinner would be ready? She might have taken Cato's place in a cage.

Vivian crept forward, her eyes trained on the folder tucked under her mom's elbow. She held her breath, watching Madison's face as she took the corner and patiently worked it from side to side until it came free. Madison inhaled deeply and stirred. Vivian froze. She held her breath, but her mom didn't wake. Vivian backed away with her trophy, not daring to breathe until she was back in the kitchen.

She set the folder on the table and went to the doorway to flick the light switch. When she turned back to see the lonely kitchen table, bare except for that forbidden folder, an overwhelming sadness weighed her down.

She pulled out the chair and seated herself. It wasn't eagerness that had driven her to steal this from her mom, not even curiosity, but a need for the truth. She took a few extra minutes to compose herself before she was ready to read the print on the cover. She pressed the flesh of her finger against the words in the upper corner: ***Subject: 5292***. She slid her finger down to the printed words beneath it. ***Project: Classified***.

Vivian retracted her hand, as if doing so might uncover more words. *Classified? Why is it classified?*

She gazed at the folder, her heartbeat loud enough to shake the still house. Now that she had it, she was afraid to open it. Trey had been haunted ever since he went to the AGC. He'd learned something horrible that had happened to Cato, something that might be right here in the folder lying in front of her.

Nothing added up. It all fit somehow, she was sure, but the puzzle was still scrambled. Her brother's death was no accident; she was convinced that Kovak had orchestrated it. But why would the Agents want him dead? Why was their ultimate weapon against ghosts being built on the pain of ghost kids younger than herself? Why was Kovak so desperate to get them back? What was his endgame, and how did a half-human fit into the master plan?

Vivian drew in one shaky breath, held it, then let it sigh back into the kitchen. She opened the folder and skimmed over test results that meant nothing to her. DNA analyses, biopsies, blood tests, charts, diagrams, all useless to her until she reached a section of handwritten notes. Heart pounding, she leaned forward and read:

Day 1: Bypass Retention. Sent through Detox and electroshock test. Fitted for NMS, branded. Standard preliminary tests. Samples taken from Subject include blood; marrow from spinal column, pelvis, and rib cage; biopsies of lung, skin, muscle, brain, nerve, liver, and gastrointestinal tract; full-body scan, MRI. More to come.

Day 2: Subject exposed to weaknesses. Able to withstand temperatures up to 68.3°C. Subject started shivering at –72.2•C and succumbed to hypothermia at –102.7•C before collapsing. Successfully revived both times.

Day 4: First muscular electroshock test. Results inconclusive.

Day 7: Subject refused to participate in first NMS test. No notable results.

Day 13: Operation yielded no new results compared to other Subjects from Project Omega. Subject is in recovery.

Day 17: Subject released from Quarantine.

Day 20: Subject has become increasingly uncooperative and hostile. Handlers have been authorized to use extreme but nonlethal force to transport Subject.

Day 29: Subject admitted to Quarantine for hunger strike, attempted suicide. Dehydrated. Placed on feeding tube and IV until deemed healthy enough to return to Project for further testing.

Vivian closed the folder. She couldn't read any more. Why tarnish the pure memories with thoughts of suicide attempts? What could have happened to Cato in a month's time to make him give up?

She tapped out an irregular rhythm with her fingernails, perturbed. The file was way too thin. Kovak had to have collected more information than this. Even his notes seemed hollow, as if he'd censored most of them and left the bare bones. What Vivian was looking for, she wasn't sure, but she hadn't found it. She was left with more questions than answers. Was that why her mom dwelled in the reclusive basement laboratory all day and night? No, their questions were different. Madison was interested in the test results, the data. Vivian wanted the bigger picture, starting with which Project at the AGC Cato had been sent to. *Classified.* That didn't bode well, but that answer alone would tell her more than this whole file.

Trey was right; Finn and Reese must know, she realized. But even if she could convince them to say "hi" aloud to her, which by itself was an impossible task, she had no doubt they'd been well-conditioned to keep classified information a secret. Maybe the other Alpha ghosts knew. Sure, Jay had denied actually meeting Cato at the AGC, but even prisoners gossiped, right? If anything was worthy of being a rumor, it would have been the captivity of a half-human in the lab. They wouldn't have had to meet him to know which Project he was in, and that would be a start.

Vivian turned the corner of the folder until the edge aligned with the table. Seph had been in Phantom Heights before. That news still surprised her and didn't at the same time, not when she thought about the familiarity he'd shown toward her and the contempt he'd demonstrated toward her mom. Now that she reflected on her midnight conversation with Seph when she'd been held hostage, she remembered that he'd known she had a younger brother but seemed surprised to learn of his demise. Seph had probably been the mastermind behind her kidnapping, not Jay as she'd originally assumed.

The enemy of my enemy is my friend.

But the enemy of my family can't be trusted.

Troubled, she tilted the folder, then straightened it again. By helping the Alpha ghosts, she might very well have aided her mom's enemy, and that thought turned her stomach. But Seph, even if he'd been an enemy back then, could be a connection to a piece of the past. He might be able to help her find the truth.

Vivian picked up the folder and wandered to the doorway to return it, but she hesitated, hugging the file against her chest for an extra moment. Madison would never know she'd borrowed the folder.

Tomorrow, Vivian would look for Seph. She needed more answers.

— Chapter Forty-One —

Shadow

I passed beneath the warm glow cast down from the streetlight on my way back to Saros Manor.

Phantom Heights was asleep. Each time I left another pool of light, I imagined I was slipping into Chelvistin's dark lake where everything was quiet and peaceful, where nobody expected anything of me.

"You'd drown," the sirien had told me. She didn't realize I was already drowning.

I closed my eyes, and I saw the green light. Somebody was there, a silhouette. Madison? It must be. Her form was wrong. Bulky, amorphous. Was she facing me, or was I looking at her back? I couldn't see. Just the silhouette in an instant before the light blinded me.

The Flash itself was a broken memory; the moments leading to it had been eradicated no matter how hard I tried to dredge them from the depths of my subconscious. I'd already triggered one Spasm on the walk back, and the worsening headache warned I was instigating another, but . . . if only I could remember what preceded the light. Had I gone downstairs by my own will, or had Madison lured me down?

Even if the Flash itself had been an accident, there was still a strong possibility that she'd realized what she'd done to me. If she knew what I was—and I still wasn't certain she did—then she had been a convincing actress. And yet, now I thought back and wondered if all those times she'd fought me, maybe she'd been purposely challenging me, testing me, all to make me grow so she could study me from the shadows until I was ripe enough for *Him*, like fattening a pig for slaughter. I was sure Trey wasn't willingly a part of it, but what if she'd manipulated him, too? What if all those secrets we thought we were keeping were actually ideas sowed by the ghost hunter? Was I a science experiment?

The uncertainty was driving me slowly but surely insane. I couldn't ask the only person who knew the truth.

Unless there was another person who might know. A Seer. But what was I going to do? Venture into the Ghost Realm alone to find one? All I knew about that Realm was drawn from Ero's stories. It was a land I didn't know filled with creatures I didn't understand, and I had no money to pay for a Seer's services.

Besides, I couldn't leave. The family was mine to guide and protect, and here I was wallowing in my own troubles. Chasing answers to a possible conspiracy would put my family in danger. I couldn't allow myself to be distracted, at least not until I was able to pass the burden of leadership back onto Jay again. Then maybe I'd part ways with my lab-family for a little while. The money might not be a problem. The city of Phantom Heights was paying us now, and Wes could probably convert our money into whatever currency was used in the Ghost Realm. Maybe I could pay him to be my guide.

The next streetlight I walked under was flickering. I paused and tilted my head back to look up at the sputtering bulb, which brightened back to life and steadied. Something moved in my peripheral. I turned slowly, my alarm minute. I hadn't sensed a ghost, and I didn't see anyone, just my own shadow on the wall.

A sinking sense of foreboding settled in my stomach. My eyes narrowed. Again, I looked up at the streetlight. It wasn't flickering anymore. But it was above me, casting light straight down. How could my shadow be on the wall?

As if it knew what I was thinking, my shadow shifted. It crossed its arms over its chest. I took a horrified step back, but it didn't mirror me anymore.

"Did you think I would forget about you?" a deep voice said. It was a voice I recognized, one that gripped me in the clutch of panic.

"Azar?" I whispered, a question that was really an acknowledgment. It wasn't actually Azar. At least, I didn't think it was.

Instinct made me immediately take stock of my environment to calculate the best escape route and search for any people nearby. I cast a look down the street in each direction, channeling cold power into my left hand.

"Are you planning to run?" my shadow taunted. "Where can you hide from the darkness at night? And do you think you can outrun your own shadow?"

My fingers twitched with the thought of sending a distress signal to call my lab-family, but instead, I curled them into fists. No, I wouldn't lead any of my siblings to danger. This was my redemption, my second chance to confront the Warden. I would succeed or fail without Jay. He had taken on Azar head-to-head; surely I could face the enemy's shadow.

I mustered every ounce of confidence I could gather and asserted, "I've been living in the shadows. If you think I'm afraid of the dark, you're wrong."

"Hmm, what an interesting statement. Why do you think you *need* to be afraid of the dark?" Perplexed by the question, I simply stared at my shadow.

He continued, "You took shelter in my darkness when your enemies hunted you. You covered yourself in my shadows to hide from the searchlights. You've always felt safest in the dark, haven't you? And now the Dark offers you sanctuary, and you reject it?"

"You hurt Jay, and I will never forgive you for that."

A cold laugh answered. "You must look like you've lost your mind, standing here talking to your shadow."

Paranoid, I wrapped my arms around my torso and checked the deserted street again to see if anybody was watching.

Azar's silky voice mused, "Now, which one are you, I wonder. Son without wings? Child of beast? Or perhaps the blinded who sees."

I shouldn't tease the ruler of the Ghost Realm, but I couldn't stop myself from muttering, "Between the two of us, I'm not so sure *I'm* the insane one."

I was braced for a spark of temper, but instead he chuckled, and this laugh was genuine, lacking the hard mockery he'd possessed before. "You've got some spirit left, don't you, Prisoner? Tell me, what's your name?"

"Seph." I blinked, surprised by how easily the name slipped out. It was starting to feel real, as if I truly was becoming Seph.

"And your number?"

This time I hesitated, not because my number was a secret, but because I was afraid of the Mark beneath my gauntlet becoming my identity. *They* had tried very hard to convince me it was my name. This word grated through my teeth much slower than my previous answer: "Seven."

My shadow straightened. I thought it must be staring at me—at least, it would be if it had eyes. Azar murmured, "Seven . . . could it really be that simple?" He waited a few more seconds, motionless, before saying, "You said your name was Seph?"

I was as puzzled as I was unnerved by his sudden interest. Even without an expression to read, I felt certain he was sizing me up, scrutinizing me, debating whether I was a threat or an asset. "Well," he finally said. "That's very interesting. *Seph.* See, I was looking for Jay tonight, but I think I was fortuitous to cross paths with you instead. I am curious, though . . . How *did* Jay escape from me?"

I could hear the desperation burning in his question, the hunger for an answer. "He outsmarted you," I said boldly.

The shadow stirred. "Yes, he did, didn't he? I'm sure he had a good laugh about it, too. But he won't be laughing at our next encounter."

"King of the Ghost Realm or not . . . We aren't afraid of you."

"Hmm. King of the Ghost Realm," Azar repeated, rather amused. "There was a king once, a long time ago. I wouldn't dare claim that title from him. Tell me, do you think this is a game?"

"No," I whispered, the only word I could force out.

"No?" my shadow echoed. "Ah, but it *is* a game. And with every game, there are winners and losers. You don't want to be on the wrong side, do you?"

I backed away. "I don't want to play your game."

"But it isn't *my* game." The shadow was growing taller, losing the shape of my body to form into Azar's physique. "I'm just a player, like you, except I don't think you've figured out the rules yet." The shadow split into two—mine and Azar's. He'd bent the light so my real shadow, under my control again, defied natural order and remained on the wall. His life-size shadow seized the arm of mine.

I felt him. His strong, cold fingers pressed into my biceps. I brought my hand to my arm, but when I touched the place where his shadow was holding mine, I felt nothing but my own skin. Now high on panic, I balked, trying to squirm away, but he held me tight. I was bound by my shadow.

"I will not let you go," the Shadow Ghost seethed, the vice tightening. "It's your choice—you can stand before me and we can talk as equals, or you can be dragged in chains to fall at my feet."

I writhed in his grip, boots sliding on the concrete, but there was no enemy for me to strike. What good was ice against a shadow?

Azar, losing patience with my struggles, morphed his shadow again. In his free hand sprouted a sword. "You're an insolent child," he snarled. "I find it hard to believe you're destined to have such an impact on the Realms." He drove the blade into the stomach of my shadow.

The gasp pulled from my lungs was equal parts shock and pain. The blade—I felt its cold edge pierce my flesh, drive deep into my body, ripping, twisting, and then it was yanked out, and I felt that too, the slide of it against my insides, cutting as it left me. I felt blood vessels burst. I felt my intestines rupture. I didn't scream; I was too surprised, and I didn't have enough breath in my lungs. Instead, I coughed and shuddered as I collapsed onto my knees. Azar's grip kept my arm elevated to prevent me from wilting into a fetal position.

Tears pricking my eyes, hands shaking, I sobbed and yanked up my shirt to see the wound.

I touched my trembling fingers to my smooth, pale abdomen. No cut, no blood, not even a bruise. But the feel of metal slicing through my stomach had been no illusion.

It still hurt; I couldn't catch my breath.

Azar was hauling me back onto my feet. In desperation, I threw my free hand straight up and sent green ectoplasm smashing into the streetlight above. There was an explosion of sparks, and I cowered as glass fell on me in the sudden darkness. My shadow was gone, and so was Azar's grip.

A cold, manic laugh made my hair stand on end. Before, his voice had come from the shadow he was animating, but now it echoed from every direction. I turned in circles, unsure where to look for him. "You're trying to fight me in my own element? I am the Darkness. I am all around you."

"Y-you aren't really here," I stammered, more to remind myself than tell him. "You can't turn into your element."

"Are you sure about that?"

I took two steps back.

"Can't you hear me?" Azar asked. His voice echoed from multiple directions. "Can't you feel me?" Something stirred my cloak.

I spun, only to feel fingers trail over my shoulder. I whirled and slashed my icicle wildly, striking nothing but air.

I couldn't fight darkness. I retreated a few more steps, about to sprint until I was safe in the brightest place I could find, but then I froze. A smoldering arc of red-orange light curved across the night sky. Ash. It was her distress call.

Azar's laugh cut through the darkness again. "Oh, that's right—I did put a price on your heads, didn't I?" he mused.

I bolted. All around me from every direction echoed Azar's laughter. Panic strangled the breath from my lungs. I pounded through the pools of light down the street, but I felt as though I were moving against a conveyor belt. He taunted me every step of the way. "Too slow . . . You aren't going to make it in time . . ."

Town square, the Rip. That was where the distress call had come from. Azar's claim of "uh-oh, you're too late!" only made me run faster until I was punishing the asphalt of Main Street. I whipped around the corner and halted. Figures moved in the dark amid flashes of red light, feminine laughter, grunts of exertion. I needed a full minute to fully grasp the situation.

Ash and RC had engaged a group of Shadow Guards.

Two Guards—a man and a woman—were lying on the ground, either dead or unconscious. Ash was the one who had sent the distress signal; I found her first. She had a short-haired, dark-skinned woman in her sights and was firing shot after shot of ectoplasm at her. Every single one missed. I'd never seen Ash so off her game, and it was showing; her eyes blazed with frustration, and steam was starting to rise from her body. Her target was giggling, skipping, turning cartwheels, and dancing around Ash's attacks, fueling my lab-sister's anger. Meanwhile, as Ash tired herself out, three more Guards were watching, edging closer and closer, slowly surrounding her while her attention was focused on the twirling woman.

Ash had thrown at least ten misses in a row since I arrived. The Guard returned fire. Ash tried to spin away, but not fast enough; she was nailed in the arm hard enough to stagger before resuming her attack.

I didn't understand. I'd trained with Ash, dueled her in the Arena, fought Scouts beside her, and I'd never seen her have such bad . . . *luck*. As soon as the thought took root, my suspicion was confirmed. Finally fed up, Ash rushed at the giggling Guard, swinging her fire staff with all her might. The Guard ducked, and Ash's staff smashed through the glass of the window display in one of the shops. A security alarm blared.

When Ash tried to pull her weapon free, she discovered it was stuck in the broken pane, so she gave it a hard yank to free it. Too hard—it slipped from her fingers and careened over her shoulder, spinning until it struck the fountain at just the right angle to bend one of the water jets and send a stream of cold water back at Ash, who squealed in displeasure as billows of steam erupted from her hot skin. The Shadow Guard pointed and laughed at her. Now Ash was soaked, weaponless, and livid.

Tychokinesis. It must be; I didn't know how else Ash could possibly have such bad luck while her opponent couldn't be luckier. The trajectory of her staff had been too perfect. I doubted even RC could have replicated those results if he'd steered the staff with telekinesis.

Remembering RC, I located him doing battle with what appeared to be shadowy demon creatures. Jet-black beasts of various sizes and forms—some loping on four legs, others leaping on two—were rushing him from every side while a handful of Shadow Guards observed and waited patiently for an opportunity to move in.

RC's disks didn't seem to be doing any good; I watched one slash straight through the center of a four-legged animal. The beast didn't break stride. It wasn't even injured; its mass immediately reconnected where the blades had severed. RC was forced to use his telekinesis to repel the creatures, but they were rushing him so fast that he barely had enough time to throw one away when two more leapt at him from behind.

I'd never seen monsters like these before. Had Azar summoned them from some kind of shadow world? Did Netherkinetics have the power to do that?

RC sent a silver disk zipping between two shadow monsters. The weapon missed, or so I initially thought—it kept going until meeting its intended target, clipping the arm of a Shadow Guard. She shrieked in pain, and one of the creatures collapsed in a splash of black ink on the cobblestones.

Finally, I understood. These weren't beasts from a shadow world— they were made of ink. They must have originated as tattoos on an Animator. The only way to kill them was to damage the original canvas where the art had been created or take out the Animator, but the brutal assault wasn't leaving RC an opening to get a clean shot.

I didn't know who to help first. What would Jay do? He'd analyze, taking a fraction of the time I'd already wasted, decide who was in the most trouble, and then swoop in. But my feet were stuck to the cobblestones. I was so scared of choosing the wrong sibling to aid that I couldn't decide who needed me more.

RC caught a glimpse of me hesitating from the corner of his eye.

"Not *us*!" he snapped, flinging his hand to send a beast flying away from him.

What? I skimmed the plaza again, and then I saw her. Kit was entangled in a net, thrashing with wild, angry frustration under the watch of two captors. To my horror, one Guard drew a shock rod. His shadow fell over her terrified face as he loomed over my lab-sister, poised to strike. To stop her struggles.

To hurt her.

"*NO!*" I screamed.

And the whole world exploded.

— Chapter Forty-Two —
A Just Killing

It was an accident.

I hadn't meant to use that Divinity. It was one shout, one shock wave rocketing outward from the epicenter—me.

Glass erupted all around me and continued to explode in a ripple effect as the shock wave expanded outward.

Everyone—the Shadow Guards, Ash, RC, Kit, even the ink creatures—cowered as slivers showered through the air and the ground trembled. I stood in the middle of it all, horrified and entranced by the shards falling like sharp rain in the night.

Quiet fell in the wake of destruction, just a tinkling sound of glass, water splashing in the fountain, and the distant sirens of car alarms.

Kit reacted first. With her captors distracted, she donned her fur in a swirl of smoke and slithered through the net, then darted for the street.

The nearest Guard pounced on her, grabbing her tail. Her howl morphed into a bloodcurdling scream as she reverted back to skin. It was an eerie sound, a wailing note of wild panic I'd never heard before.

He seized a fistful of her hair, and she turned on him, squealing, scratching, and kicking. She screamed again, cut short by his meaty hand around her throat.

I tried to move, but I was too slow. The weight was shifting off my foot, and when I blinked, Axel was already there. The air buzzed with energy.

Snarling, eyes blazing bright red, excess power flickering around his clenched fists, he ripped the man away and held him one-handed off the ground. *Don't touch my sister!* He threw the Shadow Guard with all his might.

The moment the fabric of the man's cloak left my lab-brother's fingers, I knew something was about to go horribly wrong. I'd always known Axel possessed incredible strength, but I'd never witnessed it firsthand. The ghost floundered through the air and crashed into the Fruth building. But he didn't just hit it and crumple to the ground; his body crashed right through the brick wall. And he kept going.

Through countless walls within the building, and still, he didn't stop. The battle ceased as every one of us stared openmouthed at the poor man crashing through wall after wall. I couldn't count how many. There was no possible way he survived.

Though Axel didn't move, the remaining Guards eyed him in horror. They backed away from us.

RC was the one who seized advantage of their hesitation to reengage the attack, although I shouldn't have been surprised by his quick response after all the time he'd spent with Jay. Rather than blindside his opponent with ectoplasm or one of his disks, he used his telekinesis on Ash's staff still lying in a puddle next to the fountain. It rocketed through the air like a chopper blade and cracked the Animator upside the head at full speed, sending her crumpling to meet the cobblestones. Her ink creations splattered. The staff continued its trajectory until it reached Ash, who caught it in one hand.

Inspiration prompted me to step forward and point at the hole in the building across the street.

"Who wants to meet the same fate?" I shouted.

The Guards backed away as if afraid to turn their backs on us in case we went berserk and attacked from behind. I should have felt some satisfaction as I watched them scramble to collect their fallen comrades and retreat through the Rip, but an acrid taste was foul in my mouth, and my stomach was queasy. It was a victory, I supposed, but it was messy and unorthodox and . . . a disaster.

Ash, RC, and Kit gathered to me, but Axel was still staring at the hole in the wall. "I just killed someone," he whispered in a hoarse voice. How ironic that the half-nydæa, bred to slaughter, had until now a body count of zero on his conscience while Jay, Ash, RC, and I were stained with the blood of many victims.

"You took a life to save Kit," RC reasoned. "It's okay."

Based on the blank look on Axel's face, I wasn't sure the half-breed heard him. "Ax," I said, setting my hand on his shoulder. He flinched away from me with a snarl and backed away from us. "Axel," I called again. He shook his head, and then he was gone.

A small body stepped away from the group to stand in Axel's place. I circled in front of her, knelt down, and placed my hands on her shoulders. She gazed at me with soaked eyes. "Kit, are you hurt? Did they hurt you?"

She sniffled and wiped the back of her hand across her nose, shaking her head. "Axel saved me." She blinked and smiled through her tears. "That means he loves me, right?"

I opened my mouth, but I couldn't force myself to say yes.

Love. Axel didn't love.

I stared beyond Kit, searching for a neutral answer, but my train of thought derailed. Slowly, I rose. I turned in a horror-stricken stupor, engulfed by destruction in all directions. Before me yawned the gaping hole where a body had been pulverized. The waning moon glistened on the facets of glass that covered the concrete, as if reflecting on water.

Every window of every office building and shop was gone. Every streetlight was dark.

Axel wasn't the only one horrified by his strength. I'd done this. One scream. That was all it had taken to unleash this force inside me. More screams, or a longer one with more power behind it, would have devastated this place, maybe even leveled it.

People were emerging in the streets, blinking their wide eyes and staring at the sea of glass glittering in the moonlight. "Cato, come on," called Ash.

I didn't move. I couldn't.

"Cato!" A hand seized mine and yanked me away to break the trance. "Let's *go!* Madison is coming!"

That was all I needed to hear. I turned my back on the eerily beautiful demolition and sprinted in Ash's and RC's shadows, Kit already gone in smoke and a streak of fur.

Only once did I look over my shoulder.

First, I noticed the Fruth building. The silhouette of a man, a giant, eclipsed the entire front of the building. If shadows could emit fury, this one succeeded.

My attention fell to the figure below. Hands on her hips, surveying what I'd done, Madison Tarrow locked her furious gaze onto me in the instant before we rounded the corner.

We were all trembling and panting by the time we snuck across the front lawn of Saros Manor. The door was locked; we had to use our power reserves to phase through, and then we stood in the dark foyer taking solace in the quiet.

I was still trying to process the shock from tonight. All this time, I'd thought Jay was a pushover for letting Axel refuse to uphold the deal. Axel was the strongest, the fastest, the most powerful. That should have equated to being the best fighter.

Now, though, I understood. He wasn't a fighter; he was a killer. Fights drew blood, which lured the monsters out, and Axel was, at heart, a monster. Jay was wise in yielding to Axel's rebellion. It had taken me this long to figure that out; I felt like an imposter wearing the leader's whistle.

"I'd like to speak with Jay alone," I announced. My exhausted voice didn't sound like my own.

The kitten was nestled in Ash's arms being comforted by gentle caresses. Ash and RC granted my request with nods and quiet mutterings of "Sure" and "I understand." I breathed in the familiarity and safety of this place and then glided up the stairs, my thoughts faster than my body but trapped in the past as I replayed tonight again. How could it have gone so horribly wrong?

I could have sworn I'd taken only two steps before I was standing in front of our door on the third floor. Maybe I Blinked. Nothing would surprise me after tonight.

Jay was curled up beside Finn and Reese, their breathing deep and peaceful and synchronized so perfectly that I wondered if the twins had subconsciously connected to Jay. I stood over them, casting a shadow on their pale faces. I didn't want to bother Jay with troubles I should have been able to deal with on my own, but I was flailing in the dark, screaming on the inside while silently watching everything fall apart in front of me.

I knelt beside him, watching him sleep. He stirred, and the rhythm of his breathing broke with one deep inhale. He let it out slowly, eyes still closed, face still expressionless with slumber.

"I screwed up," I blurted. "Everything happened so fast, and I didn't think, and then someone was dead, and then Axel was gone, and I lost control, and . . . I . . . I screwed up, Jay."

My voice trailed to silence. Jay didn't respond. I wasn't surprised; I hadn't expected him to hear me. I'd just needed to say it out loud.

His eyes opened. I deserved criticism at the very least, and yet all he did was stare at me, his silver eyes still dull and groggy with sleep. He wasn't visibly angry, but that didn't lessen my shame. I hung my head and mumbled, "I told you I wasn't cut out to be the leader," as if this were all his fault for putting me in this position in the first place.

He blinked slowly. "What happened?"

He sounded ancient. Vulnerable. As if he might break if I loaded the weight of any more problems onto him. I wrung my hands and admitted, "Axel killed somebody. Not just *somebody*, either—he killed a Shadow Guard. I don't think Azar's the type to let that go unpunished."

Jay seemed to have expected an answer that differed from the one I'd just given him. His eyebrows crept closer together, indicating more alertness. "He lost control?"

I was about to start babbling about what Azar might do to punish us, but Jay's question made me hesitate, mouth still slack. He didn't seem to care about Azar. I shook my head, my fingers traveling to the hollow piece of metal dangling on the cord around my neck. "No," I whispered. "Axel didn't lose control. I did."

I took a deep, shaky breath, still unnerved by that extraordinary release of power. "I screamed."

"So I heard," Jay muttered, glancing at the cracked window. "Where's Axel now?"

"I don't know."

Saying it aloud filled me with icy terror. "I don't know," I said again, making the statement even more concrete. "I don't think he's in Phantom Heights anymore, but I don't know where he went or if he was even stable . . ." My next thoughts I didn't say aloud because I feared if the words escaped, they'd become true.

I pulled the cord over my head and held the whistle in my palm for a minute. The power to incapacitate A6 in such a tiny, seemingly insignificant piece of metal.

"Bloody Scout," I whispered. *What if Axel isn't stable?* Jay had promised to stop him at any cost, and then I'd made the same commitment.

The whistle didn't belong with me. The false symbolism of leadership made me sick. I let it fall, caught by the cord around my fingers so it dangled before Jay. "Take it. Please. We need you back. I can't do it anymore."

Jay closed his eyes again and heaved a long sigh. "Okay."

As the whistle settled in his open palm, the crushing weight finally left my shoulders.

— Chapter Forty-Three —

Unnamed

"Good morning!" Bridget sang.

Agent Byrn disregarded the perky receptionist with an irritated wave of his hand. He was too preoccupied to be bothered with her chipper attitude. *Morning people.*

Normally he'd be trudging to his office, bleary-eyed and still half-asleep, a coffee mug clenched in one hand and his briefcase in the other after another long night of investigating empty leads about his fugitives from Project Alpha. Today, he didn't need coffee to keep his eyes open, and he'd left in such a rush that he'd forgotten his briefcase. He never ran, but he did speed-walk through the ultraviolet chamber and rush to his partner's office, barely glancing at the handlers and techs who darted out of his way and then stared after him.

Breathless, he appeared in the Head Agent's doorway. "I've got . . . good news . . . and bad news," he said between gasps.

Kovak, who was scribbling notes in a folder, frowned and held up one finger. His partner scowled but leaned against the doorframe to wait. He tried his utmost to keep his huffing and puffing quiet and not double over with his hands on his knees. *Good lord, I'm out of shape.*

The intercom on the desk beeped. Kovak pressed the button and snapped, "What, Bridget?"

"Sir, there's an investor on line three," her cheery voice announced.

Agent Kovak sighed and rolled his eyes, finally setting the pen down. Byrn shifted, annoyed with the delay, but he held his tongue and used the time to catch his breath as Kovak picked up the phone and said, "Kovak speaking." A brief pause, then, "Oh, Mr. Jeong. Um . . . *konichiwa.*"

Byrn shook his head and whispered, "That's Japanese! Mr. Jeong is from South Korea."

Kovak shot him a dirty look. He scowled and nodded, although Byrn knew perfectly well his business partner couldn't understand a word the man on the other line was saying. Kovak said, "I apologize, I'm afraid I can't hear you. We'll talk later. Uh . . . *s-sayonara.*"

"Oh my god," Byrn muttered under his breath. "Please tell me you didn't just insult and then hang up on one of our key investors."

Irritated, Kovak snatched his pen to resume writing. "Did you need something?"

"I have some bad news, but it might be good news for us."

"What?" Agent Kovak asked, barely glancing up from his paperwork.

"Bodies were found this morning. Bad news—a whole town was slaughtered in a small farming community. Every victim was torn to shreds."

Kovak's pen stopped moving. He looked up. "A6?"

Byrn grinned and answered, "That's the good news."

Agent Kovak leapt to his feet, eyes shining. "How far away?"

"About two hundred miles, south. Stupid brute didn't go for the Rip."

Kovak strode to the door. "Let's check out the site," he said, fingering the whistle around his neck. "And hopefully bring our troublesome demon back home where he belongs."

Phantom Heights was in an uproar.

The emergency town meeting had become a protest of many causes. Town square was packed. So many people were yelling and arguing and waving signs that I could hardly determine who was protesting what. Some were in favor of instating S-O-S while others waved signs with the Alpha symbol emblazoned on them. The shouts rang in the streets—feet stamping, voices chanting—an eerie, rhythmic battle in the air.

Madison had been at the podium beneath City Hall's portico pleading for the crowd to settle down and listen to her, to no avail. Right now, she seemed to be arguing with Wes, who was standing in the front row next to Ero.

I watched the madness unfold from inside City Hall with my lab-family. A familiar face through the window jolted me. My blood-sister was standing at the forefront of the protests holding a sign that read: **WE WILL NEVER SUPPORT SOS**.

She was rebelling against our mother. That made me smile. She wasn't an aggressive protestor; she was just standing there waving her sign in time to the chanting. Her expression had a peculiar vacancy to it, as though she was going through the motions but not really paying attention.

Jay said, "Let's go. We have to do damage control."

If I were still leader, we would have barricaded ourselves in our room instead. I didn't like Jay's edict, but I was the one who had willingly relinquished leadership back to him, so now I had no choice but to follow.

The moment we stepped out onto the portico, we were met with an immediate roar of noise. I tugged at the mask over my nose. Apprehension was a parasite eating my innards away bite by bite. Jay kept telling us not to worry. *"Everything will be fine. We'll adapt, just like we've done since the day we escaped."*

At least, those were the words out of his mouth. He could soothe Kit, but the rest of us saw the cracks in his illusion. This morning when we'd woken and started to gear up for training, Jay had something else in mind. Finn and Reese had, per Jay's request, conjured an impressive three-dimensional holographic map of Phantom Heights from ECANI. The map had been layered with data from security cameras and photographs and blueprints and satellites so the whole miniaturized town was hovering over the carpet in real time; I could even see people walking in the streets. Instead of the usual training workout, Jay had spent the morning going over our best escape routes to the Rip.

"But don't worry," he said.

At least he was finally back on his feet, although he was wearing the sling to keep his arm still. His eyes were alert again, if still a little duller than I knew them to be. The swelling in his nose had receded, the color faded from purple and blue to more of a yellow-green.

Still in too much pain to hassle with contorting his arm into a shirt, Jay had opted to go shirtless, the black cloak over his bare shoulders accompanied by the hood up to shadow his face. The result was a startling juxtaposition. On the one hand, Jay looked so strong; every muscle carved into his core proved his physical prowess. But on the other, his pale skin, naked and unprotected now, made him appear so much more vulnerable, especially with the sling cradling his arm and—although I'd always thought he was practically untouchable—a timeline of bruises marking his torso.

Guilt kept me subdued. I couldn't look at anyone. I'd lost control of the team, lost control of myself, and now Jay was going to have to deal with the repercussions of my blunders. What a leader I'd made.

Madison faced the restless crowd. "Okay, everybody just shut *up* for a few minutes, all right? We need to sort this out before any decision is made. I mean it. Emerton? Please have your team remove anyone who causes trouble." She pivoted to face us. "*So*," she said.

I hated that word. No, I didn't hate the word; I hated the way she said it.

"You might as well take off the hood, Jay."

At first, I didn't think he would obey, but then he reached up and pushed the hood back, shaking his gray hair from his eyes. In a low, deadly voice, Madison said, "I had a long meeting with city council this morning. They've given me the responsibility to decide what to do with you. Honestly, I don't know yet." She gestured at the protesters. "I will take all of these opinions into account, but in the end, it's *my* decision. I am the only one you need to appeal to right now if you want to keep our deal in place."

Jay muttered at the ground, "I don't see why anything has to change."

"Explain."

"Explain what?"

"You can start by explaining why you lied about your age."

"I didn't. You never asked my age."

"But you purposely hid your faces so we wouldn't know. I want the truth—are you the oldest?"

Jay shifted, then nodded.

Madison's stern voice softened to a tone that almost sounded compassionate. "Come on, Jay, why are you here? Your family must miss you."

"I don't have a blood-family to return to," he replied despondently.

Madison studied Jay for a long moment, and then her gaze drifted across the rest of us. "That can't be the case for all of you."

I hung my head, the unbidden hurt needling my heart. My eyes burned to find my blood-sister in the crowd again. I knew where she was. I also knew it was better not to look at her.

Quietly, Jay said, "Mrs. Tarrow, if we had families in the Ghost Realm who wanted us, do you really think we would've stayed here?"

"You could have told us you were kids. Did you think we'd be heartless enough to withhold the medicine for Finn and Reese?"

"Yes."

She acted taken aback by his unflinching answer. "And what gave you that impression?"

Jay's top teeth touched his lower lip as he started to say, "Pha—" before he stopped himself and shook his head with a scowl and a roll of the eyes.

Madison folded her arms. "I'm sorry, I didn't catch that."

He ground his teeth.

"Jay—"

"Why does this suddenly matter? We're no less capable now than we were a week ago. All that's changed is your perception of us. You never asked my age, and I didn't know, okay? I didn't know how old I was until Axel said it."

Silence. At first, Madison appeared doubtful, but then her stern expression turned to pity. "How could you not know?"

"There were no windows in that place. No consistent schedule to measure time. I don't know how long I've been locked up, or where I was born, or what my mom looked like, or even my . . ." He trailed off, cheeks flaming.

"Your what?"

Flushed, Jay stared at nothing. "Name."

It was a whisper I barely heard. I stared at Jay, and once again, I felt as if I were looking at a total stranger.

"What?" Axel blurted.

Ash said, "Your name isn't Jay?"

He winced. He didn't have to answer. "You're one of the Unnamed," I said. The look in his eyes told me I was right.

RC said, "You never told us that." His wounded voice cracked.

Jay swallowed and turned to face us. "My name is Jay. That just . . . isn't my original name. By the time I realized I'd forgotten . . ." He tenderly touched Reese's shoulder. "I gave myself a new name when I gave them theirs."

I'd heard of the Unnamed—the prisoners locked away for so long they responded only to their Marks—but Jay had always been Jay. I never would have guessed he was one of the Unnamed. I had so many questions to ask him, but Madison wouldn't let me. Her voice weighted with weariness, she said, "Whatever your real name is, do you realize that in the past twenty-four hours, you've somehow managed to break every piece of glass in a five-block radius and put a hole through the solid walls of three buildings downtown? I don't think you take into account that it costs money to fix what you break."

Jay mumbled, "We're just doing our job."

"Do you think you can do your job without destroying Phantom Heights? That's another factor I have to take into consideration."

Eyes downcast, Jay muttered, "I accept full responsibility."

"Oh, do you? Because I find it very hard to believe that a Blinker contributed to this damage, especially considering you've been out of commission."

"My team. My responsibility."

"You sure don't act your age, do you, Jay? But you can't be reckless and then apologize for the casualties afterward. *If* I decide to continue this arrangement, and if this happens again, we're going to have to start deducting damage costs from your paycheck. Am I clear?"

"Yes."

She rubbed her temples as if staving off a headache. "What, dare I ask, *did* crash through those buildings?"

Statue-like Axel finally shifted. Jay fidgeted. "A . . . ghost."

His answer stirred the crowd. Madison's stunned expression might have been comical if I weren't so worried about how much trouble we were in.

"A *ghost*? You shot a *kálos* through fourteen solid walls? How?"

"Ah, well . . ."

He cleared his throat and sent a guilty one-shouldered shrug at his interrogator.

Madison heaved a sigh of exasperation. I prayed that was the end of it, but her hard eyes told me the scolding was far from over. Sure enough, her hands found her hips. "*Now.*" Her tone darkened. "We have another topic to discuss before I make my decision. Where. Is. A. 6."

My head jerked up. I looked at Wes, suspecting that he'd had a hand in this after our discussion at dinner, but he acted just as confused as the rest of us, although even as I watched, I saw the puzzlement transform into intense interest. His fascination with A6 was disturbing. My stomach sank. Why would Madison ask us about A6 *now*?

Unless . . . had something happened last night?

The crowd before City Hall was dead silent, waiting, finally united to hear the answer. Jay shrugged noncommittally.

"Oh, no," Madison snarled. "Don't give me that crap, Jay. You know where A6 is, and I want to know *now*."

"Why?"

"*Why*? Because you promised it was under control, that's why!"

Jay's jaw clenched. He shot a furious look at Axel. "What has A6 done?"

"Nothing," Axel hissed between his teeth so quietly I barely heard him.

Madison glanced out at the people standing in the plaza. "An entire town was slaughtered last night. Bodies were literally torn to pieces. Do you understand what I'm saying, Jay? There are no survivors. The news is calling it a freak animal attack." Madison swallowed the lump in her throat. "That was no animal attack, was it? The Agents are at the crime scene. A6 did this."

"That's not true," Axel snarled, red ectoplasm crackling around his knuckles.

"They're trying to piece body parts together just to get an estimate of how many people died. Where is A6? I know you know."

I couldn't help it; I was staring at Axel in horror. He hadn't really done that . . . had he? What if his animal half had taken over and he'd gone on a killing spree last night while I slept? I didn't know where he'd gone, and he'd been so shaken up after killing that Shadow Guard . . . Once blood was spilled, maybe he couldn't stop. Nausea gripped my stomach with the sickening realization that this tragedy might have happened on my watch.

Jay left me in charge. I had the only weapon capable of incapacitating A6. Are all those senseless deaths on my conscience because I failed as leader?

Axel was still growling, his fury beyond words. He bowed his head and turned to Jay, muttering too quietly for Madison to hear, "I swear I didn't do it. Arena's Honor. You believe me, don't you?"

Jay pondered for a moment. He took the time to study our lab-brother carefully before he nodded and said, "A6 wasn't responsible for that tragedy."

I wanted to believe that, I desperately did, but I couldn't help but wonder—how could Jay be so certain? He had no proof beyond Axel's word.

"Nothing else could have," Madison countered sharply.

"A6 may be the only half-breed, but purebloods exist in the Ghost Realm, along with plenty of other types of monsters."

My sick stomach eased a little. Axel wasn't the only nydæa, and nydæa weren't the only monsters, and the Rip wasn't the only Tear. Then the nausea returned with fresh guilt that I'd almost believed *her* over Axel. Shame warmed my cheeks. I still wasn't totally convinced of Axel's innocence, but even if he was guilty, his brotherhood was more important to me than the lives he might take. I knew that was wrong, but I didn't care.

The ghost hunter, still rattled by the massacre, didn't seem to accept Jay's suggestion. "I don't care if A6 actually did it or not. I want to know where it is *right now*, Jay."

"And what will you do if you know?"

"I haven't decided yet."

"Will you call *Them*?"

Madison didn't answer, silently reiterating her original statement.

Ash touched Axel's shoulder in wordless support. RC slipped his hand into his pouch. The twins looked troubled, which was unusual considering their normal composure. The Jay I knew was back as he lifted his chin and stated, "A6 is our lab-brother."

"Your *lab-brother*?"

"Yes."

Madison glanced at the crowd again. I thought she had been looking for general support, but now I noticed her gaze kept gravitating to the same place every time. It was almost as if she was seeking approval from someone before she continued. "This isn't a game, and you're testing my patience. People died. Now. Where. Is. It."

"He," Jay corrected. "Not 'it.'"

"Fine. Where is *he*?"

"You can't let *Them* take him back to that place."

"I most certainly can."

"That would violate the terms of our agreement."

Madison, mouth open to argue, hesitated. "What?"

"You promised to protect us in return for our services. Everyone in Project Alpha falls under that protection, including A6."

My eyes widened. I thought back to the moment we'd first struck the deal. Jay was right; at no point in time had we ever excluded A6 from the terms.

The crowd stirred, and people muttered among themselves.

Madison had been struck speechless. Wes, the concoctor of the original deal, marched up the steps and argued, "Wrong. A6 isn't part of this. He isn't fighting. He doesn't get our protection."

"The twins don't fight, either. Are they not protected under our deal?"

Ero smirked in appreciation of Jay's cunning. Poor Wes was fighting a losing battle and probably didn't even realize it. He was visibly flustered, trying to outmaneuver Jay's counterargument. "When we made this bargain, we . . . uh, I . . . I mean, it was supposed to apply to only you seven. A6 was never a factor."

Jay fired back, "You never specified that A6 was exempt, nor did you say that we all had to fight for the deal to be valid. You promised to protect us, and A6 was a member of Project Alpha, so if he's captured, that breaks our deal."

"What the hell?" Wes muttered, more to himself than anyone else as he scratched his head.

Madison demanded, "Why are you protecting that monster?"

Jay met her critical gaze. "You call him a monster, but you don't know anything about him."

"I know enough. And what I don't know is because of your lies."

"I don't lie. You draw incorrect assumptions."

She retorted, "Misleading is a form of lying, no matter how you skew it into rationality."

"My word has been good from the beginning. Why can't you just trust that the way I handled the situation with A6 was for the best?"

"Because trust doesn't work like that, Jay! It's supposed to be mutual, give and take, and you've been doing an awful lot of taking without giving anything back. If you want to continue being a part of our community, you better open up right now. This is your last chance to convince me that you can be honest and our deal should stay in place."

He turned away from her to face us. I'd never noticed the weariness before, not until bearing the weight myself. He wanted to protect every-one from everything, and someday he'd have to acknowledge that he just couldn't.

"Okay," he said, nodding. He faced her again but kept his eyes downcast. "Okay. But you aren't going to like the truth. A6 was sedated when the truck crashed. We could have left him behind, but I carried him."

"What? *You* let it escape?"

As if she hadn't interrupted, he continued, "We left him in a safe place so he wouldn't kill us when he woke." He raised his head to meet the ghost hunter's perturbed stare. "I was aware of the risks when I chose to free A6."

"Who gave you the right to decide the freedom of that monster was worth the lives of innocent humans?"

"Obviously, you disagree with my choice, but I have no regrets. I accept full responsibility for A6."

Axel crossed his arms and grumbled, "How noble of you. But A6 ain't a child who needs someone to take responsibility for him."

Jay glared at him sidelong. "A6 doesn't always think with his head." He faced Madison again and said, "You really want the truth? RC, take off your hood."

The Telekinetic hesitated, waiting for the leader to change his mind. "W-what?" His gaze wavered uncertainly between Madison and Jay.

"Take it off."

Slowly, giving Jay time to issue a new order, he raised his hand and pushed back his hood. Wavy locks of brown hair fell over his eyes—one bright, one dull and marred by a scar.

Madison stared at him. I thought she was starting to comprehend, although she was still trying to deny the only logical answer.

"You're . . . but . . . Agent Kovak said *one* of you is blind. Then, doesn't that mean . . . ?"

"Axel isn't," Jay finished for her. "But he can navigate without his eyes. He can feel movement, hear echoes bouncing off walls, smell things even Wes can't smell."

The blood drained from Madison's face as she finally grasped exactly what Jay was saying. Still, he continued, "I didn't finish my story; not long after we parted ways, A6 tracked our scent and found us in the woods. We've been together ever since. You want to know if A6 killed all those people? You can ask him yourself."

On cue, Axel reached up, pushed the hood back, and pulled the blindfold from his glowing red eyes.

Terrified whispers rustled through the crowd. Jay ordered under his breath, "Hold your hands up."

"Why?" Axel grumbled.

"Because I said so."

Axel rolled his eyes but did as he was told. "This is stupid."

Despite Axel's gesture of surrender, people backed away from us. Madison stared, too stunned to react. Trey drew his ectogun but held it loosely in his hand, unsure what to do.

These reactions were logical. The one that caught me off guard was Wes. The werewolf burst into laughter so boisterous he doubled over and fell to his knees. "*Please*! You're serious? Axel? *Axel* is A6?" He clutched his sides, lost again to laughter.

"Not what you expected, mongrel?"

The werewolf was wiping tears from his eyes, but he sobered enough to answer, "And here I thought you didn't have a sense of humor, Jay. This is a joke. Axel can't be A6."

Ero, contrastingly calm in the thick tension of the audience, intervened, "Perhaps you should allow Axel a chance to explain."

Madison finally reacted. It happened so fast I almost missed it. In one smooth move, she drew her ectogun, leveled, and fired. If I'd been the one at the end of her sights, I wouldn't have processed quickly enough to do anything except flinch. But by the time the ectoplasm reached Axel, he'd already formed a highly concentrated Grade A ectoplasm shield in front of his body.

Madison's shot struck his shield in a burst of red light.

With a snarl, he retaliated by throwing out his arm. The shield flew straight at Madison.

My eyebrows shot up. Forming shields was easy enough, although condensing one to Grade A was still beyond my limits, but I couldn't maintain a shield so far away from my body. I honestly wasn't sure what Axel was capable of with the immense amount of power at his disposal. Rarely had I ever witnessed him demonstrate even a small sample of his power except in brief moments of anger when he lost control and leaked raw ectoplasm.

Axel's shield collided with the startled ghost hunter. She was thrown back and pinned between the pillar and his translucent barrier, her gun now useless.

A deafening explosion followed. There was no time to react. No time to process. Just a single moment to stare at the crowd and realize the horror unfolding at the end of the firing squad's sights as the police in town square unleashed a barrage of bullets at my lab-brother.

Humans screamed and fell to their knees, cowering with their arms over their heads. I wanted to scream too, but I couldn't breathe.

I wanted to squeeze my eyes shut, but they wouldn't close.

A few seconds.

Then it was all over.

— Chapter Forty-Four —

Unraveling

Axel stood frozen in place as the last gunshot echoes faded to silence.

Through the mind-numbing fog of shock, I cursed myself for my slow reaction time. I should have created a wall of ice between Axel and the incoming bullets. I should have protected him. It was just so fast . . . there wasn't time.

But Axel was faster than me. He could have dodged the bullets, but he didn't, and in my dismay, I was swept up in a hot flash of anger that burned green. *Why didn't he move?* I was waiting to see the blood well up from my lab-brother's pockmarked body, to watch him fall forward, dead.

But he just stood there, his left arm extended, shield still pinning Madison.

Except now I noticed that he *had* moved; he was holding his right fist out to the side. Had the bullets bounced off him? No, I didn't see any littering the ground. Unless they all somehow missed, they must be lodged in his body, and yet he showed no pain, no wounds, no blood. Could he bleed? I didn't even know what color his blood was.

In a low growl that somehow carried across the entire plaza, he said, "You're all really starting to piss me off."

He opened his right hand. The bullets fell to the ground, clinking like metal hail by his boot. From the corner of my eye, I noticed a rippling effect in the crowd. The humans were bordering on panic. The police, their magazines empty, didn't know what to do.

Madison squirmed, but she was held fast. Axel seethed, "You think your shoot-on-sight ideology will work on *me*? And you, Tarrow, you're more of an idiot than I thought if you actually believed your human-made ectoplasm could harm me. 2C? That's the best you can throw at me? I'm insulted." His gloved fingers splayed farther apart. The shield pressed harder against Madison's body, evoking a gasp.

A flash of bright light made me jump. A hole had appeared in Axel's ectoplasm around Madison's gloved left hand, which was smoking. Barely a second later, the barrier had repaired itself.

Madison squirmed again. "You're . . . an Ectokinetic?"

He smirked. "Ectokinesis? You don't give me enough credit. This is just my basic power."

"All right, I yield. Let me go."

Axel glowered at her. He didn't move.

"Axel," Jay said sternly. "Enough." Finally, the hybrid let his arm drop, and his shield dissipated.

Madison fell forward and landed on her knees. She dropped her ectogun, and then her hand was rifling in the pouch on her weapon belt. She drew a small object that flashed silver in her fingers. If bullets couldn't hit him, I wasn't concerned about any weapon she could draw, but Axel went stiff beside me with a ferocious growl.

Jay had already reacted. Before Madison could bring the whistle up to her mouth, he was beside her. He snatched it out of her hand and vanished, then reappeared almost instantly beside Axel, who demanded, "Where the *fuck* did you get that?"

"Give it back," she ordered, leveling her ectogun at Jay with both hands.

He held up the whistle. "Axel has the right to decide who's entrusted with this."

Without a word, Axel took the second whistle between his thumb and forefinger. He rolled it into a tiny ball as if it were made of clay, and it landed with a *ping* at his feet. Madison's shoulders sagged as she let out a sigh, her arms falling until her weapon pointed at the ground.

"Axel," Ero said gently, "an explanation is in order, agreed?"

"No."

"Come now, that is not fair. A misunderstanding of this depth deserves answers." Axel scratched his head, mussing his unruly hair, and then folded his arms with a cross huff. "*Axel*," Ero said sternly.

Axel sent an annoyed sigh toward the sky before he leveled his glare at the crowd and smirked. "I bet *They* told you all about how dangerous and scary I am, didn't *They*? The big bad monster on the loose. Not quite the truth, but not intentionally a lie, either. I put on a very convincing act. Shutting down Project Delta really wasn't hard; all I had to do was crouch on all fours and growl like an animal so *They* would think I was a failed experiment."

The sneer faded, and he sighed, as if doing so relieved the building pressure within. I'd always tried to avoid imagining what his life in Delta must have been like. The little glimpses I'd seen of his act in Alpha had been hard enough to watch. He wasn't gloating; he really did make a convincing monster. But it came at a price. More than once, I'd witnessed him "attack" and throw himself at the bars of his cage, knowing he was going to be electrocuted. But at least in Alpha, once *They* left, he'd had us. In Delta, he'd had nobody but his venom-brothers for company.

Axel locked his chilling red eyes on the ghost hunter, challenging her. "So," he murmured. "What're you gonna do now?"

Silence answered him. I wished I had the twins' Divinity so I could know what was going through Madison's head. Her expression was hard, cold. Unreadable. Finally, she holstered her ectogun. "Why didn't you tell us?"

"*Why?*" Jay repeated incredulously. "You just tried to execute him. If I'd told you A6 was in Phantom Heights, you would've broken our deal."

"So, you lied to us. Again."

"*No.* Not once did we ever tell you he was blind—that was your own conclusion—and referring to Axel as A6 sometimes is not a lie because it's his lab name."

"How long did you think you could play this game before we figured it out?"

"Longer than this," Jay muttered under his breath.

The ghost hunter was even angrier than she had been before. Her cheeks were flushed, and her voice wavered under the strain. "All this time . . . I am so *sick* of these games, Jay. We've been completely transparent to you, but everything we thought we knew about you has been either a secret or a lie!"

Jay dropped his gaze. "You know the truth now. I don't know what else you want."

Wes broke the uncomfortable silence by scoffing. "A6. You must transform into some terrible beast, because you look way too scrawny to be super-strong."

He wasn't wrong. Axel looked sickly, terminal even. His youth, too, was misleading. Wes asked, "You're half-kálos, right? What else are you mixed with?"

"Something you don't want to run into in the dark."

"You're really a Level 9?"

"Don't be an idiot," Axel retorted. He grinned slyly and added, "Level 9 doesn't exist."

"So, you're a super-soldier."

That evoked a genuinely pissed snarl from the hybrid. "I am *not* a soldier. I don't fight for humans."

Madison demanded, "What do you mean you don't fight? You're bound to our deal, same as the others."

"That wasn't the case five minutes ago when you thought I was blind and A6 was some wild monster out there killing people."

"Now that we know, you have the same obligation."

"Or what?" Axel challenged. "I ain't your soldier or your pet or your fucking slave."

"*Language*, Axel! Bloody Scout!" Jay exclaimed. He hastened to add, "He doesn't have to fight. The rest of us pick up his slack."

Axel blatantly snorted, and Jay glared at him. Even with two functional arms, Jay wouldn't have a right to make that claim.

Giddy from Axel's threat, Wes interrupted before Madison could answer: "If you're even half as strong as Agent Kovak claims, you're the most powerful being to ever walk the Realms. Show us. Give us a demonstration."

"Do I look like some plaything that performs on command? Go to hell."

Madison was either very brave or very stupid as she shouldered past Wes to circle my lab-brother, eyeing him head to toe. His narrowed eyes followed her path, but he remained otherwise motionless as the prey circled the predator.

"I was expecting something much more . . . sinister. Scales, fur, claws . . . not a kid. Do you know how old you are?"

"Fourteen from the day I was born. Seven from the day I was *reborn*." His hands rose. Madison immediately set her hand on her gun, but Axel just smirked at her and unlaced the gauntlet on his forearm. Unlike me, Axel bore two Marks there—D5, and beneath that, A6. He held his fist up so she could see.

Madison scrutinized the tattoos. She reached for him, then hesitated and drew back. Axel snickered. He didn't move, but she was still uneasy when she brushed her fingertips across his skin to authenticate the tattoos.

"Is that good enough for you?"

Touching his skin once wasn't enough; she pressed harder, studying the texture of his arm. "You feel . . . normal," she noted, surprised. Her gaze shifted up to his face. She was wearing an expression I didn't trust, one *They* often donned when studying us. I had to remember that she was a scientist too, like *Them*, and maybe that was a subconscious part of why I feared her. "And your eyes," she whispered. "If you're a half-breed, then shouldn't they be . . . ?"

Axel was boring into her with his clairvoyant stare, and yet she maintained eye contact—an impressive feat, I'd give her that. "We half-breeds can't all have such fascinating eyes. I lost my purity in a very different way than the person we both know you're thinking of. I was the *first* hybrid."

Breath held, I waited. Axel, whether he'd intended to or not, had set the perfect bait. Would she acknowledge me? What she did to me? I needed something—an admission of guilt, or acceptance of responsibility for the Flash, or even denial that she would dare pass a fleeting thought to the creature she'd made, born of green light and then condemned to hell. But all she asked was, "Did Kovak make any more hybrids?"

"Just me. Not for lack of trying, though."

"For what purpose?"

Axel smiled, as if she'd just told a joke. "Are we going to pretend you don't already know?"

"I don't," she insisted.

His smile widened. "C'mon, really? I was designed to be a new breed of ghost hunter." Axel's lips covered his sharp teeth again, but he was still wearing a crooked smirk. "Specifically designed to hunt down and slaughter ghosts. Good thing I made sure Delta failed, huh? I might have put you out of a job."

Madison's eyes narrowed marginally at his claim, but that was the only reaction I could see. Hesitantly, she raised her hand. "May I touch your face?"

"I don't recommend it. I've been known to bite."

Her hand retracted immediately, her fingers curling inward like a dying spider. "You have venom in your fangs."

"Mmm, better not risk it then, huh?"

She should be afraid, and for a moment she was, but the fear hardened into something else, something more like a cross of hatred and anger. "Did you kill those people?"

"Fuck you. I had nothing to do with that. I was here in Phantom Heights all night."

"Then what did?"

"Didn't you hear me? I wasn't there. How the hell should I know? Maybe a Tear opened up and something came through, but it wasn't me. There are a lot more monsters out there than you know, and they don't all have my good looks." He flashed her a fanged grin and a wink, to which she replied by scowling and folding her arms. Axel inspected his Marks as he laced RC's gauntlet over the ink. "Anyway, I ain't gonna go sniffing around to find out with *Them* in the area."

"What, *you're* afraid of the Agents?"

"*They* created me. *They* know how to destroy me."

"You better not be lying to me."

"I told you, I never killed a single . . ."

He hesitated, and Madison's eyes narrowed dangerously. Axel grudgingly admitted, "The only person I killed was that Shadow Guard last night. But that was an accident."

"*You* did that?"

"I said it was an accident!" He shifted with guilt, finishing in a mumble, "I didn't mean to throw him so hard."

Madison went deathly white, so pale so quickly that I actually tensed, expecting her to pass out. "The glass breaking . . . was that you, too?"

Axel looked her in the eye. "So what if it was?"

A girl's voice sliced through the quiet: "Where's the last ghost?"

Her words hung in the air like fog. I blinked, then turned to face Vivian in the front row. Everyone redirected their attention to the ghost hunter's daughter, though the humans around her stepped back as if her interruption had contaminated her with the plague.

"What?" asked Madison.

Vivian leaned the edge of her sign on the cobblestones and pointed at us. "Eight test subjects were in Project Alpha, right? We assumed seven were here because A6 split from the group. But he didn't, so there's one unaccounted for."

Madison's eyes bulged. I silently cursed Vivian's skills of perception, and by the way Jay drew his lips into a tight line, I bet he did, too. The ghost hunter wheeled to face us. "Well?" she demanded. "Where is it?"

The crowd stirred. People turned their heads in all directions, as if expecting someone to magically appear out of thin air. Axel rolled his eyes. "Damn a Scout to Omega."

"Watch it," Jay predictably warned, maintaining eye contact with Madison. He exhaled slowly—we were caught. Again.

Madison set her hands on her hips. "Another secret, what a surprise. Is this kálos in Phantom Heights?"

"Yes," Jay admitted.

Wes folded his arms, bearing a surprising resemblance to a stern father. "Jay, I believe I made it a condition that all of you were supposed to present yourselves if you wanted to live in Saros Manor."

"Seven," Jay muttered without looking at Wes. "You specifically said seven of us had to be there."

Wes cursed under his breath and rubbed his forehead as if battling a building headache.

Madison announced, "I want to meet him or her. *Now.*"

I glared at the ghost hunter, my power pulsing. I didn't want her anywhere near little Kit. Axel, sensing my sudden irritation, glanced over at me, and I understood his look. I scowled and poured more power into the ice in my closed hand. The green power, which had started to rise, settled again.

Jay rubbed the ports across his forehead. "Jay," Madison murmured, her voice soft but deadly with an air of both reassurance and underlying threat. "No more secrets. We have to have an open relationship if we're going to continue our deal."

He hung his head, defeated. "Kit, please change and come here."

For a moment, nothing happened. The humans grew restless and continued to glance around while Madison stared Jay down. Axel folded his arms, fixing the ghost hunter with an icy glare of his own now that his chilling red eyes were visible. RC drew a disk but kept the blades closed. Ash pulled her staff free from the harness on her back.

I shivered when Kit drew near enough for me to sense her, which meant she'd done as Jay had requested and changed from fur to skin. I glanced over my shoulder just in time to see her peer around the last column. She took a deep breath, as though about to dive underwater, and then she vanished. Jay's cloak stirred a few moments later, and then I noticed her bare feet appear next to his boots. Jay moved his arm, holding the edge of the cloak away from his side.

Madison gasped as soon as she saw the golden eyes peering up at her. Kit's ears fell back. Slowly, Madison lowered herself to one knee.

"Hello, there."

Kit shrank away, her small hand clenching Jay's waistband as she pressed her face into his side for protection. "I won't hurt you, darling," Madison promised. Her voice had lost its cold, commanding edge, and now she spoke softly, gently, like a mom.

Jay nudged Kit, who stepped forward while maintaining her grip on him. The crowd murmured as the little girl entered their view. I kept a wintry glare on Madison as she smiled and requested, "Can you tell me your name?"

Kit pondered, then shook her head shyly. Jay encouraged, "Go on, tell her your name." She shook her head again and buried her face in his cloak. "Kit," he answered for her, stroking her hair.

Wes tilted his head, his focus trained on the pendant around Kit's neck. "Oh, King," he whispered as wonder lit his face. "She's an Amínyte."

My foot moved half a step forward. *Damn it.* Of course he'd recognize her Name. She wrapped her fingers around the ivory tag, glancing up at Jay.

The way Wes's gaze roved greedily over my lab-sister made a bubble of unease expand in my stomach. At least he hadn't seen her in her fur. "Kit looks like a domestic to me—feline, I presume. I've always wanted one, but, well, they're expensive and hard to come by in the slave trade. The domestic ones, anyway." He smirked and folded his arms. "No wonder you've been so successful. You have A6 at your back and an Amínyte spying for you."

Madison said, "No more games. Ash, Seph, hoods off. Now."

No more games? Azar himself said it was all one big game. I crossed my arms, feeling bolder than usual now that the humans knew A6 protected us. "No," I said.

Ash was more gracious than I. She tilted her chin down and timidly added, "I'm sorry, Mrs. Tarrow." She had nothing to hide; she was keeping her hood on for my sake. If she showed herself and I still refused, the spotlight was going to be shining right on me.

But Vivian knew more than she should, and that was all my fault.

She drew my attention like a magnet. I couldn't expect her to keep the whisper, and I was waiting for her voice to come down like a guillotine again. I was the final secret. Once that was severed—once I had to stand before the humans of my past without my mask—our time in Phantom Heights would be over.

Vivian was watching me. She made a point to roll her lips together and incline her head, a silent promise. Trey kept glancing between us and his ghost-hunting master, waiting for directions, but Madison just stood there, her brows drawn in deep thought. Finally, she lifted her chin. "I've decided. The deal's off."

A group of protesters yelled their approval, waving their signs again. Others shook their heads and booed. Jay gave Kit a gentle shove in our direction, and I welcomed her small body under my arm.

Madison was resolutely facing us, as if making a point to not look at whoever had been giving her cues before.

Jay's voice cracked with frustration when he said, "I don't understand. I did everything you asked. Why are you punishing us?"

The ghost hunter, even though she'd been prepared for an argument, blinked in surprise at Jay's response. "This isn't a punishment."

For the first time since I'd met him, Jay was so flustered he was having a hard time finding words. He ran his hand through his hair. "But . . . we've done a good job. I saved your apprentice, and your daughter, and—"

Madison's cold voice sharpened into a blade when she interrupted, "I didn't ask you to save them."

Jay's expression was wounded from her callous dismissal of his sacrifices. He could have died if that bolt had struck him just a little more to the right. He could be in Prison right now being tortured by an Inflictor if his escape had gone even marginally wrong. And he hadn't taken those risks for Madison. He'd done it for me. Maybe that was why her disrespect cut me so deeply, why the green rage was starting to boil beneath the frozen surface of the blue ocean I'd been feeding from.

"Ungrateful," I seethed, rather startled to hear the word escape from my thoughts. I shuddered as heat cracked the ice. "Then where were you?" Madison's hard eyes locked onto me, and I imagined that she saw me lined up within crosshairs. My powers were reacting strangely, as if the green had fractured the frozen blue surface and formed a current, rearranging the ice plates into armor around my heart. I nudged Kit toward Ash.

Madison didn't answer me.

"Why won't you just admit that you're a failure when it comes to protecting the people you claim to care about? That's not our fault."

As if in a trance, her hand drifted up and settled on her ectogun, conforming to its shape.

I wasn't done. She could shoot me if she wanted, or at least try. At this point, I felt as if the plate tectonics happening inside me had coated me in invincible armor she couldn't penetrate. That wasn't true—physically, I was just as exposed as I'd been before—but the anger had put me in a reckless state of mind. I knew how to hurt this enemy without leaving any physical wounds. I'd almost destroyed her when I stole Vivian, and this time, all I needed was a few deadly words to wound her again. "Since you're advocating an open relationship, why don't you tell us what happened to the rest of your family?"

She finally reacted, though her movements were oddly jerky, as if her brain had switched to autopilot, her glassy gaze trained on me. She drew the ectogun and raised it while moving forward to close the span between us. I stepped up to greet her in battle.

Wes lunged and grabbed her extended arm, then swept it to the side before she had a chance to shoot me. "Seph, you are *so* far out of line," Madison seethed, trying to break free from his grip. She actually wanted to fight me, and I was more than happy to oblige. My heart raced. I hadn't realized how much I wanted to fight her, too.

I strode forward just as Madison managed to duck and slide her arm free. My metaphorical armor wasn't imaginary anymore; ice had coated my hands and forearms.

"*Stop!*" Jay commanded.

It wasn't his authority that made me halt. My hand was outstretched, frozen in place, though my fingers twitched with effort.

I bared my teeth and growled with strain. What was happening? Yes, Jay's voice had been like thunder, but I couldn't move.

Madison seemed to be suffering from the same effects. She had leveled the gun once more, but although her finger wavered over the trigger, she couldn't overcome the force to pull it. As if someone had attached an invisible tether around each of our waists, we were both yanked back, our soles sliding across the marble. *RC*, I finally realized.

"That's enough," Jay said. "We have to settle this, and ripping each other apart isn't the way to solve it."

I almost didn't hear Axel mutter under his breath, "Too bad."

Madison's body slumped when RC released her, as if gravity had doubled. Her ectogun was pointed toward the ground, but she didn't holster it. Her sparkling eyes finally broke away from me to focus back onto Jay, who finished, "The past is behind us. Can we move on and talk about right now?"

"Right now? Sure. As of *right now*, our deal is expired."

The subtle pressure in my navel withdrew. RC had let me go. I simmered in silence, only slightly contented by the knowledge that I'd been able to hurt Madison, even if we hadn't gotten our chance to fight. Not today.

"Wes?" Jay implored, turning to the werewolf. "We made the deal with you."

Under immediate fire from Madison's death glare, Wes chuckled nervously and raised his hands in surrender. "Whoa, now—"

"Do *not* undermine me," Madison snapped. "He made the deal under *my* authority."

Jay argued, "But this isn't fair! We have nothing else to trade. Our service is the only way we can pay you for the medicine for Finn and Reese."

I blinked. So much had happened that I'd almost forgotten *why* we'd been fighting. Her voice gentle again, Madison said, "When I said the deal was off, I didn't mean we'd stop providing you with supplies. You can still live here."

My heart sank. Our deal had never been perfect, but it was always balanced so each side owed the other. If we were no longer contributing value, this mutual deal would become nothing more than charity, and that certainly wouldn't last long. I bowed my head and focused on making the ice that had crept up my forearms converge into my palms.

Jay wasn't ready to give up the fight yet. "We've done a good job. You can't deny that."

"Yes, you have. But Kit, Finn, and Reese are way too young, Axel doesn't fight, you're still in recovery . . . That leaves three teenagers—well, I *assume* you're teenagers considering you're still hiding your faces—putting themselves at risk, and I can't in good conscience allow that."

Axel scoffed and snapped back, "I thought you were supposed to be a ghost hunter, Tarrow. You could pull a little more weight yourself. And what about your pet dog? What does he do all day, sit around and lick his balls?"

Wes's eyebrows shot up. "Hey, I don't . . ." He trailed off when he saw that try as Madison might, she was losing the battle to contain her grin. His face turned vermillion. "I have *never*—"

"What about your apprentice?" Jay interrupted, visibly annoyed by the topic shift. "He's our age, and he fights."

"Under my supervision," Madison answered, recomposing herself.

"And Phantom? Did he fight under your supervision?"

A few voices called out from the crowd, but I couldn't tell if they were supporting Jay or condemning him. That was probably too far. I'd already crossed one line, and Jay was pushing the boundary of another.

My creator bristled at my alter ego's name. "First of all," she said, a vein pulsing in her neck, "Phantom was before your time here and is not a part of this. Second, nobody knew Phantom was as young as he was. And third, if I had known, I wouldn't have allowed him to fight, either."

My green power flared, and the ice in my hands exploded. "You wouldn't have *allowed* him?"

"Seph," Jay warned, "don't."

I took a step forward, halfway expecting RC to hold me back again.

My sonokinesis was stirring again. I forced it down and drew upon the cold power of cryokinesis instead. Ice crusted the exterior of my wrist gauntlets once more. "What do you mean you wouldn't have allowed Phantom to fight?"

"Phantom," she said, "was a mistake."

Jay threw his arm out in front of my chest, reclaiming control as I stiffened, mouth hanging slack behind my mask. *A mistake. What does that mean?*

I tried to push Jay's arm aside. "But you—"

Created him, I wanted to finish, although my mouth was forming the word *hunted* instead. As soon as I started to struggle, Jay whirled on me and shoved me back with one hand. "Now isn't the time."

Wes cleared his throat. He edged forward and said, "Speaking of Phantom, I, uh, I brought something I think you should see."

I was both annoyed by his interruption and curious as he produced a drawstring bag. Before showing us what was inside, he said, "Maddie, I hope you'll forgive me. I borrowed something from the museum."

Intriguingly enough, the ghost hunter went rigid with something akin to pain and disapproval. "Please tell me you didn't steal what I think you stole."

"*Borrowed,*" he corrected. "We, ah, we were talking last night, and our friends raised the concern that what happened to Phantom is going to happen to them."

Murmurs broke the tense quiet, and the hard lines I was so used to seeing in Madison's brow softened to the point of genuine compassion. She stared at us, heartbroken. "Okay," she whispered. Now my resentment had melted into wonder as I stared at the bag that must contain something very important. Madison held her hand out to Wes. "Then let me."

He handed it over without complaint.

We watched, mesmerized by curiosity, as the ghost hunter gingerly removed black fabric from the bag. "Wes is right. I think it will benefit you to see this. It was—"

"Phantom's uniform," I blurted in wonder.

The words slipped out before I could even get a good look at what was in her hand, and yet, I knew exactly what it was. Madison paused in surprise. "Yes."

Her mouth was still moving. But someone had hit the mute button and reset time to slow motion. I watched her pull out pieces of the costume one at a time. She set a pair of black boots on the ground, draped dark pants on the podium, spread out a sleeveless athletic shirt on top, a pair of gloves, and finally the mask, and then she stepped back and gestured to it so we could approach. In a trance, I moved forward.

My fingers trembled as I brushed them across the fabric of the shirt. Lightweight, breathable, form-fitting, easy to wear under my school clothes. I never needed anything warmer in the wintertime because of my high tolerance to cold. I remembered long hours mastering my intangibility power until I could phase out of my jeans and T-shirt in a second, leaving the black running pants and sleeveless shirt on, stuffing my school clothes into my backpack, fastening the mask . . .

The mask. My gaze flitted to the mask beside the shirt. I reached for it, then drew back. It seemed sacred, as though I shouldn't touch it.

But it's mine.

I slid my hand beneath the mask and raised it up so I could better study it. Crafted of two layers, it had a metal band over the nose and twelve holes on each side to reveal the blue-gray fabric lining underneath the neoprene. The mask was form-fitted, much more practical than the stifling cloths we'd been wearing.

Jay was standing beside me. He studied my old wardrobe but didn't touch any of the clothing.

Madison said, "You need to understand what happened to your predecessor."

While her frigid exterior had melted away, mine hardened. I narrowed my eyes, curious to hear the ghost hunter's rendition of Lastday while bracing myself for the lies I knew were about to come. My fingers tightened around the mask.

She began, "Phantom . . ." She picked up the shirt and stared at it sorrowfully, then tried again: "See, the Agents were here studying the

Rip. When Phantom fell in battle, they got to him before we'd even realized what had happened. But I give you my word—you have my protection."

"Why didn't Phantom have your protection?" I demanded.

She shot me a look of daggers. "Because he didn't ask for it."

Realizing that she'd lashed out, she sighed and pinched the bridge of her nose while hanging her head. "That's all in the past. I can't have peace of mind knowing that kids are putting their lives on the line for us. It's over. No more negotiations."

The silence exploded into sound. Protestors were making so much noise I couldn't think straight. Madison screamed for order, but her voice was drowned in the cacophony. They were fighting over us, as if they had the right to decide our future. I backed away from the crowd. I felt sick. I hated humankind. I hated them all.

Kit pressed her palms over her velvety ears. Finn and Reese were cowering together, watching with wide blue eyes while Jay observed the crowd with stony disapproval. Axel's mouth was turned down in absolute disgust. Ash clutched her staff as if it were a lifeline tethering her to sanity in this chaos, and then the magnesium alloy clenched in her grip burst into white-hot flames.

People were so worked up they didn't even notice that reading glasses, keys, wallets, and other small objects were levitating into the air. My body was numb, but I didn't realize how cold I was until I saw my breath fog in a cloud before me. Since I'd suppressed one Divinity, the other had swelled in response to my stress and fury. The sudden drop in temperature cooled the arguments and incurred puzzlement as people finally noticed the miscellaneous objects rising above their heads. A few people jumped to snatch their possessions.

"What in the world?" Madison whispered. Ice crystals were creeping up the stone columns and down the steps, filling the gaps between the cobblestones and creating a cracking, grinding sound. She watched one of her own ectoguns float past her face.

Jay's irises were ablaze. Silvery-white ectoplasm sparked around his clenched fist. "You respected us when you thought we were adults."

Ash's cloak ignited, and then the podium a few feet away exploded in a burst of smoke, flames, and splinters. Wes rushed forward to stomp out the flames licking Phantom's black uniform.

"Okay," Madison said, snatching her ectogun out of the air and backing away while staring at the hurricane of possessions swirling over town square. "Okay, just calm down."

"You can't treat us like we're helpless kids now," Jay continued. "That's not fair. We've bled for you."

The humans in town square were shifting in fear. Wes, however, was as calm as could be, hands in his pockets, smoking fabric sitting in a heap at his feet, his dark eyes observing everything. The small sneer at the corner of his mouth revealed just how many details about our carefully guarded Divinities he'd already deciphered.

Madison shivered. "*All right*!" she cried. "I'm sorry! You have to control your powers before somebody gets hurt! Please."

I don't believe it. She apologized.

The swirling mass came to an abrupt halt. RC bowed his head and exhaled, and all the objects fell. Ash had a harder time calming down; she sank to her knees, one end of her fire staff resting on the marble so it was erect in both fists. She stared at the flames, which reflected in her smoldering eyes. She was murmuring to herself. I couldn't hear the words, but I knew she was counting backward from a thousand in increments of seven. It was a technique we'd used at that place when we needed to ground ourselves to prevent the pain from swallowing us whole. The flames around her dimmed, flickered, and finally died, erased in curling wisps of smoke.

I cut back my own power, letting the ice melt until all that remained was a small orb in my hand. In the last twenty-four hours, I'd lost control of both my divine powers. Stupid, stupid, *stupid*!

"May I intervene?" asked a masculine voice. Ero had been quiet so far, observing without interference. Only now did he face Madison. "You have made your opinion clear. Has anyone asked them what they want?"

He smiled at us with so much warmth that his words melted the ice sealing my heart. I blinked at him in surprise, the simplicity of his question driving away the heat of the frustrated scream locked inside me. I'd never appreciated him more than at this moment. Jay inclined his head in silent thanks.

Madison eyed Ero, then turned to us. "Okay," she said slowly. "What *do* you want?"

Jay lifted his chin, his silver eyes flashing. "Humans have dictated everything about our lives. When, if, and what we eat. When we sleep. When we can relieve ourselves. When we fight. When we feel pain." He took a deep, shuddering breath. "We want the freedom to make our own choices. You gave us the option to accept your bargain, and we did. So now, we want you to respect our decision."

"But I don't understand; I'm freeing you. I thought you would be relieved."

I jumped when something brushed my hand, but it was only Kit reclaiming her place beside me. Jay replied, "If this deal has to end, we want it to be on our terms, not yours. If you insist on ending the deal, we're leaving."

Madison folded her arms and cocked her weight on one hip. "And where will you go?"

"Don't know."

She jabbed her finger at the twins and snarled, "You are *not* taking them to live on the streets again. They'll die—don't you understand that? And while you're busy making enemies with Azar, you're putting them in more danger."

"Azar wanted us before we ever made this deal with you," Jay retorted.

My fuse had been burning for a long time, and it had finally burned to the quick. No, I didn't want to be bound to this place, but I didn't want our deal to end like this. Not like *this*—deemed incompetent for no reason other than our youth. I'd always let Jay fight all our battles, but I was no longer content standing silent. I took a brazen step forward and announced, "So, you're saying the truce with humankind is over."

The ghost hunter's cold glare locked onto me, and for a moment, my confidence wavered. Jay was always in front of me, even if only by half a step. Now, he was a full step behind me. There was no one between me and the ghost hunter. I'd thought I was afraid of her, and yes, to an extent I still was, but this feeling was something else, something I couldn't name. It had been building all this time and was only now starting to break the surface after I'd taken Jay's place.

I was angry, not only at this injustice, but also at the collection of wrongs that had buried me ever since Lastday.

Her words still rang in my head: *Phantom was a mistake.* My stiff fingers unlocked, and his mask fell. "I bet we could destroy Phantom Heights in an hour." I'd never felt so rebellious. My heart was flying so fast it was humming. "What do you think, Ax?"

"Oh, less than that," said my lab-brother, grinning devilishly. He strolled to the nearest column and set his palm against the stone. With barely any pressure, a terrifying cracking sound groaned from the roof as a dusting of stone snowed from the capital.

"*Stop it!*" Madison cried, taking a step and reaching out in wild desperation. Axel smirked and retracted his hand, point made.

Terrified murmurs rose from the crowd, and several people called out, "Stop! We don't want them to be our enemies!"

Madison's gaze darted to someone in the crowd again, as if she was embarrassed that she was losing control. When she redirected her glare back onto me, the fierceness had been renewed. The intensity made me take a step back so Jay was ahead of me again. I cursed myself for the lapse in courage.

Madison shook her head, somewhere on the spectrum between disbelief, horror, and rage. "I was afraid this would happen. You're out of control."

"*Control,*" Axel repeated. He scoffed. "You say that as if we were ever under your control. I don't think you get it, *Maddie.*" She cringed at the nickname but didn't dare correct him. "You really want to know why we were chosen for Project Alpha? You think breaking windows was the worst we could do? Come on, Jay, let me finally have some fun. The truce is over."

Jay surprisingly didn't break the uncomfortable silence ringing in the wake of Axel's unsettling request. He pretended—at least, I hoped he was pretending—to consider while people shifted on the verge of panic. I chewed on the inside of my cheek, nervous about Axel's direct reference to the sonic scream I'd unleashed earlier. It wasn't a common power, and I was afraid if more attention was drawn to it, people might start to wonder how exactly one of us had caused that kind of damage.

Paranoid about my eyes, I hid my fist behind Kit's back and worked a piece of ice in my hand, watching Madison. We'd outright challenged her authority in the most public way possible. Her face was so red she looked like she might spontaneously combust.

Jay's soft but deadly voice pressured, "What will it be, Mrs. Tarrow? Are you sure you want to end our truce? I can't guarantee anyone's protection if you do."

"You haven't left me much choice, have you?"

"Is our deal still in place?"

Only with great reluctance did she heave a defeated sigh. "Yes. But I'm not happy about it."

There was no applause. Only whispers of uneasy acceptance.

Madison shook her head and glowered across town square. She couldn't even look at us.

Kit tugged at my cloak until she won my attention. I glanced down at her, and she tugged the fabric again until I knelt so she could whisper into my ear, "Cato, can we go now?" She kept shooting anxious glances at the audience.

I scooped her up, and she wrapped her arms around my neck.

"Jay," I called. My voice was quiet, calm, and emotionless. But he knew. Somehow, he always knew. He turned his back to Madison and strode over to the twins, took Finn's hand, and pulled him to his feet, then did the same to his blood-brother.

The ghost hunter said, "I didn't give you permission to leave yet."

Jay paused. Still facing away from her, he stared straight ahead for a moment. He gazed down at the twins, and then the three of them vanished in one last act of rebellion.

RC and Ash backed away from Madison, leaving Axel standing before her to guard us. I held Kit close as the four of us retreated. I expected an attack, and yet Madison just stood there, staring at Axel. Her final statement went ignored.

523

— Chapter Forty-Five —
Dishonor

Behind LeahRae Harris High School, Shannon gathered an armful of signs.

Two slipped out of her grip, and when she tucked the stack under her chin and crouched to reach for them, the others spilled from her arms. Shannon balanced on the balls of her feet, tears brimming, and then she bowed her head and squeezed the frustration out of her eyes. *Damn it. Why am I crying all the time?*

"Shannon?"

She jerked her head up and swiped at her eyes as she stood.

"Vivian," she acknowledged, taking another moment to compose herself before she turned around to face the last person she wanted to catch her with tears on her face.

The ghost hunter's daughter lingered uncertainly near the dumpsters. Shannon knelt again to collect the signs. "Let me hel—" Vivian offered, but Shannon snapped, "I got it, thanks." She scooped them into her arms and transferred them into the dumpster.

Vivian rubbed the back of her neck. "I, uh, I just wanted to say you did a great job." Shannon nodded, but she couldn't speak. She wiped the back of her sleeve across her nose. Vivian added, "But your mom doesn't agree, does she?"

Shannon stared at the pile of signs in the garbage. They were all anti-S-O-S and pro-Alpha. She was always early to school, and Mrs. Dermody's otherwise empty classroom was where Trey and Vivian had found her this morning. Trey had announced, "We need the help of the student-body president," while Vivian, who clearly hadn't been happy about enlisting Shannon's assistance, had sulked behind him. His request had been simple enough: they wanted a mass movement to support the Alpha ghosts at the town meeting.

Shannon had known that her mom was looking for the right opportunity to advocate S-O-S again. As soon as the Alpha ghosts made a fatal mistake, Holly intended to push her political agenda forward. She was ready for humankind to take over its own battle instead of relying on mercenaries who were likely to betray them when the war against their kin began.

But Shannon didn't agree with her, and Trey had raised a good point when he'd claimed the town hadn't felt this safe since Cato put on Phantom's mask. "With Cato gone, we need the Alpha ghosts," he'd said.

Shannon had looked over his shoulder to make eye contact with Vivian. "And you agree?"

"I do."

"What about your mom?"

Vivian had looked away. "Doesn't matter. What about yours?"

"Doesn't matter," Shannon had echoed. "So, where do I fit into this?"

Trey's eyes had lit up instantly. Thrilled that she was on board, he'd rushed to explain, "Your Safe Haven campaign was genius! You got a lot of people involved, and you did it all behind the scenes. But if we want to stop S-O-S, we need to be loud. The Alpha ghosts are about the same age as us—and Cato—so even though they aren't human, I think our peers will stand behind them. How many students can you organize to make a scene at the town meeting?"

Shannon had smiled her coy, confident smile and accepted the challenge with grace. This wasn't unfamiliar territory; she'd organized several intense protests in the wake of Cato's arrest. People didn't like to talk about him because deep down, they were angry. Anger was a good call to action.

By the time the final bell rang, Shannon had accrued a crowd behind the school. She stood on one of the lunch tables to address her audience. "Cato was one of us. And I don't just mean human. I mean he was a friend, a student, a kid—just like us. He walked beside us through these halls. He made a real difference in the world, something many of us have dreamed about but never accomplished. When the Agents took him away, we let them. Because they were in a position of authority, and we were just kids, and when they said there was nothing we could do, we believed them."

Not a single voice had interrupted her pause. "When city council told us they were negotiating on Cato's behalf, we listened to them. We let the adults handle the problem because we were just kids. What could we do? When our parents told us to have faith in the system and our elected leaders, we trusted them. Because they were our parents, and we were just kids, so they must know best. We wrote letters to the AGC, to city council, to Congress, even to the White House, but we were too quiet. Our voices were only the whispers of invisible children."

She'd cried, "We let them silence us! We swallowed their bullshit that kids had no right to try and make a difference! But guess what? We 'kids' grew up real fast in those two years inside City Hall. We carried dead friends. We were brave. We were raiders. We were survivors."

A boy's whoop had immediately been followed by a handful of cheers and smattered applause. Shannon had paused until all was quiet again before she'd continued, "I know the Alpha ghosts are not like Cato. They're not human. But regardless of how this deal started, they've carried his mantle in a way that makes me proud, a way that should make all of us proud. They may be 'just kids,' but they changed our lives. And now, here we are, right back where we started—adults making all the decisions and trying to brush us aside again. Our opinions matter! Do you support the Alpha ghosts?"

The answering cheers had made the schoolyard ring.

"Then let's make sure our voices are heard this time! We are not 'just kids.' We are a force to be reckoned with! Our lives are at stake, too! I, for one, am not going to just stand in silence and watch history repeat itself. Are you with me? Let's be loud! Let's shake Phantom Heights! Let's remember Cato's sacrifice! Let's defend the ghosts that now wear Phantom's mask!"

Shannon could still, even now, hear the echoes of the wild cheers. As volunteers had crafted protest signs in the gymnasium after school, Trey had declared, "Some team we make, huh? A ghost hunter's daughter, an apprentice, and the daughter of the lead anti-kálos councilmember, all advocating on behalf of a group of ghosts."

Vivian had folded her arms and grumbled, "We're not a team."

Shannon had simply smiled. Vivian might not have agreed with Trey, but there was something pleasant in the way he'd proclaimed their union. It made Shannon feel like she was finally making a real difference.

As it turned out, she'd been right. When the town meeting had evolved into a massive protest, she'd noticed the age discrepancies. The people crying for termination of the very deal that had spared them from death and disease in City Hall were from her mom's generation, so deeply seated in its distrust of ghosts.

The students of LeahRae Harris High, who remembered Cato as a friend, who had idolized Phantom and watched the news every night hoping for a glimpse of him, had dominated the front of the crowd in opposition, and their voices had been heard.

Shannon closed the lid of the dumpster. She'd been successful in her endeavors. There had been no doubt; once she put her mind to something, she rarely failed. But it had cost her. "Mom isn't speaking to me."

"I'm sorry."

"Don't be. I knew what I was getting into. Mom and I are fighting the same battle in different ways."

"Don't tell me you're actually justifying her."

Shannon shrugged. "You know when you're a little kid and you believe your parents are omniscient and always right?"

"And now you've grown up enough to realize that's not true?"

Shannon raised her head and forced a pained smile. "I understand that Mom sometimes makes the wrong decisions with the right intentions." She picked at the peeling paint on the corner of the dumpster. "I see why politics appeal to her. I like fighting these kinds of battles. I want to fight with words, not guns."

Vivian leaned against the wall and muttered, "I'm just tired of fighting, period."

A single chuckle jerked Shannon's diaphragm. "Trey once told me that I wasn't a fan of breaking the rules. And he's right. But I realized I'm really good at bending the rules as far as they can go without actually breaking them." She shoved her hands deep into her pockets. "Look, I know you still don't like me, but—"

"We did make a good team," Vivian finished with a hesitant but genuine grin.

***

Captain Hassing knocked on the door.

"Enter," came Azar's voice.

Hassing opened the door and gestured inside. Officer Jana hesitated, then stepped over the threshold. Hassing followed, then closed the door behind, but he stayed back with his hand on the ornate knob, leaving poor Jana to approach Azar's desk by herself. She stood at perfect attention and performed the Guard's salute, resting her right fist on her heart and her left in the small of her back.

Azar surveyed her for several tense heartbeats before murmuring, "At ease." As Jana relaxed her militant stance, he solemnly gestured to a glass of water. "Thirsty?"

"No, sir."

"Are you sure?" She maintained her stony silence. "Officer Jana. I don't think we've ever had the pleasure of speaking face-to-face, have we?"

She shifted. "No, sir. My orders have always come directly from Lieutenant Cisco or Captain Hassing." She chanced a brief glance over her shoulder.

Hassing inclined his head. *You're doing fine*, he thought in encouragement, as if she could hear him.

Azar opened a folder and skimmed the contents. "Remote-viewing runs in your family, correct?"

"Yes, sir."

"Your grandmother, your father, your sister." Azar peered up at her without raising his head. "You have an impressive track record when it comes to catching fugitives. I see why Captain Hassing was so quick to recommend you. Can you tell me why you were unable to perform basic reconnaissance on the Alpha fugitives?"

Hassing swallowed hard. *Curse King's grave. Does he know?* He cast a bitter look at Rayven on his perch. *Did the damn slave tell Azar that I ordered him to deliver an incomplete report?*

Jana faltered. "I-I . . . uh . . ." She glanced helplessly at Hassing. "I had no knowledge of the fugitives' identities. It's nearly impossible to find someone if you don't know who you're looking for. I was unable to establish a full link. Just . . . just glimpses. Nothing concrete enough to report."

Azar closed the folder. "Tell me about your sister."

Even from behind, Hassing noticed how Jana's body stiffened. "I haven't seen her in several years. She disgraced our family when she violated Law."

Azar interlocked his fingers and rested his hands on the folder, leaning forward. "What about her son?"

Jana shifted again. "Sir? I don't understand."

"Answer the question."

Jana's blue-eyed gaze darted toward Hassing again before she said, "I . . . I don't know. I haven't had any contact with them. I swear on my honor."

Azar leaned back in his chair and opened the folder again.

"I believe you. I do find it interesting that Vera's offense occurred right before your promotion to officer. That wouldn't have had any-thing to do with her decision to flee instead of face the charges, would it? Because if she'd been convicted, you never would have made rank."

"As I already stated," said Jana through clenched teeth, "my sister was a disgrace. Is the point of this questioning to ascertain my loyalty? I promise, my allegiance is to you and the Shadow Guard. If you want me to apprehend her, I will track her down and bring her to you for judgment. Just give me the order."

"That won't be necessary, although with this file right here—" he held up the folder "—I could strip you of your title and put you in Prison for the crime your sister committed."

Hassing tightened his grip on the brass knob. He'd had no idea why Azar had requested Officer Jana for a private meeting, but to arrest her? He never would have guessed that. He clenched his jaw, mentally preparing himself to do what had to be done. Too bad. Jana was a loyal and valuable officer.

Even from his position by the door, he could see her whole body trembling. Rather than give Hassing an order, Azar set the folder down on the desk again. "Vera and Simial took their son into Cröendor to hide from the Shadow Guard. I have reason to believe they had the misfortune of crossing paths with the Agents." Azar narrowed his eyes in a way all too familiar to Hassing; he was gauging Jana's reaction.

"Is my sister dead?"

"I believe so. But I think her son survived."

Jana was frozen, probably brain-locked in shock.

Azar continued, "In fact, I have reason to believe Axel was one of the fugitives you failed to retrieve. Which brings us to the point of this questioning."

"To test my loyalty?" Jana said again, though much weaker. Azar simply gave her a polite grin and tilted his head. Jana released a shaky breath and dragged her fingers through her short blonde hair. "Axel was so young the last time I saw him. He must have . . ."

"Fourteen years now," Azar finished.

"Are you sure it's him?"

"I suppose you would be the one who could positively identify him. But that brings me back to my original problem. You said you didn't know the identities of any of the fugitives. Now that you do, it should be easy to establish a remote link to your own flesh and blood, am I right? All you have to do is hold something of his to strengthen the connection—a toy, a shoe, perhaps. Surely you have something that belonged to him."

Jana stared at Azar, mouth open, not even trying to form words. Hassing cleared his throat. "Ah, sir?" Azar's intense red eyes locked onto the captain, who suddenly felt much smaller. "I have a confession. By my direct order, Officer Jana's report was not entirely complete. She did establish a remote link to one of the fugitives for a few seconds. However . . . I ordered her to cease reconnaissance."

Azar's eyebrows crept up. "Oh?" he said softly, dangerously.

Sweat trickled down the back of Hassing's neck, but he didn't move a muscle. "The fugitive was somehow aware that she was watching him."

"That's not possible."

"That's what I told her at first. She insisted."

Jana nodded weakly. "It's true, sir. When I made the connection, his back was to me. It was as though he felt me watching. He turned around, looking for me, and then he found me. His eyes weren't glowing. But I swear, he was staring *right at me*. He told me he could see me."

Azar said, "And you chose to leave this out of your report . . . why?"

"I apologize, sir," said Hassing. "I . . . I didn't think such a minor detail was relevant. I ordered Officer Jana not to reengage the remote connection at the risk of the targets feeding her false information."

"As far as the Alpha fugitives go, I don't want censored reports. I will be the one to determine which details are relevant and which are not. Am I understood?"

"Yes," said Jana at the same time Hassing said, "Perfectly."

Jana rolled her shoulders back and stood straight again. "I apologize for my momentary indecision. Will Axel's capture absolve me?"

"I think that would be a fair trade. You don't have any reservations about turning your own kin over to the Shadow Guard?"

"No, sir. We don't both have to pay for Vera's crime, and he's already a fugitive who has broken your Law multiple times. Let me redeem my family's honor."

— Chapter Forty-Six —

Heartbeat

"Cato. Cato, wake up. You're going to be late for school."

"Mm-hmm, 'kay."

Her voice at the bottom of the stairwell was so far away. "Cato . . . let's go, Cato."

I rolled over, eyes squeezed tight.

"Cato . . . you have to get up. I can't wait all day for you."

Panic was ice water through my veins. I had the sudden terror that if I didn't get up in time, if I made Mom wait any longer, she'd walk out the front door and I'd never see her again. "Wait," I whispered, reaching out in the dark. "Mom, wait, don't go yet . . ."

Green light.

"Cato? Cato! Can you hear me?" The world started to come into focus, not enough for me to truly see, but just enough to distinguish the blurry figure of a person kneeling over me.

Rewind. A closed door with green light leaking around the edges. The door opened, and the light was bright, brighter, blinding; the Flash filled my vision again.

Downtown, screams. Glimpses of people running, looking over their shoulders. I was thrown backward . . . the wall slammed into me . . . warmth and red in my eyes . . .

Eyes. Blue eyes. Ero? No, this was a woman. Pointed ears. Fangs. Short, bleach-blonde hair. A small scar on her chin. "Who are you?" she demanded. She seized my mask and pulled it away . . . just as the news camera was trained on me.

"Cato!" Vivian cried, trying to push her way through the crowd to reach me. Her voice was far away, haunting, distant. I couldn't focus.

She couldn't force her way through the figures that blocked her path. They swallowed her.

The stunned look on Madison's pale face, her gun held limply in one hand, pointed at the ground. Trey, he just stood there, horrified. The crowd, the eyes, all those eyes, staring at me, watching, uncomprehending . . .

"Mom?"

She was crying. "He was born human! He should be protected by human rights!"

"I'll come get you, Cato! Be strong. I'll get this mess straightened out."

A hand in my pocket. I turned, but no one was there, only a tear-choked voice echoing, "I love you! Don't you ever forget!"

I bolted upright. Where was I? Where were all the people?

All was quiet. I was in a room with tan walls.

I was in Saros Manor.

I squeezed my eyes shut and pressed the heels of my trembling palms against my pounding temples. Half-dried tears itched my cheeks.

A pair of golden eyes watched me in the dawn. Kit was balanced on her hands and the balls of her feet, brows drawn in sorrow and worry, ears pinned back. I swallowed once, hard, and held out my shaking hand. "Hey," I called in a hoarse whisper. She hesitated, then crawled into my lap, curling up in my arms and resting her head on my chest.

She gazed up at me with her golden eyes and gently reached her small hand up to my face, then wiped away a tear with her thumb.

"What were you dreaming about?"

I closed my eyes and leaned my cheek on the top of her head. "Lastday."

"Oh." She sighed and snuggled in deeper. Her small, warm body nestled against mine brought me comfort. "I don't like it when you have bad dreams."

"I know. I'm sorry."

We were silent for a few minutes. "Hey, Cato?"

"Huh?"

"I can hear your heart beating."

"Yeah?"

She shifted and tilted her head up to gaze at me. "Yeah. But . . ."

"What?" I asked, peering down at her.

"I don't know. It sounds the same as mine."

I frowned. "Why wouldn't it?"

"Because it's a human heart."

"All hearts beat the same, Kit."

She pondered my answer. "Then why do humans hate us?"

I sighed. "I don't know, Kit-Kat. I guess because we can do things they can't, and that scares them."

Kit reached out and took my hand in hers. "I hated that bad place, but it wasn't all bad, because I met you there. And now I have a family." She closed her eyes and nuzzled against my arm. "I love you, Cato."

I was silent for a long moment. Kit's words, kind and sincere as they were, shredded my heartstrings. She hadn't been forced to leave any loved ones behind from her old life. That was a blessing; I shouldn't envy her for that. I stroked her long black hair, causing her to sigh in contentment. "I love you too, Kit."

She burrowed deeper into my arms, sucking quietly on her thumb. I hummed the melody I remembered from childhood, the one I still couldn't put words to except for one line. Quietly, I sang, "You make me happy when skies are gray. You'll never know, dear, hmm hm hmm hm hmmm . . ." I trailed off, pleasantly startled by the four extra words that had floated to the surface.

I gently cupped Kit's pendant in my hand and held it up. Clean lines had been dissolved into the otherwise smooth ivory on one side, forming the three-pointed symbol of the Amínytes set in a circle divided into thirds. Her name on the other side, in comparison, had been crudely carved. Her Breeder hadn't taken much care in etching it. I'd been told before that it was a sacred ritual for all Amínytes, even those bred in captivity like Kit. Without a name carved into the pendant they were born holding, they wandered through life like zombies, never answering to a name, making them worthless merchandise in the slave trade.

Kit reclaimed her Name and stared at it with her ears back. After a minute, she tilted her head to look at me. "What's wrong?"

"Nothing."

The wrinkles drawn in her forehead deepened. "Yes there is."

I soothed, "Everything is going to be all right. I'll protect you, okay? You don't have any reason to worry, Kit-Kat."

"You're worried."

"Yeah, but I'm your big brother. It's my job to worry."

Kit leaned against my chest again. This time, she was the one who started to hum the melody, the sweet innocence of her youth lending heartbreaking beauty to the song, even though neither of us knew most of the words. We remained in that position for a while, simply enjoying each other's company. Kit seemed happy just to be with me, but my mind was far away, replaying the final moments before my old life ended. Dawn was turning to day when the others stirred.

My head wasn't in the training this morning. The sparring matches passed in a fog as I contemplated how to plan a trip into the Ghost Realm to find a Seer. Maybe Axel would accompany me. I couldn't ask for a better bodyguard than him. Then again, it might not be such a good idea to bring Axel into Azar's domain with my lab-brother still hungering for revenge. I supposed my first move should be to ascertain whether this would even be a worthwhile endeavor. Ero might be able to provide me with the name of a Seer to contact, maybe even a map, and if not him, then Wes. Strange, to realize I actually had contacts and resources at my disposal.

"Something on your mind?" Jay asked.

I flinched, jolted out of my guilty thoughts. We were walking Home, and apparently I'd been trailing far enough behind the group that the leader had dropped back for me.

I'd never been ashamed to share my thoughts with Jay, no matter how reckless or idiotic they might be, but I wasn't ready to seek his blessing to enter the Ghost Realm, at least not until I'd spoken to Ero and had a semblance of a strategy worked out. I knew Jay would try to talk me out of it, and if I didn't have a concrete plan already conceived, he most certainly would. The best way to redirect the conversation was to blurt something else that had been tickling the back of my mind: "Do Finn and Reese know?"

The surprise was genuine; for once in my life, I'd managed to catch Jay off guard. He faced forward. "No," he said, understanding the question without any need for elaboration. "And it isn't in my file."

"But how can the twins not know your real name? They remember everything."

"Now, sure, but they were even younger than Kit is when I first met them. And besides, they accepted my number as my name." He scratched his head, tousling his ashy-gray hair. "I noticed my memories were fading, but I didn't realize my name was gone until one day I just . . . drew a blank. Nobody called me by my name. Finn and Reese wouldn't speak to me, the handlers and techs called me by number, and there was no one else to talk to. I endured the NMS experiment so often that sometimes *They* didn't even remove it when I was put back in my cage. The constant exposure made my memories disappear faster."

I stared at my boots as I walked. No wonder he forgot his own name. I remembered what Jay had told me when I was freshly Marked. He'd asked my name, and when I told him, he'd said, *"They'll try to take it away from you. They'll try to unname you and make you believe you are A7, not Cato. Don't let* Them. *You have to remember who you are."*

He'd been speaking from experience, and I'd brushed off his advice with such carelessness. I owed him my name, among all my other debts to him. I couldn't imagine the sear of panic that must have ripped him apart the moment he realized he was unnamed. Would I have remembered who I was without my lab-family calling me by name on a daily basis? Without them, my name could have slipped from my grasp with the rest of my memories until I was A7-5292, one of the Unnamed.

"Do you ever wonder what your name really is?"

"I used to, but I haven't in a long time. It's not really important anymore."

"What made you choose the name Jay?"

He frowned, pondering. "I'm not sure. It seemed kind of familiar. I wonder if I once knew someone named Jay."

"And Finn and Reese?"

"The same, I guess," he said with a little shrug. "I was looking at them together in their cages, trying to think of names, and those are the ones that came to me. *Finn* and *Reese* felt right together."

"You kept it a secret," I gently accused. "Why?"

"It was easier for me to accept my new name if that was the one you knew me by. This doesn't change anything. My name is Jay. Whoever I was Before is gone. I'm okay with it, really. I've accepted it and moved on."

"I've accepted it and moved on . . ."

I repeated his words all day while Ash and I scouted Phantom Heights. How could he accept it? If I were in his situation, I'd never be able to let it go. It would torment every thought, the name I'd lost, and I'd drive myself to the brink of insanity trying to remember. I was teetering on the edge of sanity as it was with my own unanswered questions about my past.

Ash stopped short. I lifted my head and halted to face Axel, who announced, "There's trouble at the Rip."

I fired back, "And you're sending us to do the dirty work again because you won't help humans?"

I couldn't see his eyes—he was wearing the blindfold even though his identity had been revealed—but I could feel him glaring at me, and, taking extra effort to keep his voice level, he said, "Actually, jackass, Jay sent me to find you." He pivoted and strode away.

"He did?" I asked as Ash and I followed him. "Why?"

Axel's grim answer of silence nurtured a rapidly growing pit of anxiety in my stomach. I chewed the inside of my cheek, afraid of where he was taking us. Was a whole army waiting up ahead?

I wouldn't be surprised. We had been dancing just out of Azar's reach, stoking his rage. Killing his Shadow Guard must have been the last straw.

As if he could read my thoughts, Axel stopped in his tracks. I collided with his rock-hard body. I grunted; I might as well have run into a statue. As I stumbled back in surprise, he said quietly, "Cato, you know I didn't slaughter those humans, right?"

He was still facing forward, not even looking at me, and yet my gaze fell away from him. He turned, visibly affronted by my silence. "You don't believe me."

"Just tell me where you went after the fight."

He stared at me long and hard through the blindfold, waiting until I lifted my head to meet his scrutiny before saying, "I climbed to the top of the bell tower and sat there all night, thinking."

I nodded. "Okay."

Axel's expression was as unreadable as ever, and yet, something in the tone of his voice made me believe him. This seemed ridiculous, but I didn't think he'd be wearing the blindfold if he'd been responsible for the massacre. He would have been healthy. Maybe that was what Jay saw when he'd studied Axel and decreed his innocence.

"We believe you, Axel," Ash said quietly.

He turned away from us and tilted his head back as if staring at the black bird with a white-tipped wing circling Phantom Heights. "Not that I'm trying to prove my innocence, because I shouldn't have to, but you should know that slaughter was overkill. One nydæa wouldn't have done all that. My guess is that town became the hunting ground for a whole clan, if it even was nydæa."

"I thought they lived in the Ghost Realm," said Ash.

"Yeah, they do, but Tears open up all the time, and human blood smells . . ." He smiled in a way that made my stomach instantly ill. "So *enticing*. They probably came through to feast on humans, then returned to their Realm before the Tear closed."

I shouldn't, but I asked, "Have you ever, you know, fed on a human?"

"No."

And yet, he injected such lust, such bitterness in that one word that I subconsciously put another step between us. If it had truly been a clan of nydæa that destroyed that town . . . and to think Axel was capable of that too . . .

He hadn't stayed with us again last night. Jay had asked the twins, "How is he? Psychologically, I mean."

"Not great," was Finn's answer.

Reese had added, "And lately he's become more photophobic."

At our horrified confusion, Finn had explained, "Sensitive to light."

"He prefers the dark."

"The sunlight has been hurting his eyes."

"Is that normal?" I'd inquired. "Are the other two Deltas like that?"

They'd looked at me incredulously, and Reese had said, "Project Delta was shut down seven years ago."

"Yeah, so?"

Finn, his voice slow with patience, had reminded me, "We were three."

Oh, right. Still Gamma kids back then. Reese had admitted, "We weren't involved with Delta; all we know about nydæa is what we read in Axel's file. We can't give you any answers."

After the twins' lesson, Jay and I had asked Ero if he knew anything about nydæa. "Regrettably little," had been his answer. "Nydæa are . . . difficult to study, shall we say. There are stories, and there are theories, but few verified facts. To be honest, I would love to ask Axel some personal questions. He could dispel many myths about nydæa."

"Is sensitivity to light normal?" Jay had asked.

"It would not surprise me in the slightest. Keep in mind that Axel's nydæa kin are nocturnal predators, and their hunting grounds in Avilésor offer no light—no moon, no stars—only pitch-black wilderness unless they prey upon a town. They rarely hunt during the day, and even if they do, remember that the sun never shines in Avilésor. I myself struggled with the change for my first few days here until my eyes adapted. Your sun is very bright."

Jay had replied, "But Axel never used to be photophobic. It's a recent development. Do you think it's cause for concern?"

To that, Ero had no answer.

I remembered right after our escape, how Axel had squinted in pain the first time he saw the sun. But after a few seconds, his pupils had constricted, and he'd adapted well enough to see, even in bright sunlight.

He couldn't anymore because his pupils were always dilated, even when he returned from his trip at the end of each week. Whatever "medicine" he was taking, it wasn't working. Axel was losing his daytime eyes, which made me fear he was deteriorating into a monster that thrived in the darkness. I did believe Axel hadn't killed those humans, but why he was so determined to convince me of that, I wasn't sure, unless . . . he was afraid we might not walk away from this battle and he didn't want me to blame him at the very end.

Axel, afraid? I scrutinized him. His mouth was drawn in a tight, grim line, but I couldn't tell if he was scared.

Ahead, screams pierced the quiet. Humans were running past us, their eyes wide with fright. I felt as if I were back in my dream, reliving Lastday. The deep shiver down my spine was the first warning. When we joined Jay and RC at the edge of the plaza and, invisible, peered around the corner, I understood why the humans were fleeing.

At least fifty Shadow Guards stood in perfect formation. Hassing was at the center, but the captain wasn't what commanded my attention. It was the creature he was mounted upon.

Titon was a striking beast, as tall as a draft horse but with the long legs and slender build of a thoroughbred. He towered over the Guards standing on either side of him. His long mane cascaded over his chiseled shoulder, and protruding from the forelock spiraled a white horn to contrast his sleek obsidian coat. His feathered wings were folded against his sides. Everything about Titon radiated impressiveness. He seemed to know it, too; his head was arched, and his very poise was a boast that said, "Look at my magnificence and envy me."

Hassing even looked different. He was proud and confident on

Titon's back, posture perfectly straight, and he had a smug, superior look on his face. I remembered Wes's warning that unicorns—and therefore valdenars as well—could break a skull with one kick. I believed that claim; I was certain Titon would shatter my body if he so much as stepped on me with one of his massive hooves. That horn looked sharp enough to pierce metal armor. If Titon charged me, he would crash right through my ice and barely notice the hindrance.

Next to the valdenar stood a smaller palomino unicorn with a creamy mane and tail and a white blaze down its face. Its rider, a man who looked vaguely familiar, leaned toward Titon and spoke, his voice carrying quietly across the plaza: "Captain, shouldn't we try to flush them out?"

I squinted at him. Why did I feel as though I'd seen him before?

Hassing's green eyes were trained straight ahead. "No," he replied. "They'll come to us."

As far as I could tell, the Shadow Guard hadn't attacked anyone. Humans were fleeing in fear, but I saw no bodies on the ground. The Guard wasn't even on the move; it just stood there in formation, waiting. I pulled back around the corner and whispered, "So . . . this is it. The first strike against humankind."

"No," said Axel. Although we all turned to look at him, he seemed to be gazing beyond us at the Shadow Guard. "No," he said again, "this has nothing to do with humankind. This is still about us."

"All this is for us?" Ash whispered.

A shudder of terror racked my entire body. Why were we so important? I knew why *They* wanted us, but Azar was unleashing full forces for the eight of us? Could we really have that much value to him? *Looks like he's making good on his threat to throw us at his feet in chains if we won't willingly come to him.*

I peeked around the corner again. Titon was restless. He pranced in place, tossing his head up and down. Hassing had a firm hold on the reins, but he was struggling to keep his mount under control. The valdenar pawed at the ground and backed up a step, pulling his wings away from his body as though about to unfurl them.

Hassing scowled and summoned a glowing green whip in his right hand, which he brought down on Titon's flank in demand of obedience. Something seemed to have spooked the steed; Titon reared, ears pinned as he landed on all fours again and pivoted in a tight circle on his back heel. Livid, Hassing whipped him again, and the valdenar quieted, although he continued to swish his tail and strike the ground with his cloven hoof.

Titon's unease was contagious; the palomino danced beside him. "Whoa, Sun. Hey! Whoa, Sundance!" its rider ordered, keeping his mount on a tight rein.

Jay turned to us, grim. "Listen up. Azar wants us alive, so we'll use that to our advantage. They'll hold back; we won't. We're going to face this together. Win or lose, we might be separated for a little while, but I promise I won't stop until we're together again. We've been training for this, right? Are you with me?"

"To the end," I promised. Ash and RC nodded weakly.

Axel announced, "I'm with you too this time."

Jay set his hand on Axel's shoulder and warned, "Be careful."

Why the leader told that to Axel and not the rest of us, I couldn't fathom, because Axel was about as close to invincible as a person could be. He was the last one to worry about.

Jay was gone.

I peered around the corner to see him standing alone before an army, head held high. Hassing sneered down at him while the Guards stirred, waiting for orders. Axel appeared beside Jay.

Ash was deathly pale, lips drawn, as if about to throw up. I gently touched my knuckles to the back of her hand squeezing the metal staff. "You good?"

Her grip tightened on the weapon. "I'm in control," she whispered. "Come what may."

"Come what may," I echoed under my breath with a nod. I pushed my shoulders back and strode toward Jay and Axel, Ash twirling her staff on my left, RC drawing his disks and unlocking the blades on my right. We reached our leader and stood as one united front before the

Shadow Guard.

Titon whinnied. I didn't know much of anything about horses, but I could tell something was wrong. Hassing looked as though he wanted to speak to us, maybe try to negotiate, but he was too busy trying to tame his mount, and the unicorn was just as skittish.

Axel tilted his head as if pondering a puzzle, and then he took two bold steps toward Titon. The stallion balked, throwing his head up and showing the whites of his eyes. As Hassing labored to keep the terrified valdenar under control, I finally understood the reason for Titon's odd behavior. He was afraid of Axel. Titon was, after all, an animal, and his instincts identified Axel as an immediate threat to his life. He feared Axel more than he feared Hassing's whip.

Axel grinned devilishly and unleashed a truly terrifying guttural snarl. Titon reared and squealed, pawing at the air as his great wings unfurled like sails. The Guards ducked and leapt away as the stallion raised his feathered wings and beat them down in a strong gust of wind. Hassing yanked the reins with a curse and brandished his ectoplasm whip, but Titon paid him no heed. The valdenar pushed off from his powerful hind legs and rocketed into the air, taking his rider with him.

On the ground, Sundance reared with a piercing whinny. The rider tried to keep his balance, but he floundered and fell from the unicorn's back. He landed hard on the cobblestones. Guards dove out of the way when the unicorn pivoted and bolted through the Rip, leaving its rider lying on the ground.

Axel sank to all fours, his head tilted back to watch the retreating valdenar carry Captain Hassing away. "Should I bring them down?" he asked.

"No," Jay replied.

Axel deflated with disappointment, but he straightened.

Sundance's rider scrambled to his hands and knees, his eyes locked on the half-breed. "What in King's name are you?" he whispered. He glanced back at the Shadow Guards, some watching him, others eyeing us, the rest looking skyward to where Hassing and Titon were nothing more than a black speck on a cerulean backdrop.

I studied him closely—the shoulder-length blond hair, the trimmed beard shadowing his square jaw, the glint of his violet eyes—and I remembered. I'd fought him the night I first met Captain Hassing.

He staggered to his feet and dusted imaginary dirt from his shoulder, clearing his throat to command attention.

Jay acknowledged, "You must be Lieutenant Cisco."

"And you must be Jay. By the Warden's orders, I'm authorized to take you all into custody."

"I warn you now—we will not go peacefully."

Cisco sent Jay a look of disappointment. "Your cooperation would be much easier for us all," he said. "Our orders were clear; we aren't leaving this Realm without you." He made a hand signal behind his back, and the flanks edged forward.

"Axel," Jay muttered. "You're up."

The hybrid pressed his palms together and pulled them apart, revealing red energy between his hands, so bright it was blinding. He rotated his wrists and swept his arms out.

I caught my breath in awe. Axel had produced ectoplasm in a form I'd never seen before—a wave, as if he'd created a beam between his hands and forced it outward in a devastating attack. So much power, and he did it so effortlessly.

The Shadow Guards in front had only seconds to react. Their eyes widened; they stopped short and tried to retreat, but they backed into their comrades rushing from behind. Intangibility didn't work on ectoplasm, and except for a lucky few with quick reflexes and the sense to dive to the ground, most were struck by energy so concentrated the impact must have felt like being hit by a car. The Guards toppled backward in a tangle of bodies trapped in a domino effect.

Cisco was one of the few to escape Axel's attack. He rose, raised his hand high over his head, and slashed forward, yelling, "Go! Take them!" The rear guard roared battle cries and leapt over their fallen to charge us.

My fingers closed around lengthening ice blades.

"Come what may," I whispered.

— Chapter Forty-Seven —
A Sea of Blood

Time became a curious abnormality.

I stood beside my lab-family, waiting, watching the first wave of Shadow Guards charge toward us. My mind processed my surroundings so fast that my enemies seemed to be moving in slow motion, and I wondered if this was how Axel always perceived the world around him.

The yells were odd echoes that rang between my ears. Staring at the intimidating wall of bodies bearing down upon us filled me with an overwhelming feeling of dread, but when I focused on the single Shadow Guard who was poised to strike me first—a woman, lithe and strong, shaved head, long limbs, dark skin, gold eyes—my nerves settled. One opponent. One point to focus on in the approaching chaos.

On my left, Axel's growls were deep, primitive, rumbling in my ear like thunder below the battle cries. I'd never seen Axel fight. Actually, I didn't think he knew how to, at least not in the sense I did. Mastering combat moves was an irrelevant skill when he had the speed, strength, and instincts of a nydæa.

On the one hand, I felt empowered knowing I had an unstoppable whirlwind beside me about to be unleashed. On the other, thorns of unease prickled as I watched the Shadow Guards descend upon us. Axel wasn't a team player. He didn't think through his consequences, and if he wouldn't listen to Jay during peacetime, I feared his total disregard for orders during battle might incur a steep price.

And then there was no more time to think. The wave crashed into us, and time snapped back to normalcy. It was a chaos in which I must find order. Fundamentally, this was no different from fighting RC and Ash in the fire-lit warehouse.

Battle was a dance, and there was a rhythm; I just had to find it.

In seconds, I was surrounded by bodies, and what frightened me most was not the Guards trying to overwhelm me, not the shock rods they were trying to jab against my body, not the battle cries deafening me, not the claustrophobia that seized my lungs. I was afraid of how quickly I'd been separated from my lab-family. Already, there was an insulation of at least three bodies between us, and the rift was growing.

I ducked as a woman swung a shock rod at my head. One strike was all it would take to bring me down. From the corner of my eye, I saw RC hold out his hand, and the nearest trash can lid zipped through the air to meet him. He leapt onto it and rocketed straight up out of reach above the battle.

I was trying to move in the direction of Jay and Ash, but more and more Guards were filling the distance between us, driving us farther apart. A flare of bright light—Ash had ignited her magnesium staff. White-hot flames licked the air as she twirled the flaming weapon, forcing her attackers back even though she was surrounded.

Jay was right; the Shadow Guards were definitely holding back. Their strategy seemed to hinge upon overwhelming us with numbers until a lucky shock rod could find its mark. Grade G ectoplasm was, after all, a surefire way to incapacitate a victim, and much less likely to be lethal than a misjudged Divinity that might have accidental consequences in the heat of battle. One miscalculation or poorly timed attack could be disastrous, and I certainly wouldn't want to be in the position of someone who killed something Azar coveted.

Three ghosts were charging me at once from different directions. I threw my hands out to either side, forming a domed ectoplasm shield around myself. Green energy surrounded me when their weapons hit.

My shield dissipated within seconds of making contact with the shock rods, but I was quick to summon another, this time cold instead of warm. I formed the ice shield on my arm like an ancient gladiator and smashed the broadside into one Guard, forcing him back. I spun and whipped the shield around, straight through one intangible Guard before cracking the edge into the side of another man's head. He crashed to the cobblestones. My third opponent rushed me, but I crouched low, ready for the impact. With a strained grunt, I used his momentum and leveraged my shield to heave his body over me. The Guard fell in a heap, and I showed him no mercy; I shot an ice projectile through his eye as coolly as if this were nothing more than target practice. This was war. No holding back.

I went down on one knee, raising my ice shield, bowing my head, and bracing myself when the colorful flashes of ectoplasm collided with my shield. I pressed my left palm against the stones and let the cold flow. Ice crystallized in a circle around me. I focused on my center, on the point of blue light within me, and then I let it expand. The ice rapidly grew like roots between the cobblestones, filling the gaps and spreading across the surface, leaving me inside an island of bare cobblestones in the center of a slick, smooth ice rink.

I stopped the spread before it reached Jay and Ash. The shots against my shield ceased; Shadow Guards were slipping and flailing to keep their balance. Watching them crash onto their backs was almost comical.

I curled my fingers into a fist and let my head hang for a moment. I felt a bit light-headed. *Gotta be careful.* I had to pace myself; I couldn't afford to use up too much power in one attack and then burn out.

Slowly, I stood, observing the chaos around me. One loud heartbeat pulsed in my ears.

Duh-dun.

I stared across the battlefield. RC was levitating above the skirmish on his lid, directing his silver disks through the air with his open hands and stripping Shadow Guards of their shock rods with telekinesis.

Duh-dun.

I blinked, eyes wandering to Ash twirling her fiery staff as she crouched low to deliver a blow.

Duh-dun.

My gaze settled on Jay, who turned his head in my direction. Our eyes locked, and I knew we were both thinking the same thought—we were too far outnumbered to protect our wards of this town. Jay inclined his head.

He vanished from sight.

I witnessed all of this in three heartbeats. By the fourth, everything halted.

The stoplights at the street intersections went out. Lit windows went dark. A siren pierced the air, and everyone ceased fighting to look up at City Hall looming above us where the alarm was originating.

On the tip of the clock tower's spire, a green spark flared to life. It arched down like a falling curtain, the transparent green shield encasing the white building until the Dome was whole once more, a glorious and spellbinding feature dwarfing us all.

The trance broke.

A Guard lunged at me, and I spun away, deflecting the shock rod with ectoplasm as I stole another glance at the great Dome. On the outskirts of our great battle, Jay had created a safe haven for the humans we were hired to protect.

The siren continued to blare through Phantom Heights.

***

Pencil tips scratched—the only sound in the silent classroom besides the steady ticking of the clock on the wall. "Ten minutes," Mrs. Snyder warned, triggering a series of quiet groans and frustrated sighs.

Vivian scowled, the tip of her tongue poking out from the corner of her mouth as she scribbled the same equation for the fifth time along the side of her test. She kept finding seventy-eight as the answer to the solution—a number that was not an option listed on the multiple-choice assessment.

The overhead lights went dark with a loud and sudden *click* an instant before a wailing siren shattered the quiet.

Vivian jumped, leaving a thick mark across her paper. She and her classmates gazed around in confusion, uncertain of where the sound was originating. It wasn't the fire alarm or severe-weather warning. Students began to murmur with unease.

Mrs. Snyder was the first to realize what was happening. She stood from behind her desk and announced, "Okay, everyone, please stay calm. I think that's the ghost alarm. We need to get to City Hall now, so please proceed into the hallway calmly and—"

The students bolted, only to find themselves fighting to squeeze through the door before their teacher could finish. Vivian was swept up in the mob, caught in a mass of bodies.

Below her, on the ground level in another classroom, Shannon gasped at the sound of the alarm. She twisted in her seat to stare out the window as if expecting to see an army marching.

Trey was on his feet already. "Shit," he whispered. He fumbled to draw an ectogun from his belt. "I gotta find Madison!"

Madison Tarrow was in her lab, the AGC's folder spread open before her. She was scribbling in a notepad, completely absorbed in her research when the lights clicked off. She jerked her head up, frowning and tilting her head to listen. No doubt—that faint sound in the distance was her siren.

She rose so quickly that the stool tumbled to the ground behind her. The ghost hunter blindly felt her way along the table, her wrist knocking something over the edge and sending it crashing to the floor.

"Damn it," she muttered, reaching the corner and shuffling through total darkness with her arms held out. Her fingers met the door and slid down the wood to fumble for the knob, and then she dashed up the steps two at a time and entered the kitchen, where the alarm was an ear-splitting shriek through the open windows.

"Vivian," she whispered in terror, sprinting through the living room and yanking open the front door. She collided with a body in her path. Madison grunted and reeled back. "Wes!"

The werewolf was glancing around with shifty eyes as Madison's neighbors emerged from their homes. People were running down the street in a panic. Madison's gaze followed. She caught her breath when she saw the shimmering green entoplasm shield arching above the rooftops.

"Who activated the alarm?" she demanded.

Wes shook his head without an answer.

"Well then change and get down there! I have to get to the school and find my daughter!"

"I'm sure Vivian is fine; she's a resourceful girl. You're needed downtown."

"But—"

She was interrupted by a *boom* that rocked the ground and made the buildings tremble. People in the street who had been making their way toward the entoplasm shield stumbled and fell. Madison rushed to a woman on her hands and knees on the sidewalk.

"Holly," she said, grasping the councilwoman's arm and helping her to her feet, "are you okay?"

Holly opened her mouth and started, "I—"

Another *boom*, and the ground heaved.

The blast exploded a few yards away, throwing me off balance. I landed on my hands and knees in a daze. My right ear was ringing, and my cheek stung from tiny bits of ice shrapnel. I didn't even know what had caused it. A Clapper making a concussive blast by smacking his hands together? A Detonator self-destructing? Whatever it was, it had shattered my ice trap, exposing stone for boots to gain traction.

I pressed my hand to the deep gash in my arm, freezing the blood. The nearest Guard scrambled to his feet and brought his shock rod down on me. My eyes widened, taking in the fanged snarl and scruffy face behind the assault, the spittle in the corner of his mouth, the wrath in his blazing red eyes. I rolled to the side; the heat of the electric rod sizzled the threads of my cloak as it barely missed me. I brought my hand up, closing my fingers around an icicle, and then I stabbed down, driving my blade through the Guard's boot. He roared in pain, giving me time to leap to my feet.

Another was lunging at me, shock rod brandished, and I crouched, my hand glowing green with ectoplasm. I threw out my hand, about to strike.

But when the Guard swung his weapon at me, he missed. Instead of jabbing the end of the rod into my side, he thrust past me and shocked another Shadow Guard who had been approaching from behind.

I paused, stunned by the fortunate accident and prepared for him to whirl and try again. To my absolute confusion, he turned his back on me and struck down two more of his comrades.

I let the ectoplasm dissipate as I stood in place, dumbfounded. The traitor turned his head and fixed one glowing blue eye on me briefly. "You seemed as though you could use some assistance."

"Do I know you?" I asked.

He smiled and nodded to the side. Sitting on the edge of the fountain and observing the battle without a care in the world was Ero. He winked at me, and my eyebrows shot up in respect and awe.

I formed another icicle, then ducked and drove my cold blade between a man's ribs. "Will Finn and Reese be able to do that?" I asked the eclipsed man.

"Perhaps someday," the stranger replied. He pretended to rush me, but now that I knew he was really an ally, I spun out of range so he could deflect another Guard without singling himself out as an obvious traitor.

I hit the ground as two Guards swung their rods at me from opposite directions. The rods collided in the air, and sparks erupted a moment before the two stunned men fell. An acrid smell filled the air.

I scrambled to my feet again. "How many Guards are you controlling?"

"Three."

I skimmed the battlefield and deduced that the Telepath's commandeered Guards were assisting Jay and Ash as well. "Can't you make the Shadow Guard retreat?"

"There are too many. I am preventing anyone from using an active Divinity against you, but I have reached my limit."

Ero's power was awe-inspiring. Not only was he eclipsing three ghosts simultaneously from a distance, but he was also coordinating each individual fight and having a conversation with me through one of his victims, all while skimming the minds of every enemy so he could neutralize the direct threats. I'd thought it was strange that a Hemokinetic hadn't downed me by now, or an Illusionary hadn't trapped me in a hallucination, or . . . well, my imagination as to how I would fall was nearly limitless. So, this was what a powerful Telepath with more than three centuries of training could do. I was grateful that he stood beside me as an ally. As an enemy, Ero would scare the hell out of me.

"What about Cisco?" I asked. "Can't you force him to give the order?"

"Lieutenant Cisco has spent centuries training to fortify his mind. Breaking his barriers is possible, but it would take time, power, and my undivided attention. I would not be able to assist you in the meantime."

The Guards had finally realized that their own comrade had turned against them, and multiple shock rods connected with the man Ero was controlling. I squinted across the square at Ero to see if he was hurt. He didn't make eye contact with me this time. His head was down, deep in concentration, and a trickle of blood crept from one nostril.

"I felt nothing," a woman said from behind.

I jumped and turned to find a woman with blazing blue eyes standing beside me. "That poor fellow, though, will be sore when he wakes up."

I heard a shriek of pain, one that was all too familiar to me. "Help!" a girl begged.

I whirled. Ash had fallen and now was desperately swinging her extinguished staff to keep enemies at bay. She spotted me and pleaded, "Help me!"

I rushed toward her, but Ero's Guard said, "Cato, stop! That is not Ash!"

I hesitated. She was crying in terror, and she called for me again. My personal Guard said, "Look at her eyes."

I halted in my tracks. "They're . . . glowing blue," I realized.

"She is a Shifter." The Guard raised a shield to protect me from a strike.

I sent a painful but nonlethal wave of ice needles into the bodies of three Shadows Guards at once, then cast a suspicious look at the woman claiming to be Ero's consciousness in another's body. "How do I know you aren't a trick?"

"I called you by name. How many Outsiders know who you are?"

Okay, good point.

A sudden *crack* made me instinctively duck. I wasn't the only one, either. The Shadow Guards around me looked as confused as I was until I spotted the source. Police officers had joined the battle, and a Guard was dead with a bullet through his ear.

"I need to get to Jay," I announced.

The woman nodded. She assumed the role of a buffer to help me slowly but surely bend, twist, sidestep, duck, shove, punch, kick, and leap my way closer to my lab-siblings. When she fell, another took her place until I was near enough to reach out and touch the real Ash's fingers.

Above us, a woman leapt up to RC and latched onto the bottom of his lid, crouching upside down. Her tail whipped around and swiped my lab-brother in the side of the head. She threw her weight, tipping the lid, forcing RC to bail. He made a wild leap, then landed gracelessly between Ash and Jay.

Axel called, "RC, can you get us some distance?"

The Telekinetic crossed his wrists and then threw his arms apart. An invisible wave of telekinetic energy expanded outward; I felt it stir my cloak. The Shadow Guards caught in RC's radius were thrown away from us. As they floundered on the ground, Axel held out his hands, and a brilliant red dome of ectoplasm surrounded us so we could regroup.

The enraged Shadow Guards howled and beat at his shield with fists and shock rods, but it held. Ectoplasm orbs of all colors exploded against it. We were lucky Axel's power reserves were practically limitless.

Axel growled under his breath and curled his fingers into tight fists; a layer of excess Grade G energy crackled along the smooth, solid surface of his Grade A shield, whipping and snapping like red lightning, shocking anyone too close. *Wow.* His shield was the most impressive display of ectoplasm I'd ever seen. Captain Hassing was the only one who might be able to break it.

Jay fell to his knees, clutching his injured arm. He asked Axel, "Are you okay?"

Jaw locked, Axel muttered, "Fine . . . for now."

"I need you to protect the humans trying to reach the Dome."

"No."

Jay shot Axel a withering glare, which the half-breed returned in a silent challenge. His mind was set; not even Jay could persuade him. He wouldn't leave us to guard humans.

A woman's voice called, "I will do it." We all turned to look at a Guard standing near the edge of Axel's shield, her blue eyes bright. "But I will have to leave you."

"Go," Jay ordered with a wave of his hand. The woman's face went blank. Her eyes turned from blue to violet, and she blinked in bewilderment. Beyond her, Ero was ushering humans to the edge of the Dome.

"Why draw this out?" called Lieutenant Cisco, stepping in front of his Guards to stand before us. Jay staggered to his feet to face him. "Look at you; you can barely fight. We have you outnumbered. Just come quietly and—"

He was interrupted by a blast of red ectoplasm to the jaw. Stunned, he stumbled a few steps to the side, his hand flying to his face. He whirled, eyes blazing as they settled on Madison Tarrow. "Get her!" he shouted, then waved his hand at us and said, "Now!"

Ash was no longer beside me. A man had taken her place.

He jabbed his shock rod at me, but even in my surprise, I was quick enough to sidestep and drive an icicle through his forearm as his hand passed by. He drew a sharp intake of breath, but before he could even regain his balance, RC struck the blunt edge of his disk into the Switch's temple.

Damn it, that was stupid. I shouldn't draw blood so close to Axel.

Ash was on the wrong side of Axel's shield, standing in the Switch's place. Too disoriented after Switching, which I assumed must be a sensation akin to Blinking, she had already been swarmed, and she fell to several shock rods.

Axel's shield dissipated, and then he was crouched over Ash's still form, snarling viciously. One Guard brought his weapon down on Axel, who reached up and caught the rod in his fist. Wispy tendrils of blue ectoplasm attacked his hand and snapped up his arm, and yet he didn't flinch. The whites of the Guard's eyes grew wide in the brief instant before Axel yanked the weapon away and shoved the ghost into the throng, sending a whole group sprawling on the ground. We were separated again as the Guards closed in on Axel and Ash.

A powerful howl sent a thrilling chill through my bones; Wes was here. He bounded into the fray, baying and snarling, teeth snapping. There was a wildness in him I'd never seen before, as if he were channeling his wolf ancestry and unleashing the ferocity of an entire pack. He must have been knocking into dozens of shock rods with his recklessness, but he was big enough to tolerate the zaps that were little more than bee stings in his tough hide.

Reinvigorated by the reinforcements, I charged back into the fight. It was a blur of motion and movements I was only semiconscious of making. I'd changed since Phantom's time. The Arena had taught me to sense without seeing, react without thinking.

I was separated from Jay and RC again by a flow of moving bodies. Wes passed me, swiping an opening as he moved by, and I stopped to take advantage of the brief reprieve to catch my breath. A hefty man detached from the mass, his focus on me. I summoned ectoplasm to life in my hands, but before he could take another step, he was downed by green ectoplasm that sent him to his knees, followed by a sharp *crack!*

He collapsed, splayed lifelessly across the ground with a red mist hovering for one last heartbeat in the air before it dispersed.

On the other side of Wes's wake stood the ghost hunter, now connected to me by the open swath in the middle of this chaos. She gripped an ectogun in each hand, both still aimed at where the now-dead Shadow Guard had been standing. The weapon in her left hand was dark, single barrel; the other was silver and sleek with two barrels, and I knew that the symbol ζ of Project Zeta was emblazoned into the handle.

Two Guards bore down on Madison from different directions, shock rods brandished. My brain was processing in hyperdrive again. I already had ectoplasm crackling in my hand, licking through the gaps between my fingers. I had the opportunity to shoot.

Madison's analytical gaze skipped over both incoming ghosts. She glanced at me and then made the decision to pivot, aiming both guns in front of her with her arms level to the ground. She discharged both weapons at one Guard to double her firepower. He staggered behind a shield under her onslaught, and she turned her head just enough to make eye contact with me with a nod, counting on me to take down the second Guard now that she had left herself exposed.

She trusts me.

The realization made me sick to my stomach.

I lowered my hand, closing my fingers into a fist to extinguish my ectoplasm.

Madison's eyes widened in the instant before the second Guard shot her down. I watched her flail through the air, and a wicked satisfaction coursed through me like a disease I knew was killing me and yet I couldn't help but relish.

I shouldn't have done that. But if I was being honest with myself, I didn't regret my action, or rather, inaction. I was a mercenary. Not a hero, but not a villain, either. I was something in between. I wasn't obligated to protect the woman who had cursed me. She had no right to put her trust in me.

I turned my back on her to face the battle.

The amount of carnage spread before me was all wrong. Only a minute had passed since the last time I'd surveyed the battlefield, if that. Too many bodies littered the ground, not enough standing.

And the blood. So much blood.

RC was squaring off against Cisco. The lieutenant formed small, quick shields that appeared and vanished in an instant to counter RC's wicked spinning disks attacking from every direction. I wouldn't say my lab-brother was necessarily winning the match, but RC was forcing Cisco backward as he advanced, showing no mercy with his blades.

Cisco's level of control over his ectoplasm shields was impressive, and despite the steady retreat, his narrowed eyes as he analyzed RC's moves made me suspect that he was biding his time on defense, waiting for the exact moment to execute his counterstrike.

RC swept his arm to the side, guiding one disk away in a wide arc to build up speed on its return orbit while the other two disks continued their barrage to keep Cisco occupied.

The lieutenant smiled.

He blocked one disk, ducked below the other, and rushed my lab-brother to take advantage of the brief opening. He was quick; RC didn't have time to react. The lieutenant's hand darted like a striking serpent. From my vantage, it didn't look like a particularly hard hit. His fingertips jabbed RC in the chest, right next to his shoulder. RC barely even faltered. But his disks dropped out of the air as if the telekinetic strings holding them had just been cut.

RC's eyes widened the instant before Cisco drove a shock rod between his ribs. Degraded violet ectoplasm swarmed my lab-brother, and he went down hard on his knees.

Cisco pulled the rod back and seized the front of RC's cloak in his other hand to hold him upright. But then, he froze. Horror-stricken, he gazed beyond his opponent, finally seeing the carnage.

Dozens of his Shadow Guards lay strewn across the cobblestones, all dead, all missing chunks of flesh, some decapitated, others with their chest cavities pulled open and their broken, bloody ribs littering the massacre. Most didn't even have the chance to scream.

Standing in the middle of it all was Axel.

The blindfold had been stripped away. His irises were bright red, his pupils constricted and once again responding to light. Crimson dripped from his chin, his fingertips, his cloak, his hair, as if he'd taken a bath in blood. He stood still in the sea of twisted bodies, head down, haunted eyes trained on Lieutenant Cisco.

His immobility was actually a consolation. Axel's nydæa half wouldn't have been able to remain motionless; he would have been a feral thing crouching, snarling, feeding on bodies or hunting new prey.

No, the bloodlust had passed. A6 had come and gone, and Axel was back.

Cisco let go of RC, who fell onto his backside but was somehow still conscious and able to remain sitting up. The Shadow Guard lieutenant took a panicked step back. "Retreat!" he called to the survivors.

They scrambled over their fallen comrades, slipping in the blood, tripping over each other to reach the Rip. Raiders followed them with their guns. Wes maintained a low, warning growl. Cisco was the last one to reach the Rip. He paused to give us a measured glare, silently promising revenge before he vanished in the distorted air.

As soon as he was gone, Axel's shoulders slumped. He dazedly surveyed the carnage, and based on the blankness in his eyes, I suspected he didn't remember killing these people. He'd awoken from a nightmare to find it was very real. The war between his mind and his demons would always rage on, but the animal was never here for very long. It just left an impressive wake of death in the short time it manifested. This time, it had all happened so fast I hadn't seen him do any of this. Last I saw, he was tackling the Shadow Guards who had attacked Ash . . .

Ash!

I rushed forward, the blood slippery underfoot. "Axel, where is she?" I cried, feverishly skimming the bodies. "What did you do to Ash?"

"Ash?" he repeated, as if the name were unfamiliar. He wiped his jaw, but his glove was so saturated that rather than wiping blood away, all he did was leave finger tracks smeared in the red.

I couldn't catch my breath. Axel wasn't capable of identifying allies or enemies when he was in a bloodlust. Only killing. That was all his nydæa half knew how to do.

I kicked and shoved bodies in search of my missing lab-sister. RC and Jay were searching, too. I was going to throw up. With each body I turned, I wanted to find her while hoping I wouldn't.

Axel just stood there, shell-shocked, not even watching us. "Damn it, Axel, *help us*!" I yelled.

He didn't react. On some level, I understood that this tragedy, as horrifying as it might be, was the only reason we'd been victorious. And yet, I would rather be dragged through the Ghost Realm in chains than kneel over the broken body of my lab-sister.

"Her heart is beating."

I whirled to Axel, who was still standing in his stupefied trance. Had I imagined that he'd said that? His gaze was near me but not on me, not focused. He seemed to be staring blankly into space. When I followed his line of sight, I spotted a hand, fingers curled and limp from a black glove that ended below the first knuckle. I scrambled over and heaved a body off my lab-sister. As soon as the weight left her chest, she stirred and took a deep breath.

"Ash," I whispered in relief, sliding my arms beneath her and pulling her into my lap. Her eyelashes fluttered at the sound of my voice. Jay and RC were beside me, Jay squeezing her hand, RC touching her hair. She was bloody, but the blood wasn't hers. How lucky she was, so very lucky, to have been struck down before Axel snapped. His primal awareness had been focused on the prey that was moving and running and attacking, not on the unconscious girl lying on the ground.

"I'm okay," she whispered. "It's okay; I'm okay." She struggled, and I helped her sit up. I registered movement all around us, and I tensed, expecting another attack.

The figures were humans. They were wandering from City Hall, almost as zombie-like as Axel as they took in the five of us in the debris of mangled corpses. A modest group of raiders with weapons still drawn were grouped together on the far side of the plaza but moving toward us. We were being surrounded.

Jay quietly urged, "Get up." He took Ash's arm and half lifted, half dragged her to her feet. She swayed, and RC had to support her while Jay seized my hand and helped me rise.

The wolf was standing at the edge of the crowd, a few steps forward so he wasn't part of it but close enough that he wasn't isolated like we were. His hackles were raised along his spine, but he wasn't growling or baring his teeth. Just staring. Not at the carnage, not at

Axel soaked in blood.

He was staring at me.

I stared back. We were connected by an invisible tether; I couldn't look away. There was something eerie about the way he was watching me with such burning intensity, every muscle stone still, ears pricked forward, tail rigid.

"*Seph*!" a woman screeched.

I turned. Madison was shoving her way through the crowd. Loose strands of dark-brown hair had pulled free of her ponytail and drifted over a deepening bruise on her cheek. She stepped into the circle, and we faced each other with a sea of blood between us.

— Chapter Forty-Eight —

Duel

"What the *hell* is your problem?"

I stared at her, impassive, disturbed by how satisfying it was to see her so angry. No, *angry* wasn't a strong enough word. Madison was seething.

I tilted my head and replied, "What?"

"You had the shot! Why didn't you take it? I thought we were on the same team!"

I shrugged. "I don't know what you're talking about."

Wes, who had reverted to his human form and was now zipping a pair of pants taken from a dead Shadow Guard, was still staring at me. "Maddie . . ."

She ignored him, and so did I.

I turned toward Ash, but Madison commanded, "Stop! We're not done! Seph, don't you turn your back on me when I'm talking to you!"

I was still charged from the fight and the terror of almost losing my lab-sister. My power flickered in my center, green and hot. I whirled. "I don't have to obey your orders!"

Madison's fingers clenched into fists tight enough to turn the knuckles of her right hand white and strain the fabric of the glove she wore on her left. "I get it—you hate me."

"Maddie," Wes interrupted again.

"Not now, Wes!"

"But Maddie, I think that's—"

"Later!"

Something was wrong with his voice. One glance at Wes, and my stomach sank. He hadn't stopped staring at me with wide, disbelieving eyes, his face pale, his jaw agape, as if he'd seen a moorlin.

He knows.

I returned his stare, brain-locked. I didn't know what to do.

Madison paid him no heed. "You listen to me, Seph." I blinked and turned to face her again. "This feud between us ends now. *Right now.* You understand?"

Wes's epiphany rekindled my hatred to a heightened level. Why hold back when I had no secret to protect anymore? Why not face my creator and finally unearth the answers I needed? She had to pay for what she'd done to me.

I lunged for the ghost hunter, but Ash and RC seized my arms, keeping me at bay.

"It's not worth it," Jay said.

I stopped struggling against my lab-siblings. Every muscle in my body quivered under an overdose of adrenaline, lungs heaving with fury and hatred. "Argh, she makes me want to scream."

RC warned in a low undertone, "Don't."

Ash whispered, "Cay, your eyes are green—"

"I don't care." Madison was so preoccupied that she hadn't noticed, and I wasn't going to bother trying to suppress my rage. RC and Ash reluctantly let go, watching warily, ready to grab me again if I tried to rush forward.

Jay gripped my arm, leaning in close and hissing into my ear, "Getting into a fight isn't going to solve anything."

He was wrong. Everything was falling apart. We'd built our new life on a web of twisted half-truths and secrets, and it was unraveling fast.

"It's too late," I said. "Wes knows."

Jay's eyes widened. He shot a glance at the pale werewolf, then nodded in understanding. "Okay." Defeat dragged his voice to a low I'd never heard. "I think it's time to go."

Go. Time to leave Phantom Heights, just as we'd planned. After what Axel had done, the humans were probably about to drive us out anyway, and there was no way to shut Wes up. Jay's fingers tightened on my biceps, but I recoiled from him. "No. You can't do that to me."

"Cay—"

"No!" I jerked free, surprised to semiconsciously realize that I was gripping an icicle in my hand, ready to strike my own lab-brother. He noticed, and a wounded expression shadowed his face. "You can't make me leave. Not now. I need closure. Please don't hold me back. I promise if you let me do this, I'll go anywhere you say, but I can't leave Phantom Heights without answers. I have to know what happened, Jay."

"Will that satisfy you? Is it going to change anything?"

"*Please*. I need this."

He nodded slowly. "Okay." He took a step back, but not before whispering, "I'll bring Kit and the twins here, and the second this takes a wrong turn, we're going through the Rip. If it looks like you're going to lose, I'll have to take you. Good luck."

He was gone.

My opponent narrowed her eyes. "You want to fight me," she stated. Our conversation had been out of her earshot, but the ensuing actions must have been clear enough for her to draw the right conclusion. My answer was to take a step toward her. My icicles lengthened. Crude armor was forming outside of my conscious creation.

Madison continued, "We saved the twins' lives, gave you your powers, and welcomed you into our town when you had nowhere else to go. Apparently, the concept of gratitude is lost on you."

"You want me to be grateful? You cost me *everything* I had Before! You destroyed my life!" Excess ice was forming on the ground at my feet, spreading outward between cobblestones in crystallized tendrils. The right side of my face was cold, although my core remained hot.

Madison let out a mocking scoff. "You need someone to blame for all your misfortune, and you've chosen me. You came here through the Rip, didn't you? Did I fight you? Is that why you're so mad at me? Do you think it's somehow *my* fault you ended up at the AGC?"

She was so calm, so irritatingly composed, and it was the steadiness of her words that made them bite. She was wrong—I didn't *choose* her.

Her mistake cost me my humanity. My life.

The icicles were gone, and my hands were hot with ectoplasm waiting to be released.

So I did. Straight at the ghost hunter.

She hadn't expected the sudden assault and didn't have time to react. The potent green energy sent her flailing. She crashed hard on her back several yards away from where she'd been standing, and the rush of air out of her lungs was lost in the crowd's collective gasp. The ghost hunter lay still, staring at the sky.

A body slammed into me from the side. As we fell, I criticized myself; I knew better than to be so singly focused on one opponent that I didn't pay attention to my surroundings. At first I thought it must be Wes, but it wasn't. My assailant was a human, smaller than the werewolf.

The shock took only a second to wear off, and then I reacted, twisting in the air so I already had momentum to roll when the ground met my shoulder.

We tumbled in the grass . . .

We tumbled across the cobblestones.

He landed on top of me . . .

I landed beneath him, his weight settling on my body.

I lay still, pinned . . .

I threw my weight to the side, bucking beneath him, using our collective momentum before he had a chance to find his balance. In one smooth move, I rolled, taking him over with me as I kicked away from my attacker. I was on my feet again. Trey scrambled up rather gracelessly after me and took a wild swing.

He hadn't gathered his balance before rushing. As he lunged at me, I had a microsecond to realize this was it. This was the moment I'd feared, although it wasn't playing out the way I'd envisioned. There was no standoff. I'd imagined standing in front of him facing his gun, leaving him with the choice to pull the trigger. This was happening too fast. No time for choices. No time for thinking, and my thoughts were still on Madison, not him. Perhaps this wasn't the moment after all.

Trey was fighting Seph, not Cato. He was just an interruption.

Instead of dodging or pushing him away, I caught his fist and seized his shirt in my other hand. I pulled him close. "If you're going to be a ghost hunter," I seethed in his face, "you'd better figure out a better way to catch a ghost."

I didn't know why my statement had such a profound effect on him, but he stopped dead in his tracks. Every muscle went stiff beneath my grip, his frozen punch slack in my hand. He gaped at me, wide-eyed. "What?"

That was all he had time to say. I let go of his shirt and lunged forward, my metal-studded fist sinking into his abdomen to make him double over my arm. I summoned ectoplasm, and in a burst of green light, he was thrown away from me. He didn't land on his back like his ghost-hunting master. He struck the ground and slid, rolling across the bloody cobblestones that bit at his bare arms. "Wait," he cried, flopping like a fish out of water to rise again before he'd even stopped falling. "Wait—"

RC pounced on him. He hauled Trey up and flung out one arm. Whatever Cisco had done to disable RC's telekinesis seemed to have worn off, and once again, the apprentice was thrown through the air until he collided with the wall of the nearest shop, where he was pinned a few feet above the ground by telekinetic force. "Don't interfere," RC said.

"But—"

RC flicked his hand, and the end of Trey's shirt was pulled up and shoved into his mouth, gagging him. He hung there, too stunned to struggle, his lean abdomen pulsing with quick breaths.

Trey also had questions to answer. He betrayed me too, but it wasn't his turn. No, before I dealt with him or the custody contract, I had to start at the very beginning with a flash of green light. I had to know the truth, once and for all, how I'd come to be. The rest would follow.

I surveyed my arena. Kit, Reese, and Finn were huddled nearby while my other lab-siblings were stationed with their backs to my opponent and me to prevent any further interference from humans in the crowd. Nobody else was going to stop me from getting my revenge and my answers, but I knew Madison wasn't going to tell me anything until I'd defeated her. If I lost this fight, I'd have no one to blame but myself. I didn't intend to lose. I couldn't face my mother until I'd beaten the ghost hunter. I had to win; only then would I have the right to ask what happened to me, and why.

Madison had only just caught her breath and risen to her feet, but she saw that I'd assaulted her apprentice, and I could see the fire in her eyes. Her anger excited me. As satisfying as it had been to purposely let her be injured by an enemy on the battlefield, a personal shot from my own hand had felt even better. I wanted her to fight back so I could have the excuse to do it again. I smiled coldly behind my mask as she obliged me.

Madison drew her Zeta gun. She wasn't playing around; that gun had both ectoplasm and bullets. She could kill me with it.

Vivian, shivering in the cold air, took a nervous step past Ash, who allowed her to enter the circle. Vivian reached out to touch Madison's shoulder. "Mom, please."

Madison shrugged her off. "Stand back. Winning duels is how ká-los determine respect in their Realm, so that's what it'll take to put Seph in his place."

Wes tried to pass Axel, but he was held back with a savage snarl from the blood-soaked hybrid. The werewolf called, "Maddie, you're making a mistake!"

"My only mistake was letting this insubordination and disrespect go unchecked for so long."

"Please, listen to me! You're going to regret this because I think Seph is actually—"

"Shut up, Wes," I snapped.

His eyes widened again as he gawked at me. My command seemed to have confirmed his suspicion. He shook his head in astonishment. "You're . . . I don't believe it . . ."

My eyes still on Madison, I threw my arm out to the side, palm out, releasing a burst of ectoplasm at the werewolf. He gasped when it struck him square in the chest, and he was knocked backward with a grunt, then landed with a soft moan. That would leave a bruise and knock the wind out of him, and it should keep him quiet, at least for a little while. Long enough for me to deal with Madison. I trusted my lab-family to keep him out of my way if he tried to interrupt again.

I closed my fingers into a fist, savoring the delicate sound of ice cracking. The loose tendrils of ectoplasm flickering around my hands kept the ice from creating a thick coating, but I was releasing enough power that a thin layer survived despite the heat. I was so high on the thrill of battle that I saw the muscles in Madison's finger tighten over the trigger.

And it began.

I charged her. She leveled her gun and fired brilliant red energy directly at me. I conjured my own condensed ectoplasm in the form of a green disk to shield myself.

On some level, I was aware of the concentration of ectoplasm that just dissipated against mine. I was stronger. The human-made ectoplasm from the Zeta gun was only half as potent as mine. I could blast her into oblivion, and she would have no way to make a shield.

But that would be too easy. I wanted to draw this out. I wanted to feel her body and spirit break. Mercy was weakness that had been driven out of me in all those Arena matches when I'd hurt my own lab-siblings for a bowl of white rice, or when I'd struggled for my life against a Scout trying to kill me just as desperately as I was trying to kill it. I'd learned not to hold back in the Arena, even when sparring against friends and allies—I certainly wasn't going to hold back against Madison.

She had time to fire only one more shot before we collided, and then her gun was useless. I was too close, too fast, and for her to have any chance, she was forced to take a defensive stance and block my strikes. Wes was staying quiet. He seemed to be waiting . . . waiting for proof beyond a doubt. But in his heart, he knew, and I understood this. The final cord of the complicated web of deceptions we had constructed to build our new life had just been cut. No more secrets. No more hiding. No more holding back.

"You're wrong about me, you know," Madison said, shielding her head to protect her face. "I've killed ghosts, and I've driven them back to their Realm, but I've never turned any over to the AGC."

She ducked, and I found myself staring down the barrel of her gun. I summoned a transparent green ectoplasm shield between us, but her shot didn't come. Her left hand was moving, coming toward me in a palm strike.

When her glove met my shield, the metal nodes on her fingers flared with crackling light, and my ectoplasm burst before my eyes. A point of red light had formed at the back of the barrel. I whirled; red filled my vision, a sizzling heat grazing my ear as I twisted and went down.

My hands met the ground and pushed my body back up immediately, completing the rotation. I was off balance for only a few seconds, but in that time, Madison had transferred the ectogun to her gloved left hand. Her right hand smacked my arm as I came up.

Her slap itself didn't hurt; it was the ectoplasm drawn from the little gadget stuck on my skin that felt like white-hot needles.

Damn it!

One second.

I went down hard, screaming as my own degraded ectoplasm electrocuted my body, the highest concentration attacking my arm at the source. That tiny device was a cruel invention, hurting me with my own power while simultaneously weakening me by draining my reserves.

Two seconds.

I was at her mercy. She could shoot me while I was helpless, or attach more of those gadgets to extend my suffering and make me burn out.

Three seconds.

Through the green haze, I reached for my center beyond the mind-numbing pain. Controlling the flow was harder than usual, as if the device on my arm had rusted the faucet so I couldn't turn the stream off while this thing pulled the power out of me.

But finally, I succeeded. I extinguished the warmth in my chest as if blowing out a stubborn candle and watching the glowing ember on the tip of the wick fade.

Four seconds.

The pain stopped. My gamble had paid off. The Dome didn't affect me in my human form, and apparently neither did the gadget that fell off my arm now that the ectoplasm current holding it in place was gone. An offensive smoky smell, like melting plastic and scorched flesh, assaulted my nose when I drew a ragged breath, although I couldn't tell if it was caused by the thing that had zapped me or Madison's glove when she'd dissipated my shield.

Madison gawked at me, stunned. "What—?"

I launched myself at her with a primitive growl.

She didn't stand a chance. All of my hatred was unleashed upon her. I didn't even need my powers; simply beating the ghost hunter with my fists was satisfying enough.

Truthfully, she wasn't a bad fighter. She might be human, but she was fast and resourceful. She had trained to hunt supernatural creatures like me.

Unfortunately for her, I was in a bloodlust of my own. Axel feared his creators because he knew *They* could destroy what *They* had made. It was time I tested my own creator. One of us was destined to destroy the other today.

For a while, Madison tried to retaliate. She punched and kicked; I dodged and blocked, countering each of her blows with a harder strike. The warmth returned to my core, now blazing hot with devastating power that was mounting rapidly.

Her gun fell as she raised her hands to protect her face. She took a step back. When I advanced, my boot kicked the gun, which skittered out of reach behind her.

She wasn't fighting back anymore.

But I didn't stop. The anger and frustration building inside of me like a thunderhead had finally been unleashed. The raw power coursed through me and fueled my fury, ice and ectoplasm around my hands and arms, hot and cold, wild extremes colliding inside me like the storm of all storms.

My creator had brought me to the brink—to the unexplored limits of my abilities. How fitting that she would be the one to draw this new-found power out of me. An unprecedented phenomenon, both of my Divinities were active at the same time. My cold hands collected ice without my conscious control, and the hurricane of energy inside me was gathering into what was doomed to be a devastating scream if I let it out. With both divine powers awakened, I was certain my eyes were blazing different colors—one blue, one green.

But Madison was covering her face with her arm, and she didn't see.

Vivian cried out for her mom. When I paid her no heed, she called out to me instead. "Seph, *stop*!" she screamed. Ash gently pulled her back to the outside of the circle, and although Vivian didn't resist, she called, "Please, I'm begging you!" Her voice should have brought me back to reality, but it didn't, even though I knew she would hate me forever if I killed her mom.

I formed a dagger of ice in my hand and swung it in an arc across my body. Madison registered the gleam of my incoming weapon just in time and leapt back so the tip of my icicle nicked her shirt but didn't make skin contact. She drew another ectogun but had no time to shoot before I attacked again, forcing her to deflect my ice with the butt of her gun. Thrice more she blocked me before I grew frustrated and flicked my free hand, freezing a sliver from the air and shooting it into her leg.

She cried out and limped backward in an attempt to escape me. I wouldn't let her retreat. My heart was flying with adrenaline, like a predator going in for the kill. I could send a thousand ice needles into her skin. I could freeze her, limb by limb, until she confessed to her sins. The possibilities were limited only by my imagination.

I threw my ice weapon aside; it broke on the cobblestones. "Is that the best you've got? Come on! I want a fight, Madison! Why! Won't!

You! *Fight*! *Back*!" I yelled, punctuating each word to match my fist striking her body.

Her next step changed everything.

She stepped back, but her foot didn't touch the ground. Her heel landed on the ectogun she had dropped earlier. As she fell, her fingers latched onto my cloak.

She was pulling me down with her, and I panicked. I turned intangible for a fraction of a second, just long enough to free myself of the cloak.

She landed on her backside. The fabric settled in her hands.

She looked upon my face for the first time, and immediately, the blood drained from her cheeks, turning her pasty white. I'd seen that look of shock before—the day the town of Phantom Heights learned I was half-ghost.

Now, finally, she saw standing in front of her the masked Phantom dressed in an Alpha uniform. Wes remained silent, but the corner of his mouth was pulled up in a smug smirk.

People began shifting and whispering.

"Look!"

"Doesn't he look like Cato?"

"He's the spitting image!"

"That kid was right!"

"It's Phantom!"

"No," Madison whispered. "It's not possible."

— Chapter Forty-Nine —
Creator

"Oh, so you *do* remember me." I yanked the mask away and threw it at my feet.

Madison quailed on the ground. "You . . . you can't be here."

I'd been wavering on the edge, but that was the final crack that made the dam fail. The currents of raw power circulating in my core consumed my entire body, numbing my senses—a rushing roar in my ears, a steadily collapsing tunnel encroaching on my vision. The cold air turned frigid. "You're not happy to see me?"

"W-what? No, that's . . . that's n— that's not what I said . . ."

Degraded ectoplasm crackled around my hands, my arms, my eyes. I'd never been this charged in my life; it was simultaneously terrifying and exhilarating. The heaviness lifted from my shoulders.

"Do you have any idea what I went through because of you?"

Madison scrambled to her feet. I advanced menacingly; she backed away. "C-Cato . . . if . . . if it really is you, y-you have every right to be angry."

"You're damn right I do!"

"Okay, let's just be rational, and, and we can talk . . ."

"Talk?" I snarled. "Oh no, we're *way* past talking."

"Please, just listen—"

I flicked small bursts of ectoplasm at her feet as she retreated, forcing her to hop back. "Now wait . . . just . . . w-wait a minute . . . Cato, I'm sorry—"

"*TRAITORS*!" I screamed.

Any remaining glass shattered in my echoes. The ghost hunter, who had been standing in front of me and received the full brunt of my scream, was flung backward. She crashed into the wall behind her and then cowered as debris poured down.

Concrete cracked. Buildings heaved as though in the throes of an earthquake. I heard the splintering of wood, followed by a crash as the nearest telephone pole snapped like a toothpick and fell in an explosion of sparks.

"*All* of you! You're all traitors! I became a hero, and that still wasn't good enough!" My unfortunate victim opened her eyes and slowly pulled her hands away from her head to listen. "So how about now? Do I make a better villain than a hero?"

I crossed the distance between us in a few long strides, then seized the front of her jacket and hauled her to her feet with alarming effortlessness. "Fight me."

She shook her head. "No. I won't."

I stared at her. She *wouldn't*? After every possible way she'd hurt me in the past, *now* she wouldn't fight? My disbelief morphed into rage. I finally had the opportunity to let out all of my frustration, to release my pent-up anger at the ghost hunter who had ruined my life, and she was cheating me. Again, she was ruining *everything*!

I couldn't see straight. The ectoplasm was crackling all around me, and it was so hot, pulsing in my core, tingling my skin, charging my wrath. "Fight me!" I shouted, shaking her.

"No," she sobbed.

With a half-growl, half-scream, I converged the wild energy to my hands and then released it in an explosion of green light. Madison flew back and struck the wall with such force that I was surprised not to hear the snapping of bones. She crumpled to the ground.

I couldn't . . . see . . . in the haze . . . I was drowning. The hot power peaked again, higher than before, overpowering the cold. Shuddering, I seized fistfuls of my hair, squeezed my eyes shut, and tried to contain it behind my teeth. But it expanded. I had a brief surge of panic in the moment I realized this force was going to kill me if I didn't release it. My head tipped back.

And I screamed.

I screamed as I'd never dared to before. It was a wail of anguish, of pain, of betrayal, of heartache, of frustration. I released it all, lighting every fiber of my being until it swallowed me and I ceased to exist. I was energy. I was power. I was . . .

Out of control.

The moment I realized this, clarity struck a note in the chaos.

I opened my eyes. No one was left standing. I saw the blood of Axel's victims and accepted the certainty that I'd slaughtered everyone, including my lab-family.

But then figures shifted, moaned, sobbed, called for loved ones in the wreckage. Dazed, they rose to look around with horror equal to mine.

City Hall's portico—or at least, what was left of it—was balanced precariously on two stone columns. Most of the outer walls were gone, leaving only structural supports so it loomed like a skeleton over the plaza, which was littered with loose cobblestones and debris. The stone steps, half-buried beneath part of the portico, had been cleaved in two as if from the ax of a giant. The air was choked with dust. Whole office buildings had collapsed, shops obliterated. Jets shooting water from a mound of rubble were all that remained of the fountain.

No. No, no, what have I done? All I'd wanted was the truth.

Instead, I'd become the monster I swore I would never be. I had proved that *They* were right and I belonged in a cage. And . . . I understood. I knew why my mother sold me. Why I'd been locked in a cage and sealed away from the Outside world.

Horror in fury's wake was dangerously cold. I shivered. The cold seeped through every part of me, filling me with emptiness as penance. I could feel the sudden shift from hot to cold, as if feeling the very transition of my green eyes turning blue. Snow swirled around me.

I clutched my heart, certain it was freezing and I must be dying. The snow thickened, big flakes spinning into a vortex that expanded over the whole town. Ice crystallized on surfaces, on clothing, on skin, icicles dripping from overhangs, filling cracks, expanding, breaking apart stone and cracking wood and broken glass. A biting wind kicked up in the cloudless storm.

Axel wasn't the only one with an inner demon. People were afraid of me. They'd known, even when I hadn't, that this thing was inside of me. If I couldn't be kept under control, I had to be contained, and *He* had offered that very solution. So this wouldn't happen.

But it wasn't my fault! Didn't they understand I was just as scared as they were? I hadn't meant to do this. It wasn't my fault. It was . . . Madison's. She made me into this.

I found her pushing away shingles and siding covering her legs. Snow had drifted in the crevices of her clothes, and flakes clung to her dark hair and eyelashes. *She* had done this.

When I parted my lips, people gasped and cringed, afraid I was going to scream again. "I want you to fight me," I stated, voice hoarse. Madison was too stunned to do anything but shake her head in refusal.

I marched through the blizzard and kicked her in the ribs, evoking a grunt of pain. "You selfish *bitch*! After everything you took away from me, why can't you give me this one thing? Fight me, or I . . . I'll . . . I'll scream again. There won't be anything left of Phantom Heights!"

Shivering, she continued to shake her head back and forth. "I don't care. I won't do it. I won't fight you."

She crawled backward, away from me. I advanced on her.

"Cato, you have to stop this."

My steps didn't falter.

"I know you didn't mean for this to happen. It was an accident. I can help you."

"Help me? You mean neutralize me, right?"

"No. That's not what I meant! Listen to me! Please, Cato, stop! It's not too late to make this right!"

I held my hand out, palm facing her, green light growing brighter between us. She must have seen the resolve harden in my eyes, because she rose to her knees.

"That's enough! *Cato Jaxon Tarrow*, I said *STOP*!"

— Chapter Fifty —

Carrion

Agent Kovak held a mask over his nose and mouth.

He'd witnessed plenty of gruesome scenes over the course of his career, but this made even his stomach turn. Byrn had already bolted after getting one whiff of the flesh baking in the afternoon sun and then contaminating the crime scene by vomiting.

The county authorities had been all too relieved to pass the investigation off to the AGC, and now dozens of Agents in hazmat suits were picking their way through the corpses, trying to avoid stepping on body parts. A few deputies were still lingering by the general store, the lights from their vehicles flashing red and blue while they leaned against the hoods and answered questions.

Kovak carefully made his way to a man kneeling over the body of a young girl. Her throat had been ripped out, but she was the most intact body he'd seen yet. "Sorry to pull you away from your work, Doc."

Anders glanced up through the clear faceplate of the hazmat suit. "Eh, well, I needed a break anyway."

"What's the verdict?"

Dr. Anders settled back on his heels and draped his arms across his knees while he worked a piece of gum between his molars. "You want to know if A6 did this."

"Did he?"

Anders shrugged. "Maybe. Maybe not." He set his hands on his knees and rose with a soft groan. "The way they were slaughtered fits his killing method. Problem is, he'd need only a handful of victims at most to satisfy his bloodlust and sustain himself until his next feeding. If this was his doing, he killed the rest of these people just for fun."

"Any idea of the death count yet?"

"According to the last census, the town's population was three hundred and eighty-seven. You want my best guess? That's your death count, give or take anyone lucky enough to be out of town. It'll take a long time to piece every corpse together to give you an exact count."

Crows and vultures were plucking at the body parts. Kovak swallowed the bile at the back of his throat. "If this was A6, it's the first slaughter we know of. Is it possible he's made it this long without feeding, and this overkill was the result?"

"I don't think so. We had him on a biweekly feeding schedule. I doubt he could have survived this many months without sustenance." He met Kovak's gaze. "I don't have any proof A6 did this. It could have been something else entirely."

Kovak nodded. "Send me your report when it's ready." He turned on his heel and navigated through the remains. As much as he didn't want to look down at the bloody remnants, he would most certainly throw up if he accidentally stepped on a body part.

He didn't dare remove his mask until he was in the woods beyond the massacre and upwind from the nauseating stench. He tossed the mask on the ground and wandered through the slender trees. A dry creek bed riddled with boulders half-buried under a layer of dead leaves carved a meandering path. A lone figure sat hunched over on a stone slab.

Kovak approached from behind. "Did you find something?"

Without turning around, Byrn answered, "Whatever did this is long gone." He held up a scanner. "It's degrading fast. A few more minutes and it'll be gone."

Kovak squinted at the creek bed.

There, by the bend, now he saw it—a faint shimmering in the air, like heat waves over a road on a hot summer's day.

Byrn cradled the scanner in his lap to watch the readings. "Still think it was A6?"

"I don't know. It's an awful lot of carnage for him to leave by himself. It's possible that . . ." An ominous shadow temporarily blocked the filtered sunlight overhead, causing a sudden eruption of goose bumps on the back of Kovak's neck.

"What?" Byrn pressed when he trailed off.

Kovak scanned the treetops. He glanced at the Tear, and then movement to his right caught his eye. "Get down!" He threw himself forward, seizing Byrn's jacket and dragging him down, too. They rolled off the rock and landed in the leaf litter of the creek bed. A massive animal glided over them.

Byrn instinctively cowered and threw his arms over his head. "What the hell? What the hell!" he whimpered.

Kovak scrambled to draw an ectogun. He rolled onto his belly, took aim, and fired three shots of ectoplasm at the black, four-legged creature bounding deftly across the tops of the boulders on cloven hooves, wings still spread wide. The beast's rider barely glanced at the Agents, but the ectoplasm blasts, which had been on a true course, veered away from their target and shot off into the trees.

And then, as quickly as they'd come, they were gone. Steed and rider had both vanished.

Kovak lay frozen, his weapon still aimed at the fading Tear until the final shimmer was gone and the barrier between the Realms was solid once more. Byrn was sniveling in the leaves beside him.

"Get up," Kovak snapped, jabbing him with his gun. "Have a little dignity."

Byrn rubbed his face and dared to open his eyes. He sat up, staring at where the Tear had been. "What was that thing?"

"Don't know, but it's gone now." Kovak stood and holstered his ectogun. "Damn."

Byrn scrambled up into a low crouch, his beady eyes darting skyward as if he were afraid of another ambush.

"Let's go," said Kovak as he strode away. "We're done here."

— Epilogue —

"Stop . . ."

". . . Stop . . ."

". . . Stop . . ."

My mother's shout echoed through the icy streets until it faded to dead silence.

The vortex of snow stilled. Fat white flakes hung in the air, as if the whole world had stopped turning and we were in a snow globe frozen in a single moment forever.

She said my full name.

I couldn't breathe.

Finally, she saw me. She saw *me*—not Seph. Not A7. Not Phantom. Her son. Her greatest mistake.

The crackling ectoplasm in my hand flickered and dissipated into nothing. My arm fell to my side.

Axel was right—I'd never know the truth if I was afraid to search for the answers. No more cowering in the shadows. No more hiding.

I stood, maskless, in the frozen blood and ruins before the judgment of Phantom Heights to claim the truth I deserved by right.

I was finally ready to face my ghosts.

To be continued

Acknowledgments

Writing is a solitary craft, but it takes a network of supporters to bring a story to life and publish a book. My heartfelt thanks to:

My talented editors, Kayla M. Ware and Nikki Mentges, for their talents and time to polish this novel into something I'm proud to share with the world.

Jason Anderson for his time and attention to detail while formatting the ebook.

My awesome team of beta readers—Gordon Glanders, Jo Pilecki, Lorraine Tighe, and Kim Noë—for providing honest feedback on the rough draft and being a part of this journey with me.

Cindy Sullivan, my wonderful photographer who captured my author photo in snowy Bendix Woods.

My friends, family, and fans—everyone who has found a place in the pages of my novels—who have offered endless support and encouragement in both dark times and success.

My early fans who appreciated my writing before I was published, and the Sandcastle Writers who lifted me up with encouragement and challenged me to keep writing. Special thanks to the Lubeznik Center for the Arts for giving us a home and a sanctuary where we can write.

Sara A. Noë is an award-winning author, photographer, and artist. She lives in a little cottage in Indiana with her cat, Calypso. Sara's writings have appeared in various anthologies and literary journals since 2005, and her poetry is available in the Indiana Archives. Her photography has been exhibited in galleries and featured on the cover of *Voices* literary journal. Sara designs and creates her own book covers, graphics, and artwork for her novels.

A Fallen Hero, her debut novel and Book I in the Chronicles of Avilésor: War of the Realms series, has been critically acclaimed by *The Prairies Book Review*, *Literary Titan*, *NAM Editorial*, and *Chronicle Focus Editorial*, among others, since its 2018 release. The debut novel made book reviewer Lauren Gantt's Top 10 Favorite Books of 2019 list and won *Literary Titan*'s Gold Book Award in May 2020.

Phantom's Mask followed in its predecessor's footsteps and received the Gold Book Award in September 2020, less than two months after the novel's official release.

THE STORY WILL CONTINUE WITH
BOOK III:

Blood of the Enemy

www.ingramcontent.com/pod-product-compliance
Lightning Source LLC
Chambersburg PA
CBHW031043110726
47900CB00003B/788